FREE...TO FEED!

That hunger gnawed at the ghoul's empty belly, a cold, hollow craving that it had no means of satisfying.

Until two weeks ago, when it was finally freed.

Then it had made up for lost time, and at long last, satisfied its appetite.

That night, after the sigil was accidentally broken, after the gravestone had cracked and fallen to the earth, it awoke fully, and became aware. Aware of the human standing above it. The creature could smell him—the stink of his man-sweat, the alcohol oozing from his pores, the fear in his heart, and the anger in his head. The ghoul could smell it all, and more, smell the dead in the cemetery. The creature growled along with its stomach.

The man's head was like a hive of enraged bees, and the ghoul could sense it.

Above the grave, the man moved. Mumbled something angry and unintelligible, voice slurred by alcohol. Cursed the fallen tombstone, even though he'd been the one to knock it over. Lit a cigarette.

The ground shifted.

The ghoul surged toward the surface, cleaving the soil like a shark through water. Its long, bony fingers erupted from the earth....

Other *Leisure* books by Brian Keene:

THE CONQUEROR WORMS
CITY OF THE DEAD
THE RISING

HIGH PRAISE FOR BRIAN KEENE!

THE CONQUEROR WORMS

"Keene delivers [a] wild, gruesome page-turner...the enormity of Keene's pulp horror imagination, and his success in bringing the reader over the top with him, is both rare and wonderful."

—Publishers Weekly

"Basic and beautiful, simple yet sublime. Keene is a virtuoso writer of...descriptive talents who can also trip out on the minimalism of American Gothic... *The Conqueror Worms* is a...thoroughly enjoyable novel grounded in Keene's fantastic control over his material."

—Fangoria

"Incredibly fast-paced, emotionally charged and gruesomely entertaining... Fans of post-apocalyptic thrillers will enjoy Keene's newest—gloriously horrific!"

—B&N.com

CITY OF THE DEAD

"In the carnival funhouse of horror fiction, Brian Keene runs the rollercoaster! The novel is a never-ending chase down a long funneling tunnel...stretching the reader's nerves banjo-tight and then gleefully plucking each nerve with an off-key razorblade... There aren't stars enough in the rating system to hang over this one-two punch."

—Cemetery Dance

"[*City of the Dead*] will force even the most sluggish readers to become speed demons in the quest to reach the resolution. The pacing is relentless, the action fast and furious."

—Horror Reader

"Brian Keene has given zombies their next upgrade! A major new horror novelist."

—Cemetery Dance

"Keene reminds us that horror fiction can deal with fear, not just indulge it."

—Ramsey Campbell

MORE PRAISE FOR BRIAN KEENE!

THE RISING

"[Brian Keene's] first novel, *The Rising,* is a postapocalyptic narrative that revels in its blunt and visceral descriptions of the undead."

—*The New York Times Book Review*

"[*The Rising* is] the most brilliant and scariest book ever written. Brian Keene is the next Stephen King."

—*The Horror Review*

"*The Rising* is more terrifying than anything currently on the shelf or screen."

—*Rue Morgue*

"*The Rising* is chock-full of gore and violence...an apocalyptic epic."

—*Fangoria*

"Hoping for a good night's sleep? Stay away from *The Rising*. It'll keep you awake, then fill your dreams with lurching, hungry corpses wanting to eat you."

—Richard Laymon, author of *The Beast House*

"Quite simply, the first great horror novel of the new millennium!"

—Dark Fluidity

"With Keene at the wheel, horror will never be the same."

—Hellnotes

"Stephen King meets Brian Lumley. Keene will keep you turning the pages to the very end."

—*Terror Tales*

GHOUL

BRIAN KEENE

LEISURE BOOKS NEW YORK CITY

For Brian Dubs, Steve Gingerich,
Joe Messersmith, and Jesse Watson.
One last raid on the prep school...

A LEISURE BOOK®

February 2007

Published by

Dorchester Publishing Co., Inc.
200 Madison Avenue
New York, NY 10016

ISBN 0-8439-5644-5

The name "Leisure Books" and the stylized "L" with design are trademarks of Dorchester Publishing Co., Inc.

Printed in the United States of America.

Visit us on the web at www.dorchesterpub.com.

ACKNOWLEDGMENTS

Thanks to Cassandra and Sam; Don D'Auria; Tim, Brooke, and Brianna; Bob Ford and Whutta Design Agency; Kelli, Tod, Mark, and John; Kelly for the fallacies; Bob, Jim, Benjamin, and the rest of the staff at Borders Books in York, PA, for allowing me to set up temporary shop in the café when I lost my office; my father, Lloyd Keene, and father-in-law, Glenn Burnham, for building me a new office; Don Coscarelli, Brian Hodge, John Skipp, and Jim Moore; Pete Zedlacher and Monica Kuebler; and the message board regulars at BrianKeene.com.

AUTHOR'S NOTE

Although this book takes place in the year 1984, I have taken fictional liberties with some of the pop culture of the period. So if a character is listening to a song that wasn't popular until months later, keep in mind that it's a fictional timeline. This is 1984 as I remember it. Your memories—and mileage—may vary.

Although many of the Central Pennsylvanian locations in this novel are real, I have taken certain fictional liberties with them. So if you live there, don't look for your church or cemetery. You won't like what you find living beneath them.

PROLOGUE

Pat Kemp had his T-shirt off before he'd even closed the car door behind him. The night's breeze brushed against his back. He tossed the shirt onto the car's still hot hood. By the time they reached a good, flat, secluded spot, Karen had slipped hers off, too. Pat's eyes were drawn to her again and again. She spread the blanket out on the wet grass, right between the tombstones, while Pat pulled another beer off the dwindling six-pack of Old Milwaukee pounders. The cans were starting to get warm in the muggy June heat. He popped the tab. It sounded loud in the darkness. White foam bubbled around the rim. Pat took a sip and sighed in frustration.

"This place gives me the creeps. I still don't see why we can't just do it in the car."

Giggling, Karen gracefully stepped out of her sandals and lay down on the blanket. She arched her back, thrusting her breasts forward. They swelled against the fabric of her bra. She stretched like a cat, crossing and then uncrossing her long, slender legs.

"Because I like being outside. I like the stars, and the dark. It's romantic."

The moon hung full in the sky like a watchful yellow eye. It reflected off the stained glass windows of Karen's father's church. Each window bore a scene from the New Testament; the Sermon on the Mount, Jesus walking on water, bathing someone's feet, riding on a donkey, the crucifixion and the resurrection. Hell, maybe the moon really was an eye—His eye, the Almighty Peeping Tom. Doing it in the shadow of those windows, it felt like the Lord really was watching (not that Pat believed in Him); secretly, he thought that same impression might have more to do with Karen's insistence that they do it here, in the shadow of the church, than her romantic notions ever had. This was one way of getting back at her preacher daddy—by getting back at his God. Not that she'd ever admit it. Pat wondered if she was even aware of the secret reason for her compulsion. Probably not. Afternoon Phil Donahue talk show psychology aside, she was also just as horny as he was.

But why did it have to be in the graveyard? Irritated, he glanced around at the tombstones. It seemed wrong, somehow, fucking on top of dead people. Hell of a way to spend a Friday night.

Karen licked her lips. They glistened in the darkness, red and inviting.

Pat took another sip of beer, eyeing her breasts, concealed only by her skimpy bra, and the way her long, blond hair spilled over her bare shoulders. She didn't tease her hair way up high, as most of the other girls in school were doing now, and Pat liked that. Her skin looked pale, almost milky, in the light of the moon, and that made her full lips seem even redder. Karen's nipples stiffened beneath the fabric as he watched, and despite his annoyance with her, he grew hard.

It was in his nature. Pat was eighteen.

"Besides," Karen continued, slowly unfastening her bra and tossing it aside, "we do it all the time in your car. There's not enough room. I get cramps in my neck and hips."

He glanced back at the Nova, paid for with his college money (the savings bonds his grandparents had bought for him every birthday since he was two years old), because there was no way Pat was ever going to make it to college. His dad worked at the paper mill, like most of the men (and many of the women) in town, and the union had been on strike most of last year. They were still recovering financially from that. Money was tight, and his parents couldn't afford the cost. His grades were mediocre, and so was his athletic ability—too much smoking, tobacco and otherwise. That black Chevy Nova with the chrome magnum wheels represented all he had in the world. Pat worked part-time at the hardware store, after school and on weekends, to pay for the insurance and gas. He figured he'd probably work there after graduation, too, maybe even go full-time. In fact, he was certain of it. Graduation was next week. The Spring Grove Area High School's Class of 1984 was about to be unleashed on the world. School was over, except for finals. The junior high, intermediate, and elementary schools had all finished up that day. Summer had arrived. Might as well enjoy it while he could. Pat had no illusions. He'd get a brief respite, and then it was work, work, work—until retirement or alcohol's soft middle age, whichever came first, made him old before his time.

Just like his dad. Or dead, like Pat's older brother,

who'd been killed in Vietnam two weeks before America finally pulled out the troops.

Next week, after they graduated, many of Pat's friends would head for Ocean City, Maryland, for their senior trip. They'd get drunk and stoned and laid for a week, then come home to do more of the same before college. A few of the preppie kids were going to Fort Lauderdale (he supposed the preppies would also be partying), and Dave McCormick and Jeremy Statler were going to boot camp. Hell, even some of the underclassmen were heading for the beach to party, including his friend Nick Wagner, who wouldn't graduate until next year—but even *he* was going. While everybody else was having fun, doing something exciting, going through the ritual passage from high school into young adulthood, Pat was staying home to work. This moonlit tryst with Karen in the middle of the Golgotha Lutheran Church Cemetery was the extent of his senior trip.

And when Karen peeled off her shorts and he saw those white panties, and the soft tuft of blond hair sticking out from beneath them, he didn't care.

Karen noticed his sharp intake of breath. She smiled.

"You want me?"

Pat nodded. "You know I do."

"Only because you can sleep with me," she teased. "You don't really love me."

"Yes I do," he lied. In truth, he didn't love her, or at least he didn't think he did. Pat wasn't sure he'd ever been in love. Maybe in fifth grade, when he'd stared at Marsha Morrell all day long because she was so pretty, but that was more puppy love than the romance he'd seen in the movies and heard others talk about. Pat and Karen had been dating since their junior year. They'd gone to the prom together (at her insistence—

and oh how his buddies from shop class had laughed at him for it), and homecoming, and saw each other every weekend, but despite all that, he didn't love her. Pat stayed with Karen because she liked to have sex as much as he did.

Pat pulled off his shoes (black and white Vans with a skull and crossbones pattern) and gym socks, and stood barefoot in the wet grass. Prince's *Purple Rain* cassette played softly on the Nova's tape deck, drifting through the night. Personally, Pat fucking hated Prince, almost as much as he hated Duran Duran and Culture Club. But right now, Prince was hot. Smoking hot. He was all over the radio and MTV (Pat didn't have cable yet, but one of his friends did, and they spent a lot of time getting stoned and watching MTV). Karen loved Prince. She'd made him take her to see the movie three weeks earlier, and he'd almost fallen asleep (except during the part when Apollonia got naked and the segments with that bad-ass purple motorcycle). He was into Iron Maiden and Judas Priest and Quiet Riot and his brother's old Deep Purple and Black Sabbath albums. Those albums were all Pat had left of him. But if you lived in the suburbs, you were practically issued a copy of *Purple Rain* or *1999*, and besides, the chicks dug Prince, especially Karen, and especially *Purple Rain*, so he kept a copy hidden under his dash. Nothing put Karen in the mood quite like beer, a little weed, and "Darling Nikki."

Just like now.

"Come here. Lay down with me."

Smiling, she reached up and took his hand. Her fingers were cool. Sensuous. The light touch of her fingernails tickled his skin. He felt himself stiffen in response. Karen began to sing along with the song, something about masturbating with a magazine.

Draining the beer and tossing the can aside, he let Karen pull him down next to her on the blanket. They embraced, lying side by side, legs entwining around each other, arms and hands exploring, mapping, and pleasing. She kissed him hungrily, her mouth open and wet, her tongue gliding across his. Her hands slid down to his jeans, while Pat gently cupped her breasts, feeling her nipples stiffen between his thumbs and forefingers. Karen unbuckled his pants, unzipped his fly, and Pat arched his hips so that she could remove his jeans all together. His penis poked out of his boxer shorts, and Karen's eyes sparkled.

Jesus, he thought. *She gets hornier every time we do it.*

She removed her panties, then lay back and spread her legs. Her wetness glistened in the moonlight. Hastily, Pat fished a condom out of his discarded pants and tore at the wrapper. He couldn't get it open. Frantic, he ripped the cellophane with his teeth.

Karen giggled, her hand stroking him, keeping him hard.

Pat put on the condom and moved between her legs, then slid inside and sighed. He closed his eyes as her warmth surrounded him.

Did he love her? No. But he loved this. Loved being inside her. And if these really were the best days of his life (as his boss at the hardware store kept insisting they were), then this was a fine way to end them.

On the Nova's tape deck, "Darling Nikki" blurred into "When Doves Cry."

Karen watched him as he slowly thrust in and out of her in time with the music (though she doubted he realized it). Pat never looked at her when they made love. Oh, he kissed her, held her close, whispered her name. When he came, he'd squeeze her so tightly that she couldn't breathe. Occasionally, he'd talk to her;

breathless, nonsensical promises and praise, all uttered in the heat of the moment. Pillow talk, her girlfriends called it, though Karen had always thought it sounded more like baby talk.

But when he made her feel the way she felt now, Karen didn't mind—even if the act itself turned him into a child, rather than a man—because this was when she felt alive. Her best friend, Becky Schrum, had asked her several times over the past year why she dated Pat. Karen could have her pick of any guy in school. Why stay with this shop class loser whose main activities involved smoking marijuana behind the shop class and listening to Mötley Crüe tapes all night long? It was because of the way she felt when he touched her. Pat's fingers were electric. His eyes drank her in, worshiped her. Let her know she existed, was the center of his attention.

Karen Moore was a middle child. Her older sister, Kathy, was in her third year at Boston College, much to the delight of Karen's mother. Her younger sister, Katie, eleven years old, was heavily involved in the church youth group, which pleased Karen's father, the Golgotha Lutheran Church's minister. Karen's interests and activities excited neither of her parents. Her good grades were met with casual disinterest rather than enthusiasm. The school plays she participated in (*A Midsummer Night's Dream* this year and *Dracula* the year before) were not attended by either of her parents, who always cited previous obligations with their other two daughters. *Have a nice time dear, and break a leg.* The only time her father took an interest in her was when he cautioned her, frequently, against the perils of premarital sex and taking drugs, and how listening to Madonna and Prince was a fast track to hell. They'd had an argument about those very things earlier that evening.

Pat paid attention to her, and more, he provided the very same things that her father warned against—sex and drugs. She knew he didn't love her, but that was okay, because Karen didn't love Pat, either. He was a means to an end, a stopgap measure. Someone to hold her over until she left for college in the fall (no Boston for her—Karen was attending York Community College). Between now and then, she hoped to get an apartment in York and move out from under her sisters' shadows. Eventually, she hoped to meet someone else in college, someone who really loved her and who she really loved, someone who could take her away from all of her indifference once and for all.

Becky's boyfriend, Adam Senft, had jokingly asked Karen the other day if she felt like an adult (Becky and Adam wouldn't graduate until next year). Karen had said no, that she didn't feel any different. No different at all.

And she didn't, except now, when Pat tensed, muscles coiled as he approached orgasm. It was times like this that she felt something. Felt noticed. Needed. Wanted. That she was valued and important. It was that emotion, that sense of worth, that urged her own orgasm along.

A rock dug into her back from beneath the blanket. She barely felt it.

Karen closed her eyes and held her breath as she came.

Pat opened his own eyes, his head thrown back against the night sky, his breathing harsh, his moans drowning out Prince.

Karen's hips bucked beneath him as she felt him explode. Pat's body went limp, sagging against her. Karen lay still, panting. She nuzzled his chest. Pat flipped his sweaty bangs away from his eyes and sighed.

"That was all right."

She giggled into his chest hair.

Pat wondered where he'd left his cigarettes. Still lying on top of Karen, he glanced around—and froze.

Somebody was watching them.

A figure crouched atop a tombstone twenty yards away. The darkness hid its features. Pat couldn't tell if it was male or female, young or old. It sat still, frozen like stone. Despite the shadows surrounding it, the voyeur seemed to give off a pale, faint glow.

Karen felt Pat's entire body stiffen, but this time, it was very different than when they'd been making love. Pat pulled out of her and she gasped. She hated that sudden empty feeling.

"What's wrong?"

"Someone's watching us. Spying."

"Where?"

"Over there."

He peered into the darkness, trying to discern a face, even just the eyes, but the figure was still concealed in shadow. Again he noticed the muted glow. It seemed to be coming from the figure itself.

"Hey," Pat shouted at the voyeur. "What the hell you doing, man?"

The figure didn't respond, didn't move.

Karen sat up and grabbed her shirt, trying to cover herself with it.

Pat jumped to his feet, his hand curled into fists. "What's your problem, pal? You looking to get your ass kicked?"

Somewhere in the forest bordering the cemetery, an owl called out. The chirping insects fell silent.

Karen looked at what Pat was shouting at. Then she began to laugh. She slapped the blanket with one palm and howled.

"You think this is funny?" Exasperated, he glanced down at her.

Laughing louder, Karen pulled on her panties and fastened her bra. Pat's penis was already going limp, and the condom drooped the end. The sight brought a fresh round of giggles.

"What's wrong with you?"

"It's a statue, dummy." She pointed. "I saw it when we came in. One of those stone angels that people put on top of their tombstones. A life-sized one."

On the tape deck, Prince's "When Doves Cry" segued into "I Would Die For You."

"A statue?" Embarrassed, Pat looked back at the carved figure.

It was gone.

"It's not there anymore."

Not looking up, Karen said, "Quit messing around. I'm losing my buzz."

"I ain't—"

Then the stench hit him.

When he was ten years old, Pat rode his bike to the Colonial Valley Flea Market one Sunday afternoon, where he bought Bucky Dent and Rick Dempsey rookie cards for five cents each. On his way home, the cards slipped out of his bag. He'd stopped to gather them, and noticed a soda bottle along the side of the road. A mouse, attracted by the sweetness inside, had crawled into the bottle, but was unable to get out. Eventually, it died in there, and the hot sun had cooked it along the side of the road. When Pat experimentally tipped the bottle upside down, the mouse turned to liquid and oozed out of the opening. The stench was incredible, strong enough to make his eyes water. He'd picked up his cards and rode home, sick to his stomach for the rest of the day. He'd never smelled anything more revolting in his life.

Until now, and this was much worse.

It smelled like something rotting in an open grave.

Karen's eyes grew wide, staring at something behind him. She screamed.

Before Pat could turn around, something slammed into him from behind, knocking him to the ground. A crushing weight bore down on his back, pressing the air from his lungs. He struggled, but couldn't move. The stench was overpowering now. A massive, clawed hand closed around his head and smashed his face into the ground. Before the dirt obscured his vision, he caught a glimpse of wicked black talons, long and curved and caked with dirt. Mud filled Pat's ears and nose as his face was pressed deeper into the earth.

Karen's screams grew frantic.

Pat managed to get his head free. He opened his mouth, drew a breath, and tried to shout at Karen, to tell her to run, to head for the caretaker's house and call the cops, but before he could, the hand returned. It was cold against his cheek; the flesh felt like cottage cheese. The hand was also coated with translucent slime.

His attacker bashed Pat's head against a tombstone, once, twice. Hard. His face went numb and his vision blurred. It didn't hurt, really, which surprised him. On the third strike, Pat heard a cracking sound, and wondered what it was. The sound was very loud. He felt warm—and sleepy. And then he knew no more, and the best days of Pat Kemp's life became his last.

Karen screamed in terror, watching her boyfriend's brains drip off the bloody tombstone. The bloated figure laughed, looming over her, naked flesh pale and white in the moonlight. Slime dripped from its malformed limbs. Something monstrous dangled between its legs, bobbing and swaying like a hairy serpent. The attacker was human in shape—two arms, two legs, a head. But that was where all similarities ended. Its smell assailed her senses.

"P-please . . ."

The thing between the creature's legs stiffened, pointing toward her like a magnet. Whimpering, Karen shrank away, scampering backward like a crab.

She did not get far.

In the darkness, Prince sang, but only the dead were around to hear it.

An hour later, another figure crept through the cemetery, carrying a flashlight. The auto-reverse feature on the car's stereo had recycled the Prince cassette back to side two again. The title track's mournful guitar solo wailed at full volume, reaching its thunderous crescendo. Grumbling, the figure turned the stereo off. The cemetery was silent once more. The figure searched the tops of the tombstones until it found what it was looking for: jewelry—most belonging to the two teenagers, and some to others. Pocketing the loot, the figure turned to the task at hand.

A cloud passed over the moon, and the night grew darker. The figure glanced upward and shivered.

Then the figure collected their gore-covered clothing and blanket, empty beer cans, cigarette butts, and other belongings, and put it all in the trunk of the car. The few remains of Pat's body were tossed on top of the pile, and the figure slammed the trunk. Then it scrubbed Pat's blood and brains off the tombstone. Its stomach churned as it completed the grisly task. Red water turned pink, then clear. Finished, the figure emptied the bucket far away from the crime scene. Returning, it got behind the wheel of the Nova, started the vehicle, and drove away. The headlights were off. The driver went slowly, so that there would be no need for the brakes, and therefore no telltale flashing brake lights, which might be glimpsed by a late-night passerby—somebody coming home from a late shift at the paper mill, or last call at the Whistle Stop, or kids sneaking around when they should be in bed.

Darkness swallowed the car. The only sign that it had ever been there were two deep tire ruts in the grass. The graveyard was deserted again, and when the owl hooted a second time, there was nobody around to hear it.

Not even the dead.

CHAPTER ONE

It was the first day of summer vacation, and Timmy Graco's mind swam with the possibilities. Excitement and fun and really cool adventures awaited him for the next three months. There were miles of forest yet to be explored, bike rides to make down to the newsstand to buy his weekly fix of comic books, fishing to do at the local pond, camping out and telling ghost stories—and especially hanging out in the clubhouse.

And it all started with this—Saturday morning cartoons.

The milk in his bowl had turned into sugary, multicolored sludge. Timmy ate another spoonful of Fruity Pebbles, stared at the television with rapt attention, and tried to ignore his father.

"Timothy, did you hear me?" Randy Graco raised his voice, competing with the television's volume.

Timmy nodded, pushing his dark bangs out of his

eyes. "Yes, Dad. Weed the garden. I'll do it when *Thundarr* is over."

Thundarr the Barbarian was Timmy's favorite Saturday morning show, having replaced *The Herculoids* and *Tarzan, Lord of the Jungle* before them, and *Land of the Lost* before that. (*The Bugs Bunny and Daffy Show*, of course, remained his all-time reigning champion, however.) Two of his favorite comic book creators, Steve Gerber and Jack Kirby, worked on *Thundarr*, and Timmy was addicted to the program. Many of the kids at school argued that *He-Man and the Masters of the Universe* was better, but Timmy merely laughed at them. They were novices. He was a cartoon connoisseur.

"No," his father argued, his tone still patient, but bordering on something else. "You'll do it now. No arguments."

"Dad . . ." It was very hard to hear the TV.

"If you want an allowance to buy comic books and play those stupid video games, then you're going to have to work outside and around the house. Those are the rules."

Timmy's grandfather, who sat next to him on the couch, sighed.

"Oh, why don't you lay off him, Randy? It's the first day of summer vacation. Thundarr and Ookla the Mok are fighting the Rat People. He can weed the garden later."

"You stay out of this. I'll decide what's best for my boy."

"I can't stay out of it," the old man said. "You're doing it in here while I'm trying to watch my cartoons. I can't hear anything with you talking."

A commercial came on for a toy Timmy didn't want.

He watched it anyway, feigning interest. He felt the tension in the air. His father and grandfather glared at one another. Then his grandfather coughed and looked back at the television.

Timmy's father spoke slowly, the same way he did to Timmy when he was in trouble. "Dad, I really wish you wouldn't undermine my authority around the house. We agreed that if you were going to live here with us, that you'd respect Elizabeth's and my—"

"Shush." Timmy's grandfather cut him off. "How many times do I have to tell you? We can't hear this with you talking."

Timmy suppressed a smile.

"Never mind," Randy Graco grumbled. "I'll do it myself." He glared at them both and stomped to the door. "But this isn't over. I'm not putting up with this all summer."

After he was gone, Timmy and his grandfather glanced at one another and laughed. In the kitchen, Timmy's mother's radio played softly, a song by Dolly Parton, one of Elizabeth Graco's favorites. Outside, they heard Randy open the garage door.

"Thanks, Grandpa."

"Don't mention it. Besides, this is more important. Wish they'd had stuff like this when I was your age."

"What did you watch on TV?"

"Watch? We didn't watch anything—didn't even own a television. We listened to the radio. We had programs, too, but not like this."

Timmy frowned, trying to imagine listening to *Thundarr* on the radio, rather than the stuff they usually played—Michael Jackson and Cyndi Lauper and Huey Lewis and the News and Journey and "Come On Eileen" by Dexy's Midnight Runners. Timmy was just starting to discover music. Iron Maiden. Twisted Sister. Sugar Hill

Gang. Duran Duran. The Eurythmics. Van Halen. And new underground metal bands like Metallica, Slayer, and Anthrax, which some kids from shop class had turned him on to. Older stuff like Rush's *2112* and Black Sabbath's *Mob Rules* and Dio's solo material. One of the kids at school had shown him that if you turned Dio's album cover upside-down, it spelled out "Devil." Timmy wasn't sure what particular type of music he liked yet, but he knew it wasn't "Come On Eileen." That song was only good for dirty jokes on the playground.

"Nope," his grandfather repeated, "no shows like this."

"What kind of programs did you have?" Timmy asked.

His grandfather frowned. "Well, let's see. There was *The Shadow*. You would have liked it. *Green Hornet* and *Lights Out*. *The Lone Ranger*. *Amos and Andy*. Oh, and *Superman*, of course."

"Superman was around then?"

"He was indeed. No Thundarr, though."

"You like him better?"

"Oh, yeah." His grandfather's voice dropped to a whisper. "Superman's a pussy."

The two laughed at the forbidden word.

Timmy's grandmother had passed away five years earlier. Although he didn't admit it out loud, Timmy sometimes had trouble remembering her, especially her voice, and that made him sad. Dane Graco, father of Randy and grandfather to Timmy, had been living with them for the past nine months. A misstep on a ladder while hanging Christmas lights had led to a broken hip, followed by a near fatal bout of pneumonia. Compounded with his heart condition and general waning health, Timmy's parents had moved him into their house rather than having him live by himself, or

worse, putting him in an old folk's home. He'd taken
the spare room at the end of the hall, right next to his
grandson's.

Timmy loved his grandfather and enjoyed spending
time with him. He seemed so cool, so different than
other adults, especially other old people. He didn't talk
down to Timmy or treat him like a kid. His grandfather still had a sense of humor. He spoke to Timmy as
an equal, and was genuinely interested in the things
Timmy liked. Watching Saturday morning cartoons together was just one of their weekly rituals.

Timmy's father, Randy, worked seven days a week
shift work at the paper mill, the same place most of the
men in town found employment. Mr. Messinger, who
owned the newsstand where Timmy and his two best
friends, Doug Keiser and Barry Smeltzer, bought their
weekly fix of comic books, had once told them that if
the paper mill went out of business, the entire town
would dry up and blow away. All of the other busi-
nesses in town, the dry cleaners, the bars, Genova's
Pizza, the grocery store, the post office, the hardware
store, Old Forge Service Station, and even the
churches, lived and died on how well the mill was doing. If it had a bad quarter, the town itself had a bad
quarter. The union had gone on strike last year, and
when management hadn't budged, the walkout had
stretched on for ten months. Timmy remembered riding his bike through town and seeing his father walking the picket line. He'd seemed tired and beaten;
shuffling along like the zombies in a movie Timmy had
watched late one night on Channel 43, *Dawn of the
Dead*. Timmy remembered his father complaining
about scabs, and how he'd thought it funny at the time,
until they explained to him what scabs actually were.

Timmy still wasn't sure he understood it all. The scabs had families, too, and needed to work to support them.

When the strike was finally over, the Gracos' savings, like the savings of so many others, had dwindled down to nothing. As a result, for the past year his father had been working the extended shift, eagerly taking all the time and a half he could get (while still working seven days a week) in an effort to earn back the money they'd lost. His father was only home a few hours a day, and then he was either sleeping, working outside in the garden, mowing the lawn, or taking care of their chickens and other livestock. (Randy Graco played at being a part-time farmer and beekeeper.) As a result, Timmy didn't see much of him. His mother, Elizabeth, was usually busy with housework, playing Bridge with her friends, or participating with the Spring Grove Ladies Auxiliary. As a result, he spent more time with his grandfather than his parents. Despite Dane Graco's flagging health and how quickly he grew tired, his grandfather took him fishing along Codorus Creek, for walks in nearby Bowman's woods, and played *Pitfall*, *Asteroids*, and other video games on the Atari video game console.

Occasionally, when he was feeling up to it, Dane would drive the two of them into town and treat for two slices of pepperoni pizza at Genova's, where they'd feed quarter after quarter into the *Galaga*, *Paperboy*, and *Mappy* arcade machines until his grandfather ran out of change—usually after ten dollars or so. Once, when his father was in a particularly good mood and had a rare day off, the four of them had driven to Baltimore to watch the Orioles play the Yankees. He and his grandfather had jeered the opposing team until his mother had made them both hush. On the way home, the two of them had fallen asleep in the back of his parent's Aries K car.

When Timmy looked back on these moments, he smiled. He hoped that he never forgot them, the way he'd forgotten his grandmother. Forgetfulness seemed to be something that came with adulthood. Sometimes, when Timmy asked his parents about certain things from when they were growing up, they'd say that they couldn't remember. He'd noticed that other adults did this, too—except for his grandfather. Timmy wanted to be just like him, and never forget. Not remembering his grandmother was bad enough. He couldn't imagine forgetting the times spent with his grandfather, too.

Timmy knew how lucky he was. Yes, his father was stressed-out over his job, and that made him grumpy. And yes, his mother probably conceded to his father a little too much, especially when it came to decisions that affected Timmy—decisions with which she often disagreed. But Timmy knew they loved him, just as his grandfather loved him. Things could be worse. At least his parents were still there, and at least they paid attention to him. His friend Doug Keiser's father had run off three years ago, vanishing from the Whistle Stop bar one night with a waitress in tow, as well as the family car and the contents of their checking and savings accounts. Doug's mother had started drinking after that, and these days, that's all she seemed to do. She didn't work, just collected welfare checks—and newspapers. And magazines. Soda cans. Junk mail. Coupons. Empty bottles. Like a pack rat, she stacked them up in ever increasing piles all over the house. The towering, precarious walls of debris formed pathways through the living room, dining room, and hallway. Except for Doug's bedroom, their entire home smelled like booze and mildew, and she kept the windows and shades closed all day, preferring the darkness. If Doug's mother still loved her son, she had a funny way of showing it. She barely registered his presence most days, unless it was to holler at him for something. Doug was able to come and go as he pleased, simply because his mother didn't notice he was missing. Worse, she paid more attention to Timmy and Barry— too much attention. Sometimes, the way she touched them, or the way she smiled, or the things she said— Timmy knew it was wrong. Fingers lingering on their arms just a little too long or licking her lips when she talked to them, arching her back to push her sagging breasts out. It was like the beginning to one of those letters in the *Penthouse* magazines they sometimes read. Probably their imagination. They knew that. And Doug certainly hadn't noticed (or if he had, he'd never mentioned it). But still, sometimes it seemed like Carol Keiser was hitting on them. And that was just weird, because Carol Keiser was a grown-up.

Any time Timmy got mad at his parents, all he had to do to put things in perspective was think of Doug's mother. That made things better, made him grateful for what he had. And if that didn't work, there was always Barry's mom and dad to consider.

But none of the boys talked about what went on inside Barry's house. Especially Barry. Timmy and Doug both knew, or could guess. If Timmy thought about it too long, he wanted to cry. But the facts themselves remained unspoken between them, just like Doug's mom's odd behavior when drunk.

It was better that way. Some things were better left unsaid.

Doug and Timmy pretended they didn't see the bruises and cuts.

"And now back to . . . Thundarr the Barbarian!"

The music swelled. With the commercials finally over, they turned their attention back to the screen.

"Haven't seen this one before," his grandfather grunted.

"I have. It's a rerun. The Rat People live down under the ground."

"Kind of like that underground clubhouse you boys built up there in the cemetery?"

Timmy was too startled to reply. Nobody, especially grown-ups, was supposed to know about the Dugout. It belonged to him, Barry, and Doug. They'd spent most of last summer building it; digging a hole deep enough to stand in and wide enough to give them all elbow room, covering the hole with thick wooden planks, designing the trap door, putting in an old stovepipe so that they'd have air, and then covering the planks up with canvas they'd swiped from the Bowman's barn and laying sod over the planks and canvas so that it was hidden from view. Someone walking by wouldn't have known it was there. They'd worked on it every day, from early in the morning until sundown. The boys were proud of their engineering marvel, agreed that it was the finest clubhouse ever built, and had spent their weekends last fall and this spring sitting inside it, reading comic books and back issues of *Hustler* and *Gallery* that Barry had stolen from his dad. Nobody else was supposed to know it existed.

His grandfather winked. "Don't worry. Your secret is safe with me. I won't tell anybody."

"But how did you know about it?"

"Been taking my evening walk around the graveyard, cause that's what the doctor said to do, and mostly to give your mom and dad a little time to themselves while you're doing homework. Few weeks back,

I saw a covered stovepipe sticking out of the ground, right between the cemetery and Luke Jones's pasture. Wondered to myself, what was that doing there? When I walked up to it, I noticed the ground seemed kind of springy under my feet. You can hear those planks thud, even with the sod on top of them. So I poked around some more and found that leather strap sticking out of the dirt. Pulled on it, and low and behold, there's a secret hideout down under the ground."

"Man," Timmy whispered. "We thought nobody knew about it."

"They don't. Just me. Far as I know. And like I said, I won't tell. Left you boys a present. Didn't you wonder where the card table came from?"

He had, now that his grandfather mentioned it. Timmy had assumed that Barry or Doug rescued it from the town dump, another of their favorite hangouts. Unbeknownst to Timmy, they'd assumed the same thing about him. None of them had mentioned it, accepting the new addition with the disregard common to all twelve-year-old boys.

"Thanks, Grandpa! That's awesome."

"Don't mention it. Though, if you don't mind, I might stop in from time to time and take a peek at those dirty magazines you boys keep in that box. The ladies never looked like that back in my day."

They both laughed at this, and when Timmy's mom came into the living room and asked them what was so funny, they laughed harder. She walked away shaking her head.

"Listen," his grandfather said. "Don't be too hard on your old man. He means well."

Timmy frowned. "I know. But weeding the garden sucks."

"It does, indeed. But I used to make him do the

same thing when he was your age. He's just trying to do what he thinks is right. Trying to be a father. That's hard work. And meanwhile, you're trying to be a boy, and do what you think is right. That's hard work, too. And those two things, being a father and being a son, they never seem to agree. Certainly didn't when your father was twelve."

Timmy tried to imagine his father at his age, or his grandfather at his father's age, and found that he couldn't.

They watched Thundarr, Ookla, and Princess Ariel kick mutant butt, and both grinned. Outside, they heard Elizabeth calling for Randy.

"Orwell was wrong," his grandfather said.

"Who's that?"

"George Orwell. He was a famous writer. You'll probably learn about him when you get a little older. He wrote a book called *1984*. Took place now, but back then, it was the future, of course. Society was supposed to be a bad place by the year 1984. Not a good time to be alive. But he was wrong. These are the best times of them all."

Ten minutes after *Thundarr* ended, there was a knock at the front door. Timmy answered it. Doug stood in the doorway, panting and out of breath. His white, mud-splattered BMX Mongoose bike lay on its side in the yard. At twelve, Doug had boobies, just like a girl, the result of too many Kit-Kat bars and bowls of Turkey Hill ice cream. They jiggled as he shuffled his feet. There were dark circles under the armpits of his T-shirt. His thick glasses were fogged, and his forehead covered with sweat. His freckle-covered face looked splotchy.

Doug held up a long, black plastic tube, waving it around with excitement.

"I finished it," he gasped. "Worked on it all night long. You gotta see!"

"Well," Timmy said, "take it out."

Still trying to catch his breath, Doug shook his head. "At the Dugout. Let's get Barry and look at it there."

Timmy glanced back inside. His grandfather was still on the couch, but there was no sign of his parents.

"I can't right now," he whispered. "Dad says I've gotta weed the garden. He's already up there doing it. If I don't help, he's gonna be mad."

"Go ahead," his grandfather said. "This sounds more important. I'll handle your father."

Timmy smiled. "Are you sure? I thought you said he was doing what he thought was best."

His grandfather waved his hand. "Sure I'm sure. Just because he thinks it's for the best doesn't necessarily mean it is. Hell, it's the first day of summer vacation. Boys your age should be out playing and discovering. You shouldn't be working. There'll be enough of that when you're older. You boys don't know it, but these are the happiest days of your lives. Enjoy them while you can."

He paused, coughed, and flexed his fingers as if his left hand had gone to sleep. Shaking his head, he continued. His voice sounded weaker.

"And besides, your mom always says you should be outside anyway, instead of sitting in front of the television watching cartoons and playing Atari. Right?"

"Right!"

"Go on, now. You boys have fun. Later on, I'll whip your butts at *Pitfall*. I finally figured out how to get past those darn scorpions."

"Thanks, Grandpa!" Timmy started out the door, and then, on impulse, he did something he didn't do much anymore since turning twelve. He turned around, ran over to his grandfather, and gave him a sudden, fierce hug. His grandfather groaned in mock surprise and squeezed back with one arm. He was still flexing his free hand.

"I love you, Grandpa."

"I love you, too, kiddo."

He kissed Timmy's forehead, and Timmy caught a whiff of pipe smoke—another one of Grandpa's secrets, since the doctor and Timmy's parents had forbidden him to smoke.

"Are you okay?" Timmy asked.

"Sure," he wheezed. "Just a little short of breath this morning. Might lie down and take a nap while you boys are gone. Run on now, before your mom and dad come back inside. And make sure your dad don't see you leaving."

He ruffled his grandson's hair, which was cut just like Kevin Bacon's in *Footloose*, which Timmy and his family had seen just a few months before.

"Looks like a porcupine died on top of your head."

"At least my hair is still brown instead of silver."

"Wait till you're my age." His grandfather flexed his hand again. He made a face like he had indigestion.

"You sure you're okay, Grandpa?"

"Positive. Now go on. Get out of here."

"Love you," Timmy called again over his shoulder.

"Love you, too."

Timmy followed Doug outside into the front yard. Timmy's own BMX Mongoose was parked next to the sidewalk, its kickstand sinking into the grass. The boys hopped on their bikes and sped down the driveway.

"Did anybody else see it?" Timmy asked.

Doug shook his head. "My mom's still passed out."

"Why are you so out of breath?"

"Catcher was waiting for me when I went by. He came flying out of the driveway and almost bit my ankle."

Catcher, the bane of their existence (along with the occasional hazing from the neighborhood bullies Ronny, Jason and Steve), was a black Doberman pinscher that belonged to the Sawyer family. The Sawyers owned a dairy farm along the road between Doug's house and Timmy's. Bowman's Woods bordered the other side of the road. The boys had to pass through Catcher's territory any time they went to Doug's house or vice versa. The dog was usually near the farmhouse, but when they rode their bikes by, no matter how quietly, some sixth sense alerted him to their presence. If he was untied—which was often—he'd charge down the driveway, barking and growling. Each of the boys had ripped sneakers and torn socks as a result, and Barry had a scar on his calf from when the dog had latched onto him almost two years ago.

It was one of the few scars on Barry of which the other boys could actually identify the source.

"I hate that dog," Timmy mumbled as they reached the end of the driveway.

"Yeah. One of these days we'll teach him a lesson."

Timmy nodded. Over the last few weeks, he'd been formulating a plan to do just that, but he hadn't yet told the other boys about it.

The Graco home, a one-story, three-bedroom rancher with two acres of land, was built on the side of a hill. The garden was at the rear of the property, near the top of the hill, bordering Barry's parent's home and Bill and Karen Wahl's house—an elderly couple with no children left at home. Normally, Timmy and Doug would have just gone through the backyard and up the hill to Barry's. But with Timmy's dad in the garden, pulling weeds that Timmy was supposed to pull, they followed his grandfather's advice and took the long way around.

Pedaling out into the road, they turned right onto Anson Road, a narrow two-lane stretch of blacktop that cut through the countryside, giving drivers a back road shortcut from Route 516 to Route 116. They followed that to the edge of the Graco's property, past the acre lot his father had turned into a hillside pasture, complete with a small, two-stall barn for their one cow and two sheep. To the left was Laughman Road, which led to Doug's house—if you made it past Catcher—and on their right was a narrow strip of woods. "Our woods," the boys called it, though technically, it belonged to the church. Passing these, they turned right again onto Golgotha Church Road, an even narrower road that went straight uphill. On their left stretched the cemetery. The bottom of the hill was filled with old graves and crumbling crypts from the 1800s. The upper portion of the hill and beyond was covered with newer, more durable monuments. On their right lay the woods and Timmy's parents' property. The trees kept them hidden from Randy Graco's sight.

This was their playground—the woods, the cemetery, the Dugout. Occasionally, they made an excursion to the town dump to find treasures or shoot at the rats with their BB guns, or went over into Bowman's Woods to catch minnows and crayfish in the creek and shoot water snakes, and once a week they rode their bikes into Spring Grove to buy comic books at Mr. Messinger's newsstand (they left their BB guns at home, then), but for the most part, they were content to not stray from the cemetery and surrounding forest. Over the years, this area had served as everything from the Death Star to a pirate ship to Amazonian jungles—

complete with imaginary dinosaurs—to the battlefields of World War Two.

This was their world, and they ruled it; three kings who would never grow old, but remain twelve forever. Summer was just beginning, and the days were long and endless, and their cares and fears seemed like small things when cast against the backdrop of the deep blue sky overhead.

Doug wiped the sweat from his eyes. "You know the *Frogger* machine down at the Laundromat?"

"Yeah."

"I got the high score yesterday. But then Ronny Nace unplugged it and erased everything."

"Ronny's a dick."

"Yeah. He was pissed because I played that new Toto song on the jukebox."

They hopped off their bikes and walked them to the top of the hill. Timmy could have pedaled it, but Doug was obviously tired.

Their noses crinkled as they passed by a dead groundhog, its midsection ruptured by a car tire, its fly-infested innards exposed to the sunlight and open air. Maggots squirmed through rotten meat. Though it was a disgusting sight, neither one of them could help but study it closely.

"God," Doug panted. "That stinks."

They hurried past the road kill.

"You know what's weird?" Timmy fanned the air with his hand. "That's the only one we've seen in a week. Usually, there's two or three per day—possums, skunks, groundhogs, squirrels, cats, snakes. Now, there aren't any at all, other than that fresh one."

"Maybe the state is cleaning them up. Sending a road crew around or something."

"Yeah, maybe."

And though the boys wouldn't notice, the dead groundhog they'd just passed by would be missing the next day as well. Rotted and putrescent, it was food for something. Fodder.

"Glad my grandpa let us sneak out," Timmy said.

"Your grandpa is so cool," Doug said. "I wish mine was like that."

"Isn't he?"

Doug made a sour face. "No. When we go to visit him, all he does is preach to us about the Bible and fart a lot. My dad used to say that's because he was full of hot air."

Timmy laughed obligingly.

Doug talked about his father all the time, and it made Timmy sad. Doug seemed to believe that his dad was coming back for him, any day now, and that they'd go live in California together. According to Doug, his father called or wrote to him every week, told him stories about Hollywood, how he'd gotten a job as a stunt man, the movies he'd worked on, the famous actors he'd met, the things he'd seen; but none of it was true. Last fall, Barry and Timmy had discovered that their friend was lying. His mother had let it slip when she was drunk. Taunted Doug with it. There were no letters or long distance phone calls. They hadn't heard from Doug's father since he'd left town. Too embarrassed for their friend, Timmy and Barry never brought it up, allowing the charade to continue. No sense confronting him with the truth. If it made Doug feel better to believe that his father had found a career as a stunt man and that he would one day return, then that was good enough for them.

Timmy was about to ask Doug if he'd gotten any new letters when something in the cemetery caught his attention. Near one of the cracked, mossy crypts, two of the older tombstones had sunken into the earth. Only their lichen-covered tops were sticking out. The ground around them was also depressed, as if a giant groundhog had burrowed under the grass.

Weird, he thought. Had they been like that yesterday? He didn't think so.

"I don't know," Doug whispered. "Sometimes I think about what it would be like if my grandpa died, and when I do, I don't feel sad."

"What do you feel?"

He shrugged. "Nothing. I don't feel anything. Is that weird?"

"Yeah, but that's okay, 'cause everybody knows you're weird anyway."

Scowling, Doug punched Timmy in the arm. Timmy laughed.

As the road leveled out, they hopped back onto their bikes. The Golgotha Lutheran Church sat to their left, and Barry's house was on the right—a red-brick, one-story home with a white garage off to one side and a rusted swing set in the backyard, facing Timmy's house on the hill below. The church parking lot served as its driveway. Barry's father, Clark Smeltzer, was the church caretaker and groundskeeper for the cemetery.

"Besides," Timmy continued, his laughter drying up, "at least your grandpa's not as bad as . . ."

He didn't finish, and instead, just nodded his head in the direction of Barry's house.

"Yeah," Doug agreed. "Nobody's as bad as that."

They wheeled into the parking lot and dismounted, propping their bikes against the side of the Smeltzer's white garage. Doug still clutched the plastic tube. They approached the house, making sure to avoid the side of the garage closest to Timmy's house, lest his father, still working in the garden, looked up over the hill and saw them.

As he knocked on the door, Timmy wondered who would greet them this morning—their friend, his mother, or the monster that lived with them.

It opened, and Barry's mother, Rhonda, smiled at them through the screen door. The boys cringed as they always did when she smiled. One of her front teeth had been missing for the past year. They heard the soft sounds of a Barbara Mandrel song coming from the radio in the kitchen.

"Hi, Mrs. Smeltzer."

"Good morning, b—"

The radio shut off.

"Who is it?" Clark Smeltzer barked from behind her.

Rhonda's smile instantly crumbled, her happiness melting as quickly as a popsicle on a summer sidewalk. Timmy noticed something odd; diamond earrings sparkled on her ears. The Smeltzers didn't have a lot of money, and Timmy had never seen her wear something like that.

She scrambled out of the way and Barry's father replaced her in the doorway. He glowered at them, obviously suffering from a hangover. His eyes were bloodshot, and there was something dried and crusty in his mustache and beard. He wore yellow-stained boxer shorts and an olive work shirt, unbuttoned. Black lint poked out of his swollen belly button. Despite his slovenly appearance, a gold watch adorned his wrist, replacing the Timex he usually wore. Timmy frowned, backing away a few steps. Mr. Smeltzer stank of sour sweat, booze, and despair. Timmy wondered if he was still drunk.

"What the hell do you two want? Ain't you got jobs this summer?"

Timmy shook his head, his spirits sinking. Clark Smeltzer's slurred speech answered his question.

"No, sir. We were just looking for Barry."

"You woke me up. Didn't go to bed but an hour ago."

"We're sorry," Timmy apologized. "We didn't know."

"Banging on the door this early in the morning. The hell's wrong with you? Ain't you got nothing better to do?"

"We just wanted to show Barry something," Doug explained, holding up the black tube.

Clark Smeltzer eyed it and frowned. "What's that? Poster?"

"A map," Doug said. "I made it."

"Should be playing baseball or football, instead of drawing. That's queer shit. You a fag? Ain't no wonder your old man took off."

There was a shocked gasp of dismay behind him. "Clark! Don't say such things to that boy."

"Get the fuck back in the kitchen, Rhonda, if you know what's good for you!"

Timmy started to turn away. Doug looked like he was ready to cry. His bottom lip quivered, and his ears and cheeks had turned scarlet. The color made his freckles seem more numerous than ever.

"Where the fuck you going?"

"Sorry we woke you up, Mr. Smeltzer," Timmy apologized again. "Can you tell Barry we stopped by?"

"He ain't here. He's over in the cemetery, working. Same way you boys should. Kids today are lazy. Don't know how good you got it. Ought to get a damn job."

Timmy froze. "If we're so lazy, how come Barry's out doing your job, while you're sleeping off last night's bottle?" The words left Timmy's mouth before he could stop them.

Clark Smeltzer stared at him in angry surprise. His eyebrows narrowed. Both Doug and Barry's mother groaned.

"You know what your problem is, Graco? You're a fucking smart-ass. Got a real attitude problem."

Timmy didn't respond.

"I've got a good mind to tan your hide."

Mr. Smeltzer shoved the screen door open and stepped out onto the porch, towering over the boys. His hand curled into a fist. Doug retreated into the yard. Timmy held his ground.

"Go ahead," Timmy challenged. "You lay one hand on me and I promise you'll regret it."

Barry's dad charged. Timmy stood his ground.

"Clark!"

Barry's mother rushed outside and grabbed her husband's arm, wrestling him away from the boys. He shook her off and grinned humorlessly. His flashing gray teeth reminded Timmy of a shark's.

"Bet your father will want to hear about this, Graco. He won't be too goddamned happy when I tell him how his son is smarting off to adults."

"Go ahead and tell him. He's right down over the hill, working in the garden. In fact, I'll go with you."

Timmy knew that his father despised Clark Smeltzer as an abusive, bullying drunk, but furthermore, Clark Smeltzer knew it, too. Timmy wasn't worried.

"Come on, Doug." He turned his back on Barry's parents.

"You get out of here," Mr. Smeltzer hollered. "And don't go bothering Barry, either. He's got work to do!"

The boys ignored him.

"And stay out of that cemetery. You hear me? I don't want to see you playing there no more."

Doug stopped. "But we always play there, Mr. Smeltzer."

"Not no more you don't. Stay clear of it. I've told Barry the same thing. He's not to be there except for when he's helping me, and never after sundown. Those are the new rules. Gonna put up signs this week saying so."

"You don't own the cemetery," Timmy said. "You're just the caretaker."

"Don't matter. You mind me, boy. I catch you there and it'll be your ass. That's a promise."

Without glancing back or responding, the boys hopped on their bikes and pedaled away, still careful to stay out of Randy Graco's line of sight. Timmy wondered if his father had heard Mr. Smeltzer's outburst, and then decided that he didn't care.

"Jesus," Doug panted as they reached the end of the parking lot. "You're crazy, Timmy. You know that?"

"Why?"

"Mouthing off the way you did? Being a smart-ass? I thought he was gonna lay you out cold, man. One of these days you're going to get smart with the wrong person."

"You sound like my mom."

"I'm just saying, is all."

"It's bullshit, and I'm not going to take it. He's not gonna push me around the way he does Barry."

Doug stopped pedaling and slammed on his brakes. His back tire skidded on the pavement. Balancing the plastic tube, he cleaned his glasses on his shirt.

"You okay?" Timmy asked.

"Yeah. Why wouldn't I be?"

"Well, what he said about your old man . . ."

Doug shrugged. "Oh, I don't care about that. I

mean, it's not true. You know? My dad loves me. When he comes back from California, everyone will see."

"Yeah."

Timmy glanced back at the house. Barry's parents had gone back inside. He wondered what price Barry's mother would pay behind that closed door, perhaps right now, for stopping her husband from hitting him. Then he wondered why she didn't do the same when he hit Barry. If she'd stuck up for her son's friends, couldn't she stick up for her own son as well?

Doug put his glasses back on and smiled. It looked false. Strained. They coasted into the road. Timmy's handlebars were sweaty. So was Doug's shirt, especially around his armpits.

"What are you thinking about, Timmy?"

"Did you notice that both of Barry's parents had new jewelry on? It looked really expensive."

Doug shook his head. "No, I didn't see it. But big deal. As bad as he treats Barry and his mother sometimes, we should be happy he's spending money on them at all."

"Yeah, I guess you're right. I don't know. Just seemed weird. He never does stuff like that. Barry has to bum money from us for lunch at school sometimes."

"Maybe Mr. Smeltzer got a raise."

Timmy shrugged. "Yeah, maybe."

"It's not really any of our business."

"I guess not."

"So what now?" Doug asked.

"Let's go find Barry."

"You heard Mr. Smeltzer. He said we weren't supposed to play over there anymore. Said he'd kick our ass."

"The heck with him. He ain't watching us right now.

Probably went back to bed by now. Let's find Barry. I want to see this map you made."

"But what if someone else spots us?"

"Who's gonna see? Other than Barry, there's nobody out there this morning."

"Except for the dead people."

Timmy grinned. "Well, yeah, except for the dead people. They're always there. Wouldn't be a cemetery without them."

"Yeah," Doug agreed. "It would just be a bunch of empty holes in the ground."

CHAPTER TWO

After making sure Barry's parents weren't watching them from the windows, the boys crossed Golgotha Church Road and wheeled around the church and into the cemetery. To their left, down over the sloping hill, were the old graves. Timmy noted again how two of them had sunk into the ground. In front of them, sprawling out behind the church, was the more modern portion of the graveyard. This part stretched nearly a quarter-mile to the west. It was split into three large sections by narrow, cracked blacktop roadways, each barely wide enough for a single car to drive on.

The first road, off to their left, separated the older graveyard at the bottom of the hill from the more modern cemetery above. Halfway along this path was an old yellow clapboard utility shed with a rusty tin roof that was covered with fallen tree branches and leaves. Beyond the shed was another stretch of woods. The boys often played inside the old shed, gaining access,

when they didn't have Barry's dad's keys, through a
boarded up window at the rear, half hidden by a massive pile of dirt left over from new graves. Inside was a
small backhoe, a riding mower, two push mowers, a
grass catcher, winch, shovels, rakes, pickaxes, hoes,
wooden planks and plywood to cover up open graves,
canvas tarps, stone markers, plastic flowers and
wreaths, vases for the graves, and little flags for Veteran's and Memorial Days. Because of the dirt floor, it
always smelled musty inside. Barry, Doug, and Timmy
often waited with their pump-action BB and pellet
guns until a rat or groundhog burrowed up through
the floor. Then they'd nail it. Barry especially enjoyed
this activity since it was one of the few times his father
seemed genuinely pleased with him; they were taking
care of the rodents that plagued the graveyard. This
morning, the shed's doors hung open, swaying slightly
in the breeze, and the tractor was missing—both signs
that Barry had been there earlier.

The path to their right bordered the northern end of
the cemetery. On one side were gray and brown tombstones carved from granite and marble. On the other
side was a long, sloping pasture in which beef cattle
grazed. An electric fence kept the cows from wandering into the graveyard. Last summer, Barry and Doug
had dared Timmy to pee on the fence, offering up back
issues of *Man-Thing*, *Defenders*, *Captain America*,
and *Kamandi* from their collections, as well as one of
Doug's *Micronauts* action figures (a blue Time Traveler) and some of Barry's extra *Wacky Packages* cards.
It was a hard deal to turn down, especially because
Timmy collected *Defenders* and it was an issue he
didn't have—the one where Hulk, Dr. Strange,
Valkyrie, Nighthawk and the rest of the team fought a
villain called Nebulon, and Chondu the Mystic pos-

sessed the Hulk's pet fawn. So, steeling himself, he'd peed on the fence, got the shock of his life, and had endured two days of not being able to sit down comfortably along with the jeers of his two best friends. His testicles had turned black and blue, and after returning from the doctor's office, his parents had grounded him for two weeks. By that time, it didn't matter. Admitting to his parents what he'd done had been, until that point, the most mortifyingly embarrassing moment of Timmy Graco's life.

And it had totally been worth it.

At the bottom of the hill, beyond the lush, rolling pasture, was a small hollow with a thin stream running through it's center, emptying into a deep pond, complete with diving board, boat dock, and a tire swing hanging from a drooping willow tree. Next to the pond stood Luke Jones's three-story farmhouse and a long barn, both white with green tiled roofs. Several other outbuildings sat clustered around the two larger structures. The view beyond the farm was clear for miles and miles—the paper mill's stacks belching white smoke into the sky, the twin towns of Colonial Valley and Spring Grove, and in the distance, on the horizon, the forested tops of Pigeon Hills and the radio transmitter tower for 98YCR nestled among them. On a quiet day, visitors to the cemetery could hear the distant whine of traffic on Route 116, which cut through Spring Grove and passed by Colonial Valley on its way to Hanover and Gettysburg.

The far end of the cemetery was bordered by a cornfield, which bridged the pasture to the side with the older graveyard, shed, and vast forest beyond them. It was at the intersection of the cemetery, cornfield, and the electric fence that the boys had built the Dugout. It sat only a few feet away from the blacktopped cemetery path, invisible to passersby (except, apparently, Timmy's grandfather), and the electric fence skirted the fort's far edge. They weren't sure whose property it was on, the churches or Mr. Jones's—and in truth, they'd never stopped to consider it. At twelve, they saw all of the area as theirs, and begrudged the adults their usage of it. Had Timmy been able to figure out a way to tax all the grownups for their usage of the surrounding countryside, he'd have happily done it.

They rode down the pathway, searching for Barry. The smell of fresh cut grass hung thick in the air. A bird chirped happily overhead. White and yellow butterflies hovered over a puddle leftover from the rainstorm two days before. Honeybees buzzed in a patch of clover.

As he pedaled, Timmy watched the gravestones flash past; SARAH MYERS 1900–1929; ABBY LUCKENBAUGH 1922–1923; BRITNEY RODGERS, AGE 5; BRETT SOWERS 1913–1983, WWII VETERAN; KENNETH L. RUDISILL 1923–1976. He'd spent so much time amongst these markers that the names and dates were as familiar as the kids in his class. A lot of the people buried here were children, many of them infants, many more around his age. That had always disturbed him. Timmy normally felt immortal, like the *Eternals*, another of his favorite comic books. He didn't like to think about the alternative—that somebody his age could die. But here was proof, carved in stone, that it happened all the time—that kids his age died. His grandmother was buried in this section as well. Timmy didn't remember her very well, just vague impressions. Her perfume, the way she'd always tried to get him to eat more when they visited, how she'd squeezed him when they hugged. He often had to look at photographs just to remember her face. Next to her grave-

stone was a matching marker for his grandfather;
Dane Graco's name and date of birth were already engraved in the marble, just waiting on his death to complete the inscription. Timmy didn't like to think about
that either, and as a result, he avoided his grandmother's grave whenever possible. Seeing his grandfather's name along with that blank date, as if the stone
were just waiting for Dane Graco, gave Timmy the
creeps.

Behind them, five arch-shaped stained glass windows on the rear of the church stared out, overseeing
the cemetery. They'd also always given Timmy the
creeps. Often on Sunday mornings, when the sermon
was especially boring, he'd stare at the windows and
make up spooky stories about the scenes depicted in
them. Sometimes he even wrote them down in the
margins of his church bulletin, much to his mother's
chagrin. She told him it was disrespectful, bordering
on blasphemous. Timmy didn't understand that. The
Bible was full of scary stories and characters—witches
and black magic, zombies and demons, giants and sea
monsters, murder, even cannibalism. Why were his little tales any worse? Why wouldn't God like them? He
told some of the stories to Barry and Doug, and they'd
asked him for more. Their eagerness had inspired
something inside Timmy. He thought that when he
grew up, he might like to write comic books. Not draw
them, of course. He was lucky if he could draw stick
figures. Doug was the artist in their group. He'd been
working on the map for the last four months, and
couldn't wait to unveil it. Timmy couldn't wait, either.
Doug was much more talented at drawing than
Timmy, but Timmy could write, and comic books
needed writers to tell the artists what to draw. Maybe

he'd grow up to be like Steve Gerber or J. M. DeMatteis or even Stan "the Man" Lee.

At twelve, Timmy's entire world pretty much revolved around comic books. His father had bought him his first two when he was six—an issue of *The Incredible Hulk*, in which the jade-jawed giant fought a group of villains called the U-Foes (before that, Timmy's only exposure to the Hulk was the television program on Friday nights, and the Hulk hadn't been able to talk in that) and an issue of *Star Wars* that featured a blaster-toting, man-sized, talking bunny rabbit named Jax who had helped Han Solo and Chewbacca ward off a bounty hunter.

After finishing these comics, he was hooked. Like any other young boy's hobby, it soon became an obsession.

Each week, he rode his bike down to the newsstand and bought his weekly fix of comics. His selections varied, but his favorites were *Transformers, The Incredible Hulk, Sgt. Rock, Marvel Two-In-One, The Amazing Spider-Man, Moon Knight, The Defenders* and *Captain America*. He supplemented his newsstand purchases with mail-order comics from a company called Bud Plant. He preferred underground books like *The First Kingdom* and *Elfquest*, and wished he could figure out a way to get their X-rated, adults-only material like *Omaha the Cat Dancer* and *Cherry Poptart* without his mother's knowledge. In addition to the new monthly issues, he bought every back issue he could find. Sometimes he saw advertisements in the backs of comics for comic book stores, but the closest one was Geppi's Comic World in Baltimore, and he'd only been there twice (but the visits were enough to impress upon him that the proprietor, Steve Geppi, was a god among men). The next closest was in New

York City, four hours away. Instead, Timmy scrounged back issues at yard sales and the Colonial Valley flea market. On Sundays, he'd ride his bike there and buy old back issues for fifty cents each. The woman who ran the flea market had roughly 5,000 comic books at home ranging from the 1950s to the mid-1970s. According to popular rumor, they'd belonged to her son, who was killed in Vietnam. Timmy didn't know much about Vietnam, other than that both his father and Barry's had fought there. Timmy's dad had been in the Airborne and Clark Smeltzer served on a riverboat. Timmy was sorry her son had died, but he liked to think that whoever the guy was, he'd appreciate his comic collection now being enjoyed by kids like he once was. Every Sunday, she'd bring in a new box. She was beloved by all the neighborhood children, and loathed by their parents, whom the kids begged for more money.

Last Christmas, his grandfather had bought him a copy of the *Overstreet Comic Book Price Guide*. When Timmy saw what some of his comics were worth, it fueled his obsession even more.

Needless to say, Timmy had amassed quite a comic book collection. His father often groused about getting rid of them, that they took up too much space, and that a boy his age should be more interested in sports than reading "funny books," which is what Randy Graco insisted on calling them. But Timmy had no interest in playing professional sports. Anybody could throw a football or baseball, but making up a story about how the Devil had taken over Earth, like J. M. DeMatteis had done in *The Defenders #100*—that took real talent.

Riding beside him, Doug panted, out of breath. His bike's spokes flashed in the sunlight.

"You need to lay off those Twinkies," Timmy teased.

"Screw you."

"Your Calvin Klein's are sticking to your thighs, man. Gross."

"Least I got designer jeans. You're wearing those same old Levis from last year."

"Only reason you got Calvins is because your mom bought them at the thrift store. It's not like she shops at Chess King."

"Bite me."

Laughing, they punched at each other, almost crashing their bikes in the process.

They found Barry near the end of the cemetery, right on the border between the graveyard and the budding cornfield. Over the next three months, the stalks would go from ankle-high to towering over their heads. Barry was raking two car tire tracks out of the grass, smoothing out the damage. He waved as they approached, and flipped his long blond hair out of his face. Even at twelve, his lean muscles flexed beneath his black Twisted Sister T-shirt, the result of many days of hard labor. Although they'd never admit it, both Timmy and Doug often felt self-conscious when standing next to their blue-eyed friend. The girls at school paid attention to Barry, and ignored them, for the most part.

As they got closer, Timmy could hear the tinny strains of Def Leppard's "Die Hard the Hunter" coming from the earphones around Barry's head.

"Hey guys." Barry stopped his Walkman and removed the earphones, letting them dangle around his neck.

Timmy and Doug skidded to a stop.

"What happened here?" Timmy stared at the rutted ground.

"My dad says some teenagers must have drove through here last night. Went off the road and through this section of grass where there aren't any tomb-stones, and then kept on going right on through the corn."

"Mr. Jones is gonna be mad when he sees that," Doug said, eyeing the bent and broken stalks. "They messed his field up."

"Nah. Corn grows back so fast, he won't even notice it. By this time next week, the stalks will be twice the height they are now.

Timmy and Doug agreed that he was right.

"How'd you guys know I was here?" Barry asked.

Timmy nodded back toward the church. "Your dad told us."

Barry's face darkened. "Oh. Did he say anything else?"

"Yeah."

"How bad?"

"Well, he was pretty angry . . ."

"He was up late," Barry apologized. "I went to bed after that special Friday night *Family Ties* was off, but I couldn't sleep. I was in bed listening to Doctor Demento on the radio. I heard Dad get up around mid-night and leave the house. He didn't come back till early this morning. Said he'd chased some kids out of the cemetery. Same kids that did this, I guess."

Timmy shrugged. "Was he drinking?"

"I don't know. He stayed awake long enough to tell me what he wanted me to do today. Then he went to bed."

Barry refused to meet his stare, and Timmy knew then that he was lying.

"He was pretty pissed off," Timmy repeated. "More than usual."

"I don't want him anymore pissed than he already is," Barry said. "My birthday's coming up, and he said I could get a Yamaha Eighty dirt bike if I listened."

Timmy frowned. Since when did the Smeltzers have the money for a dirt bike?

"Was he angry at you guys for waking him up, or just angry in general?"

"Both," Doug said. "He called me a fag, because I don't play baseball and stuff. Said that's why my dad left."

"I'm sorry, man. You know that's not true."

"I know," Doug said softly, "but it still hurts sometimes. Just cause I don't play sports, that's no reason to say mean things like that."

Barry squeezed his friend's shoulder. "I feel bad. He was probably just really tired."

"He was acting weird." Timmy refused to let Barry make excuses for his father's behavior. "Said we weren't allowed to play here anymore, and you weren't allowed here, either, after sundown."

"That's true," Barry confirmed. "Some new rule about trespassing. Guess these teenagers were the last straw. Nobody is allowed in here after dark. He called the church board this morning, right before he went back to bed. Sounds like they were in agreement. He got permission to get some signs made up and everything."

Doug dismounted. "What about during the day?"

"Well," Barry said, finished with the raking, "he told me we weren't allowed to play around here anymore, especially not after dark. The way it sounded, he didn't want me here at all, except to work. No bike riding. No skateboarding."

"That sucks," Timmy spat. "What's the big deal?"

Barry shrugged.

Timmy felt his summer slipping away, and it angered him.

"Where are we supposed to hang out instead?"

"The dump?" Doug suggested. "Or over in Bowman's Woods? I bet Mr. Bowman wouldn't care. Or Mr. Jones's pond?"

"No way." Timmy slid off his bike and flicked a bug off the front mag wheel. "Only thing we can do at the pond is fish. We can't swim in it with all those snapping turtles and water snakes." He shuddered at the mere thought of snakes, then continued. "And too many other people go through Bowman's Woods— hunters, hikers, older kids. Besides, it's too far to go every day. The Dugout is right here. We're just going to abandon it?"

"We could build a new one. A *better* fort." Doug segued into the introduction from *The Six Million Dollar Man*. "We can rebuild it. We can make it better than it was before. Better. Stronger. Fas—"

"Shut up," Barry said, rolling his eyes. "Retard."

Doug pouted. "Then how about a tree house?"

Timmy scoffed. "A tree house? Get real, man. Those are for pussies. It's too easy for other kids to raid. You guys want Ronny, Jason, and Steve stealing our stuff when we're not around?"

Ronny Nace, Jason Glatfelter, and Steve Laughman, each a year older and a grade higher than the boys, were the town bullies—and their sworn enemies. They lived beyond the Jones farm, along Route 116, but often road their bikes up the hill and into Timmy, Doug, and Barry's territory. Presently, an uneasy truce existed between the two trios, but all of them knew that before the summer was over, because of slights real or imagined, a new war would break out. The last time, it had been because Ronny and Jason had thrown rocks at Doug and called him fat boy when he rode by their homes on his way to the Colonial Valley Flea Market.

The time before that, it had started because Barry shot Steve in the butt with his BB gun.

Although none of the boys would have admitted it out loud, they looked forward to the yearly wars. The familiarity was comforting.

Barry wiped his sweaty brow with the back of his hand. "Look. If we're inside the Dugout, then my dad can't see us, anyway. He'll never even know that we're over here. I don't see the point in moving. And besides, when we sneak out at night, it ain't like nobody knows. We can play over here then."

All three of them were experts at sneaking out, crawling through their bedroom windows after their parents had gone to sleep and getting into midnight mischief; or at least Barry and Timmy were. Doug often used the front door rather than the window, since his mother never seemed to care if he was home or not.

Agreeing that Barry was right, they turned toward more pressing matters. Timmy decided to keep quiet about the fact that his grandfather was aware of the Dugout's existence. He wasn't sure how the guys would react.

"Is that the map?" Barry asked, pointing at the tube in Doug's hands. "You done with it?

Grinning proudly, Doug nodded.

"Let's see it."

Doug glanced around furtively, as if expecting Barry's father, or perhaps one of their archenemies, to be lurking behind a tombstone.

"Let's take it to the Dugout first. Safer there."

With Barry perched atop Timmy's handlebars, they rode over to the fort, and stowed their bikes in the tall weeds, obscuring them from view. They made sure no one was in sight, and then pulled up the trapdoor, quickly climbing down the ladder and disappearing into the hole. Once they were settled, Timmy pulled the trapdoor shut, plunging them into darkness. Barry clicked on the flashlight and shined the beam around until Timmy struck a match and lit the rusty kerosene lamp they'd salvaged from the dump. The soft glow filled the underground space, flickering off the moldering centerfolds of naked women and posters torn from the pages of *Fangoria* and *Heavy Metal* hanging from the tan-colored wood paneling, which had been rescued from the dump and pinned to the soil with twelve-penny nails, clothesline, and generous amounts of duct tape. (The most important thing that Timmy's father had ever taught him was that duct tape could be used for anything—from battlefield triage to plumbing to hanging pictures.)

Doug moved a stack of comic books, *Hustler*, and *Cracked* magazines off the card table and pulled the cap off the plastic tube, while Timmy and Barry fished cans of Pepsi out of an old Styrofoam cooler. With something bordering on reverence, Doug took out the map, unrolled it, and spread it across the table.

"Wow," Timmy exclaimed after a moment's pause.

Barry whistled in appreciation.

"You guys like it?"

"Totally." Barry's attention was glued to the map.

"You did good, man." Timmy clapped Doug on the back. "It's amazing."

Spread out before them was a scale depiction of their world, their domain. Doug had captured everything in loving detail: their homes and the roads between them, the surrounding forests, the cemetery, the homes of their enemies, and the location of the Dugout. The area devoted to Bowman's Woods was filled with hand-drawn trees, each one meticulously rendered. The graveyard had hundreds of tiny tomb-stones. Catcher's driveway had an illustration of a growling dog along with the words, *Here There Be Monsters*.

"How long did this take you?" Barry asked. "You must have worked on it, like, forever."

Smiling, Doug shrugged. "It was easy. I did a lot at night, after my mom had gone to sleep or was watching TV. I stayed up late. It was fun. Used a whole box of colored pencils."

Timmy's eyes shone. "This is so cool. We can mark off stuff as we discover it. And you even left room around the edges."

"Yeah. I figured when we explore those places, we can add it to the map."

Timmy's index finger traced the roads. "Cool. You even added Ronny, Jason, and Steve's forts."

"The one's we know about, at least."

"We can use this to plan our strategy before we raid them. Make sure we have escape routes and stuff like that."

"That's what I figured," Doug agreed. "We can hang it up, and you can mark stuff on it, just like a real general would."

Timmy smiled. "General Graco. I like the sound of that."

"How come you get to be the general?" Barry flicked Timmy's ear with his thumb and index finger. "I didn't vote for you."

"You don't vote for generals," Doug said.

"Yeah, well, I outrank you, even if Timmy's the general."

"No way."

Timmy turned their attention back to the map. "Hey, we could even—"

"Listen," Barry whispered, interrupting. "You guys hear that?"

"What?" Doug asked.

They tilted their heads upward, straining to listen.

"Timmmmmyyyyyyy!"

The voice was faint, but drawing closer. It was his mother.

"Timmy? Where are you?"

"Oh, man," Timmy moaned, "if she finds out about this place, she'll never let me play here again."

Barry rolled up the map. "Why not?"

"Because she'll freak out and worry that it will collapse on us or something."

"What do you think she wants?" Barry stuffed the map back in its protective tube. "It ain't lunch time."

"Probably wants me to help my dad. Let's just stay down here till she's gone."

"Timmmmmyyyy? Timmy, answer me!"

Barry slapped his forehead. "Oh shit. The bikes are up there, man. If she sees them, she'll know we're around here somewhere."

"So? We're underground. She can't find us."

"Yeah, but if she's looking in this spot, she might notice the stovepipe, and figure it out."

"Shit. You're right." Timmy thought of his grandfather. The stovepipe had given the fort's location away to him as well.

Quickly, they blew out the lantern and clambered up the ladder again, scrambling for the bikes. Timmy's mother stood about fifty yards away on the cemetery's lower road. Her back was turned to them as they approached. She called out again, hands cupped around her mouth.

Timmy pedaled towards her before acknowledging her cries.

"I'm here, Mom."

Elizabeth Graco spun around, and Timmy was surprised to see that she was crying. Black mascara ran down her cheeks. Her eyes were red and puffy. Her expression was frantic and worried.

"Timmy, where were you? We've been looking all over!"

His spirits sank. He was in trouble now. It appeared that his grandfather had been unsuccessful in convincing his father to let Timmy have the day off.

"I—I was just . . ."

"Come home, now. Your father's on his way to the Hanover Hospital."

Timmy's pulse accelerated. "The hospital? What happened? Is he okay?"

"It's your grandfather." She took a deep breath. "He . . . he had a heart attack."

"Grandpa?"

Sobbing, his mother nodded.

"What's wrong with Grandpa?"

"The paramedics think it was a heart attack," she repeated.

"Is he going to be okay?"

She began sobbing again.

"Mom? Is he all right?"

"No . . . He's gone, Timmy. He passed away."

CHAPTER THREE

Dane Graco had suffered a massive heart attack just after Timmy and Doug left the house. He was dead before the paramedics arrived. Timmy's mother had found him slumped over on the couch when she came into the living room to tell Timmy to go help his father in the garden.

Although the next morning was Sunday, the Graco's didn't go to church, the first time since winter of the previous year when they'd all had the flu. Elizabeth went to church every Sunday because she believed. Her belief was sincere. Randy went out of deferment to his wife. His belief was one of convenience. Timmy went because he wasn't offered a choice. He didn't know what he believed yet.

For the next few days, they moped around the too-quiet house. It seemed empty without Dane Graco's lively presence. Randy and Timmy were too stunned to do more than stare at the walls. Both cried off and on, and Elizabeth did her best to console them, trying to stay strong for her husband and son. It wasn't enough. Randy took a few days off work from the paper mill, contacted his father's friends and distant relatives; he made the funeral preparations and tried to keep busy. It wasn't enough. Timmy stayed in his bedroom a lot, consoling himself with comic books, trying to escape his grief by escaping into stories of men in brightly colored costumes so that he wouldn't have to think about his own reality. It wasn't enough.

The funeral was held the following Tuesday at the Golgotha Lutheran Church. The weather was chilly for summer. The sky was gray and overcast, and a cold light drizzle fell all morning long. It suited Timmy's mood. When he walked inside the church for the viewing, Timmy heard muted voices. He followed his parents through the vestibule doors and into the church itself, and stopped in the doorway. He was stunned by the turnout, and for a few moments, the crowd's size took his mind off the fact that his grandfather was lying in a casket at the front of the church. Everybody was there. Barry and his parents. Clark Smeltzer appeared sober and sincere, and offered his condolences to the Gracos, shaking Timmy's hand as if nothing had happened between them the Saturday before. Timmy noticed that in addition to his new gold watch, Barry's father was also sporting an antique-looking solid gold tie clip. Doug and his mother, Carol, who wore a skirt several inches too short and dark sunglasses to hide what were no doubt even darker circles beneath her eyes, were there, as were Bill and Kathryn Wahl, the elderly couple who lived next door to the Smeltzers. There were several distant relatives of his grandfather whom Timmy had either never met or barely recalled. He hadn't even known his grandfather *had* cousins until now—his grandfather had never mentioned them. Others in attendance included Luke Jones, who owned the farm bordering the cemetery and the Dugout, and some fellow Freemasons from his grandfather's lodge. Dane had achieved the rank of a fourth-degree mark master in life. There were friends of his grandfather's from within the community, church members, and the LeHorn family, who attended the Brethren church in Seven Valleys. Mr. LeHorn's father had been a good friend of Dane Graco's. Even Mr. Messinger, who ran the newsstand in town and sold the boys their comic books and cards, was on hand, looking both solemn and uncomfortable in his suit and tie.

Reverend Moore was there, too, along with his wife, Sylvia, and their youngest daughter, Katie. She looked pretty. She always did in Timmy's eyes. Her flowing brown hair was hanging down over the back of her long black dress; not what she normally wore to school, or even to church. Katie was one year younger than the boys, and though she didn't hang out with them, Timmy had started to notice her more and more often, and found himself thinking about her when she wasn't around. Surprisingly, he also found himself attending more and more youth group functions lately, just so he could spend time with her. Timmy didn't see Karen, the Moore's older daughter (whom he, Doug, and Barry had spied on from the bushes with Doug's binoculars last summer while she was sunbathing topless). The Moores seemed sad—not just solemn, but genuinely depressed, as if affected by something more than just one of their parishioner's death.

Katie caught his stare, smiled, and quickly looked away. Her cheeks turned red. Timmy blushed and felt his ears begin to burn.

Spotting Timmy when he entered with his parents,

Barry and Doug walked over to him, and the three boys moved to the rear corner of the church. They made small talk, each uncomfortable with mentioning why they were there. Curious, Timmy asked them about Karen Moore's whereabouts.

"You didn't hear?" Barry sounded surprised.

"No. What?"

"She skipped town with Pat Kemp. Nobody's seen them since Friday night. Took off together in his Nova. People are saying maybe they eloped."

"No way. Seriously?"

Doug nodded. "Reverend Moore called the cops and everything."

Timmy was mildly surprised, but not shocked. Pat Kemp was about the coolest older kid they knew, and Karen had a wild reputation as the stereotypical preacher's daughter. He could easily see the two of them running off together.

"Where did they go?" he asked.

"Nobody knows for sure," Doug whispered. "California, maybe?"

Timmy wondered if his friend was basing that on something he'd heard, or on his own wish fulfillment regarding his father.

Somebody sobbed loudly near the front of the church. The boys fell quiet.

"Sorry about your grandpa, man," Barry finally said, staring at the floor.

Doug nodded. "Me, too. He was cool."

Timmy mumbled his thanks, and then glanced around the church for his parents. They were near the front, shaking hands with mourners. His father was dabbing his eyes with a handkerchief. As he watched, the crowd parted, and Timmy got his first real glimpse of his grandfather's casket. He bit his lip, drawing blood, and his hands clenched into fists. The thing inside the coffin didn't look like the man he remembered. That man had been full of life, even in old age. He'd been funny, always smiling or telling jokes. The pale, waxy figure lying in the coffin wasn't smiling. It looked like a department store mannequin. Even his grandfather's hair was combed differently. His Freemason's ring adorned his hand, the stone glinting under the lights. He was dressed in a suit. When had his grandfather ever worn a suit? Never, at least as far as Timmy could remember. He wore slacks and buttoned shirts with the sleeves rolled up. Even when he went to church, his grandfather had preferred sweaters to suits.

Doug sensed his friend's discomfort. "You gonna go up there? Your dad looks really upset."

"I don't want to. Guess I should, though."

His mother caught his eye and smiled sadly. Her expression alone beckoned him, a unique form of telepathy shared only by parents and their children. Reluctantly obeying the command, Timmy stood up.

"I'll see you guys later."

He shuffled forward, weaving his way through the adults. They offered condolences as he passed by them, along with condescending pats on the head, as if he were six years old rather than twelve. Timmy did his best to be polite to them, but inside, he barely acknowledged their presence. His attention was fixed on the figure in the coffin, the thing that was supposed to be his grandfather.

Barry and Doug watched him go. Barry tugged at his tie. His collar felt like it was choking him, and even with the air conditioning turned on, the church was still hot inside.

Doug leaned over and whispered in Barry's ear.

"This sucks. I feel bad for him, but I don't know what to say."

"Me neither. I've helped my old man with dozens of these. It's always weird, and you feel bad for the people, but there's not really anything to say. 'Sorry' just doesn't seem to cover it. Especially this time."

"Why now more than the others?"

"Because Timmy's our friend. And because his grandpa was pretty cool."

"Yeah," Doug agreed. "He was. I liked him."

"Sometimes," Barry said, "I think he was the only cool grown-up I knew."

When they looked up again, the crowd of adults had swallowed Timmy whole.

Timmy had walked the red-carpeted church aisle hundreds of times. He'd walked it for communion and on Youth Sunday when it was his turn to take the offering and when the youth group put on the annual Christmas pageant. Last year, he'd been Joseph and Katie had played the part of Mary and all of the adults had remarked how cute they looked together. Timmy had thought he might die of embarrassment, and die all over again when Katie squeezed his hand while they took their bow as the parishioners applauded. He knew the aisle like he knew the cemetery outside, but the aisle had never seemed longer or more crowded than it did at that moment. The heat was cloying, made worse by the crowd, and his suit felt like it was stuck to his skin. The air was a mixture of cologne and perfume and candle smoke. He pushed his way through and emerged at the front.

He stood in front of the coffin, looked down at his grandfather's corpse, and did his best not to cry. It was even worse up close.

Timmy closed his eyes, trying in vain to get rid of

the image. The thing in the casket even smelled different. His grandfather had always smelled like Old Spice aftershave. This still figure had no smell. He opened his eyes again and glanced at the corpse's hands, folded neatly across its chest. His grandfather's skin had always felt rough and warm his hands deeply callused from years of hard labor. He wondered how they'd feel now. Shuddering, Timmy took a deep breath and held it. His ears rang, a high-pitched, constant tone, and his mouth felt dry. His heart thudded in his chest. He let the air out of his lungs with a sigh.

His mother put her arm around him and kissed his head. She smelled of lilac soap and hairspray.

"You okay, sweetie?"

He nodded.

"They did a real good job. It looks like Grandpa's just sleeping, doesn't it?"

Timmy wanted to scream at her. No, it did not look like Grandpa was sleeping. It looked nothing like that at all. In fact, it didn't even look like Grandpa.

At twelve, Timmy was well aware of the fallacies adults sometimes used. "Do as I say, not as I do" was a big one. Many times, he'd overheard Mr. Smeltzer promising Barry that he'd tan his hide should he ever catch Barry and his friends drinking or smoking cigarettes, yet Clark Smeltzer started and ended each day drunk as a skunk and smoked two and a half packs before nightfall.

"It's for your own good" was another. When he was younger, Timmy used to believe that he had an invisible accomplice named U'rown Goode who only his parents could see. Timmy had once shot a dove with his BB gun, and his father had grounded him and confiscated the weapon as a result (shooting doves without a license was illegal in the state of Pennsylvania).

Two days later, his father had left to go deer hunting in Potter County. He'd returned home bragging about how he'd shot three deer, one over the legal limit, and had given the third to a friend. Why was Timmy grounded for shooting the dove without a license while his father had basically done the same thing? It was for U'rown Goode. Had his invisible friend actually fired the fatal shot?

Santa Claus and the Tooth Fairy and the Easter Bunny were adult fallacies, as well. Grown-ups encouraged their kids to believe in them, only to yank the wool from their eyes and chuckle over the joke when they got older, killing whatever belief in magic the child still clung to. Killing their innocence. Sometimes, Timmy wondered if maybe God was just another fallacy, too. After all, his parents insisted that He was real, just like Santa Claus. Both of them lived at the top of the world and kept track of everybody, judging the populace on whether or not they'd been good or bad. The only Santa Timmy had ever seen was at the North Hanover Mall, and that guy was a phony. The only God he'd ever seen was the one that hung from the cross at the front of the church. He'd never seen God, but was expected to believe in Him just the same. As he got older, would they tell him that God didn't really exist either, and that it really didn't matter if he wrote scary stories during church service? Part of him expected just this. Of course, he never said it out loud, not even to Doug or Barry, because if God was real, then thinking something like that was a sure way to get on His bad side. Timmy was more afraid of God than anything else in life, with the possible exception of snakes and Catcher. You could shoot a snake or a neighborhood bully or a mean dog with a BB gun.

But not God . . .

And now, there was a new fallacy. "It looks like Grandpa's just sleeping." The biggest fallacy of them all, because Grandpa wasn't sleeping, he was dead. He was never going to wake up again. There would be no more walks or games or Saturday morning cartoons or long talks about things that mattered to Timmy, things his grandfather seemed interested in, too, because they were important to his grandson. His grandfather was dead, so why couldn't his mother just say it out loud? Why did she treat Timmy like he was a little kid? Next, would she tell him, "Guess what, it turns out Santa Claus is real after all"? Of course she wouldn't, because it wasn't true. Santa Claus wasn't real, U'rown Goode was actually Timmy's own good, and . . . Grandpa wasn't coming back again.

Timmy opened his eyes. Tears rolled down his face. He balled his fists at his sides and wept, and his mother and father held him between them, crying as well.

He cast one last glance at his grandfather's body, and then looked no more. He didn't have to. The image was burned into his retinas.

Grandpa wasn't sleeping.

After the viewing, there was a short break before the funeral service. Timmy's parents and some of the distant family members stayed at the casket, saying their final good-byes before the lid was closed. Timmy elected not to join them, and slipped away through the crowd. The other adults went outside to smoke, or mingled between the pews, talking softly. Timmy, Doug, and Barry wandered aimlessly around the church, ending up downstairs in one of the Sunday school rooms. Barry sat on top of the table, his legs hanging over the side. Timmy stood in the corner. Doug had found a Hot Wheels car, left behind by a younger child, and was running it aimlessly back and forth over the tabletop.

"You guys want to do something after this . . . is over?" Timmy asked. "I really need to get my mind off things."

"Sorry, man, but I can't," Doug apologized. "My mom drove, and my bike's at home."

"So? You could walk back to your house. It's not that far."

Doug shuddered. "And go by Catcher's driveway? No thanks, man. It's bad enough when he chases me on my bike. No way I'm letting him go after me when I'm on foot. He'd kill me. Besides, it's raining outside. I'd get wet and catch a cold. Nothing worse than a summer cold."

"Wimp." Timmy turned to Barry. "How about you?"

"I can't either, man. I've got to . . . well, you know."

"What?"

"I've got to help my dad with your Grandpa, after everyone else leaves."

"Oh . . ." He'd forgotten about that. It seemed weird, somehow, that his best friend would help to bury his grandfather. Fresh grief welled up inside him, and Timmy sighed.

Behind them, someone cleared her throat. The boys turned around. Katie Moore stood in the doorway to the Sunday school room. Timmy's heart beat a little faster, the way it always did when Katie was around. Sometimes, Timmy hated the way Katie made him feel. It was exciting, but scary, too. On Sundays, during the sermon, he found his gaze invariably drawn to her. Next year, she'd be starting sixth grade, and would go to the junior high school with them. He wondered what that would be like, and if they'd see more of each other then, and if so, if the possibilities of them hanging out together more often would increase. Thinking about it made his stomach hurt.

"Hey Katie," Barry said.

"Hey." She smiled sadly. "Hi Timmy."

Timmy responded with what could only be described as a garbled squawk.

"What's up, Katie?" Doug asked.

"They sent me down here to find you guys," she explained. "The funeral is getting ready to start."

"Oh."

Timmy's apprehension returned at the thought of sitting in the front pew, staring at his grandfather's not-sleeping corpse while Katie's father droned on about ashes and dust and walking through the valley of the shadow of death. "We'll be right up."

"I'm sorry about your Grandpa, Timmy. He was a nice man."

Doug's Hot Wheels car made scratching noises in the background. Barry cleared his throat and loosened his tie.

Timmy realized Katie was staring at him, and that he hadn't responded.

"Thanks." He searched for something else to say to her before she left, anxious to keep the conversation going for just a little longer. "I'm sorry to hear about your sister. I hope she's okay."

"Yeah, me too. I miss her."

"Do you guys know where she went?"

Katie's voice grew quieter. "No. Mom and Dad are really worried. She got in a fight with Dad before she left the house. He didn't want her going out with Pat. She did anyway. The township and state police said they'd tell us when they heard something, but that's about all."

"Well, I'm sorry," Timmy said again, and meant it.

"So am I." She smiled again, but this time it wasn't quite so sad. Their eyes lingered for a moment. Then Katie blushed and turned away. They heard her shoes clomping up the stairs two at a time.

Timmy's face and ears were scarlet.

"You like her," Barry teased, shoving him playfully.

Grinning, Timmy pushed him back. "Screw you. I do not."

"Why not? She's cute, man."

Timmy's stomach sank. Did Barry like Katie, too? He'd said hi to her first, while Timmy was still struggling to talk. And if so, did Katie like Barry more than she liked him?

"Not as cute as her sister, though," Barry added quickly, as if sensing his friend's thoughts.

Doug stood up and slipped the toy car into his pants pocket. "I guess we better go upstairs."

"Yeah," Timmy sighed. "I guess we better."

Then he thought of his grandpa again, and started crying.

It was starting to sink in that he'd never see him, talk to him, or hear his voice again. Timmy remembered the last time he'd seen him, Saturday morning when they'd been watching cartoons together. He'd hugged him good-bye and then gone out to play with Doug. He'd been anxious to go outside and enjoy his summer vacation. If only he'd known then what he knew now. He would have stayed behind.

Summers were endless. Life was not.

He was still weeping when he took a seat between his parents in the front pew, and when Reverend Moore began the service.

"Friends, would you please bow your heads in prayer." The preacher's voice was soft, and the sobs echoed over it.

The tears kept falling, and Timmy wondered if they'd ever stop.

They did stop, though, after the service, when the coffin was carried to the hearse. The sudden lack of tears surprised him, and for a moment, Timmy felt guilty. The emotions drained from his body as the tears dried up. Timmy felt empty. Hollow. He watched the pallbearers—his father among them, tears streaming down his face—load his grandfather's casket into the back of the hearse and experienced only a numb sense of finality.

The rain had stopped, too. Beams of sunlight peeked through the dissipating cloud cover. White and yellow butterflies played in the puddles. Sluggish earthworms, forced topside by the rains, crawled and squirmed on the blacktop.

The mourners walked slowly along behind the hearse, following it down the cemetery's middle road. They talked softly among themselves, murmuring gossip that had nothing to do with the deceased; President Reagan and William Casey and Ed Meese, the godless Communists, the godly Pat Robertson, who was going to see the Charlie Daniels Band at this year's York Fair, what had happened on last week's episode of *Hill Street Blues*, how Charlie Pitts had been able to afford that big new satellite television dish when he was still on disability, and the twelve point buck that Elliott Ramsey had poached out of season in Mr. Brown's orchard, and whether or not the Orioles would make it to the World Series (even though they lived in Pennsylvania, Southern York County was close enough to the Maryland state border that most of the residents rooted for Baltimore's teams). Timmy felt like hollering at everybody to shut up, but he didn't. Instead, he tried to ignore the whispers, and looked down over the hill. Far below, in the old part of the cemetery, he noticed again that another gravestone had sunken down into the ground. He'd seen two more like that the day Doug unveiled the map—a day that seemed like an eternity ago, even though it had been less than a week. It was hard to tell through the drizzle, but it looked like in addition to the sinking grave markers, a few more headstones might have fallen over onto the grass, too. Barry's dad was letting the cemetery fall into disrepair. Despite the man's misgivings, it was unlike him. Even if he was laid up drunk somewhere, he'd crack the whip, making sure his son covered for him. Maybe he just didn't have enough time to keep up with the sinking tombstones.

The funeral procession halted. The coffin was unloaded from the hearse while the crowd circled the open grave. Timmy's breath caught in his throat.

Barry and his father had dug the grave that morning. The top of the hole was framed with a brass rail and covered with a white cloth. A mound of fresh, reddish, clay-like dirt lay piled to one side, along with squares of sod. Deep backhoe tracks marked the grass, but Clark Smeltzer had moved the machine back into the utility shed so that it wouldn't loom over the service.

This was it, his grandfather's final resting place—a long, rectangular hole in the ground, right next to his grandmother. Now, every time Timmy came here to play, they'd both be nearby. The morbid strangeness of it all was not lost on him. This was both his playground and his grandparents' burial ground. If not for the Dugout and the fierce pride he took in its construction, he'd have suggested to Barry and Doug that they'd been right before, and maybe they should play in Bowman's Woods more often, or settle for a tree house somewhere else.

After the graveside portion of the service, Timmy trudged home with his parents. They walked in silence, not speaking, emotionally and physically exhausted.

For the first time in his life, Timmy felt two new sensations.

He felt old.

And he felt mortal—even more now than when he did playing among the graves of kids his own age.

He didn't at all like feeling either one.

Grandpa wasn't sleeping. He was dead. That was that. Sooner or later, everybody died.

And one day, it would be his turn.

The cemetery had a new permanent resident.

After everyone else went home, Barry and his father went back to their house, changed from their suits into work clothes, and then returned to the grave. Slowly, they lowered Dane Graco's coffin into the hole via a winch rope and pulley system. The casket was heavy, and Barry's arms and back ached afterward. His father didn't allow him to take a break once the coffin rested at the bottom of the grave. Instead, Barry began shoveling dirt back into the hole while his father retrieved the backhoe. The clouds had finally cleared, and the temperature rose. It was hard, sweaty work, and Barry was glad that evening was drawing closer. It would have been even hotter had the sun been in the sky, rather than setting on the horizon. His calloused hands blistered beneath his leather work gloves.

Barry hated this; hated working for his father, slaving away every day, mowing and digging and raking while his friends enjoyed the summer. Nobody else's fathers made them work like this. Randy Graco didn't force Timmy to go to the paper mill with him every day. Why should he be stuck doing this stuff all summer long, just because his father was a drunk? *Chores,* his father called them. Barry knew about chores, and this wasn't it. Timmy had chores; weeding the garden and sweeping out the basement, stuff that took him an hour or so to complete. Timmy bitched and complained about it, but Barry could only laugh. Timmy had no idea how lucky he was. He didn't have to bust his rear just to cover for his old man's laziness.

Barry didn't know what he wanted to be when he grew up, but it certainly wasn't his father.

Buzzing gnats flew in front of his face, darting for his eyes and ears. He waved them away and dropped another shovel full of dirt onto the coffin, listening to it hit the wood and trickle down the sides.

Minutes later, another sound echoed across the graveyard, the roar of the backhoe's powerful diesel engine as it sputtered to life. Slowly, his father backed it out of the utility shed and drove over to the grave, carefully weaving the big machine through the tombstones. Barry backed out of the way, grateful for the short break, and wiped the sweat from his brow. Using the scoop, his father quickly filled the hole with dirt. Then he shut off the backhoe, hopped down, and lit a cigarette. Smoke curled into the sky. The tip glowed.

Barry thought his father seemed nervous.

The sun edged closer to the horizon.

"No screwing around now," Clark grumbled. "Let's get this done quick. Your mom's got dinner waiting."

"Yes, sir."

Barry tensed. His father's tone was all too familiar. It meant trouble tonight. For him, for his mother, for anybody who did anything to piss him off. Barry wondered whose turn it would be this time.

He hated his father. Sometimes, late at night when everyone was asleep, Barry imagined what it would be like to kill him. He thought about it again now. To hit him over the head with the shovel, dig up the dirt and throw him down on top of Dane Graco's coffin, then fill it all in again, burying his old man alive. He grinned, even as sour bile rose in his throat. He knew it wasn't right, thinking that way. He knew that God could see inside his heart, just like Reverend Moore said. But he couldn't help it. Besides, if God really cared, then why didn't He step in and help them? Why did He allow Barry and his mother to continue living this way? He imagined his father in the hole, gasping and sputtering as the dirt hit him in the face. His smile grew broader.

"What are you grinning about?" Clark grunted. "You laughing at me?"

"No."

"Then what you grinning about?"

"Nothing."

"Wipe that damn smirk off your face and keep working."

"Yeah . . ."

"Yeah? Yeah what?"

Barry lowered his eyes. "Yes, sir."

They replanted the squares of sod on top of the grave, as they'd done so many times before, and neither said a word to the other as they worked. Barry watched his father out of the corner of his eye, trying to determine if he was drunk yet. He knew that his father kept a bottle of Wild Turkey hidden in the shed, and it was very likely he'd taken a few swigs while getting the backhoe. Barry hadn't told Timmy and Doug about the secret stash. They might want to try some, the way they had last summer when they'd found a six pack of Old Milwaukee beer that Pat Kemp had left in the creek to stay cold (the oversized pounder cans). Secretly, Barry was terrified of alcohol and its effects. He'd seen firsthand what it did to his father, turning him into someone else, into a monster, and he had no desire to do the same. Barry's biggest fear was of becoming his father. He'd heard other adults say that happened—as you got older, you became your parents. He'd vowed that in his case, he'd make sure that didn't happen. Never. He hated it when some well-meaning adult patted him on the head and said, 'Why, you look just like your father.'

His father was an abusive drunk, and Barry had the scars, both physical and mental, to prove it.

But his father didn't seem drunk now. He seemed . . . apprehensive. And as the sun sank lower, his agitation increased. He kept glancing around the cemetery, as if looking for something . . . or someone.

"You okay, Dad?"

Clark frowned. "Course I'm okay. Why? You saying I don't look okay?"

"No. It's nothing."

"Well, then quit dicking around."

"Yes, sir."

Finished with the job, they tamped the sod down firmly, and then stepped back.

Clark Smeltzer mopped his forehead with a red bandanna. "Let's get home."

"Don't we need to water the sod first?"

"No." He glanced up at the advancing twilight. "We'll do it tomorrow. Been a long day."

"But—"

"None of your lip." A vein throbbed on his father's forehead. "I said we're leaving. Now."

"Sorry."

"Shut up."

They went home. Barry's mother had fixed pork chops, green beans, and mashed potatoes. Barry did his best to eat, but he had no appetite. When his mother asked him what was wrong, he didn't reply. The look on his father's face halted further discussion.

After dinner, Barry tried to watch television. He couldn't focus on the show.

Later on, his father got very drunk, split Barry's lip open with a backhand slap, and chased his mother around the house with a belt, laughing and shouting. Barry fled for the safety of his bedroom, and put his fingers in his ears to block out the sounds of leather meeting flesh, and of his mother's screams, and his father's curses. He'd tried to help her once before, and as a result, had been out of school for a week until the bruises faded. Afterward, his mother had made him promise never to do it again.

And he hadn't. Not because of his promise, but because he was afraid.

Afraid of what his father would do the next time.

So he did nothing.

Under his pillow was a BB pistol, powered by a CO_2 cartridge. It looked just like the gun Clint Eastwood used in his *Dirty Harry* movies. Barry often wished it were the real thing. Sometimes, when his father was passed out drunk and there was no danger of waking him up, Barry would creep up beside him in the darkness and point the BB pistol at his head.

But not tonight.

Barry cried himself to sleep; hot tears, full of shame and anger and hopelessness.

He dreamed of monsters.

Doug cowered in bed; dirty flannel *Spider-Man* sheets pulled up over his head, he listened to his mother pawing at his doorknob, pleading drunkenly, her speech slurred by vodka, whispering the things she wanted to do to him, things Doug had read about in *Hustler*. Dirty things. He'd never told Barry or Timmy, but those things filled him with dread. The same pictures of naked women that his friends drooled and snickered over made him feel queasy. He'd seen those private feminine parts in real life, and it was horrible. The thing his mother had between her legs looked nothing like the women in the pictures. It didn't offer the same promise. It was a dark place, full of shame and guilt and nausea.

"Doug? Dougie? Come on, baby, open the door for Mommy."

"Go away," Doug whispered. "Please, go away."

Over his bed were three movie posters from *Friday the 13th*, Parts 2, 3, and 4. Though none of the boys were old enough to see the films at the theater, they all knew the story. Doug stared at the sinister image—the killer, Jason, with his bloody machete. It was preferable to what waited outside his door.

"Doug? I know you're awake. Open up."

"Go away and leave me alone."

"I've got a present for you. It's a surprise."

He bit his lip and fought back tears.

"Can you guess what it is? I'm wearing it. Let me in and we'll do some new things."

He stayed silent.

"Doug? Open this door. Quit being a baby. I've told you before. You're not Mommy's little boy anymore. You're Mommy's man. And Mommy needs a man. Mommy needs a man bad."

She shoved against the door with all her weight, but the deadbolt he'd installed held firm. He'd purchased the lock at the hardware store; paid for it with money he'd earned raking the neighbor's yards last fall. Timmy and Barry had teased him about it, not knowing its real purpose.

"Douglas Elmore Keiser, you open this door right fucking now."

She hammered on the door with her fists. Doug heard a glass bottle roll across the floor. He stifled his sobs so that she wouldn't hear. He plucked a tiny yellow Lego block from the floor and squeezed it until his knuckles turned white. The hard plastic contours dug into his palm.

Eventually, she stumbled back into the living room, but not before telling Doug through the closed door that he was just as worthless as his no-good, limp-dick father.

Doug knew why his father had left, knew why he'd run off with that waitress. It didn't matter what he told his friends; he told himself the same lies during the day.

At night, he understood the real reason.

He fell asleep, crying and nauseated.

He also dreamed of monsters.

Timmy lay in bed with his headphones on, tuned in to 98YCR out of Hanover, but they were playing "Pass the Dutchy" by Musical Youth, which he hated, so he switched over to 98Rock out of Baltimore, and listened to "Yeah, Yeah, Yeah" by Kix instead. That was much better. His parents didn't like him listening to that type of music, especially Ozzy Osbourne (whom Reverend Moore had deemed a Satanist)—so, of course, Timmy listened to it every chance he got. Kix had played at the York Fairgrounds the year before. He'd begged his parents to let him go, and of course, they hadn't.

Earlier, he'd been watching a movie on his little black-and-white television, *The Car*, which had been corny but sort of cool, too. At least it had taken his mind off things for a while. But then his mother had told him to turn it off and go to sleep. He'd obeyed the first command, but found the second one impossible.

He was exhausted, both physically and emotionally, but Timmy couldn't sleep. His mind kept running through the day's events, playing back the funeral. When he closed his eyes, he saw his grandfather lying in his coffin. His mother's voice echoed in his mind. *"It looks like he's sleeping."*

Timmy turned on his flashlight, careful not to let the beam shine under the crack of his door, which would alert his parents to the fact that he was still awake. He shined it around the room. *G.I. Joe* and *Star Wars* action figures stared back at him. A toy motorcycle and his baseball glove stuck out from under the bed. Posters adorned the wall; *Star Trek II: The Wrath of Khan* and *The Empire Strikes Back*, Madonna lying on her back, pouting for the camera; Joan Jett, sexy with a guitar; the album covers for Iron Maiden's *Powerslave* and Dio's *The Last In Line* (much to his mother's chagrin); all of the heroes and villains that populated the Marvel Comics Universe, as depicted by John Romita, Jr.; dinosaurs pulled from the pages of *National Geographic*.

His bookshelves overflowed with books, magazines, and comics; Hardy Boys hardcovers, Paul Zindel paperbacks (Zindel was the boys' version of Judy Blume), back issues of *Boys Life*, *Mad*, *Crazy*, and others. Other treasures sat atop his dresser—a model of Spider-Man fighting Kraven the Hunter that his father had helped him build, his piggy bank that doubled as a globe, a blue glass race car that had once held Avon aftershave, and a small wooden box that his grandfather had given him. Inside were his most secret possessions: a wooden nickel and pocketknife (also both given to him by his grandfather), a rubber whoopee cushion, faux-gold collector's coin featuring the Hulk, the rattle from a rattlesnake his grandfather had killed while hunting, marbles, some of his father's old fly lures from when he was a boy, and buried in the bottom, a dried dandelion and a note. Katie Moore had given him the last two items at a church picnic when they were much younger—first and second grades, respectively. The note simply said, in a childish scrawl, *I like you Timmy*. He'd been embarrassed by it at the time, still under the firm belief that girls were infected with cooties. Despite that, he'd never thrown it out, nor shown it to anyone else.

In the darkness, he reread the latest issue of *G.I. Combat* with a flashlight, until his eyes finally drooped, then closed. The flashlight slipped from his limp hand and rolled onto the floor. Eventually, the batteries died.

Timmy's breathing grew shallow. Tears soaked his pillow as he slept. He dreamed about his grandfather, and in the dream, Dane Graco's grave was an empty hole in the ground. In the distance, he heard a woman screaming. Closer to him, something growled.

Although he didn't want to, Timmy shuffled closer to his grandfather's empty grave.

When he looked closer, he saw that it wasn't empty after all.

The hole was full of monsters.

CHAPTER FOUR

The dead slept, too, but did not dream.

James Sawyer was forty-three when he died of complications from Hodgkin's lymphoma. Before that, he'd worked second shift at the paper mill, where he operated a forklift in the shipping and receiving department. In his spare time, he enjoyed going deer hunting and putting model cars and airplanes together with his sons, Howard and Carl. He'd met his wife, Marcia, in high school, fell in love with her instantly, and had never been with another woman. Never even considered it. He was active in the Golgotha Lutheran Church, and in the local Lion's Club. He never smoked and rarely drank. James was a man of gentle humor, and his spirits remained high, even in the final stages when the cancer ravaged his body. He passed away in a sterile, bland room at the Hanover General Hospital. James and Marcia were holding hands when it happened. He gave her one last squeeze, whispered that he loved her, and then he was gone. His family laid him to rest in the cemetery; he was buried in a gorgeous mahogany casket, beneath a black marble stone with gold lettering that proclaimed him a loving husband and father.

George Stevens's death was more sudden and less peaceful. He drowned in the old abandoned quarry located halfway between Spring Grove and Hanover on the summer of his fourteenth birthday. He'd been swimming there with friends, and earlier, they'd shared their first beer—piss-warm Michelob, stolen from one of their older brothers. There were rumors that the old quarry was haunted; that the remains of a mining town still stood at the dark, murky bottom, and the spirits of the townspeople still lurked in the waters, waiting to drag unsuspecting swimmers beneath the surface. Will Marks, his voice slurred by the beer, had told them about how he'd seen a figure under the water once—a boy their age, pale and bloated. George didn't believe the story, so when Will Marks dared him to dive down and see for himself; he did it, egged on by his friends and the warm, fuzzy feeling with which the beer had left him. He leapt from the tire swing and into the inky depths, unable to see anything, plummeting ten feet before striking his head on an old refrigerator that someone had thrown into the quarry. Even underwater, he heard his own neck snap. It was the last thing he heard. His friends pulled him out of the water, but he was already dead, and they never found out if George saw the ghostly aquatic townspeople or not.

Cathy Luckenbaugh, a bright, cheerful twenty-one year old who was loved by everyone who knew her, had spent the Christmas holidays with her family and was on her way back to the Penn State campus when a drunk driver crossed the yellow lines on Route 30 and hit her head on at seventy miles per hour. Part of her went through the windshield. The other half, everything from the abdomen down, remained inside the car. Her death was quick and relatively painless, despite the severe trauma. Cathy had been studying English literature, and hoped after college to get a job as a teacher, and to marry her boyfriend, Ken Bannister, whom she'd met the previous semester. Her family buried her in the Golgotha Lutheran Church Cemetery, near her aunt and grandparents. Ken married another girl he met after college. Many years later, Cathy's image was used in a television commercial for Mothers Against Drunk Driving.

Damon Bouchard started stealing when he was eight. His first heist was a pack of baseball cards from the Spring Grove newsstand. By the time he was twelve, he'd been busted twice for shoplifting. Two times being caught versus the hundreds of times he'd done it? Damon was happy with those odds. He graduated to breaking and entering, did a brief stint in York County Prison, and died two nights after his release. He'd just come from a meeting with his parole officer, returned to his third floor apartment, passed his neighbors on the way up the stairs, watched them pull away from his kitchen window, and broke into their apartment. In the dark, he'd tripped over the cat and fell face first into a glass coffee table, slicing his head and throat to shreds. He'd felt the blood gush from his wounds, as well as his mouth and ears, and his last impression was one of anger, wishing he'd had time to kill the stupid cat. Damon's long-suffering parents buried him next to their plots. They rarely visited his grave.

Britney Rodgers was five when her father started

climbing into her bed at night, and seven when he smothered her with a pillow to keep his awful secret. Her mother had died while giving birth to her, and her only friend had been her stuffed rabbit, Mr. Bun. Her father said it was her duty. At night, while he grunted and sweated above her, reeking of booze and sour sweat, Britney would hide Mr. Bun's face beneath the pillow so the rabbit wouldn't have to see. Britney's father buried her body in the woods behind their house, and the police found her four days later. She was given a proper burial next to her mother. A police detective made sure that Mr. Bun accompanied her into the ground. Her father was killed during the Camp Hill prison riots, and was buried in a potter's field near Harrisburg. The detective who arrested him visited his grave every year on the anniversary of Britney's death—and pissed on it.

Raymond Burke lived a long, full life and died in his sleep at the ripe old age of eighty-seven. His wife of sixty-two years, Sally, had passed away three months earlier, and as far as Raymond was concerned, he died with her on that day. They'd never had children, or even a pet, and he felt totally abandoned. He'd never been by himself, and didn't know what to do. The house was too quiet, and the silence amplified his loneliness. After Sally's funeral, he'd gone home to wait to die, cursing each morning when he woke up alone instead of finding himself with her, until the morning when she finally was. They were buried side by side.

Stephen Clarke was thirteen when he first had sex with the family dog, Trixie, and fourteen when his older brother Alan found out about it. Their parents had been gone for the day, dining with another couple at the Haufbrau Haus in Abbotstown. Alan walked into his brother's room without knocking, only to find Stephen sitting naked on the floor, his back against the bed and his legs spread. Trixie was between them, busily licking peanut butter off Stephen's erect penis. Disgusted, embarrassed, and enraged, Alan had threatened to tell their parents as soon as they got home. Stephen pleaded with him, but Alan refused to listen. As his parents pulled into the driveway, Stephen ran to his parent's bedroom, unlocked his father's gun cabinet, pulled out a Winchester 30.06, loaded one round into the weapon, put his mouth over the barrel, and squeezed the trigger. He was buried in the cemetery, and in the years immediately following his death, his family visited his grave with a mixture of grief and unspoken shame. Eventually, they stopped visiting. A car ran over Trixie two years after his death.

The moon shined down upon their graves.

The dead kept their silence; kept their secrets. Young and old, good and bad, innocent or guilty, loved or unloved, it didn't matter what they'd done in life, how they'd lived it, or how they'd ended. In death, they were the same. In death, they found rest beneath the newer portion of Golgotha Lutheran Church Cemetery.

Something else was in the ground, too. Something that was not dead, yet not really alive. For years, it had slept beneath the soil in the old portion of the cemetery at the bottom of the hill, the section where the names and dates on the cracked tombstones were faded and covered with moss. The forgotten area, where the dead received no visitors (other than the caretaker), because all those that remembered them were dead, as well. The creature slumbered beneath an old granite marker with an even older symbol carved into the stone. Both the symbol and the creature were ancient.

The creature in the ground had no name, at least none that it could remember. None of its kind did. They were low things, cursed by the Creator long ago to dwell beneath the surface; white and wiggling like carrion worms. Not the Great Wurms, like Behemoth and his ilk, but low things; condemned to dirt and shadow, condemned to walk and breed in darkness, condemned not even to feast off the rich lifeblood or the warm, still-living flesh of the Creator's beloved children (the way the others, the Vamphyir and the Siqqusim, did), or to act as the planet's antibodies like the ancient race of subterranean swine-things had done during times of world strife. His race was not smiled upon by Him like the angels and small gods were, nor did they enjoy the autonomy and freedom from His gaze the way the Thirteen did. No. His kind were condemned to feed on the cold, rotting corpses of the dead—the scraps from the Creator's table. Warm flesh was forbidden to them, and they could only shred it with their claws, empty it of blood and organs and wait for it to turn rancid. The Creator's commandment was that they not taste warm blood or flesh. They could slay, of course, in self-defense or just sheer malice. But they could not feast upon the living. They were cursed to eat carrion, commanded to clean up after death.

There was no air in the subterranean prison, but the creature did not need to breathe. It wished, at times, for death, but death would not come. Its kind were impervious to the weapons of man. Guns and knives meant nothing to it, other than a temporary wound, which would soon heal. It could have slashed its own throat with its claws, but that would not have ushered in oblivion. Only the sun's rays could destroy it, and the sigil kept it from reaching the light—kept it from doing anything but lying there.

The thing was a ghoul, and quite possibly, as far as it knew, the last of its race. It had been nearly two centuries since it had encountered another of its kind, and that had been on another, faraway continent. Its loneliness simmered inside its clammy breast.

The ghoul had no idea how long it had lain there, imprisoned and unable to move or to feed, bound by the symbol on the gravestone above it, trapped by magicks now forgotten, by sigils borrowed from books of power like *The Daemonolateria* and *The Long, Lost Friend*, mystic symbols copied and etched by men long dead, men who'd lain moldering, turning to dust and bones in nearby graves, rotting in peace while it half-slumbered in boredom and despair—and suffered from an overwhelming hunger. Realistically, the imprisonment hadn't been long, not by the ghoul's standards. One hundred years. Maybe a handful more. A blink of the eye for its kind, but the hunger had made it seem longer.

It was lonely.

It was angry.

And above all else, it was ravenous.

That hunger gnawed at the ghoul's empty belly, a cold, hollow craving that it had no means of satisfying.

Until two weeks ago, when it was finally freed.

Then it had made up for lost time, and at long last, satisfied its appetite.

That night, after the sigil was accidentally broken, after the gravestone had cracked and fallen to the earth, it awoke fully and became aware. Aware of the human standing above it. The creature could smell him—the stink of his man-sweat, the alcohol oozing from his pores, the fear in his heart, the anger in his head. The ghoul could smell it all, and more, smell the dead in the cemetery. The creature growled along with its stomach.

The man's head was like a hive of enraged bees, and the ghoul could sense it.

Above the grave, the man moved. Mumbled something angry and unintelligible, voice slurred by alcohol. Cursed the fallen tombstone, even though he'd been the one to knock it over. Lit a cigarette.

The ground shifted.

The ghoul surged toward the surface, cleaving the soil like a shark through water. Its long, bony fingers erupted from the earth. The filthy, curved talons on the tips of its fingers were cracked and peeling. Its arms thrust forward, white and cold. Its thick, fleshy hide was hard and greasy. The ghoul's hands curled around the startled man's ankles, gripping him tight, holding him in place. Then the thing's hairless, pointed head emerged from the rippling dirt like a pale, rotten, oversized gourd. Its yellow eyes bulged. Sharp teeth, blackened with decay in some spots, flashed in the moonlight, wicked incisors glinting beneath black, rubbery lips.

The man screamed, cigarette falling from his mouth. His cries echoed through the empty graveyard with no one else to hear them.

Laughing, the ghoul pulled itself from the grave and rose to its full height. It was completely naked, its body almost entirely devoid of hair except for a tangle between its legs and a few wayward strands along its body. The man was too frightened to flee. A wet stain spread across the crotch of his pants. A half-empty bottle of Wild Turkey slipped from his grasp and rolled across the wet grass. He trembled as the creature shook the dirt from its body. It was thin, almost emaciated. Its bones were visible beneath the hairless skin. The ghoul licked its lips, the tongue slithering across its face like a gray snake.

Despite his terror, the man gagged and coughed, recoiling from the creature's stench. It smelled like strong cheese, left out in the summer sun for too long. Pungent. Spoiled. Bad milk spilled inside a Jiffy John.

"Oh, Jesus . . . Somebody help! Help me!"

He backed away, his foot colliding with the bottle.

The creature hissed, its breath like a sewer.

"Help!"

The ghoul paused, studying the terrified man's dialect. Though it knew most of the languages of men, it had been some time since it had spoken them.

"What is your name, human?"

"Christ. It's a flashback. Agent Orange or something—"

"Silence. I am no vision or dream."

The man flinched. "Y-you're real?"

"Of course I am real. Again, what is your name? What are you called?"

"C-Clark S-S-Smeltzer."

"What are you doing here?"

"I'm the c-caretaker. I was drinking, and I-I was mad. Angry. I kicked the tombstone. I'm s-sorry. Was it yours?"

The ghoul glanced down at the shattered fragments. The marker had cracked in half, the sigil cracking with it; thus, freedom.

The man's eyes grew wider. "It w-was, wasn't it? Oh God . . ."

The ghoul grinned. The caretaker began to sob.

"Puh-please . . ." Clark started coughing again.

"Please, what?"

"I'm sorry. P-please don't k-kill me. . . ."

The ghoul's laughter was like a hissing steam kettle. "Kill you? I am not going to kill you. I can see inside your mind. You will be useful."

Clark nodded furiously. "Yeah, that's right. I-I am useful. I can f-fix your tombstone good as new."

"You misunderstand. I am hungry."

"Oh, shit . . ."

"You bury the dead?"

Clark nodded, recoiling from the ghoul's stench.

"Tell me, son of Adam. Have you ever seen the fruits of your labor? Have you ever viewed a corpse after it has ripened beneath the soil? Seen the earthworms and millipedes crawling over and through it? Smelled the aroma of grave mold, or warmed yourself in its luminous glow? Wallowed in the rich, fatty stew of decomposition?"

Clark retched. "No."

The ghoul patted its stomach. "It is a treat. My kind was not supposed to enjoy it. It was our curse, to eat the dead. But in time—in time, we grew to relish it. Savor it."

"Y-you eat dead people?"

"Yes, and you are going to feed me."

Clark Smeltzer's bladder let go again, further soaking his pants. "B-but you said you weren't gonna k-kill me!"

"I am not. I will allow you to live, so that you can continue to do your job. You will bury the dead, so that I can feed. You will also keep my existence a secret. For this, you will be richly rewarded. And there is something else you will do for me, as well. I require something else, in addition to sustenance. I am lonely."

Swallowing hard, Clark stared in horror, listening as the creature spoke.

It talked for a long time, and when Clark returned home, it was almost morning. The ghoul returned to the grave, hiding beneath the soil, sheltering itself from the sun. Waiting. No longer imprisoned, but free to come and go under the shelter of darkness.

When it was night again, it began to dig. And to plan. First, it satisfied its hunger. That was an immediate need. It devoured the nearby dead, eating whatever flesh remained on the bones, and then the bones themselves, leaving nothing behind but whatever they'd been buried in—jewelry and scraps of moldering clothing. Sated, the ghoul focused on fulfilling its longing for others of its kind—a family.

The caretaker was supposed to find it a mate, for its kind could mate with human females and had done so in the past. But the caretaker had not yet procured one. So when the boy and girl mated in the darkness, lying together on a blanket spread out between the tombstones, the ghoul had watched them from the shadows, and saw its chance. It had killed the boy, obeying the commandment and not partaking in the pumping blood or still-warm flesh, and had taken the girl below. She was ripe and fertile. The creature could smell it on her. The ghoul wasted no time.

Over the last two weeks it had created quite a den. The warren was centered in its original grave, but it had tunneled out in all directions, a spiraling labyrinth that grew larger and more complex. The girl was kept in the main chamber, in a nest the ghoul had built for her. It didn't have to worry about her fleeing—her mind was too far gone for that, and even if she had been able to reason, she wouldn't have been able to navigate the pitch-black maze of tunnels.

It ate every night. At first, it had feasted in the nearby older graves, devouring the few human remains still left after one hundred years of interment, and snacking at night on nearby road kill, left to rot in the sun along the roads that bordered that portion of the cemetery. Then it had branched forward, burrowing up the hill to where the new graves lay. There, night after night, it had eaten its fill, rooting through the graves of James Sawyer and George Stevens, Cathy Luckenbaugh and Damon Bouchard and Britney Rodgers, Raymond and Sally Burke, Stephen Clarke, and many others.

The dead could not scream.

This night was no different. Dane Graco's corpse was devoured within ten hours of its interment. The ghoul was displeased at the chemicals in the body, embalming fluid and the like. It longed for the old days. But food was food, and it was hungry.

The next day, after the Gracos had buried their dearly departed and tried to move on with their lives, Clark Smeltzer checked a preappointed spot and found a new collection of graft, including Dane Graco's Freemason ring. He started thinking again about all his newfound wealth. He wasn't doing anything wrong, he reasoned. He wasn't digging up corpses and robbing them. And it wasn't like the dead needed that stuff anymore. Why shouldn't he be able to turn it into money at the pawnshops? Even so, he had to be careful. Something like this ring, he couldn't sell it locally. He'd have to drive to Harrisburg or Baltimore to unload it.

Beneath the small pile of jewelry and coins was a note, scrawled on a scrap of white cloth—cloth ripped from someone's burial clothes. The note was brief, only seventeen words, but Clark had to struggle to read the handwriting.

CONTINUE TO TELL NONE OF MY EXISTENCE
BRING ME MORE WOMEN
YOU WILL CONTINUE TO BE REWARDED

He put the items in his pockets and his pants sagged from the weight of the coins and jewelry. Clark pulled them up, readjusted his belt, and walked away.

He tried very hard to ignore the faint female screams he heard coming from beneath the ground.

By noon he was drunk again, and nothing else mattered.

CHAPTER FIVE

Two weeks had passed since Dane Graco's death, and life went on for everyone else. Timmy's grief subsided, Barry's bruises healed, and Doug's guilt faded. The boy's fears seemed to dry up, if only temporarily, in the warmth of the summer sun. They were twelve, after all, and resilient, still able to employ the defense mechanisms of childhood. Timmy still thought about his grandfather every day, especially if he passed by his grave, and he still experienced moments of deep heartache and bouts of crying. But the two weeks of summer vacation's start were like a new lease on life; afternoons spent fishing at the pond (Barry and Timmy caught sunfish and blue gills, while Doug usually caught sticks, and once, a turtle), hanging out together inside the Dugout, reading comics and girlie magazines, playing with Timmy's *Star Wars* Death Star play set, complete with foam garbage for the trash compactor. They'd walk the railroad tracks and finding iron spikes, which they carried back to the Dugout. They spent time shooting rats at the town dump with their BB guns, and retaliating to the opening volley of a new war with their archrivals. Ronny and Jason had stumbled across Doug on the far side of Bowman's Woods and had tried to beat him up, chasing him all the way to Barry's house; the boys had retaliated by stealing Ronny's bike and hiding it on the railroad tracks behind the paper mill. They waited and watched with a giddy mixture of excitement and dread as the coal train ran it over.

During the mornings, Barry helped his father, mowing the grass in the cemetery and cleaning the inside of the church. Timmy helped out at home, doing his daily chores without complaint. His father had been nicer and more patient during the past two weeks, telling Timmy that he loved him more often, and actually taking the time to talk to him about things. He was working more hours at the paper mill again, but when he got home, he made an effort to spend time with his son. Timmy wondered if maybe all the overtime his father was working stemmed from a desire to not think about his own father's death. But he didn't ask. Instead, he weeded the garden and mowed their yard. He was glad that his father had taken an interest in him again.

With no chores to perform or a father to please, Doug spent his mornings by himself, or helped Timmy with his own duties. As in previous summers, when they'd finished, they'd ride their bikes over to the cemetery and give Barry a hand (if his father wasn't around) so that the three of them could hang out sooner. It was during one of these moments when the three boys were clearing the dead floral displays from the graves that they discovered the first hole.

Clark Smeltzer was working in the lower section of the graveyard, at the bottom of the hill where the older tombstones were located, fixing the sunken grave markers. He was out of sight and out of earshot when it happened.

Barry had hooked a small wagon up to the back of the riding tractor. He drove it between the rows, humming a Billy Idol tune and thinking of maybe asking his mother if he could cut his hair short and spiky to match the singer's, while Doug and Timmy gathered the dead plants and tossed them into the back of the wagon. When they were finished, they would dump the debris in the mulch pile behind the shed.

"Han Solo is a pussy," Doug said, clutching a handful of withered flowers. "The Doctor would totally kick his butt. You guys are high."

"The Doctor doesn't even have a real spaceship," Timmy said. "He flies around in a telephone booth."

They were arguing about who would win in a fight, Doctor Who or Han Solo from *Star Wars*. Barry revved the tractor, drowning him out in midsentence.

Then Doug shouted in fright.

They didn't hear his cries at first, over the roar of the tractor's engine. Doug shouted louder. Barry engaged the parking brake and leapt off the tractor, and Timmy whirled around, expecting to see Ronny and the others giving Doug an atomic wedgie or something. Instead, their overweight friend had cast his dead flowers aside and was pawing at the ground. His left leg had disappeared into the earth from the knee down. His screech echoed across the graveyard.

"Relax, man." Barry ran over to him and extended a hand, while Timmy turned off the tractor. "My old man will hear you."

"Get me out of here. Something's got my ankle!"

"It's just a groundhog hole."

"Something's biting me!"

Timmy and Barry suppressed their laughter. The entire scene looked pretty comical, Doug floundering, his arms flailing wildly, his glasses sliding off his sweaty nose, and his leg deep inside the ground.

"It's not funny, guys. It hurts!"

"Take my hand."

Doug grasped Barry's outstretched hand desperately, and Barry pulled him up. Fresh soil clung to his pants leg and sock. His sneaker had come off, and remained beneath the surface. There was blood on his sock.

From deep inside the hole, something squealed. It sounded angry.

"Jesus Christ!" Doug collapsed onto the grass and drew his wounded leg up, slowly peeling off the tattered sock. Five shallow but ragged scratches marked the flesh around his ankle and calf, as if he'd been raked with long fingernails or claws.

"Are you okay?" Timmy asked, concerned.

"No, I'm not okay. I fell in a hole and something bit me. Look at my foot, man. Does it look okay? I'm bleeding."

Barry and Timmy glanced at each other, ashamed of their initial reaction.

"Didn't you see the hole?" Barry asked.

"There wasn't one," Doug said. "The ground just caved in. Like it was a trap or something."

Timmy and Barry examined the hole. It didn't look like a groundhog's den. The size was wrong. It was too big for a mole, but too small for any other type of burrowing mammal. Furthermore, it didn't look like it had been dug from above the ground. There was no dirt piled off to the side of the hole. It appeared to have been dug from beneath the earth, as if something had tunneled up from below, and this small portion had then collapsed. Timmy knelt by the hole. A subtle breeze blew against his cheek. He wrinkled his nose.

"There's air down there. I can feel it on my face. But it stinks."

"Who cares?" Doug rocked back and forth. "Look at my ankle. I could get rabies."

"Your ankle is fine, man. Just put some Bactine on it or something."

"But that won't stop rabies. That kills you. You foam at the mouth and stuff."

Tuning him out, Timmy focused on the strange opening. The odor was terrible, but he couldn't look away.

"You guys heard that noise, right? It didn't sound like a groundhog. I wonder what this is?"

"Sinkhole," Barry said. "Graveyard's been full of them lately. My dad says there must be a cave or something below. We've had little holes like this opening all over the place. Sunken tombstones, too. They fall right down halfway into the ground. That squeal was probably just air rushing out."

"Air?" Doug sighed in exasperation. "Then what bit me, you moron?"

Timmy ignored them both. His mind swam with the possibilities. An underground cavern! Maybe even a whole network of them. If they could get inside and explore, there was no telling what they'd find. They'd be famous. Last winter, he'd read a book about caverns, and had become enamored of the idea of finding a cave near their homes. It would be even cooler than the Dugout.

He leaned closer, winced at the stench wafting up from the hole, and fanned his nose.

"It doesn't smell like a cave. Smells like a sewer."

"We're in a cemetery," Barry reminded him. "It's probably someone's body, decomposing and stuff."

Timmy bolted away from the hole in disgust. For a second, he thought of his grandfather. Was that what was happening to him right now? He closed his eyes and tried not to think about it.

"Oh, man," Doug moaned. "If it was a sewer or a dead person, I could get infected."

"Look," Timmy said, "just go home and get it fixed up. If you take care of it now, you're not gonna get infected."

"I can't go home now. Not with my foot like this. I won't be able to pedal my bike fast enough to get past Catcher."

"Catcher." Timmy curled his fingers into fists. "Always something with Catcher. Things would be a lot easier without him."

"Aren't you sick of that dog?" Barry asked Doug.

"Well, sure I am. But what can I do? I told Mr. Sawyer that Catcher had been chasing me, and my mom has called him a bunch of times, and he still won't tie him up. The dogcatcher hasn't done anything, either. Mom says that's because he's friends with Mr. Sawyer. They hang out together down at the VFW."

Timmy smiled. "I think it's time we took care of Catcher on our own. I'm tired of him chasing me every time I go to your house."

"What?" Doug's eyes grew wide, his injury forgotten. "You talking about bumping him off? I don't know if I could do that."

"No, I'm not talking about killing him. We'd get in trouble for that, man, and I don't feel like spending the rest of the summer being grounded. But we can get even. I've been thinking about this for a while now, and I know how to take care of him. We can make sure he thinks twice before messing with any of us again."

Doug stopped sniffling, put his sock back on, and stared at Timmy with interest. "How?"

"Squirt guns."

Barry snorted. "Squirt guns? Are you nuts? You nail him with water and you're just gonna piss him off even more. This is Catcher we're talking about, not a cat."

"Yeah," Doug said. "I don't know, Timmy. I don't think Catcher is scared of a little water."

"No." Timmy's smile grew broader. "Probably not. But I bet he's scared of vinegar."

"Vinegar?"

Timmy nodded. "Vinegar. Lemon juice. Stuff like that. We can get some from my mom's kitchen, put it into the guns, and nail him when he comes after Doug. He gets it in his eyes, and he'll never chase us again. Guarantee it."

"Gasoline," Doug said. "That would do the trick."

Barry shook his head. "No, that would eat through the plastic. And besides, we don't want to kill him. Just teach him a lesson. It's got to be lemon juice or something. Maybe mix it with vinegar."

"So you guys up for this?" Timmy asked.

Barry and Doug agreed that it was a good plan. They usually did, no matter what Timmy proposed. He could summon them to the Dugout and state his desire for them to travel to Mars by the end of the summer, and the boys would agree that it was a solid plan. Timmy had read *Tom Sawyer* when he was younger, for a fifth grade book report assignment, and the character's ability to sway others was not lost on him. He found a familiar poignancy to many of the scenes, especially the whitewashing of the fence and Tom's ability to convince his friends to take part in his adventures, no matter how dangerous or ill-advised. Timmy often secretly fancied himself a modern Tom Sawyer, with Barry and Doug as his Huckleberry Finn and Joe Harper. (Barry's dad even fit the role of Huck's own abusive father.) Some of the older kids listened to a band called Rush, and they had a song called "Tom Sawyer" that made him feel the same way. He didn't understand all the lyrics, but he knew enough of them to know that it echoed his own thoughts.

"What are you going to do about your shoe?" Barry asked Doug. "You can't limp around with just one."

"I don't know, but I'm not putting my hand back down in that hole. Whatever it was that bit me is probably still inside."

Timmy got down on his hands and knees and peered inside the hole. It was pitch black inside, and he couldn't see anything but dirt. He got the impression that the crevice was deeper than it looked. Another gust of foul air drifted out, and he cringed.

"I don't see it, man. Want to borrow a pair of mine instead?"

"That would be cool. Thanks."

"Sure. While we're there, we'll get my mom to fix you up. She'll probably insist on it anyway—she freaks out over infection and stuff. Just like you."

Barry laughed. "Why do moms do that, anyway? Mine would do the same thing."

"Mine wouldn't," Doug whispered. "I'd be lucky if she noticed."

Timmy wondered if maybe that was why Doug had reacted the way he did to his own injury—because he knew his mother wouldn't.

"Come on," he said, trying to cheer Doug up. "Today's the day Catcher bites off more than he can chew. You should be happy."

"Hate to be a downer," Barry reminded them, "but I can't go anywhere until I finish up here. My dad will have a fit if I leave in the middle of this."

"We'll help you," Timmy said. "We're almost done, anyway."

Doug glanced down at his shoeless foot. "Better let me drive the tractor. The bleeding's stopped, but I don't think I should walk on my foot for a bit."

Barry double-checked, making sure his father was still occupied in the lower portion of the cemetery. Then they hurriedly finished the job at hand, emptied the wagon onto the mulch pile behind the utility shed, and headed for Timmy's house, taking the long way around the cemetery to avoid Barry's dad. They stopped at the Dugout and collected their bikes. Doug slowed them down, unable to pedal his bike without hurting his foot. He coasted along, instead. As they rode past his grandfather's grave, Timmy skidded to a halt. His back tire fishtailed, and he almost wrecked.

Barry slid to a halt behind him. "What's wrong, man?"

Gasping, Timmy pointed at his grandfather's grave.

The grass on top of the fresh sod had withered and turned brown, and the soil had sunken almost a foot, leaving a deep, rectangular depression.

Barry glanced at his friend, then to the grave, then back to Timmy.

"The dirt settles after a week or so. Happens all the time."

"Yeah, but not *that* much. Look at it! It's caving in."

Barry shrugged. "Well, like I said, my dad thinks there might be a sinkhole."

"That's a big cave, man." Doug shook his head in disbelief.

"Underneath the entire graveyard?" Timmy exclaimed. "This is bullshit, Barry."

"Hey, don't get mad at me! It's not my fault."

"Sorry." Timmy's voice grew softer. "I was just shocked, is all. What's your dad gonna do about it?"

"I don't know," Barry admitted. "There's not much he can do, except to add extra dirt to the sinking areas, and straighten up the headstones. If it keeps happening, I guess the church board will have to do something."

They crossed the road and cut through Barry's yard and over the hill into Timmy's backyard, all so that Clark Smeltzer wouldn't see them and find something else for Barry to do. Then they went inside Timmy's house. His mother made a big production over Doug's injuries, and made him sit down while she attended to him with cotton swabs and disinfectant. Doug beamed at the attention and concern, happier than his friends had seen him in weeks. They shook their heads, saddened and bemused. The simple attention of a mother—any mother—changed his entire mood.

"What in the world did you do?" Elizabeth asked him. "How did you cut it like this?"

"I don't know, Mrs. Graco. I think it was a rock or something."

"You think? These scratches look like claw marks, Doug."

"It was a bunch of sticks. I cut it when I fell. Sticks or a rock. I didn't really look to see."

While Elizabeth was distracted with Doug, Barry and Timmy snuck into the kitchen and borrowed a bottle of vinegar and a plastic container of lemon juice. They turned up his mother's radio to cover the noise—Olivia Newton John moaned about getting physical. Quickly, they filled up their squirt guns, laid the plastic weapons out on the patio, and then returned the items just as Elizabeth and Doug were finishing up. They walked into the kitchen. Doug was wearing Timmy's old pair of Vans, from last year when he'd gone through a skateboard craze. They barely fit, and the laces were undone.

Timmy's mother sniffed the air. Her nose wrinkled.

"It smells like vinegar in here."

The boys glanced at one another. Doug's smile vanished.

"Really?" Timmy's voice cracked. "I don't smell anything. You guys smell anything?"

Barry and Doug shook their heads.

Shaking her head, Elizabeth turned down the radio. "You guys want to stay for dinner? We're having hamburgers and French fries. Randy's grilling when he gets home from work."

Doug grew excited. "Sure, Mrs. Graco. That would be great."

"I'd better not." Barry's eyes fell to the floor. "Don't want to leave my mom home alone."

Elizabeth frowned at the odd statement, but said nothing. She winced again at the sharp tang of vinegar in the air. Motherly instinct told her that Timmy and his friends were up to something, but it also told her that it probably wasn't something that would get them hurt or killed or in trouble, and therefore, she decided to let go. Letting go was something she struggled with. No matter how old Timmy got, she still thought of him as her little boy, and she still worried. She supposed she always would, even when he was an adult.

"Hamburgers and French fries," Doug said. "That'll hit the spot. What's for dessert, Mrs. Graco?"

"Blueberry pie." She patted Doug's head. "I'll call your mother and make sure it's okay."

"You don't have to," Doug said. "She's probably not there to answer, anyway."

"Oh?" Elizabeth arched her eyebrows. "Did she start back to work? Good for her!"

"No, she just spends a lot of time sleeping."

"Oh . . ."

"Mom," Timmy interrupted, sparing his friend further embarrassment, "we'll be back in time for dinner. Right now we've got to go do something."

"What?"

"Can't tell you. It's top secret."

His mother smiled. "Be back by four. Your father will be hungry, and if you're not here to eat, you'll make him grumpy."

"Will do."

The three ran outside, collected their armament, and walked down Timmy's driveway, heading in the direction of Doug's house.

Barry glanced behind them. "Won't your mom wonder why we left our bikes behind?"

"No," Timmy said. "She knows Doug can't pedal with his foot like that. She'll just think we headed for the creek or something."

At the edge of Timmy's property, they turned left and started up Laughman Road, which climbed steadily uphill before leveling off after a half-mile. Thick forest bordered both sides of the road, with Bowman's Woods on their right. If Timmy's mother were indeed watching them from the window, she'd assume they were going to the creek, just as he'd planned. But instead of following the thin footpath into the woods, they continued up the hill and passed from his mother's view. The road grew darker, shadowed on both sides by the tall, arching trees. They seemed to loom directly overhead, as if trying to block out the sunlight. It was cooler in their shade, but unsettling, as well.

Doug limped, slightly dragging his injured foot.

"You okay?" Timmy asked.

Smiling, Doug flashed him a thumbs-up. "Never been better. Your mom fixed me up good. She's so nice."

"You say that now," Timmy scoffed. "But I bet you'd change your tune when she made broccoli for dinner and told you that you couldn't watch *The A-Team* until you'd finished."

"*The A-Team* is stupid. Ever notice they fire like ten thousand frigging bullets at the bad guys, but never manage to hit anything? Nobody ever gets killed or wounded."

"So? I like it."

"Well, I like broccoli—and I like your mom."

"Want to trade?"

Doug's smile disappeared. "I don't think you'd want to do that, Timmy."

"Why not?" Timmy teased. "You change your mind?"

"No. I just don't think you'd like my mother very much. . . ."

"Yeah." Timmy's voice grew softer. "I guess you're right."

They walked on in silence.

At the top of the hill, Laughman Road leveled out, providing a straight shot to Doug's house. To their left, the forest disappeared, giving way to acres of fenced in pasture. They'd yet to climb the fence and explore the territory, due to Catcher. Mr. Sawyer's dairy cows roamed and grazed among the fields. Several of them stood close to the road, staring at the boys on the other side of the fence with wide, unblinking eyes. Timmy had once heard his father say that cows had the stupidest expression of all God's creatures, but Timmy disagreed with that. He thought the cows looked sad. To him, their eyes held longing, a wish that they could go beyond the fence and graze on the other side of the road. The grass of Bowman's Woods must have looked greener to them.

"Moo," Doug called out, his spirits lifting again. "Mooooooooo!"

"Knock it off," Timmy warned him. "If Catcher hears us, he'll come running."

"But don't we want that this time?"

"Yes. But I also want to be ready for him. This is a sneak attack. Don't holler for him until we're all set."

Nodding, Doug moved away from the cows and began quietly humming a song by Morris Day and The Time. His limp grew more pronounced and his pace slowed as they neared the Sawyer's home.

"Maybe we should wait," he suggested. "Come back another day."

"Screw that," Barry said. "We've got the squirt guns, and we've come this far. What are you—scared?"

"No."

"Yes, you are. Admit it. You're scared of Catcher."

"Screw you, dipshit." Doug's face grew red. "You're scared of him, too."

Barry held his hands up in mock surrender. "Yeah, okay. Guess I am."

The Sawyer's farm grew visible in the distance, sitting far back from the road and connected to the world by a narrow, winding lane. The boys knew that lane well, and viewed it as the gateway to hell. A grain silo and the top of a red barn jutted above the rolling hilltops.

"Okay," Timmy muttered. "This is it."

They lined up side by side at the entrance to the lane.

"Okay," Doug whispered. "I admit it. I'm scared."

"Of what?"

"Catcher! What if we miss?"

Barry grinned. "Don't."

"Wait until you see the whites of his eyes," Timmy advised them. Then he placed his feet squarely apart, cupped one hand to his mouth, and shouted for the dog.

"Oh shit," Doug whimpered. "I'm not ready. You said we'd wait until we were ready."

Timmy stared straight ahead. "Too late."

His cries for the dog did not go unheeded. Within seconds, the three boys heard an all too familiar snarling coming from the distant farmhouse. A flash of black fur appeared at the end of the lane and rocketed toward them. Catcher's growls split the air like artillery shells. As the dog drew closer, Doug took a step backward.

"Don't you move," Timmy warned.

"But—"

"Come on, Catcher," Barry taunted the enraged Doberman. "We've got something for you!"

Foam and spittle flew from the dog's jaws as he closed the distance between them. Catcher paused for a moment, as if surprised to see his rivals on foot and standing their ground rather than on bikes and fleeing. Surveying them with his dark eyes, the dog lowered his head and growled again, deep and menacing. He bared his white teeth. The boys trembled. Warily, he took another step forward. His hackles were raised.

"Come on," Timmy shouted, his voice cracking. "Come take a bite out of Doug."

Doug shot a terrified look at his friend. "W-what?"

Still suspicious, Catcher barked. His muscles rippled as he flexed his haunches.

Timmy stomped his foot at the dog.

Doug's eyes grew wide. "Oh, Jesus . . ."

Suddenly, Catcher darted forward, open jaws pointed directly at Doug's crotch.

Doug screamed.

Catcher moved quickly, but Timmy was quicker.

"Now—fire!"

They did. All three aimed their squirt guns directly at the charging Doberman's eyes and unleashed a stream of vinegar and lemon juice. The effects were instantaneous. Catcher stopped in midcharge and spun around, trying to avoid the stinging barrage. Yelping, he darted away, weaving back and forth as if he were drunk.

"It worked," Barry hollered. "Holy shit, it worked!"

Laughing with triumphant glee, the boys continued their assault, squeezing their triggers again and again, releasing all of the squirt guns' potent contents. Catcher's tortured whining grew louder. Fleeing, he ran onto the grass and rolled onto his back. He squirmed, yelping and snapping at the air. Flipping over onto his belly, the dog pawed at his eyes.

Still firing, Timmy inched closer. Barry and Doug followed along with him. Their bravery grew with each step until they stood over the thrashing canine. Catcher looked up at them, unseeing.

All three boys continued laughing.

"Eat shit." Doug leaned over and fired directly into the dog's left eye at point blank range.

Catcher let out one long, mournful howl, and then Barry kicked him.

"Take that, dickhead."

Timmy and Doug's laughter dried up. They stared in shock and surprise.

Barry kicked the dog again. The tip of his sneaker drove into Catcher's side, right between his ribs. Catcher snapped at his foot, but Barry easily side-stepped him and lashed out a third time.

Timmy's heart sank. Catcher, their personal demon, the dog that had terrorized them for all these years, that had made the simple act of going to each other's homes a living hell, suddenly seemed pitiful. Timmy was horrified. He felt sorry for the dog, and ashamed at what they were doing. This had been his idea. The guilt was overwhelming.

Barry kicked him again. Blood trickled out of Catcher's nose.

"Stop it, man," Timmy cried. "You'll kill him!"

"So?" Grimacing, Barry wiped the sweat from his eyes. "We won't have to worry about him chasing us . . ."

Kick.

". . . ever . . ."

KICK.

". . . again."

Catcher wailed. Not yelped—*wailed*. Timmy had never heard a dog—or anything else—make that noise before. The sound filled him with dread. Catcher's nose and muzzle were covered with blood now. The dog's bladder let go, flooding the ground with urine.

"Bite me now, fucker! Cocksucker. Son of a bitch."

Timmy had never heard so many curse words come out of his friend's mouth at once.

"Barry," Doug pleaded. "Stop. You'll get us in trouble."

Timmy grabbed his friend's arm, but he was no

match for Barry's superior strength and size. Grunting, Barry pushed him to the ground.

"Get off me, Graco, unless you want some, too. *This was your idea!*"

"Not like this . . ."

Taking advantage of the distraction, the wounded dog jumped to his feet and fled across the fields, his tail tucked firmly between his legs. He was limping badly, and dog shit ran down his hindquarters.

Out of breath, the three boys stood there looking at each other. Each of them was exhausted. Timmy felt sick to his stomach. The strength seemed to drain from his limbs. What had just happened? And how had it happened? He'd daydreamed about this plan a dozen times, but never with these results.

He shook his head at Barry. "What got into you, man?"

"My father," Barry panted, his hands on his knees. "Oh Jesus, just like my old man . . ."

Misunderstanding, Doug pointed back toward Timmy's house. "Let's go. If we leave now, your dad will never find out."

Barry stared at him and said nothing.

Timmy picked up the fallen squirt guns. "He's right. We need to get the hell out of here before Mr. Sawyer finds out what happened to his dog. If he sees us standing down here, we're screwed. He'll tell our parents for sure."

"Sorry I shoved you," Barry apologized. His cheeks were wet with tears.

"Don't worry about it. Let's just go, okay?"

The three of them cut across the road into Bowman's Woods, far enough inside the treeline so that they couldn't be seen. They wound their way through the forest, pushing aside low-hanging limbs and slashing the clinging vines and poison ivy out of the way with long sticks. When they reached the creek, they stopped to rest and catch their breath. Doug kneaded his sore ankle and swatted at the swarming gnats. Timmy washed the squirt guns out in the cold water to get rid of the evidence, the lingering smell of vinegar. Barry was silent and morose.

"I don't know what happened," he said after a few minutes. "I just . . . snapped."

Timmy picked up a pebble and threw it into the creek. "It's okay, man. We all kinda did. We could have blinded him."

"Seriously?" Doug asked.

Timmy shrugged. "Sure. He was certainly acting like we had. Guess I didn't think about that when I came up with this plan."

He'd heard the expression, "Things can change on a dime" before. His grandfather had said it all the time, but until today, Timmy had never really understood it.

"Well," Doug said, "we shouldn't be too hard on ourselves. Remember all those times he chased us? Remember in school, when we were studying mythology? That dog that guards the afterlife? Cerebus? He was a monster, and so was Catcher."

A monster, Timmy thought. *Was he really?*

He tossed another stone into the water and watched the ripples spread. The concentric rings lapped against the creek bank.

Is Catcher the real monster, or are we?

CHAPTER SIX

"Shit." Barry stopped suddenly in the middle of the trail and threw his hands up in despair.

They'd been following a winding deer path through the middle of Bowman's Woods, taking the long way back home so nobody would see them. Timmy and Doug halted and turned. Barry was frantic, his expression one of sick fear.

"What's wrong?" Timmy asked.

"My watch . . ."

"You break it?"

"No. I think I lost it."

Timmy felt a surge of panic. "Back at Sawyer's place? Oh man, if they find it . . ."

"I know." Barry finished his thought. "Then we're screwed. My name's engraved on the bottom. Mom got it for me for my birthday last year. God damn it, I don't believe this."

"We've got to go back and get it," Timmy said. "We can't just leave it lying there."

"Are you crazy?" Doug swatted a mosquito. "We can't go back there. Mr. Sawyer probably already called the cops."

"Well, I can't go home without it," Barry said. He sounded terrified. "My old man will have a cow if he finds out I lost that watch."

"You took it off while we were working," Doug told him.

"Are you sure?" Barry asked, sounding hopeful.

Doug shrugged. "Pretty sure. Kind of. Well, maybe . . ."

Timmy thought for a moment. "You know, now that he mentioned it, I don't remember seeing it on your wrist after that. Did you take it off in the graveyard?"

"I don't know. I can't remember. Sometimes I do, because my arms get sweaty and the band slips off. So, maybe."

"Well, if you did take it off, where would you have left it?"

Barry sounded very close to tears. "On one of the tombstones, or maybe inside the shed."

Timmy turned to Doug. "How's your ankle?"

"It feels better. Burns a little, but I'm okay."

"Good." Timmy was surprised. The fact that Doug hadn't taken the opportunity to complain about his injury and make it out to be worse than it really was meant that he understood the gravity of the situation. "Okay, Barry, don't worry. We'll help you look for it. It's got to be around there somewhere."

"I hope so. Otherwise . . ."

He trailed off, but they heard the fear in his voice.

Timmy thought again of Barry's outburst during their attack on Catcher. Despite the fact that Barry had a scar on his calf from when the dog had latched onto him almost two years ago, what had happened today hadn't been Barry's fault. It had been his father's. Barry's body had plenty of scars and bruises, and only one of them was from the dog. Sometimes in the afternoon, Timmy's mother watched talk shows (more often now that they'd just installed the new cable television with nineteen channels); on the talk shows, they talked about abused kids and how they lashed out at others as a result. It was their way of dealing with it, of feeling powerful instead of helpless. Sometimes, they turned into school bullies. Other times, serial killers. Barry wasn't either of those, but his actions that afternoon had definitely been a warning sign. They'd never discussed it, but Timmy and Doug both knew what Clark Smeltzer did behind closed doors. And what they didn't know, they could guess.

And Doug's mom—something was up with her, too. Timmy wasn't sure what, but he had his suspicions, and they turned his stomach. Certainly, it was more than just ignoring her son. Indeed, he was pretty sure that when she was drunk, Carol Keiser paid *too* much attention to her son, the kind only hinted at in the stack of *Penthouse Forum*'s that lay hidden inside the Dugout. There was a word for it, and that word was incest. He'd seen that on the talk shows as well.

Monsters? They weren't monsters. And Catcher wasn't a monster, either. For all they knew, Mr. Sawyer beat the dog. Trained him to be mean, to attack. It wasn't like the dog's behavior was anything new. He'd been chasing them, chasing anyone who passed by the lane, for years, and Mr. Sawyer had been told about it repeatedly. He'd done nothing, refusing to tie the dog up or install a pen or fence. Was that Catcher's fault? No, Catcher wasn't a monster. Neither were they.

Adults were the real monsters. Maybe not his own parents, and maybe not Reverend Moore or some of the others, but still, there were a lot of them around. He saw them every time he watched the news (unlike most twelve-year-olds, Timmy's mother had instilled in him an appreciation and interest in current events, and encouraged him to watch the evening news and read her weekly copies of *Time* magazine, which he did.) He saw them, too, in his comic books and Hardy Boys mysteries.

Saw them when he looked into his two best friend's haunted eyes.

"We better get going," Doug said. "It's getting late."

They continued along the narrow, winding trail, ducking under tree limbs and pushing past thorns and vines until they reached the edge of Bowman's Woods. Then they crossed Anson Road and made their way through the lower portion of the cemetery. Barry's father was nowhere in sight, but there were signs he'd been there. The gravestones had been returned to their upright positions and fresh earth had filled in the holes. A careless cigarette butt, one of Clark Smeltzer's brand, lay nearby.

"Looks like my old man's done for the day," Barry observed. "Hope he's not in the shed."

Silently, Timmy and Doug both wished for the same thing.

The boys crossed the cemetery and cautiously approached the dilapidated yellow utility shed. It was deserted; there was no sign of Clark Smeltzer. The doors were shut, and Barry's father had the key to the padlock, so they went around to the back. There, half hidden by a pile of red clay leftover from the new graves (the same dirt Clark Smeltzer had used earlier to shore up the sinking tombstones) was a boarded up window.

Unbeknownst to Barry's father, two of the boards were loose, and had been further loosened by the three boys with the help of a claw hammer and crowbar.

In the woods beyond the shed, a twig snapped. Their heads swiveled toward the sound.

"Just a squirrel," Timmy guessed.

Turning back to the window, Barry pulled the boards away. The rusty nails screeched as they parted the wood. He pulled himself through and crawled inside. Timmy followed right behind him. Then they pulled Doug, who couldn't squeeze into the narrow space by himself, through the window as well. With a great effort, he clambered inside, gasping for breath and complaining about his injured foot. His friends disregarded it. Had his foot not been injured, Doug would have complained about his nonexistent asthma, or his back, or anything else that could be aggravated by the physical act of climbing.

There were no lights inside the shed, and the only illumination came from the paltry light filtering through the missing boards, cracks in the wall, and a second dirty window. The tin roof sagged in places, and water leaked down onto the rotten timbers when it rained. Clark Smeltzer had twice petitioned the church board for a new, sturdier, prefabricated shed, but they'd told him the funds weren't currently available. He'd grumbled about how maybe the congregation should start chipping in more when Sunday's offering plates were passed around. Sure, it was God's money, but the church was God's house, and God's house needed a new shed. They'd smiled politely and moved on to other business.

The floor was hard-packed dirt, pocked here and there with groundhog and rat holes. In the center of the floor lay a pile of lumber, mostly plywood and two-by-fours, and several lengths of rusted pipe. The shed was crammed full of equipment: the small backhoe, riding mower and wagon, two push mowers (one relatively new and the other one in even worse shape than the shed), a grass catcher, winch, various shovels, rakes, pickaxes, hoes, and some canvas tarps. Several dozen stone markers were stacked in the corner, and the other corners held plastic flowers and wreaths, cheap plastic vases, and little flags for Veteran's and Memorial Days.

A few sparse clumps of mold clung to some of the walls and scrap wood. Because of the dirt floor, it always smelled damp and musty inside the shed, but as they stood there, letting their eyes adjust to the gloom, Timmy smelled something different—the same stench he'd noticed earlier, coming from the hole Doug had slipped into.

"Whew." Doug fanned his nose. "Which one of you farted?"

"You smell that, too?" Barry asked. "I thought maybe a possum had crawled up your ass and died."

"Eat me."

"Something did die in here, though." Barry crept forward. "Smells horrible. Must be a rat or a groundhog or something. Probably lying underneath this wood."

He stepped onto a piece of plywood that was covering the dirt floor and the board sagged under his weight. Barry jumped backward, clearly startled.

"What's wrong?" Timmy asked.

"The floor—it ain't there!"

Doug frowned. "Say what?"

Barry bent over and grabbed the edge of the plywood sheet. "Give me a hand with this."

Physically stronger than either of them, Barry clearly

didn't need their help. Timmy thought that perhaps the real reason was that he was scared. And that scared Timmy.

He gave his friend a hand while Doug hung back and watched.

"Watch out for snakes," he cautioned.

Ignoring him, they slowly lifted the plywood, and then heaved it forward, sending it crashing onto the rest of the woodpile.

All three boys gasped at what was revealed.

There was a hole underneath, tunneling right through the center of the utility shed's floor. Judging from the way the soil was scattered, it looked as if it had been dug from beneath the ground, as if something had burrowed upward. But this was no mole or other rodent. The hole was far too big for that, much bigger than even the hole Doug's leg had slipped into earlier. The opening was large enough for a full-grown man to easily fall inside. The stench wafted up from the chasm.

"What the heck?" Timmy asked. "Did your dad do this?"

Barry shook his head, perplexed. "No way. My old man would be pissed as shit if he saw this. I don't know what this is."

"It stinks," Doug croaked, pinching his nose. "That's where the smell is coming from, all right. Just like that other hole earlier, out there in the graveyard."

Timmy's eyes sparkled. "It's the caves you were talking about. Has to be! Another sinkhole opened up right here, and you and your dad didn't know about it because it was underneath the woodpile."

Barry looked doubtful. "You think?"

"Sure I do. No animal dug this, and like you said, your dad wouldn't have, either. It's got to be a cave entrance."

"But they're made out of rock, not dirt."

"Not always," Timmy disagreed, even though he wasn't sure himself. He wasn't about to let science get in the way of what could be their coolest summer adventure ever. "We've got to explore it, guys. Claim it before anyone else finds out. We could be on TV, man!"

He searched the floor, found an old rusty nail, tossed it down into the hole, and listened.

"We can't explore it now," Doug reminded him. "It's almost dinnertime. You know what your mom said."

"Yeah," Barry added, "and we still haven't found my watch."

In his excitement, Timmy had forgotten about both. Disappointed, he reluctantly conceded that they were right.

"We'll come back tonight," he said. "Sneak out after our folks are asleep. Doug, you're staying for dinner, anyway. Might as well spend the night. We'll wait till like one o'clock, and then meet up here. We'll have to remember to get the flashlights and lantern from the Dugout, and maybe the map, too."

"What do we need the map for?" Doug asked.

"So we can outline this tunnel on the back of it. If we've got the surface mapped out, we ought to do the same for below."

"Then we'll need some clothespins, too."

Timmy frowned. "For what?"

"To cover our noses with," Doug replied. "I'm not breathing in whatever that is if we go down there."

Chuckling, Timmy turned to Barry. "You gonna be able to get out tonight?"

"Yeah, I guess. If I don't get killed for losing my watch first."

"Well, then let's find it before your father finds us."

They covered the tunnel entrance back up, making

sure the plywood concealed the entire opening, and then searched the rest of the shed for the missing watch. Doug's suspicions proved to be correct. They found the silver watch hanging from the riding mower's gearshift. Sighing with relief, Barry fastened it around his wrist.

"All's well that ends well." He grinned.

"Sure is," Doug agreed.

They noticed that Timmy hadn't responded, and when they turned, they found him staring down at the plywood.

Barry groaned. "Come on, man. Let it go for now. We'll see it tonight. And since you're so eager, you can go first."

Timmy looked up at them, smiling. "Sounds like a plan."

In truth, he'd have had it no other way. He was eager to be the first one to step inside the subterranean chamber.

"I still don't think it's a sinkhole," Doug said. "It looks dug, not sunken. And that smell—God!"

They crawled back out the window and fastened the boards back into place, tapping the rusty nails into the rotten wood with a rock. Over the sounds of pounding, they didn't notice when another twig snapped in the nearby tree line.

"Okay," Timmy said, "so we meet at the Dugout after our parents are asleep, and then we'll explore the underground. Lets say one o'clock in the morning."

Doug and Barry agreed. Then they went their separate ways, Barry to his house and Timmy and Doug to the Graco home.

On the way back, Timmy wondered what they'd find inside the tunnel, deep below the earth.

* * *

After the boys had departed, a slender figure emerged from the shadows of the trees behind the shed. It had been watching them the entire time. Now that they were gone, it crept forward and investigated the loose boards around the window. Then it crawled inside the shed.

Rustling sounds drifted out of the building—wood sliding across wood. Then came a gasp of surprise.

Minutes later, the figure re-emerged into the sunlight. Blinking, it let its eyes adjust again. Then it ran across the cemetery as fast as it could. Its expression was one of satisfied determination.

CHAPTER SEVEN

"It's gonna rain," Steve Laughman complained as they trudged across the field. The tall grass swished against their blue jeans. "The weatherman on Channel Eight was calling for it tonight."

"Quit fucking whining," Ronny Nace said. "Christ, you're like a little girl, man."

"They said there was a severe thunderstorm warning until six in the morning. Gonna rain buckets."

"So? A little rain never hurt nobody."

"We could catch pneumonia," Steve said. "I don't want to be sick in the summer."

"Shut up."

"Or maybe even a tornado could blow through. Wouldn't want to be out here if that happened."

"If you don't shut the fuck up," Ronny warned, "I'll shut you up for good."

Steve's open mouth snapped shut. He knew better than to cross his friend.

"We finally got a chance to get even with those shit-heads," Ronny said, "and you want to cancel all because of the weather."

They continued walking through Luke Jones's pasture, cloaked in darkness and keeping a wary eye out for the farmer's two bulls. Luckily, the cows were all lying down, clustered together on the far side of the field. Thick, obsidian clouds blanketed the night sky, blocking out the moon and stars, and even muting the floodlights on the paper mill's smokestacks and the blinking, red airplane warning lights on the distant radio tower. They lit their way with a flashlight stolen from a drawer in the kitchen of Steve's house.

"You know what's weird?" Jason Glatfelter asked. "Ever notice how people will run through the rain, instead of just walking? Like if they're coming out of a store or something, and it's raining, they'll run to their car instead of just walking like normal. Why do they do that? It ain't like they're gonna get any less wet. Same amount of rain is gonna hit you either way."

Ronny stepped over a groundhog hole. "What the hell are you talking about?"

"Think about it. Whether you walk or whether you run, you're still gonna get wet. So why run? In fact, I bet more raindrops hit you that way."

"Dude," Ronny snorted, "you've been hitting the bong way too fucking much."

They neared the fence line, and spotted the graveyard beyond it.

"Well," Steve said, "I'll tell you guys one thing. If it starts raining, I'm running my ass home. I'll be in enough trouble if my mom finds out I snuck out. It'll be ten times worse if I come home soaking wet."

"Pussy." Sneering, Ronny flipped his long bangs out of his eyes. "We should have just left you at home."

"Easy for you to say," Steve replied.

"What's that supposed to mean?" There was an edge to Ronny's voice that hadn't been there a moment before.

"Nothing." But secretly, Steve knew exactly what he'd meant. He'd wanted to say that it was easy for Ronny not to worry about his mother catching him sneaking out, because his mother worked the eleven-to-six shift at the shoe factory in Hanover and wouldn't be home until seven the next morning; since Ronny's dad had died from complications of Agent Orange five years before, there was nobody else there to worry about Ronny. This was what he'd meant, but of course, he didn't say it. The last two people that had mentioned Ronny's father were Andy Staub and Alan Crone, and Ronny had split both their lips and fractured Andy's nose.

On the other side of the pasture, a bullfrog croaked in the darkness, letting all know that it ruled the Jones pond. Nothing challenged in reply. Then the night was still again.

"Fucking pussy," Ronny said again, apparently dissatisfied with Steve's silence. "Guess we shouldn't expect any less from a guy that listens to Hall and Oates."

"I don't listen to Hall and Oates."

Jason grinned. "And Michael Jackson. You gonna do the moonwalk, Steve?"

"Screw you both."

Jason began singing Jackson's "Thriller" in a screeching falsetto, disturbing a flock of crows that had roosted for the night. They took flight, squawking in irritation.

"Go on home if you want to," Ronny said, nodding his head back across the field. "Fly like those birds. Jason and I will do it by ourselves. Those shitheads stole my bike and left it on the train tracks. It's payback time, man."

"Don't forget," Steve reminded him, "I'm the one who found out about this in the first place. Wasn't for me, we wouldn't even know about it."

Ronny and Jason didn't reply. Secretly, Ronny knew that Steve was right, and that pissed him off, because he hated it when he was shown to be wrong about something. He was the leader, damn it, and they should listen to him without question. And Jason stayed silent because he knew better than to go against Ronny, even when it came to something as innocuous as agreeing with Steve in this case. Last time he'd done that had been last Christmas, when the three had vandalized the widow Rudisill's front yard nativity scene. Even though she'd lived alone, her son came over every November and decorated the outside of her house for Christmas. He hung lights from the gutters and shrubbery and set up a small plywood nativity scene, complete with plastic light-up statues of Joseph, Mary, the Wise Men and the shepherds, several animals, and the baby Jesus himself, lying safe in a wooden manger stuffed with straw from Luke Jones's farm. People would slow down in their cars as they drove by, stopping to gawk in appreciation at the display—until the three boys had put a stop to it once and for all. To this day, Jason couldn't have told you why they did it or what sparked the idea. They'd been sitting around in their fort in the woods behind Ronny's house, smoking weed and snickering over a crude cartoon in a *Hustler* magazine, when Ronny had suddenly suggested it. They'd waited until after dark and then raided the nativity, smashing Joseph and a plastic lamb, tossing Mary and one of the Wise Men out into the road, and stealing the baby Jesus, which they'd later hung from a tree along Route 116. During the rampage, right about the time Ronny was heaving the statue of Mary over his head, Jason had suggested that it was wrong, and that Mrs. Rudisill had never done anything to them, and that maybe they should stop. That little mutinous outburst had resulted in Jason being frozen out of the group for almost a month. Ronny and Steve were his only friends, and while it sometimes felt as if Ronny was the general and he and Steve were merely soldiers, he didn't like being lonely, being an outcast.

So now he said nothing. Like tonight, for example. Yes, Steve had been the one to overhear Graco and his buddies. He'd been out hunting squirrels with his old man's Mossberg .22 (illegally and out of season, of course) in the woods bordering the graveyard when he'd come across Timmy Graco, Doug Keiser, and Barry Smeltzer. Steve had hid behind a tree and eavesdropped on their three adversaries, and after they'd left, he'd looked inside the shed for himself, confirming what they suspected. They'd first heard the rumor about the three boy's underground clubhouse last winter, but so far, they'd been unable to confirm its location, or even its existence.

But while Steve had finally done that, he'd delivered the information to Ronny and then conceded. Ronny called the shots. This raid was his idea. Steal their stuff. Trash the rest, including the fort.

Jason's mother had once asked him (after he, Ronny, and Steve had gotten in trouble for throwing rocks at cars) if he'd jump off a bridge if Ronny told him to do it. "No" had been his sulking answer.

But the truth was something different.

Yes, if Ronny ordered him to jump off a bridge, Jason probably would, if reluctantly, do it. What he wouldn't do was talk back or disagree with him until they were on their way down.

"So are you going home or what?" Ronny asked Steve.

"No, I'm staying. I want to see this fort, too."

"Gotta tell you," Ronny admitted, "I thought the whole thing was bullshit. Keiser told Andy Staub, who told Erica Altland, who told Ramona Gerling, and she told Linda Paloma, who told me when we were making out behind the shop class."

Jason interrupted. "Linda's hot. You made out with her?"

Ronny nodded. "Yeah. She's got nice tits. Let me feel them. But I didn't really believe it when she told me. Didn't think those three had it in them. Graco's a runt, and Keiser's a fat sack of shit. Only one of them with any meat on his bones is Smeltzer."

"The hole is huge," Steve said. "Wait till you see it. Fucking massive, man! Must have taken them forever to dig it, though. Keiser's titties must have been jiggling like Jell-O while he worked that shovel."

"Well, after tonight, they'll have to dig another one."

He laughed, and Steve and Jason dutifully joined him.

They reached the fence line and climbed over it. In the darkness, they didn't notice the old stovepipe jutting from the ground less than ten feet away. Had they seen it, they might have investigated and learned of the underground fort's true location. Instead, they crept through the cemetery toward the utility shed.

They weaved between the tombstones, keeping an eye out for headlights or anyone else, but the graveyard was empty. An owl hooted from somewhere to their left. Crickets chirped in the grass. A tractor trailer rumbled by in the distance, rocketing down Route 116 to parts unknown.

Jason suddenly stopped.

"You guys hear that?" he whispered.

"What?" Ronny turned around, annoyed.

"Sounded like . . . sounded like a woman screaming."

"It was a fucking owl, dipshit."

Jason shrugged. "Maybe. Yeah, I guess you're right. Just sounded weird, is all. Like it was coming from under the ground or something."

Ronny started walking again. "Dude, you need to listen to Nancy Reagan."

"Nancy Reagan?"

"Yeah. President's wife."

"I know who she is. But what did she say?"

" 'Just say *no* to drugs.' "

Steve laughed at Ronny's joke, eager to score some points over Jason. When their backs were turned, Jason shot them both the finger. Then he hurried to catch up, trotting along behind them. He noticed that several of the graves had a sunken look, as if the dirt were collapsing in upon the coffins beneath the surface.

"Smeltzer's old man is really letting this place fall apart," Jason observed. "Frigging shame."

"What do you care? You ain't got no family buried here." Ronnie plucked a fistful of wilting flowers from a graveside vase and threw them into the air, scattering them. "You don't even go to this church—any church, for that matter. And besides, Mr. Smeltzer's a drunk. Everyone knows that. He's a loser, just like his son."

Chuckling, he grabbed the vase and flung it skyward as well. It soared over their heads and then plummeted back to the ground, shattering on a bronze memorial plaque.

"Dude," Steve whispered. "We're gonna get caught, you keep making noise like that."

"Nobody's gonna catch us. It's after midnight. Everyone's asleep."

"You never know. Someone could be watching."

"What—you worried God is gonna get pissed?"

"It just don't feel right."

"Shut up. Let's go." Ronny kicked a plastic wreath like it was a football and then stalked forward again, leaving destruction in his wake—uprooted flags, scattered floral arrangements, broken glass. Jason and Steve nervously followed. But when Ronny stopped at a sagging tombstone and began to push against it, they quickly joined him despite their misgivings. It was easier that way. The three managed to push it over, and then jumped out of the way.

"Look at that," Ronny said. "Damn thing sank right into the ground. Spot must be muddy."

Steve shined the flashlight on the spot. "It looks dry."

"Then why'd the ground give in so much?"

"Maybe their tunnel goes all the way out here."

"No way." Ronny shook his head. "There's no fucking way those three wimps dug all the way out here. Keiser's a fat piece of shit. Graco might weigh a buck oh five, soaking wet. The two of them couldn't do ten pushups if their lives depended on it. And Smeltzer didn't dig it himself. I'm telling you, the ground must be soft from rain or something."

Afraid to disagree, Steve cast a nervous glance upward and noticed that the storm clouds were growing denser and darker. They looked swollen, heavy, as if they were about to fall out of the sky. He kept it to himself, rather than risk another round of ridicule from his friends.

Ronny started humming Judas Priest's "Breaking the

Law" and Jason accompanied him on air guitar. Both of them whipped their heads back and forth, their long hair flying like wind-tossed straw.

They reached the rear of the shed and made sure they were still alone. Satisfied that they were the cemetery's only occupants, Ronny motioned to Steve. All three of them were excited now at the prospect of getting back at their three enemies, and any individual misgivings they had vanished. Steve showed them the loose boards. Quickly and as quietly as possible, they worked the nails free and then clambered inside. Steve shined the flashlight around the interior. All three wrinkled their noses in disgust.

"Jesus Christ," Ronny whispered. "What the hell is that?"

"I don't know," Steve said, "but it's worse now than it was today. I noticed it when I found the hole, but it's stronger now."

Jason gagged. "Smells like something died. Man, that's *foul*."

"So where's the entrance?" Ronny pinched his nose shut and his voice sounded funny.

Steve trained the flashlight's beam over the pile of wood. "Under there."

"Give me the light," Ronny ordered. Then, after Steve complied, "You guys pull those boards up."

Steve and Jason did as commanded, grunting with the effort. Then they stepped back from the edge. With the plywood out of the way, the nauseating stench grew even thicker. Ronny shined the light down into the hole. Darkness stared back at them.

"How deep is it?" he asked.

Steve shrugged. "I don't know. I didn't go down inside."

"Well, go now, stupid. We ain't got all night. Gotta

make sure you're home before it rains. Don't want you melting or anything."

Moving with obvious reluctance, Steve stepped toward the tunnel entrance, leaned out over the opening, and looked down inside. He snorted, and then spit. The wad of phlegm and saliva vanished into the darkness.

"Didn't hear it hit bottom." He grinned. "Maybe it's a bottomless pit, like in *Raiders of the Lost Ark*."

Ronny didn't say anything. His glare was enough to prod Steve into action. Steve turned around, knelt on the dirt floor, and lowered his legs into the hole. Then he inched himself backward. His waist was even with the floor, then his chest. His fingers clutched at the ground, clawing for purchase. Then his chin was even with the ground and still his feet hadn't touched bottom.

Ronnie shined the light directly into his eyes. "Anything?"

"No . . ." Blinking, Steve raised a hand to shield his face from the bright beam, forgetting that both his hands were digging into the dirt, holding him aloft. With a yelp, he slipped. His fingers left deep trenches in the floor. He vanished from sight. His screams were followed by a muffled thump.

"Holy shit." Jason ran to the edge and peered over. Chuckling, Ronny joined him. Steve stared back up at them from approximately ten feet below. His face and hands were covered in dirt. He brushed soil from his hair.

"You asshole, Ronny. Why'd you do that?"

"I'm gonna kick your ass when I get down there if you call me an asshole again."

"Sorry, dude. But that wasn't right, man. I could have broken my leg or something."

"Fuck you, crybaby. What do you see?"

Steve shook the rest of the dirt from his hair and then peered into the darkness. "Not much. Looks like it goes both ways. The smell is definitely coming from down here, though. God, it makes me want to puke."

"Maybe they're pissing down there," Jason suggested. "Shitting, so they ain't got to run home when they need to go."

"The walls are slimy," Steve called. "There's some kind of . . . goo. What is this shit? It's sick."

Ronny shook his head in disgust. "Do you see their stash or anything?"

"No. You've got the flashlight, man."

Without warning, Ronny tossed the flashlight down to him. Instead of catching it, Steve threw his hands over his head to protect himself. The flashlight thudded onto the tunnel floor. The beam went out.

"Shit! Pick it up, man."

Plunged into total darkness, Steve knelt and frantically felt around for the flashlight. The hard-packed dirt on the tunnel's floor felt slimy, too. His fingers brushed across the flashlight and he turned it back on, but nothing happened.

"It's broke," he called. "Get me out of here. I can't see shit, and it stinks."

"Because you're under a graveyard." Jason giggled.

"Come on, dudes. Pull me up."

They heard his hand flailing around in the darkness, slapping at the moist, earthen sides of the pit.

"Goddamn it," Ronny muttered. "Do I have to do everything myself? All we're supposed to do is trash three geeks' stupid clubhouse. Get them back for what they did to my bike. That's it. And now look at us. You guys would fuck up a wet dream. I swear to fucking Christ, sometimes I feel like Boss Hawg, surrounded by a bunch of idiots." He reached into his pocket and pulled out a cigarette lighter. Handing it to Jason, he said, "Go help him."

Swallowing hard, Jason turned and lowered himself into the pit.

"Look out below."

Steve called up, "What? It's hard to hear down here."

"Move out of the way, dipshit."

Feet dangling into empty space, Jason let go and dropped to the bottom, landing in a crouch. He sprang to his feet, brushed himself off, and then thumbed the lighter wheel. He sighed in relief at the sight of the orange flame. The brief darkness had seemed like a solid thing. Next to him, Steve was visibly grateful as well.

"Coming down."

Ronny landed with a grunt. The floor squelched beneath his feet. The flame on the lighter wavered, then resumed. The three teens glanced around. They stood in the center of a tunnel, running roughly in the direction of the cemetery's lower half, where the older graves were, and in the direction they'd come from, towards Farmer Jones's pasture. The walls were smooth. The floor was smooth, too, although piles of soil lay scattered along it—debris left behind from the digging. The passage was roughly circular, wide enough to walk single file, and varied in height. Their heads brushed against the ceiling, but none of them had to crouch or slump forward.

"This is fucking disgusting." Ronny wiped slime from his hair with his fingers, then flung it away. It dripped from his fingertips like translucent mucous. "What the hell is this shit?"

"Snail snot?" Jason suggested.

Steve and Ronny blinked at him.

"Snail snot?" Ronny snickered. "That would have to be one big fucking snail."

Steve covered his mouth and nose with his hand, trying in vain to block out the stench. He immediately pulled it away. The traces of slime left on his hand smelled even worse than the air. "So what now?"

The lighter was growing hot. Wincing, Jason switched it to his other hand and sucked the tip of his burned thumb.

"Well," Ronny said, no longer bothering to whisper. His voice echoed in the subterranean chamber. "Their clubhouse has to be in one of these two directions. You go that way," he pointed toward the old grave-yard, "and Jason, you go the other way."

"What about you?" Jason asked.

"Somebody's got to stay here and be on the lookout. What if Old Man Smeltzer shows up? Or the cops? Who's gonna warn you? Now get going. Time's a wastin'."

"Fuck that," Steve said, taking a rare stand. "I ain't going anywhere without a light."

"Yeah, Ronny," Jason dared to agree, bolstered by Steve's bravery. "In fact, maybe we ought to bag this whole thing. We don't know what this slime is. Could be toxic, like that chemical dump they found in Seven Valleys, with all the illegal waste. And these walls and roof don't look too sturdy. There's no beams or sup-ports or nothing. Could come crashing down like that." He snapped the fingers on his free hand.

Ronny sighed. "Nothing's gonna happen. Quit worry-ing."

Steve stared at his sleeve, coated with slime from brushing up against the tunnel wall. "You really think this shit could be toxic?"

Ronny's patience wore thin. "If you'd get to it, we wouldn't be down here long enough for it to bother us, even if it was poisonous or something. Look, if you need your little night-light, both of you go in one direction, then. Fucking pussies."

They glanced at one another, sighed, then set off into the darkness. Jason led the way, Steve slinking along behind him.

"Stinks worse back here," Ronny heard Jason mumble. "It's like a cloud."

Steve coughed. "Bet we're heading toward the old part of the graveyard. Maybe it's bodies we're smelling."

The lighter's flame got dimmer as they kept moving forward. Their voices grew faint, and Ronny had to strain to hear them. One of them, he couldn't tell if it was Steve or Jason, said something. The dirt walls seemed to swallow the words up.

"Can't be that far," Ronny called. "Look for their shit. Comics. Porno mags. Stuff like that. If it ain't there, then it's down the other way."

The flame was a distant pinprick now, and the shadows closed in on Ronny, surrounding him. In his mind, it felt like the darkness was pushing against his body—a tangible thing. The air inside the tunnel grew colder.

"Guys? Hey, Steve! Jason! Did you hear me, fuckers? It must be this way."

The tiny flame disappeared completely. Ronny gasped, and closed his eyes for a second. When he opened them again, it was like they were still shut. He wiggled his fingers in front of his face, but couldn't see them.

"Hey, dickheads! Get back here with the goddamn lighter! I can't see shit."

The darkness became a wall. A cocoon. Something cold and wet dripped on his head.

"Jesus Christ . . . hey, Jason? Get the fuck back here now, you son of a bitch! This shit ain't funny, man. Not one fucking bit."

There was no response.

"Steve?"

His annoyance turned to anger, then fright. Not fear. Not terror. Not yet. But he was frightened. He was shivering and it had nothing to do with the chill in the air. No way he wanted to stay down there in the dark, especially not when the whole place smelled like shit. He couldn't go find them. Without a light, he could trip or stumble into a wall or something and knock the whole tunnel down on top of them, burying them alive.

"Jason? Steve? Come on, you guys, answer me."

"me . . . me . . . me . . ."

His voice echoed back to him, taking on an odd, muffled quality. The stench, that open sewer smell, grew stronger. "Quit fucking around, goddamn it! I know you can hear me. You ain't gone that far."

"far . . . far . . . far . . ."

"I'm gonna beat the living shit out of you both if you don't get back here with that lighter right fucking now."

"now . . . now . . . now . . ."

The echo died, and was followed by a new sound. A grunt.

"The fuck was that?"

He wondered if there could be an animal down there with them. Maybe a fox or a skunk, maybe with rabies. Ronny shivered, then got pissed off all over again. He shifted his weight, and his foot collided with the discarded flashlight, knocking it farther into the darkness. He bit back a yelp. Enraged, he took a deep breath, preparing to shout at the top of his lungs, to yell and holler at them like never before, to put the fear of *Ronny Nace* into them.

That was when the screams started.

"Oh shit . . ."

Muffled. Faint. But despite the distance, there was no mistaking the terror in them. Or the pain. No illusions; they weren't just fucking around or playing a joke. Something was wrong.

"Jason?" Ronny's voice became a hoarse whisper. "S-Steve? Please come back. Please . . ."

"Ronny, run! R—arrggh . . ."

"Guys? What's happening?"

"Ronnnnyyyyyyyyyyyyyyyyyy . . ."

He couldn't tell if it was Steve or Jason, or maybe both of them. It was too high-pitched, too feminine. He'd never heard either of them scream like that before. He'd never heard *anyone* scream like that.

". . . yyyyyyyyyyyyyy . . ."

"Guys," he sobbed. "I-I can't see you . . ."

". . . yyyyyyyyyyyyyy . . ."

The scream had turned into one long, warbling wail. Then, almost lost beneath it, was another grunt—a raspy sort of snuffling sound, like a cross between a bear and a pig. Abruptly, the screaming stopped. The tunnel was silent for a brief second, and then footsteps pounded toward him. The stench grew even more overpowering. Ronny glanced up at the top of the hole, but could barely see the outline. Something hissed in the darkness, a teakettle set to boil or a locomotive building up to full steam.

The running footsteps drew closer. Ronny peered into the darkness, trying to determine if it was Steve or Jason.

It was neither.

Whatever it was, its laugh was guttural, like gravel. Both the hissing sound and the stench were all around Ronny now. Suddenly, even as his stomach churned and his nose burned from the acrid odor, Ronny realized what the sound reminded him of. Several years before, when he was younger, Ronny's favorite Saturday morning show had been Sid and Marty Krofft's *Land of the Lost*. In it, there had been an alien race of lizard-like beings called the Sleestak. They'd terrified him; equipped with huge, black, bulbous eyes, claw-like pincers for hands, scaly green bodies, and pointed heads and tails. But the worst part, the scariest part of all, was the sound they'd made: a reptilian hissing that went on and on with no pause.

That was the sound he heard racing down the tunnel. Racing toward him.

Then the figure became discernable. Human-sized; two arms and legs, and alabaster skin—white almost to the point of albinism. Ronny blinked, then realized why he could see it. Whatever this thing was, it gave off its own luminescence. Not much, but enough to make out its features. He willed himself to move, but his feet disobeyed him.

The creature drew closer, swinging long, dangling arms that hung down past its waist. On the ends of those monstrous appendages were oversized hands with talon-tipped, bony fingers. The thing seemed to be entirely hairless, and in the middle of its pointed head was a tiny face; yellow pinprick eyes, a slit for a nose, nonexistent chin, all dominated by a huge, grinning mouth full of yellow and black teeth. Slime—the same slime that covered the tunnel—dripped from its pores.

It was the stench of the creature that broke Ronny's

paralysis, a smell so brutally strong and rancid that his eyes watered and burned. Cringing, he leapt upward, hands grasping the sides of the wall, clutching the slimy dirt. He slid back down. Felt the creature's breath on the back of his neck. It was close enough to bite him, but for some reason, it didn't. Instead, it raised its clawed hands and swiped. Dodging the razor-sharp talons, Ronny jumped again. This time he found purchase. He managed to get both arms out of the tunnel, grabbed a piece of wood on the shed floor, and pulled himself up. His head emerged from the chasm, then one shoulder, then both.

Suddenly, pain ripped through his ankle. He looked down. The creature's claws were flaying through the skin, and his white sock and shoe had both turned red. It burned—a white-hot, searing agony. The monster looked up at him and grinned. Its small eyes grew larger, bulging from its head. Screeching, Ronny slid backward, his fingers slipping in the dirt.

"No, no, no, no . . ."

The creature lashed out again, slicing through the denim and into his calf. Despite the burning sensation in his leg, the monster's grasp was ice cold. Gritting his teeth, Ronny pulled himself up higher, kicking out with both feet, freeing himself again. The thing in the tunnel grunted, then roared in anger. Ronny kept pulling. His fingers burrowed deep into the dirt, trying to maintain his grip. His chest lay on the shed floor now, followed by his waist. Blood dripped from his wounded leg in bright red ribbons.

And then the thing spoke, and somehow, that was more terrifying than its appearance.

"You have invaded my home. Forced me to break the commandment."

Ronny tried to answer, but found that he couldn't.

There was a jingling sound from outside the shed. Keys. The lock jiggled. The doors swung open and a bright flare of brilliance temporarily blinded the screaming teen. A figure stood in the open doorway, a silhouette clutching a powerful Mag light—the kind used by cops and firemen. Then the light shifted away and Ronny saw who it was.

Clark Smeltzer.

"Oh, God," he babbled, a mixture of terror and relief. "Mr. Smeltzer, pull me up. There's something down there!"

The caretaker crossed the shed floor in four quick strides and glowered down at Ron. His face seemed drawn and haggard, and his eyes were red.

"Hey, man," Ronny pleaded. "Pull me up! *Please?*"

"I know you. You're the one that beat up my boy a few times. Made me whip him myself, just so he'd go back out and whip you."

Ronny clutched the dirt floor, holding on for dear life. "Pull me up, man."

"You're trespassing."

"Mr. Smeltzer, there's something down here. Pull—"

"You shouldn't a come here, boy."

"What—"

Clark raised one booted foot and stamped on Ronny's left hand. Bones snapped beneath his heel. The horrified teenager screamed. Then he stamped on the boy's other hand, pulverizing his fingers.

Ronny fell into the darkness, a look of disbelief in his eyes. He landed with a thud. The ghoul roared in triumph. Its claws descended. It tore into the teenager like a buzz saw through wood.

Clark turned away from the ripping and tearing sounds, and threw up on a pile of tiny American flags. While the screaming continued, he fetched his bottle of Wild Turkey from its hiding place and washed the taste of puke from his mouth.

The screaming stopped, but the sounds of slaughter continued.

Clark tipped the bottle up and drained it, gasping as alcohol dribbled down his whiskered cheeks and chin. He tried to pretend he wasn't crying, and told himself the tears were from guilt rather than just fear.

Finally, after what seemed like an eternity (a cliché Clark heard people use in movies all the time, but in this case, it happened to be true) the sounds stopped, and the ghoul crawled out of the charnel pit. Its white skin was streaked with blood and gore, and bits of skin and fabric hung from its claws.

Clark silently wished for another bottle, if only to wash the image from his mind. He'd drunk more than ever these last few weeks, walking around as if with alcohol-induced amnesia. Another lie he told himself, because deep down inside, he remembered everything. Every detail. Every scream.

The ghoul handed him three wallets. Two were made of black leather; one with the initials VH and the other with KILL 'EM ALL. The third wallet was red plastic and stamped MADE IN TAIWAN. He didn't even bother to look inside them; just stuffed them in his pockets.

"That it?"

"They had no other valuables. No trinkets or baubles. Such things are wasted on the youth. Did you know the boy?"

Clark shrugged. "Seen him around. He tussled with my own boy a time or two."

"Indeed?"

"Yeah." Clark ran a hand through his greasy hair. "Him and his two friends. The three of them against my boy and his two pals. They down there, too?"

The ghoul nodded. "You hold their coin purses in your hand."

"What about the bodies? You need me to, uh . . . get rid of them?"

"No need for you to dispose of their corpses. Let them ripen. In a few days they will be like sweet fruit on the vine. Then I can feast, in accordance with the Law set forth by Him."

"What do you mean?"

"My kind is forbidden to eat warm flesh or drink hot blood. We must wait."

The creature wiped its mouth with the back of its hand.

"However," it continued, "I had a little taste just now. Just a little, as I killed them. Something to whet my appetite."

Clark gagged, and fought to keep from throwing up again.

"You did well," the ghoul said. "What brings you here at night? Were you attracted by these trespassers, or do you have another for me?"

Clark swallowed the lump in his throat. The creature's raspy voice gave him the creeps. Hell, the whole damn thing gave him the creeps.

"I got another. Outside. We got to be quick. I don't want anyone to see me. Would be hard pressed to explain what I'm doing out here this time of night."

"But you are the caretaker. You are in charge of this necropolis. Who better to stalk its grounds late at night?"

"Necro what?"

"Never mind." The ghoul dismissed the question with a wave of its hand. "Show me what you have brought. I can smell it from here."

They walked outside. Clark had parked his car next

to the utility shed. The lights and motor were off. A muffled thump echoed from inside the trunk. He fumbled for his keys, realized they were still hanging from the shed door, and retrieved them. His hands shook so badly that he had trouble sliding the key into the trunk lock. On the third try, the key slipped in. He turned it, and the trunk sprang open.

The ghoul sighed with rapture. "Excellent. You have done well."

A terrified young woman stared up at them, eyes bulging from her sockets, big hair plastered to her scalp in a mix of sweat and blood. She screamed around the dirty rag that had been stuffed into her mouth and then secured with a strip of duct tape. More silver duct tape bound her wrists and ankles together.

The ghoul cocked its head and studied the woman with obvious appreciation. Its long black tongue slithered across its lips. "She is a pretty one, like a fresh plucked flower. Do you know her?"

Clark nodded reluctantly. "Deb Lentz. Her aunt's buried here. Found her earlier, on my way home from the bar. She had a flat tire, on the back road down near the Porter's Siding Sawmill. I gave her a ride. Nobody saw. There's nobody else on the road this time of night."

"You have done well, indeed. Tomorrow, you shall find more spoils."

"More than the normal stuff, right? I mean, this is kidnapping. Ain't like I'm just covering up for you anymore. Shit's getting hairy."

The ghoul laughed. "Yes, yes. More than your usual payment. These grounds are rich in plunder. I shall see to it that you are paid handsomely. Now, away with you. I must take my new bride below."

Clark hesitated, his reactions slowed by the alcohol in his system.

The ghoul reached for the woman in the trunk, and she cringed. She tried to scream again, but all that came out around the gag were choking sounds. Snot bubbled from her nose. Her eyes were so wide that Clark thought they might pop. Hissing, the creature traced one talon along her creased forehead. She shuddered at the hideous caress, and then her bladder failed. Clark winced at the stench.

"Goddamn it," he slurred. "Now I got to clean the trunk out, or else somebody will smell it and start wondering what happened."

The ghoul ignored him. It reached into the trunk again and extracted the squirming woman. Flinging her over one shoulder, it started back toward the shed. The terrified woman made squealing sounds.

"There now," it whispered almost lovingly. "You will not be harmed. I have other intentions for you. I fear that I may be the last of my kind. You will aid me with that, just as my other wife has been."

Deb Lentz went limp and slumped over his shoulder, mercifully unconscious.

Clark didn't watch it return to the tunnels. After it was gone, he shut the shed door and locked it tight. The breeze rustled through the tree limbs over the building. Dead leaves danced in the wind, forming mini dervishes. The air felt electric and held the sharp tang of ozone. The hair on his arms and what little remained on his head both stood up. Static crackled. A storm was coming, that much was for sure.

Clark had done some bad things in his life. He knew that he wasn't going to win any awards for Father or Husband of the Year. He'd done bad things. Killed people in Vietnam—some who'd deserved it and some who hadn't. He'd cheated folks, stolen money. Lied. Been unfaithful to his wife. But he'd never done anything like he had tonight. Kidnapping a woman from the roadside and handing her over to that . . . thing.

He needed a drink.

Leaving the car parked where it was, so as not to risk drawing attention, he walked back over to his house, crept into the garage, and collected a bucket, rags, soap, and a new stainless steel combination lock that he'd bought for a different task—but now had a new, more urgent use for it. He also took one of his emergency bottles of Wild Turkey, which he'd stashed in the garage's rafters for safekeeping. He took a long pull on the bottle, but barely tasted the alcohol.

Then he returned to the cemetery. He drank as he worked, and the bottle's contents quickly disappeared. He washed out the trunk as the first rumble of thunder rolled overhead. By the time he was finished, the rain had started to fall, sporadic, but promising much more to follow. Lightning flashed across the night sky. Not wanting to get caught out in the storm, Clark hurried. He drained the last drop of Wild Turkey, dumped the soapy water from the bucket, threw the pail and the empty liquor bottle into the trunk, and slammed the lid. Then he ran over to the shed, removed the old lock, and snapped the combination lock on instead.

How'd those kids get inside? he wondered. *Ain't like they picked the lock.*

He walked around the outside of the building, investigating all the walls, until he found the loose boards over the window. He grimaced.

Got to fix that first thing tomorrow. Wouldn't do for Barry or one of his bratty friends to find it.

Then something else occurred to him. He'd rarely seen the three boys who were killed tonight in the cemetery. Maybe once or twice before, and both times had been when they were mixing it up with Barry and his friends. But his son, along with that smart-mouthed Graco and the fat kid—they were in the cemetery almost every day.

He looked back at the window and his fists clenched.

Another blast of thunder shook the sky, and then the rain began to pour. Cold droplets pelted his skin, bouncing off like lead pellets. Clark Smeltzer ran to his car, got behind the wheel, and wept. Then he drove back home, sneaked inside the house, and collapsed into bed. Rhonda stirred next to him, and he glowered at her. One of her eyes was swollen shut from when he'd hit her earlier in the evening, when she'd asked him why he had to go out again. She mumbled something as he slipped beneath the covers, but Clark didn't answer. Seconds later, he passed out.

Outside, the storm began to rage.

CHAPTER EIGHT

Timmy and Doug stared out Timmy's bedroom window, watching the torrential downpour. Rain fell in sheets and the winds whipped the tops of the trees back and forth like springs. They listened to his mother's wind chimes, ringing and spinning uncontrollably as the roaring winds battered them about. Tomorrow morning the ground would be littered with fallen branches and leaves. Both of them wondered if the power would go out, but so far it had stayed on. Timmy's digital clock glowed in the darkness. The raindrops beat against the roof like hailstones.

The thunderstorm had blown in just after one in the morning, forceful and angry and demanding attention. Despite this, it hadn't woken Randy or Elizabeth, who slept right through the cacophonous explosions, nor had it woken the boys, because they'd already been awake. Indeed, they'd yet to fall asleep. They'd read comic books and played a game of Monopoly (arguing over who got to be the banker and who got to use the car as his playing piece), and had watched *Phantasm* on the late night movie. The film appealed to them both, not only because it was a horror movie, but because of the protagonist. He was a mirror image of them, complete with a cemetery to play in. Doug had been pretty freaked out by the flying silver spheres, which sliced and diced their victims, and the gruesome, hooded dwarves, and the film's ghoulish main antagonist, an otherworldly funeral director known as the Tall Man. Timmy had just been mad that all of the good stuff was cut out, and wished again for a VCR so he could watch movies unedited. He didn't understand why Loni Anderson could parade around in a swimsuit on *WKRP in Cincinnati*, but blood and guts weren't allowed to be shown.

When Elizabeth peeked her head in at eleven and told them lights out, they'd obeyed the letter of the law, if not the spirit. They'd retired—somewhat reluctantly— to their beds and spent the last two hours talking in hushed tones over a flashlight beam, until the storm interrupted them.

"Well," Timmy said, disappointed, "so much for exploring the tunnel tonight."

"You think Barry will still sneak out?"

"Not in this. Guess we'll have to explore it tomorrow. How's your ankle feeling?"

"Better. I think it will be okay. Still like to know what the hell bit me, though."

"Ah, it wasn't anything to worry about, I'm sure."

Timmy was sitting cross-legged in his bed, wearing a pair of plaid pajamas. Doug was stretched out on the floor, in the bed Timmy's mother had made up for him, clad in his boxers and one of Randy Graco's ratty old T-shirts, since Timmy's shirts wouldn't fit him. The shirt proudly proclaimed IPW LOCAL 1407 and on the back it said, AMERICAN MADE IS UNION MADE. He propped himself up on his elbows and stared out the window again.

"Boy," Doug whispered so as not to wake Timmy's parents, "it's really coming down out there. Look at it bouncing off the yard."

"Yeah. This keeps up, the Codorus Creek will flood for sure. We can go inner-tubing tomorrow."

"What about the tunnel?"

"We can still explore it tomorrow night. It's probably better to wait for night, anyway. Less chance of getting caught."

"Where will we get the tubes from?"

"Barry's dad has some in their garage. I saw them when Barry and I were looking for his football. Four tire tubes off a tractor—big ones, like you'd get at a construction site."

"Where did he get them?"

"I don't know." Timmy paused. "Speaking of which, you noticed anything about Barry's dad lately?"

"Other than the fact that he's meaner than usual? No."

"He's had a lot of stuff that they didn't have before."

"What do you mean?"

"It's like he has more money or something. Mrs. Smeltzer's been wearing new jewelry. Barry's supposed to be getting a Yamaha Eighty dirt bike. The way Barry talks, they've been going out to eat and stuff a lot more often."

"You mentioned it before. The day your grandpa . . . well, that day."

Timmy felt a twinge of sadness at the mention of his grandfather. "Yeah, but I've noticed a lot more of it since then."

"Maybe his dad's just trying to make up for some of the crap he's pulled. Trying to buy them off."

"Yeah," Timmy said. "Maybe. But that still doesn't explain where he's getting all this money. They were never poor, but he was always bitching about how the church didn't pay him enough."

A flash of lightning reflected off Doug's face. "Maybe he got a raise."

"I guess. But you'd think Barry would have said something about it. Last time the union got my dad a raise, we went to Chuck E. Cheese to celebrate."

"Never mind all that," Doug said. "How he got the inner-tubes doesn't matter. How are we going to get them out of the garage without him knowing?"

"If we think he'll have a problem with it, we'll just wait till he's busy working—or until he's passed out inside. Then, all we gotta do is inflate them, and we can use the air pump down at the Old Forge service station for that."

Doug's face brightened. "I can get some Hershey's bars while we're there. And they've got *Sinistar* and *Golden Axe* and *Spy Hunter*. And those cool old pinball machines like our dad's used to play when they were kids."

"Your dad played pinball?"

Doug shrugged, and then started humming the theme to *Spy Hunter*.

Timmy shook his head. "Dude, forget about all that. You want to play video games all day, or do you want to go tubing? We can float all the way from Bowman's Woods down through Colonial Valley and into the paper mill's pond. Then we can just walk home. Just have to make sure we don't go by Ronny or Jason's houses. It'll be fun. We could even take our fishing rods, and catch carp and suckers while we're floating downstream."

"What about snapping turtles? Creek's full of them. And water snakes. You don't like snakes."

"I'll take my BB gun. If we see one, I'll shoot it before it even gets close."

"If your mom lets you, that is."

Timmy shrugged. "What she doesn't know won't hurt her. I don't see why I should have to report every little thing I do during the day. This ain't Russia."

"Sometimes I wish my mom *would* ask me where I was going and what I was doing. It would be nice to know she cared."

Timmy wasn't sure what to say. "She cares, man. She just . . . has a funny way of showing it."

Right away, he realized how insincere he sounded.

Doug didn't reply. He stared out at the falling rain, watching it run down the windows and pour off the roof of the Graco's shed.

"Seriously," Timmy said, even though he didn't believe it, "you know she loves you, right?"

Slowly, Doug looked at him. His bottom lip quivered and there was a haunted, feral look in his eyes that Timmy had never seen before. His face had gone pale.

"That's just it. She loves me too much. She . . ."

He sobbed, unable to finish. Sniffling, he turned away. His hands curled into fists, and he slammed them into his legs again and again.

Timmy reached out his hand. "Hey."

Doug's entire body began to tremble. He made a sound like a wounded animal.

"She . . ."

"Doug, what is it?"

Part of Timmy was already afraid he knew the answer, and another part of him was even more afraid—afraid of having those suspicions confirmed, afraid of what it might mean for his friend, and for them all. A loss of innocence, a dark passage from boyhood into the beginnings of manhood. He couldn't articulate it, not even to himself, but the emotions were there, deep down inside, bubbling to the surface and now spilling out over the brim.

"Whatever it is, you can tell me."

"She . . . oh, God."

Tears rolled down both of Doug's cheeks. When he spoke, he started slowly, each word, each syllable, choked out with an agonizing slowness. But the more he talked, the faster the rhythm—and the confirmation of everything that Timmy dreaded—became.

"She . . . she comes to me at night. In my room. When I'm sleeping. She t-touches me. Down there. And I don't want to like it. I don't want to, you know—get hard. But I do anyway. Deep down inside, a part of me does want to. I can't help it. Can't control it. She puts her mouth on my . . . on my thing . . . and I can't stop her. And then things start happening. I don't like the way it feels, but I let her do it anyway."

Doug shuddered at the memories, and Timmy found himself doing the same.

"How long?"

Doug looked at him in confusion. "How long is what?"

"How long has it been going on?"

"It started after my dad left. Seems like forever. Sometimes it's all a blur. You know? She lost her nursing job at the private school. Dad left around the same time. Instead of getting a job as a school nurse somewhere else, Mom just stayed home and started drinking. She'd sit there in front of the TV, just staring and crying, or lock herself inside her bedroom for twelve hours at a time. Eventually, she started staying awake all night, usually drunk, and then sleeping all day. And that was when she started coming in my room at night. Timmy—the things she says. The things she does. They sort of feel good, and that's the worst part of all, because they shouldn't. You and Barry joke about them when we're in the Dugout, reading those magazine letters and stuff, but in real life . . . In real life, those things are horrible. You don't want to hear those things. Not from your mother. Not from . . ."

Tears eradicated the rest. He hung his head and sobbed into his chest. After a moment, Timmy slid out of bed and padded over to him. He sat down, hesitated, and then put his arm around his best friend. Doug stiffened, but didn't move. They sat like that for a long time. Occasionally, Timmy would squeeze his shoulder.

Outside, the thunder rolled. Another ominous blast rattled the windows. Both boys jumped at the noise, and then were still again.

"That's why I put a lock on my door from the inside," Doug said, wiping his nose with his shirt. "That deadbolt? You and Barry laughed at me about it, but you didn't understand. You didn't know. It was to keep her out. She'd come in when I was sleeping. I'd wake up and she'd be standing there in the moonlight. Naked, sometimes. A few times she had on stuff like the centerfolds wear. Or worse, she'd already be in the bed with me. Under the covers . . . doing stuff."

Timmy nodded, sick to his stomach. He pictured Carol Keiser doing the things Doug was describing, and then immediately wished he hadn't.

"She always made me promise not to tell. Said it was our secret, that no one else would understand, and that if I told anybody, my dad might never come back, or that they'd take her away from me, too."

"So what did you do?"

"What could I do? I didn't do anything. I just laid there and . . . took it."

"Jesus."

"When it was over, sometimes she'd go back to her room or out into the living room. A few times she passed out. Right there in my bed. That's how drunk she was. Couple times, she called me by my dad's name, and once, she called me by someone else's."

"Who?"

"Someone I don't know. Some guy. Harry. Who knows? Could have been an old boyfriend of hers, or maybe she was running around on my dad."

Or maybe, Timmy thought, *it was another kid. Someone just like you, Doug. After all, she was a school nurse at a private boy's school.*

Doug got to his feet and pulled a tissue out of the box on Timmy's dresser. He blew his nose, then sat back down again. His hands kneaded the crumpled tissue, rolling it, then balling it up, and then rolling it again.

"A few times," he continued, "she said I should have you guys spend the night more often. You and Barry. Said if I convinced you, and you promised not to tell, that she'd let you guys do things to her, too. Let you touch her, and . . . stuff. I never told you guys, because I was afraid you might tell somebody, or that you might . . ." He paused, and shook his head.

"Might what, Doug?"

"Nothing."

"Come on, man. You can tell me. You told me this much already."

"And I shouldn't have. You can't tell anyone, Timmy. Not a soul."

"I'm not going to say anything. You thought Barry and I might what?"

"Promise you won't get mad?"

"Sure. I promise."

"You've got to swear it, Timmy. You've got to cross your heart and hope to die."

Despite his friend's traumatic confession, Timmy found himself chuckling at this. "And stick a needle in my eye while I'm at it? Come on, Doug. What are we, back in Mrs. Trimmer's fourth grade class? I swear it already. Cross my heart . . . and hope to die."

Doug licked his lips, nervous. "I . . . I was afraid you guys might do it."

"Oh, dude! You thought we'd do your mom? Man, that's sick."

"Lower your voice." Doug reached out and clamped a sweaty hand over Timmy's mouth. "You'll wake up your parents."

He removed his hand, and put his finger to his lips as a reminder. Outside the window, blue lightning flashed across the sky, making it daylight for a brief instant.

"Sorry," Timmy said. "But man, dude, I mean . . . how could you think something like that about us? We'd never do that to you. It's disgusting. It would be like doing that Jane Fonda chick that Mr. Messinger down at the newsstand thinks is so hot. Yeah, like maybe thirty years ago she was. Gross! Your Mom's like . . . old. And she's your *mom*, for Christ's sake."

"I know, I know," Doug whispered, ashamed. "But I was . . . jealous, I guess. I know that sounds weird, I mean, what with all she was doing to me. But despite all that, she's still my mother. I still want her to love me. Just not in that way. I thought that if you guys did it with her, that she might not love me at all anymore."

He started to cry again. Timmy sat there in stunned, silent disbelief—and despair. There was a word for what Doug had been forced to do with his mother, and that word was *incest*. Timmy had read about it. It was disgusting. But as sick and as wrong as it was, some part of Doug still loved his mother. He was more worried about her leaving him than he was about the vile things she was doing to him.

"It was nice," Doug said. "Being here tonight, with your mom and your dad. Eating hamburgers and playing games and watching movies—it felt so real. It felt like a regular family must feel, you know? I wish I had that."

Timmy nodded.

"You're a lucky guy, Timmy. I know you're still sad about your grandpa, and I know you argue with your parents sometimes, but you don't know how good you've got it. You should be grateful, man."

"I am," Timmy said. "Believe me, I am."

"I don't want to go home tomorrow. I wish I could stay here."

"Well, look. When we get up in the morning, let's talk to my parents about it. Maybe we can—"

"No!" Doug's shout was lost beneath the thunder, but both of them paused anyway, listening to see if it had awoken Timmy's parents.

"No," Doug said again, whispering this time. "You promised that you wouldn't tell anybody. You can't. Nobody else can know. Not even Barry."

Timmy felt torn. On the one hand, he wanted to tell his parents. This was too big for him to try and keep it bottled up inside. His parents would be able to help. He was worried about Doug, worried about what this would do to him emotionally. Obviously, it had already had some effect. Maybe his parents would let Doug stay with them. But on the other hand, he'd made a promise to his friend, and he couldn't just break it. He didn't want Doug to be mad at him.

While he struggled with these conflicting emotions, Doug excused himself and crept down the hall to the bathroom. Timmy heard him running water in the sink. His mother snored softly and his father farted in his sleep. The lightning flashed again, but the storm's power seemed to be lessening. The rain slowed to a drizzle, and the thunder was distant now, muted.

Doug came back into the room and tried to smile. He shut the door behind him.

"Sorry. I'm done crying now."

He sat back down, and Timmy squeezed his shoulder one more time.

"It'll be okay, Doug. You'll see. It'll all be okay."

But in his heart, Timmy knew that nothing would ever be okay again.

It was a long time before dawn arrived, and Timmy was still awake when the first rays of sunlight crept over the horizon.

CHAPTER NINE

When they got up for breakfast the next morning, they were surprised to learn that Timmy's father hadn't yet left for work. His truck was still in the driveway, and they heard him talking to Timmy's mother in hushed, serious tones. Timmy's first thought was that someone else in their family had died, maybe one of his aunts or uncles. His second thought was that maybe his father was sick. If that were so, it would have to be something very serious. Randy Graco had gone to work with the flu and a high fever before. He'd even gone in every day when he broke his leg while out deer hunting four years ago. Things like illness didn't stop him when it came to putting food on the table.

"Wonder what's happening?" Timmy said.

Doug didn't respond. He'd woken taciturn and withdrawn, and Timmy wondered if perhaps he was regretting telling the truth about what was happening between him and his mother.

"You okay, Doug?"

"Didn't sleep too good."

"Yeah, me either." Timmy pulled a clean pair of socks from his top dresser drawer. "Listen, about last night—"

"Let's not talk about it right now."

After getting dressed, the boys walked into the living room, and immediately, Timmy noticed the grim expression on both his parent's faces. His father looked shocked, and his mother was pale. At first he was afraid they'd overheard Doug's late-night confession, but then he realized that they were both staring at the television, which was tuned to the local news. They hadn't even looked up to acknowledge the boys' presence.

"What's going on?" Timmy asked. "What's wrong?"

Randy looked up from the newscast and blinked in surprise. "Hey guys. Good morning."

"Don't you have to work today, Dad?"

"I'm going in late. Wanted to talk to you guys first."

"Did you boys sleep okay?" Elizabeth sipped from a coffee mug. "Or did the storm wake you up last night?"

"We heard it," Timmy said. "Sounded pretty bad. Is that what's on the news?"

"No," she said quickly, glancing at her husband. "It's just . . ."

She shook her head and took another sip of coffee.

"Just what?"

"Maybe you two better sit down," Randy said, waving his hand at the couch.

Shit, Timmy thought. *They did overhear us last night.*

Doug shuffled his feet. "Um, are we in trouble, Mr. Graco?"

"No, Doug. Not at all." He gave a short, uncomfortable laugh. "But we do need to talk."

Timmy and Doug took seats on opposite ends of the couch. Timmy glanced at the television. A reporter was standing alongside a road. There were woods behind him, and a car parked along the side next to the trees. The entire area had been roped off with yellow police tape. Timmy frowned.

"What's going on, Dad?"

Randy stood up and turned off the television. Then he turned to his wife. "Hon, can you get me some more coffee?"

"Sure." Elizabeth got his mug and disappeared into the kitchen.

Randy leaned forward in his chair, folded his hands together, and stared at them both without speaking. He seemed to be considering something. Timmy and Doug both twitched nervously. Randy opened his mouth to speak, but the phone rang, interrupting him. In the kitchen, Timmy heard his mother answer it.

"Hello? . . . Oh, hi Brenda. . . . Yes, Randy and I were just watching it on the news. . . . Terrible."

Randy cleared his throat. Timmy and Doug turned their attention back to him.

"Boys," he said, "I don't know how to say this, so I'm just going to say it. I know you've had some trouble in the past with Ronny Nace and Jason Glatfelter and Steve Laughman. I know they're not exactly friends of yours, but—well, there's been some bad news."

Timmy twitched, wondering if his parents had found out about Ronny's stolen bike, and what they'd done with it.

Doug looked relieved. "Are they finally in jail for something?"

"No. They're missing."

In the kitchen, Elizabeth told Brenda good-bye and then hung up the phone.

"Missing?" Timmy glanced at the blank television screen. "Like they ran away?"

His father shook his head. "I guess it's a possibility, but the police don't seem to think so. Their parents reported them missing this morning. Another woman is missing, too. An adult. Deb Lentz. They found her car abandoned out near Porter's Sawmill. And there's even speculation that maybe Karen Moore and her boyfriend didn't run off, either."

"A serial killer?"

"I don't know, Timmy." Randy Graco scowled. "That's a little extreme, don't you think? Ask me, you've been reading too many comic books."

"But it could be."

"Yeah, sure it could. I guess. But they don't know that yet. All they know is that there are a lot of people missing all of the sudden. That doesn't mean it's a serial killer. Where do you get this stuff? I wasn't thinking about serial killers and monsters when I was twelve. I was busy playing football."

That's because you didn't get clobbered every time you played, Timmy thought to himself. *And you didn't live next door to a monster or down the road from one, either. The bad people aren't just in my comics. They're in the real world, too.*

Elizabeth returned with two fresh mugs of coffee for Randy and herself. Then she sat back down in the rocking chair.

"That was Brenda," she told her husband. "She and Larry are going to do the same thing with their kids."

Nodding, Randy sipped coffee.

"Do what with us?" Timmy didn't like the sound of this—whatever it was.

"Well," his mother said, picking up where Randy had left off, "the reason your father stayed home this morning was because we wanted to talk to you about this. We've discussed it, and came to a decision. Your father and I think it might be best if you stick close to home for the next few days. You too, Doug."

"But it's summer," Timmy said. "We've got stuff to do. Important stuff. We're not babies. We can watch out for ourselves."

"Even still," Elizabeth insisted, "you're not to go anywhere by yourself from now on—until the police find out what's happened. No going off to the woods or the dump or the pond, and no riding down to the newsstand, either."

"But I've got to go to the newsstand every Wednesday, or I'll miss the new comics."

"You've got enough comics," Randy said. "Won't hurt you to miss a few. You should save your money, anyway. In four more years you're going to want a car and—"

Timmy cut him off. "If I miss the new issues, then I'll have gaps in my collection, and won't find out what happens next."

"I'm not going to argue with you, Timmy. We've all been under a strain lately since—well, since Grandpa's death, and I've tried to take it easy on you. But don't fight me on this."

"It isn't fair." Timmy crossed his arms over his chest and sank back into the cushions. "Why should we be punished just because some other people are missing?"

"You're not being punished," Elizabeth said. "We're just worried about your safety, is all. We're worried about you—both of you. I bet Doug's mother will say the same thing. Try to see it our way. It's for your own good."

Timmy stifled a laugh. There was his old friend, his invisible accomplice, U'rown Goode, making another appearance.

"I've got to ride my bike past Bowman's Woods to get here," Doug said. "What should I do?"

"Well," Elizabeth said, "for the time being, maybe your mom can drive you over here when you want to visit?"

"I don't think so, Mrs. Graco. My mom doesn't leave the house much."

"Oh. Well, maybe Timmy's father can pick you up and take you back."

"Wait a second," Randy said. "I've got to work."

"Well then, you can make special trips when you're home."

Randy started to protest, but Timmy cut him off again.

"This sucks."

"Language," his mother warned.

"Well," Timmy said, "it does suck. Our whole summer is ruined because of Ronny, Jason, and Steve."

"Timothy Edward Graco!" Elizabeth's voice boomed across the living room. "Those boys are missing, and Lord only knows what's happened to them. You should try to be a little more understanding and sympathetic. We raised you better than that."

"Sorry," he said, feeling anything but.

"You should be."

He forged ahead. "Well, what about Barry? Can we still hang out at his house? He's right over the hill, and we only have to go through our backyard to get there."

"You can still play with Barry," Randy said. "But no further until we say otherwise. I mean it."

"And we can help him work in the cemetery?"

Randy sighed. "Yes, as long as you're not by yourself. But no further. Understand me?"

"Yes, sir."

"Doug? How about you?"

"Yes, Mr. Graco. You don't have to worry about me. If some sick perv tries to snatch me, I'll kick him in the balls and run!"

Elizabeth gasped. Randy struggled to suppress his laughter. A moment later, all four of them started laughing. Privately, Timmy wondered why he got hollered at for saying "sucks" but Doug could get away with "balls." But he didn't ask. It was good to hear Doug laughing, especially after last night.

"What do you boys want for breakfast," Elizabeth asked when she'd regained her composure. "There's Count Chocula or Trix, or oatmeal."

Both boys made a face at the mention of oatmeal.

"Or, I guess I could make pancakes."

"Pancakes," Doug said. "Yes, please. That would be great. Can you put blueberries in them, too?"

She smiled. "I think we can do that. It just so happens I bought some at the store this week."

"Awesome."

Timmy raised his hand without much enthusiasm. "Me too, I guess. With bacon."

"That makes three of us," Randy said. "With eggs."

While she cooked, Timmy and Doug watched *The Transformers* while Randy got ready for work. They ate, and Timmy listened to his parents talk without really hearing them, and his mother's blueberry pancakes, usually his favorite, had no taste. The new set of rules and boundaries really chafed at him. Sure, unbeknownst to his parents, they still had the Dugout to play in, but that somehow wasn't enough. The most desirable horizons were the ones you were forbidden to reach, and the thrill of exploration was what lay beyond those known borders. He thought about Doug's map, useless for all intents and purposes now. The blank space all around the edges would stay blank now.

Doug chatted with Randy and Elizabeth, and ate three helpings of pancakes.

Timmy sulked. He tried very hard to ignore the fact that his best friend's mom was having sex with him, and that people were missing, probably abducted by some serial killer, and that his summer vacation was not turning out to be a vacation at all, but a prison sentence. It was like one of the storm clouds from the previous night had settled over him, dark and foreboding.

It felt like he was in a tunnel and the walls were closing in.

He shivered.

After breakfast, Randy left for work and the boys went outside to play. They grew bored after an hour and decided to go to Barry's house and see what he was doing—after assuring Elizabeth that they'd stray no farther and come straight home when they were done. They left their bikes behind, and doing so filled them both with sadness. What good was a BMX with mag wheels and thick tires and racing stripes if you couldn't ride it anywhere and show it off? It was like Batman without a Batmobile or Han Solo without a Millennium Falcon.

As they trudged through the backyard and up the hill toward Barry's, Timmy picked up a stick, left over from the storm, and in a fit of anger snapped it in half and tossed the pieces aside.

"So much for going tubing. This bites. This whole summer just keeps getting worse and worse."

"Could be much worse," Doug said. He was still wearing Randy's old shirt, and had put on his jeans from the day before, along with a pair of Timmy's socks.

"How could it be any worse?"

"The police could be trying to find out who beat Catcher, instead."

"True. I guess they've got more important things to worry about now."

"Or it could be us that was missing."

"Yeah . . ."

"I just hope Ronny and those guys are okay," Doug said. "I'm a little worried about what could have happened to them."

Timmy stopped walking. "Are you crazy?"

"What? I'm concerned, is all."

"Doug, how can you say that? Are you forgetting about everything they've done to you? The pink bellies and the wedgies and swirlies? How they made you wear girl's underwear on your head that time on the school bus? Or how Ronny used to squeeze your . . . well, your tits, until you cried?"

"I don't have tits," Doug said. "And I cried because it hurt. And no, I haven't forgotten about any of those things. How could I?"

"Exactly. So why worry about them?"

"I don't know. I just do."

"Those guys are jerks. They picked on you constantly."

"Yeah, they're jerks, but that doesn't mean I want some crazy guy to kidnap them and do stuff to them. That's wrong, man. Nobody deserves that."

They started walking again. The wet grass soaked through their sneakers. They passed by Randy Graco's grapevines, which had been flattened by the storm. To their right, at the top of the hill, the Wahl's cherry tree was spilt in half, the unfortunate victim of a lightning strike.

"I just hope they come home safe." Doug stepped over the drooping vines. "That's all I'm saying."

"They deserve whatever happens to them," Timmy said. "Serves them right. I don't care."

"Yes you do," Doug said. "You're just pissed off right now."

"So? I'm serious. Why should I care what happens to those assholes?"

"You cared about Catcher when Barry started beating on him, and he was just as mean to us as Ronny and those guys were."

"Catcher didn't know any better. He's just a dog, and he was just doing what all Dobermans do. They're attack dogs. It's instinct."

"Not necessarily. The guy that lives next door to me used to have a Doberman, and it was nice, because he'd trained it to be nice. Catcher was mean because Mr. Sawyer didn't teach him any different."

"So Ronny, Jason, and Steve's parents taught them to be assholes?"

"Maybe." Doug paused, choosing his words carefully. "Look, with everything I told you last night, I know I've got problems. But when Barry started kicking Catcher the other day, who did he remind you of?"

He shrugged, and then mumbled, "His father." Timmy wondered how his friend could be so nice, how he could keep such a positive attitude with all that had happened to him. But even so, Doug was right. He was about to admit that he'd been thinking the same thing, that maybe grown-ups were the real monsters, when they reached Barry's house. Timmy decided to wait until later.

They slowly approached the front door. The window shades were still closed, and the house looked dark.

"Go ahead," Doug whispered. "Knock."

"You knock. It's your turn. I knocked last time."

Doug rapped on the door twice. They heard shuffling sounds inside. Then the door opened, the rusty hinges squeaking. Mrs. Smeltzer peered out at them through one good eye. The other one was swollen shut and looked black and purple. Timmy and Doug gasped in surprise, but she just smiled.

"Hi, boys."

Timmy thought she sounded sad—and maybe a little relieved as well.

"Um, hi Mrs. Smeltzer. Is Barry home?"

She nodded toward the cemetery. When she tilted her head, Timmy noticed that another pair of new earrings sparkled in her ears.

"He's out helping his dad. You might not want to go over there this morning, though."

"Why not?" Timmy stared at her black eye.

"Well, Mr. Smeltzer didn't get much sleep last night. He was out late. He's a little grumpy."

Neither of them replied. Doug stared at his feet. Timmy couldn't look away.

"You okay, Timmy?"

Am I okay? he thought. *You're the one with the black eye, lady.*

"Yeah, I'm fine. Didn't sleep much last night, either. The storm kept me awake."

She smiled at them again. "Well, I'll tell Barry that you stopped by."

"Thanks, Mrs. Smeltzer."

She closed the door, and they turned away and started back down the sidewalk.

"Jesus," Timmy whispered. "Did you see that shiner?"

"See it? How could I miss it? The whole side of her face is swollen up. What do we do?"

Timmy sighed. "Nothing we can do, except maybe tell my parents, and if we do that, Barry might get pissed at us, or they might say we can't hang out with him anymore. Let's just not think about it. We'll go find Barry. Make sure he's okay. If he doesn't have to work, then maybe we can explore the tunnel today after all. If not, then we'll just hang around inside the Dugout until he's finished."

"Maybe we better not. Mrs. Smeltzer said Barry's dad was in a bad mood. The way her face looked, I'd say she was right."

"Screw him. I'm in a bad mood, too."

He crossed the road. Doug followed after a moment's hesitation. They passed by the newly installed NO TRES- PASSING sign and went around the side of the church.

"I noticed something else," Timmy said. "She had on another new pair of earrings. I'm telling you, man, something weird's going on. Something more than just him hitting them."

"But, like you said, there's nothing we can do. Barry's dad is a grown-up. We're kids."

Timmy kicked a stone. It shot across the church parking lot, careened off a telephone pole, and rolled away.

"He's no adult. He's a monster. Barry should tell somebody."

"Maybe he's afraid to."

They reached the rear of the church and started down the cemetery's center road. There was no sign of Barry or his father, and they didn't hear the sound of lawnmowers or anything else. This morning, even the birds and insects seemed silent. It was almost as if all the wildlife had abandoned the grounds.

"Why would Barry be afraid to tell?" Timmy lowered his voice, in case Mr. Smeltzer or Barry were within earshot. "He'd be safe. Him and his mom both. The cops would lock his old man up in a heartbeat."

"Maybe he's embarrassed—like I was." Doug sighed. "I still can't believe I told you last night."

"Are you sorry that you did?"

"No." Doug hesitated. "But I am afraid that you'll tell somebody. Your parents, or Reverend Moore."

Timmy clapped him on the shoulder. "I promised that I wouldn't tell, and I won't. But you've gotta do something, man. You can't just stay there and let her keep doing this to you. It's not right. She's no better than Barry's dad."

"I know, I know. It's just—she's all I have left, Timmy. I can't just leave her."

"But you have to. You have to get out of there."

"I can't. I know it's wrong. I know it's doing something bad, like the time we put the shotgun shell on the railroad tracks to see what would happen when the train ran over it."

Timmy shook his head. "It's a little worse than that, Doug."

"I know. All I'm saying is that I know it's wrong, but I can't stop it, other than locking my door."

"Do you like it? Do you want it to keep happening?"

Doug looked horrified. "No. Of course I don't like it. I hate it. I told you that."

"Then get some help."

"I can't. It wouldn't be—"

"She's a monster."

"She's also my *mother!*"

He shoved Timmy, hard. Timmy stumbled backward, almost tripping over a low gravestone. Doug advanced on him, meaty fists raised in defiance.

"She's my mother and don't you dare call her that, you jerk. Don't you dare!"

"Hey—"

"Shut up. It's not for you to say."

Timmy held his hands up in surrender. "Okay, okay. Take it easy. I'm sorry. Seriously. I shouldn't have said anything."

Doug's face had turned reddish purple, and the veins stood out in his neck. Another one throbbed on his forehead, pulsing beneath the skin. He dropped his fists to his sides, clenching and unclenching his fingers. His jaw hung slack. His breath came in rapid, labored gasps. He turned his back and walked away.

"You okay?" Timmy asked.

Without looking back, he nodded, still hyperventilating. His shoulders sagged.

"Where you going? You're not going home, are you?"

Shaking his head, Doug bent over, hands on his knees, and threw up. Timmy didn't know if he should help him or just give him some space, so he just stood there, watching.

"Don't bring it up any more, Timmy."

He took a few more steps and then vomited again.

"Doug," Timmy said, "I really am sorry, man. I didn't mean to piss you off."

"I'm sorry, too." Doug stood back up, wiping his mouth with the back of his hand. "Just let me deal with it. Okay? It's my problem and I'll deal with it. I don't want people finding out. They pick on me already. Can you imagine what they'll say if they find out about this? Can you imagine what they'd do to me? To my mom? I don't have anything. My dad's gone. All I have left is her, and even if she is . . . disgusting, I still don't want to lose her. Can you understand that?"

Timmy nodded, somewhat reluctantly.

"So let me handle it my way, okay?"

"Okay."

"You promise? You won't say any more?"

"Yeah, man. Sure."

They walked on in silence, past the debris left behind in the wake of two storms—the thunderstorm from the night before, and the emotional storm brewing between them. They passed earthworms wiggling helplessly at the bottom of rain puddles, and graveside floral arrangements that had been blown over by the storm, their petals and stems scattered across the cemetery. A green Styrofoam wreath lay in the middle of the road. Timmy picked it up, examined it, then tossed it aside like a Frisbee.

They avoided two mourners, who were gathered around a single gray stone, and nodded hello to a jogger, Mrs. Nelson, who lived on the other side of the Wahls and gave out the best candy on Halloween. Apparently, Mrs. Nelson had ignored the NO TRESPASSING sign as well. Timmy wondered aloud if Mr. Smeltzer had hollered at her about it. But other than the graveside visitors and the jogging woman, the cemetery was deserted. Finally, they spotted Barry and his father. They were using a chain hoist to lift a fallen tombstone.

"Wow," Doug said, speaking for the first time since their argument. "The storm must have been even stronger than we thought."

Timmy nodded, only half-listening. He was studying Clark Smeltzer's posture, looking for clues to his demeanor. All signs pointed to bad. Barry moved like a whipped dog, and even from this distance, they could hear Clark shouting orders at him.

"We can't get to the Dugout with them working down there." Timmy picked a blade of grass and put it in his mouth, chewing the tip. "Mr. Smeltzer would see us for sure."

Neither Barry nor his father had spotted them yet. They were too absorbed in their task. The mourners had gotten back into their car and left, and Mrs. Nelson was all the way on the other side of the cemetery now.

"Come on," Timmy said. "Let's sneak over to the shed while they're busy. We'll take a look at the cave entrance."

"What if he catches us? If we're down inside the tunnel, we might not hear him coming."

"We'll hear him. Besides, it's not like we can actually go inside it right now, anyway. We promised Barry that we'd wait for him. I just want to check it out a little more."

"Okay," Doug agreed, still sounding unsure.

They cut through the grass, ducking behind tombstones and monuments, trying to stay out of Clark Smeltzer's line of sight. Timmy noticed more sunken graves, and when they passed by his grandfather's plot, he was dismayed to see that the dirt had fallen in even more. For a moment, he imagined himself exploring the caverns below, and stumbling across his grandfather's coffin—or even a body. A hideous image, but one he'd seen a thousand times before in the pages of *House of Secrets* and *The Witching Hour*.

They were almost to the shed when Mrs. Nelson circled round again, this time on the road that ran between the old portion of the cemetery and the new one. They hid behind a monument until she'd passed by, and then darted out and crossed the path. They ducked behind the shed and knelt at the window.

"What the hell?" Timmy pounded his fist against the new boards that had been nailed up overnight. "Barry's old man must have found out. No wonder Mrs. Smeltzer said he was pissed off."

Doug slapped at a mosquito. The squished insect left a red smear on his palm. "Oh, man. Wonder how much trouble Barry got into?"

"God," Timmy said. "I don't even want to think about it. Depends on whether or not his dad figured out we were the ones climbing through there when he wasn't around."

Timmy paused to lace up his Converse All-Stars, which had come undone, while Doug inspected the window.

"I don't see what the big deal is. Barry's allowed in there when he has his old man's keys."

"Yeah, but nobody's supposed to be in there when he isn't around—especially us. And besides, when have any of Mr. Smeltzer's rules made sense? He makes a big deal out of everything."

"If he does know, you think he'll tell our parents?"

"I don't know," Timmy said. "I doubt it. He knows that my dad doesn't think much of him."

Doug poked the dirt with a stick. "You don't think . . . you don't suppose he'd hit us? The way he does Barry?"

"I'd like to see him try," Timmy said. "I'd kick his drunken ass."

From behind them, Clark Smeltzer said, "Is that so?"

Timmy and Doug both jumped, and Doug let out a frightened squawk and dropped his stick. Mr. Smeltzer seized them by the ears, pinching and twisting the cartilage. The boys shouted for help as he yanked them to their feet and spun them around.

He grinned. "Kick my ass, will you?"

"Let go," Timmy demanded. "You're hurting us."

Doug started to whimper. Timmy silently willed him not to cry, not to give Barry's father the satisfaction.

"You're hurting us," Timmy repeated.

"You're goddamn right I am, you little brat."

He released them both and took a menacing step forward. Crying out, Doug scrambled backward, tripped, and tumbled over onto the dirt pile, landing flat on his back. Timmy shrank against the wall of the shed.

Clark Smeltzer glared at them both. His eyes were red and rheumy, and an unlit cigarette dangled from his mouth. He chomped the filter furiously. Barry stood behind him, lingering in the background, looking at his friends in dismay. His eyes were wide. He said nothing.

Timmy glanced around in fright, hoping that Mrs. Nelson would jog by again, see what was happening, and rescue them. But Mrs. Nelson was nowhere in sight, apparently done exercising for the day. The cemetery was deserted. Somewhere in the distance, one of the neighbors started a lawnmower, and he heard the faint drone of it, but as far as Timmy was concerned, the lawnmower and its owner might as well have been on the moon.

Clark spat out the cigarette. "I figured it was you two that was sneaking in here, as well. 'Couldn't just be them other boys,' I thought. Looks like I was right. Thought I told you two that I didn't want you playing in this graveyard no more."

The boys said nothing. Doug was too busy fighting back tears and Timmy was afraid his voice would betray him. His legs trembled and his face was flushed. His lips felt heavy. Swollen. His heartbeat throbbed inside his head.

Barry took a timid step forward. "Dad . . ."

Clark whirled on him. "You shut your goddamned mouth, boy. I don't want to hear a thing from you. You were probably breaking in here with them, weren't you? What'd I tell you about being out here without me? Huh?"

He raised his hand and Barry cringed. Timmy stepped forward.

"Why don't you just leave him alone, you son of a bitch?"

Clark turned, slowly, his mouth hanging open in disbelief.

"What'd you just say?"

Timmy swallowed. "You heard me, asshole. You're good at hitting women and little kids. Why can't you beat on somebody your own size?"

The color drained from Mr. Smeltzer's face. His open hand curled into a fist.

"I've warned you before, Graco. Somebody needs to do something about that mouth of yours."

"Go ahead," Timmy challenged. "Hit me."

"Timmy," Barry said, "Shut up. Don't—"

Clark lunged. Timmy tried to dodge him, but the angered man was quicker. He seized Timmy's T-shirt with both fists and lifted him off the ground, slamming him into the wall of the shed. Timmy's feet dangled off the ground. The boy was too terrified to speak. Timmy's anger vanished, replaced with fear.

"Dad," Barry pleaded, "put him down."

"P-please," Doug said, "please Mr. Smeltzer, don't—"

"Barry, I told you to shut your fucking mouth. You too, fat boy."

He turned back to Timmy, his leering face only inches away. Despite his terror, Timmy winced at the man's foul breath—a miasma of cigarette smoke, coffee, booze, rotting teeth, and bleeding gums.

I won't cry, Timmy thought. *I won't cry, I won't cry, I won't.*

And then he did.

"Now, Graco," Clark snarled, "you listen up and you listen good. If I see you or your tubby friend in this cemetery again, I will tan both your goddamned hides so bloody that your mommas won't recognize either one of you. And you know what? I'll get away with it, too. You're trespassing, and that's against the law. It ain't like I didn't warn you before."

As if to emphasize, he slammed Timmy against the wall, hard enough that his teeth clacked together. Then he let him drop.

"There's a new lock on this shed, and I'm the only one that can open it. It's all boarded up nice and tight. Anybody else gets in, I'll know about it. Don't let me catch you here again. And as for you," he turned to Barry, "you ain't to hang out with these two no more. They're trouble. Up to no good. You think they're your friends now? Just you wait. Get a few years older, they'll want nothing to do with you anymore. They'll think they're better than you. Their kind always does. Just like Graco's daddy. Ol' Randy thinks he's better than me cuz' he's got that high-paying union job down at the mill and all I do is dig graves and mow grass."

Timmy stirred. "That's not true."

"Shut your face. Now you mind me, Barry. You see these two riding down the street, you go the other way. They come to the house, you don't answer the door. I catch you playing with them again, you know what will happen."

"Yes, sir . . ."

While Mr. Smeltzer was distracted, Timmy crawled over to Doug's side. The two boys squeezed each other's hands. Timmy thought he might throw up.

"No more," Clark said. "Am I understood?"

Tears filled Barry's blue eyes. "But Dad—"

"No 'buts' about it."

"But they're my best friends. I don't have anybody else."

Clark lashed out, slapping him across the face with the back of his hand. Timmy and Doug gasped. Barry's cheek turned red.

"Go ahead," Clark said, his hand still raised. "You go ahead and back talk me again, you little punk. I dare you."

Weeping, Barry stared at the ground. Clark turned back to the others.

"Wipe your noses and run home to your mothers. I don't want to see you here again."

"Barry?" Timmy reached for their friend.

"I said *go!*" Clark kicked out. His heavy, steel-toed work boot slammed into Timmy's tailbone. "Get the fuck out of here."

The boys' last bit of resolve shattered. Both Timmy and Doug fled. They couldn't go in the direction of Timmy's house, because the utility shed and Mr. Smeltzer both blocked their way. He stood there, hands on his hips, the look on his face just daring them to pass. So instead, they ran in the other direction, toward the cornfield at the far end of the graveyard.

A rock bounced off Doug's shoulder blade. He cried out, but didn't look back.

"That's right," Clark Smeltzer shouted, "Just keep on running. If I see you here again, it'll be both your asses!"

His laughter hounded them as they reached the edge of the cemetery and stumbled into the cornfield, heedless of the damage their pounding feet were doing to Luke Jones's crop. Halfway through the field, Doug paused, gasping for breath.

"Let's stop a minute," Timmy suggested, wiping the remaining tears from his eyes. Sweat poured down his forehead.

Doug nodded, unable to speak. He sank to his knees and closed his eyes.

"That . . . jerk . . ." He gulped air. "He can't . . . do that. Barry's our friend. He can't . . ."

Timmy stripped off his T-shirt and mopped his

brow. "Save your breath. He just did. And we let him."

"We could have stopped him. We could have fought back."

"No we couldn't have. Come on, Doug, who are we kidding? We're two kids, man. When it came down to it, and he literally had us backed up against the wall, we did everything but piss our pants, we were so scared."

Doug's face, already purple from a combination of crying and running, now turned violet. When he spoke, his voice was barely a whisper. "Too late."

"Oh no. Please tell me you didn't."

"I did. Just a little bit. When I fell. Some squirted out."

Timmy snickered, then chuckled, then turned his face to the sky and howled. He pointed at his friend, tried to speak, and only laughed harder. He stretched out on his back and giggled.

"It's not funny," Doug said, but he was smiling, and a second later, he started laughing as well. "Look at us," he said. "We almost get beat up by our best friend's dad, and then, just a little while later, we're sitting in a cornfield laughing because I peed myself."

Timmy sat up. "It's a defense mechanism. Like Spider-Man. Ever notice when he's fighting Doc Ock or Hobgoblin, how he cracks jokes all the time? That's because he's scared. It's how he deals with being afraid. It helps him face the monsters."

"Too bad we couldn't do the same back at the shed."

"Yeah." Timmy took off his Converses and shook dirt and pebbles from them.

"I mean, why did we have to be so chicken?" Doug shook his head in shame. "We weren't afraid of Catcher. Well, maybe a little. But that didn't stop us from standing up to him."

Timmy slid his shoes back on. "And look at what happened when we did."

"That wasn't really our fault, though. Barry was the one who snapped."

"I read this issue of *The Defenders* once. Nighthawk, Gargoyle, Dr. Strange, and Son of Satan had to travel to this other dimension to rescue Valkyrie and Hellcat. There was a line in it that said, 'When you look into the abyss, the abyss also looks into you.' I didn't understand what it meant, so I asked my grandpa. He told me it was from some philosopher. I can't remember the guy's name. Nacho or something. He was German, I think."

"Nacho doesn't sound very German."

"It doesn't matter. Anyway, Grandpa explained it to me and then told me a few other things this guy had said. I always remembered the one, because I thought it sounded cool."

"What was it?"

"When you battle monsters, you have to be careful or else you'll turn into a monster yourself."

Doug mouthed the words, silently repeating them to himself. Then he frowned. "I don't get it. What's it mean?"

"Think about it. We fought Catcher and what happened? For a few seconds, Barry acted just like his father. And me, earlier. What I said about Ronny and those guys. You're right—it was a stupid thing to say. The kind of thing you'd expect *them* to say, rather than one of us. Maybe it's better that we don't fight our own monsters. Maybe we're better than them."

"Maybe," Doug agreed. "I don't know. I still wish we'd have done something. Poor Barry. I'm worried about what's gonna happen to him now."

"We'll still see him. Dude, he's our friend. I don't care what his old man says. He can't stop the three of us from hanging out together. We'll sneak out tonight and then all three of us can hang out in the Dugout—or look for another way into the cave, since we can't get into the shed."

Doug looked frightened again. "No way. After what just happened? I'm not setting foot in that cemetery anymore. And besides, that's not what I mean."

"Well, what do you mean, then?"

"I'm worried about what his dad is going to do to him after all that."

"Yeah." Timmy sighed. "Me too, man. Me too."

"Mr. Smeltzer was always kind of weird, but he's really starting to lose it. Who knows what he could do? And did you notice something else? When we were at the shed, he said, 'I figured it was you two that was sneaking in here, as well. Couldn't just be them other boys.' Who do you think he was talking about?"

"I don't know," Timmy said. "I can't even think about that right now. I still feel like I'm going to throw up."

"What if it was Ronny, Jason, and Steve? What if Mr. Smeltzer knows what happened to them?"

"Barry's dad is a serial killer?"

"Well, no—probably not. But you saw what he did to us today. How he acted. Sure, he's hollered before, but he never laid a finger on us. Not like this. Today was different, and the way Barry's mother talked, he was like this last night, too. Maybe he caught them trying to sneak in the shed and . . . lost control?"

"You think he killed them?"

Doug didn't reply.

"He wouldn't have done that," Timmy said. "He's crazy, but killing them? That seems a little far-fetched. He's just an abusive jerk, not some psycho. Much as I hate the guy, and as much as I think my dad's wrong, and that there really is a serial killer running around, I don't think it's Barry's old man."

"Yeah," Doug said, nodding. "I guess you're right. I hope you are, anyway. So what do you want to do now? We can't go back to the cemetery and we can't go anywhere else, either. We can't even get our stuff out of the Dugout."

"Let's finish catching our breath first. My stomach and my head still hurt."

"Did he hurt you when he slammed you against the shed?"

Timmy shook his head. "No. Not really. I think it's more nerves than anything else."

Timmy lay back on the ground, careful not to squash the budding corn stalks. Clouds drifted slowly by above them, and he wished that he could hop on one and ride away. He'd always been mystified by clouds. They looked like solid things—islands floating above the earth. Meanwhile, Doug reached into his pocket and pulled out a plastic egg of Silly Putty. He began playing with it, rolling it in his hands and then flattening it out, while Timmy watched the sky and tried to figure out what they could do. The sun felt good on his face. He wished they could just stay there in the field for the rest of the day. He turned to his friend.

Doug found an anthill and began picking up the scurrying insects with his wad of Silly Putty, pretending it was the Blob and that the ants were frightened townspeople. He'd always been able to entertain himself like that. One summer, he'd enlisted Timmy and Barry's help in collecting empty locust shells from the trees and shrubs. They'd spent an entire day gathering the bug-eyed, creepy looking husks. Then, overnight, Doug had set them all up on top of a train table in his basement. He'd placed his green plastic army men in the diorama as well. The next day, the boys had reenacted a fantastic battle between the U.S. Army and some alien bugs from outer space. Watching him now, as Doug transformed his Silly Putty into yet another alien menace, Timmy grinned.

Then the memory of Clark Smeltzer's voice—and the look on Barry's face—made his grin vanish as quickly as it had appeared.

Timmy stood up and brushed the dirt off his pants. "Let's walk over to the woods. Maybe we can find a hornet's nest or something cool."

"But we're not supposed to. Your parents said."

"Yeah, but they didn't know that Mr. Smeltzer was going to chase us out of the boundaries anyway. I mean, we're already beyond where my mom and dad said we could be. Might as well make the best of it. It's not like we'll get caught or anything."

Doug put his ball of Silly Putty, now embedded with ants, back in the plastic egg and slipped it into his pocket. Timmy gave him a hand and helped him to his feet. Then the two of them set off for the tree line. As they neared the edge of the forest, they noticed four turkey buzzards circling in the sky. The carrion birds were hovering over a specific spot in the woods.

"Something must have died in there," Timmy said, nodding toward the birds. "Maybe a deer or a pheasant. We should check it out."

"What do you want to see an old dead deer for? That's gross."

"I don't think so," Timmy said. "Sometimes, it's kind of cool."

They pushed through the thick tangle of thorns and branches growing around the edges of the forest, and stepped beneath the leafy canopy.

The temperature was cooler in the woods, and rainwater from the previous night's storm still dripped off the limbs overhead. It was darker under the trees. The woods were alive with sound, birds and insects, squirrels barking at one another, dead leaves and pinecones crunching under their feet. Flowers burst from the dark soil, lining the trail with different colors and fragrances. A chipmunk sat on a mossy stump and watched them go by. A plane passed overhead, invisible beyond the treetops. Timmy glanced upward, but he could no longer see the circling buzzards.

They didn't often come to this section of forest and hadn't fully explored it, and despite that morning's terror, their spirits lifted slightly at the opportunity to do so now. They'd only gone a few yards in, and were still standing in an area where the undergrowth was sparse and the trees were spaced far apart, when Doug spied the raspberry bushes.

"Awesome!"

He ran over to the thick stand of bushes and began picking raspberries, greedily popping them into his mouth and relishing the taste. Juice dripped from his lips.

Timmy heard the unmistakable squawk of a turkey buzzard overhead, but the leaves still hid them from sight. He sniffed the air, but didn't smell anything dead.

Doug groaned with delight. "My mom never buys these at the grocery store. Says they're too expensive."

"My mom says the same thing. I was surprised she actually had blueberries on hand this morning for the pancakes."

"Try some." Doug held out a handful of berries.

Timmy strolled over, but before he could join in, something behind the bushes caught his eye. The sun shined down through a break in the trees, and the sunlight glinted off of something bright and metallic.

He tapped Doug's shoulder. "What's that?"

Doug looked up. His face and fingers were stained red from berry juice. "What?"

"There," Timmy said, pointing. "On the other side of the bushes. The sun is reflecting off something. See it?"

"Metal . . ."

"Sure looks like it."

"What do you think it is?"

"Could be anything," Timmy said. "A tree stand left behind by a hunter, or someone else's fort, or an old junked refrigerator or something."

Or a crashed UFO, he thought, *or maybe the hatch to a secret underground government base. Or what those birds are looking for . . .*

He glanced down at the forest floor, found a long, straight stick, and picked it up.

"Let's find out."

Swinging the stick like a scythe, Timmy slashed at the clinging berry branches, cutting a path through the thicket. Doug followed along behind him, still picking raspberries and stuffing them into his mouth. They waded through the undergrowth and reached the object. Standing in front of it, the boys saw obvious signs that someone had gone through an awful lot of trouble to conceal it. Tree branches had been cut and laid over it, and dead leaves had been heaped on top of those, all in an effort to camouflage the mysterious object.

Doug's nose wrinkled. "Smells like something died around here all right. Those turkey buzzards must be right overhead."

Timmy had noticed the stench as well. It wasn't like what he'd smelled coming from beneath the graveyard. This was sharper. Muskier. Fresher, the way a dead groundhog smelled after lying in the middle of the road for several days. This was the aroma of death and decay.

Ignoring the foul odor, Doug grabbed another handful of berries. He stepped to the left, spotted a patch of poison ivy, and quickly jumped behind Timmy again.

Timmy grasped a pine branch. Sap still leaked from the end of it, and the bark stuck to his hand. He pulled the limb away, revealing a glimpse of what lay beneath.

"Is that . . . ?"

Doug nodded, his berries forgotten. "Yeah. I think it is."

Without another word, both boys stepped forward and began clearing away the debris. Beneath it lay Pat Kemp's black Chevy Nova. Enamored of Pat as they were, the boys would have recognized it anywhere. Chrome mag wheels; big tires, shiny and black; the Thrush high-powered muffler sticker on the back window; a chrome blower sticking up through the hood like some space-age coffee maker; an AC/DC bumper sticker, complete with a cannon and the slogan, FOR THOSE ABOUT TO ROCK; and the waxed, flawless body—so dark that the viewer was left with the impression that it absorbed light. The paint was now dirty and sticky with sap, and some of the branches had left long scratches.

Timmy leaned forward and peered through the driver's side window. Cassette tapes lay scattered on the seat—Ratt, Motorhead, Ozzy Osbourne, Dio, Dead Kennedy's, Black Flag, Iron Maiden, Autograph, Suicidal Tendencies, and curiously out of place (in his opinion), Prince's *Purple Rain*. A crumpled pack of Marlboro cigarettes and a pair of black sunglasses sat on the red vinyl dashboard. Empty beer cans littered the floor. Each one had been crushed. Timmy breathed through his mouth. This close to the car, the stench grew stronger. Doug pushed up beside him and peeked through as well.

"Why would Pat have a Prince tape?" he asked. "I thought he was a metal head."

"You like Prince," Timmy reminded him.

"Yeah, but I'm not cool like Pat. What do you think his car's doing here?"

"I don't know, but it ain't good. Whoever put it here went through a lot of trouble to hide it."

"Do you think he's okay?"

Timmy shrugged, then straightened up and looked around. "I don't see any sign of him. Or Karen. But look over there." He pointed to another section of the forest where the undergrowth was sparse and the trees were spaced far apart. "If you look carefully, you can see tire tracks going back up to Mr. Jones's cornfield."

"You remember the morning after Pat and Karen ran away, Barry was smoothing out tire tracks? They went off into the cornfield."

"Yep. So somebody drove it from the cemetery to here."

Both of them heard the sound of buzzing flies.

Doug peered back inside the car. "So maybe Pat and Karen were parking in the graveyard. Somebody found them, did something to them, and then hid the car here."

"Could be," Timmy said, "or maybe they hid the car so people wouldn't find it, and then walked out."

"You don't really believe that, do you?"

"No," Timmy admitted, remembering the circling carrion birds. "There's no way Pat would have ever left his car behind. He loved this thing. But a good detective considers all possibilities before coming to conclusions. That's what the world's greatest detective would do."

Doug seemed puzzled. "Who's the world's greatest detective? Sherlock Holmes?"

"No, you idiot. It's Batman."

Doug wiped the window with his sleeve. "Well, I don't think they ran away. Ronny, Jason, and Steve. That lady on the news this morning. Now we find Pat and Karen's car? I think it all adds up."

Timmy didn't reply. Secretly, he was thinking about Katie Moore, wondering how she'd react to this news regarding her sister's disappearance. He walked around the car, studying it, looking for clues. The smell got stronger as he neared the abandoned Nova's rear. The buzzing flies grew louder.

"You think I'm wrong? You think Pat and Karen are alive, and that they really did run away together?"

Timmy staggered backward, his hand over his mouth.

"Timmy? What's wrong? What is it?"

Unable to speak, Timmy raised his hand and pointed. Doug hurried around to the back of the car, and gagged. They'd discovered the source of the stench. A thick, viscous liquid leaked from the trunk and pooled onto the forest floor, sticking to the leaves and pine needles. Maggots and other small insects wallowed in the slop. It was dark in color, and there were tiny bits of pink matter floating in it. The smell was incredibly strong, almost overpowering. Bloated, black flies swarmed over the trunk, crawling into the car through the same small crevice the slime was dripping out of. Whatever was inside had rotted to soup and was now spilling out of the trunk.

"No," Timmy said. "I don't think you're wrong. I think that's them. I think they're inside the trunk."

Then he leaned over and threw up.

CHAPTER TEN

They fled from the woods, not bothering to mark their location so they could find the car again. The buzzards, still swooping around above the trees, would do that for them. Not wanting to risk encountering Mr. Smeltzer, they cut through the woods and followed Anson Road, avoiding the cemetery. Then they walked along the side of the road the whole way back to Timmy's house. Timmy had puke on his shirt and jeans, and Doug's face was stark white.

They burst through the door, and at first, Elizabeth assumed that one of them had been injured. She flew out of the kitchen, where she'd been balancing the checkbook, her pulse racing. The boys weren't hurt, not physically at least. But they appeared absolutely terrified. At first, Timmy was too shocked to speak, and all Doug would say was, "It was spilling out." He kept repeating it over and over, and each time he said it, Timmy looked like he was about to vomit.

When they finally calmed down and told her of their discovery, she immediately called Reverend Moore and informed him. Then she called the police. She was so upset and concerned for the boys that she didn't even question what they were doing in the woods after having been forbidden to go that far just hours before.

The township police arrived at the Golgotha Lutheran Church, and the boys were there to meet them, along with Timmy's mother, Reverend Moore, Sylvia Moore, and Katie. Mr. Smeltzer, spying the adults with the boys and assuming they were there for what had happened earlier, made Barry go inside. Warily, he walked over to them as the police got out of their vehicles.

"I done told them boys several times not to be playing here. Even posted these signs. It ain't my fault what happened."

"What in heaven's name are you talking about, Clark?" Reverend Moore frowned. "The boys discovered something in the woods, on Luke Jones's property."

"Oh." He shut up after that. Timmy thought he would have been relieved, but instead, he seemed even more nervous than before. The township police walked over to the group. Clark excused himself, saying he had to go wash up for lunch.

Reverend Moore watched him go, and muttered, "That's odd."

Soon after, the state police and a team of paramedics arrived on the scene. Then Timmy and Doug led the township officers, the state police, and the paramedics to the car. The boys were nervous, but their excitement at being involved in a police investigation—at being the ones to discover the car—overrode all other emotions. Timmy was thrilled, and he found himself comparing the events to Tom Sawyer again. This was just like when Tom solved the mystery as to the whereabouts of escaped murderer Injun Joe.

First, they stopped in the cemetery, and the boys showed them where the tracks had originated. The investigators found remnants of tire tracks in Luke Jones's cornfield, as well. Finally, the boys led them to the woods. The birds were still circling. Once they'd arrived, the police sealed it off as a crime scene. They dusted the Nova for fingerprints, meticulously took photos of both the car and the surrounding area, and combed through the leaves and detritus on the forest floor for clues. Timmy and Doug watched with rapt attention, and basked in the reciprocal attention showered on them by the police. Despite the morning's bad start, they were surprised to find themselves having fun.

Then a bulky state trooper opened the trunk and the fun stopped.

Pat Kemp's half-liquefied remains splashed out onto the ground, splattering across the trooper's boots. The man's face turned white. Everyone else scrambled backward. The stench was revolting.

Doug screamed, and almost fainted. Timmy bit his thumb to keep from vomiting again.

This was their hero. The cool older kid who was always willing to stop and talk to them, who treated them like little brothers, gave them advice on girls and bullies and turned them on to good music. The guy they'd all wanted to be when they reached high school. The cool kid who smoked and drank and had the fastest car in town and was dating a fox like Karen Moore—that cool kid was now a waxy, congealing, rancid stew of tissue and bone and squirming maggots.

A state police detective led the boys out of the

woods, back to the edge of the cornfield, right next to the cemetery, where Timmy's mother and the Moores had been interviewed by another officer while they were waiting. The farmer, Luke Jones, had also arrived after being contacted by the officers when it was determined that the car was on his property. There was no sign of Barry or his father.

Timmy noticed the sad, fearful look in Katie's eyes, and wanted to talk to her, wanted to tell her that it was only her sister's boyfriend's body that had been found, and maybe Karen was still alive, but before he could, the detective asked Elizabeth's permission to question the boys, then took them aside and did so, one at a time. When they were finished, the detective took them back over to the other adults and told them they were free to go. He asked Timmy's mother if she'd be willing to let them contact her son later if they had any more questions, and she agreed.

While they were talking, Timmy glanced over at the Moores again. Both Reverend Moore and his wife, Sylvia, were crying. She clung to her husband, his shirt balled up in her fists, her black mascara staining the material. Great, uncontrollable sobs racked her body. Reverend Moore's tears were more controlled, but no less heartbreaking. He looked like he'd aged ten years in the last three weeks. Katie stood beside them, alone, frightened, and seemingly forgotten.

"I don't feel so good," Doug said, clutching his stomach. "When they opened the trunk . . ."

Elizabeth put her arm around the shaken youth. "I'll take you home, sweetheart. Can you make it back to our house?"

Doug nodded. "Yes, Mrs. Graco. I think so. But maybe I could stay at your house for a little bit longer? Maybe spend the night again."

"I don't think that's a good idea, Doug. We'd love to have you stay, but I'm sure your mother is already worried about you. And we need to tell her about what happened. She'll need to contact the detective. He gave me a business card to give to her."

"Please, Mrs. Graco? Pretty please? Just one more night?"

Timmy noticed the desperate pleading in his voice, but his mother did not.

"I'm sorry, Doug, but I just don't think you'd better tonight."

He can't go home, Timmy felt like shouting. *Don't you understand, Mom? What's waiting for him at home is ten times worse than what we found in the woods.*

But she was already offering her condolences and prayers to the distraught Moores. The adults exchanged hugs, and once again, Timmy's eyes were drawn to Katie. Summoning up his courage, he smiled at her. She smiled back. Sadly.

A tow truck from Old Forge service station arrived, and Mr. Jones got into an argument with the driver about the man tearing up his cornfield, until one of the officers intervened.

Elizabeth returned to the boys. "You guys ready to go home?"

"Mom," Timmy lowered his voice to a whisper. "Maybe I should stay here and talk to Katie for a little bit. You know, cheer her up?"

Elizabeth glanced over at the girl, then back at her son. She smiled knowingly.

"I think that's a very nice gesture, Timmy. As long as Doug doesn't mind?"

"No." Doug spoke with the air of a condemned man

who knows he can't escape his fate and is resigned to it. "I guess not."

Elizabeth turned to leave. Timmy quickly pulled Doug aside.

"If you need me—if anything starts to happen—call our house. I'll come up right away."

"You can't. Your dad said you weren't supposed to go that far by yourself. Your curfew—"

"Screw my curfew. This is more important. If I have to, I'll sneak out."

"Doug," Elizabeth called, "you ready to go, hon?"

"Coming, Mrs. Graco."

Timmy grabbed his arm. "Remember. If you need me, I'll be there."

"I will." He tried to smile, but it came off as a grimace. His eyes were tired and haunted. "Gotta go. Your mom's waiting."

"See you later, man."

"Not if I see you first."

They both chuckled, and then Doug ran to catch up with Elizabeth. Timmy turned back to Katie. He willed himself to walk over to her. Slowly, his feet obeyed.

"Hey." He tried to say more, but his tongue suddenly felt like cement.

"Hey."

"I'm, uh . . . I'm sorry about . . . well, you know."

"They said there's no sign of my sister. She might have been abducted. Like in the movies. She might be . . ."

Katie trailed off, fighting back tears.

Timmy nodded, unsure of how to respond.

A white news van arrived, and slowly rolled across the field. Luke Jones shook his fist at them and ran to-

ward the vehicle. His cornfield was beginning to resemble a parking lot.

Katie moved closer to Timmy. "Thank you for what
you did today."

He felt his cheeks begin to burn. "Oh, well . . . I didn't
do anything, really. All we did was tell our parents."

"You found Pat's car. That might help the police find
Karen. And it's not just that. You were nice to me at
your grandfather's funeral. Even though you were sad,
you still made time for me."

Timmy's voice betrayed him. He opened his mouth
to thank her, and "Would you like to go for a walk?"
came tumbling out instead.

Katie smiled, and this time, it was genuine. Some of
her sadness seemed to lift.

"I'd love to go for a walk. That would be fun."

"Cool."

They heard voices, raised in anger. Luke Jones
shoved the cameraman. The cameraman pushed back.
Both men were cursing. A township officer ran to
break it up, shouting at them to knock it off or he'd arrest them both.

Katie tugged on her mother's sleeve and asked for
permission to go for a walk. Sylvia Moore turned to
her husband, seeking his approval as well.

"Sure," Reverend Moore told them. He looked over
at the arguing men and frowned at their language in
disapproval. "Go ahead. That might be for the best.
They're getting ready to tow the car out. I'll come get
you when we're ready to go, so don't stray too far."

Katie and Timmy strolled off together, walking between the tombstones. He glanced around for Clark
Smeltzer, worried that he might spot them, and then
decided it didn't matter. Let him try to keep them out
of the cemetery with their parents and all the cops

around. Timmy noticed that many more of the graves had now sunk the way his grandfather's grave had done. It was almost as if a giant groundhog had burrowed beneath the graveyard, tunneling off in every direction. He wondered just how big the cavern beneath the cemetery actually was. He felt a pang of regret. With everything that had happened, he'd probably never get a chance to explore it now. He started thinking about Tom Sawyer again, and how Becky and Tom had gotten lost in the cave. He glanced over at Katie.

She smiled. Her teeth were white and perfect.

He smiled back.

And when she reached out and touched his hand, he thought he might die. His feet stumbled, his heart pounded, and he began to sweat. He was speechless—and the feeling got worse when her fingers wrapped around his and squeezed. She did not let go, and his discomfort grew.

It was the most wonderful thing he'd ever felt in his life.

And then Katie started to cry. She was still holding his hand, clutching it now, squeezing his fingers tight. Timmy wasn't sure what to do, so he squeezed back.

"It'll be okay," he said.

"I miss her." Katie sniffed. "At first, I told myself she just ran away. That she was tired of living with our dad's rules. He never liked Pat. But three weeks later, we hadn't heard from her. She would have called. Karen wasn't mean. She wouldn't let us keep worrying. She would have called."

Timmy nodded.

"Something bad has happened," Katie continued. "I know it. She's not coming back."

"She could still be okay," Timmy said, trying to sound

hopeful. "Maybe she got away from whoever did that to Pat. Maybe she's lost or has amnesia or something."

Katie sniffed again, and then wiped her eyes with her free hand. She gave him another squeeze.

"Thank you, Timmy. I don't believe it, but thank you for trying. Nobody else has paid much attention to me during this whole thing."

He was surprised. He'd always thought the Moores doted on their youngest daughter.

"Not your parents?"

She shook her head. "Nope. Too worried about Karen, I guess. It's like I'm invisible."

Timmy was speechless, and Katie misinterpreted his silence as disapproval.

"I'm sorry. That probably sounds horrible, doesn't it? I don't mean it to be."

"I don't think it sounds horrible at all."

"I'm just hurt, you know? It's like I don't exist. They miss Karen, and want her to come home, but they forget that I'm feeling those things, too. Your parents are supposed to make you feel better. They're supposed to tell you everything's going to be all right. The only person that's told me it would be okay is you."

"Yeah, parents are weird sometimes. I'm learning that more and more."

They walked on, still holding hands and a little closer together. Katie smelled good, like strawberries and shampoo, and Timmy shivered a little. He wondered what he could do to cheer her up.

"Karen used to play Easy-Bake Oven with me," Katie said. "We'd make cupcakes and little pizzas and stuff. I keep making things now, hoping she'll come back. Isn't that stupid?"

"I don't think so," Timmy said.

They started down the cemetery's rear pathway. Farmer Jones's cows stood grazing in the field. As they passed by, the cows raised their heads and stared at them blankly. Timmy noticed that none of the animals would come near the fence line, which was unusual. Most days, they'd stick their head under or through the fence, trying to feed on the cemetery's greener grass. Now, it was as if they were afraid to draw near.

Timmy spotted the Dugout's stovepipe sticking up out of the ground, and suddenly, he had an idea of how to cheer Katie up.

"Want to see something cool?"

She smiled. "Sure."

"Okay. But it's a secret, so you've gotta promise not to tell anybody. And you have to close your eyes, too."

"Is it your clubhouse?" Her voice was innocent but her eyes glinted mischievously.

Timmy gasped. "How do you know about that?"

"Everybody knows about your fort." Katie shrugged. "Erica Altland told me about it at school."

"Erica—how does *she* know? It's supposed to be top secret!"

Katie giggled. "I think Doug let the secret slip."

"Oh, man." Timmy groaned. "That dipshit."

Immediately, he felt his ears burning, and worried that he'd offended her. But Katie was laughing.

"I'm sorry," Timmy apologized. "I shouldn't have said that."

"That's okay. I don't mind."

He smiled, relieved. "So . . . you want to see it?"

"I better not." She squeezed his hand reassuringly. "Not today, at least. If what Erica said is true, your clubhouse is underground, and if my dad comes looking for me and can't find me, he'll be mad. Maybe you could show it to me during church some Sunday?"

"Sure. But won't he be looking for you then, too?"

"Not if we play hooky from Sunday school."

She shoved him playfully, and then dashed off through the graveyard.

"Hey," Timmy shouted. "Where are you going?"

"To show you something else that's top secret. Catch me if you can."

Curious, Timmy ran after her. She led him on a chase around the graves, weaving around tombstones and darting behind statues. When they reached the older portion of the cemetery, she slowed down. Timmy caught up with her, winded, but trying hard not to show it. He reached out and tapped her shoulder.

"Tag. You're it."

"You're out of breath," Katie teased. "What took you so long? Can't keep up with a girl?"

"No. Just didn't want to make you look bad."

Laughing, she took his hand again and led him forward. Their fingers entwined. No longer stunned by the display of affection, this time he was able to enjoy it more. It was quite possibly the best thing he'd ever experienced. He liked how soft her skin was, and how tiny her fingers felt next to his, and the way her red fingernails brushed against his skin when she moved.

They came to a circular depression, almost thirty feet in circumference, where the ground had collapsed—tapering from several inches on its outer edge to three or four feet in the center. The grass in the circle was wilted and brown.

"Wow," Katie said, "what is this?"

"Sinkhole," Timmy said. "Haven't you noticed how some of the graves are sinking?"

"Yeah. My dad was complaining about it earlier. He said he needed to talk to Mr. Smeltzer about it. What's making it happen?"

"We think there's a cave underneath the cemetery. Barry, Doug, and me found a tunnel."

"Really?"

"Uh-huh. We were gonna explore it, but then . . ."

"What?"

"Well, some other stuff came up."

Sensing his sudden sadness, she led him onward, skirting around the edge of the sinkhole.

"So, what's this big secret?" Timmy asked. "Don't tell me you've got a clubhouse down here, too."

Katie giggled. "Not quite. My clubhouse is in our garage. But there is something cool that I've always wanted to show you."

She stopped in front of two old gravestones, which had also begun to sink. The lichen-covered limestone surfaces were pitted and worn by time and exposure to the elements. The dates of births and deaths were faded and unreadable, but the names and epitaphs were still apparent.

"Timothy Rebert," Timmy read out loud, "and Katie Rebert. Beloved husband and wife."

He scratched his head.

"Don't you see?" Katie said. "They have the same names as us."

"Kind of creepy."

"I think it's sweet."

"If you say so."

"I do. It's sweet—just like you."

Timmy fumbled for words. "So, does this mean . . . like . . . you want to . . ."

Katie laughed. "It doesn't mean anything, other than

I noticed the names a long time ago, and I always thought it was nice. They were married and they had the same names as we do."

"So why didn't you ever tell me before?"

"I was afraid you didn't like me. You never talk when I'm around. Barry always talks more."

Timmy blushed. "I didn't talk because I was afraid you didn't like *me*. I figured you liked Barry more."

"I don't. I like you."

Timmy swallowed, and his stomach fluttered. "You do?"

Katie nodded.

"Um . . ."

"Well," she tapped her foot, "is that all you can say?"

"No," he blurted. "I . . . I like you, too. I have for a long time."

"Good."

"It's kind of like that note you made for me when we were little."

He blushed, immediately regretting saying it. She probably didn't even remember what he was talking about.

Katie smiled. "I was in first grade and you were in second. It said 'I like you, Timmy,' right?"

"Yeah. Wow, I'm surprised you remember it."

"I'm surprised you do, too."

"I still have it, actually. In my room."

Now it was Katie's turn to blush. "Well, I meant it then and I still do. I like you, Timmy."

They both stood silently, staring into each other's eyes.

"So," Timmy stuttered, "does this mean we're going together?"

Now it was Katie's turn to blush. "If you want to."

"I'd like that."

"I'd like it, too."

Timmy wanted to kiss her, and it seemed like Katie was waiting for him to. She looked at him expectantly; her face turned upward, lips slightly parted. But he couldn't bring himself to do it. Pat Kemp would have done it in a heartbeat, so why couldn't he?

An image of Pat's corpse—what had remained of it—flashed through his mind, and Timmy scowled. Katie noticed it and asked what was wrong.

"I'm sorry," he said. "For a second there, I was just thinking about Pat. And your sister."

"Yeah." Katie nodded. "I've been trying not to. Being with you helps."

"Good. I'm glad."

And he was. He was glad being with him helped her, and he was glad to just be with her. Ecstatic. What had started out as the worst day of his life since his grandfather's death was now turning into something special—something he'd longed for for quite a while.

They strolled on together, hand in hand, and easier with one another than they'd been before. Timmy picked a full, yellow dandelion and gave it to her. She clutched it to her chest and smiled.

"I'll keep it forever."

"Well, not forever," Timmy said. "Nothing lasts forever."

"Flowers do, if you press them in a book. My mom showed me how."

"Cool."

They continued on their way. Timmy wondered how much longer their parents and the police would be. He didn't want the day to end.

Katie looked up into the treetops. "You know what's weird?"

"Hmm?"

"There aren't any birds around. I haven't seen or

heard a single one since we left my parents. No squirrels, either."

Timmy thought again of the cows in the field, and how they'd been reluctant to approach the border with the cemetery. Could they sense the cave somehow? Did they know the ground was weakening, and they avoided it? He'd read in school about how some animals could predict earthquakes and tornadoes. Maybe this was something similar.

They passed by a broken tombstone. It had fallen to the ground and cracked in half, its marred surface so worn with age that most of the writing was illegible. The only thing they could still make out on it was an odd symbol—one half of it on each section of broken stone. Playing in the graveyard, Timmy had seen plenty of symbols on the stones before—crosses and hands clasped in prayer and lambs and open bibles. But he'd never seen one like this. It looked like the sun, rising over a hill. In the middle of the sun were two crosses, one upright and the other upside down. The image, shattered as it was, filled him with dread, but he didn't understand why. Katie must have noticed it too, because she shivered against him.

"Never seen one like that before," Timmy said. "Wonder what it is?"

"It's ugly. I don't like it."

"Why not?"

She shrugged. "I don't know. I just don't. It makes me feel . . . weird."

"Yeah," he admitted. "Me too."

There was some faint writing carved directly beneath both halves of the symbol, barely discernible beneath the clinging green lichen. Timmy brushed the crumbling moss aside, pushed the two pieces of limestone together, and tried to read it.

I.

N.I.R.

I.

SANCTUS SPIRITUS

I.

N.I.R.

I.

"What's it mean?" he asked.

"How should I know?" Katie teased. "You're a grade ahead of me. Have you studied Latin yet?"

"No. We don't get Latin. Just Spanish, French, and German—and I'm not taking any of those. I just figured you might know, your dad being a preacher and everything. It looks religious."

Katie studied the faded letters, tracing them with her fingers. "I-N-I-R-I . . . that's what's on the pulpit at the front of the church, right?"

Timmy nodded. "I think so. Something like that. Do you know what it stands for?"

"No. I guess we learn that in catechism class, and we don't take that until we're fourteen. I wonder what knocked the tombstone over?"

"Oh, it happens a lot, especially in this section. They get old and fall over, or people push them."

"People knock them over on purpose?" She sounded surprised.

Timmy nodded. "Sure. Ronny and those guys knocked a bunch over last Halloween. It took Barry's old man a week to put them all back up again. Some of them couldn't be fixed. The church had to pay for new ones."

"Why didn't they make Ronny, Jason, and Steve pay?"

"Couldn't prove it was them, I guess. But we knew. They bragged about it one day when they cornered us while we were sledding. Anyway, these things fall over all the time. Could have been the way the ground's settling, too. Might have shifted and knocked it over."

Then they heard Reverend Moore's voice, calling for Katie. They looked up and saw him at the top of the hill, near the utility shed. Timmy's heart sank, knowing that their time together was at an end. Spotting the two of them, Katie's father walked down the hill toward them. Immediately, Katie let go of Timmy's hand. He felt an immediate longing for contact again, but restrained himself. He'd already been in enough trouble today. He didn't need Reverend Moore getting mad at him, as well.

"There you are," the preacher said as he drew closer. He looked tired and beaten. His face was puffy and sweat poured off his forehead and cheeks. His thinning hair was plastered against his scalp. "You ready to go, sweetheart? Your mom is in the car already. She's pretty tired."

"Yeah, I'm ready, I guess." She glanced at Timmy and smiled. "Thanks again, Timmy. For everything."

He returned the smile, and tried to keep his feet on the ground.

"Yes, Timothy," Reverend Moore said, sticking out his hand, "thanks for taking care of my little girl. You're a fine boy. Your parents should be proud."

Timmy shook his hand, trying to keep a firm grip. "Thanks, sir."

The preacher noticed the broken tombstone. "Good Lord. That's the third stone I've seen like that today. Not to mention how the ground is sinking. Have you noticed it?"

Timmy nodded. "Yeah, it's happening all over the cemetery. We think there's a cave underneath."

Reverend Moore arched his eyebrows. "Really? Well, it wouldn't surprise me. This whole area is riddled with limestone. But I would think Mr. Smeltzer would have let the church board know. To be honest, I'm disappointed in the cemetery's general appearance lately. After all, it's not only a place for our loved ones, but a reflection of the church, and of God himself."

Timmy wasn't sure of how to respond, so he tried to look thoughtful and concerned.

Laughing, Reverend Moore gripped his shoulder and squeezed. "I'm sorry, Tim. These are matters for adults, not for you. There will be plenty of time to worry about things like this when you're older."

"Reverend Moore, can I ask you something before you leave?"

"Of course you can. What is it, son?"

Timmy pointed at the broken tombstone. "Well, Katie and I were wondering what that meant. It's weird looking."

The preacher knelt beside the marker and studied the faded symbol and writing. "Why, it's an old powwow charm. I didn't even realize we had anything like it here on the grounds. You don't see many of these anymore."

"Powwow?" Timmy had visions of Indians dancing in a circle to the beat of drums.

"I suppose they don't teach you about that in school," Reverend Moore said. "Powwow is something our ancestors believed in. I guess some of the older folks in the county still believe in it today, too. This part of Pennsylvania was mostly settled by the Germans, English, and Irish. When they came here, they brought their own customs and folklore and beliefs. They were all good Christians, of course. But in many cases, they had no place of worship, and no minister to see to their faith. Some towns had a preacher like myself travel through once a month, but he had many other towns to see too, and so the settlers were pretty much left to their own devices.

Sometimes they strayed from the Lord's teachings. That's how powwow came about. It was a mix of Christianity and their own folklore. Some folks call it white magic, but you know what the Bible says about that."

Timmy, who spent most sermons writing stories in the margins of the church bulletin, didn't know what the Bible said about white magic, but he nodded as if he understood because he wanted Katie's father to like him. It had never mattered to him before, but now that they were officially going together, it seemed very important.

"Thou shall not suffer a witch to live. Of course, powwow isn't really witchcraft, at least not by my definition. It's more superstition than anything. I only know of one person in the area who supposedly still practices it, and that's Nelson LeHorn over in Seven Valleys. And he seems like a nice gentleman. Doesn't attend our church, of course, but we can hardly cast doubt on him just for that. My interactions with him have always been pleasant. He seems to know God's love."

Timmy shifted uncomfortably, and the preacher seemed to realize he'd gotten off subject.

"Anyway, there's an old wives' tale about our churchyard. The old gate over there, the one you boys play on, is all that remains of the original Golgotha Church. Ours was built after the first one burned to the ground." He chuckled to himself. "I haven't thought of this story in years. Supposedly, our ancestors—Golgotha's first congregation—were bedeviled by a demon that had followed them here from the Old World. They'd called upon the Lord to help them defeat the beast, and buried it in a chamber somewhere behind the church, which, of course, would be somewhere in this portion of the cemetery. A tombstone was erected on the site, so that no one would disturb the earth, and it had powwow symbols carved on it to keep the ghoul trapped. Like I said, it's just a story. There's no such thing as monsters. They're make-believe, unlike the very real evils in this world."

Timmy stared at the cracked marker with renewed interest. He thought the story was just about the coolest thing he'd ever heard from Reverend Moore, and wondered why he didn't talk about things like that during his Sunday morning sermons. If he had, Timmy would have paid more attention.

"Well, Katie, we'd better be going. Your mother is still waiting. She's very tired. We all are, I guess."

"Okay, Daddy." She cast one more glance at Timmy, and her expression was a mixture of sadness and excitement. "Bye, Timmy. See you on Sunday?"

"You bet. Wouldn't miss it for the world."

Her father gave them both an odd, puzzled look. His stare lingered on Timmy a moment longer. He seemed perplexed. Then, without a word, he led Katie back up the hill.

The shadows grew longer as the sun moved toward the horizon.

Timmy walked home, and though the day had been long and unsettling, his step was lighter. He was heartsick about Barry and worried about Doug and furious with Mr. Smeltzer and shocked over Pat Kemp's fate, and the possible fates of the other missing people—but he was also exuberant. Katie liked him. Katie had said they were going together. Katie had held his hand. Somehow, the other things paled in comparison.

Life was not endless. He knew that now. But summers were. Or, at least it seemed that way.

Fear was a strong emotion, but so was love.

He looked at his open hand, and marveled over how, just a short time ago, it had been holding Katie Moore's.

CHAPTER ELEVEN

When Doug got home and went inside, his mother was sprawled out in her recliner, watching a syndicated rerun of *Three's Company*. The volume was turned up loud and the sound of a canned laugh track filled the house. She barely acknowledged him as he walked into the living room. Carol Keiser wore the same nightgown she'd had on two days before, and her hair was tangled and unwashed. An empty bag of Utz potato chips lay beside her, and crumbs dotted her lap. A bottle of vodka sat on the floor, snug against the chair.

"I'm home," Doug said.

Her eyes flicked toward him. "Where you been? I hollered for you earlier. I wanted you to ride your bike down to Spring Grove and pick me up some things."

Her speech was slurred, her movements jerky. Doug glanced down at the bottle and saw that it was almost empty. He knew from experience that it would join the other empty bottles tossed about all over the house, and then she'd start a new one.

"I wasn't here, Mom. I spent the night over at Timmy's."

"You were gone last night?"

"Yeah." Then he thought to himself, *Did you miss me?*

Grunting, she turned her attention back to the television.

Doug cleared his throat. "Have you watched the news?"

"No," she said. "Why? Are you on it?"

He sighed. "Maybe. I'm not sure, really. Some bad stuff happened."

"What did you do? You steal something?"

"No. Some kids from my school are missing. A few other people, too. The police might call here. They might need to talk to me some more."

Now he had her attention. She picked up the massive remote control and turned the volume down. Then she studied him with drooping, bloodshot eyes.

"Why do they need to talk to you? Are you involved, Dougie?"

"No. I didn't do anything. But Timmy and I found something today. Pat Kemp's car. Out past the graveyard, in that little stretch of woods next to Mr. Jones's cornfield. It was . . . pretty gross. The police think—"

"Are you in trouble? Are the police coming here?"

"No, Mom. I told you—"

"Then don't worry about it. You don't tell the police anything."

"But—"

"No arguments. I don't want you talking to policemen. They might trick you. Make you tell them things that aren't true or say things you don't mean. And I especially don't want them coming here. You understand me?"

"Yes, ma'am."

"Good boy. You know I love you, Dougie. I only want what's best for my little boy."

He nodded.

She smiled. "You hungry?"

Doug paused. He wanted to talk about his day, about what they'd found. Seeing Pat's remains had disturbed him deeply. Mrs. Graco had listened to him on the way home, and talked to him in soft, reassuring tones. She'd cared. He wanted the same thing from his own mother.

He opened his mouth, intent on telling her that, but instead, he said, "I'm a little hungry, I guess."

"There's chicken in the fridge. Stay out of trouble with the police. Remember, I don't want them coming here, and I don't want you talking to them."

She turned her attention back to the television and fumbled for the remote.

Doug's shoulders slumped; he walked into the kitchen and opened the refrigerator. The aroma of cold chicken wafted out of the door. His stomach churned. He thought again of Pat—what he'd looked like, how he'd smelled. Deciding he had no appetite after all, Doug closed the door and walked back down the hall to his room.

"Maybe you and your friends should play here for a few days," his mother called after him. "I'll keep the three of you out of trouble."

"Yeah, maybe." Sour stomach acid burned the back of his throat.

"Barry and Timmy don't come over here much anymore."

"They've been busy, Mom."

"You should invite them over. They can spend the night."

He unlocked his bedroom door and slipped inside, closing and locking it behind him. Then, still dressed and without even bothering to remove his muddy shoes, he lay down on the bed, curled into a ball, and stared at nothing.

Sometimes he felt very old—much older than twelve.

And sometimes, he felt like dying.

Timmy was in his room when his mother returned from dropping Doug off. He sat cross-legged on the floor, listening to a Cheap Trick cassette that Pat Kemp had once given him. "You'll like it," the older boy had promised, and he'd been right. Now, Timmy let the music wash over him and thought about the day's events. It seemed a fitting tribute.

"Mommy's all right. Daddy's all right. They just seem a little weird . . ."

He chuckled. "Boy, ain't that the truth."

There was a knock on his bedroom door. Timmy turned his stereo down until it was barely audible.

"Come in."

The door opened and his mom peeked her head inside. She smiled.

"You okay, hon?"

He nodded. "Yeah, I think so."

"Can I come in?"

"Sure."

She walked into the room and sat down on his bed. "What you doing, kiddo?"

"Just listening to some tapes. Pat gave this one to me. I was just thinking about that. I mean, we weren't exactly friends or anything, because he was older than us. But he was always nice to us. He treated us like little brothers, I guess."

"I see." She paused. "Do you want to talk about what happened today?"

Timmy shrugged. "I think I'm okay, Mom. I mean, it just sucks. Pat was a cool guy, and I feel bad for the Moores,"—*especially Katie, he thought*—"but what can I do?"

"Doug said it was pretty bad, when the police opened the car's trunk. Did you see much?"

His face paled at the memory. "Yeah."

"Do you want to talk about that?"

He breathed a heavy sigh. "It . . . it wasn't like in comic books and movies. The smell was the worst. The sound of flies. And the . . . maggots. I've seen maggots before, like when there's a dead groundhog on the road. One time, we were riding our bikes down to the dump and Barry stuck an M-Eighty in a dead groundhog and blew it up and there were maggots everywhere. That was kinda cool. But this was . . . different."

She frowned. "You boys blew up a dead animal?"

"It was cool, Mom. But that wasn't anything like this. This was . . ."

Still frowning, she nodded with tentative encouragement.

"I know that's just a part of the process," Timmy continued, "the maggots and stuff. But it made me think about Grandpa, and about what really happens to us after we die. And that freaked me out. You think about dead people going to heaven, but not about what happens under the ground. Like I said, it freaked me out for a little while. But Katie . . ."

He trailed off, suddenly nervous and uncomfortable.

He was embarrassed to tell his mother anything about Katie.

Elizabeth waited patiently. "Yes? Katie what?"

"She cheered me up. I'm okay, now."

"Well, good." His mother rose, and patted him gently on the head. "I'll leave you alone. If you want to talk about it though, I'm here. Your father is working late, since he went in late this morning. Are you hungry?"

"Not really."

"Well, if you get hungry, let me know and I'll put a pizza in the oven or something."

"Okay, Mom. Thanks."

She started to leave, then turned. "Timmy? You know we love you, right? Your father and I?"

"Sure. I know."

"It's been a really hard summer so far, what with your grandfather and the extra hours your father is putting in at the mill. But you seem . . . different, the last few weeks. Withdrawn, like something's on your mind. Is there anything else that's bothering you? Something else that you want to talk about?"

Sure, Mom. I'm going with Katie Moore now, and I can hardly believe it because it seems like a dream, and meanwhile, Barry's dad is an abusive asshole and I think he's up to something and he has forbidden us to hang out with Barry anymore and Doug's mom is having sex with him.

"No, Mom. Honestly, I'm okay. Like you said, it's just been a weird summer. I can't believe I'm saying this, but I'll be kind of glad when it's over and school starts again."

"Okay. Well, I'll leave you alone. Your father will probably want to talk to you when he gets home. Be patient with him. He's tired and stressed. I guess we all are."

"Yeah."

"You and Doug might be on the evening news. Want to see?"

"No. I think I've seen enough for one day."

"Love you. Try to get some rest, okay?"

Timmy nodded, and she closed the door. His mother's footsteps faded down the hall. He reached over and turned the stereo back up. Cheap Trick was still playing.

". . . but don't give yourself away . . . away . . . away . . ."

He sat there for a few more minutes, remembering Pat and thinking about the day's events. Over and over again, his mind was drawn to Katie—the smell of her hair and the touch of her hand, and the way her eyes had sparkled in the sunlight. He missed her already and couldn't believe he'd have to wait until Sunday to see her again.

After a while, he pulled a box of comic books out from under his bed and began flipping through them. His nostrils flared as he breathed in the comforting, familiar smell of old paper. He came across a tattered issue of *House of Secrets* that he hadn't read in a long time. The bottom section of the cover was missing and the paper around the staples was brown with age. He leaned back against the bed and began reading it.

On the top of what was left of the ragged cover was the title, along with the logo:

There's No Escape From . . . THE HOUSE OF SECRETS.

In the left hand corner was the circular *DC* logo, as opposed to Marvel's. In the right hand corner was the issue number—135, along with the price of thirty-five cents. It was a late seventies back issue that he'd picked up at the flea market. Timmy grinned, nostalgic. In 1978, comics had cost a measly thirty-five cents. Now, in 1984, they cost fifty cents, or sometimes more. It was a shame. On the cover, a man in a cape stood atop a coffin. A group of men were gathered around him. "In one minute," the man told them (via a word balloon), "I'll prove my power and bring Jennifer back to life!" The ghost of a blond woman, supposedly Jennifer, floated behind him.

Timmy opened the comic. The cartoonish host (named Abel), talked directly to the reader from the first page, introducing each gruesome tale (his brother Cain was the host of DC's sister publication, *House of Mystery*). The first story was called "The Resurrection Business" and pretty much followed the events depicted on the front cover. The second story, "Don't Look Now," was about some underground cave explorers fighting a group of monsters called Cypors. Timmy wasn't impressed with either the writing or the artwork, and figured he and Doug could do better. Tempted to return the comic to the box and select something different, he flipped to the last story, "Down With the Dead Men." It took place in a cemetery, which piqued his flagging interest. A ghoul was on the loose; eating the bodies of the dead and hording the gold and jewelry with which they'd been buried. In the comic, a group of villagers trapped the creature in a crypt and destroyed it by waiting for the sun to rise, then allowing the sunlight to shine through the crypt's small window.

Timmy bolted upright against the bed and stared at the last panel. He shut the comic book with trembling hands.

Earlier, Reverend Moore had said that the church's original founders had imprisoned a demon in the cemetery. The demon had supposedly followed them from the Old World and had been causing trouble. What if the demon had actually been a ghoul, just like in the comic book? What if they'd imprisoned it in the grave, and bound it in place with the magic powwow symbol? And then, when the grave and the symbol were destroyed, the ghoul had been freed?

Timmy had always been fascinated by the supernatural, and believed a lot of it. When they were six, he and Doug had thought they saw Bigfoot near the creek in Bowman's Woods. It had turned out just to be a tree, but Timmy still believed it was possible, and that perhaps one day they would come across Bigfoot in the forest.

He believed in Bigfoot. He believed in ghosts. He believed in flying saucers and sea serpents and demonic possession. Timmy believed that people really did disappear inside the Bermuda Triangle and that some dinosaurs probably escaped the Ice Age and were still alive in the deep, dark corners of the world—in places like Loch Ness and Lake Champlain. He believed in pyrokinesis, telekinesis, extrasensory perception, and remote viewing. He didn't know where these beliefs came from, just that he had always had them. The bookshelves in his room were full of books on the topics. He'd always viewed the world with wide-eyed fascination. He'd noticed over the last few years that many of his friends at school—friends who had once believed just as fervently as him—no longer considered the possible existence of ghosts or monsters. Perhaps they viewed them as fallacies, the same way he viewed Santa Claus and the Easter Bunny. But while Timmy no longer fell for those parental inventions, he still believed in the supernatural. He believed in monsters. Maybe it was because he'd retained that sense of wonder that so many others his age seemed to be losing. Or maybe it was because of what he read and what he wrote.

The monsters were real, and not all of them were adults or attack dogs.

Just because he couldn't see them, it didn't mean that they didn't exist.

Timmy believed because he wanted to believe, and if growing up meant that time dulled your perceptions and eradicated that belief, erased the possibility of magic and monsters, then he wanted to stay twelve forever.

He thought over everything he'd ever read about ghouls, both from this particular comic book and others. They lived in tunnels and warrens beneath cemeteries and burial grounds. They were nocturnal and hated sunlight. In this particular story, the ghoul had been destroyed by direct exposure to sunlight. It was that way in most of the other comics, too. On a few occasions, they'd been destroyed by fire, and once by being dropped into a vat of acid, but daylight seemed to be the only sure bet. Ghouls ate the dead, which was why they dug beneath graveyards.

The Golgotha Lutheran Church cemetery was collapsing in spots. The ground was sinking. There was a tunnel entrance inside the utility shed. Supposedly, according to Clark Smelter, there was a cave running beneath the grounds. But what if it wasn't a cave? What if it was the ghoul's tunnels, as it burrowed from grave to grave devouring the dead? Somehow, the sigil keeping it imprisoned had been shattered. It had begun feasting on the dead, first in the old part of the cemetery and then up into the new section. That would explain the steadily sinking ground, and why they'd first noticed it around the older graves.

He thought about his grandfather's sinking grave. Could it have . . . ?

Timmy shuddered, unable to complete the thought.

Ghouls ate the dead. All of the stories agreed on this. In some of them, they ate living humans as well. That would explain some of the recent disappearances. Maybe not the woman on the news, Deb Lentz (her car had been discovered all the way over in Porters), but possibly Ronny, Jason, and Steve—maybe they'd been partying in the graveyard. And it certainly fit with Pat and Karen's disappearance. It seemed pretty certain they'd been parked in the graveyard. Maybe the ghoul had eaten Karen and stuck Pat's body in the trunk for safekeeping, intending to eat him later.

There was only one problem with that theory. Could ghouls drive cars? Timmy looked at the comic again. If they had long claws in real life like they did in fiction, then probably not. Which meant that someone else had hidden the Nova.

In some of the comics, the ghouls had used human helpers, sort of like Dracula's assistant, Renfield. They worked for the creatures, did their bidding, helped to conceal their existence, and were paid with money and jewelry stolen from the dead—extra baubles from the creatures' treasure hoard. In one back issue of *Vault of Evil*, the villagers had hung the ghoul's human familiar from an old tree in the graveyard.

If there was a ghoul beneath the cemetery, did it have an assistant, and if so, who was it?

It didn't take him long to come up with an answer. It was Barry's father who'd suddenly forbid them to play in the cemetery, who'd put up the NO TRESPASSING signs and had blown off the sinking graves by suggesting there were sinkholes. He'd had more money than normal, and Mrs. Smeltzer was wearing lots of new jewelry—some of which seemed really old, like the antiques at the flea market. He was angrier and more violent than ever, like he was suffering from stress or guilt or something. And Barry had mentioned several times that his father was out late at night.

So if he was right, then how could he go about proving it? If Barry's father found out he suspected, there was no telling what could happen. But if Timmy could prove there was a ghoul, if he could get evidence without Mr. Smeltzer finding out, then maybe people would believe him. He'd have to tell Doug and Barry his suspicions. If he was right, they couldn't just waltz down into the tunnel beneath the utility shed. That would be suicide. They'd have to be better prepared than that. He thought of Doug's map. Tomorrow morning, if Mr. Smeltzer wasn't around, he'd get the map from the Dugout and try to figure out exactly how far the ghoul's tunnels reached, based on where the graves were sinking. That was the first step.

When his mother knocked on the door and told him to take a shower, brush his teeth, and get ready for bed, Timmy was so preoccupied with planning that he barely heard her.

He rushed through the bathroom, barely allowing the water to hit his body before he was out of the shower and toweling off. He made quick work of putting on his pajamas and ran the toothbrush across his teeth once or twice. Then he went out into the living room.

His mother was curled up on the couch watching a sitcom. She looked up from the television.

"You ready for bed?"

Timmy nodded.

"You want to watch TV with me until your dad gets home?"

"No, that's okay. I thought I might read for a while."

"Alright." She paused, studying him. "You sure you're okay, Tim?"

He smiled. "Positive. Everything's going to be just fine."

"May I be excused?"

Rhonda Smeltzer glanced over at her son's plate. His food—pork chops, mashed potatoes, and lima beans—had barely been touched. Barry had taken a few bites and then pushed the rest around with his fork. He hadn't spoken during the entire meal. Indeed, he hadn't spoken since returning home from the cemetery. When the police had shown up and questioned Clark, Barry had stayed in his room. His face was pale, and there were dark circles under his eyes.

They matched the circles beneath her own eyes.

"Aren't you going to eat, sweetie?"

"No." Barry shook his head. "I'm not that hungry."

"Eat your supper." Clark shoveled a forkful of mashed potatoes into his mouth.

"I don't feel good."

"None of your lip. Eat your goddamn food. When I was in Vietnam, I saw a hundred starving kids that would have given their left arm to have just a mouthful of what you got on that plate."

Barry put his fork down. "That's a shame. Why don't you send mine over to them?"

Clark choked on his food. He grabbed his glass, took a quick drink, and then slammed it back down on the table. Milk sloshed out.

"What did you say?"

Barry sat back in his chair and crossed his arms over his chest in defiance. "I said why don't you send my dinner over to them. Then they won't be starving anymore."

Clark started to rise, but Rhonda reached out and placed her hand atop his clenched fist.

"Dear," she pleaded, "he's just upset. We all are. The police were here for so long, and it's been—"

Clark tore his hand free of hers, picked up his glass, and threw the milk in her face. Rhonda gasped in surprise. Milk dripped from her nose and chin.

"That's where he gets it from," he said. "Boy talks back and doesn't listen. Acts like a smart-ass because his bitch of a mother is the same way."

"You motherfucker." Barry jumped to his feet, sending his chair crashing backward to the floor.

Fists clenched, his father rose to meet his challenge.

"You sit the hell down, shut the hell up, and eat your goddamned supper, or so help me God, you won't sit down for another week."

"Fuck you, you son of a bitch. I hate you. I hate you and I wish you were dead!"

Barry's hands curled into fists, just like his father's. Hot tears of anger, not shame, coursed down his face. He shook with rage. Clark studied him for a moment. Then he stepped around the kitchen table.

"Reckon you're a man now, huh? All grown up and cursing like an adult. Figure you can kick my ass?"

"I would love to."

His mother jumped to her feet, hands flailing like frightened birds. Her wet bangs were plastered to her forehead and milk still dripped from her face.

"Barry, no. Clark! Please!"

Ignoring her, Clark swung around to Barry's side and stood right in front of him. Barry resisted the urge to step backward, and held his ground. His father leaned down and thrust his chin out.

"Go ahead, boy. Take your best shot. Better make it a good one."

Trembling, Barry said, "Why are you like this? Why can't you be like Timmy's dad?"

Clark laughed. "That what you want? Randy Graco don't know the first thing about being a father."

"He's better than you'll ever be. You're a drunk and an asshole. You don't let Mom or me have any friends. You don't let us go anywhere. I can't even be next door anymore unless you're with me."

"I told you," Clark said. "It's for your own good. Nobody is allowed in the cemetery after—"

"Shut up," Barry shouted. "I'm tired of your shit. Tired of the way you treat us."

"Barry," his mother cried. "Please, stop this now. Sit back down."

His father smiled. "Then like I said, take your best shot."

Barry stared at him. His entire body quivered. The anger felt like a solid thing, deep down inside him. His pulse throbbed in his ears, and his lips felt swollen and full.

"Pussy," his father teased. "I knew you didn't have it in—"

Barry swung. Swung with all his might. His fist plowed forward with the weight of twelve years of abuse and cruelty behind it, twelve years of anger and tears and frustration. Twelve years of hell. It rocketed toward his father's stubbly, unshaven chin and he felt a surge of vindication. Importance. A fiery, testosterone-driven right of passage into manhood. In that brief second, he understood the magnitude of his actions, and how they'd change the course of his life.

And then he missed.

Arm extended, body swerving with the thrust, stepping into the punch just like Luke Cage-Power Man did in the comics—and yet, despite all this, and despite the poetic justice he felt flowing through his veins—his fist sailed by his father's jaw and clipped the older man's shoulder.

His father didn't even blink.

Still grinning, Clark swung his own fist. It smashed into Barry's mouth, and immediately, the boy tasted blood. His lips were crushed against his teeth, splitting open. Blood flowed. The warmth squirted over his tongue, and Barry's stomach rolled. He spat blood, and the simple act of doing so left his mouth in agony. In the background, his mother was screaming. He stared at the bright red spot, and didn't notice the second blow coming. Clark's other fist clobbered the side of his head. Barry became woozy. His vision dimmed on the sides and it seemed as if he were looking down a tunnel. Stunned, he kept staring at the blood, even as more of it filled his mouth.

He noticed something else. A flash of color, glinting off his father's ring finger. It had just left an imprint on his face—a ring. A Freemason's ring. Barry had only seen one like it before, and that was buried with Timmy's grandfather.

"That's what you get," his father said. "I told you before to not talk back to me. This time, you ain't gonna forget it."

His fist—and the ring—came down again, but Barry's knees gave out before it could connect. The blows followed him all the way to the floor, and continued as he wavered on the edge of consciousness. Blood—his blood, he realized—flowed into his eyes. The last thing he heard were his mother's screams.

Barry tried to speak, and then he passed out.

Mercifully, he did not feel the next punch.

When Timmy's father arrived home at a quarter past ten, Timmy was sequestered in his room, lying in bed, surrounded by books and comics. He had his Trapper Keeper notebook in his lap. He-Man's arch-nemesis Skeletor graced the front cover. Timmy was taking notes on ghouls. He'd pulled out every reference he could find, from the *House of Secrets* comic to his *Dungeons and Dragons Monster Manual*. He wasn't sure the latter was entirely accurate, because it dealt more with the game than it did mythology or legend.

He heard his father's pickup truck pull into the driveway. Glen Campbell's "Wichita Lineman" drifted softly from the cab's radio. Then he heard the garage door opening. Moments later, his father came inside. The television snapped off. In the living room, his parents talked in hushed tones, and though Timmy strained to hear them, he couldn't make out their words. Instead, he turned back to his research.

A few minutes later, there was a knock on his door.

"Timmy?"

He closed the notebook. "Come on in, Dad. I'm awake."

His father entered the room, looking exhausted and smelling of sweat. He sat down on the edge of the bed, and patted his son's knee through the blankets.

"You okay? Your mom says you and Doug had quite the day."

"Yeah, it was something, all right. But I'm fine."

"Well, it must have been pretty scary, I guess."

Timmy shrugged. "Kind of. It's scary to know that somebody did this. When you see it on TV, it's always in faraway places like Los Angeles and New York. And I'm sad about Pat and the others."

"I shouldn't have hollered at you this morning, about the serial killer thing. I'm sorry about that. Looks like you may have been right."

"That's okay."

Randy glanced down at the books spread out all over the bed. "So what's all this? You working on a D&D game for your friends?"

"No," Timmy said. "Just doing some research."

"On what?"

"Ghouls."

Frowning, his father picked up the *Monster Manual* and began flipping through it.

"Ghouls, huh? You know, Reverend Moore says that some kids get too wrapped up in this game. Can't tell fantasy from reality anymore. A couple college kids supposedly died . . ."

He trailed off, put the book down, and nodded at the Iron Maiden poster on the wall. "That, too. The Number of the Beast? That's satanic, Timmy. Don't you think?"

"Isn't that what they used to say about the Beatles when you and Mom were kids? And Elvis?"

Randy nodded, obviously reluctant. "Yes, you're right. Some people did say that. Especially when John Lennon joked that the Beatles were more popular than Jesus Christ. But that's different, Timmy. Elvis and the Beatles never sang songs about the devil. They certainly never had album covers like that. My parents would have kicked me out if I'd had something like that hanging on my wall. It's just evil looking."

"Come on, Dad. You know I don't worship the devil."

"I know. You're a good kid, Timmy, and I'm very

proud of you. I just worry sometimes. Your attraction to stuff like this and your infatuation with monsters and things—it just isn't normal for a boy your age. You should be playing sports—"

"I hate sports."

"—and be more interested in girls than you are little green men."

"I am interested in girls," Timmy said, feeling defensive.

Randy paused, surprise and relief both clearly visible in his expression.

"You are? Well, that's good. That's very good."

"You sound surprised, Dad."

"No. Don't think that way. I just didn't know. See, we need to talk more, kiddo. You need to know that you can tell me things like that."

"Okay," Timmy said. Secretly, he wished his father would just kiss him good night and go to bed, so that he could get on with his research. It had been a long day and he still had lots to do.

Randy made no move to leave. Instead, he winked and said, "So, is it anybody I know?"

"Who?" For a moment, Timmy thought his father was talking about the ghoul.

"This girl you like. Is it someone your mother and I have met?"

"Yes," Timmy mumbled.

"Who?"

"Aw, come on, Dad. I don't want to say. It's embarrassing."

"You can tell me. I won't say anything to your mother. Is she cute?"

Timmy took a deep breath. "It's Katie Moore."

Grinning, his father slapped his knee in delight. The bed springs groaned from the sudden movement.

"Katie, huh? That's great. She's going to be a knock-out when she gets older. Does she know you like her?"

"Yes. We're going together. We talked about it today."

"Going steady?" Randy reached out and ruffled Timmy's hair. "Well, how about that. My little guy is finally growing up."

Despite his embarrassment, Timmy smiled. Once he'd finally admitted it, he was surprised to find that it actually felt good to share the news with his father. Maybe his dad was right. Maybe he should talk to him about things like this more often. Like Doug had said earlier, Timmy was pretty lucky. He had a father, unlike Doug, and his father was pretty cool most of the time, unlike Barry's.

Still grinning, Randy got to his feet. "Well, I'll let you get back to your reading. Still wish you'd read about other stuff, for a change. Don't stay up past eleven, okay?"

Timmy decided to take a chance.

"Dad, wait. Can I talk to you about something else?"

"Sure." Randy sat back down again. "What's up?"

"Well . . . I'm not sure where to start. This may sound kind of weird."

"Try me."

"Okay." Timmy swallowed. "I think I know what happened to Pat and Karen, and all the others."

His father blinked. "Well, Timmy, I know it was traumatic finding Pat's body the way you boys did, but according to your mother, the police have cautioned against assuming the other disappearances are related."

"Do you believe that, Dad?"

"I think it's safe to assume that whoever killed Pat probably killed . . . that the same thing might have happened to Karen. But we just don't know about the others yet."

"But this morning, when you warned us to stay around the house, I thought you were assuming the same thing."

"Maybe I was. Look, Timmy, I don't have all the answers. I'm just worried about you—and your friends. Something's going on and I don't want it to affect you any more than it already has. Whatever it is that's happened to the others, I don't want it happening to you. Let's just let the police find out who's responsible."

"But, Dad, that's just it. I know who it is! I know who's behind this."

"Who, Timmy? And how do you know? Is there something you didn't tell the detective when he interviewed you?"

"No. I figured it out later, when I got home. That's why I'm doing all this research."

Randy's face grew concerned. "What do you mean?"

"The person that killed Pat isn't a person at all. It's a ghoul."

His father didn't speak, and Timmy assumed he was too shocked to reply. Gathering his courage, he pressed ahead.

"You said I could talk to you about what's going on. Well this is what's going on."

He proceeded to tell his father about all that he suspected, blurting out a breathless, excited litany of the past month's chronological events and how they connected to facts regarding ghoul legends. Occasionally, to clarify a point or back up a position, Timmy would rifle through the stack of comics and hold one up for verification, pointing to the specific panels where he'd gotten the information. Randy kept quiet, listening with rapt attention to all that his son had to say. He started to interrupt once, when Timmy voiced his suspicions about Clark Smeltzer, but then he fell silent again. His mouth was tight, his face grim. When Timmy had finished, he was speechless. Timmy waited expectantly for some sort of response—anything—but none was forthcoming. His father merely stared at him.

"Dad?"

Blinking, Randy shook his head slightly, as if waking up from a daydream.

"Dad," Timmy said again, "what should we do? Do you think we should tell the police?"

"No." His father's voice was sad and hoarse. "No, Timmy, I don't think we should call the police."

"But why not? It could be out there right now."

"That's enough, Tim."

"But Dad, you said that you'd listen to me. You said I could talk to you. What's wrong? Don't you believe me?"

Randy sighed. "No, Tim. I don't."

Timmy's heart sank.

"But . . . but it all makes sense. Even Grandpa's grave."

Randy tensed. "Stop it, Timothy. Just stop this right now."

"Don't you care? The ghoul could have tunneled into his coffin."

"I said stop it."

"It could have eaten Grandpa."

"I said stop it!"

In the living room, Elizabeth heard the outburst. Gasping, she ran down the hall. She flung the door open and stared at them, frightened. Tears rolled down her son's face. He was sitting upright against the headboard, shrinking away from his father. Her husband looked angrier than she'd seen him in a long time.

"What on earth is going on in here? What's wrong?"

"Tell your mother," Randy spat. "Tell your mother the same nonsense you just told me."

"I . . . I . . ." Timmy trailed off, stifling a sob.

Randy stood up, fists clenched at his sides. Elizabeth touched his shoulder, but he shrugged her away.

"Randy, what is going on?"

"Our son," he said through gritted teeth, "thinks that a monster is on the loose next door in the cemetery. He says that it's in cahoots with Clark Smeltzer, and that the two of them are robbing graves. He thinks that this monster, this *ghoul*, is eating people. He thinks that it ate . . . my father."

Elizabeth's eyes went wide with shock. Her head whipped back and forth in denial.

"Timmy," she cried, "why would you say such horrible things?"

More tears rolled down his face. "Because it's the truth, Mom. I can prove it."

"Honey, you know it's not the truth. There is no such thing as monsters. And Mr. Smeltzer? I'll admit, he has problems, but Barry's father is—"

"Barry's father is a monster," Timmy shouted. "Jesus Christ, are you both blind?"

"Don't take the Lord's name in vain."

"Mom, don't you know what Mr. Smeltzer does to Barry and his mom? He's evil, and he's working with that thing out there. That ghoul."

"Timothy Graco," Elizabeth snapped. "You stop talking like that this instant. There is no monster living in the cemetery. You know that."

"It's these funny books," Randy said, seizing a handful off the bed. He crumpled them in his fist. "This garbage. I told you Reverend Moore was right. We shouldn't be letting him read this bullshit. These comics are where he gets these ideas. They're a bad influence."

Timmy cried out as his father continued to squeeze, crumpling the comic beyond any hope of repair.

"Your father is right," his mother said. "Like earlier, when you said that you and your friends blew up a dead animal. That type of behavior just isn't acceptable."

"I'm sorry," Timmy said. "We won't do it again. But I'm not lying about the ghoul."

"No more," Randy said. "I'll have no more of this nonsense. It's not normal, Timothy. These things you believe in—normal people don't think about monsters and demons."

He tossed the comics on the floor and stalked out of the room. Timmy leapt out of bed and scooped them up. He flattened the comic books out on his mattress and tried to smooth them.

"Look at this," he sobbed. "Look what he did. He ruined them."

Elizabeth tried to soothe him. "Timmy. Calm down, sweetie. Your father is very angry right now, and he's had a long day."

"I don't care. It isn't right."

"Honey, did you really say that about your grandfather?"

"Yes."

"But why? Can't you see how hurtful that is to your father? How wrong it was to make up such a horrible story?"

"It's true!" Timmy looked up at her with red-rimmed eyes. "See for yourself. His grave is sinking."

"That's normal, Timmy. Graves settle after a few weeks, especially if it rains like it did last night. You can't make up lies like that."

"It's not a story, and he didn't need to do this." He

continued smoothing the comics. "I hate him. I'll never forgive Dad for this."

"Timmy, that's not true. You love your father, and he loves you very much."

"If he loved me, then why won't he listen? Why did he do this?"

"You have to look at it from his perspective."

"Why? Why do I have to? Because I told the truth?"

"But you didn't, Timmy. You're telling stories. Fiction. You're confused right now. Upset with all that's happened."

"No, I'm not."

Randy walked back into the room with a huge cardboard box in hand. He sat it down on the floor and then, without a word, he began dropping Timmy's comic collection into the box. Timmy gasped. The comics folded and bent as they were dumped inside.

"Dad, what are you doing?"

"Something I should have done a long time ago. Elizabeth, pull those long white boxes out from under his bed."

"Randy, I—"

"I said to do it."

She took a deep breath and complied. Not once did she look up at her son.

"What are you doing?" Timmy asked again. "What is this?"

"Follow me."

Randy turned and stomped down the hall, hefting a box under each arm. Timmy ran after him, demanding to know what was going on. Elizabeth trailed along behind them, carrying the last box. When they reached the kitchen, Randy set down a box, opened the basement door, and motioned for Timmy to go through.

"Downstairs."

Timmy did as he was told. His father's voice was cold and emotionless. He'd never heard it sound this way before.

His parents followed him. When they reached the bottom of the stairs, Randy made Timmy sit down on a wooden stool that he pulled out from under his workbench. He sat the boxes of comics next to him. Then he pulled over a large, empty trash can and put a fresh garbage bag inside it. Only then, after he'd finished this task, did Randy finally speak.

"Elizabeth, go back upstairs."

"Randy, don't do this. Please. You know how much he loves those books. Please? I'm sure he didn't mean it."

Silently, Timmy prayed she'd convince his father to stop before it was too late.

Randy sighed. "Honey, do as I asked you to. Please, just this once? This is hard enough."

They stared at one another for a moment, and then she turned and went back upstairs to the kitchen. She shut the door behind her. Randy pulled out another stool and sat down facing his son.

"Dad . . ."

"Timmy, I love you. I need you to know that."

His voice cracked. He paused, taking a moment to compose himself, and then continued.

"Sometimes it's hard, being a parent. When you have a kid, it's not like buying a new car or an appliance. There's no instruction manual, and you get so scared of making a mistake. Get scared of screwing your kid up. Your generation has it pretty easy. You don't have Vietnam or the Depression to go through. But it's still tough, these days. We want the best for you. Your mom and I have tried very hard to give you the things we didn't have at your age. Things like good food and clothes. Your bike. That Atari in the living room. And you deserve them. I meant what I said earlier—I'm proud of you. But this lying has got to stop."

"I'm not lying, Dad."

"You know very well that story isn't true. Don't act like you don't know what I'm talking about. I'm going to give you one last chance, Timmy. One last chance to take it all back."

"But, Dad—I . . ."

His father sighed. His shoulders slumped.

"Okay. I didn't want to do this . . ."

"What?"

"I'm grounding you for disobeying me this morning. Yes, I know you boys found Pat's car, and that's a good thing for all concerned. But you still disobeyed me. You went beyond the boundaries your mother and I set for you."

"We had to. We were—"

"I don't want to hear any more lies. It doesn't matter. You're grounded for a month."

"A month? But that's half my summer vacation!"

"I'm sorry, Timothy. You should have listened."

"But the ghoul—"

"There is no such thing as monsters, Timmy! Stop it. Stop making up bullshit stories!"

Flinching, Timmy reared back on the stool in fright. His father's anger seemed to roll off him in waves, almost tangible.

Randy picked up the first comic book, *Avengers Annual #10.* His hands shook.

Timmy's eyes grew wide.

"Don't speak, Timothy. Don't say a word, because all you're doing is lying more. I gave you a chance. And don't you dare look away. If you look away, I'll ground you for another month."

"Dad," Timmy sobbed, "please don't do this. I'm sorry. I'm sorry!"

"I'm sorry, too, son."

He tore it in half, slowly. A single tear rolled down his cheek.

"No," Timmy screamed, "please, Daddy, don't. Please? I'm sorry, I'm sorry, I'm—"

The torn halves were tossed into the trash can, followed by an issue of *Marvel Two-in-One*.

"Stop it, Daddy! Please, just stop."

"It's too late for that." An issue of *Fantastic Four* was next. Then a mint copy of *Justice League of America* that Timmy hadn't even had a chance to read.

"I hate you," Timmy screamed. "I hate you and want you to die."

More tears spilled from both of their eyes as Randy tore up a copy of *The Defenders*.

And another.

And another.

And an hour later, when the boxes were empty and his entire comic book collection—his entire childhood— was destroyed, Timmy still had plenty of tears left.

There is no such thing as monsters, his father had said, but his father was wrong.

Timmy was looking at one, and at that moment, he hated his father far worse than he'd ever hated Barry's.

CHAPTER TWELVE

Doug pedaled down Laughman Road. The spokes on his wheels hummed quietly as the tires went round and round. His bike's white reflectors flashed in the darkness when the moonlight hit them. He sped by Catcher's driveway, but if the Doberman was awake, he didn't give chase. Breathing a big sigh of relief, Doug coasted on.

He'd woken, plastered in sweat, as his mother's mouth closed over him. Somehow, she'd already succeeded in pulling his pajamas down while he slept. Frightened and disoriented, he'd jerked away from her and glanced around his bedroom, wondering how she'd got in. Then he saw. Though he'd invested his meager savings in a lock for the door, he'd forgotten to lock his window. It hung open and the screen was missing. Drunk as she was, his mother had managed to remove the screen. Then she'd crawled inside while he'd slept, exhausted from the day's traumatic events.

She reached for him again. Doug fought her off, managing to get his pajama bottoms back up while she sat on the floor and cried. Then he comforted her, holding her close and whispering consoling words until she passed out, drooling on his shoulder. As soon as she began snoring, he'd slipped out from beneath her, got dressed, and left. It was a quarter till midnight. With any luck, Timmy would still be awake, probably reading comic books under the covers with a flashlight. Doug could bang on his window and spend the night.

Bowman's Woods were different at night. Scary. The tree limbs seemed to reach out over the road, grasping for him. The darkness between their trunks was a solid thing, and strange noises came from within its shadowy confines. Night sounds: snapping twigs, rustling leaves, a chirping chorus of crickets, something that could have been an owl—or laughter.

Shivering, Doug pedaled faster.

To his left, another twig snapped, as if something were following him. Then another. The faster he went, the faster the snapping sounds increased.

His mind conjured up images of Jason and Michael Myers and every other movie maniac he'd had the misfortune to see. What if Pat's killer was in the woods right now, watching him, lying in wait? After all, it had been him and Timmy that had discovered Pat's car—and Pat himself.

He increased his speed yet again, and the wind ruffled his hair, cooling the sweat on his forehead. His pedals beat a steady rhythm, clanking against the bike's faulty kickstand. He'd been meaning to get it fixed, maybe have Timmy's father install a new one, but he hadn't yet come up with the money to get it, since most of his savings went toward candy and video games.

Eventually, the snapping sounds faded. Doug chided himself for being silly. It had probably just been a deer or a squirrel.

Somewhere deep inside the forest, a whippoorwill called out—a mournful, lonely sound. Doug had heard the old wives' tales about them—if you heard a whippoorwill late at night or just before dawn, it meant that somebody close to you was going to die. As the bird sang out again, Doug hoped those stories weren't true. There were enough people dead. He didn't need any more.

Sometimes he thought about dying. What it would be like. If it would hurt. If anything happened afterward, like Reverend Moore promised, or if there was nothing but oblivion. Of the two choices, he preferred oblivion. Sleep was good. Doug enjoyed sleeping. It was the only time he didn't have to think; didn't have to feel.

Doug reached the intersection with Anson Road and paused to catch his breath. With relief, he noticed that the Graco's living room light was on, which meant that at least one of Timmy's parents were still awake, and maybe Timmy, as well. Both vehicles were in the driveway. Everyone was home—the whole family.

Family.

Doug wished he had one. He spent his time alone daydreaming about when his father had still been around. He often wished that he'd appreciated those times more while they lasted. His parents had seemed happy, at least to him. And they seemed to be happy *with* him, as well. His Dad said, "I love you." They did stuff together. Talked about things. His father had never called him fat boy or tub-o-lard or faggot, like the kids at school or Barry's father did.

The last month he was with them, things changed.

Subtly. Doug hadn't seen it at the time, but it was clear in hindsight. His father had seemed withdrawn. Distant. Irritable. At first, Doug had figured it had something to do with his mother losing her job. But the uncharacteristic behavior continued. Those last few weeks, Doug and his mother ate dinner alone. His dad didn't come home after work—didn't come home at all, sometimes. Spent the night somewhere else. He never said where, at least to Doug. He'd heard his parents arguing about it, but at the time, he hadn't understood what was going on and was too afraid to ask. He thought maybe it was something that he'd done.

And then, one night, his father didn't come home again, and the next morning, he was still gone. He never came back. Never said good-bye. Never explained it to Doug or told him where he was going or that he loved him one last time.

He was just . . . gone.

His father abandoned him for a waitress that Doug had never met. Worse, his father had left him alone with his mother, knowing full well what she was capable of.

Ever since then, Doug had felt hollow and empty. Dead.

So maybe oblivion wasn't such a bad alternative after all, if he was already dead inside anyway.

At twelve, Doug felt eighty.

He hopped off his bike and pushed it up the Graco's driveway, trying his best to be quiet. The chain rattled softly and the spokes clicked. He gently laid the bike down in the yard and then crept around back. The grass brushed against his shoes, the dew soaking his feet. The breeze picked up for a moment, and Mrs. Graco's wind chimes rang in the silence. Doug willed them to be quiet, and the wind died down again. He started toward

Timmy's window, tripped over a stick, and froze, waiting to see if he'd been heard. He noticed that Timmy's bedroom window was dark, as were the rest of the lights in the house except for the living room, its soft yellow glow peeking out from beneath the shades.

Doug paused, wondering what to do next. Somebody was obviously awake, but it probably wasn't Timmy. Even if Timmy was still up, his parents didn't know about it because his light was out. If he knocked on Timmy's window, he risked the possibility that whoever was still awake might hear him. If Mr. or Mrs. Graco caught him, not only would Timmy get in trouble, but they'd also insist on either calling his mother or taking him back home themselves. No way was he going back home tonight.

He crept back around the side of the house and sneaked up to the living room's large picture window. Pressing his nose against the glass, Doug peeked through a space in the shades. Timmy's father was sitting on the couch. A half-empty bottle of Jack Daniels sat on the end table next to him. Doug's eyes widened with surprise. Mr. Graco rarely drank, especially on weeknights. But what shocked him the most wasn't the alcohol. It was the look of absolute anguish etched into Randy Graco's face. Timmy's father was weeping; large, fat tears that made his cheeks shiny and wet. His eyes were red and his body shook each time he sobbed. Doug had never seen him show so much emotion—not even at Dane Graco's funeral. He looked scarred. Tortured. In a weird way, it almost looked like he was laughing instead of crying, since there was no sound. But the haunted look in his eyes was a dead giveaway that this was a man in pain.

Doug backed away from the window. It felt wrong, somehow, spying on his best friend's father at such a private and darkly intimate moment. Something was definitely wrong, but whatever it was, Doug would have to wait until tomorrow to find out. There was no way he could risk waking Timmy now. And going to Barry's house was obviously out of the question. He couldn't go home. He couldn't spend the night with friends. And so, he was left with only one option.

The Dugout.

Sighing, Doug collected his bike. He coasted down the driveway and onto Anson Road. When he was out of earshot, he began pedaling again. He slowed as he reached the cemetery. Even though they'd played there after dark often enough, it was still spooky at night. Spookier than even Bowman's Woods. Especially when he was alone. Light wisps of mist curled around the bases of the tombstones and trees. The moon seemed frozen overhead, bright and full, offering radiance, but no warmth. Unlike Bowman's Woods and the rest of the countryside, the graveyard was quiet. No crickets chirped. No birds sang. Not even an owl or a whippoorwill. It was weird, as if Mother Nature were holding her breath.

The cemetery felt empty.

Despite the humidity in the air, Doug shivered.

He slogged up the hill, out of breath, hot and sweating hard. The bike seemed heavier than normal, and he wished that he had the leg strength to pedal it uphill, rather than push it. He avoided going anywhere near Barry's house, and instead, turned off the road and into the old portion of the graveyard. Even though it was still uphill, the going seemed easier. The ground was softer, and the wet dew soaked through his sneakers and cooled his feet.

He reached the top of the hill and paused to catch his breath. Then he hopped back on the bike. To his left, the dilapidated utility shed loomed in the distance. Just the sight of it filled Doug with dread and sadness. That morning's memories were still fresh. He imagined that he could still hear Clark Smeltzer's cruel, mocking laughter and slurred speech, as if he were nearby. It seemed very real, as if Mr. Smeltzer was still there.

And then, with a jolt of panic, Doug realized that he was.

Clark Smeltzer leaned against a tall, granite monument near the utility shed, in the newer portion of the cemetery. Despite the solid support, the drunken caretaker swayed back and forth. One arm hugged the stone. The other waved around in agitation. He clutched a bottle in his hand, and the liquid sloshed in time with his jerky movements. His voice was animated—loud and angry. He was talking to someone, but from his vantage point, Doug couldn't see who it was. He strained to hear. The wind shifted toward him and he picked up a snatch of conversation. The breeze carried something else, too—a foul odor, similar to the one they'd smelled wafting from the hole beneath the shed floor. Doug assumed that was where the stench was coming from.

"You leave them out of this," Mr. Smeltzer threatened whomever he was talking to. "That wasn't part of the deal."

He lurched to the side, still holding onto the grave marker, and Doug caught a glimpse of the stranger. Whoever it was, they appeared to be naked and almost hairless, except between their legs. His eyes widened. Yes, the person, whoever it was, really was naked, and definitely a man. Their skin was very pale, and seemed to be . . . *glowing*?

That couldn't be right.

He squinted, trying to see clearly. His pulse raced. A lump rose in his throat. If Mr. Smeltzer turned around now or if the stranger spotted him over the caretaker's shoulder, he'd be caught. He'd already seen just what Barry's father was capable of in broad daylight. There was no telling what he'd do under the cover of night, especially as angry as he sounded right now.

Slowly, carefully, Doug turned the bike to the right and began heading for the church. He held his breath, hoping the chain wouldn't rattle. The spokes clicked softly. He prayed they wouldn't notice the bike's reflectors. His plan was to cut around it, letting the structure block him from their view, and then take the lower cemetery road—the one that bordered Luke Jones's pasture—to the Dugout. If he needed to, he could even go the long way around and cut through the pasture itself. Once inside the fort, he should be safe. There was no way they could stumble across it in the dark.

Swallowing hard, he tried to calm his fears, tried to make a game out of it. He was Han Solo, sneaking around onboard the Death Star and hiding from the Imperial storm troopers. His BMX was really the Millennium Falcon, the fastest bucket of bolts in the entire galaxy. He tried to think of the film's line about the Kessel Run, but he was too scared to remember it.

Inching farther away, he climbed onto the bike, breathed a silent prayer, and coasted away. His feet slipped onto the pedals and he gently pumped them. The pedals went round in a circle—and clanged against the faulty kickstand.

Ka-chunk.

Doug whimpered.

Behind him, something squealed like a monstrous, enraged pig.

"Oh, shit." Doug pedaled as fast as he could.

The bike picked up speed, rocketing toward the church. The tires crunched through the gravel, and the bike's chain rattled. Clark Smeltzer shouted in confusion, but Doug didn't bother to turn around. He heard feet slapping the ground in pursuit, coming hard and fast. The horrible stench seemed to be following him as well, getting stronger. He bent over the handlebars, gritted his teeth, and pedaled with all his might. Another terrible cry sounded from behind him, and then the sounds of pursuit faded. He rolled into the parking lot, and out onto the road, passing between Barry's house and the church. The windows were dark inside each, reinforcing in his mind just how late it was.

I'm all alone out here, he thought. *If something happens now, nobody will ever know.*

Risking a glance over his shoulder, he saw no sign of either Barry's father or the mysterious, howling stranger. He took a deep breath, held it, and listened.

Silence.

Who sounds like that, anyway? Not even the guy who does all those sound effects in the Police Academy movies could make a noise like that. It was more like an animal than a person.

He waited a few seconds longer, his muscles tensed, ready to flee if there was any sign of pursuit. No one came. Apparently, they'd given up. Relieved, Doug reached down and patted the bike's crossbar.

"Good girl," he whispered. "Got us out of that one, for sure. Need to get that kickstand fixed, though."

He rode on into the night. He'd decided that maybe death and oblivion weren't really what he wanted after all.

* * *

Smeltzer had become a problem. Angered, the caretaker was suddenly making demands, and refusing to follow the ghoul's commands. He was inebriated almost to the point of incoherency, and threatening to expose the ghoul's underground warren—breeding pit and all. There was dried blood on the caretaker's fists, and it had belonged to the man's whelp, judging by the scent. In this drunken, unreasonable state, Smeltzer was no longer useful. The ghoul had been about to kill him when the child interrupted them.

The creature had commanded Smeltzer to bring it more females, and warned him that if he didn't, it would have no choice but to take Smeltzer's own woman, as well as the women living in the homes nearby. Despite this, the gravedigger had refused. Finding courage from his bottle, he'd grown belligerent. He'd complained about the police presence, and how the law was asking questions. The ghoul had known nothing of this, having spent the daylight hours asleep deep beneath the graveyard. It was displeased to learn that its first victim—the youth whose mate he'd stolen—had been found, and even angrier to learn that Smeltzer had not properly disposed of the youth's body. Once again, the ghoul gnashed its teeth in annoyance at the Creator's commandment—not to taste living blood, nor to eat living flesh.

It grinned, remembering the child whose foot had fallen through the tunnel roof. The ghoul had only clawed him, but it had heard the child on the surface above, telling his companions that he'd been bitten. The ghoul wasn't positive, but he thought that it might have been the same child who'd interrupted them tonight. The scent was similar. It should have bitten him. It hadn't broken the commandment until the three young men had invaded its underground home. Even then, it hadn't consumed their bodies immediately. It had enjoyed merely a small taste. But that was in the process of defending its lair, and the ghoul felt justified.

In hindsight, it should have done the same when this drunken fool, Smeltzer, first freed it from its prison. It should have ignored the Creator's law when it came across the young couple rutting in the cemetery. When it slaughtered the male and took the female as its first mate, it should have devoured the youth's carcass. It hadn't, and because of that, because it had left the matter of disposing of the body in the hands of a human accomplice, its home and security were now threatened. Its family—the ghoul's new family—was now endangered.

Or maybe this was all happening as a result of the ghoul's breaking of the commandment in the first place. Maybe the Creator was displaying His displeasure.

It had intended to kill its human accomplice, to rip Smeltzer's head from his body and bathe in the warm, red fountain, but the child had interrupted those plans. And now the child had escaped, and could tell others. Soon men would come, armed not with torches and magic. Not this time. But armed nevertheless. It did not fear their guns and ammunition. It feared discovery before it had the chance to become a parent. Relocation would delay those plans.

The ghoul stopped in its musings, pausing in front of a black marble gravestone, the ornate lettering gilded in gold. A cross symbol dominated the stone's center. It had been carved with obvious craftsmanship and care. Beneath the engraving were the words, *He is Risen.*

Snarling, the creature lifted one leg and urinated on the symbol. The pungent stream splattered over the tombstone and ran down onto the grass, steaming in the darkness.

"There is what I think of your commandment. *He is risen?* Bah. He would not have risen, had one of my kind been in the tomb with him. He would have been another meal. Nothing more. Then where would your great plan be?"

The ghoul gnashed its teeth in frustration. The child was gone, vanished into the night. But his scent was familiar. The ghoul was positive now. It had smelled this scent several times before: the day the boy's foot had fallen through the tunnel, and most strongly from a separate warren on the graveyard's edge—a den manufactured by children's hands. Smeltzer's son, the child from this evening, and one other. It had discovered the hole during the previous evening when it was foraging in a nearby grave, but had thought nothing of it at the time. Now, it knew better.

Snorting, it leapt over the tombstones and bounded back to Smeltzer. The man had slumped over to the ground, his back propped up against a statue. His eyes were slits, his breathing troubled. The bottle was still clutched firmly in his hand. The caretaker muttered something under his breath.

The ghoul knelt beside him and took his chin in its clawed hands. The long, black talons dimpled Clark's grizzled cheeks, drawing small beads of blood. He tilted his face upward.

"Tell me who that child was."

Clark winced. The creature's breath woke him up; it stunk like rancid meat, and there were bits of decayed flesh between its teeth.

"Who?"

The ghoul squeezed, impatient. "The child. The boy I just pursued. What is he called?"

"Doug," Clark slurred. "Doug Keiser. Faggoty . . . lil' fat kid. 'S nuttin' to worry about."

"I will be the judge of that. Twice today my safe haven has been compromised. I cannot allow this to stand. It is important that I see my race live again. All that matters is my children."

"Kids ain't . . . shit." Clark belched directly into the beast's face, and then took a drink of Wild Turkey. His breath reeked almost as bad as the ghoul itself.

"You test my patience, grave digger."

Ignoring the creature, Clark continued. "Kids jus' don' lishen. Got to show 'em who's . . . boss. Knock 'em around a bit."

The ghoul released his chin. "Does this Keiser child dwell nearby?"

Shrugging, Clark lifted the bottle to his lips again. With a low, rumbling growl, the ghoul smacked it away. The bottle shattered against a tombstone. Clark pouted at the loss.

"My patience wears very thin. Listen carefully. Does the child live nearby?"

"Yeah, up past Sawyer's place. He comes and goes. Shumtimes . . . sometimes he stays wit' my boy and the Graco kid. Livsh down over t' hill."

Pausing, the ghoul sniffed the air.

"Ain't enough," Clark stammered. "Whatchu giving me, it ain't enough. At night . . . when I try t' sleep . . . I hear those women screamin'. In my head."

"Silence."

The ghoul's nostrils flared, catching a scent. The boy was back. Not close by, but still near enough for the wind to carry his scent. Perhaps sneaking into the graveyard from the other side, intent on cowering inside his little den. Grinning, it turned back to the caretaker.

"You are displeased with our arrangement? Then rejoice."

"Why? Ain't got nuthin' to be happy 'bout."

"Indeed you do. It is time for our dealings to come to an end, as you wished."

"What'sh that mean?"

In answer, the ghoul uttered a savage growl and lashed out. Its talons ripped through Clark Smeltzer's face, flaying the skin on his cheek, nose, chin, and throat. Red-hot pain overwhelmed the muting effects of the alcohol. Shrieking, Clark brought his hands to his ruined flesh. His fingers brushed against the ragged flaps of skin. He pulled his hands away and stared in disbelief at his dripping red fingers, wondering whose blood it was.

By the time he collapsed, slipping into unconsciousness, the ghoul was already speeding toward the tunnels.

Commandments be damned. It was weary of feasting on the dead.

It wanted blood.

Inside the Dugout, Doug pulled out his neon green Duncan Imperial yo-yo and did a few tricks while he tried to calm down. Eventually, he got his breathing and heart rate back under control. He was safe now. No way could Barry's father or that weird guy *(thing?)* he'd been hanging around with find him down here. The stranger had actually scared him worse than Mr. Smeltzer had. That horrible squeal, the way his naked skin had looked in the moonlight, the sounds he made when he'd given chase. None of those things were normal.

So what the heck was he?

He wished Timmy were there with him. Timmy was smart. He knew everything there was to know about monsters and stuff.

Monsters. Could the guy have actually been a monster? That was just silly.

Doug put away the yo-yo. He unwrapped a Kit-Kat bar and turned up the lantern. He tried to laugh. It sounded more like a sob.

"It wasn't a monster," he whispered aloud, the sound of his voice soothing his frazzled nerves. "More like a molester. Just some guy painted up so his skin would glow or something. A nut. Likes to run around naked at night. Mr. Smeltzer's crazy. Figures he'd have crazy friends."

Munching his crispy chocolate bar, Doug flipped through an issue of *Boy's Life* magazine, skimming an article about model rockets, but he found it hard to concentrate. Instead, he reached for the rusted coffee can in which they kept all sorts of assorted junk, and plucked out a sharpened pencil. He spread the map out before him and felt a sense of pride. It didn't matter what people said about him. None of them could make something like this. He began to work on it some more, adding the section of forest where he and Timmy had discovered Pat Kemp's Nova—and what was left of Pat. He drew it by memory, and hoped he was getting the details right. He wanted to finish it by morning. Then he could show it to Timmy. That might cheer his friend up. He didn't know when Barry would have a chance to see it. Sneaking out to see him at night seemed awfully risky, especially since his father apparently hung around the graveyard with a naked, glowing man all night long.

Doug breathed a heavy sigh. The three of them had

been hanging out together since the first grade. It seemed inconceivable that Barry was no longer allowed to see them. There had to be something they could do other than clandestine late-night meetings in the Dugout. In a way, Doug was actually looking forward to school starting again in September. They could hang out together at school without Clark Smeltzer's watchful eye knowing about it. And besides, this summer had been kind of a bust, anyway. He'd be glad to see it end.

His chocolate-covered thumb left a smudge on the corner of the map, but Doug didn't acknowledge it. He drew the outline of a pine tree, then another. He clenched the tip of his tongue between his teeth, focusing on the task at hand. Content, he hummed quietly to himself—the chorus from a John Cougar song. He drew another tree, and then filled it in.

"Life goes on," he sang softly, "long after the thrill of living is gone."

The only time Doug was ever truly happy, other than when he was hanging out with Timmy and Barry, was when he was drawing something. The simple act of sketching, then adding detail, bringing something to life on paper, calmed his mind like nothing else. It was a form of escape. When he was drawing, his mind went into hibernation. He didn't think about his parents or his troubles at school or the things people said about him. None of those things mattered, or even existed. He was consumed with creation, blocking out everything other than the picture in his head. In a way, it was much like the oblivion he craved. He became totally absorbed in it and tuned out the rest of the world.

Which was why when a few small pebbles and loose soil on the Dugout's floor began to quiver, it didn't register with him. He barely noticed when the card table began to wiggle. He just assumed he'd accidentally bumped against it with his knee.

Until it wiggled again, this time more noticeably.

Doug dropped the pencil and sat back, moving his knees away from the card table's legs.

It shook again, more violently this time. The pencil rolled across the map and fell to the dirt floor.

"What the heck?"

Still seated, Doug bent over to retrieve the pencil and noticed that it had rolled to the center of the floor. So had several other objects—a marble, a Matchbox car, several loose BBs that had fallen out of someone's gun, a dud M-80 that Timmy had told them he wanted to take apart, but had apparently forgotten about. As he watched, all of these and more slid to the middle of the Dugout's floor, as if the floor itself were caving in—just like the graves in the cemetery above.

"Oh, man. The sinkhole!"

Doug heard a muffled rustling sound from somewhere beneath his feet. He jumped out of the chair and sprang for the hatch door. The sound grew louder. Closer. A small hole appeared in the center of the floor, and the soil began tumbling into it, like sand through a sieve. Eyes bulging, Doug fumbled with the door's pull-rope. His fingers were slicked with sweat and chocolate, and the rope slipped out of his grasp. Behind him, the card table toppled over, spilling the lantern and the map. The light went out, plunging him into darkness. Terrified, Doug began to cry.

He smelled the now all-too-familiar stench. It burned his nostrils. He heard more dirt falling into the hole. The entire floor was caving in.

"Please," he prayed aloud, "I don't want to die. I really don't."

The darkness was replaced by a faint, eerie luminescence. Not enough to really see by, but still noticeable. The glow was coming from the hole. The foul odor grew stronger.

Something hissed.

This wasn't some underground crevice opening up. Something was alive down there, beneath the Dugout, and it was tunneling up from below.

Desperate, Doug reached for the trapdoor again. Behind him, the hissing was replaced with cruel, wicked laughter. Crying now, he closed his eyes. When he'd been little, Doug used to lie in bed at night, fearful of the monster he was convinced lived in his closet. When he thought the monster was near, he'd close his eyes. He was pretty sure that if he couldn't see the monster, then it couldn't see him.

"Daddy," he whispered. "Come back now. Please? Come back and save me from the monster."

He opened his eyes.

The floor exploded upward, showering him with dirt and rocks. The card table and a stack of comics and porno magazines tumbled into the crevice. A long pair of pale, sinewy arms thrust toward him, barely visible in the gloom. Hands grasped his legs, just as his mother had done earlier in the evening. Doug beat at the clawed hands, but they held firm. The monster pulled him into the hole. He didn't even get a chance to scream.

Plunging downward into darkness, Doug thought about his father, and wondered if he still loved him.

Just like before, his father hadn't shown up to save him from the monster.

CHAPTER THIRTEEN

Barry waited until his mother was asleep before he got up. His alarm clock showed that it was 2:23 in the morning. He reached above him and turned on the small lamp sitting precariously on his headboard. Just this simple movement caused new agony, and the light hurt his eyes. He groaned, and that hurt his mouth.

His body was sore and battered. It hurt just to breathe. If he moved too quickly, he felt a sharp, stabbing pain in his side. His father's fury had left no part of his body untouched. His bottom lip was split wide open in the middle, and simply touching it brought tears to his eyes. One eye was swollen, the other blackened, and Dane Graco's Freemason ring—which had somehow ended up on his father's hand—had left ugly, purple indentations on Barry's cheek and forehead. The ring had gouged a ragged furrow in his other cheek. The deep cut would leave a permanent scar; just one more scar to add to all of those left by his father. His shoulders and kidneys ached, and his stomach, back, and sides were covered with welts and bruises. Portions of Barry's scalp were raw and bleeding, where his father had pulled his hair out. His left forearm had five finger-shaped bruises on it. The other had been burned with a cigarette, and the open wound wept. He dimly remembered that—it had been the burn that brought him back to consciousness. Even his groin throbbed. His father's last act had been to kick him there, after he was already down and about to pass out a second time. Barry was covered in dried blood, all of it his.

He eased himself off the bed, went to the door, and listened. The house was quiet. His father had left many hours before, stomping out into the night without a word. His mother had either cried or drank herself to sleep. Probably a combination of both. After his father was gone, she'd tried to help Barry, wept over him and tried to soothe his pain, but Barry had pushed her away. Now he felt guilty about that. He'd shouted at her, told her he hated her. The look in her eyes had been the same one she gave his father, when the old man was hitting her. Feeling a savage twist of vindication, Barry had said it again. But it wasn't true. He didn't hate his mother. He just no longer cared. Not about her or his father or anything else. Not after tonight. His physical pain was immense, but inside, Barry felt emotionally numb.

His mother had taken a beating as well, after Clark was finished with Barry. At one point, Rhonda had scrambled for the phone, threatening to call the police. Clark ripped it out of the wall, and then did the same with the one in the bedroom. He'd put his foot through both jacks, so that the phones couldn't be plugged back in. Then he'd laughed, hands on hips, defiantly daring them to run for help.

Slowly, Barry opened his bedroom door and peered

out into the hallway. The house was still silent. He crept into the bathroom, turned on the light, and shut the door behind him. Bending over to lift the toilet seat caused fresh pain. He whimpered while he relieved himself. The act made his kidneys and groin ache even worse. Alarmed, he saw that his urine was dark in color. He wondered if that meant there was blood in it, and if so, what he should do about it. He realized there wasn't really anything he could do. If he went to the doctor, there would be questions. He might get placed in foster care. That would be just as bad as this. It would interfere with what he'd decided to do.

Finished, he left the seat up and didn't flush, afraid that the sound would wake his mother. Then he opened the medicine cabinet. The door squeaked, but his mother slept on. He dry swallowed two Tylenol caplets to help ease his pain. Then Barry doctored his wounds as best he could, wincing when the hydrogen peroxide hit his cuts, and nearly screaming when he put it on his split lip. The disinfectant bubbled and fizzed like acid. Pain coursed through him like liquid fire. But this pain was different. Good, somehow. Better. Because this was the last time he'd ever allow himself to feel pain like this, and knowing that strengthened his resolve for what was to come.

Several months ago, Pat Kemp and some of the other older kids had gone to see Quiet Riot and Slade opening for Loverboy at the York Fairgrounds. They'd been there for the opening acts and left when Loverboy took the stage. A few days later, Pat had told Barry, Doug, and Timmy all about it when they ran into him at Genova's Pizza. As a result, Barry had picked up a Slade cassette. Experience had taught him that if Pat Kemp liked a band, he probably would, too. Slade had been no exception. Now, as he bandaged his cuts, his favorite song by them ran through his head. He sang it softly, whispering the chorus. It hurt his mouth, but he did it anyway.

"See the chameleon lying there in the sun . . . Run, run away. Run, run away . . ."

He'd overheard the cops when they'd come to the door and questioned his father earlier. He knew what had happened to Pat. Barry had always looked up to him—wanted to be him. The whole thing sucked.

"Run, run away."

He grinned, and doing so reopened the gash in his bottom lip. Fresh blood dribbled down his chin. Despite the searing pain, his smile didn't fade. He liked the way it looked.

"Run, run away . . . Run, run awayyyyy . . ."

That was what he was doing. Running away. He'd made up his mind. Never again would he allow this to happen. Never again would his father lay a hand on him. Because if he stayed around, and it did happen, Barry was sure he'd kill the son of a bitch. His fateful punch earlier in the evening had missed. Next time, he wouldn't. He could get a gun, easily. He knew where his father kept his pistol. Timmy's father had a gun cabinet full of hunting rifles, and the boys could get access to the key. If he stuck around, next time his father came after him, he'd squeeze a trigger rather than his fist. And that would be murder, and they put people in jail for that. Put people to death for it, too.

Barry did not want to die, especially now. He felt reborn. He wasn't sure where he'd go next, or what he'd do, but it felt like the whole wide world was open before him. Anywhere was better than here. He never wanted to see this house or his parents or the cemetery and church again.

After the worst of the pain had subsided, Barry

turned off the light and tiptoed back out into the hall. He peeked in on his mother. She lay on her back, mouth open, snoring softly. He felt the urge to go to her, to kiss her forehead and tell her he was sorry, but he squashed it down. Pulling her bedroom door shut behind him, he made his way back to his room and rummaged through the closet until he found his book bag. His bare foot came down on a *Star Wars* action figure—Greedo, complete with blaster—and he bit his lip to keep from hollering, which hurt him even more. Fresh blood flowed. He wadded a tissue against it.

Barry slipped on his shoes and went into the kitchen. He began gathering items he'd need. The combination can and bottle opener from the utensil drawer, along with a single fork, knife, and spoon. Then he raided the cupboard. He stuffed his backpack with potato chips, Twinkies, Hershey's kisses, and Fruit Roll-Ups, along with canned goods—peas, corn, baked beans, succotash, tuna fish, sauerkraut, Vienna sausages—and some Ritz crackers. He tested the weight and was surprised to find that the backpack was still relatively light. He added some more Twinkies, then closed the cupboard door and moved on to the fruit bowl, which was sitting out on the counter. He selected a few small apples and dropped them into the book bag. He avoided any of the citrus fruit, worried that it might go bad before he had a chance to eat it.

Finished with scavenging the kitchen, he moved on to the living room. It was littered with empty beer cans, dirty coffee mugs and overflowing ashtrays. His mother had never been much of a housekeeper, and it had only gotten worse as his father got worse. Barry found just over ten dollars in quarters, dimes, and nickels in the large dolphin-shaped ceramic ashtray his parents used to hold loose change. He remembered the day they'd bought the souvenir, during a family trip to the National Aquarium in Baltimore. He'd had a good time. Thought the day might turn out okay. Then, on the way home, his father had backhanded him for talking while he was trying to drive. Frowning at the memory, Barry dropped the coins into his pockets. His jeans sagged a bit from the weight. His parents wouldn't miss the money. Lately, his father had seemed to have more cash than usual. After seeing Dane Graco's Freemason's ring on his father's hand tonight, Barry suspected he knew how his father had gained these new riches.

Grave robbing.

Barry returned to his bedroom and closed the door behind him. He opened his Baltimore Orioles bank and dumped out his life savings—twenty-two dollars and ten cents—then added the bills to his pockets. Combined with the money he'd stolen from the living room, he assumed he'd have enough to live off of for a while. If money and food ran out, it was summer, and he could always eat by raiding people's gardens at night. He debated on whether or not to bring his fishing pole, but decided it would be too cumbersome.

He also grabbed his flashlight, a pocketknife, his BB pistol, extra CO_2 cartridges and BBs for the pistol, and his jean jacket from the closet. It was warm outside, but he didn't know where he was going, and he might need it sooner or later. Plus, he could use the jacket as a pillow or blanket. He tied the jacket around his waist and stuffed the pistol behind his back, making sure it was snug inside his waistband. Then he dropped the other items into his book bag. Finally, he opened his dresser drawers and grabbed several pairs of underwear, socks, shirts, and another pair of jeans, and crammed those into the book bag as well. Stuffed to the brim, the bag's fabric bulged at the seams, and he had a hard time zipping it shut. When he slipped the straps over his bruised shoulders, the extra weight pulled at him, magnifying his pain all over again.

He patted his jingling pockets and glanced around his bedroom, trying to decide if there was anything else he was forgetting. Barry wondered if he should feel sad or nostalgic. After all, this was the last time he's see his room and all of his stuff. But he didn't feel sad. He didn't feel anything, other than an urgency to leave. The stuff was just that—stuff. Bought for him by two parents who smiled when they handed it to him, despite the nightmares that would follow. None of it meant anything to him. Shaking his head, he closed the door behind him.

He left no note. He had no good-byes to say.

Except for two.

He couldn't run away without saying good-bye to Timmy and Doug. They were his best friends, the only good things that had ever happened to him. What had happened today, out behind the shed, had broken his heart. He had to see them one more time.

Taking as deep a breath as he could without hurting his sides, Barry crept to the front door and slipped outside. There was no need to go out his bedroom window, the way he usually did when he snuck out at night. His father was gone, his mother was passed out, and he was in too much pain to crawl through the window, anyway.

A chorus of crickets greeted him. The stars sparkled overhead, and the yard was bathed in moonlight. The church loomed across the street—dark, gloomy and menacing. Beyond it, the cemetery sprawled out into the darkness. Barry wondered if his father was in there somewhere, beyond the shadows, even now looting another grave as he'd done with Timmy's grandfather's. Barry thought it over. Dane Graco had been buried with the ring on his finger. He'd seen it before they closed the casket. The funeral procession went out into the graveyard. The casket was lowered into the ground. The mourners tossed in flowers and the first few handfuls of dirt. Everybody left. Barry and his father had gone home, changed clothes, and then returned to fill in the grave. They'd been together the whole time, so there was no way his dad could have stolen the ring then. His father had been in a hurry to leave. He remembered thinking it was as if the old man didn't want to be in the graveyard after dark. But maybe it had been something else. Maybe he'd just been anxious for the sun to go down, eager for night to fall, so that he could dig Timmy's grandfather back up under the cover of darkness. Barry had noticed other trinkets and baubles—new jewelry, much to his mother's delight, and the extra cash in his father's pockets. Now he knew where it was all coming from.

The thought filled him with dread. It was horrible. Sick.

But so was his father.

All he had to do was look in the mirror to see the proof of that.

"Good riddance," he whispered. His busted lip throbbed. Barry winced.

He walked through his backyard and started down over the hill to Timmy's house. The lights were out, but he figured he'd just knock on Timmy's window and wake him. He went slowly, his body still aching. He pulled the bloody tissue from his lip and tossed it onto the ground. He readjusted the book bag so that his bruised shoulders wouldn't chafe more from the straps. He was carrying a lot of weight.

But the heaviest burden of all lay behind him.

Barry did not turn around.

He smiled again, and this time, it didn't hurt as much.

* * *

Timmy lay in bed, staring at the ceiling. His alarm clock said it was a quarter till three in the morning, and he still couldn't sleep. His father had finally gone to bed about an hour ago, after sitting in the living room by himself, crying his eyes out. Timmy had heard him through the walls, weeping and talking to God, but he hadn't cared. Let his father cry. Timmy was finally out of tears. He'd shed enough. He would shed no more. He was emotionally spent. Nothing mattered now. His grandfather's death, Katie Moore, Pat's body, what had happened to the others, the ghoul, Mr. Smeltzer, Barry and Doug's problems—all seemed to pale in comparison to what had happened down in the basement that evening.

His childhood, his fondest memories, the very things he loved the most, were ripped to shreds and lying in a cardboard box. And he still didn't understand the reason for it. Timmy had seen enough afternoon talk shows to know that this would scar him for the rest of his life. He wasn't being melodramatic. It was the simple truth. Surely his parents must have known that, too. They knew how much those comic books meant to him. So why mete out such an unjust punishment? Why punish him at all? He'd told the truth. Instead of disregarding what he'd had to say, they should have investigated his claims. After all, these were the two people who had always told him he could come to them with any problem. That he could tell them anything. Drugs. Alcohol. Sex. Whatever the problem, they'd assured him time and time again that they would listen to him. Be there for him. That he didn't need to be afraid of talking about it.

But they'd lied.

Lying there in the dark, he was no longer filled with sadness. He was consumed with rage.

After the very last comic book, an old *Classics Illustrated* adaptation of *Ivanhoe*, was destroyed, Timmy's father had sent him to his room. As he'd slunk through the living room, Timmy looked at his mother for support, for a condemnation of what her husband had just done, for some inkling that she disagreed or felt sorry for her son. But instead, his mother had merely dabbed her eyes with a tissue and turned her head away.

He interlaced his fingers behind his head and stared at the ceiling. *Go ahead and cry,* he thought. *Both of you. Just wait until I prove you wrong. I'll show you. I'll prove I wasn't lying. Then you'll* really *have something to feel bad about.* He'd show them all. He might be grounded now, but when that was over, he'd get the proof he needed.

If it wasn't too late by then. . . .

He thought about it some more. It probably would be too late by then. He couldn't wait. He'd have to sneak out at night, after his parents were asleep, and get the proof he needed. Maybe he could get a picture of the ghoul. That should be enough to shut everyone up. But not tonight. It was too late, now. He'd have to wait one more day. And besides, he couldn't do it alone. He'd at least need Doug with him, and preferably Barry as well, especially since his father was involved.

His thoughts focused on Barry. Timmy closed his eyes. He was wondering how his friend was doing, and how he was coping with everything, when there was a light tap at his window. Timmy's legs jerked in surprise, and his eyes popped open. The tap came again, still light, but more urgent.

He slipped out of bed, went to the window, and opened the shades.

Something that looked like Barry stared back at him, but it couldn't actually be Barry, unless he'd just gone ten rounds with the *X-Men's* Juggernaut. His friend's face resembled a package of hamburger—raw and pink and bloody. Despite this, Barry smiled.

Timmy put a finger to his lips, advising his friend to be quiet. Then he opened the window and the screen.

"What happened," he whispered. "Are you okay?"

"Do I look okay?" Barry's voice sounded funny. Slurred. "I've had better days."

"Your dad did this." It wasn't a question.

Barry nodded. It looked like he was about to start crying.

"Jesus Christ, man." Timmy ran a hand through his hair. "You need to go to the hospital."

"No way." Barry shook his head. "No doctors. No adults. I'm out of here, dude."

"What do you mean?"

"I'm leaving. Running away."

"You're hurt. You can't just run away."

"Well, I am. I can't take any more of this shit."

And then Barry did start crying, and somehow, that scared Timmy worse than his appearance did. His split lip quivered and tears spilled from his swollen eyes.

Timmy sighed. "Hang on. I'll be right out. Just stay quiet. If my parents wake up, we're both screwed."

Sobbing, Barry nodded again, and then slipped off his book bag and crouched down by the side of the house.

As quickly and silently as possible, Timmy changed out of his pajamas and into some clothes. He checked on his parents, making sure that they were both asleep and their door was shut. Satisfied that they were, he grabbed a flashlight and then climbed out the window. He left the screen and the window open a crack so that he could sneak back in.

He stared at Barry. Barry stared at him.

Then they hugged. Spontaneously. Uncharacteristically. But the gesture was real all the same. Timmy patted his friend's back, and Barry winced, and then pulled away.

"Ouch."

"Sorry," Timmy apologized. "He messed up your back, too?"

"He messed up my whole body. Even my bruises have bruises."

"You really should see a doctor, man."

"No. That would just be one more delay, one more excuse. And then I'd be stuck here again tomorrow night. If I don't leave now, I might not ever."

"But your face . . ."

"I'll be okay. It's not as bad as it looks."

Timmy disagreed with his friend's diagnosis, but didn't argue.

"What set him off? Was it what happened earlier, at the shed? If so, I'm really sorry. I shouldn't have gotten smart with him."

"No, it wasn't that. Who knows? It started because I didn't want to finish my dinner, but if it hadn't been that it would have just been something else."

Despite his friend's obvious suffering, Timmy felt an immense surge of relief. Finally, after all these years, they were actually talking about the abuse. It was out in the open. No more excuses. No more pretending that it wasn't going on. Now, maybe they could finally get Barry some help.

"Can I ask you something?"

Barry nodded. "Sure. What's up?"

"How long? How long has this been going on?"

Barry looked at the ground. "As long as I can remember."

"Shit."

"Yeah."

"Why didn't you ever tell somebody?"

"Who would I tell?"

Timmy shrugged. "Well, on those after school specials, kids tell their teachers. You could have told Mrs. Trimmer."

"Mrs. Trimmer hates us. No way I was telling her."

"You could have told me and Doug. We kinda knew about it anyway."

"You guys couldn't have done anything. Not really. It just didn't seem fair to get you involved. And besides, Doug's got his own problems."

They sat in silence, huddled together against the side of the house. Elizabeth's wind chimes rang softly. The notes seemed melancholy. A dog barked, far away into the night.

After a few minutes, Barry said, "You know what the first thing I remember is? I mean my very first memory? I was like two or three years old. I was sitting on the kitchen floor, underneath the table, playing with one of those plastic telephones. Remember the ones with wheels on the bottom, and the smiley face and eyes that moved when you pulled it on the string?"

Timmy nodded, smiling at the memory. He'd owned one, too.

"Well, I'm sitting there playing with that thing, calling Daddy on the telephone and pretending to talk to him. And then my old man comes home. He'd been working all day. Back then, I was too little to understand that he just worked across the street. All I knew was that I missed him. So he comes in and sits down at the kitchen table, and he's talking to my mom. I think they were arguing. I'm not sure, but they probably were. And meanwhile, I'm trying to get his attention. Trying to get him to pay attention to me, because I'd missed him all day. I'm still under the table, tugging on his leg, and he's just ignoring me. So I bit him."

"You bit him?"

"Yeah. Like I said, I was just little. I don't remember why I did it. Just seemed like a good way to get his attention, to let him know I was down there. It wasn't hard. I mean, I just had baby teeth, right?"

"And what did your old man do?"

"He kicked me across the room. I can still see that very clearly. He hollered something and then kicked me across the room. And that's my very first memory."

"That's messed up."

"Yeah, it is. And every day since then has been the same. I'm not putting up with it anymore. I can't."

"And you're really planning on running away?"

Barry pointed at the overstuffed book bag. "Not planning. I'm doing it. Tonight. I just wanted to tell you first, you know? I didn't want to leave without saying good-bye. But now that I'm here . . . well, good-bye sucks, doesn't it?"

"Then don't say good-bye." Timmy's voice cracked. "Stay. We'll figure something out."

Barry began to cry, softly. "How?"

"I don't know. But we will." Timmy's eyes filled with tears. "We'll figure it out together. Me, you, and Doug— the Three Musketeers. We're like Luke, Han, and Chewie, man. You can't break up a good team like that."

"Only if I get to be Han."

Timmy smiled. "Sure. I'd rather be Luke, anyway, and Doug's obviously a good pick for Chewbacca."

Both of them wiped their eyes and then laughed.

"Jesus Christ." Barry groaned. "It hurts to laugh. But it feels good, too."

Timmy appraised his friend's face. "He really cut up your cheek. What did that? A knife or something?"

Barry's expression darkened. "No. It was a ring."

"A ring?"

"Yeah." He paused, unsure of how to continue. "Timmy, I need to tell you something. It might make you angry."

"Dude, I couldn't be any more pissed off at your old man than I am right now."

"Don't be so sure." He took a deep breath, kneaded his ribs, and then continued. "Your grandfather had his Freemason's ring on when he was buried, right?"

"Yeah. Why?"

"Because that was what cut my cheek up tonight. My old man was wearing it."

To Barry's chagrin, Timmy seemed only mildly surprised.

"Aren't you pissed off?" Barry asked. "He stole your grandpa's ring, man!"

"I've got something I need to tell you, too," Timmy said. "I suspect that your dad's taken a lot more than just the ring."

Barry was shocked. "What are you talking about? You mean you knew he was robbing dead people? You didn't say anything?"

Timmy stood up, peered through his window, and made sure his parents were still asleep. He didn't hear them moving around, and there were no lights on. Assured they were safe, he knelt back down and told Barry everything he suspected and everything that had transpired since their fight with Barry's father behind the utility shed. He started with the legend that Reverend Moore had related to Katie and him, and then worked his way chronologically through the past month's events, lying out the supporting evidence and bolstering it with his research. Finally, Timmy voiced his suspicions regarding Mr. Smeltzer's compliance, and added Barry's admission that his father had stolen Timmy's grandfather's ring as further proof. He left out his suspicions that it had also been Barry's own father who hid Pat kemp's body, because he wasn't sure how Barry would react to that. Grave robbing was one thing. Accessory to murder was another.

When he was finished, Timmy braced himself, expecting Barry to scoff just like his parents had. But he'd forgotten something. Barry was his friend—and Barry believed him without question.

"I knew about the old church," he said. "My old man told me about it once. If you look carefully, you can still see some of the foundation stones. The grass has pretty much grown over them, though. There are pictures of it down at the library. Never heard about the ghoul, though."

"Well, for whatever reason, they imprisoned it, rather than just killing the thing. I don't know why. But now it's loose again."

"Okay," Barry said. "What are you going to do about it? Have you told your parents about the ghoul?"

"Yeah." Timmy's voice grew sullen. "They didn't believe me. Dad grounded me and . . . ripped up my comic collection."

Barry gasped. "Holy shit! All of them?"

Timmy nodded. "Every last one."

"Oh, man. That's . . . I don't know what to say. My old man, I could see him doing that. But your dad? Never in a million years."

"Well, believe it. The proof's sitting in the basement right now."

"I'm sorry about that, man. What are you going to do?"

Timmy shrugged. "Nothing I can do. And it's not like I can run away with you. Not now. Not after . . ."

"Katie?"

"Yeah. You can understand that, right?"

Barry spoke slowly, choosing his words with care. "I guess. I mean, she's cute and all. I don't know. Just seems like me, you, and Doug have been hanging out longer. I'd think we would come first."

Timmy's temper flared. "I'm putting everybody first. If I don't do something about this ghoul, then everyone's in danger. Katie. Doug—"

"Not me," Barry interrupted. "I'm out of here, man. Tonight."

"What about Doug?"

"I'm stopping at his house next. It's on my way. Who knows? He might want to go with me, crazy as his mom is."

Timmy's spirits sank even lower. He hadn't considered the possibility that both of his friends might want to leave.

"Doug won't go. He'd chicken out."

"Probably," Barry agreed, "but I at least want to tell him bye."

"Then what?"

"Figured I'd walk to Porters or Jefferson and hop a freight train. They're both close enough that I could make it before dawn. Then I'll just hide out in the woods along the tracks until a train comes by. I don't want to grab one here in town because all of the ones that come into the paper mill are either coal trains or log carriers, and it would be too hard to hide on one of those. Dangerous to hop, too."

"So you'll hop a train. And go where?"

"Wherever it takes me. Hanover is too close, but maybe Westminster or Baltimore or down into West Virginia or Ohio. Wherever. As long as it's away from here, I really don't care."

"Barry, you just had the shit beat out of you, man. You can barely talk. You're moving like you're eighty years old. There's no way you can hop a train tonight."

"Well, then what do you suggest I do, Timmy? Hitchhike? Get picked up by some psycho, and dumped alongside Interstate Eighty-three? No thanks. Or maybe busted by the cops and then brought back home to my old man?"

"Stick around for another day. Rest up a little bit. Recuperate. Doug and I will hide you. When your mom reports you missing, we'll say we don't know anything about it. At least get better before you leave."

"Where are you gonna hide me? The Dugout? No way I'm staying there. Not if there really is a ghoul on the loose. And I can't stay here. Your parents would want to call the cops and stuff."

"And then your dad would go to jail."

"Probably not. This isn't TV. And even if the cops did put him in jail, what if they took me away from Mom and stuck me in a foster home? That would be just as bad."

"How about you hide at Doug's house?"

Barry snorted in derision. "Yeah, right. With his mom? Get real. Would you spend the night there?"

"No."

"I'm sorry, Timmy. I really am. But this is the way it's got to be. I can't stay around here another night. If I do, I'll never escape. I don't want that."

They fell quiet again. Somewhere in the night, out on the main road, a car backfired. An owl hooted closer to them. The crickets had grown quiet.

Barry slowly stood up. "Well, I guess this is it."

He stuck out his hand. Timmy stared at it. After a moment, he took it. Their grips were firm. Then Barry pulled him to his feet.

"See," Barry said. "I'm feeling better already. Told you it wasn't as bad as it looks."

Timmy didn't respond.

"You gonna be okay?" Barry asked.

Timmy nodded. He was afraid to speak, afraid that he might start crying again.

"Seriously, the pain isn't as bad now," Barry said. "My lip still hurts, and my cheek. But the aches and stuff are going away."

"That's good. Maybe you can take another break when you get to Doug's."

"Yeah."

They stood there, neither one knowing what to say, and neither one wanting to be the first to turn away from the other. Finally, after what seemed an eternity, Barry spoke.

"I'm gonna miss you, man."

"Yeah . . ." The lump rising in his throat cut off the rest of Timmy's reply.

They hugged, quick and hard this time. When they disengaged from one another, Timmy stared at the ground and Barry looked into the night sky. Then, shuffling his feet in reluctance, Barry picked up the book bag and sighed.

"Take it easy, Timmy."

"You too. You got my address, right?"

"Sure do. I'll write to you."

"Okay. Be careful, dude."

"I will. Nothing out there can be any worse than what we've got right here. I'll be all right."

"Well . . ." Timmy paused, and then looked him in the eyes. "You're the best friend I've ever had. You and Doug. Never thought we'd leave each other. I love you, man."

Barry smiled, sadly. "I love you, too. And I will always be your friend. Even when you do grow up and become a rich and famous comic book writer."

He smiled. Timmy tried his best to return the gesture, but found that he couldn't. It was more of a grimace than a grin.

Then Barry turned to walk away.

Timmy watched him go. His fists balled at his sides.

Barry kept walking. His shoulders were slumped. He stared at the ground.

Suddenly, Timmy lurched forward and grabbed his arm.

"Look. I can't do this without you, man. You're my best friend in the world and I need you. Please stay. Just long enough to help me beat this thing in the cemetery? Please? I need your help."

Barry grinned. "It's hard being your friend sometimes, Graco. You always have to be the one in charge."

"Yeah, but this time I mean it. I need your help. I can't do this by myself."

"Well, since you're admitting that you can't do it without me, then I guess I have to, don't I?"

Timmy gasped, relieved. Then he laughed with joy.

Barry set the book bag down. "So, what's the plan, oh fearless leader?"

"I thought you'd never ask."

"Squirt guns with lemon juice again?"

"Nope. Something better. Let me take a leak real quick and I'll tell you all about it."

CHAPTER FOURTEEN

"Are you insane?" Barry shouted. "It will never work."

"Yes, it will," Timmy said. "And keep your voice down. You want somebody to hear us?"

"Yeah, if only to stop us before we get killed. This is a dumb idea."

"As long as you guys listen to me, there's no way we can fail. What's the worse that could happen?"

Sputtering, Barry raised his arms to the night sky. "Didn't you just hear what I said? We could get killed! What's the worse that could happen? How about the ghoul eats us for breakfast, man? How about all three of us end up like Pat? You don't think that's bad?"

"None of that is going to happen. You've got to trust me."

"Last time we trusted you was with Catcher, and look what happened."

Timmy stopped walking. "That was your fault."

Barry grew sullen. "Okay. You made your point."

They continued on, crossing from Timmy's yard into the Wahl's. The first part of Timmy's plan was simple. They intended to go the long way around to the Dugout, avoiding Barry's house and the church and the cemetery. Instead, they'd cut through the Wahl's, cross the road, and then walk through Luke Jones's pasture. Hopefully, the bulls were penned up for the night. When they were near the Dugout, they'd come back up to the fence line. Timmy insisted that they needed the map for his plan to work, and that they couldn't wait until daylight to get it because Barry's dad might see them—not to mention that Timmy was grounded and Barry would soon be listed as a runaway. Timmy had tried one more time to convince his friend to go back home for the evening, but Barry refused. Instead, he would hide out in Bowman's Woods for the day, while Timmy plotted their next course of action.

Timmy's intent was simple. Tomorrow, he would use the map to chart out the possible locations for the ghoul's network of tunnels. He'd start with what they knew—the hole in the utility shed and the places where the ground was sinking, and mark those on the map. Then he'd connect the dots, and that should give them an idea of where the tunnels lay. While he was doing this, Barry would sneak off to Doug's house and inform him of the plan, then go back into hiding in the woods. Tomorrow night, the three of them would sneak into the cemetery and, utilizing Mr. Smeltzer's picks and shovels, would dig up the tunnels in various locations, flooding them with daylight when the sun rose.

They crept through the Wahl's yard, skirting around their swimming pool. Inside the house, the elderly couple's miniature Schnauzer yipped in alarm.

"Shit." Timmy urged his friend on. "Pookie's awake. Go!"

They hurried on, crossing the road and jumping the fence. Barry, normally much stronger than Timmy, had trouble keeping up. Once they were safely out of sight and in the pasture, they stopped to take a rest.

Barry sighed. "Wish I'd left this book bag back at your place. It's getting heavy."

"Leave it here. We'll get it on the way back."

"Good idea." He unzipped the bag and ruffled around inside it. He pulled out the flashlight and his pocketknife and then zipped it back up.

"You ready?" Timmy asked.

Barry nodded.

They walked on. Almost an hour had passed since Barry had first shown up at Timmy's bedroom window, and it was now well after three, the longest part of the night, yet neither one of them were tired. They should have been. They knew this. Both boys had been through more that day than the combined events of the summer so far. Yet they weren't fatigued. Far from it. They were both excited and angry and a little bit scared, and the adrenalin kept them moving. Especially Barry, battered as he was.

"So, tomorrow night," Barry said, "what if the ghoul shows up while we're digging? What happens then? You said daylight was the only thing that would kill him."

"Don't worry about that. I'll take care of it."

"You've got a plan for that?"

Timmy paused. "No. But I will by tomorrow night. I'm sure there's something in one of my comic—"

He stopped, jarred by the knowledge that his comic book collection no longer existed.

"I'll come up with something."

They continued through the pasture and then turned toward the fence, coming up behind the Dugout. They carefully scanned the cemetery beyond, but there was no sign of monsters—parents or otherwise. Everything was silent. They approached the Dugout. The clubhouse lay hidden in shadows, invisible from their vantage point. They checked again to make sure the coast was clear, then opened the trap door. Timmy turned on his flashlight and swung around, preparing to climb down the ladder.

Barry grabbed his arm. "Wait a second."

Timmy paused. "What?"

"Thought I saw something in your flashlight beam."

Barry turned on his own flashlight and shined it down into the hole. Both boys gasped aloud.

The Dugout was gone. The roof was still there, still concealing it from the outside world. The stovepipe still jutted from the ground, providing fresh air below. But the ladder led down into darkness. The fort was now a gaping chasm. The entire floor had disappeared, and all of their belongings had apparently gone with it. The tunnel dropped straight down for about five feet before sloping away into parts unknown. It looked like it ran in the direction of the cemetery, but they couldn't be sure from where they stood.

At the same time, they both said, "Oh shit . . ."

Perched on the ladder, Timmy shined his flashlight around, studying the damage. He noticed a few random items at the mouth of the crevice, caught at the tunnel's bend—an issue of *Cracked*, a plastic Spider-Man cup from 7-11, an old shotgun shell they'd found in the woods.

A discarded Kit-Kat wrapper.

The map.

"Shine your light down there," Timmy told Barry. He set his own flashlight on the ground and then started down the ladder.

"Are you nuts? What are you doing?"

"I'm going in."

"No you're not. This isn't a comic book, dude. You and I both know what did this. You were right. This is our proof. Let's get the hell out of here and call the cops."

"You didn't want to call the cops before."

"That was about my old man. And besides, we didn't have any hard proof before. We do now. They can't ignore this."

"I'm going down there," Timmy insisted. "You just stand guard for me."

"Timmy!"

Ignoring his protests, Timmy started down the ladder. Without even thinking about it, Barry pulled the BB pistol out of his waistband with his free hand and pointed it down the hole. Just holding the weapon made him feel better.

When Timmy reached the bottom, he dangled his legs over the hole and glanced around, unsure of what to do next. His pulse pounded in his ears, drowning out Barry's alarmed whispers. Swallowing hard, he closed his eyes and let go of the rungs.

Barry gripped the flashlight and BB pistol and watched in terrified amazement.

Timmy plummeted downward and landed with a smack, sending a cloud of dirt into the air. Immediately, he began to slide down into the tunnel. He scrabbled, grasping at the soil, trying to arrest his fall. Above him, Barry struggled to see. The swirling dust blocked his flashlight beam. When Timmy reached the curve, he stopped sliding. Inching forward, he grabbed the map and the candy wrapper. Then he crawled back to the ladder. He slipped a few times, and each time he did, his heart leapt into his throat. When his hand closed around the rung, both boys breathed a sigh of relief. Timmy stuffed the rescued items in his waistband and then climbed back up.

"You okay?"

Timmy nodded, out of breath.

"That was really stupid, man."

"I know. But we need the map."

"Let's get the hell out of here now. Okay? This whole thing gives me the creeps. It's too quiet, like in a movie."

"Hang on one second. I just want to make sure the map is okay."

Timmy unrolled the map and spread it out on the ground. He paused, his fingers tracing over the topography. Then he looked up at Barry. His eyes were wide.

"What's wrong?"

Timmy pointed. "There's some new stuff on here that wasn't on it before."

"Where?"

Timmy showed him, pointing out the section of woods where they'd found Pat Kemp's abandoned Nova. The area around the edge, which had been left blank before, was now partially filled in. The illustrations were obviously made by Doug's hand, and it looked as if he'd stopped drawing mid-tree.

"So Doug stopped by and worked on it," Barry said. "Good. Now let's get out of here."

"Don't you see? The only time he could have done this was earlier tonight. Look at this thumbprint. That's chocolate." He scraped at the smudge with his fingernail. "And it's fresh."

Agitated, Timmy pulled out the candy wrapper and sniffed. "This is fresh, too. There are still crumbs inside."

Barry turned pale. "You don't think . . . Doug was in there when . . . ?"

Timmy swooned. The Kit-Kat wrapper slipped from his hand, fluttering to the ground. He knelt, his face in his hands.

"My mom took him home when the cops were done. He'd spent the night before, so he didn't have his bike. That was around dinnertime. He would have had to come back here between then and now."

"And he would have rode his bike," Barry said. "I don't see it here. Maybe he'd already left when this happened."

"Maybe." Timmy sounded unsure.

"Look, we need to get out of here, man. This is too close to the cemetery. If that thing is still around, or even if my old man is out here, we're sitting ducks. Let's at least go down into the pasture or something."

Nodding in agreement, Timmy stood up and brushed himself off. His jeans and T-shirt were filthy.

"My mom is gonna freak out if she sees this."

"Why? It's just dirt. You get dirty all the time."

"Yeah, but if she sees these tomorrow, she'll know I snuck out. I'll have to hide them in the bottom of the hamper."

Timmy turned his flashlight back on, and the two of them started toward the field. Barry's light beam flashed off something white, hidden in the weeds.

"What's that?"

He trained the flashlight on the object and it shined back in his eyes.

A reflector.

Both boys ran over to the weeds and pushed them aside. Doug's bike lay on its side, abandoned.

Timmy moaned. "Oh, no."

"This doesn't mean he was here," Barry said. "Not Doug. He wasn't here. He just wasn't."

Timmy's voice was barely a whisper. "Yeah. He

was. He was in the Dugout, eating a candy bar and working on the map when that thing came up out of the ground and got him."

"Not Doug. We don't know that for sure."

"Stop it," Timmy cried. "Just stop it, Barry. I know you're scared. I'm scared, too."

"What are we going to do?"

Taking a deep breath, Timmy strode back to the trapdoor.

"You're going to get your old man's keys, get the backhoe out of the shed, and then start digging this whole place up."

"I am?" Barry scoffed. "And what are you going to do?"

"I'm going down there. I'm going after Doug."

"Yeah, right!"

"I'm serious, dude. Go get your dad's keys and start the backhoe up."

"I'm not going back to my house. What if my old man is there?"

"Then make sure he doesn't see you."

"No way. No freaking way, Timmy. Not on your life."

"Barry, we've got no choice."

"If I got the keys and if my old man didn't see me, I still can't start the backhoe. It's nuts. Running that thing in the middle of the night? Somebody will hear us for sure, and call the cops."

"Good," Timmy argued. "Let them. The more the merrier."

"But a few minutes ago, you didn't want the cops here."

"I don't care anymore. Doug is gone, man. Don't you see? Can't you get it through that thick head of yours? He's down there, right now, with that thing, and he could be hurt. For all we know, he could be *dead*. We can't wait any more. We don't have time to make a plan. We can't rely on the grown-ups. We have to do something *now*. You promised that you'd help me, so help me goddamn it."

Scowling, Barry kicked the ground. His mouth was a thin, tight line, and his bottom lip had started bleeding again. The red gash on his cheek stood out in stark contrast to his pale, moonlit skin.

"Okay. I'll do it. But you're insane, Graco."

"No, I'm not, and neither are you. We're not the crazy ones."

"Then who is?"

Timmy didn't respond. He simply stared at Barry, impatient.

After a moment, Barry understood what he was implying. "Oh, yeah. Them."

"Get going," Timmy said. "Once you get the backhoe running, just start digging everything up between here and the shed. Any place where the ground is sinking—that's where you'll want to dig. It's got to be close to four o'clock now, if not a little after that. Sun usually comes up around five-thirty. That gives us like an hour and a half or so."

"Yeah, but the sunlight isn't really shining bright until around six-thirty or seven. What if the light isn't enough?"

Then we'll just have to go with Plan B."

"And what is Plan B?"

"Just get going." Timmy pointed in the direction of Barry's house.

Barry stayed put. "You don't have a Plan B, do you?"

"No," Timmy admitted. "I don't."

Timmy stepped to the ladder's edge and peered nervously into the darkness. He took several deep breaths and then said, "Okay. Here I go."

He didn't move. Neither did Barry. They stared at each other.

"Aren't you going?" Barry asked.

"Aren't you?"

"Yeah. I will. I just wanted to make sure you made it down safely."

"I'll be fine," Timmy said. "You be careful."

"You too."

They both continued standing still.

"You scared?" Barry asked.

Timmy nodded. "I've never been more scared in my life. But Doug is down there somewhere. We owe it to him. We owe it to ourselves. I . . . I need to prove to my dad that he was wrong. Does that make sense?"

Barry glanced off into the distance. "It makes perfect sense. More than you know."

"I'll try to keep the ghoul distracted while you open the tunnels up. Don't let me down, okay?"

Barry turned back to him. His expression was grim. His fingers tightened around the BB pistol.

"I told you, man. We're friends for life. You can count on me."

"Okay. Seriously, let's do this. Before it's too late."

"Here." Barry held out his pocketknife. "You might need this."

"Thanks." Timmy stuffed the knife in his pocket and then stepped onto the ladder.

"Be careful," Barry called.

Nodding, Timmy climbed down the rickety ladder.

"Here I come, Doug," he whispered. "Just hang on man, and please be all right."

He went slowly, carefully watching his footing. When he reached the bottom, he let go of the rungs and tumbled once more into the darkness. Barry watched the hole swallow him up, until he could see him no more. Even his flashlight beam had vanished. Timmy was gone, into the monster's lair.

"Be careful," he whispered. He didn't know if Timmy heard him or not.

Barry turned toward home—a monster's lair of its own—and wondered if either one of them would actually still be alive come dawn.

CHAPTER FIFTEEN

The first thing Timmy noticed was the stench. It hung thick in the air, like an invisible fog, and he could taste it in his mouth when he breathed. It was just like what they'd smelled before; coming out of the holes around the cemetery, but it was much stronger now; highly concentrated. It burned his nose the way the smell of bleach did when his mother was doing laundry.

Make it a game, he thought. *I'm Luke Skywalker, sneaking through the Death Star, trying to rescue the Princess.*

He stumbled over a thick tree root jutting up from the soil and reached his hand out to steady himself. The tunnel's walls were cold and damp, and covered with some type of slime. Timmy jerked his hand away and shined the flashlight on it. His fingers were webbed with something that resembled milky snot. Disgusted, he wiped them on his jeans before continuing.

The passageway wound into the darkness, and his

meager flashlight beam did little to penetrate the gloom. And yet, Timmy had the distinct impression that he could actually see farther than he should be able to. As his eyes adjusted, he realized why. It was the slime. The stuff was glowing—barely noticeable, but giving off a faint, eerie radiance all the same. He wondered what it was. Living within twenty miles of both the Three Mile Island and Peachbottom nuclear power plants, Timmy was very conscious of radioactive waste, even at twelve. Several times over the last five years, there had been news stories about barrels of waste found dumped in creeks and streams, or off dirt logging roads way out in the wilderness. But this wasn't anything like that. The substance coated everything— walls, ceiling, and the parts of the floor not covered up with piles of loose soil. It had to be the ghoul. Maybe the creature exuded the slime from its pores. Maybe the stuff aided the ghoul in digging, or allowed it to see much better below ground.

And maybe, the thought occurred to him, he didn't know nearly as much about ghouls as he'd assumed, and perhaps he should just turn around right now and go call the police. But then he thought of Doug, who'd been let down by everyone in his life, except for Timmy and Barry. He couldn't just abandon his friend down here. As scared as he was, he had no choice.

Timmy pressed ahead, feeling less like Tom Sawyer or Luke Skywalker and more like the very frightened twelve-year-old boy that he was. He pulled out Barry's pocketknife and opened the blade. He clutched it with one hand and held the flashlight in the other. Neither item made him feel more courageous. He wished his father were here with him. Timmy's hate and anger were forgotten. He wanted the safety net he'd grown accustomed to over the years—knowing that no matter how bad the danger was, his parents were always standing by, ready to take care of him. Shelter him. Keep him safe from the monsters. He remembered when he was little, and had been convinced there was a monster under his bed. He'd cry out at night, and his father was always there, turning on the light and checking the closets and beneath the bed.

And now his father wasn't there.

Timmy went on. He'd never felt more alone. Even thinking of Katie didn't help.

The passage was roughly circular, and varied in height and width. At some points, he had to duck his head or pull his arms tight against his sides to avoid brushing up against the walls. Other stretches were wide enough to walk comfortably in. He tried to guess in which direction he was traveling, but it was impossible to tell. Eventually, other tunnels began branching off the main passageway. He decided not to venture down them, for fear of becoming lost. His progress was slow. He kept the light trained on the floor, looking for signs of where Doug might be—footprints, candy wrappers, blood, anything. He found nothing.

The maze of tunnels was silent. The only thing Timmy heard was the sound of his own panicked breathing. His mouth felt dry, and his pulse throbbed in his neck and temples. He felt a momentary urge to call out, to shout for Doug, just to break the stillness, and the thought frightened him even more.

Where are you, Doug? Please be okay. Just hang on a little bit longer.

Biting his lip, Timmy forced himself not to cry.

The passage sloped downward, and Timmy followed it, deeper into the earth. The spoiled milk stench grew stronger—and now there was another smell mixed with it. Rot. Decay.

Death.

Barry rushed through the field. His wounds and pain were forgotten, and he urged himself on. Dew-covered weeds whipped at his legs, soaking his jeans and shoes. The crickets and other insects grew louder, disturbed by his passage. He went by the spot where he'd left his book bag, but didn't bother stopping to retrieve it. When he reached the road, he crouched close to the ground and stared at his house. All of the lights were still off, which meant anyone inside was probably sleeping. The car was still in the driveway, but that meant nothing. When his father had left earlier, he'd departed on foot. Which meant he was probably in the cemetery somewhere.

He hoped.

Swallowing nervously, Barry rushed across the road and into the yard, moving as quickly but silently as possible. He opened the screen door, silently willing the hinges not to creak, and then slowly turned the doorknob. Meeting no resistance, he stepped inside.

The house was quiet. He paused, listening. After a moment, he heard his mother's soft snoring coming from his parent's bedroom. He was tempted to creep down the hall and peek, see if his father was lying next to her, but he decided not to chance it. Timmy was counting on him. He had to hurry.

He moved over to the hat rack hanging above the kitchen door. His father only had one hat, a faded, weather-beaten Skoal cap that he sometimes wore. The rest of the rack was used for keys and umbrellas. Both the hat and the umbrellas were there, hanging from their pegs, as were his mother's keys. But his father's key ring was missing.

"Shit." His voice was louder than he'd intended, and Barry jumped, frightening himself.

It made sense, of course, and he cursed himself for being so stupid. His father would have taken the keys with him when he left, even if only to get inside the utility shed where he stored his emergency bottles of Wild Turkey. He should have thought of that when Timmy came up with this stupid plan.

Frustrated, Barry checked his parent's room after all. His mother slept soundly. His father's side of the bed was still made up. Untouched. And with the car still sitting next to the garage, that meant there was only one possibility: his father was still in the graveyard, probably drunk, and Barry would have to find him, face him, and somehow get his keys.

He ran out of the house and prayed he could do it all in time. The horizon was tinged with a faint trace of bluish-white. Not a lot—just a hint of the dawn's impending arrival.

"Hang on, Timmy," he panted. "I'm coming."

Timmy traveled steadily downward. At times, the tunnel sloped so steeply that his feet slipped and he had to struggle to maintain his balance. In addition, the maze had become more bewildering than ever. When Timmy was seven, he'd had a pet hamster named Milo that he'd won at the York Fair. He'd kept the hamster in his room and set up a Habitrail for him. Timmy had assumed that Milo would love running around inside the multiple plastic tubes and paths, but the hamster had seemed terrified of them. Now, he understood how Milo had felt.

Soon, the purpose of the branching passageways and multiple crossroads became clear. Each new path led upward to a grave. The further he went, the more of them he encountered. The tunnel was littered with empty coffins, smashed into kindling and tossed aside, along with scraps of clothing and other unwanted items that had held no value to either the ghoul or his human assistant—teeth, toupees, and something that Timmy realized with dread was a pacemaker. In some areas, the main tunnel was so clogged with discarded coffins that he had to crawl over the wreckage. At one point, teetering on the edge of a silk-lined casket, he dropped both the flashlight and the pocketknife. The beam went out and the flashlight rolled away, plunging Timmy into total darkness. Frantically, he dropped from the coffin and felt around for them. Tears welled up in his eyes. His breathing came in short, quick gasps. Then his fingers closed over the flashlight. Mouthing a prayer, he turned it on. It still worked. After a few moments, he recovered the pocketknife as well, and then continued on his way.

"Thank you," he whispered. "Oh, thank you, thank you, thank you. Now just let Doug be all right and let us get out of here and let Barry get the backhoe and everything will be okay."

Timmy stopped in the middle of the passage. He suddenly felt as if someone had dumped a bucket of cold water over him. He remembered Clark Smeltzer, standing over him behind the utility shed, bragging.

"There's a new lock on this shed, and I'm the only one that can open it."

Both Timmy and Barry had heard him say that. How could they have been so stupid? How was Barry supposed to get inside the shed if he didn't know the combination? His father's keys were useless.

So, he thought, *Barry will just have to bust the window in or something. He won't let us down.*

Eventually, after a long, descending walk, the tunnel evened out again. At the same time, it grew wider and taller. He noticed that the surface was more smoothed and rounded, as if extra care had been taken in finishing this part. The side-tunnels became nonexistent. Timmy wondered why at first, and then figured it out. He must be getting close to the older portion of the cemetery. There was an area between the two sections, right along the hill separating them, where there were no graves—ancient or modern. He must be beneath that now. Just today he'd been there with Katie, walking hand in hand, when they'd seen the big depression in the earth. He closed his eyes, remembering the way she'd smelled. It already seemed like a million years ago, and he wanted very badly to see her again at that moment. He felt that if he could hold her hand again, everything would be okay.

He paused and listened, but heard nothing. If his suspicions were correct, and he was nearing the older part of the graveyard, then he must be very close to where the ghoul had originally been imprisoned. The smell was at its strongest now. He'd grown used to it during his journey, been almost able to ignore it, but now he noticed it again. His fears, which he'd managed to set aside, came creeping back now. Every bit of him wanted to turn around and flee, but the thought of Doug, trapped in this impenetrable darkness, rooted his feet to the ground.

As if in response to his mounting terror, something grunted in the darkness. An animalistic sound, like a boar or a bear would make. Timmy let out a frightened yelp and spun around. It was impossible to tell for sure where the sound had come from, how near or far, but he thought it might have been behind him. He shined the light back the way he'd come, terrified of what it might reveal, but the tunnel was empty. He waited for the noise to be repeated, but the silence returned.

"Oh, Jesus . . ."

He resisted the urge to run, and hurried ahead instead.

From its hidden nook in a side tunnel, the ghoul listened to the boy go by. The child was heading deeper into its warren, nearing the main lair, which was exactly what it wanted. Once there, the intruder would be cut off. The boy would have to come back through this same tunnel to exit the burrows, and the ghoul could catch him unawares.

Its initial urge had been to kill the boy as soon as it had caught his scent and then heard him coming. But it had waited, intrigued that such a young human could display a courage and determination not found in many of his elders (at least, from the ghoul's experience with humans). It had let the child pass simply because he might provide good sport. As an afterthought, it had let out one short grunt, simply to spur the child onward and intensify his fear.

Meat was much sweeter when it had been marinated in fear.

And besides, it was still consuming the first one.

Grinning, the ghoul returned to its meal. The still-warm flesh felt solid—real—between its teeth—not disintegrating or turning to mush the way decaying flesh did. The ghoul relished every bite. It sighed with delight as its incisors sank into a thigh. The blood was sweet and thick, and it eagerly lapped it up. The boy had been blessed with an extra layer of fat, and the ghoul greedily dug into the yellow curds with both hands.

It cracked open a bone and sucked out the marrow, and wondered if this new child intruder had been a friend of its current meal. The new boy's scent was familiar, possibly from the children's clubhouse it had ransacked earlier. What was it that Smeltzer had said? The Keiser child, who currently lay spread out and open before it, had played with the gravedigger's son, and one other. The ghoul searched its memory for the name. Draco? Mako?

Graco.

The ghoul raised its hands to its face. Its long, black tongue flicked, licking bits of flesh from its gore-encrusted talons. It burrowed its snout into the boy's stomach, and even as it did, the creature's stomach growled at the promise of more to come. And it didn't even have to move or hunt. It could wait here, finish this appetizer, and then trap the main course before the boy escaped.

Barry found his father beneath a marble monument—a tall, monolithic spire nearly eight feet high. His father sat propped up against it, eyes shut, reeking of booze. Shattered glass lay nearby, the remains of a Wild Turkey bottle. At first, Barry thought he might be dead. He was covered in blood and his face and neck were sliced open pretty bad. He didn't stir when Barry prodded him with one foot. Hands trembling, Barry brought out the BB pistol and fired one round at his father's unmoving body. The projectile bounced off his shirt. Still he didn't move.

"Shit."

Barry wasn't sure what he was supposed to feel. He was no stranger to grief. He saw it all the time, whenever there was a funeral at the church. He'd seen every reaction imaginable, from sadness to dark gallows humor. He guessed perhaps he should feel sad, although that seemed stupid, considering all his father had put him through.

The only emotion Barry felt was an overwhelming surge of relief.

It quickly turned to anger—and fear—when his father opened one eye and stared at him in surprise.

"B-Barry? Wha . . ."

That was all. He closed his eye. Barry stepped backward, making sure he was out of reach, and then he shot him again. This time, his father's hand twitched feebly. Barry sat the flashlight on a tombstone and approached him cautiously, ready to run if the old man showed any sign of moving more than he had. He didn't. His chest rose and fell very slightly, but that was all. Barry shoved the barrel of the BB pistol in his face, just inches from his eye. He knelt in the grass, careful to avoid the shards of broken glass. Slowly, he reached into his father's pocket with his free hand and retrieved the keys. They jingled. His father groaned, but lay still. Barry stood up and hurried away. He grabbed the flashlight and headed for the utility shed.

The faint glow on the horizon was spreading.

Barry reached the shed doors and fumbled for the right key. He held it up to the lock and then cursed out loud. In their panic, in their hurry to rescue Doug, both he and Timmy had forgotten about the new lock.

He threw the keys at the shed. They bounced off the wall and landed in the grass. Barry ran back over to his father and knelt beside him. He grabbed his father's face in his hands, careful not to touch the wounds, and shook him.

"Dad, what's the combination to the shed?"

His father didn't reply. His eyes twitched, but he made no sound.

"Dad! Wake up. What's the combination?"

Clark mumbled, "S' 'nother bottle inshide."

"Goddamn it!"

Barry stood up, stalked back over to the shed, and surveyed his father's repair job. The old window had been boarded up, and the plywood sheeting looked thick and strong. He glanced around for something to pry it with, but the ground was barren. His eyes settled on a metal plate stuck into the ground at the foot of a grave. The plate informed him that the man who was buried there, Mick Wagner, had died in service to his country in Korea. Barry ripped the plate from the ground. The edges were blunt and narrow. He wedged it between the boards and pushed. The nails creaked. The board moved. Spirits rising, Barry dropped the sign, stood back, and kicked the plywood. The sole of his sneaker absorbed most of the impact, but his foot throbbed. The pain was nothing compared to how the rest of his body felt. Clenching his teeth, he kicked the board again. The plywood clattered to the floor inside.

Barry grabbed the flashlight, clicked it on, and cautiously crawled through the window. He'd been inside the utility shed thousands of times, but it had never scared him until now. In the darkness, once familiar shapes now became something sinister lurking in the corner.

He stood overtop the hole in the center of the floor and listened, hoping to hear an indication that his friends were still down there—and alive. Instead, he was greeted by silence.

He found the crowbar, went back outside, and pried the hasp off the doors, lock and all. The doors swung open. Barry retrieved his father's keys, climbed up onto the backhoe, and crossed his fingers. Taking a deep breath, he inserted the key into the ignition and turned it.

The backhoe roared to life.

Exhaling, Barry turned on the headlights and drove it out into the graveyard. Awoken by the rumbling engine, his father stirred, glancing about slowly.

Shit, Barry thought, *if he regains consciousness he could screw this whole thing up.*

Leaving the engine running, he put the backhoe in park and hopped down. He ran back into the shed, found some long black bungee cords, and wrapped them around his father's chest, abdomen, and shoulders, tying him to the monument. After making sure they were tight, Barry stood back and smiled.

His old man had fallen unconscious again.

Barry spit in his face.

The sky grew lighter.

The tunnel broadened and all at once, Timmy found himself stepping into a large, roughly circular chamber. He gasped, not so much from fright, but from the scene before him. The dirt floor was littered with bones and other body fragments. A shattered skull stared back at him. His flashlight beam disappeared into its hollow eyes. The ceiling was high, much higher than in the network of tunnels, and Timmy got the impression that he was deep below the cemetery now. It felt like the earth itself was pressing down on him. But neither the bones nor the atmosphere were what made him gasp.

It was the women.

There were two of them. Katie's older sister, Karen, and another woman whom Timmy didn't recognize. He assumed that she was the missing woman he'd heard about on the news. Both of them were dressed in rags, their clothing soiled and torn to shreds. Despite his overwhelming dread, Timmy felt a dark thrill go through him at the sight of Karen Moore's breasts. He immediately felt guilty, but his eyes were drawn back to them again. They were covered with red scratches. Both women's hands and feet were bound with thick roots and vines, tied together in crude knots, and then looped around large, heavy logs, insuring that they wouldn't escape. A corner of the chamber was covered with feces; most of it theirs, he assumed. The larger piles probably belonged to the ghoul itself. The two women huddled together on a pile of straw and grass, staring at Timmy with wide, horrified eyes.

"Um." He wasn't sure what to say.

"I . . . know you . . ." Karen spoke haltingly, hesitant, as if she'd forgotten how to talk—or was afraid to. Her voice was hoarse and scratchy. "From . . . church?"

Swallowing, Timmy nodded. "Yeah, you do. I'm Timmy Graco, Randy and Elizabeth Graco's son. I'm your sister's . . ."—he started to say boyfriend, but caught himself—". . . friend."

The other woman said nothing. She simply stared at him, that frozen, horrified expression never leaving her face.

Timmy smiled, trying to reassure them.

"Are you okay?" he asked Karen.

She nodded slowly, as if unsure what the word meant. "I . . . we—it hurt us. Did . . . things."

Karen began to make clicking sounds in her throat. She looked as if she might start screaming. Slowly, Timmy stepped toward them. The other woman shrank away, pressing her back against the dirt wall.

"Look," Timmy said, keeping his voice calm and soft, "I've come to rescue you. I'll get you out of here."

Both women whimpered. Tears rolled down Karen's

dirty face. The other woman fixated on the knife in Timmy's hand.

"It's okay," he whispered. "I'm just going to use it to cut you free."

She shook her head, trembling harder.

"Her name is . . . Deb," Karen rasped. "Her first night here . . . all she did was scream. She . . . hasn't said anything since."

Timmy sawed at Karen's bonds first, so that with any luck, Deb would see he didn't mean them any harm. This close to them, he tried to ignore their nudity. It was easier than he'd imagined. Both captives stank of unwashed bodies and something else— something fishy, almost like almonds or ammonia. He was afraid to ask what it was. Their pale skin was covered with cuts and scratches and a fine sheen of dried blood and the ghoul's slime. When he was finished freeing her, Karen rubbed her wrists and ankles. Both had red circles where the vines had rubbed the flesh raw. As her circulation returned, he moved over to the other woman. She cowered, moving as far away from him as she could.

"It's okay," Timmy said. "I promise. I'm just going to get you loose, like I did her."

She shook her head and turned away from him, squeezing her eyes shut.

Timmy sighed in exasperation. "Why doesn't she believe me?"

"Because," Karen said, "she thinks you're going to . . . do what he's been doing to us."

"Who?"

Karen frowned. "That thing."

"The ghoul?"

She nodded. "Is that what it is?"

Rather than answering, Timmy tried again to free the frightened woman.

"Don't scream," he told her. "I'm not going to hurt you."

He raised the knife, and she whined, the start of a shriek building in her throat.

"Okay," he said, and dropped the knife again. "Shhh. Don't scream. It's okay. I put it down."

Her scream turned into a fearful sigh.

Timmy turned to Karen. "Do you know where it is now?"

"It feeds at night. Usually comes back just before dawn. That's when it . . . that's when it happens. After that, it sleeps."

Timmy paused, listening for the sounds of the backhoe. He didn't hear anything. He wondered if he'd even be able to hear it this far below the surface.

"The sun will be up soon," he told Karen. "We've got to get you both out of here before the ghoul comes back. See if you can help me cut her loose. Then the two of you head straight down that tunnel. It goes for a long way, but keep following it."

"What about you?"

"I've got to find my friend, Doug Keiser. Do you know him?"

She paused; then nodded. "Fat kid? Yeah, I know him. Hangs around with you and the Smeltzer kid. I remember now. All three of you guys used to talk to Pat . . . he liked you. I'd forgotten. Forgot about . . . Pat."

Her face blanched, and Timmy thought she might scream. Instead she swooned. He propped her up while she shook against him, her entire body quivering.

"Is he okay?" she asked. "Pat—is he alive?"

"Yeah," Timmy lied. "Sure. Help me get Deb loose and we'll go see him, okay?"

She nodded. Steadying herself, she rose to her feet.

Timmy shined the flashlight back to Deb. This time she met his gaze. Her lower lip trembled.

"Please," Timmy said. "I need to help my friend. Let me help you first, okay?"

Her nod was barely perceptible, but she consented in silence. Timmy began cutting her bonds.

"Hurry," Karen urged.

"I'm going as fast as I can. This knife wouldn't cut a wet monkey."

Karen frowned at the odd statement. Timmy grinned, and tried to squelch the sudden sadness that overcame him. It had been a long-time private joke between him, Barry, and Doug. Doug had first uttered it one night when they were camping out, and the phrase had never failed to make all three of them laugh.

Now, it just made Timmy want to cry.

"Have you seen Doug down here? I can't leave without him."

The vines and roots around Deb's wrists and ankles fell away. She still looked afraid. Trying to ease her fears, Timmy sat the pocketknife down and backed away from it, still crouched at eye level with the frightened woman.

"We haven't seen him," Karen said. "But why would he have been down here in the first place? Was he helping you?"

Before Timmy could respond, there was a rustling sound behind them. Deb screamed—a hoarse, wretched sound, like gargling with glass. She clawed at the dirt and stared over Timmy's shoulder. At the same time, Timmy became aware of a faint illumination spreading throughout the chamber. It wasn't much, but it was definitely noticeable—a pale, flickering luminescence, much like the light cast by the slime. The foul stench that permeated the entire tunnel network suddenly became stronger.

And then something hissed. It sounded like air rushing from a punctured tire.

Karen shrieked. Deb pressed against the wall. The hairs on the back of Timmy's neck prickled. He was afraid to turn around, afraid that if he did, he might pee his pants.

But he did anyway, and came face to face with Doug.

His best friend's disembodied head swung back and forth like a pendulum, dangling from the ghoul's left hand. Its long, curved talons gripped Doug's hair. The creature stood in the entranceway to the chamber, blocking their escape. It looked nothing like the monsters depicted in Timmy's comic books. Naked, its body was almost completely devoid of hair, except for between its legs and a few long strands along its body. It was thin, but its limbs were knotted with corded muscles and its stomach bulged considerably, as if it were pregnant. Its white skin was covered in filth, and yet still shone with an eerie incandescence. It had yellow, baleful eyes, a pointed head, and thick black lips that resembled two pieces of raw liver. Its mouth and face were slicked with fresh blood. The ghoul's gray tongue flicked out and licked some away. Then it grinned, revealing pointed teeth. They looked very sharp.

"Are you looking for this, child?" Its voice was like sandpaper.

Timmy couldn't speak.

The ghoul held Doug's head aloft. "A friend of yours, yes? He was succulent. A fine repast, indeed. The fat melted in my mouth. For too long I have fed on carrion. I wonder how you will taste."

Timmy shouted at Karen to run, but even as he did, he realized there was nowhere to run to. His voice sounded very small and afraid. He couldn't take his eyes off Doug's head.

"You are trespassing in my home," the ghoul said. "Disturbing my mates, and threatening discord amongst my tribe. You should not have come here."

Growling, the ghoul flung Doug's head at them and then leapt. Timmy flung his hands up in front of his face and dodged right. Karen jumped to the left. The head bounced off the wall, knocking soil loose, and then rolled across the floor. The ghoul followed behind it, landing in front of Deb. Teeth snapping, it whirled toward Timmy.

With a frantic, shrill scream, Deb seized the pocket-knife with both hands and plunged the blade into the creature's groin. The ghoul shuddered, then howled. Its hands cradled its wounded testicles. Blood spilled through its fingers. Timmy stared at it in horror, then glanced back down at Doug's head. His dead, sightless eyes seemed to be staring right at Timmy.

"Run!" Karen grabbed his arm and led him toward the exit.

As they fled, Timmy glanced over his shoulder. Bellowing with pain and rage, the ghoul ripped the knife free. Still on her knees, Deb lashed out with her bare hands, striking at the creature. It struck back, knocking her to the floor with one swipe of its massive hand. Then it turned and faced them.

"I will kill you slowly, boy."

Timmy ran.

The backhoe's front scoop gouged at the earth. The engine coughed, but kept running. Barry dropped the dirt to the side and then dug up another scoop full. A yawning crevice appeared beneath the soil—a tunnel, sloping downward at a sharp incline. He'd decided to use the front scoop rather than the back scoop to save time, and the results were worth it. Behind him, the cemetery looked like it had been infested with giant groundhogs. Holes and collapsed graves dotted the landscape. He drove on a few more yards, his progress slowed by weaving the big machine around the tombstones, and then started digging again.

Barry glanced at the sky and saw that it was getting brighter. The first true rays of sunlight crept over the horizon. But here on the ground, it was still dark. He tried to go faster. The backhoe's oversized tires ran overtop a small gravestone. He began digging again, dragging the scoop through the dirt, making trenches instead of holes.

The back end lurched and Barry glanced around. The left rear tire had fallen into the earth. The dirt had collapsed beneath it, and Barry saw that he was sitting on top of a tunnel. Trying to maneuver away before the entire thing caved in, he gunned the engine. The motor thrummed.

When his father began shouting, Barry didn't hear him.

Timmy and Karen plunged through the darkness, running as fast as they could. The flashlight beam bounced off the walls and floor, jostled by the exertion. Timmy let Karen lead the way, but her captivity had left her weak, and she kept stumbling and slowing down. Timmy urged her on. Behind them, he heard the sounds of pursuit. The ghoul howled, sputtering curses and threats. Its feet pounded on the dirt floor. The tunnels echoed with its harsh, ragged breathing.

Karen clambered over the splintered wood from a

broken casket, and Timmy urged her to move faster. He cast a terrified glance over his shoulder and saw the ghoul narrowing the distance between them. It ran hunched over, one hand still cradling its wounded groin. It looked like a ghost, the phosphorescent slime glowing all around it as it neared them.

"Hurry." Timmy pushed her legs.

"I'm trying."

They cleared the barrier and kept running. Karen stumbled over a rock, but regained her balance. She gasped for air. Timmy was tiring as well. Despite days spent riding bikes and hiking through the woods, he was at the limits of his physical endurance. His lungs burned, and his leg muscles were beginning to cramp. A sharp pain jolted through his ribs. Clenching his teeth, he rubbed the side-stitch and tried to keep moving.

"Wife," the ghoul screeched. "Return to me, now. You cannot forsake me. My kind must live."

Karen sobbed, but didn't look back. Behind them, they heard their pursuer crash into the pile of shattered timbers.

"Woman, I will not warn you again."

Desperate to put more distance between themselves and the creature, Timmy and Karen pushed on while the ghoul clambered through the wreckage. They reached a crossroads, with side tunnels branching out in three different directions. Over the ghoul's enraged shouts, Timmy heard a new sound—the muffled rumble of a diesel engine. It was the backhoe. It had to be. Sure enough, farther up the tunnel, dirt showered down from the surface. Confused by the falling debris, Karen weaved right and darted into one of the side tunnels.

"No," Timmy shouted. "That's the wrong way!"

If she heard him, she gave no indication. She passed

beyond the reach of his flashlight beam. He paused for just a moment, unsure of what to do. The ghoul growled, and then surged forward. It reached for him, talons clicking together. Timmy ran after Karen. Bones crunched under his feet.

The tunnels began to shake.

The first thing Clark Smeltzer was aware of was the noise—a loud, steady rumble that made his head throb and his teeth ache. It thrummed through the very earth and cleaved the air around him. A machine, by the sound—maybe a motor. The second thing he noticed was that the pain in his head was minor compared to the rest of him. Each breath brought fresh jabs of agony in his chest and sides. His face and throat felt like they'd been burned. He tried to move and found he couldn't. He'd been tied up with bungee cords. Clark took a few shallow breaths and then leaned forward, trying to loosen his bonds. His muscles screamed, and so did he. His voice was lost beneath the din of the machine.

The bungee cords tightened, then went slack, tightened and slacked, as he slowly rocked back and forth. The rubber bands squeaked against the tombstone's marble surface. Finally, they slipped down his body. He pulled his arms free and unfastened the cords.

Clark squinted at his hands through crusted eyes, saw half-dried blood, and then touched his cheek. He shivered. The action brought more pain. His fingers came away red, fresh blood coating the already dried blood.

Fucked me up, he thought. *Damn thing fucked me up good.*

He shuddered. It was very cold. But that couldn't be right, could it? Cold—in the middle of June? His teeth wouldn't stop chattering.

He forced his eyes open further. Only one of them obeyed. The other stayed shut. He turned his head slowly, seeking the source of the rumbling noise, and more pain ripped through him, causing his entire body to spasm. Clark clenched his hands into fists and forced his head to turn. His remaining good eye widened in surprise.

Somehow, Barry had gotten inside the utility shed. The little bastard had picked the lock and hijacked the backhoe. As Clark watched, the scoop threw another clod of earth into the sky. He was digging up the cemetery—obviously taking revenge for the beating Clark had handed down to him earlier.

"Hey!" he shouted. "You little fuck. What are you doing?"

Barry ignored him.

"Don't pretend you can't hear me, you son of a bitch. Get off that fucking backhoe! I mean it."

The engine revved higher. The machine rolled forward, the front end bouncing over a tombstone.

"Barry! You mind me, boy."

Fists still clenched, Clark stumbled to his feet. So his worthless son was pissed off about getting his ass beat? He'd teach him now. This was vandalism, plain and simple. Barry was about to get a beating he'd never, ever forget.

"Okay. I warned you. You still ain't learned. This time, you don't get another chance."

Clark staggered forward, grinning through the pain. Blood ran into his one good eye, and he saw red.

Karen moaned.

Timmy turned around and pointed the flashlight back the way they'd come.

"Oh God . . . Oh God . . ."

Karen kept repeating it over and over. Timmy wasn't sure if she was praying or just going into shock. If it was a prayer, it had gone unanswered. They had reached a dead end—a mound of dirt and rock sealed the side tunnel off from the surface. An ash-gray bone protruded from the center of the pile. All around them, the walls trembled. Timmy could hear the backhoe very clearly now, and it was easy to figure out what had happened. This tunnel had led to a grave. With Barry digging above them, the soil around the grave had collapsed, sinking down into the chasm below. Now they were trapped.

Timmy stared back down the tunnel. It curved away into the darkness, sloping downward. He wondered if there was time to run back out to the main passage and find another route. But even as he considered this the pale luminescence thrown off by the ghoul's body lit up the tunnel walls beyond the bend. Timmy shrank away, placing himself between Karen and their pursuer. She reached out and took his hand. Numb with terror, he barely felt it when she squeezed.

He thought of Katie, and how her hand had felt in his. He thought of his parents, and wished he could see them again, one more time, if only to tell them that he was sorry. He thought of Doug.

"I don't want to die," Timmy whispered. "Please."

The walls around them shook and rumbled. Dirt spilled down on them, showering their hair and shoulders. Coughing, they brushed it off. A cloud of dust filled the narrow passageway, obscuring the flashlight beam. Their hands squeezed tighter. When the dust cleared, the ghoul had rounded the corner and stood several yards away. The creature cocked its pointed head and laughed.

"There is nowhere left for you to flee. You have offered good sport, boy, and for that I am grateful. But it is time to end this charade. I will make your death quick, not out of kindness or pity. Believe me, I would relish the chance to flay your skin slowly for your transgressions. But I must still deal with what is transpiring on the surface. Did you and the grave digger's son really think to shake the foundations of my kingdom?"

Timmy licked his lips, too frightened to respond. His nostrils and the back of his throat tasted like dirt. His mouth was dry.

"Never mind," the ghoul said. "Tonight, you shall both feed me. And feed my wives, as well."

Karen squeezed Timmy's hand so hard that his knuckles popped.

The ghoul raised its claws and took a menacing step forward. Timmy's eyes were drawn to the knife wound—or where the knife wound should have been. It had healed already, and the only sign that Deb had even stabbed the creature was the dried blood on its thighs and legs.

The tunnel shook again and the ceiling rustled. More dirt showered down upon them all. The ghoul stumbled backward. Timmy and Karen pressed themselves against the wall, holding their breath so they wouldn't choke. The sound of the backhoe's engine swelled, filling the tunnels.

You were right, Barry, Timmy thought. *We shouldn't have tried to do this ourselves. We should have just told the adults. We can't fight a monster. . . .*

The cloud of dust dissipated, and the ghoul lunged for him.

Barry struggled with the gearshift. It vibrated in his hand, refusing to budge. The backhoe rocked back and forth, the front end swaying precariously several feet off the ground. He'd spotted a fresh sinkhole and had tried to back up so he wouldn't drive over the depression. He was afraid the ground might give way. In the process of turning around, he'd driven up over a tombstone and was now stuck. He pushed harder on the stick. The gears made an awful grinding sound. Black smoke belched from the exhaust pipe.

The sunrise grew brighter on the horizon, the glowing orb now peeking over the treetops of Bowman's Woods.

Grunting, Barry tried again. As he wrestled with the gearshift, something tugged at his arm. Barry glanced down, saw a bloody hand clenching his wrist, and screamed.

His father clung to the side of the backhoe. The old man was grinning. Blood coursed down his face. It looked like he could barely stand, let alone hang on to the bucking vehicle, yet his grip tightened.

"That's it for you, boy." Clark spat blood. "Time to take your medicine, once and for all."

"Get off me." Barry jerked his arm away, breaking his father's grip. Arms flailing, Clark teetered backward, and then fell forward and grabbed the backhoe's sides. He swiped at Barry's head with one fist, but in his weakened state, his aim was off. Barry easily dodged the blow, and then struck back. This time he connected. His fist plowed into his father's already mangled mouth. Clark's lips exploded beneath his son's knuckles. More blood splattered them both. Barry's other hand slipped off the steering wheel. The backhoe careened atop the tombstone, leaning forward at a dangerous angle. Both father and son grabbed on tight, struggling to keep their balance. Pain lashed through Barry's hand. He glanced down and saw a piece of his father's tooth jutting from the knuckle of his middle finger.

Clark's hand shot forward and closed around Barry's throat. Barry tried to breathe, but couldn't. His tongue and eyes bulged. Grunting, his father squeezed tighter, his fingers digging into Barry's flesh.

"Look at this shit," Clark wheezed. "All this damage. You did this, you little punk."

Barry could barely hear him over the ringing in his ears. His head began to pound. He tried again to take a breath, but his father's grip was firm. Barry's lips started bleeding again. He reached up with both hands and clawed at his father's wrist and forearm, trying to dislodge him. He pried at the thick fingers, but his father was too strong.

"You ain't no son of mine."

Barry's legs thrashed. The ringing in his ears grew louder. His hands fell away, weakening. Clark's grip tightened.

"You ain't no son of mine," he repeated.

Metal shrieked against stone. The backhoe tilted forward, then plunged over. The motor sputtered and died. All around them, the ground collapsed, falling down into the earth with a deafening roar. The sinkhole yawned wide like an eager mouth, waiting to devour them all. The front scoop disappeared into the earth, followed by the grille, headlights, and front tires. Barry slammed against the roll cage. Wire mesh pressed against his cheek. His father's grip slipped from his throat as Clark struggled to avoid falling.

Gasping for breath, Barry held on tight as the backhoe again lurched forward. His stomach felt sick. His fingers clutched the wire mesh. His father scrabbled for purchase, clinging to the steering wheel. The backhoe tipped forward and plunged headlong into the chasm.

* * *

As the ghoul approached, Timmy tried to scream. Instead, all that came out was a muffled whine. Clouds of dust swirled in the air. The creature loomed before him, its stink filling the tunnel. Slime dripped from its pores, pooling at its feet. It raised its claws to strike—

And the tunnel collapsed behind them. Tons of dirt filled the passageway, sealing off the other end. The flashlight slipped from Timmy's grasp. He dropped to his knees, pulling Karen down with him. Both of them covered their mouths and noses as more dust filled the air. Timmy closed his eyes. A great roaring sound filled his ears, and then faded.

He opened his eyes again.

Despite the debris in the air, he could see. The ceiling was gone. Dim sunlight spilled through the chasm. The backhoe filled the tunnel, surround by piles of dirt, broken tombstones, and splintered coffins. Barry knelt in the dirt, coughing and gagging. The wound on his cheek had opened up again, and there were fresh cuts and scratches on his face and arms. His neck was bruised. The purple blotches looked like finger marks. There was no sign of the ghoul. Next to him, Karen threw up.

Timmy patted her back, unsure of what to do. "You okay?"

Gasping, she nodded. She wiped her mouth with the back of her hand.

Timmy crawled over to Barry. Despite his injuries, Barry smiled.

"You're rescued."

"What happened?"

Groaning, Barry struggled to his feet. "The ground caved in. I couldn't jump off because my old man—"

His eyes grew wide. He turned around quickly; then looked back to Timmy.

"Where is he?"

Timmy frowned. "The ghoul? I don't know. He must have took off when you came crashing through."

"No," Barry shook his head. "My old man. He was on the backhoe when it fell."

They searched through the wreckage. The backhoe had landed on its front, and the scoop was imbedded in the tunnel floor. The dirt had piled up around it, burying the entire front end. The rear scoop jutted through the crevice in the ceiling and out to the surface. They clambered over the mounds of earth, searching.

Timmy gasped. "Is that . . ."

Barry knelt in the dirt. His father's hand jutted from the soil. Dane Graco's freemason ring was still on his finger. Without a word, Barry pulled the ring free and tossed it to Timmy.

"There. You should have this."

"Thanks." Timmy put the ring in his pocket. "Are you gonna be all right?"

Barry shrugged, his eyes not leaving the hand. "Yeah. I mean, maybe I should be sad, because he was my father, but I'm not. I don't even feel happy. I'm just . . . empty. Does that make sense?"

Timmy nodded.

Barry ran his hands through his hair, shaking out the dirt. "He said I wasn't any son of his. Right before we fell."

"That's not true."

"Yeah, it is. He may have been my old man, biologically, but I ain't his son. No way. I'm nothing like him, and I'm never gonna be. I swear it."

Karen stepped forward. "Can we go?"

"What about the other woman?" Timmy asked. "Deb? We can't just leave her down here."

"Where is she?" Barry stared at Karen's breasts, then quickly looked away.

"Back there somewhere." Timmy pointed past the pile of dirt choking the tunnel. "We'll have to dig through that."

"With what," Barry snorted. "Our bare hands?"

Karen climbed up the backhoe. "We'll get help. They can send a rescue squad in to dig her out, just like they do when a mine collapses. I'm not waiting for that thing to come back. She might not even be alive anymore. She was pretty . . . out of it. I think her mind went after the first time the ghoul . . ."

Rather than finishing the sentence, she turned her face skyward.

Timmy and Barry watched her climb. Barry leaned close and whispered in his ear.

"Do you think the ghoul is dead?"

"I don't know," Timmy said. "My eyes were shut. I didn't see where it went."

"What about Doug? Did you find him?"

Timmy lowered his head. His lip quivered. "Yeah. He's . . . I don't want to talk about it right now."

"Shit."

"Yeah."

Karen shimmied up the rear scoop's arm. When she reached the ceiling, she looked back down at them.

"You guys coming?"

Nodding, the boys climbed onto the backhoe. Barry started up first, followed by Timmy. Timmy had only ascended a few feet when he heard a soft rustling noise. He glanced down at the mound of debris. It was moving.

"Shit. Go, go, go!"

"What is it?" Barry stopped, looking down in concern.

"Just go," Timmy screamed. "Hurry!"

A clawed hand erupted from the dirt, followed by another. Several of the ghoul's talons had been ripped away, and its fingers were bleeding. Its arms thrust forward, followed by its pointed, oversized head. Its yellow eyes smoldered with rage.

Screaming, Barry began climbing again. Timmy pushed on his feet, urging him to go faster.

The ghoul sprang from the mound and shook off the dirt. Then it rose to its full height.

"My bride!" It beckoned to Karen. "Return now, and I shall not hurt you."

With a shriek, Karen pulled herself up to the surface and out into the light. Barry and Timmy climbed higher.

"No," the ghoul roared. "No, no, no, no, no. I will not allow this. My kind must live again. You will not take away my chance at parentage."

It leaped onto the backhoe. The scoop arm rocked back and forth, and both boys had to cling tight to keep from falling. Like a spider, the ghoul raced up the side of the machine, its long arms and legs scrabbling for purchase. Barry reached the top and heaved himself over the side onto solid ground. He extended his hand down into the hole and Timmy grasped it.

"Hurry," Barry shouted. "It's almost on you."

Timmy pushed with his legs and reached the top. The ghoul was directly beneath him. He could feel its breath on his ankles; hear it hissing with rage. Then it howled—but this time, the sound was different.

Timmy crawled out of the hole and glanced back down. The dim sunlight had touched the ghoul's arm, and the pale flesh sizzled. The slime coating the appendage bubbled and popped, and a thin line of smoke curled upward.

"Come on." Barry grabbed Timmy's arm and pulled him to his feet.

Timmy shrugged him off and stared in horrified fascination, absolutely transfixed as the ghoul's arm continued to smolder.

"Timmy, let's go!"

Barry shoved him forward. Timmy stumbled, and then followed. They ran between the tombstones. Karen sprinted ahead of them, heading for the church. The sun's upper half had cleared the treetops now, and the blue light of predawn had given way to the red glow of sunrise.

"No. My family . . ." The ghoul emerged from the crevice. Smoke billowed from its body as the light touched its flesh. Even as they ran, the boys heard it sizzling behind them. Still, it pursued them with determination, screaming for Karen to come back. As they neared the church, the creature's shouts faded.

Timmy turned and stared.

The ghoul writhed in the grass, its body contorted with pain. Timmy had once found a slug on his parent's sidewalk, and had poured salt over the unfortunate creature. He was reminded of that now. The ghoul's pale flesh sloughed away each time the monster moved. The muscles and tissue beneath bubbled and burned. A layer of white foam covered everything. Timmy expected the ghoul to explode, like in the movies and comic books, but instead, it simply pawed at the earth, making pathetic mewling sounds and watching Karen race away. Even after its eyes had melted and run out onto the ground, its head remained upright and pointed in her direction.

"My . . . family . . ."

The boys watched until there was nothing left but a bubbling puddle.

And then Timmy began to cry. He thought about their attack on Catcher, the guilt and shame he'd felt after the fact. Like Doug had said, the dog wasn't a monster. It was just doing what it was supposed to do. What it had been bred to do. Protecting it's home. When they'd attacked, and Catcher had run around in a circle, yelping and whining and pawing at his eyes, he hadn't looked like a monster. He'd looked pitiful.

Timmy stared at the stewing remains of the ghoul. It didn't look like a monster anymore.

"Didn't it realize? Didn't it know what the sunlight would do?"

"It must have wanted Karen that bad," Barry said. "Nothing else mattered."

"Family," Timmy whispered. "It was trying to save its family."

"Come on," Barry said. He put his arm around Timmy's shoulder and led him away.

Behind them, the sun rose into the sky. A new day had begun.

EPILOGUE

The black Toyota SUV wheeled into the church parking lot and slowed to a halt. A satellite radio antenna was magnetically affixed to the roof, and the muffled sounds of a children's program drifted from inside the vehicle. A man sat in the driver's seat, gripping the wheel tightly. A woman sat next to him. After a moment, the Toyota slowly made its way down the graveyard's middle road. The path was wider than the man remembered it being, and looked as if it had recently been given a fresh coat of blacktop.

"Is this it, Daddy?"

The man nodded. "Yep. This is it. This used to be my playground."

He shivered. His wife noticed and turned down the air conditioning. The man said nothing.

The SUV crawled past the graves, slowed again, and then stopped.

The man got out, and smoothed his suit. His tie fluttered in the warm June breeze. He took a deep breath. He hadn't been there in a long time. He glanced around. The old utility shed was gone, replaced with a more modern structure. Farmer Jones's pasture now held duplex housing instead of cattle. Things were different. He closed his eyes for a moment and heard the sound of children's laughter. Old ghosts. They'd been good ghosts, once upon a time.

Not anymore.

As an adult, the man was reminded of how children laughing often sounded like children screaming.

He opened his eyes and moved on.

Inside the vehicle, his wife and kids watched him approach the grave. Then the woman made a call on her cell phone.

The man stood in front of the grave—a fresh, open hole in the earth. A wound. It would be filled later that day, and then covered back over with sod. A brand-new tombstone sat at the head of the hole. It said that Randy Graco was a loving husband and father. Dane Graco's tombstone stood a few feet away.

"Hey, Timmy."

Tim jumped in surprise. He'd thought he was alone. He looked up. The cemetery's caretaker stepped out from behind a tall monument. A bashful young boy, around the same age as Tim's oldest son, crept out behind him, watching with curiosity. Both were dressed in work clothes, their jeans soiled with grass stains and dirt.

"Timmy?"

The caretaker pulled off his work gloves and walked toward him.

Tim frowned. Nobody had called him Timmy since he'd graduated college. Not even his parents. He didn't recognize the caretaker at first. He was bald, and his skin looked weathered from too much sun or stress—or both. There were dark circles under his eyes that most men didn't get until much later in life. But the scar was what gave his identity away: a narrow, pale line running up his cheek, carved years ago with a stolen ring—a ring that was now on Tim's right hand. The scar had happened on a night neither man would ever forget. The scar, like the memories, had faded over time, but was still there.

Smiling in disbelief, Tim stepped forward. "Barry? Jesus Christ . . ."

"Good to see you, too, man." Barry laughed. "Thought maybe you didn't recognize me."

"I didn't. At first, anyway. Took me a second. It's been a while."

"Yes, it has. Twenty years, give or take."

Still surprised, Tim was speechless.

"I keep up on you," Barry said, his voice filled with pride. "The *Hanover Evening Sun* and the *York Dispatch* both had articles on you. I hear you're a famous comic book writer now."

Tim chuckled. "Well, I wouldn't say I'm famous or anything. But I do all right."

"You and your funny books." Barry pulled out a can of Husky tobacco and loaded some into his lip. "I remember you were crazy about those things when we were kids."

"You were, too."

Barry's brow furrowed. "Yeah, I guess maybe I was. I'd forgotten about that. I don't read much of anything these days, except the paper. But man, I remember how pissed you were when your dad ripped yours up."

"I remember, too," Timmy whispered. "I don't think we'll ever forget."

"No," Barry agreed. "We won't. But shit, I didn't mean to bring up your old man. I'm sorry."

"It's okay."

Barry pointed at the grave. "I was sorry to hear about what happened. He was a good neighbor. Hell, I've been living next to him my whole life. It'll be weird not seeing him down over the hill."

Tim nodded sadly. "Yeah. It was pretty sudden. The heart attack hit him while he was watching the game. Happened quick. Mom's still in shock, I think. But at least he didn't suffer."

"Well, that's good."

"Yeah."

They stared at each other in silence, neither one knowing what to say.

Barry spat a wad of brown tobacco juice onto the grass. "That your family?"

"Yeah." Tim turned back to the SUV. "That's my wife, Mara, and my sons, Dane and Doug."

Barry paused. "Doug, huh? That's good. He'd have liked that."

"I think so."

"Wife's good-looking," Barry said, staring at the Toyota. "You done good."

"Yeah, I can't complain."

"Ever hear from Katie Moore?"

"Not since graduation. I went to college. She had another year in school. You know how it is."

"I always figured you two would get hitched. Young love and all that."

"That only happens in songs, I guess."

Barry nodded, and they fell silent again.

"That's my kid back there." Barry turned, pointing at the shy boy, who'd crept back behind the monument again. "Richie. Get your ass out here and say hello."

Tim frowned. Barry's voice had taken on a rough, unpleasant tone. The boy, Richie, slunk out from behind the marker, eyes cast to the ground, shoulders slumped. Tim finally got a good look at the kid. He was skinny, and his arms stuck out of his T-shirt like twigs. Both of them were bruised, and his right forearm had a nasty circular mark. Tim tried to keep a straight face, but inside he was shocked. It looked like a cigarette burn.

"Get over here," Barry shouted.

The boy jumped at the sound of his father's voice, and dutifully shuffled over to them. As he got closer, Tim noticed the scars.

"This here is Timmy Graco," Barry said, introducing him. "We was best friends when we were your age."

"Hi." Tim stuck out his hand.

Richie shook it. His grip was weak, his palms sweaty. He mumbled under his breath.

Barry slapped the back of his head. "Speak up. I told you before, nobody can understand shit when you mumble like that."

"Sorry," the boy apologized. "Nice to meet you."

He didn't look into Tim's eyes, but kept his gaze focused on the ground.

"Get on back to work," Barry commanded.

He prodded Richie with his boot. The boy ran off.

Barry grinned, looking sheepish.

"He don't listen sometimes. Got to teach him manners. Guess we did the same thing when we were kids."

"Looks like he got hurt recently." Tim kept his voice calm.

Shrugging, Barry looked away. "He's careless. Clumsy, like I was at that age. You know how it is. Boys have scars."

Timmy nodded, unable to speak around the lump in his throat. He stared at the faded scar on Barry's cheek.

Boys have scars, he thought. *Some of them fade— and others don't. Some scars stay with us for life.*

"Listen, Barry . . . I should get going. The kids are restless, and I want to check in on my mom. It's been a long drive."

"Sure." Barry met his gaze again, and smiled. His face was sad. "Funeral's tomorrow. You gonna stay in town long?"

"A few days, probably."

"Well, let's get together. Have a few beers. I'll have to show you how I fixed up the house, since the last time you saw it."

"That sounds good. It will depend on Mara and the kids, of course. And Mom. I want to be there for her."

"You can make time for a beer with your old bud."

Timmy nodded.

Barry wiped the sweat from his brow. "Good seeing you, Timmy."

"You too, man."

Tim started to turn away, but Barry called out to him, his voice soft and sad. For a brief moment, he sounded like the old Barry, the Barry Tim had known from childhood.

"What happened to us, Timmy?"

"What do you mean?"

"We were supposed to be best friends. Remember? We promised ourselves that we wouldn't let each other down. Best friends for life."

"I remember."

"So what happened?"

Tim shook his head. "I don't know, Barry. Life happened, I guess. We grew up. Grew apart. I think of you a lot, though. You and Doug."

"Yeah." Barry wiped his eyes. "Me, too."

They said good-bye again, and Tim headed back to the Toyota. He hadn't lied. He did think of Barry and Doug, and Katie, too. Almost every day, in fact. But in his memories, they were twelve—and immortal. And they would be twelve forever, living out the happiest days of their lives over and over again. They were who they'd been at twelve and not who they were now.

He'd come to the cemetery and found new old ghosts. The happiest days of their lives had been nothing more than a defense mechanism.

Tim opened the door and slid into the driver's seat.

"Who was that?" Mara asked. "Old friend?"

"Yeah." Tim turned the key. "An old friend. My best friend, actually."

"What's his name?"

"Barry. We used to run around together. Me, him, and our friend Doug."

In the backseat, Dane pressed buttons on his handheld video game, oblivious to the conversation. But Doug leaned forward in the seat. "You mean you had a friend named Doug, just like my name?"

Tim smiled. "I sure did."

"And the three of you were best friends, just like me and Joey and Jesse?"

Tim nodded. He blinked the tears away so his family wouldn't see them. Mara noticed, reached out, and patted his leg.

"Sit back, honey, so Daddy can pull out."

Doug complied. As he fastened his seat belt, he said, "I miss Joey and Jesse. It's summer. I want to get back home and play."

"You will soon," Mara said. "You've got the whole summer ahead of you."

"I guess you're right," Doug said. "Summer's last a

long time. And me, Joey, and Jesse are best friends forever, so they'll be there when I get back."

Tim sighed. He wanted to promise his son that yes, summers were endless and that his best friends would be his best friends forever, but the truth was, life didn't work out that way. When he was twelve, Tim had believed that summers were endless and so was life. But he knew better now. Nothing was endless. Nothing lasted forever. Nothing was eternal. Not life. Not summer. Not friendship. Not even love. Because the ghouls would gnaw away at those things until there was nothing left.

The only things that lasted forever were scars—and monsters.

*Turn the page for an advance look at
Brian Keene's next terrifying novel…*

DEAD
SEA

COMING AUGUST 2007

I didn't shoot the bitch until she started eating Alan's face. Before this whole thing began, I'd never shot anyone in my life. Not once. Never held a gun until a few weeks before Hamelin's Revenge started. Hell, I never even referred to women as bitches. But that's what she was. And I had the pistol in my hand.

And I shot her.

Cue "Hey Joe" by Jimi Hendrix.

This thing . . . this plague; it changed people. Not just the dead ones, either. It changed everyone. Changed me. I'm a different person now. Listen . . . you never know what you'll do until you find yourself in an impossible situation, so don't ever say never. Survival instinct is a real motherfucker, and when your back is against the wall, everything changes. *Everything.* I know. It did for me.

My name is Lamar Reed and this is the way the world ended.

It started with the rats. They swarmed out of the sewers about a month ago. Well, maybe *swarmed* isn't the right word. Swarm indicates speed, and the rats were anything but fast. The first attacks took place in New York City during the evening rush hour. Imagine it. Sidewalks bustling with activity, the crowds of people rushing to catch subways and trains and buses; streets choked with gridlock, taxicabs weaving in and out of traffic, horns blaring, manhole covers clanging as trucks drive over them. And then, in the middle of all this chaos, the rats slowly crawled out of a sewer grate on Thirty-first Street and attacked people— climbed up legs, raked at stomachs with their sharp little claws, sank their yellowed incisors into cheeks and thighs and necks; anywhere they could find a soft morsel. The rats fed.

And the rats were dead. I should mention that. Wasn't weird enough that rats attacked commuters en masse. They were *dead* rats; guts hanging out, limbs and tails falling off, and big, ulcerated wounds on their sides, infested with maggots. Rotting meat on the run.

Oh, we didn't know it at first. I remember watching it on the news that evening. Sitting on my couch in East Baltimore, eating bologna straight from the package and ignoring the stack of overdue bills. Watching the news, wondering when the cable would get shut off for nonpayment. Wondering where the hell my unemployment check was. The mail lady hadn't brought it yet, and things were tight. I'd come up with some cash a few weeks before, but it all went to my mortgage. Like sticking one finger in the dam while three dozen more leaks sprang up.

The news caught my attention because of the fucked-up factor. Rats attacking pedestrians? Crazy shit. But when the first reports started trickling in that they were dead rats—not dead as in some frantic stockbroker flung one to the ground and stomped it—but dead as in the living dead? That shit was off the hook. People scoffed, the media's pundits argued, and the authorities refused comment. The cable news channels carried live footage. MSNBC called it a riot. CNN speculated about a possible terrorist attack. I don't know what Fox News called it because nobody I know watched Fox News. One thing that appeared clear was that nobody knew what the fuck was going on. New York's hospitals filled up with wounded pedestrians. Most of them suffered bites, and others had been injured in the chaos that followed—trampled on as people fled. A few suffered heart attacks, brought on by the stress. The people who'd been bitten got real sick. Then died. Then came back. Just like the rats.

They were dead, but they still came back.

Hamelin's Revenge, the media called it. They came up with the name almost immediately. Hamelin's Revenge: the return of the rats the Pied Piper was hired to get rid of. But in that old story, when the mayor refused to pay, Hamelin—the Pied Piper—came up with another plan. Hamelin's Revenge was when the Piper decided to get even. He took all the kids away and returned the rats to the village. Now the fairy tale had come true. The rats returned all right. And hell followed with them. Just like the Bible verse or the song. Hell.

By midnight, New York City's hospitals became slaughterhouses. Like I said, the infected died, and then came back. And they came back hungry, man. Zombies. The White House press secretary actually used the word during a news conference. Until then, the media were calling the attackers cannibals. But after the government confirmed it, *zombies* was the buzzword. They attacked the living just like the rats had done. They bit and clawed and fed, gorging themselves on the flesh of the living. The victims who managed to escape got sick with Hamelin's Revenge a few hours later, just like their attacker had. Then they died and came back. And the ones who got ripped to pieces, the ones who ended up (for the most part) inside the zombie's bellies? What was left of them came back, too. They didn't need arms or legs or internal organs. As long as there was a brain left attached, something to control the motor functions and impulses, the remains came back. A CNN anchor actually walked away from the news desk after they showed footage of an armless corpse wandering the streets, trailing intestines behind it like a dog leash. You could hear her sobbing off camera, and some producer or technician begging her to go back on the air. She never did.

The chaos spread throughout the five boroughs. By dawn, the National Guard locked down New York City and quarantined everything. Blockaded the bridges and tunnels and left folks to die. A few soldiers even fired on civilians as they were trying to escape—gunned them down in the dawn's early light. It was for the good of the country, the media assured us. New York was a biohazard area. Nobody could get in or out. But Hamelin's Revenge managed to escape. Hamelin's Revenge said "Fuck you" to the barricades and armed guardsmen and quarantine signs. The disease raced like a California brushfire. Cases popped up in Newark, Delaware; then Trenton, New Jersey; and then on to Philadelphia, Pennsylvania. By the next evening, it had arrived here in Baltimore. Martial law was declared nationwide and the army was mobilized. That was like pouring perfume on a pig. The troops were good at killing zombies, but they couldn't shoot a disease. All it took was one bite from an infected mouth. And you could get it even if you weren't bitten. One drop of blood, sprayed from a bullet's exit wound. Pus from an open sore, splattering on you as a zombie attacked. Inhale it or ingest it; get it on your lips or in your eye and that was it. Say good-bye. You got sick. You died. You returned. Folks that died from heart attacks or cancer or stabbings or car wrecks—they stayed dead. But anyone who came into direct contact with the zombies—anyone who managed to get infected—they joined the ranks of the living dead.

And those ranks swelled quickly. First the rats. Then people. The disease jumped to dogs and cats in the second week. A few other animals, too. They said on television that a cow attacked an Amish farmer in Lancaster, Pennsylvania. It sounds kind of funny until you think about it for too long. Then it just becomes a mind-fuck. Zombie cattle . . . this time, the hamburger eats you. A pack of undead coyotes ripped a mother and her baby to shreds in the Hollywood hills. Gruesome shit. At least it didn't spread to the birds. If it had, well . . . for years we'd worried about the avian flu. The idea of birds spreading Hamelin's Revenge was terrifying, because birds are everywhere. Ain't nowhere you can run where a bird can't find you. The birds didn't catch it, at least that we'd seen, but many other animals did. Not all of them, but enough. Sheep caught it, but not pigs. Horses were immune, but cattle were not. Apes—death equaled zombie. Deer—their deaths were old school.

And of course, some species that seemed immune at first later became vulnerable. Squirrels didn't seem affected at first, which was weird, since they're just rats with fluffy tails. But later, they caught it, too. With all the cross-species jumps, there was no stopping the disease. It happened very quickly. America fell. South America. Canada. Then Hamelin's Revenge made it overseas and infected Europe and Asia and Africa. Last thing I saw before the power went out for good was grainy footage of a million zombie rats swarming over a million humans in Bombay.

Suddenly, I didn't have to worry about past due utility bills or if the cops had figured out that I was the one who robbed the Ford dealership during that test-drive. I didn't have to think about whether or not I had the balls to do it again. I had more important things to focus on, like staying alive and not getting eaten by my neighbors—or shot by some stupid motherfucker.

See, it wasn't just the zombies we had to watch out for. If it was, and if the president and Homeland Security and the Centers for Disease Control and the rest of our government had acted quickly, maybe none of this would have happened. But they didn't. Just like Pearl Harbor and 9/11 and Hurricane Katrina and all the other national disasters; when faced with an unimaginable crisis, they failed to respond in an accurate and timely manner. Maybe they couldn't. I mean, there's probably no FEMA playbook for what to do when dead folks start running around eating people. Not the sort of thing the government plans for.

In the weeks that followed there were dangers other than just the zombies. Looters and gangs of armed thugs roamed the streets. Cops and National Guardsmen who'd gone off the deep end shot the dead and living indiscriminately. America returned to the glory days of the Old West. Things like innocence and guilt didn't matter. The only law that mattered was the law of the gun. They evacuated Washington DC, and sent the president and his cabinet and all of the king's horses and men who worked in the House and the Senate off to secure underground bunkers in Virginia and Maryland and Pennsylvania. They were supposed to be able to run the country from there. They didn't. Things fell apart.

Our cities and towns resembled Somalia or Beirut. Well, to be honest, my neighborhood had been like that even before Hamelin's Revenge. Only difference was now the rest of the country got a taste of what it was like to live in the ghetto. Instead of drug gangs and tweaked-out freaks on crystal meth or crack, we now had vigilantes and zombies. Not much of a change, and in either case, the cops didn't show up when you called them.

I remember a press conference with the secretary of state. He was sweating like a pig. Looked nervous. He assured the reporters that President Tyler, the vice president, and cabinet members were all fine—and that the crisis was passing. Things would soon be under control, and society would return to normal. Until then, martial law would remain in effect as a cautionary measure.

Except that nobody was calling the shots. The person in charge was the guy with the most firepower, and that changed from moment to moment. People didn't aspire to cure the disease or stop it from spreading. They only aspired to not get eaten by a zombie. They'd always worried about their careers and homes and favorite television shows and what their most-loved Hollywood starlet had done. Now, the only thing they worried about was staying alive. And the worst part was, if you'd asked people, they probably couldn't tell you why they bothered resisting. Did it matter? What was the point? The zombies outnumbered the living. Why not surrender, or eat a bullet? Like I said earlier, survival instinct is a motherfucker.

Some people had higher aspirations, of course.

When there's blood on the streets, there's money to be made. That's an eternal law in the ghetto, and the rest of the world learned it soon enough. Stocks, bonds, shit like that—worthless. Cold hard cash ruled the day, and price gouging was common. Twenty bucks for a gallon of gas or a bottle of water. And when the cash became as worthless as the paper it was printed on, the barter system took over.

The madness continued. Last bit of the news I saw, in Pennsylvania, a National Guard officer had reportedly ordered the death of civilians by firing squad. They were accused of looting. In Miami, zombies overran the airport. A popular television preacher committed suicide, believing that the Rapture had occurred and he'd missed it. In China, a nuclear reactor went into meltdown. Chicago and Phoenix were on fire. The military finally retreated from New York City after losing control and admitting defeat.

More people died every day. Then they came back. And every day there were less of us.

I stayed inside. Didn't have any family. My mama died years ago. Breast cancer. Our health insurance sucked. There wasn't much they could do, in any case. Found a lump during a routine exam. Three months later, she was gone. I never knew my old man. Heard he was useless. That's all I knew of him. "Mama, tell me about my dad." "He was useless." I had a brother, Marcus, who lived in California. Hadn't seen him in years, and when the phones went down, I had no way of contacting him. I hadn't been in a serious relationship in a long time—not since my last partner, Louis, moved to New Orleans. I had no one to worry about. So I hid. I was safe inside my home, and had no reason to leave.

The big thing I had to deal with was time. Trapped

inside the house all day and all night with no television or Xbox or stuff like that. I had to find things to occupy my mind, because otherwise, I'd get very depressed and start thinking about walking outside, finding the nearest zombie, and letting them have a bite. The loneliness was the worst part, and that's why I was glad when I found out Alan was alive and he joined me (even if he was hopelessly straight). Alan was my neighbor. Nice enough guy. He'd worked at the plant, too, and got laid off the same time as me. Alan took a gig with a temp agency. Did odd jobs like flagging traffic and loading trucks. Some days they had work for him, some days they didn't. He barely scraped by, but he'd never once let his spirits get down. He was a funny, jovial person. After he'd moved in (because his house wasn't as secure) my loneliness vanished.

. But eventually, with his added presence, supplies went quicker than I'd imagined. With the power out, the food in the fridge had spoiled and the kitchen smelled like the zombies. I still had plenty of beer, canned goods, and packaged foods. Had plenty of water, too. We pissed in empty beer bottles so that the toilet water would remain untainted. I figured we could drink from the commode if necessary.

When we ran out of food, we had to venture out.

We showed up at the Safeway's parking lot in the middle of the night and found a dozen other well-armed people with the same plan. We grabbed two shopping carts and joined in before the shelves were picked clean. The cops weren't around, and neither were the zombies. The other looters ignored us, busy making due for themselves. Four of them stuck together in a group. The others appeared to be loners.

The meat department and the produce aisles

smelled like an open sewer. The stench of rotting vege-
tation and spoiled meat hung thick in the air. I heard a
droning buzz, and noticed that the butcher's display
cases were covered with fat, sluggish flies. Thousands
of tiny white worms burrowed through rancid steaks
and hamburger and pork chops. I remember wondering as I watched them if Hamelin's Revenge could
spread to insects—mosquitoes, ticks, or other blood-
suckers. I hoped not. If it could spread to them or to
the birds, then we were pretty much fucked.

But then again, we were pretty much fucked anyway.

The fruit and vegetables in the produce department
were covered with fuzz and slime and more flies. We
held our breath when we passed through the aisle, and
again when we cut through the dairy products section.
Exploded cardboard milk cartons were thick with
green-blue mold, and the stench was overwhelming. A
fat man in a soiled T-shirt sat on the floor, his back
against one of the coolers, and ate spoiled milk with a
spoon, scooping it from the carton like cottage cheese.

"Hey," Alan said, "you're gonna get sick, dude. That
shit will kill you."

The man smiled sadly. "I hope so. I ain't got the guts
to shoot myself, or to let one of those things bite me."

"Suicide?" I frowned. "Why die at all?"

The man shoveled another spoonful of sludge into his
mouth. It dribbled down his chin as he replied. "Don't
you guys see? We only got two options. We can join
them or we can feed them. Either way, we're dead."

A tear slid down his cheek. We walked away without another word.

"He's just given up," Alan said when we were out of
earshot.

"Fuck that," I said. "I'm going to fight."

"You ever wonder why?"

"Why what?"

"Why we fight? Why we sit in your house going stir crazy? I mean, what's the alternative? Shit ain't gonna get better. It's just gonna get worse. Why bother?"

I didn't have an answer for him.

Alan and I filled our carts with bottled water; canned vegetables, fruit, and meat; dry goods like cereal and oatmeal; batteries; aspirin; hydrogen peroxide; anti-bacterial cream; bandages; vitamins; cigarette lighters; matches; and other things we could use. He grabbed a few small propane cylinders for my grill, but I made him put them back. Even if we'd had fresh meat or veggies to put on the grill, the smell of cooking would attract predators—living and otherwise.

A fly landed on Alan's forearm as he reached for a box of granola bars. He gave a small, disgusted cry and slapped at it. When he took his hand away, the insect was squashed all over his arm. He let it fall to the floor, and then wiped his arm on his shirt. I wondered if he'd been thinking the same thing I had about the bugs.

"You ready, Lamar?" He shoved his cart forward.

"Yeah," I said. "Let's go home."

"Home?" He snorted. "Is that what it is these days?"

I didn't answer.

We now had enough goods in our two carts to last us a month. Maybe more if we rationed. I figured we'd hunker down and stay barricaded inside my house and wait to see what happened next. On our way to the exit, I added a case of warm beer almost as an after-thought. We passed by the cash registers. It felt weird, not paying. Then we got the hell out of there. Our fellow looters weren't arguing with each other, but the whole place had an underlying mood of fear. It felt like any moment, the whole store could explode.

Or the zombies could show up.

We were on our way back home. The streets were deserted, except for abandoned vehicles; most of them wrecked or shot up. The damp pavement shined; it had rained earlier in the day. With the power out, there were no lights to mark our way, but the moon was full and round. Its dull glow was strangely comforting. Broken glass crunched under our feet. The wheel on Alan's cart squeaked. Somewhere, a dog barked. A distant gunshot echoed off the buildings. A plane passed overhead, red and blue lights blinking in the darkness. I wondered who was on it and where they were going. The wind shifted, bringing the smell of decay. It was early August and the days were sweltering, the nights barely tolerable. The heat really compounded the stench of the dead, but that was a good thing. You could smell them coming before you saw them. We sped up our pace.

An undead cat lay twitching in the road, unable to move. Its spine had been crushed and a fresh tire tread stood out in its burst stomach. On the sidewalk, something that might have been a dead crow had congealed into a puddle of tissue. Nose wrinkling, Alan steered his shopping cart around the mess, and the squeaky wheel squealed in protest. I glanced at the worms squirming in the bird's remains and wondered again if they were alive or dead.

The short breeze died down and the heat returned—as did the stench. We stayed aware, and kept looking over our shoulders. The wheel on my shopping cart kept going crooked, making it a real pain in the ass to push. Every time I hit a stone or piece of broken glass,

I had to shove extra hard. When we came across a cracked and rutted section of sidewalk, I wheeled the cart into the street. As we passed by a sewer drain, I noticed a severed head lying against the curb, right over the grating. A few flaps of flesh hung below the chin, but that was it. Water swirled past the head, trickling down into the drain. As we watched, a black tongue slithered from its mouth like a slug. The blue eyes turned up to watch us pass.

"Should we kill it?" Alan asked.

"It's already dead."

"You know what I mean."

I shrugged. "Why bother. It can't hurt anybody. It's just a head."

"Fucking creepy."

"Yeah."

"How long you figure it can survive like that?"

"Until it rots away, I guess. It doesn't have a stomach or anything, but look at it. I bet if we stuck our fingers down there, it would snap at us. Whatever this disease does, these things operate on instinct. Kind of like a shark. All a shark does is swim and eat. All these things do is walk and eat. It can't walk anymore. But it's still hungry. Bet it stays hungry until its brain dissolves."

Alan stared down at the head. "Wonder if they think."

I didn't reply, because I didn't know. Alan cocked his foot back and kicked the head like a football. It sailed off into the night. There was a wet splat as it bounced off the hood of an abandoned car.

"Field goal." Alan grinned. "I should play for the Ravens."

"Come on," I said. "Let's get this stuff home while the coast is still clear."

We'd gone two more blocks when it happened. Alan

was armed with a sword. He'd picked it up during a vacation in Tijuana. It was a cheap piece of junk, but he'd sharpened the blade and practiced with it in my kitchen. He was pretty good at slicing cantaloupes in half, but he hadn't had the opportunity to try it on a zombie. I was carrying a pistol. I don't know what kind. As I said, I was never much of a gun aficionado. During the dealership robbery, I'd used a Ruger .22 pistol, purchased hot downtown. Bought a box of ammo to go with it. I'd thrown both into the harbor afterward. When things broke down a few weeks later, I'd wished I still had it. This new gun was a revolver. I knew that much. Didn't know anything else, except that if I pulled the trigger, I'd shoot something. I'd picked it up off a dead guy lying in the middle of the intersection. We'd come across him on our way to the grocery store. After some experimentation, I figured out how to get the cylinder open. There were four bullets inside.

Like Alan and his sword, I hadn't had to use them yet.

Until that zombie bitch shuffled out of the bushes . . .

Here's the thing about zombies. You can get the fuck away from them easily enough. They're usually quiet, but they're also slow and stupid. You see them coming, so it's real easy to run away. And like I said earlier, even if you don't see them, you can usually smell the fuckers. Ever smell roadkill? It's the same thing, except mobile. But that night, the breeze kept shifting. First, it would blow off the Chesapeake Bay and away from us. Then it would switch, but that was no better, because the stench of decay would get so strong you couldn't tell if it was a zombie approaching you or just the city itself—a giant graveyard full of rotting corpses.

We passed by a small row house with a withered, brown hedge out front. The windows were broken. The aluminum siding was splattered with gore. The zombie must have come from behind the hedge, because that was the only spot to hide. We didn't see her, didn't smell her, until she'd latched on to Alan.

He was behind me, talking in hushed tones about getting out of the city and heading for the wilderness—the woods in Pennsylvania or southern Maryland or maybe down to Ocean City. I was against it. Thought we should just stay inside my place. We didn't know shit about what was going on elsewhere. What if the woods were full of infected animals? I waited for Alan to reply. His shopping cart coasted past me and out into the street. At the same time, he started screaming.

I let go of my cart and whipped around. The zombie clung to Alan, scratching and biting. This close, her stench made me gag. She wrapped her swollen, rotting arms around Alan like an exuberant lover and then clambered onto his back. She held on tightly. He buckled under her weight, but managed to maintain his footing. Her feet dangled off the ground. She wore no shoes or socks and her toes were caked with filth.

Alan dropped his sword. It clanged onto the pavement. Panicked, I could only watch as he hunched over, beating at the harpy clinging to his back. The zombie moaned and he shrieked. Her cracked fingernails raked at his arm and neck, ripping his skin. She leaned forward and her teeth snapped shut on his cheek. The zombie jerked her head back and Alan's flesh stretched like soft taffy. Alan screamed again, and even in the darkness, I could see the blood welling up inside his mouth. His skin stretched even farther, pulled taught, and then tore. His flapping cheek dangled from the zombie's clenched teeth. His screams turned into a gurgle. The entire time, the zombie didn't make a sound.

It was then that I remembered the gun. It had been clenched in my hand the whole time, but I'd been so fucking overwhelmed with shock and fear that I'd forgotten about it. The zombie's head was thrown back away from Alan's left shoulder. She was chewing the piece of meat while he thrashed and spun. Blood streamed down his neck, soaking his clothing. His skin looked garish and pale, and I saw his teeth and his tongue flopping around in the ragged hole. Amazingly, he didn't collapse. He kept beating at her, making gobbling sounds in his throat. When he spun around again, I raised the pistol. The zombie's head darted forward for another bite.

I stepped close, put the gun against her forehead and pulled the trigger. At the same time, I turned my face away, closed my eyes and kept my mouth shut tight, pursing my lips together so that no blood would splatter into my mouth. The pistol jumped in my grip. There was an explosion. Over the zombie's stench, I smelled burned hair and gun smoke.

The zombie went limp, slumped, and then slid to the asphalt like a sack of cement. Alan collapsed to his knees. He tried to scream again, but the sound was garbled. He sounded like a wild animal. His eyes rolled up at me, wide and horrified. Sweat and blood covered what was left of his face. He tried to speak, but I could barely understand him.

"Shloo emee . . ."

"Oh, fuck." I backed away from him. Alan was dead. Even if I managed to stop the bleeding and somehow patch up his face, he'd been bitten.

Hamelin's Revenge was already coursing through his veins.

I heard the sound of tinkling glass from a nearby alley. The zombies were on the move, attracted by the gunshot.

"Laarr," Alan slurred. "Shloo eeee."

Lamar, shoot me. . . .

I raised the gun. My hands trembled.

"I'm sorry, man. I am so fucking sorry."

I did as he asked. I shot him.

Like I said, things have changed. People have changed. Me included. I didn't even look away. The gunshot echoed into the night. Somewhere, another dog barked. Another zombie shuffled into sight. When it saw me, it grinned and made a low moaning noise. Blinking away tears, I raised the pistol, and then lowered it again. The zombie was too far away to shoot with accuracy and I didn't want to waste bullets.

I forgot about the shopping carts and ran home. I saw more zombies, but stayed out of their reach. They lurched out of alleyways and stumbled out of houses. I didn't see anybody else who was still alive. When a rat skittered by me and disappeared behind a parked car, I nearly screamed. I didn't know if it was dead or alive. I wondered if I should consider myself lucky to be alive, or cursed because I wasn't dead yet. Of course, if I were dead, then I'd be a zombie. I wondered if they knew—remembered—who they'd been.

Then I decided that I wasn't ready to find out yet.

I ran on; racing death.

- SHOULD YOU IGNORE YOUR CHILD'S
  CRYING AT BEDTIME?

- IS IT ALL RIGHT TO SPANK YOUR CHILD?

- WHAT ARE THE BEST WAYS TO DEVELOP
  YOUR CHILD'S IMAGINATION?

- HOW DO YOU HANDLE TEMPER TANTRUMS?
- DOES A WORKING MOTHER JEOPARDIZE
  HER CHILD'S SECURITY?

These are only a few of the vitally important questions answered in HOW TO PARENT. Here is an eminently practical guide to dealing with every key problem you and your child will encounter in his first five years; here is an exciting approach to child-rearing that has become for the parents of today what Ginott was to the 60s and Spock to the 50s.

DR. FITZHUGH DODSON is an internationally renowned psychologist whose best-selling books *How to Father, How to Parent,* and *How to Discipline—With Love,* have received acclaim from educators and parents all over the world.

The father of a girl and two boys, Dr. Dodson draws from his parental experience as well as from his more than twenty years of professional work, both as a psychologist and an educator. He has appeared on numerous TV and radio shows, and is in great demand throughout the country as a lecturer.

A member of Phi Beta Kappa, Dr. Dodson is an honors graduate of John Hopkins and Yale universities, and received his Ph.D. from the University of Southern California.

How to Parent

by Dr. Fitzhugh Dodson

Foreword by *Louise Bates Ames, Ph.D.*
Keynote by *Charles M. Schulz*
Edited by *Sylvia H. Cross*

A SIGNET BOOK from
NEW AMERICAN LIBRARY
TIMES MIRROR

SIGNET, SIGNET CLASSICS, MENTOR, PLUME, MERIDIAN AND NAL
BOOKS *are published by The New American Library, Inc.,
1633 Broadway, New York, New York 10019*

FIRST PRINTING, FEBRUARY, 1971

19 20 21 22 23 24

PRINTED IN THE UNITED STATES OF AMERICA

Dedication

To my mother, a teacher, and my father, a stock broker, who loved me and gave me my start in life.

To my grandmother, whose prayers first directed me into the ministry.

To my grandfather, who taught me the meaning of old-fashioned integrity.

To my Uncle North, who by his own example instructed me in both courage and *chutzpah*.

To my Aunt Maryon, who showed me what true graciousness is in a woman.

To my "second mother," Adelyn Breeskin, who opened doors for me to the world of culture.

To my "second fathers":

Norman Atkins, from whom I learned much about people and my own potential self

and Howard Goheen, who taught me how to weld and work with my hands

. . . to all these wonderful parents and parent-figures, I dedicate this book on how to parent.

Fitzhugh Dodson

"None but a mule denies his family"
—old Syrian proverb

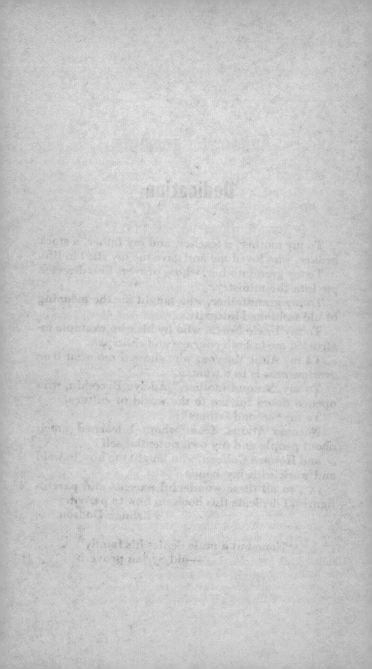

Acknowledgements

To these people, my special thanks:

Writing this book has impressed upon me the fact that no author can ever justifiably claim to be a "self-made man." Every book is the product of the thought and work of many people, and I want to express my special thanks to those persons who have contributed to my thinking in this book.

I am grateful to the thousands of psychologists and behavioral scientists in many different countries of the world who have studied children and their parents, and upon whose experimental and clinical research I have drawn in this book.

This book grew out of a series of lectures to parents at La Primera Preschool in Torrance, California, which I have given every year beginning in 1963. I have learned much from the comments and questions of all of those parents. I also learned a great deal from the mothers who took two of my courses in "The First Five Years of Life," which I gave as part of the La Primera "Coffee Cup College."

Psychotherapy has aptly been described as a "window into the secret places of the soul," and I am grateful to my patients, both children and adults, who have allowed me the privilege of looking inside that window. In the course of our work together they have taught me a great deal about the human situation.

I wish to acknowledge my debt to the late Dorothy Baruch, whose books have contributed so much to my own thinking about the science and art of parenting. And to the late Paul Tillich, with whom it was my privilege to study, and whose thinking has been the fountainhead for much of modern day humanistic psychology. I am also profoundly grateful to Dr. Seward Hiltner, who first got me interested in psychology; to Dr. Carl Rogers, from whose books and lectures

vii

I have learned a great deal about what it means to be a person; and to Dr. Volney Faw, who incorporated the principles of Dr. Rogers in his own life and teaching. I want to express my gratitude also to Dr. Lee Travis, another of my fine teachers, who taught me a great deal about dynamic psychology.

I want to express my appreciation also to my mentors in the art of writing: the late Halford E. Luccock, in whose classes I learned much about the witty and incisive use of the English language; Rudolph Flesch, whose books have been for me a lifelong course in the art of readable writing; William C. Chambliss, who taught me, along with many other things about nonfiction writing, the difference between a "letter to the editor" and a book; Bernice FitzGibbon, whose book *Macy's, Gimbels, & Me* is a one-volume encyclopedia in the art of communicating ideas; and Erik Barnouw, Al Crews, Frank Papp, and Everett Parker, all of whom taught me a great deal about writing for radio and TV.

My sincere thanks to all who have helped very specifically in enabling the original rough manuscript to grow into the completed book. To Elaine Magness and Mildred Schultz, for excellent and, at times, pressure-cooker typing. To Jean Beckman for meet-the-deadline xeroxing.

To all those who have read the manuscript and made helpful suggestions: Janet Switzer, Ph.D.; Allen Darbonne, Ph.D. and his wife Ginny; Al Bach, Ph.D. and his wife Ramah; Bob LaCrosse, Ph.D. and Jean LaCrosse, Ph.D.; Digby Diehl; Mac and Kate Friedlander; Carol Kinnon; Jeanne Harris; Stanley and Maureen Moore; Tom and Gladys Eason; David and Ginger Tulk; Carl and Ann Brown; Charles and Bernadette Randall; Mel and Joan Lindsey; and George and Retta McCoy. To Sheila Weber who helped with the annotated children's book list in the appendix.

To Charles M. Schulz, who has so generously lent his name and talents to my book, so that hundreds of thousands of people will read it who otherwise would probably not have done so, a gratitude which is truly impossible to put into words.

To Bil Keane, wonderful father, loving husband, and excellent cartoonist, my appreciation for illustrating this book, because he has so perfectly expressed in carbon form what I have said in written form.

To my wife Elise and to my children Robin, Randy and Rusty, all of whom have taught me a great deal about how to parent, and to whom I can never adequately express my thanks.

And finally, to my very skillful "midwife" at Nash Publishing, my editor, Sylvia Cross, who has seen this book all the way through from conception to delivery.

I am profoundly grateful to all of these people. Without them, I could not have written this book.

FITZHUGH DODSON

MONTE VISTA

AUTUMN, 1969

Foreword

New parents have a great deal to learn from those already experienced in what Dr. Fitzhugh Dodson calls the art of parenting. And when he who already has the experience is also a child psychologist and psychological consultant of his own nursery school, he inevitably has a good deal to share.

As Dr. Dodson points out, producing a child does not automatically provide wisdom or effectiveness in the art of being a parent. To do a really good job, it is essential to know quite a bit about the way children grow.

This knowledge comes to many only through experience, and many mistakes will be made along the way. Some of these can be avoided if one knows in advance a little something about the common path which all children follow as they approach maturity.

This author tells a good deal about that common path, in solidly developmental terms. He also emphasizes that it is not enough to know about successive stages and then sit back and wait for them to occur. Knowledge is useful chiefly in that it allows a mother or father to know how most effectively to meet and deal with the behaviors which occur at each successive stage.

That Dr. Dodson and I are diametrically opposed on certain vital matters—I think breast-feeding, when possible, is essential; I consider teaching reading to preschoolers unessential—does not detract, in my opinion, from the value of his general presentation. Such differences of opinion perhaps exist between almost any two child psychologists, as they do between any two parents.

Dr. Dodson does not pretend to preach the gospel. Rather than preach, he generously shares his own experiences as a parent, and his opinions as a psychologist. He does not ask you to go with him every step of the way. Parents should use information in a book such as this *only* if it helps. I believe that much in this particular book *will* help.

Most parents enjoy general information about child behavior, but what most really search for is specific advice about what to do and what not to do. This book is generous in such advice. The chapter on discipline is especially useful in this respect. Advice about providing environmental control, about differentiating between natural and artificial consequences, and about giving a positive rather than a negative model, as well as nine recommended rules of discipline and twelve *Thou Shalt Not's*, should be required reading for every parent. And for good measure, the author throws in as a final aid to any struggling parent, a lively Baker's Dozen Guideline for raising children.

I particularly like Dr. Dodson's calm, sensible and highly rational approach to the subject of television. He clearly appreciates what TV does contribute, and does not castigate it unduly for what it does not do, does not view with alarm, does not accept the popular notion that children become violent just because they watch violent actions on the screen.

In fact, throughout, his style is calm and easy, almost belying the fact that what he has to say is of the utmost importance.

Most any parent will welcome the very real help in the art of parenting which this book provides. And children need all the good parenting they can get in these days of social change, when growing up is by no means easy.

I heartily agree with the author that "you can learn many scientific facts about children, but if you don't have the *feel of childhood* you must re-establish contact with the child within yourself, the child you once were. This is your best single guide to bringing up your own children. Without the feel of childhood we adults will misuse and distort the scientific facts because we will be viewing them entirely through adult eyes."

I further agree with and appreciate his stress on the fact that "each of your children is a unique combination of genes which has never before existed on this planet and never will be found again. . . . The most important thing you can do for your child is to stand back and allow him to actualize the unique and potential self which is unfolding within him."

The author is right when he emphasizes the fact that contemporary society gives practically no training in how to be a good parent, in spite of the fact that a parent is the most important teacher his child will ever have. He is right in his admission that there is no harder job in our society than being that unique combination of twenty-four-hour-a-day child psychologist and teacher that we call a parent.

Parenting is a learning process for us all.

Each of us has to do the job himself, but many will be grateful for the solid help offered in this vital book with its unusual title—*How to Parent.*

LOUISE BATES AMES, PH.D.

GESELL INSTITUTE

OF CHILD DEVELOPMENT

Contents

3
Toddlerhood 74

A learning stage: self-confidence or self-doubt • The Age of Exploration • Childproofing your house • Toys are the textbooks of toddlerhood: the necessity of play • Outdoor play • Indoor play • Language development: passive and active, expressive jargon • Your home—a school for learning • Feeding problems • Toilet training • Your child's attitude toward his body

4
First Adolescence Part One 98

Your child's timetable for development • A stage of transition and disequilibrium • Self-identity vs. social conformity • Acquiring a sense of selfhood • Parental control • Child discipline • The distinction between actions and feelings • Feelings cannot be ignored • The feedback technique • Temper tantrums • How conscience develops

5
First Adolescence Part Two 121

New language ability • Answering a child's questions • TV as an educational toy • Jealousy in children: sibling rivalry • Minimizing feelings of jealousy • Toilet training your child • Bowel training • Bladder control • How mothers feel about toilet training • Play equipment for the first adolescent • Learning through play • Nonverbal activities as expression of feelings • Play with other children: solitary, parallel, associate, cooperative • Quiet play • Bedtime ritual • A father's role

6

Preschool Part One 155

The three-year-old: a "Golden Age" of equilibrium • The four-year-old: "out-of-bounds" • The five-year-old: a delightful age • Fulfilling biological needs • Outlets for energy • Muscular coordination: laterality and directionality • A control system for his impulses • The parental role in impulse control • Separation from mother • The new world of his peers • Learning to express his feelings: repression vs. expression • Gender identity: male or female • Identification with mother • Sexual discovery • How to help your child develop a healthy sexual attitude • How you can help affirm the gender identity of your child • Father

7

Preschool Part Two 181

Developing basic attitudes toward sexuality • A positive sex education • Answering children's questions on sex: honesty, directness, openness • Books on sex • Sex play • Nudity • The family romance • Resolving the family triangle • How you can help • Sensitivity to intellectual stimulation • Basic learning skills • Selecting a nursery school • Criteria for selection: teachers, equipment, curriculum • Kindergarten • What your child has learned (Developmental accomplishments)

8

Can You Teach a Dolphin to Type? 203

Meaning and purpose of *discipline* • Reinforcing good behavior in your child • Nine principles for teaching your child desirable emotional habits

A Note to Parents

When you become a mother, you join the ranks of an absolutely unique, twenty-four-hour-a-day profession: a parent.

It is unfortunate we do not have a verb in our language that describes what you do day in and day out, every day of your life, as a parent. So I'm going to make up a new verb: *to parent*.

I'm going to define this new verb as a dictionary might define it: *to parent*—"to use, with tender loving care, all the information science has accumulated about child psychology in order to raise happy and intelligent human beings."

This new verb does *not* describe the simple biological act of giving birth to a child. And it does *not* describe the raising of that child by the usual trial and error methods. The raising of a child is a complex and difficult proposition. But it is one of the most fulfilling tasks in the world. The most important gift a mother can give to the world is a child who has been raised to be a happy and secure human being.

Parenting involves adding scientific information to the loving concern of a mother. The science of parenting can give you enormous help in raising your child. Armed with the accumulated knowledge of science about what goes on inside the mind of her child, a loving and concerned mother can learn how to raise that child to become a happy and intelligent adult. That's what you do when you parent.

But there's a catch to all this.

21

Our contemporary society gives practically no training in how to parent. We do not trust a secretary into an office with no training in typing or shorthand, and say to her: "You're a secretary now—go to it!" But when a woman becomes a mother, it's as if society suddenly says to her: "You're a parent now. We haven't told you much about how to parent; but go to it, and do the very best you can!"

Parenting means being a special kind of psychologist and a special kind of teacher.

You are a child psychologist because you need to understand the psychology of your own children. You may be a good child psychologist, an average child psychologist, or even a poor child psychologist. But whether you like the idea or not, that's you: Mrs. Child Psychologist!

You are also the most important teacher your children will ever have. You are their first teacher. The things you teach them (even the things you do not realize you are teaching them) will be more important "lessons" than they will ever learn in school.

But if you are like most women, you have probably had little training or background to qualify you to handle the job of being either a child psychologist or a teacher. You may have studied many subjects in school. But unless you have been extremely fortunate, you have probably studied little that would train you to understand babies and young children.

Ordinarily child psychologists and teachers work an eight-hour day. They have regular time off from their work every day and every weekend. They also take an annual vacation. You don't. That in itself makes your job much harder. In addition, child psychologists and teachers work with many different children. Their feelings about the children they work with are thus more detached than those of a mother, since their feelings are spread out over a number of children. And because the children they work with are not their own, they are also not as emotionally involved in the process of understanding them and coping with them.

There is no harder job in our society than being that unique combination of a twenty-four-hour-a-day child psychologist and teacher that we call a parent.

PARENTING IS A LEARNING PROCESS

Parenting is a learning process for all of us. When we learn any new skill—whether it is driving a car, playing a musical instrument, or raising a child—we learn by making mistakes. But the most wasteful kind of learning is sheer trial and error.

Suppose you have never played bridge in your life, and you decide to learn. It is barely possible to learn to play bridge by gritting your teeth and going at it willy-nilly. But what a miserable way for you to learn! How needlessly unhappy you would make yourself, struggling to find out the intricacies of bidding and strategy all by yourself. A much easier and better way would be to have someone with knowledge and experience teach you.

I want to pass on to you what I have learned from more than twenty years of professional work, and from my own experience as a parent.

If a book is going to be a successful communication from author to reader, it must have some of the elements of a good conversation. So I have tried to anticipate where you may have questions about what I have to say. And I have tried to guess where certain scientific facts may seem farfetched when you first encounter them.

I have tried to write this book in an informal, conversational way, as if the two of us were chatting over a cup of coffee. For example, I mention my experiences with my own children from time to time. And although this book is based upon the experimental and clinical research of many behavioral scientists, I have not documented all of the scientific evidence on which a particular point may rest. I have, however, mentioned a few key research studies from time to time; but I have kept such a documentation at a minimum. I know that most people don't like a book cluttered up with a lot of scholarly footnotes and references to scientific experiments.

I am particularly concerned with two types of mothers who will be reading this book. The first is a mother who has never had a child. In certain respects, she will be reading this book at the best possible time. She can learn many things which will be helpful to her, *before* she has to cope with the raising of a real live baby.

However, you cannot learn to raise a baby exclusively by reading a book, any more than you can learn to drive a car by reading a manual. You have to learn to *apply* the book to the actual real-life situation of your baby. And your baby is going to be like no other baby in the world. He is a truly unique creature.

This book, or any other book on child raising, can be only a rough-and-ready guide to raising your baby. A mother knows her baby in ways that no one else can know him. So if what you read goes strongly against your feelings as a mother at certain points, forget what the book says and follow your feelings.

There is a tendency in all of us when we are learning to do something for the first time to feel unsure of ourselves and to want someone else to lay down hard-and-fast rules for what we should do. As we acquire more experience, we become more confident. We see places where hard-and-fast rules need to be changed to fit individual situations.

Speaking from my own experience as a parent, I can guarantee that you will feel more confident in raising your second or third child than you will in raising your first. One of the reasons why we feel more confident with our second or third is that we have learned from raising our first. With our first child we win a few and lose a few. We make some mistakes and we have some good times. Usually we seem to make a few more mistakes with our first child than with later ones. When you first realize that you have handled something awkwardly with your child, then you know you are truly a member of the Club of Mistake-Makers that we call parents. Welcome to the club!

That brings me naturally to the second type of mother who will be reading this book. She has a child under five years of age, but also has one or more children who are older. As she reads various sections of this book, she may be thinking to herself: "I wish I had read this book a few years ago! I see now how I goofed when Jennie was a toddler. I did such and so, and I can see now that that wasn't the best way to handle the situation." Then she may start feeling guilty and blaming herself.

I hope you won't do that. No parent deserves blame. All of us are trying to raise our children as well as we possibly can. Considering the fact that most of us have absolutely no training in parenthood, I think we do a remarkably good job! Given our lack of real training for the position, it's a wonder our youngsters turn out as well as they do. So I hope you will be gentle on yourself, particularly for any mistakes you feel you have made with your first child.

I can assure you, from hard-won personal experience, that you can have a Ph.D. in psychology and still make mistakes in raising your first child. Hopefully, you will make fewer mistakes with your second child, and so on down the line. My own experiences remind me of the story of the psychologist who started out with six theories and no children, and ended up with six children and no theories! Since I have only three children, you can easily see that I still have three theories left. Parents tell me that by the time a fifth or sixth child arrives, they could care less what mistakes they are making. I personally believe that every mother of four or more children deserves an automatic Parent's Purple Heart. If all four children happen to be boys, she should get the Purple Heart *plus* the Congressional Medal of Honor.

Guilt feelings are not productive of good parenting. All of us need to take the attitude that we are doing the best we can in raising our children. The very fact that you are taking the time to read this book on child raising shows that you truly care about your child, otherwise you wouldn't be doing this on his behalf.

MISCONCEPTIONS ABOUT CHILD PSYCHOLOGY

Over the years, as parents have talked to me about child raising in my clinical sessions or in discussion periods at lectures I have given or classes I have taught, I have discovered that many parents have major misconceptions about modern psychology. I think it would be helpful for me to deal with some of these misconceptions before going any further. So before we talk about what psychology *does* teach about raising children, let's talk a little about what psychology *does not* believe.

Modern psychology *does not* believe it is good for parents to be permissive, if by permissive we mean letting the child do whatever he feels like doing. No sensible psychologist has ever advocated such a strange idea. But incredible as it may seem, I have actually known parents who let their children scribble on the good walls of their home with crayons because they thought it would be psychologically harmful to stop them! What is really happening in most of these cases is that the parent is afraid of saying no to her child and tries to use modern psychology as a rationalization for her fear of being firm with her child.

The second notion to which modern psychology *does not* adhere is that as children go through certain stages of development, the parent must sit back helplessly and let that stage of growth take its course. It is true that children typically do go through certain stages of development, especially in the preschool years. The parent who expects a four-year-old to act like a three-year-old, or who attempts to handle a four-year-old the way she handles a three-year-old, is asking for trouble. However, it is one thing for parents to recognize that their children go through stages of development; it is quite another thing for them to feel helpless and unable to *modify* that stage of development in any way. I have seen parents tolerate obnoxious behavior on the part of their children, with the rationalization, "I guess he's just going through a stage." At this point, the parent usually shrugs his shoulders hopelessly, as if to say, "And absolutely nothing can be done about it."

A parent is not helpless. How a parent handles a particular stage in a child's development has a great deal to do with how successful the child will be in coping with that stage. In this book, I devote a great deal of space to the different stages of development, because I believe it is important for parents to know as much about them as possible.

Many parents also have the impression' that modern psychology teaches that you should not spank children. Some psychologists and psychiatrists have actually stated this idea in print. However, as a psychologist, I believe it is impossible to raise children effectively—particularly aggressive, forceful boys—without spanking them. This does not mean that *any* kind of spanking is all right for a child.

I remember speaking to a parents' group one night, and then several weeks later running across one of the mothers in a supermarket. She came up to me and said, "Ever since you said in that speech it was okay to spank children, a lot of our kids have been getting it—but good!" I got the distinct impression that some parents must have felt, "Dr. Dodson says it's okay—get out the Chinese water torture and the thumb screws, Dad—we're going to fix little Murgatroyd good and proper now!"

In the chapter on discipline, I will explain just what kind of spanking is positive and what kind is negative. But spanking is a necessary and inevitable ingredient in raising psychologically healthy children.

There is another widespread notion that the "good" parent is the parent who never gets upset or ruffled. I have never met such a parent. I am certainly not such a parent myself. All parents have emotional ups and downs. There are times when we feel great inside, when we can handle smoothly even the most difficult behavior of our offspring. But there are other times when the slightest annoying thing a child does is enough to set us roaring at him.

It is important for parents to give honest expression to their feelings and emotions. Psychology *does not* say we should feel calm and serene all the time. If that were so, psychology would be demanding the emotionally impossible of parents.

People often think a psychologist will tell them how they should *feel* as parents and what scientifically sound *attitudes* they should have toward raising children. It is unfortunate that a few psychologists have given people reason to believe this. The catch is, people cannot help worrying or having any feelings other than those they have. Our feelings are spontaneous, and our thoughts come into our minds unbidden. We have no control over them.

I will make no attempt to tell parents how they should *feel*. Instead, I will tell them what they should *do*. Your actions are subject to your control; your feelings are not. I will give you information about children that will help you to better understand your own youngsters. And I will suggest that you *do* certain things in handling your children so that they will grow up to be happy and intelligent persons.

It may be that some of you simply cannot do the things suggested in this book or other books on child psychology. You may find that in spite of earnest efforts on your part, your children are out of hand and you are at the end of your rope. Such a situation indicates that you probably need professional help. It means that you need more than reading this or any other book on psychology or child raising. Your feeling of desperation shows that there are emotional blocks inside you which only a professional can help you with. If you find that this describes your situation, then by all means consult a professional in the mental-health field—a competent psychologist, psychiatrist, or psychiatric social worker.

Having dealt with these common misconceptions about modern psychology, let's now talk about what a parent needs to know about psychology.

THE IMPORTANCE OF THE FIRST FIVE YEARS

Probably the single most important fact for you to know is that *the first five years of your child's life are the most important years—the formative years.* It is not that the rest of your youngster's childhood is unimportant or that everything about him is decided by the time he reaches his sixth birthday; but there is no question that the first five years are the most important ones.

By the time a child is six years old, his basic personality structure has been formed. This basic personality he will carry with him for the rest of his life. It will determine, to a large extent, how successful he will be throughout school and in later life. His basic personality structure will largely determine how he will get along with other people, how he will feel about sex, what kind of adolescence he will have, what type of person he will marry, and how successful that marriage will be.

Not only are the first five years important in the *emotional development* of your child, but they are also important in his *intellectual development*.

Perhaps the best way to bring home to you the importance of these early years in the intellectual development of your child is to ask you this question: At what age do you think your child has developed approximately 50 percent of his intelligence? Twenty-one? Seventeen? Twelve?

The right answer is four!

Dr. Benjamin Bloom of the University of Chicago has

summarized an immense number of research studies which demonstrate the startling fact that a child develops approximately 50 percent of his intelligence by the age of four, another 30 percent by the age of eight, and the remaining 20 percent by the age of seventeen.

By the way, do not confuse *intelligence* with *information.* Obviously your child does not acquire 50 percent of the *information* he will have as an adult by the time he is four. *Intelligence* is the ability of your child to mentally manipulate and process the information he acquires. And he acquires 50 percent of his ability to mentally process information by the time he is four.

If you estimated incorrectly, don't be embarrassed. Most adults greatly underestimate both the intelligence and the learning ability of the preschool child. It used to be thought that each of us was born with a certain native intelligence, fixed by heredity, which could never be changed. Recent research shows that this is incorrect. The kind of intellectual stimulation that a child receives in the first five years of life has much to do with how intelligent he will be as an adult.

Since the first five years of your child's life are the most important years in his development, I have concentrated on early childhood in this book. Later childhood and adolescence deserve a separate book.

In the rest of this book, I am going to take a hypothetical child and trace his development from birth through these all-important early years. It would become awkward to refer to this hypothetical child as "he-or-she-whichever-the-case-may-be." So for convenience I am going to refer to the child as "he." If you have a little girl, you can mentally read "she" for "he" in the appropriate places.

And now let's talk about mothers and how they feel about a new baby.

1

Mothers and Their Feelings

Most books on raising children begin by describing what a young baby is like and how to take care of him. They overlook the feelings of the mother. I think this is a serious mistake.

Mothers I have talked to over the years, both as patients and as friends and colleagues, tell me that when their first baby is born and they bring him home from the hospital and start to take care of him, they feel very unsure of themselves. As one mother put it, "I never felt so inadequate in my whole life!"

No matter how much you have read about babies or how many Red Cross courses you have taken to try to get ready for the experience of caring for your new baby, it is still a totally new experience. The reality of it all doesn't hit you until you come home from the hospital and are actually face to face with this brand new, living, breathing thing: your new baby. There it is, twenty-four hours a day, and it won't go away!

It is a *terrific* adjustment. You have never had to cope with such a great psychological responsibility before in your entire life. It scares most new mothers to realize that for the first time in their lives they have total responsibility for the life of a tiny human being. In the face of this responsibility, which is so suddenly thrust upon them, many new mothers tend to feel inadequate and unsure of themselves.

A new mother may be so unsure of herself that every little thing tends to worry her. She has not had enough experience with young babies to know how to interpret different things that may happen. If the baby is sound asleep, he may not seem to be breathing. She rushes over to see if he's still alive! She worries if he seems to choke or have difficulty getting his milk down. Every small thing takes on great importance. A new mother is a real expert in making mountains out of molehills. She's afraid that any little deviation from what she thinks of as "normal" for a baby's eating or sleeping patterns means that something drastic is wrong! That's why many new mothers tend to phone their harassed pediatricians every hour on the hour.

The worst thing about these feelings of inadequacy is that a new mother is afraid to admit them to anybody. After all, she reasons, she's a mother now, and this is the crown and fulfillment of her life as a woman, having her first child. So what is she doing feeling so inadequate? She mentally pictures other mothers quite adequately taking care of their young babies. She thinks she must be the only one feeling this way. So she'd die before she'd admit these feelings to anybody else. If she only knew that every other new mother feels the same way, it would be very reassuring to her. Believe me, they do!

You see, the new mother has received all kinds of messages from our culture—some explicit and some implicit—which tell her that mothers are somehow magically and innately equipped with "mother love" and a "mother instinct" which enables them automatically to love and care for their babies. The trouble is that she doesn't feel that way! She doesn't feel very adequate to take care of her new baby. So she thinks that every other mother has this natural "mother instinct," and that she must be the only one that doesn't. She is so busy worrying and feeling inadequate that she is unable to sit down and reason out that there is a world of difference between *mother love* for a young baby, on the one hand, and *information* and *experience* in taking care of a young baby, on the other.

Your feelings of love for your baby will come naturally. Some mothers may feel an overwhelming rush of maternal feeling as soon as their babies are born. Other mothers may find that their maternal feelings develop more gradually. However, there is no built-in fund of information about young babies and their care which you as a woman have by "instinct." That comes from experience. And until a mother has had her first baby, she may have had very little experience in even being around babies.

In addition to feeling inadequate in caring for her new baby, there is another set of feelings which bother a new mother a great deal: feelings of resentment. Many new mothers find that they are feeling resentful of the twenty-four-hour-a-day schedule with which they are suddenly confronted. As one new mother lamented to me, "No one ever told me it would be like this!"

The new mother's whole life now seems to revolve around this little baby in the crib, and frankly she resents this. And it is entirely normal that she should. Unfortunately, nobody has adequately prepared her for the fact that she is going to feel this resentment. She thus often feels guilty that at times she actually resents her new baby, which in all other respects she loves.

The new mother needs to realize that these initial feelings of resentment toward her baby are *entirely normal*. After a period of adjustment to the unaccustomed responsibility of the new baby, these feelings of resentment will diminish and become absorbed into the overall love she feels for her baby.

There is another factor, however, which often causes a mother to resent her new baby. A mother tends to assume that a child will automatically bring her and her husband closer together. After all, they have produced this baby together, and she feels that when the baby is born, she and her husband and the baby will form a new and close-knit threesome. Unfortunately, many new mothers find that quite the opposite happens. Instead of bringing them closer together, the child seems to act as a psychological wedge which separates them. She finds that her husband is often jealous of the attention she gives the new baby. He acts more like a rival to the baby than its father. In addition, her husband may not take an active and supportive part in the psychological responsibility for the new baby. He may leave her with the feeling that 100 percent of the responsibility is hers alone. She may then resent the baby for causing this situation.

A new mother needs to work her way through these feelings of resentment and learn to accept them as a normal part of the adjustment she and her husband must make to the arrival of the baby. Each mother will need to find her own methods of bringing her family together into a new unit.

If you happen to have the kind of husband who is able to really share the psychological responsibility of your baby with you, count yourself as fortunate. Use him as a sounding board for your feelings of both inadequacy and resentment. Realize that these feelings are quite normal, and do not hesitate to talk them over with him. If you and your husband can talk out your feelings of inadequacy and resentment together, you will no longer feel that the whole burden of the new baby is resting totally on your shoulders. That in itself will be an immense relief.

Remember that for thousands of years mothers have had to overcome these twin ogres of Inadequacy and Resentment. You can do it too. It will be hard at first. You will have unpleasant times and you will probably cry a little. But the more honest you can be with yourself and your own feelings, the faster you can work your way through this period of adjustment.

Sooner or later, like millions of mothers before you, you will work your way through the psychological swamp of inadequacy and resentment and find yourself on dry land. When that happens, mother and child will assume their proper roles in a new type of "we-relationship." In the interim, there are still many things about a new baby you will have to learn by experience.

When your baby is first born he seems very tiny and fragile. Every little thing that seems out of kilter looms up in your mind as a possible major disaster. Sometimes a mother will get so panicked that she is unable to use her head or her common sense to analyze the situation. One mother said to me: "There I was a college graduate, and I spent four hours fixing a formula! I worried whether I was getting it fixed just right, and I began to doubt that I had a brain in my head."

At such times a mother is apt to forget that she has any common sense at all. So she helplessly seeks out an authority to tell her what to do. If her pediatrician isn't immediately available, she may rush to the phone and call a neighbor.

What a new mother needs to realize is that *all of these feelings are normal.* Feelings of inadequacy, panic, resentment—every new mother feels them. Welcome to the club!

It will gradually begin to dawn on you that your new baby is not as frail and fragile as you first thought. Babies have managed to survive the awkwardness and feelings of inadequacy of new mothers for thousands of years. Your new baby will survive your initial awkwardness and insecurity too.

As you gain more experience with your baby, your confidence will grow. You will hold him more comfortably and feed him more easily. By the time he's two months old you will realize that he actually is going to survive!

It is a good thing to have a relative or a paid helper come in for the first few weeks after a new mother comes home from the hospital. But even if you have help, you are simply going to have to live through the experience of assuming the psychological responsibility for your new baby essentially by yourself. Every new mother has to go through this "baptism of fire" in the first few months of her baby's life. No one can do it for her.

It helps, of course, to talk with other mothers and find out that they have the same feelings. Then you know you're not entirely alone. Expressing your feelings is good therapy for you as a new mother. So talk with other new mothers. Talk also with more experienced mothers. But don't make the mistake of trying to use your neighbor or another mother as an authority. Many new mothers, out of their feelings of panic, do precisely that. A mother who wouldn't dream of asking her next-door neighbor to diagnose mumps in her child will ask this other mother for authoritative advice about breast-feeding. Try to resist this kind of temptation. Use other mothers as helpful sounding boards for your own feelings. Don't use them as authorities. Also, don't ever forget that your baby is a unique individual. What worked just fine for Mrs. Neighbor Lady and her baby may not work at all for you.

YOUR BABY IS AS UNIQUE AS HIS
FINGERPRINTS

The uniqueness of your baby is a subject I can hardly emphasize too much. It is something I am going to stress again and again.

There is not a single other individual in the entire world whose fingerprints will match those of your baby. What is true of your baby's fingerprints is true of your baby's whole physiological and psychological being. His particular combination of genes has never before existed, and will never exist again. Don't ever forget that.

Perhaps the following analogy will help me get across my message. Suppose every single baby in the world were to be born an absolutely unique color. No two babies in the whole world would be the same. Oh, there would be similarities, of course. An orange baby would look more like another orange baby than a green baby. But every "orange" baby would be his own distinctive shade of orange. In the same way, each child in your family will be different from the others.

When I say your child is unique, I mean that he will not fit the generalized descriptions found in books on child raising. So if your baby and his behavior don't match the descriptions of the "typical" baby found in books, don't jump to the conclusion that there is something wrong with him. His eating patterns and sleeping patterns are uniquely his own. Let them be. Don't try to force him into some mental picture you have gotten from a book of what he *ought* to be like. He *is* what he is, and that's that!

Your baby is "writing" his own book on child development as he grows up. Let him do it! Each child has his own unique "life style." This life style begins as soon as he is born. My own three children, for instance, are quite different. Their differences became apparent when they were small babies.

I'd like you to stop a minute and think how wonderful it is that there is no one else in the whole world like your child. He is literally one of a kind. So learn to prize his uniqueness. Imagine that Picasso painted a special picture just for you—the only one of its kind in the world. Wouldn't you prize and cherish that picture? But even that analogy is too weak to picture adequately the uniqueness of that wonderful little baby of yours sleeping so peacefully in his crib.

However, just because I point out that your child is absolutely unique, don't get the impression that this uniqueness makes your role as a mother useless. Quite the contrary. He needs you to help him develop his uniqueness. He can't do it by himself. He needs your encouragement every step of the way. In the rest of this book I am going to help you become the kind of parent who can enable your child to develop every nuance and subtle shading of his own unique color.

The time to start respecting your child's individuality is as soon as he is born. If you can accept his own individual patterns of eating and sleeping, his babyish temperament and moods, it will be easier for you to accept his individualistic life style at later stages of development.

As a matter of fact, your child is going to be a unique individual, whether you want him to or not. Which reminds me of the classic story about Margaret Fuller and Carlyle. Margaret Fuller, in an expansive mood, once flung her arms out and exclaimed, "I accept the universe!" "Gad, she'd better!" said Carlyle.

It's that way with your child. You can't really prevent him from becoming who he really is. So why try? Interfere with his own natural life style and you will throw a monkey wrench into the works. But nevertheless, your child will still be who he is. All you will have succeeded in doing by trying to force your life style on him is to cause him to become an inhibited caricature of himself. One way or another, way down deep, he is what he is.

It will take a great burden off your shoulders if you give up trying to make your child over in your own image. Just give him the freedom to develop naturally.

The main theme of this book is that the greatest gift you can give your child is the freedom to actualize his unique potential self. He is his own unique color. Give him the freedom to be that color.

YOUR CHILD'S STAGES OF DEVELOPMENT

Before I get to your newly born baby and how to take care of him, I want to say a few words about children and their stages of development.

All children go through different stages of development. This is one of the most basic research findings of behavioral scientists in the past forty years.

The stages of development in the first five years are more dramatically different than they are in later childhood. For example, the changes that take place in a child between his second and third birthday are enormous compared to the changes that take place in a child between his eighth and ninth birthday.

Each child goes through the same general stages of development. However, each child goes through them in his own way, and on his own time schedule. A stage which one child might go through in a year, another child will go through in six or eight months. The time spent in each stage of development will vary enormously.

I want to emphasize that the stages of development cannot be rushed or hurried. A child has to go through each developmental stage at his own pace, and nothing on God's green earth can rush him. So don't try.

Each developmental stage provides a foundation for the next stage. It's like a house. The strength of the foundation will determine how the first story can be built. How the first story is built will determine the second story. What happens to a child at age one says something about what will happen to him at age two. What happens at age two will say something about what will happen at age three, and so on.

The most important developmental stages your child will go through are those which take place in the first five years of life. To use our analogy of the house, these five years form the basic foundation. It is during the developmental stages of the first five years that your child's basic personality structure is formed.

The single most important factor in forming your child's basic personality structure is his self-concept. A child's self-concept is the mental picture he has of himself. It's like a mental map. And how a child behaves depends on the mental maps by which he is guided. Your child's most important mental map is his self-concept. His success in school and in later life depends to a large extent upon it.

Recently, I gave an intelligence test to a twelve-year-old boy. Part of the test consisted of putting pieces of a jigsaw puzzle together. He tried it, but quickly gave up, saying, "I can't do it. It's too hard." His self-concept told him that if something is hard and you have difficulty with it, then you give up.

There are children who see themselves through the eyeglasses of their self-concept something like this: "I'm a good boy. I'm likable. I can do things. I can try new things and be successful." These are the kids who are no trouble to anybody, in school and out. These are the children who can learn the most.

But there are other children who see themselves through their self-concept like this: "I'm not very good. I'm not likable. I can't do things, especially new things. There's no sense trying, because I won't succeed anyway." These are the youngsters who are problems to themselves and others. These are the children who have the most difficulty learning.

Your child's self-concept will be the key idea presented in this book. Step by step, I will show you how the self-concept begins in infancy and develops through the first five years of life. And step by step, I will show you how to develop a strong and healthy self-concept in your child.

2

Infancy

Your child's self-concept begins as soon as he is born.

Think of the self-concept as a pair of eyeglasses. With each of the four stages of development to age six, your child adds a new lens to his eyeglasses. The lens of each stage of development is superimposed over the lens of the preceding stage.

Let's examine the first eyeglasses of infancy. This stage begins when your child is born and continues until he is able to walk. For most children this period will cover the first year of life. For some children who are early walkers, it will cover the first nine months; for later walkers, it will cover the first sixteen months.

Some mothers might look at a baby in this initial stage and say to themselves: "Well, nothing too important is going on. After all, a baby is just a baby. He spends most of his time sleeping. When he wakes up, he is fed. His diapers are changed. He is bathed. That's the life of a baby. He's too young to learn much. Later, he'll be able to sit up, play in a playpen, and begin to crawl; but now he's too young to learn much."

These mothers couldn't be more wrong. Far from being

too young to learn anything, *your baby begins to learn from the moment he is born.* The lenses of his self-concept have begun to form before he opens his eyes.

The most important thing your baby acquires during this stage of infancy is *his basic outlook on life.* He is forming, from a baby's point of view, his philosophy of life, his basic feelings about what it means to be alive. He is developing either a basic sense of trust and happiness about life, or one of distrust and unhappiness.

Whether your infant will develop a sense of trust or distrust is determined by the environment you provide for him. This environment will become a part of those eyeglasses of self-concept through which he will see the world. If he develops a basically optimistic pair of eyeglasses in his first year, he will grow into an optimistic adult. If he develops a pessimistic pair of eyeglasses, he will become a basically pessimistic person in later life.

This first year of life is extremely crucial—more important than all the stages of psychological development that follow—because the infant is absolutely dependent upon you for his environment. As soon as he learns to walk, he begins to have much more control over his own environment. Learning to talk adds still more control. But as a baby he can do very little about his environment. His environment will be almost entirely what you decide it will be.

What kind of environment do you need to provide for your baby? What should you do in order to insure the maximum development of your child's potentialities?

If you as a parent see that your baby's basic needs are fulfilled, he will attain the maximum development of his potentialities. So let's discuss the basic needs of a baby.

First and foremost in importance to a baby is hunger. In this respect, he can be thought of as mainly a mouth and a stomach. A baby feels hunger on an intense, *right now* basis. A very young baby, say a month old, will be awakened by hunger pangs. After he is fed, he will go back to sleep until his hunger pangs wake him up again. As a baby grows older, the periods of wakefulness lengthen; he will not go back to sleep as soon as he is fed.

How do you take care of his hunger need? Simple. You feed him! It sounds easy, and it really is, except that society has needlessly complicated what is, basically, a very simple procedure for mothers and babies.

BREAST VERSUS BOTTLE:

A NONCONTROVERSY

First of all, we have complicated the situation by the breast-feeding versus bottle-feeding controversy. It is highly unfortunate that people line up emotionally on one side or the other of this controversy. Doctors, nurses, and neighborhood "experts" often become quite heated about this subject. Sometimes, for example, mothers are made to feel guilty if they do not breast-feed their babies. People will say, "After all, breast-feeding is nature's way." This, in my opinion, is about as reasonable as saying, "If God wanted people to fly in airplanes, He would have given them wings."

The so-called breast-versus-bottle controversy can be cleared up by a single statement: There is absolutely no scientific evidence that one method is better for infants than the other, either physically or psychologically. It should be strictly up to you to choose the method you prefer.

However, if you do choose to bottle-feed, be sure to hold your baby and cuddle him just as you would if you were breast-feeding. This is not an absolute or rigid rule. It is not going to harm your baby psychologically if you prop a bottle occasionally. But in general, your baby needs the same kind of physical cuddling when you bottle-feed him that he would get if you chose to breast-feed him.

SELF-DEMAND OR SCHEDULE?

Now for the crucial question, whether you breast-feed or bottle-feed, of *when* to feed your baby. The obvious answer should be: *when he gets hungry.* Unfortunately our civilization has managed to complicate needlessly that simple and obvious answer.

Back in the 1920s and '30s many people believed it was good to train babies and young children as soon as possible. Part of good habit training, in their eyes, consisted of getting the young child on a schedule as quickly as possible. And so babies were put on feeding schedules of every three or four hours by the physician. The mother was supposed to feed the baby according to this schedule. This dreadful regime violated one of the most fundamental principles of raising psychologically healthy children: respect for the individuality of each child.

Each child is a unique individual, with his own internal time clock for hunger. How did we ever think that we could devise an external "time clock," a schedule, which would fit all babies? Whether the external time clock says "feed the baby every four hours" or "feed the baby every three hours," *it is bound to be wrong*. It can't possibly fit your individual baby. Not only is your baby different from all other babies, but even his own hunger will vary from day to day.

What happens to a baby when he is fed on a rigid schedule? When he is hungry, he becomes frustrated. A baby's hunger is an all-consuming thing. When he is hungry, he is *hungry!* He doesn't mean maybe; he wants food. Most of us, as adults, have never been hungry the way a baby is hungry. Perhaps I can give you some feeling for this by saying that if a baby has to wait a half hour for his feeding, it's as if we had to wait three days.

A baby is usually not a very polite creature. When he's hungry and you're not feeding him, he calls your attention to his hunger in the only way he knows: by crying. The more time that elapses without his being fed, the louder and more insistent his crying. It's as if he is saying to you: "What kind of a world is this? Here I am crying and crying, telling people I'm hungry, but nobody brings me any food!" As more and more time passes, the crying changes in quality and tone. Instead of merely being a loud demand for food, the crying now takes on a tone of anger and rage. Now the baby is saying through his crying: "I'm furious! I hate all of you and the whole world! I hate you for not paying any attention to me and my hunger messages!"

If a baby is repeatedly subject to schedule feeding, he begins to learn that no matter how much he cries from hunger, nothing happens. He does not get fed right away. He may react to this situation with anger, or he may become listless and apathetic, as if he had given up on getting his needs satisfied. This baby has "learned" to choke back his anger and to substitute for it a dreadful resignation. But whether the baby chooses continued anger or apathetic resignation, what he is learning is the same: a basic distrust of life. Can you blame him? To him, life is a frustrating, hateful affair.

Finally our society began to see the terrible shortcomings of schedule feeding. More and more doctors began to recommend, and more and more mothers began to use, what has come to be called "self-demand" feeding. This method is based on what *should be* a commonsense and obvious truth: Let the baby himself tell you when he is hungry, by waking up and crying to be fed.

Many mothers are plagued later on in their children's lives by feeding problems which are completely unnecessary from a psychological standpoint. Feeding problems arise in almost all cases because some sort of psychological pressure has been applied which is contrary to the simple hunger needs of the child—whether he is a baby or a three-year-old. After all, parents have a great biological ally in feeding their children: the child's own hunger. If we respect our child's individuality and see that this biological need is met, we should have no feeding problems.

It is important that a parent respect his child's individuality from birth. Yet this is often not the case. Such incidents as the following are unfortunately commonplace: The baby was fed about an hour and a half ago, and has gone back to sleep. He wakes up crying. The mother might think: "Now what in the world is he crying for? He can't be hungry because I fed him only a little while ago." How does she know? Can she get inside her baby and tell whether or not he is experiencing hunger pangs? Why can't he be hungry? (In this respect, mothers in primitive tribes are often wiser than we are, because whenever their baby cries or is fretful, he is offered the breast.)

So when your baby cries, feed him. Offer him the breast or the bottle. If he indicates by spitting or other negative reactions that he does not want to be fed, you will know that he is crying not because he is hungry, but for some other reason.

The most important thing you can do to help your baby develop a basic trust in himself and his world—the foundation of a strong and healthy self-concept—is to feed him when he is hungry. The baby who is fed when his crying signals that he's hungry will come to feel: "This is a nice world. It feels so good to be fed. I like the warmth of my mother holding me and giving me the breast or bottle. This world is a safe and satisfying place to be in, because when I let the world know I'm hungry, I get fed. I know that everything will turn out all right for me and my world."

The second basic need of a baby is warmth. We hardly need dwell on this because 99 percent of mothers see to it that their babies are warm enough and do not get chilled.

The third basic need of babies is sleep. This need will, of course, be taken care of by the baby himself. He will sleep as much as he needs. When he has had enough sleep, he will wake up. However, a few words about his sleeping habits and patterns may be of help.

It is not necessary for the house to be hushed and still for a baby to sleep. We all know the stereotype of the mother tiptoeing around the house and rushing to the door to inform callers in whispered tones, *"Shh*—the baby is asleep!"* This is really not necessary. In fact, if you try too hard to create silence, you may condition the baby so that in time he would only sleep well with this artificial lack of sound and noise. So go about your work in a reasonably normal fashion when your baby is asleep, and don't hesitate to play the radio or TV in another room if you want to.

The other thing I want to say about your baby's sleeping patterns is to remind you that they are absolutely independent of your adult sleeping patterns. When your baby is very young, he will go back to sleep immediately after you have fed him. That's convenient for you. But as he grows older he will have increasingly long periods of wakefulness after being fed. This isn't particularly troublesome during the day, but it may be difficult in the middle of the night. After a middle-of-the-night feeding, you want to get back to sleep because you've got to get up early in the morning. But the baby doesn't know that. He's been fed and is happy and contented, and he's not ready to go back to sleep yet. He wants to play awhile and enjoy the period of wakefulness.

A baby may also wake up and start crying in the middle of the night for some unknown reason. The cry may be due to colic or stomach distress, about which you can do nothing. Sometimes you will find that even physical cuddling and holding will not comfort him or stop the crying. There he is, crying his little head off, and there the two of you are, groggy and wanting desperately for him to stop crying so you can get back to sleep. At times such as this you discover that civilization is only a thin veneer covering a primitive, savage self inside of you. You may find yourself getting furious at the baby; perhaps you feel like shaking him or hitting him or yelling at him, "Shut up! Don't you know I need to get back to sleep!"

Since nobody has ever told them about times like these, many mothers and fathers are often terribly guilty about feeling this way. Actually, you are a perfectly normal parent if you feel this way. Notice I said, *"feel* this way." If you find yourself actually losing control and striking or hitting your baby, then you need professional help. You should be able to control your actions, but it is normal to *feel* frustrated and angry in such situations.

One item you may find helpful in handling your baby is an Infantseat. This is not only helpful in transporting him in a car or moving him to a different room in the house so you can keep an eye on him, but also in giving your baby a different sleeping position. Sometimes when a baby won't be able to go back to sleep in his crib lying down, he can go back to sleep at 5:00 A.M. sitting up in an Infantseat.

But remember that whatever pattern a baby's sleeping and wakefulness take, most babies will cause some trouble and inconvenience due to the difference between their sleeping patterns and ours.

THE DIAPER BRIGADE

The next basic need of your baby is to get rid of the waste products of his body through urination and defecation. Once again, this is a need he will take care of himself. You will have no real trouble on this score unless you make the unfortunate mistake of trying to toilet train him during his first year of life.

Due to your own childhood conditioning, you may have a strong aversion to messy diapers. They may seem highly offensive and unpleasantly smelly to you. If so, try not to communicate these feelings to your baby. He has no such feelings toward the waste products of his body. If you communicate your feelings of aversion to him, you will only succeed in making the job of toilet training him later on more difficult.

Many mothers, due to their negative feelings about messy or wet diapers, assume their baby feels the same way they do; and so they rush to change a diaper as soon as it has become wet or messy. You can afford to take a more relaxed attitude toward diaper changing. As long as the baby is not in a cold room, he will ordinarily not be bothered by a wet or messy diaper. I particularly mention this so that when your baby is finally sleeping through the night you will not feel that you have to get up to change a messy or wet diaper in the middle of the night.

Please do not misunderstand and change your baby's diapers so infrequently that he develops a bad case of diaper rash. All I am saying is that most parents can afford to be far more relaxed than they usually are about how frequently a baby's diaper needs to be changed.

CONTACT COMFORT

Your baby's next basic need is for physical cuddling, or what Dr. Harry Harlow calls "contact comfort." Your baby cannot know he is loved unless the love is demonstrated to him in a physical way—unless he is held, cuddled, rocked, and talked and sung to.

Various lines of research have produced evidence to prove this point. On the level of animal research, Dr. Harry Harlow studied baby rhesus monkeys reared by terry-cloth dummies, with built-in nursing bottles. Although these monkeys received adequate nourishment, they did not get adequate amounts of contact comfort, since there were no monkey mothers around to cuddle them and give other physical demonstrations of affection. The results of the experiment showed that these baby monkeys grew up to be socially inadequate adult monkeys. They were unable to mate with receptive monkeys of the opposite sex, and they showed strange and weird mannerisms, much like those observed in human psychotics.

Of course, we would not want to experiment with human babies by denying them contact comfort in order to see if they would turn out badly as adults. We do, however, have a record of one unfortunate "experiment" with human babies, carried out for quite different reasons

in the thirteenth century, which pathetically illustrates the
point we are making.

Frederick II of Prussia wanted to find out what the
"original language" of mankind was. He thought he might
be able to discover this language if he could have babies
raised without anyone talking to them. He reasoned that if
babies were raised in this way, when they began to speak
they would speak in the original language of mankind. So
he instructed foster mothers and nurses to feed the children, to bathe and wash them, but not to speak to them.
He thought that the babies, when they began to speak,
would speak Hebrew or Greek or Latin, and thus he
would find out which was the original language of man.
The unfortunate result of his experiment, however, was
that the children all died. Presumably the babies died
because they were deprived of the physical cuddling and
"mothering" that they would have received had the foster
mothers and nurses been allowed to talk to them.

Studies of infants raised in institutions underline this
same point. Although babies raised in orphanages and
institutions may be fed adequately, the attendants do not
have time to physically cuddle and "mother" them.
And so we find that children raised in the barren, unstimulating environment of an orphanage are, in varying degrees, psychologically impaired.

So do what comes naturally with your baby when it
comes to cuddling him, rocking him, singing to him, and
playing with him. Hold him! Kiss him! Hug him a thousand times if you want! You won't "spoil" him, for this is
how he will know he is loved.

HIS FIRST HUMAN RELATIONSHIP

So far, I have spoken of the basic needs of your baby as
if they were separate, isolated things. This is not really
true, for ordinarily *all* of these basic needs of your baby
are taken care of by you, the mother, with assistance from
father or other adults in your household. In other words,
it is ordinarily *one person* who sees that all these basic
needs of the baby are met. And, in doing so, that one
person, the mother, fills the baby's need for his first
emotional relationship.

You, the mother, provide your baby with this all-important first emotional relationship with another human being. Thus forms the foundation for his emotional relationships with the other human beings he will come in contact with throughout his life. If his emotional relationship with you is good, if he feels that you truly take care of him and his needs, he will have a sense of basic trust in the goodness of life. If you provide your baby with this type of mothering, at the end of the first year of his life he will have the beginnings of a strong self-concept, a feeling of basic trust and optimism about life.

INTELLECTUAL NEEDS

Your baby not only has the basic emotional needs we have just listed, he also has basic intellectual needs. In order to understand these needs we must consider how your infant perceives the world. The most important thing to remember is that the world for your baby is like a movie which is only gradually coming into focus.

For example, when you sit down in a chair to read, you know clearly that the chair you are sitting in, or the book you are reading, or the light you are reading by, are not "you." Your baby doesn't know this. He cannot at first distinguish between "what is me" and "what is not-me" in his world.

This is a difficult point for many adults to grasp, because we have spent many years being aware of the "me" and the "not-me" of our world. It's hard for us to understand that for our baby there is no "I" or "me" at first. It takes months for a baby to develop a sense of "I" or "me." This often becomes amusingly clear when you see an older baby first begin to discover with great delight that it is the "I" which can cause his toes or fingers to wiggle. He finds out that he can wiggle them whenever he chooses. Often you will see a baby sitting there happily wiggling away with his fingers, drunk with his new-found sense of power.

It is important to understand this "gradually-coming-into-focus" character of a baby's world, because by providing adequate intellectual stimulation for him, you help his world come into focus. As the French psychologist Piaget puts it: "The more the child sees and hears, the more he wants to see and hear."

A research study by Dr. Wayne Dennis in three orphanages in Teheran highlights this point dramatically. In the first orphanage, most of the infants were admitted before the age of one month. They were kept almost continually in individual cribs. They lay on their backs on soft mattresses and were not propped up or turned over until they learned to do this by themselves. They were changed when necessary and bathed every other day. Milk was given them in propped-up bottles, although occasionally they were fed semisolid food by an attendant. They had no toys or playthings. In other words, the world in which they lived was one with very little sensory or intellectual stimulation.

When these children were approximately three years old, they were transferred to a second orphanage, which had the same type of environment. Dr. Dennis found that fewer than half of these children between the ages of one and two could sit up, and none could walk. By contrast, almost all normal, noninstitutionalized American children can sit alone by the age of nine months and walk by the age of fifteen months. Of the two-year-olds in the first institution, fewer than half could stand holding on to a hand or chair. Less than 10 percent could walk alone. Dr. Dennis also found that only 15 percent of the three-year-olds in the second orphanage had learned to walk alone.

In a later study in an orphanage in Beirut, Dr. Dennis took a group of babies between the ages of seven months and one year, none of whom could sit up, and exposed them to a planned program of sensory stimulation. For one hour a day they were taken from their cribs and brought into an adjoining room. Here they were propped up in low chairs and given a variety of objects to look at and handle: fresh flowers, paper bags, pieces of colored sponge, metal box tops, plastic flyswatters, bright jelly molds, multicolored plastic dishes, small plastic bottles, and metal ashtrays. No adults worked with the youngsters or helped them play with the objects, which would have been even more stimulating to them.

Even with this minimal stimulation of one hour a day, all of the babies quickly learned to sit up independently. After considerable hesitation by some of the babies, all delighted in playing with the objects. During the course of the experiment, these babies made four times their average gain in development as a result of the sensory stimulation of playing with these objects, without the stimulation of playing with adults.

The same type of evidence shows up in studies of the cognitive development of children of disadvantaged poor parents as compared to children of relatively well-to-do parents in the United States. The children of middle-class parents are at a much higher level of cognitive and intellectual development at age three or four than the children of poor parents. Why? Because the children of middle-class parents receive greater sensory and intellectual stimulation, even as infants. They have access to a greater number and variety of objects to play with. And their mothers make these objects available to them, respond to their use of the objects, encourage further experimentation with the objects, and talk to them about such objects.

In short, the old idea that each child is born with a fixed amount of intelligence is not supported by newer research evidence. This new evidence indicates that each child inherits a certain maximum potential intelligence to which he might achieve as he grows up. One child's maximum intelligence might be that of a genius; another's maximum may be that of average intelligence; another's maximum may be that of below average intelligence. But whether or not a child will reach his maximum intelligence will depend to a great extent on how much sensory and intellectual stimulation he receives in the first five years of his life.

So you can see how important it is to give your baby sensory and intellectual stimulation. Provide objects he can play with, objects which will stimulate his senses—his sight, hearing, smell, etc. Give him objects that he can handle, mouth, chew on, take apart. These objects can be simple household materials. For example: clean cloth pieces, which he can crumple and chew on; plastic bottles and dishes, which he can grasp and bang with; clothespins and teething rings; cellophane, which he can crumple and make noise with; metal mirrors, in which he can see himself; paper bags and empty cardboard boxes; kitchen utensils and pots and pans. The list is endless. Of course, since everything goes into his mouth, you should be careful to see that he does not have access to objects which are small enough for him to choke on.

Toymakers have also come up with many ingenious devices which can be used for the sensory and intellectual stimulation of infants. Browse through your local toystore to see what they have in the way of cradle gyms or other sensory stimulation toys for infants. You should find such sensory stimulation materials for babies as mobiles, to hang above a bassinet or crib; an arrangement of rings and horizontal bars, for the baby to hit and tug at; or a clear plastic aquarium with fish inside, to hang by the baby's crib.

You can also make your own sensory stimulation toys. Any type of colorful and manipulatable object which is large enough to be safe for your baby can be used as a sensory stimulation plaything. Rummage through your house or take a trip to the dime store to see what kinds of simple, inexpensive sensory stimulation toys you can create for your baby.

Above all, however, let's not forget the best sensory stimulation toy of all. This toy, which your baby will love most of all, is a parent: a mother or father.

Talk to your baby and play with him in whatever way you feel like. Start by talking to him. Many mothers change their baby's diapers or feed him or give him his bath in silence. Why not talk to him on these occasions? Tell him what you are doing. Of course he can't understand what you're saying, but he will receive sensory and intellectual stimulation from the sound of your voice.

What should you say to him? Whatever you like. Say: "Here it is bath time again, you lucky kid you—let's see how you're going to enjoy the water today," or, "Well, it's diaper-changing time again, kiddo, so we whisk the old one off like this—and now we fold the new one and slip you into it—and pin you up. Magic, presto!" Each mother will say her own individual things to her baby. Each mother will sing her own individual songs.

When you and your husband sing to your baby and talk to him and make funny noises for him, and rock him, and play with him, you are giving him the sensory stimulation which will promote his intellectual development. And, incidentally, you should be having a good time yourselves doing these things with your baby. Many parents miss out on this kind of fun. When some parents speak of having a "good baby," they mean a baby who is quiet and doesn't demand much attention, so that mother can get her housework and the demands of other children taken care of. That "good baby" is missing out on the sensory stimulation which will enable him to develop to the maximum potential of his intelligence.

Please don't go to the opposite extreme and conclude that you must spend most of your baby's waking moments playing with him. Even if you had a housekeeper to do all of your housework and no other children to occupy you, you still wouldn't feel like playing with your baby all of his waking moments. Don't let playing with him become an obligation; keep it fun. Talk to him when you feel like talking to him. Play with him when you feel like playing with him. Cuddle him when you feel like it. That way you will enjoy him, and he will enjoy you.

A BIRD'S-EYE VIEW OF INFANCY

I want next to give you a brief bird's-eye view of your baby's development during the stage of infancy—the first year of his life. I would like first, however, to suggest that you invest in a book which will describe the development of your child during the first *five* years of life in much greater detail. This book is the result of research on literally thousands of children at the Yale Clinic of Child Development by Dr. Arnold Gesell and his associates. It is virtually an encyclopedia of the first five years of life, and I think no parent should be without it. The book is called *Infant and Child in the Culture of Today*. It should probably be titled *The Child from Birth to Five*, because that's what it's about. It describes the life and behavior of a four-week-old baby and traces the baby's gradual development until he is five years old.

This book is particularly valuable to parents who are having their first child. All parents learn about children by using their first child as a test case. I sometimes think we should be able to consider the first child an experiment, and start from scratch with the second one—now that we know a great deal more about children. (I'm sure that this thought has occurred to some of you mothers, particularly when your first child has been especially difficult to handle!) Dr. Gesell's book gives you a chance to "have a first child before you have a real first child." In other words, you can find out what children are like and what you can reasonably expect from them at different stages of development by following the descriptions given in Dr. Gesell's book. So don't use my brief bird's-eye view of child development as a substitute for a more thorough reading of Dr. Gesell's researches.

I have found it most convenient to organize this bird's-eye view of the stage of infancy in three-month periods, although I remind you at the outset that these are arbitrary divisions. I want to give you a general idea of the growth and development of your baby during these periods and to suggest specific ways in which you can provide him with an enriched play environment which will aid his intellectual development.

THE FIRST THREE MONTHS

Your newborn baby is an absolutely unique person.

Various studies have shown that newborn babies are decidedly different from one another in many ways: in passivity or aggressiveness; in sensitivity to light, sound, or touch; in the zeal with which they attack the nipple or bottle; in temperament; in the tonus of their muscles; in blood chemistry; and in hormonal balance.

The pattern of hunger and crying in my two male children was notably different when they were newly born infants. When Randy, my older son, woke up hungry, he announced this fact by letting out an ear-shattering cry which could be heard for blocks and which lasted until the bottle was in his mouth. But when Rusty, my younger son, was a baby he exhibited a completely different pattern. He woke up and played happily by himself for a few minutes. When he began to announce his hunger, he reminded me of one of those alarm clocks that purr softly at first and finally work up to an ear-chilling blast if you don't pay attention to the first gentle warning. He would begin by crying softly, and only cry in earnest if these first gentle cries were not heeded.

Here we have two children, both males, both products of the same general genetic inheritance, who are nevertheless vastly different, even from the day of birth, in their psychological characteristics and behavior patterns.

Your children will be just as different. Respect each child's individuality. None of your children will correspond exactly to the general outlines of expected child behavior at any particular age or stage of development. With that reminder of the absolute uniqueness of your baby, let's proceed to a general description of babies during the first three months of their lives.

The newborn infant spends much of his time sleeping, perhaps as much as twenty hours a day. (But, again, your baby may be different.) The baby is also generally passive and placid for the first three months; he cannot yet raise his head, roll over (except by accident), or move his thumb and fingers separately. Perceptually, the world is to him a big, booming, buzzing confusion. Although he begins almost immediately to pay attention to human faces, he cannot tell one face from another. Yet the newborn baby can register an astonishing number of things in his little brain. Recent studies by Dr. Robert Fantz have shown that newborn babies can discriminate visual patterns. He has proven that a newborn baby will spend more time looking at black and white figures than at unfigured colored areas, and that he will look at a crude approximation of the human face more often than at a nonsensical arrangement of the same features. Dr. Lewis Lipset has shown that even day-old infants can discriminate between a variety of sounds and odors, and quickly become conditioned to them when they are repeated.

The results of such research prove that your newborn baby registers in his brain what he hears, feels, and sees. He is capable of enjoying sensations as soon as he is born; and as soon as he is capable of enjoying sensations, you can begin to play with him. Not "play" in the sense of throwing him up in the air or playing peekaboo, but play at his level of development, which is still very primitive.

You can begin playing with your baby by using his ears to reach him. Young babies are very sensitive in their hearing and are startled by loud, sudden noises. But soft, gentle talking and singing appeal to them. They learn to stop crying when they hear footsteps. So use this magic gateway of your baby's ears. Talk to him and sing to him. Make funny noises for him. Play different kinds of music for him. Let him hear different sounds, such as the ticking of a clock, the sound of a metronome, or the clink of a spoon against a glass. It may not appear that anything is going on in his mind when you are doing these things, but all of this is registering inside his brain. You are giving him valuable sensory stimulation.

Skin is another magic avenue of stimulation for a baby. Babies love the skin play of being patted or stroked. Give him a little "massage" five minutes before or after his bath. Don't go about this as a grim obligation; do it only when you feel like doing it. You can also give your infant rudimentary little "exercises," a form of body play which will promote good muscle tone. When he is lying on his back, stretch his arms out to the side, and then fold them back over his chest, repeating the movement several times. You can also raise his legs and rotate them in a gentle bicycling motion. As soon as he gets the hang of it, your baby may smile or laugh, especially if you sing some rhythmic song or make some funny noises as you put him through these motions.

Your baby's eyes are another avenue of sensory stimulation. His world is his crib, and what a dreary world it is for many babies! How would you like to live in a house or apartment which contained only four unpainted walls and nothing to relieve the bleak monotony? Liven up the world of your baby's crib with visual stimulation. Get some colorful pieces of cloth, paper, or plastic with bold designs and hang them on the sides of his crib, or overhead. Buy a baby mobile, or make your own from bits of bright aluminum foil, paper, cardboard, colored buttons, or other attractive objects hung from a string or wire.

Most mothers hang baby mobiles over their babies' heads. It is a mistake to hang a mobile in this position during your baby's first six weeks. During these first six weeks, your baby lies with his head to either the left or the right when he is lying on his back. Therefore mobiles should be hung on one side or the other of the crib. It is only when your baby is six weeks old that he begins to be able, physiologically, to orient his head so that he can look up toward the ceiling.

It is also important not to leave your baby in his crib all the time. Sit him on your lap from time to time so that he can have a visual change of scene; or prop him up in the Infantseat in a different room so that he can see what's going on there. Some mothers might want to invest in an infant backpack in order to carry their babies around on their backs from time to time as they go about their work. This will not appeal to every mother, but if you like the idea it should give your baby some interesting visual variations.

You have been talking to your baby and singing to him, but he has been registering all of this quite passively and has not been responding to you. When your baby is about two months old, you may notice a change in him in this respect. Now when you talk to him or make nonsense sounds while playing with him, you may see the beginnings of efforts by your baby to "talk" back. He will work his mouth as though struggling to make sounds in response to you. Later on, this kind of response will develop into the typical "conversation" of nonsense sounds between mother and infant.

The efforts of your baby to "talk back" to you at this age are akin to another important development which takes place at about this same time: *visually directed reaching,* one of the first big breakthroughs in your baby's mastery of his environment. Visually directed reaching takes place when your baby is able to see something, reach for it, and touch it, all at the same time—an act which opens up a whole new world for your infant.

You can help this activity along when your child is approximately two months old by a simple and inexpensive homemade device. Take some infant stockings (the smallest size you can find) that are of a vivid color: bright red or yellow, for example. Cut the toes off and cut a hole in the side of the stocking for the thumb to fit through. Put them on your baby's hands so that his fingers stick out. What you have made is a colorful infant glove without fingers.

At first when your baby is flailing around with his hands, he doesn't realize that these things, these hands, belong to him. Putting these colorful "hand-stockings" on your baby's hands will enable him to recognize this fact much sooner, and will thus stimulate the development of his visually directed reaching.

Here is another simple suggestion that will enrich your baby's visual environment. Have you ever thought how dull the visual environment is for a child when his diapers are being changed on his bassinet? He sees the world lying flat on his back, looking up; and it's a very dull view! Put a mirror on the side of his bassinet so that your baby can see both your movements and his own as you change him

or give him his bath. It will greatly increase the visual
interest of his environment.

Your baby not only needs a visually interesting environment, he needs a *participating environment*. He needs to
learn that he can do things that have an effect on his
environment. I have mentioned talking and singing to your
baby. Equally important is responding to the sounds he
makes. Your baby will start playing with sounds early in
life. When he babbles and makes little nonsense sounds, it
is exciting to him for you to make the same sound back to
him. In this way he is getting feedback from his environment, and this excites and pleases him. He's like a kid with
a new toy. He will want to make the sounds some more so
that he will get the same feedback again.

Your baby is learning a very valuable lesson from this
interchange. *He is learning that he can do things that have
an effect on his environment.* He is learning that he is
living in an environment in which he can participate. This
lesson will help him build up a very primitive type of
self-confidence and outgoingness, even as a tiny baby.

Another simple, homemade device which can provide a
participating environment for your baby is a Texture Pad.
You can make this by sewing different textures of cloth,
patchwork-quilt-fashion, on a rubber pad about two feet
square. Your baby can scratch away and feel the different
textures on this pad. One small movement by him to a
different part of the Texture Pad changes the environment
he experiences, and this will stimulate him to further explore
his responsive environment.

Here is another device by which you can provide a participating environment for your baby. Take a piece of elastic
and hang different objects from it—such as a series of
spoons or a rattle or a colorful plastic bracelet—which are
not potentially dangerous to your baby. Do not hang tiny
things which he could put in his mouth and choke on.
Hang the elastic with the goodies on it right in front of him
so that he can flail away at it. Make sure that the elastic
is sturdy and thick so that it cannot become dangerously
wound around your baby's hand or fingers and cut off his
circulation. Do not, for example, use string.

By using these types of simple, homemade devices, you
are enriching your baby's growing personality by exposing
him to different objects and situations. You are teaching

him that by acting on his environment he will get a response from it.

Remember, however, that a baby of this age is very vulnerable. In fashioning these devices, you must rule out as far as possible the chances of his getting hurt.

THREE TO SIX MONTHS

Three months is a transition point.

Early in the third month a baby will usually begin to reach out to things. This action signals the transition your baby will make from a passive, helpless orientation to an active, manipulative, exploratory attitude toward his world.

In his first three months, the infant explores his environment with his eyes and ears and, of course, with his mouth, through sucking. Now he begins to explore his environment with his hands. He begins to show what Dr. Gesell calls "touch hunger." He loves to grasp, touch, feel, and manipulate objects. At around four months a baby's hands become quite important to him. Previously he had discovered through the use of his eyes that objects have form and color. Now he begins to discover through his hands that objects have other qualities: softness, hardness, and texture.

No scientist studying the physical world is more avid or eager in his research than a four-month-old baby exploring the hardness, softness, roughness, smoothness, dryness, wetness, or fuzziness of objects that he can grasp and hold. So give your baby a chance! Put lots of different kinds of objects within his grasp and let him feel and touch and manipulate them. The Texture Pad you have made will be especially appreciated by your baby at this age.

It is also about this age that everything starts to go into your baby's mouth. Indeed, it seems as if the mouth is one of the main sense organs through which a baby researches his world. This continues to be the case for several years. It's as if the baby is saying to himself: "I won't really know what this thing is like until I put it in my mouth." It is therefore important at this stage for you to childproof your baby's environment. The fragile mobiles and the pretty, but sharp or swallowable, objects that were fine for early visual exploration should now be put away. Now you need sturdy objects that the baby cannot swallow or choke on.

Rattles now come into the picture. Browse through your local toy store for a variety of rattles. Rubber squeeze toys are good at this age. Be careful of the kind with metal whistles inside which can be poked out or fall out with use. Your child could easily choke on one of these.

Your baby is now ready for soft cuddly toys or dolls. Be careful of such hazards as glass eyes, which your baby could pull loose, put in his mouth, and choke on. You can buy cuddly toys in the toy store, or you can make your own. The washable covering may be old towels or canvas or oilcloth. You can use foam rubber or kapok or even your discarded nylon stockings to stuff them.

In addition to browsing through your local toy store, browse through your local pet store! Hard-rubber crackle bones, doughnuts, and balls with bells inside are often as much fun for a baby as for a puppy.

Many babies are ready for a playpen by three or four months. It is best to put a baby in a playpen by the age of three or four months, before he has learned to sit and crawl and develop the freedom of the floor. Otherwise, if you put him in the playpen later, he may consider it a prison. Set the playpen near where you are working, in the family room or kitchen, where it gives the baby a chance to have your company and see what is going on. He can also have times in the playpen without being near you, and learn to amuse himself with the toys you have put in the playpen.

SIX TO NINE MONTHS

Characteristically, at around six months, babies begin to develop what has been called "stranger anxiety." Your baby has acquired, during his first six months of life, a scheme of what is familiar, including faces and people. He has now matured enough to realize what people and things are not familiar, and hence strange. When you are showing your baby to a new and strange person at this age you should proceed slowly. Don't rush the baby into the new situation. If the introduction results in fear and crying, your baby is telling you that he's afraid. Give him more time.

Your baby will now also enjoy babbling and vocalizing. The exchange of nonsense sounds that began at two or three months are now a stable pattern of verbal play between the two of you. Your baby's first teeth are likely to emerge during the seventh month. Teething is marked by a compelling urge to chew on things, and the baby needs chewable toys for this purpose.

It is during the period from six to nine months that the baby also begins to be fascinated by repetition. He loves to repeat things over and over and over again until he feels they are mastered. For example, he may want to bang and bang and bang again with some object on his feeding table or high chair. It is hard for an adult, who can be easily bored by repetition, to realize how much joy the baby gets out of repeating things.

From six months on, the baby begins to discover the joys of imitation. This will be one of his most powerful social motives all the way through childhood. The six-month-old baby will imitate hand gestures the parent makes, such as wiping up food with a sponge, and he will imitate sounds the parent makes. Long before the baby can talk he is able to find ways of communicating what he wants to other people. He is like a traveler in a foreign country who does not speak the language, yet who is able by grunts and gestures to indicate what he desires.

As the baby approaches eight months he will probably be able to crawl. This activity immediately makes him a more active explorer and researcher of his environment.

By the age of eight or nine months, your baby will have outgrown his Bathinette or the bathroom sink, and will be ready to take his bath in the bathtub. The water must be kept shallow, for if left untended in a bathtub he could easily drown. Put in a supply of floating water toys, washcloths, and plastic cups—and a whole new world of delight will be opened up to your baby. Water play is one of the best types of play for babies. Perhaps it is due to memory traces of their life in the amniotic fluid of the womb. But whatever the reason, water play is one of the most soothing and relaxing types of play for babies and young children.

After he has learned to crawl, your baby will now start to creep. Crawling differs from creeping in that the baby crawls on his belly, but he creeps with his torso clear of the ground. Once creeping has begun, especially if the baby can pull himself up to a standing position, it is especially important that you childproof your house. Anything that can harm your creeping baby must be put out of his reach. Floors should be carefully inspected for stray safety pins, tacks, nails, or other small objects which could be swallowed. Remember: Everything the baby finds will go into his mouth! Every projecting object is an invitation for your baby to pull at; every cord or wire will be tugged. Make sure that nothing sharp or dangerous can be pulled down onto the upturned face of your eager little explorer.

You should liberate your baby occasionally from his playpen. A corner of a room or a full room, fenced off, with nothing dangerous in it, will give him a field day for exploration. Because of his interest in finding out about his world, the six to nine-month-old can often play happily by himself for a half hour at a time. Common household objects often make the best toys for this age baby.

The exact age at which a baby is able to open his hand and release objects will vary from child to child. However, when your child reaches this milestone in his physical development it means hectic times for mother. Your baby has now discovered an entirely new game called "Dropping Things and Throwing Things." Out of his playpen they go. Off the feeding table or the high chair they crash to the floor! Your baby is *not* doing this to annoy or distress you. He is doing this as part of his general researching into the properties of the world. This is his discovery of the relation of his new hand-power to the law of gravity, even though he would not be able to put such a relationship into words.

NINE TO TWELVE MONTHS

Some babies may already be walking at nine months. Others may start at twelve months; others not until fourteen or fifteen months. But no matter at what age the actual onset of walking begins, during the last three months of his first year of life, your baby is completing his transition from horizontal to vertical orientation. No longer will he lie passive and quiet while you are changing a diaper or dressing him. Instead, he is now Mr. Wiggle-and-Squirm. On the other hand, he may begin to cooperate in a primitive sort of way in getting dressed.

It is during this three-month period that your baby is able to begin playing such advanced games as pat-a-cake and other traditional imitation games of babyhood. Although he cannot talk, by this time your baby can understand a great many things that are said to him. He can understand simple commands. He can also pick up certain words which act as cues for familiar games or routine activities such as eating and bathing.

You should now start to help your baby label his world. This is easy to do. Speak to your child in single-word sentences. Point out and identify objects and features of his world. As you give him his bath, put your hand in the water and splash it a bit and say "water." As you give him a bite of applesauce, say "applesauce." As you drive by a big truck on the highway, point to it and say "truck." This "labeling game" is one you can play with your baby anywhere, anytime. At this stage of development he may only register internally what you are saying to him. At a considerably later stage of language development he will repeat the word to you. This "labeling game" is one of the most helpful things you can do to stimulate his language development.

During the last two or three months of the first year you can begin to introduce your baby to the world of books. "Books!" some of you may say. "Books—why that's ridiculous—he'll only put the book in his mouth!" Remember, that's the way he finds out what everything—including books—is like. His first books should be either of cloth or heavy cardboard, because they will surely end up in his mouth. These books are not stories, because he is not ready for stories yet; they are pictures (along with single words) of familiar objects.

These first books are really a different form of the "labeling game." You show him the pictures and say the words out loud to him. Then he will want to handle the book himself. He will pat and stroke the pages; then into his mouth it goes! Later on, he will like to look at the pictures and croon a few nonsense syllables at the book. This, to him, is "reading." But do not scorn this; by starting his familiarity with books at this early age you are laying the foundation for his reading and developing a love for books.

Putting-in and *taking-out* are patterns for much of his play at this age. Common household objects make fine playthings. A big plastic bottle with a wide top and a group of household objects to put in and take out are loads of fun. A trash basket of discarded letters, envelopes, or fourth class "junk mail" may be endlessly fascinating to a youngster of this age.

THOU SHALT NOT'S FOR INFANCY

I have described the development of your baby throughout this first year of his life, and suggested specific things you can do which will enable your youngster to attain his maximum emotional and intellectual development during this stage. Before I close this chapter, however, I want to call attention to some things you *should not* do with your baby at this stage. In this age of self-proclaimed neighborhood "experts" (well-meaning as they may be), many uninformed mothers make serious errors in infancy by doing unnecessary and sometimes detrimental things. Here are four *Thou Shalt Not's* for Infancy:

Thou Shalt Not ignore the crying of a baby.

This seems obvious, but you would be amazed at how many mothers do exactly that—ignore the crying of a child. One of my former college students once made this interesting observation in a paper he wrote for me:

Our neighbors had a baby less than three months old, whose bedroom was directly across from our kitchen. Every night, from about six to seven o'clock, when we were eating dinner, we could hear the infant cry almost ceaselessly during that hour. This continued for months, with the screaming getting louder as the baby grew older. The parents' solution for this screaming was to shut themselves off where they could not hear him cry. They explained to us that the child was really content and that giving him attention would only spoil him.

From what I have learned in this psychology course, it seems to me that he obviously wasn't content and needed some care. I believe that the child was really at too young an age to be spoiled in the way his parents feared. It seems to me that a terrific feeling of insecurity might arise from this experience, as well as a basic mistrust of the world at large.

It is amazing that parents could be so blind to the needs of their baby that they could ignore his crying. What language can a baby use when he wants to tell you his wishes and needs? His only language is a cry. When your baby is crying, *he is always trying to tell you something.* What goes on inside him if the world continually ignores what he is trying to tell it? Sheer, absolute helplessness, frustration, rage and despair—this is what he feels if his infantile attempts at communication are ignored.

Suppose, for instance, that your washing machine breaks down a few minutes after your husband arrives home from work. The room is rapidly getting flooded, and you urgently ask your husband to do something about it. What is his response to your urgent communication? Nothing! Absolutely nothing! He goes on pleasantly about his business. You are bewildered, but you try again, speaking more urgently and loudly. He is still completely unresponsive to what you are trying to say. By now you are frantic. You are not only concerned about the washing machine and the flooding of the house, but you now have an even more pressing concern: What has happened to the communication between you and your husband? Why does he pay no attention to what you are trying to tell him? Maybe there is something wrong with you and that's why he is ignoring what you are trying to tell him. You feel absolutely lost and helpless, as if you are acting out some weird movie or TV show in which the heroine is going crazy because no one will listen to what she has to say.

This analogy may give you some idea of how a baby feels if he is left to cry and cry with no response from his parents. It's as if the baby is saying to the world: "Pay attention to me! I have something terribly important to say to you. Pay attention to me!" But nobody does pay attention. Given enough experiences of this nature, can a baby possibly develop a sense of basic trust in the goodness of life? Hardly. He will become very pessimistic about life, full of frustration and angry rage. He may possibly give up and adopt a "what's the use" philosophy of life. Feeling deeply that his needs will never be met, he may decide it's not worth it to try, and become the type of child (and later the type of adult) who is lacking in normal aggressiveness and drive.

Or he may be the type of baby who, in spite of everything, will not give up. Instead of accepting the situation passively, he may develop an intense and deep-seated drive to compel the world to pay attention to him. How often have I heard adults say of an older child who is acting up, "Oh, he just wants attention." Yes, the youngster wants attention. But perhaps if someone had given him the attention he wanted and needed as a baby, he would not be as an eight-year-old be making his parents' lives so miserable.

Sometimes a mother will say when a baby is crying: "He's been fed recently, and his diapers are changed, so he's not wet. There's no pin sticking him and he's not cold, so there's no reason for him to cry." So she ignores the crying and goes about her household tasks. She misses the point: there is *always a reason* for a baby's cry. What she should say to herself is that she doesn't know the reason why her baby is crying, for no baby cries without a reason. He is always trying to tell us something when he cries; we need to try to understand what it is he wants.

A baby may be crying because he's lonely. Babies can get lonely just as grown-ups can. If we get lonely we can ask somebody to come over and have coffee with us, or we can at least pick up a telephone and talk with someone. All a baby can do is cry. So when he cries he may be saying: "I'm lonely, and I want the comfortable feeling of being held by a nice warm body, or being soothed and sung to. Then I'll feel better."

But loneliness is only one of the reasons why a baby may be crying. Sometimes we will not be able to find out why the baby is crying. Sometimes we will not be able to relieve his distress. Feeding him, offering him physical cuddling, singing to him—nothing may seem to relieve him and stop the crying. Oftentimes this crying will be caused by stomach distress or colic, since the baby's digestive system is still quite immature. Sometimes gently massaging his stomach or giving him warm water to drink may help. Other times nothing seems to relieve his colic. Usually, however, holding a baby close to you will enable him to stop his crying even if he is still distressed by colic.

There is another type of crying mothers need to know about. This is the fussy crying which signals that the baby is tired and just about to go to sleep. A mother soon learns to recognize this distinctive crying and to know that it is nothing to worry about, for in a few minutes the baby will be sound asleep.

All types of crying are messages that the baby is sending to us. It will make an enormous difference in the psychological well-being of your baby whether you ignore his crying and the messages he is trying to send you, or pay attention to his crying, trying to find out, through these messages, what it is that is distressing him.

Thou Shalt Not try to toilet train a baby.

From time to time I meet mothers who have tried to toilet train a youngster during his first year. This is a rare but drastic error. One mother who brought her seven-year-old girl in as a patient had made this mistake. The girl was suffering from a number of psychological problems, including enormous fears of going to school, difficulty in making friends, sticking too close to her mother, and not being able to establish relationships with other children. Along with her other problems, she was a chronic bed wetter.

Whenever I find a youngster over the age of five who is a bed wetter, it is an almost sure tip-off that the toilet training of the child was mishandled in some way. Usually it means that subconsciously (not consciously or deliberately) the child is taking revenge on the parents for the indignities he had to suffer when the parents attempted to toilet train him.

This particular mother had begun the attempt to toilet train her daughter when she was eight months old. I asked the mother why she had started so early. She replied: "Well, I didn't think of it as early. She was my first child and I guess I didn't know too much about children. A neighbor down the street told me that this was a good time to begin and that she had her youngster trained by the time he was a year old. Besides, it worked out fine. I would put her on the potty right after I fed her, and after a while she would be having her BM's just as regularly as clockwork."

The mother was quite shocked when I informed her that it was she, the mother, who was toilet trained, and not the child. The child herself had not been trained to take care of her toilet needs. The child was merely responding passively to her mother, who had trained herself to take care of the girl's toilet needs. I inquired of the mother what had happened to this so-called "toilet training," since the child was now a bed wetter. Shamefacedly she said: "Well—I don't understand it—but she sort of reverted back after she learned to walk—and I had to do the whole process over again, and that's when she started wetting the bed every night." I pointed out that the little girl had not *reverted back,* because she had never actually been truly toilet trained in the first place.

For a child to learn to be toilet trained, he has to master a number of complex skills, including neuromuscular control over his sphincter muscles. This neuromuscular control is really not adequate for the task of toilet training most children until the child is approximately two years old. This is the time to start toilet training, not during infancy. You may be able to toilet train a child who is less than a year old, but you are going to have to pay a psychological price for training that early. Personally, I don't think the price is worth it.

Thou Shalt Not worry about "spoiling" a baby.

"Spoiling" means different things to different people.

If by a "spoiled" child you mean an eight-year-old who always demands his own way, cries at the drop of a hat when he does not get it, is unable to take no for an answer, is unable to share anything with other children, throws temper tantrums, and is whiny, fussy, and petulant —yes, I agree, such a child is indeed "spoiled."

So we can define "spoiling" as allowing infantile ways of behavior to persist in a child well beyond the point where the child is psychologically able to give them up. The behavior of the eight-year-old described above would be appropriate for a two-year-old, but it is not appropriate for an eight-year-old. In all probability his parents never encouraged him or required him to progress beyond the two-year-old level.

But—and this is a most important *but*—"spoiling" is *not* a concept which can be applied to babies. We are being realistic if we demand that a five-year-old give up infantile behavior, because a five-year-old is quite capable psychologically of not behaving like an infant. But we are being quite unrealistic if we demand that an infant give up infantile behavior. He is *not capable* of behaving like anything other than an infant. After all, he *is* an infant! So let's give him the right to act like one.

We would be much better off in our understanding of babies and children if we gave up the term "spoiled." The concept of "spoiling a child" is a prescientific concept, dating back to the days before we had means of scientifically studying the behavior of children. The whole concept of "spoiling" seems to imply that if you pay too much attention to children when they are young, you will ruin them at a later age. But you do not harm a child by paying attention to him at an early age. You may, however, harm an older child by overindulging him, by being afraid to be firm or set limits with him, or by letting him have his way all the time—all of which are vastly different from giving him attention. Let's leave the word "spoiled" exclusively for fruit instead of babies or children.

Unfortunately a number of mothers do worry about whether they are going to "spoil" their babies. They particularly tend to worry if one of our friends, the self-styled "expert" in the neighborhood, assures her: "You'd better stop doing that or you'll spoil your baby for sure." Or you may hear a mother say: "I just spoil my baby rotten—I guess I shouldn't, but I just can't help it." Or a father may say: "Well, you just can't pick up a baby every time he cries—you'll spoil him. After all, he's got to learn that he can't have his way all the time in this old world, and he might as well start learning it early."

All of these comments show a profound misunderstanding of the nature of babies. It is true that a child needs to learn he cannot have his way all the time. If he doesn't learn this, he is indeed "spoiled." But at what age shall we begin to teach him this? Two months or three months, or even nine months, is far too early to begin teaching him that he cannot have his way all the time. To impose frustrations on him at these tender ages with the idea that we are teaching him to cope with live's later frustrations is absurd.

Let's be very clear: *you cannot spoil an infant.* Cuddle your infant as much as you want; you won't spoil him. Feed him as often as he's hungry; you won't spoil him. Sing and coo to him as much as you want, you won't spoil him. Pay attention to him as often as he cries; you won't spoil him.

The best thing that can happen to your baby psychologically speaking, is to have as many of his needs gratified and to have as few frustrations as possible. His ego or sense of selfhood is too tender and immature to be able to cope with much frustration now. There will be plenty of time for life to teach him about frustrations when he is older.

Thou Shalt Not let father ignore the baby.

As a psychologist I must admit that I am puzzled as to why many fathers stay so far away from babies, both physically and emotionally. Mothers have been complaining to me about such situations for over twenty years. Mothers tell me: "He says the new baby is so tiny he's afraid he might drop it—he won't even hold the baby" or "He leaves everything about the baby for me to take care of" or "Him feed the baby or change its diapers—are you kidding?"

What becomes clear as you listen to these mothers is that many American fathers seem to be afraid of babies. Their response to this fear is to stay away from close contact with the baby whenever possible. We are not sure why this is so. All we are sure of is that many fathers do stay away from young babies and that it is not good for the babies when this happens. By keeping his distance from the baby, the father is effectively preventing the building of close, warm, affectionate ties between the two of them. And this gets the relationship of the father and the child off to a poor start.

The relationship with his father is the *second* most important relationship in a child's life, particularly in the first five years of life. I will be spending a good bit of time in later chapters showing the importance of the father-child relationship. Right now, I want to point out that fatherhood, like motherhood, begins the instant a child is born. (Though the way some fathers act, you would think they believed that fatherhood did not begin until the child was at least two years old!)

I want to make it clear that I am not advocating that father take the place of mother in feeding and burping the baby, giving him his bath, or changing his diapers. It would not be psychologically healthy for the family to have father come home from his day's work and be expected to take over as a full-time mother until it is time for him to go to work the next day.

What I am advocating is that fathers *learn* to do these things, just as mothers need to learn them. Nobody, male or female, is born knowing innately how to hold a baby, for example. Most of us hold babies rather awkwardly at first, until we get the hang of it. Red Cross classes are a good way for both mothers and fathers to learn how to do these things with a young baby, but the best place to learn is with your own baby. It's pretty hard to be able to feel close to an infant you have never held in your arms, never watched gurgle and coo in his bath, never played peekaboo with.

If your husband is not interested in your young baby, nobody else is ever going to get him interested if you don't. Why not begin by trying to find out *why* he's not very interested? Inquire into his own family background. Perhaps his father took little interest in him as a child, and he is merely repeating this pattern, following the inadequate model of fatherhood he got from his own father. Perhaps he feels even more inadequate than you do with a brand new baby, but doesn't want to admit these feelings to you. Whatever his reasons are, try to get him to talk about it with you. Try to help him see what he's missing. Use all of your womanly wiles to awaken his interest, as a father in your young baby. With some fathers you may have to go to pretty drastic lengths to get his attention on this subject, but it will be worth it.

The foundations of a good relationship between father and child are laid in infancy, and these years will never come back again. The father who says he's too busy with his work now, but that later he will be able to spend more time when his child is older, is kidding himself. Soon, before he knows it, the "little baby" is off to school. Then the first-grader suddenly seems to have materialized into a teen-ager, and by this time the child does not want a close relationship with his father. By then it is too late. Because the father did not take much interest in the child when he was little, the child has no interest in what the father has to say to him now that he is a teen-ager. The father is really a stranger to his own son. The communication gap between father and teen-ager depends to a large extent on what kind of a relationship the two of them had during the child's preschool years. And this relationship often goes back to how that relationship began, during the stage of infancy.

AN OVERALL VIEW OF INFANCY

I have pointed out what to do with your baby and what to avoid doing. I have tried to give you an overall view of your baby in his first year of life.

What has your baby learned in this first year of life?

If he has been fed when he is hungry he has learned that the world is a satisfying place in which to live—a place where his hunger needs will be quickly satisfied.

If he has received physical cuddling, he has learned that he is loved in the only way that is meaningful to him: contact comfort.

If you have responded to his crying as an urgent message to you, he has learned that mother will come to his rescue when he needs her.

If he has had a warm and loving relationship with a mother who has provided for all of his basic needs, then he has experienced his first deep emotional relationship to another human being. This will prepare him to make satisfying emotional relationships with the other human beings he will encounter throughout life.

If he has been exposed to sensory and intellectual stimulation through objects, activities, and experiences with his mother and other adults, then he has found the world to be a fascinating and wondrous place instead of a bleak and dull prison. Sensory and intellectual stimulation, plus freedom to explore and research his world, add up to the early development of his intellectual capacity.

If your baby has experienced all of these things by the end of his first year of life, he has developed a good sense of basic trust and optimism about himself and his world. His sense of basic trust forms the first and most important lens in the eyeglasses of his self-concept. As he leaves the stage of infancy, this sense of basic trust will give him the best possible preparation for his second stage of development: the stage of toddlerhood.

3

Toddlerhood

As soon as your baby learns to walk, he enters a new stage of development: toddlerhood. This stage confronts him with a new learning task, active exploration of his environment, with the opportunity to learn self-confidence. It also confronts him with a new specific area of vulnerability: feelings of self-doubt, if he is excessively punished or made to feel he is "bad" for exploring his environment.

The first lens of the self-concept eyeglasses came in infancy when your baby learned basic trust or basic distrust. Now in toddlerhood, your child will add a second lens to his self-concept: self-confidence or self-doubt.

Up till now, your baby's exploration of his environment has been rather limited and passive. Even when he has been creeping and crawling as a preparation for walking, he has still been fairly well rooted in one place. As soon as he realizes he can get around the whole house by himself, his exploration of the environment becomes active.

This stage is a learning stage for the mother as well as the toddler. While he is learning to explore the house, his mother is learning about all the things he can get into that she never dreamed of. She learns to become sensitive to the meaning of long periods of silence when her toddler is in another room. This silence means that the toddler is into something his mother never thought he could get into! She rushes into the silent room to find her little tyke happily festooning the bathroom walls with her lipstick or delightedly engaging in "sand play" with detergent, which now covers the floor of the back porch.

This stage in a child's development is definitely the Age of Exploration, and every mother has to make a basic decision about her house in relation to the young explorer who now occupies it. She has to decide whether she will keep a house designed exclusively for adults or a house designed to be childproof. If she decides that her home should remain a completely adult house, she will need to spend a great deal of time restraining her toddler, both verbally and physically. She will be spending much time and energy saying "No-no" to him, slapping his hands, or otherwise preventing him from getting into things.

Many mothers do exactly that. They try to raise a toddler in a house designed for adults, not for toddlers. From the point of view of scientific parenting, this is a huge mistake. To a toddler the world is an endlessly fascinating place. And the curiosity which he shows at this stage is the same curiosity which at later ages will make him successful in school and in his occupation. To have his curiosity run into what seems to him to be a constant stream of rebuffs will not only snuff out this basic motive to learning, but will also leave him with self-doubt and undermine his growing self-confidence.

Let me use this analogy. Imagine that your child is now in the fifth grade. His classroom has a number of interesting educational aids in it: books on various subjects, a microscope, an aquarium, scientific exhibits. He picks up a math book and begins to read it. Immediately, his teacher slaps his hand and says, "No-no, mustn't touch." He puts the book down. He goes over to the microscope and begins to look through it. Quick as a wink his teacher is at his side. "No-no, leave that alone." Rebuffed once more, he goes back to his seat and begins to read *Treasure Island*. His teacher is at him once again. "Stop doing that!"

It wouldn't take more than a few weeks of this restriction to thoroughly discourage the child from learning anything in that classroom. He would soon feel: "Whenever I'm curious about something and want to learn about it, she gets after me. I must be a bad boy. I'd better stop trying to learn about all these things, and then maybe my teacher will like me."

If you saw a teacher actually run a classroom in which your son was a pupil in this way, you would be furious. You would say to her: "Why, you're systematically discouraging him from wanting to learn anything. You're robbing him of his curiosity about the world and at the same time undermining his self-confidence!" And you would be right.

What many mothers do not realize is that they do essentially the same thing in the "classroom" of their home that I have pictured this teacher doing in her classroom at school. They train their toddlers to habitually stay away from the adult objects of the house—a convenience to mother as a housekeeper. What these mothers don't realize is that they are at the same time training their youngsters to establish patterns of repressing curiosity and the fundamental urge to find out all they can about their world.

As soon as your youngster becomes a toddler you will need to look at the furnishings of your house through new eyes—the eyes of a toddler. You will need to remove breakable or dangerous objects so that he cannot get to them. He should be free to roam and explore the house freely without running the risk of hurting himself or breaking some article which is dear to you. So remove the valuable vases or china or bric-a-brac, or otherwise put them high enough so that he cannot possibly reach them. A house that contains a thousand "no-no's" can't possibly be a happy learning environment for a toddler.

It is necessary for you to take special precautions at this time because from a psychological standpoint, your toddler is still a baby. The English call the toddler a "runabout baby," and that's a very apt descriptive phrase for him. His powers of observation and judgment are very limited. He cannot discriminate between what is safe and what is unsafe in his environment, and, of course, everything that he researches still goes into his mouth. And although he is still a baby, he is now able to get about. To him a bottle of household bleach makes a fine thing to dump on the floor and splash in, and he may splash it into his eyes. That's why you have to protect him from the potential dangers lurking in your house. Safety experts have estimated that 50 to 90 percent of all accidents which seriously injure or kill babies and toddlers could have been prevented if the parents had taken proper precautions and childproofed their house.

CHILDPROOFING YOUR HOUSE

Rather than provide you with an elaborate set of safety checklists, I suggest you train yourself to look at your house the way your toddler does, instead of the way you as an adult look at it. You think of the aspirin tablets in the medicine cabinet as tablets that you take only one or two at a time for a headache or muscular pain. Your toddler looks at them as a new kind of candy. And he can kill himself by eating a whole bottle full of this "candy."

Make a systematic and slow trip through your entire house, including the basement, backyard, and garage. Try to look at it through the eyes of your toddler. Ask yourself: "Is there anything lying around that my youngster could get into? Anything he could put in his mouth and swallow which could injure or hurt him?" Then remove all such objects. Here are some hints about things to look for as you make your safety inspection trip through the house.

Check your house for poisons. Keep all poisonous objects or materials out of the reach of a toddler. Investigate to see what is under the kitchen sink, what may be on a low shelf in the laundry room, what is on a shelf or lying on the floor of the garage. Does your toddler have access to any of the following poisonous materials in your house: household ammonia, cleaning bleach, ant powder, liquid car polish, cigarettes, antifreeze, chlorine, detergents, paint thinner, lead-base paint, shoe polish, pipe tobacco, weed killer, furniture polish, insect spray, mothballs, or fly poison?

Your medicine cabinet is an unusually good source of poisons for your toddler. Drugs which adults can take safely in small amounts can be fatal to young children. Your medicine cabinet will probably contain drugs such as aspirin, sleeping pills, codeine syrup, tranquilizers, camphor, as well as various bottles of old prescriptions, which were never used up but which have not been thrown out. The only absolutely sure way to protect your child against the medicine cabinet (or any cabinet containing potentially dangerous objects or substances) is to put a lock on it.

When you are the parent of a toddler, you also need to develop the habit of being eagle-eyed: of glancing around rooms (especially floors) from time to time to see that no nails, razor blades, sharp pieces of broken toys, open safety pins, or other such dangerous objects are lying around.

Now that your child is a toddler, the toys or other objects he plays with should be large enough so that he cannot put them in his mouth, swallow them, or choke on them. Make sure that he cannot find coins, buttons, pins or needles, beads, paper clips, or other such objects on the floor. Also, do not let your toddler eat foods on which he might choke, such as nuts, caramel corn, or popcorn.

When you are cooking, put the handles of your pots and pans toward the back of the stove so your child can't reach them and pull them over on himself. The trash can and the storage section under the kitchen sink are particularly dangerous places for children because we thoughtlessly discard things there which are potentially dangerous to a toddler.

Electricity, of course, is another potential danger for your toddler. Cover all normal electrical outlets that are not in constant use with safety protective caps. These safety caps will prevent your youngster from discovering what will happen if he puts a hairpin or paper clip into the outlet. Also, never leave a radio, a portable electric heater, or any other electrical appliance near the bathtub.

It should go without saying that firearms and ammunition should be locked up at all times, and that firearms should not be loaded even if they are locked up.

A home workshop is a lethal place for toddlers, and should be partitioned or blocked off so that a small child cannot get into it. Otherwise you will be allowing him easy access to such "toys" as power tools, saws, knives, paint, putty, and the like.

If your toddler is going to play out in the yard by himself (and it is a good idea for him to have the kind of a yard he can play in), the yard should be fenced off so that he can't get outside and expose himself to all sorts of potential dangers. It doesn't take very long for a toddler to wander off by himself and find dangerous circumstances. The only real precaution against your child doing this is a fence you are sure he cannot climb over or under.

Because of the well-known ability of the toddler to appear in unexpected places and to dart across a driveway before you realize what he is up to, automobiles are especially a problem. If you are driving a car when small children are around, look behind your car, underneath it, and in front of it before you start up. Be doubly careful when backing up, since many accidents happen when a hurried mother is backing a car into or out of a garage or driveway. When you park the car, be sure you set the brake and put the transmission in gear or in park. When your car is parked outside or in an unlocked garage, close the windows and lock the doors of the car. It is amazing how capable toddlers are of releasing emergency brakes, falling out of car windows, or locking themselves in. Incidentally, it is much safer to have hand-operated windows on your car than power windows. And never, but *never*, leave a baby or small child in your car while you run into a store on an errand "that will only take a minute." *Always* take the child with you.

One of the best things you can do is to sit down with your husband and think about an emergency ahead of time. The plain fact is that emergencies almost always happen when we are *not* expecting them. Most of us have probably given no thought at all ahead of time as to what we would do if confronted with an emergency. For example, would you phone your doctor or start out right away for the emergency ward of your nearest hospital? Be sure to have posted by the phone, and in your car, the telephone numbers of your doctor, the hospital, the fire department, the police, or any other number you might need in an emergency. All members of your family should be briefed on what to do in an emergency. You don't need to make this a grim and frightening thing for your older children; treat it matter-of-factly as you would a fire drill at school.

Be sure to have an adequate first-aid or emergency kit at home which is easily accessible. This kit should contain a small supply of universal antidotes for poisons. Consult with your doctor on the specific items such an emergency first-aid kit should contain.

It would be a good idea for you and your husband to enroll in a Red Cross first-aid course. The things you learn there, such as mouth-to-mouth resuscitation, might save not only your child's life but your own.

A parent needs to be *protective* of a toddler, not *overprotective*. There is a vast difference between the two. Your youngster needs you to protect him against dangers he is too naive to guard against himself. He does not need you to overprotect him against situations which hold no real danger. If you overprotect him, you will only fill him with needless fears of his environment, and undermine his growing self-confidence in his ability to cope with his world.

It may seem like a great deal of trouble to take all of these precautions in your own house and yard—and it is! But once you have taken these precautions and childproofed your house, you can feel free to let your child explore the house to his heart's content. For you will now have the security of knowing that your home is a safe environment for him.

Let us suppose that you have made your house and yard safe for your toddler. You have removed from your house, or locked up in cabinets, any potentially dangerous objects or materials your child might get into. Let's suppose also that you have decided not to force your toddler to adapt to an exclusively adult house by a constant stream of "no-no's" and hand-slappings. Instead, you have removed your expensive vases and breakable bric-a-brac so that during the time your child is at the toddler stage, the house is adapted to him. (When he is older, you can bring these beautiful, but breakable, objects back again.) Having taken out of your house the "nontoddler objects," you now have a house that is a psychologically healthy environment for a toddler to live and build up his self-confidence in. But now you need to go a step further and bring into your house new objects, toys, and materials for your toddler to play with which will stimulate his development.

TOYS ARE THE TEXTBOOKS OF TODDLERHOOD

It is unfortunate that due to our Puritan heritage many adults (especially fathers) think of play as an essentially frivolous activity. Psychologically this is not true. Play is necessary to adults, for through play, recreation, and vacations we truly re-create ourselves and are thus able to maintain a rhythm of life which enables us to function well at our work. Imagine a world with no evenings or weekends or vacations; how stale all of us would soon become. For adults, play thus serves to counterbalance work time. For children, however, especially young children, play has a different function.

For a young child, play is the means by which he learns about his world. In this sense, play is akin to work for a young child. Notice that while adults do things in play that they do not ordinarily do in their work (swim, ski, paint, watch TV, or go to movies), this is not true of young children. Children do not imitate the *play* of adults; they imitate the *work* of adults. The dramatic play of young children consists of imitating adults keeping house, cooking meals, gassing cars, repairing trucks, building buildings, flying airplanes, selling goods, or treating patients. Play is the major means by which a child educates himself about his world. To rob a child of play, or to provide him with inadequate play materials, is to rob him of his major source for learning about life at this stage in his development.

To most parents "toys" are things you buy in a toy store or the toy section of a department store. However, I would define *toy* or *plaything* as "anything your child likes to play with." In this sense, the following objects or materials are toys: household pots and pans, an old cardboard box, a trash basket full of old letters. Using this broad definition of *toy,* what toys and play materials does your toddler need in his environment?

Your toddler especially needs things to play with which will help him develop his large muscles, through running, jumping, pounding, climbing, crawling, pulling, and hauling.

Let's begin with your toddler's outdoor play yard, since this is the most natural place for many of these activities to take place. Every toddler should have some kind of climbing equipment in his play yard. In general, the best type of climbing equipment for a toddler is a low-slung jungle gym. You may, however, have trouble finding one of these, so I am going to suggest another piece of climbing equipment which is excellent for children and which will last them all the way through the preschool years. This piece of equipment is called a Dome Climber, and is based on the principle of the geodesic dome developed by Buckminster Fuller. Due to the strength of the geodesic principle of construction, it can safely hold as many children as can climb on it. You can find this in both the Creative Playthings and F.A.O. Schwarz catalogs (see Appendix A). Be sure to set up the Dome Climber on sand or grass, so that if your youngster does take a tumble from it he will have something soft to land on.

This is such a splendidly designed and constructed toy for preschool children that if I could buy only one outdoor plaything, this is the one I would buy. It does great things for your child's large muscle development, climbing ability, and self-confidence in handling himself physically. In addition, it can be covered with a tarp or piece of canvas and used as a tent, fort, teepee, igloo, or whatever type of dwelling your child's dramatic play calls for.

A second very basic item for outdoor play is a sandbox. Make it as large as you conveniently can, so that several children can get inside it at the same time. With the sandbox will go sand toys such as pie pans, cups, spoons, sifters, and cans of various sizes. Sand, to a toddler, is an inherently intriguing material, which does unpredictable, fascinating things. He loves to run it through his fingers, mess in it, build various mounds and clumps out of it, and make designs in it. Sand play encourages his spontaneous curiosity about the nature of substances in the world. The significance of sand play and backyard mud pies is far greater than most adults might think. This significance will become clear when we discuss the scientific curiosity of the child from age three to six.

Sand and a sandbox are also used as a background environment for playing with cars, trucks, buildings, and armies. Your toddler, especially if he is a boy, should have an ample supply of small, smooth pieces of wood for play in the sandbox, as well as small metal cars and trucks, plastic army men, people, animals, and dinosaurs. The plastic people and animals can, of course, be left outside in the sandbox. The metal cars and trucks must be brought in or they will rust. But don't expect your toddler to bring them in; he's not at that stage of responsibility yet.

Many a mother provides a sandbox for her toddler but

forgets about the toddler's need to have dirt to play in or dig in—just plain, old-fashioned dirt. A toddler loves to dig in dirt. All he needs is a sturdy metal spoon, a metal pan with a handle, a garden trowel or small shovel, and a plastic pail or bucket.

Just as important as sand and dirt to the toddler is water. However, many mothers do not make water play available to small children because of the mess. If water play for your toddler in warm weather repulses you because of the mess, then forget it. You will probably do more harm than good, for your own negative attitude toward it will very likely be transferred to your toddler. In this case, confine your toddler's water play to the bathroom and bath time. However, if you are relaxed enough as a person to be able to tolerate some mess and mud, by all means let your toddler enjoy water along with his sand and dirt play. But don't just give him access to a hose and forget about him. He isn't ready for that much freedom yet. Either be there yourself to supervise his water play, or let him have a large container out of which he can dip water to mix with the sand or dirt.

Another type of water play can be provided by a large container of metal or hard plastic, three or four feet in diameter, which can be filled with water to a depth of six inches or so. You can then supply your child with coffee cans, measuring spoons, plastic cups, plastic boats, and other water toys. Be there with him though; he does need supervision.

Another excellent outdoor plaything for the toddler is some sort of tyke-bike or baby walker that is geared to his age level. This type of wheeled vehicle is the toddlerhood precursor of the tricycle. Experience with a type-bike or baby walker will help him master the pedaling intricacies of the tricycle at his next stage of development.

A low slide is another much-used item of outdoor play equipment for a toddler. Avoid purchasing the typical kind of slide and swing set many families buy, however. A slide is fine, but swings are not good playthings for young children. A young child can't do much with the swing himself, and so he often demands that mother or father come and push him or swing him. Also, a swinging child can easily swing into another child—a disastrous conclusion to innocent play. In general, the best type of outdoor play equipment for a child of this age is the stationary type, on which the child does the climbing, rather than the movable type.

Large hollow blocks are good for climbing and for outdoor play. Colorful, hard, plastic containers such as are used by dairies to carry milk are also excellent. Unfortunately these are not easily available to parents who might want to buy them; but if you have a nursery school nearby which has them, you might find out from the school where you could purchase them. The hard plastic containers are superior to wooden blocks because they do not splinter or chip as wood does, and they can safely be left outside in the elements. If you can't get the plastic containers, however, and want to buy the large wooden hollow blocks, you might decide to have your husband make your own, as they are expensive. These blocks, together with a few wide planks, three or four feet long, sanded and shellacked, can be used by your toddler for all sorts of activities which help develop his large muscles.

A good way to supplement your own play yard is to take your child as often as you conveniently can to a nearby park which has play equipment. Here you should be slightly cautious and watchful. The play equipment in these parks is getting better, but many of them still contain the old-fashioned dangerous swings and merry-go-rounds.

Indoors, your child also needs playthings which will aid his large muscle development. If I could buy only one indoor plaything, I would buy the versatile Indoor Climber and Slide, which can be found in the Creative Playthings catalog. Your toddler can climb on it. He can walk up its steps. He can climb its rungs. He can slide down its slide. He can drape a piece of canvas or cloth over it and use it for dramatic play as a fort, teepee, or what have you. And it can be used throughout the preschool years.

Your toddler will also need toys and playthings which will aid his small muscle development. Toys for small muscle development include bean bags, a pegboard, hammering toys, large beads for stringing, simple take-apart toys, very simple puzzles, and a coordination board with large screws and nuts and colored squares that screw on and off. A few oblong blocks can now be given to the toddler, which he can use along with wooden cars and trucks in floor play; however, the blocks will not be used extensively at this age.

This is also the age for pull toys, particularly the kind that makes a sound as the child pulls it. Two companies that specialize in making well-designed and sturdy toys for the toddler are Playskool and Sifo.

Soft cuddly animals and dolls are very appropriate for the toddler. It is quite normal at this age for both girls and boys to play with dolls and stuffed animals and to take them to bed at night. Sometimes uniformed adults think it is not masculine for a little boy to want to play with dolls or stuffed animals at this stage. Doll play is a positive aspect of a boy's development for it encourages feelings of tenderness, care, and protectiveness. In addition, dolls and stuffed animals are used by toddlers for dramatic play. They help the boy, as well as the girl, to play out important emotions about various aspects of family life and to act out the roles of mother, father, brothers and sisters.

Where can you store all these toys and playthings? Avoid the traditional toy chest. Although convenient for a child to dump things in, it soon becomes a vast archaeological scrap heap, with layers of toys and odds and ends dating back to the Pleistocene era. A set of shelves on which you can store the toys is far better. These shelves should be low enough for the child to reach easily. This helps to develop independence, since the child can easily get his own toys instead of needing mother to get them for him. The toy shelves should be wide enough to house the largest toy your toddler might want to store. The shelves should have a retaining strip on the front edge to keep balls and toys with wheels from rolling off. Such a set of shelves in the family room or your child's room will be useful throughout the preschool years.

As an alternate possibility, you can easily build plywood boxes, approximately one foot by two feet, which can be painted vivid colors and stacked on top of one another in this fashion:

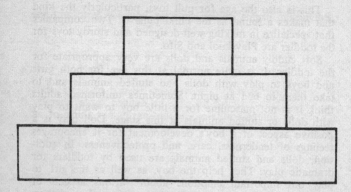

These boxes have the advantage of mobility and can thus be moved out of the family room quite easily anytime you wish.

Toys dealing with sounds and music are important at this age. Toddlers love rhythm and playing with sounds. You can buy rhythm instruments such as drums, cymbals, and triangles at a music store, or you can make your own. A series of tin cans graduated in size makes an interesting collection of drums. Metal pans make excellent cymbals. In fact, your household collection of pots and pans composes a fine set of rhythm instruments. Your local toy store or music store will also have toy xylophones, accordions, or other toy instruments that a toddler can handle easily.

Now is a good time to purchase two types of record players or tape players. One is an inexpensive type of "push-in" record player or tape-cartridge player that your youngster can operate by himself, along with inexpensive records he can play himself. Don't worry about keeping these records in good condition. He will give them a terrific beating but enjoy them hugely. He can play them himself by simply putting them on the record player and pushing them in.

But this should not be his only experience with music. Buy a good record player or tape player and get him good children's records which you play for him. Don't confine yourself just to records labeled Children's Records in the store. Try foreign and exotic music, such as African or

Polynesian drums, Indian sitar, or Japanese koto, and see if he likes it. While your child is still at this pliable and impressionable age is a good time to guide him through a broad range of musical taste. If you expose him to it, he will probably like any kind of music that has a vigorous rhythm and beat.

Books are definitely a part of his needed play materials now. Remember that *book* can be defined quite liberally to include things adults would ordinarily not think of as books, such as a Blue Chip Stamp catalog, a Sears or Ward catalog, a toy catalog, or old picture magazines. You can continue to help him to label his environment by pointing to a picture of an object or a person and saying aloud the name of that object or person.

In addition, you can actually start reading to a child at this age. He likes to listen to rhymes, in small doses, and the Mother Goose rhymes are now quite appropriate. Pick and choose among them, because some of them have really outgrown their usefulness for today's children.

The toddler still needs cloth or cardboard books because of his tendency to research the book by tearing out the pages. Simple picture storybooks geared to his level will be thoroughly enjoyed by a toddler. The Block Books published by Western Publishing are especially good for this age.

Two books are particularly helpful in teaching toddlers to label their environment and thus increase their vocabulary and foster their language development. These are Richard Scarry's *Best Word Book Ever* and Dr. Seuss's *Cat in the Hat Dictionary*. Both of these books can be used throughout the preschool years. At first the parent can point to the picture and say the word. Then as the child matures he can "find the dog, find the fireman, find the tractor." Still later, the parent can point to the picture and the child can say the word which describes the object or person.

However, books are far inferior in effectiveness to what a mother can do to stimulate the language development of a child. Continue the "label the environment" game that you started in the stage of infancy. You can do this wherever you are with him. Point to objects in the house and name them for him. When you are riding in the car, you can point out and name objects that you are passing: truck, tractor, house, church. When you take him to the market with you, you can also point out and name objects: cereal, milk, orange, apple, banana, cookie.

There are two main aspects to the language development of your child: *passive language* (understanding what is said to him), and *active language* (talking).

In toddlerhood, the passive language phase will predominate. Actually, it is somewhat misleading to label this phase "passive." For the mind of your child is *actively* reaching out to understand and piece together his native tongue, which he hears spoken all around him.

The infant begins his language development by babbling as we noted in the last chapter. Later, he begins to use what Gesell calls "expressive jargon," babbling that imitates the sounds and cadences of adult speech. He may be so good at this that it sounds like a comedian's double talk, just on the verge of being understandable as real speech. Do not hesitate to join in the "expressive jargon" game with him and babble and talk right back, just as if the two of you were carrying on a real conversation. It's not only fun, but by playing the "expressive jargon" game you are also helping his language development.

Somewhere around the time at which expressive jargon appears, the first one-word sentences also begin to make their appearance. These single words usually function as complete statements for the toddler: (I want) ... "Cookie!" or (Lift me) ... "Up!" or (I want to go) ... "Out!" It is a rare parent who is not charmed by the touching quality of communication possible through these one-word sentences. I remember when my youngest was eighteen months old and we were staying at a summer cottage on the beach. He woke me up from a nap one afternoon by tugging at me and pleading, "Outside ... ocean ... *beach!*"

By the time a toddler is eighteen months he is beginning to use spoken words instead of jargon in his language play and his social responses. His vocabulary may vary from three or four to a hundred words. He is just beginning to form occasional spontaneous two-word sentences now, such as "See that," or "Come over," or "Bye-bye in car-car," or "Gimme cookie."

How extensive his vocabulary is at the end of toddlerhood and how rich his language development will be at that time will depend to a great extent on how much you have talked to him and played with him through the medium of language. No toy or computer could possibly be designed that could teach him as much about language as you can.

Hopefully, your home is now a "school for learning," in which your toddler can happily and energetically explore his environment and learn from it. This school of learning needs only one thing to complete it: an informed teacher. That's where you and your husband come in. You need to know how your child is developing at this stage, and so you will need to follow him along in Gesell's *Infant and Child in the Culture of Today*. Here you will find sections describing in great detail the behavior typical of a child at one year, fifteen months, and eighteen months. For example, when reading about the fifteen-month-old, you will cover a section on a typical behavior day, followed by short sections on sleep, feeding, elimination, bath and dressing, self-activity, and sociality. In addition, you will want to read on into the chapter on the two-year-old, because chances are that some "two-year-oldness" will creep into the behavior of your eighteen-month-old toddler.

In addition, you will need to know which teaching methods are successful with toddlers, and which teaching methods are unsuccessful. The main thing to avoid with a toddler is forcing him to cope with a purely adult environment, with lots of expensive and breakable objects, so that he is subjected to a constant stream of negatives.

This is illustrated by a mother and child who were patients of mine. The first time the mother brought her seven-year-old girl in for child therapy she brought along her eighteen-month-old little brother. The mother and the toddler sat outside in my waiting room while I was inside my office with the older girl. The mother had brought absolutely nothing for the toddler to play with during that hour. Even though it was summer time, and my office is a five-minute walk from the beach, she did not think to take the child down to the beach where he could have played happily in the sand for an hour. I think she really expected her eighteen-month-old to sit quietly while she read a magazine in my waiting room. Of course that didn't happen. The hour that I spent in my office with the little girl was punctuated by loud crashes and shouts of "No-no!" from the mother in the waiting room. What was the mother teaching her toddler during that hour? She was teaching him: don't exercise your initiative. Be passive and quiet; sit still and don't explore your environment.

Of course you will have to use some no-no's with a toddler. But these should be reserved for things like fireplace fires and hot stoves—real hazards that cannot be removed from his environment. And when you say "No-no" to a toddler, don't just say "No-no" or "Don't touch." The toddler will not realize that this command refers only to certain things.

Instead, use explanatory words such as "No—stove hot," or "No—fire hurt baby," or "No—run in street— hurt baby." You are trying to get across to him the message that this *specific thing* (this hot stove or fire or whatever) is dangerous and will hurt him. You don't want him to get the impression that everything in his environment is dangerous and untouchable.

One of the best ways of handling a toddler who is getting into something you don't want him to get into is the method of distraction. We parents are lucky that toddlers are such highly distractible creatures, with a very short attention span. When we use distraction we are like a magician who says to the child: "Oh ho! See this amazing, wonderful, terrific thing I have for you to do over here!" (And come away from that lamp cord or hot stove that you were about to get into!)

Since the toddler is so highly motor and active in his behavior, he is bound to have a number of spills and bumps. It is important that you, as the informed teacher in his home school, not make too much of a fuss over these normal tumbles of childhood. If no one runs to pick up the toddler every time he falls, he will pick himself up. If no one agonizes over his little spills and tumbles, he will treat them merely as momentary and annoying interruptions to his vigorous play life. This will develop his self-confidence so that he can handle tumbles as part of his everyday exploration of the world.

One teaching method which unfortunately tends to be heavily used by some parents during the toddlerhood stage is that of spanking. Apart from a few very, very extraordinary occasions, there should be no need to spank a child under the age of two. If a toddler persists in running across the street, you may have no alternative but to administer a swift whack on the bottom. But ordinarily you should be able to handle the behavior of a toddler by arranging a home environment without the need for thousands of no-no's; by distraction; and by physical restraint where necessary, without resorting to spanking.

Spanking is for later ages, not toddlerhood. If you find that you are losing your patience and your temper so frequently with your toddler that you are spanking him a good deal of the time, then you need professional help to work out your own emotional problems in handling a child at this age.

One of the reasons many parents spank toddlers is that they interpret the behavior of the toddler as being willfully destructive. For example, a mother finds that her toddler has gotten into the bookcase and is tearing the pages out of one of her good books. She thinks the child is being hateful and destructive, and she strikes him. Not so. If a four-year-old did this, he would be showing hostile and destructive behavior, but not a toddler. For a toddler, tearing the pages out of a book is merely part of his scientific research into the world of books. He may not only tear the pages out, but will probably also put some of them in his mouth.

A parent should not confuse the normal behavior of a toddler researching his environment with the hostile behavior of an older child. No toddler should be punished for being normal for his age!

One of the difficult areas for many mothers in the guidance of their toddlers is eating. Many feeding problems typically develop during toddlerhood. There is no reason whatsoever for a toddler to develop feeding problems unless some physical disability is present. The only psychological reason that a toddler develops feeding problems is that his parents are not skillful teachers in this area.

Consider what often happens. Somewhere around the time he is a year old, a youngster usually becomes more choosy and finicky about his food and may eat less. This shouldn't really surprise us, because if he kept on eating at the rate he did in his first year of life, he'd soon look like a miniature version of the fat man in the circus. The child is simply developing more individuality in food preferences. Also, his appetite (like an adult's) varies from day to day and week to week. But a mother may fret that her toddler is not eating enough. So, feeling worried and insecure, she starts to put pressure on him, urging him to eat. "Finish

up your carrots, Tommy, so you'll grow big and strong."
Now the vicious circle begins. The more the mother pressures him to eat, the more balky and resistant the toddler
becomes. The less the toddler eats, the more worried and
anxious the mother gets, and the more she pushes and
cajoles him to eat. Soon the mother has a full-fledged
eating problem on her hands, where before no problem
existed.

All of this is completely unnecessary. Why? Because we
parents have a great ally on our side, if we use it wisely:
the *natural hunger of the child.* If we put a varied,
reasonably well-balanced diet before the child, and *leave
him alone,* he will eat enough of the food we put before
him to keep healthy and strong. But we have to respect
his individuality in eating habits. Allow for his taste to
change from month to month, and his appetite to vary
from day to day. If he suddenly turns against a vegetable
or fruit that he loved last week, so what? Give him the
freedom to turn against it, and don't try to force him or
wheedle him into eating it. If you present your toddler
with wholesome, varied, well-balanced meals, and let him
eat as much or as little of the meal as he wants, you
should never have a feeding problem.

Toddlerhood is the time when your child is apt to begin
dawdling and fooling around at meals. This comes about
partly because of his lessened appetite and partly because
other things than merely eating are more interesting to
him at mealtimes. By "other things" I mean such fascinating activities as messing in the food, banging the spoon on
the table, or throwing things on the floor. This behavior
can be very irritating to a mother. But it is important to
recognize that it is a normal thing for a toddler to do this.
He is not doing it deliberately to antagonize or provoke
his mother.

Nevertheless, how to cope with it? Sometimes you will
patiently sandwich in mouthfuls of food with short periods of play and distraction. Other times, when you see
that he's losing interest in his food and wants to play,
assume he's had enough. Let him down from his chair and
put the food away. If he immediately cries or whimpers
for food, give him one more chance.

Now we come to the important question: How do you
teach a toddler to feed himself? The answer is simple:
give him a chance! If you gave your six-month-old child

the opportunity to hold his own zwieback or other finger foods, you were preparing him then for learning to spoon-feed himself. The baby who has never been allowed to finger-feed himself from the age of six months to one year is probably going to be delayed in learning to spoon-feed himself.

When your child is a year old, or thereabouts, he will probably grab the spoon, or give some other indication that he is ready to have a go at feeding himself. Give him a chance. There is no doubt that you can spoon-feed him faster and more efficiently than he can, but resist the temptation to continue to feed him. It doesn't help him to develop much self-confidence and initiative if you continue to feed him. He may not be able to feed himself for the whole meal, and may still need help from you. But increasingly he will want the chance to feed himself.

It is during the early stages of toddlerhood, between twelve and sixteen months that most children *want* to learn to spoon-feed themselves. If you don't give them a chance at this age, then at a later time, say at two, it is no longer such a thrill to try to feed himself, and a child will want to have mother continue feeding him.

One training area that causes parents of toddlers a needless amount of difficulty is the issue of toilet training. Many of the books on child raising are quite vague about this. The mother who is trying to toilet train her first child is left a good bit in the dark. One key issue is when to begin toilet training. Most American mothers are in a great hurry to get themselves off the diaper detail. Who can blame them? It is inconvenient and messy to have to change diapers. It is a great day when a youngster is safely out of diapers and can take care of his own needs. But we have to consider at what developmental stage a child can reasonably be expected to accomplish this.

As I stated in the last chapter, most children do not have the neuromuscular maturation they need in order to control their bowel and bladder until they are roughly two years of age. To try to toilet train them before that time is either a psychological disaster, or just a sheer waste of time and effort for both mother and child. So drop the idea of toilet training your child until he is about two years old. We will discuss toilet training in the next chapter when we come to the next stage of development.

You may encounter mothers in your neighborhood who

proudly boast, "I trained little Homer when he was only fifteen months and had no trouble at all." You may be impressed with her statement, and wonder if you shouldn't try to toilet train your toddler at fifteen months also. What neither you or she know is that little Homer may suddenly become a bed wetter at age four or five and stay that way for many years. So sit back and relax and resign yourself to the diaper detail for a little longer; we will get to toilet training when your child reaches the appropriate age.

Now I want to discuss what is a touchy subject for many parents: a child's attitude toward his body.

Let's suppose that a twelve or fifteen-month-old toddler is being given his bath. He is delightedly exploring his body and its appendages, and discovering all sorts of fascinating things about himself. He plays with his ears and tugs at his ear lobes. Mother says, "Oh, isn't he cute the way he plays with his ears!" Then he discovers his toes and plays with them. Mother exclaims, "Oh, it's so cute the way he's playing with his toes." Then he discovers his penis and starts to play with it. Does mother say, "Oh, isn't he cute; he's playing with his penis"? Typically she does not. She may slap his hand and say, "No-no, that's not nice." Or she may distract him or do something to indicate to him that what he is doing is somehow bad and naughty. I'm afraid that some such sad sequence of events goes on in all too many homes.

What is a mother teaching her toddler if she handles the situation this way? Well, first of all, the so-called sex problem does not exist in the mind of the toddler at all; it exists only in the mind of the mother. To a toddler, his penis is no more inherently interesting than his ears or his toes. We grown-ups cause him to be morbidly interested in his sex organs by making such a big deal of it, giving him the feeling that his sex organs are a taboo part of his body.

When a mother handles the situation the way I have described, it's as if she is saying to her child: "Your ears are nice and all right to play with; your fingers are nice and all right to play with; your toes are nice and all right to play with; but there's something bad and nasty about your sex organs. That part of you is not nice."

If we wanted to, we could deliberately teach our toddlers to have the same sort of guilty (and fascinated) feelings about their toes as most children end up having about their sex organs. How would we do this? Easy. When a child first touched his toes we would immediately slap his hands and say, "Naughty, naughty; don't touch those things!" We would see to it that he kept his toes covered at all times. We would say, "Put your socks on. Do you want everybody to see your toes?" When we were teaching him the names of the parts of his body, we would deliberately leave out the word "toes." In every way possible, we would make his toes a taboo area for the toddler.

What attitudes and feelings would a child develop at later ages if he were handled in the way I have just described? For one thing, there would be an entirely new kind of "doctor" game played in a neighborhood where children were raised to feel that way about their toes. One six-year-old would shyly whisper to another, "Hey, I'll show you my toes if you'll show me your toes!" When these youngsters grew to be adults, they would go to see entirely different types of burlesque shows at bars and cabarets. Instead of "topless" shows, they would now go to see "sockless" shows. They would pay good money to see young women cavort around on a stage and slowly and enticingly peel off their stockings and reveal their toes! A ridiculous situation? Of course. But the only reason we don't have such types of adult behavior is that we are far wiser at handling our toddlers when they explore their toes than when they explore their sex organs.

How should we handle it when a toddler discovers his sex organs? No differently than when he discovers any other part of himself. That way, his sex organs will not become "taboo places," forever associated in his mind with shame and guilt. We will have taken a big step toward helping our toddler grow up with healthy attitudes toward sex and his body.

We should teach our toddlers the names for their sex organs and organs of elimination the same as we teach them the names of other parts of their bodies. Generally speaking, our culture leaves out the names of these bodily organs. Mothers love to teach the child the names of parts of his body and to play the game with him which goes like this: "Find your nose. Put your finger on your nose. Find your ear. Put your finger on your ear." But does she continue the game with: "Find your penis. Put your finger on your penis"? Probably not.

Professionals, as well as laymen, unfortunately seem to shy away from teaching the child the words for his sex organs. For example, a well-known book which advocates that you "teach your baby to read" gives the following "self" vocabulary and advocates that the mother teach the child these words: *hand, knee, foot, head, nose, hair, lips, toes, leg, eye, ear, arm, teeth, belly, mouth, elbow, thumb, finger, tongue,* and *shoulder.* Not a sex word in the lot, even though the list contains some words which are relatively sophisticated for a toddler, such as *elbow* and *shoulder.*

So we should teach our toddler words like *penis* and *breast* and *rectum* in the same way that we teach him words like *toes* and *finger* and *leg.* If we do this, he will have positive feelings of acceptance for these parts of his body. We will be helping him to avoid sexual hang-ups later in life.

Toddlers at their age and stage of development ordinarily do not have any interest in sex or their sex organs as such. We grown-ups teach them a fascinated, furtive, and guilt-ridden interest in sex when we treat their sex organs as a taboo part of their bodies. If we refrain from doing this to our toddlers, they will take no special interest in sex at this stage of their development.

We can review the developmental stage of toddlerhood in a single sentence: This is the Age of Exploration. Your toddler is a young research scientist, tirelessly exploring the environment in which he finds himself. He is exploring his physical environment, including his own body. He needs to develop his large muscles and his small muscles, and to have ample opportunity to run off all of that immense energy with which nature has endowed him. But the important, all-encompassing principle to remember is that in all of his explorations your toddler should be building up his self-confidence. He should be learning to feel confident of his growing abilities to walk and run and climb and jump; to build with blocks; to play with cars and trucks; to play with sand and dirt and water; to play with dolls and stuffed animals; to play with rhythms and sounds; to play and socialize with his mother; to babble and play with sounds and speech patterns as his language develops; to play with books and have adults read to him.

If he is allowed to play and explore freely in such a stimulating environment, he will acquire feelings of confidence about himself. These feelings will form the second lens in his self-concept eyeglasses. But if he meets a constant stream of "no-no's," he will develop feelings of self-doubt, which will be devastating to his initiative and drive as an adult.

In the Age of Exploration, the most priceless gift you can give your toddler is the freedom to explore. This will require patience and forbearance from you as a mother. You will surely have impatient moments with a house that looks at the end of each play day as though a windstorm had hit it. But remember that those beautiful, well-manicured houses you see, which look as if no children lived there, cannot possibly be developing children with feelings of self-confidence.

When a mother has a toddler in the house, she can basically make one of two choices. She can choose to have a spotless house and raise a toddler full of self-doubt. Or she can choose to have a periodically littered house and raise a toddler full of self-confidence. If you make the second choice, you will give your child the best possible send-off into his next stage of development—that of first adolescence.

4

First Adolescence

The stage of toddlerhood starts when your child begins to walk, which is approximately at one year, and continues until he is approximately two years old.

But if we tried to match my youngest child to this time-table, we would see that he entered the stage of toddler-hood at about nine months, because that's when he began to walk. Although the timetable called for him to enter the stage of "first adolescence" at approximately two years, he actually entered that stage at about twenty months. How did we know? He gave a very sure signal that he was leaving the stage of toddlerhood at around twenty months. During the stage of toddlerhood, if you asked him if he wanted something which he didn't want, he would say "No-no" in a quiet and undemonstrative tone. No big fuss or feathers about it. But when he was about twenty months old, during the course of one week it suddenly seemed as if we were dealing with an entirely new boy. Now when we asked him if he wanted something, he literally shouted "No! No! Don't wannit!"

As soon as he started to act this way, we knew that

98

although chronologically he was only twenty months old, he was now in a new stage of development. Emotionally he had reached the stage of "First Adolescence."

So the timing of these stages of development will vary with each individual child. Each child goes through the stages of development in the *order* given in this book, but at his *own rate of speed,* faster at one point and slower at another.

When I describe typical two-year-old behavior characteristic of the first adolescence stage, approximately 50 percent of the two-year-old children you might study will be behaving this way; another 25 percent will already have gone past this typical behavior; and another 25 percent will not yet have reached it.

Therefore, do not use these generalized descriptions of typical stages of development as things that your child "ought" to go through exactly as described. These generalized descriptions are only given as guides to the probable *direction* of the changes your child will go through as he matures. It is the *order* of the stages which is important for you to know. But your child will put the stamp of his own individuality on each stage as he passes through it.

Child development does not proceed smoothly and evenly in the direction of more mature behavior as your child grows older. Instead, growth and development in children generally proceed by stages of equilibrium followed by stages of disequilibrium. For example, the stage of toddlerhood is a stage of equilibrium; and it is followed by the stage of "first adolescence" (from approximately second to third birthday), which is a stage of disequilibrium. This stage in turn is followed by the three-year-old, a stage of equilibrium; followed by the four-year-old, a stage of disequilibrium. Then comes the five-year-old, another stage of equilibrium. Strangely enough, it's as if Mother Nature had arranged a simple way for us to remember these stages, in that the odd numbers (one-year-old, three-year-old, five-year-old) are ages of equilibrium, whereas the even numbers (two-year-old, four-year-old) are ages of disequilibrium.

If you want a very simple definition of equilibrium and disequilibrium that every mother can understand, it is this: When your child is generally a pleasure to have around (such as a three-year-old), he is in a stage of equilibrium.

When your child is mainly acting like an obnoxious monster (such as a two-year-old), he's in a stage of disequilibrium. Fair enough?

This first adolescence stage is a *transition* stage—the first transition stage in our story of how a child grows and matures. I have named it "first adolescence" because of the surprisingly clear analogy with the teen-age years, which we might call "second adolescence."

Teen-age is a transition period between being a child and being an adult. The pre-teen child operates within the limits set for him by his parents. He is not yet mature enough to stand on his own and set his own limits and rules. But within the limits set by his parents, the pre-teen has attained a certain psychological equilibrium. In order for him to reach a higher equilibrium as an adult, he must begin by breaking up the equilibrium of childhood. Once the parent of a teen-ager understands this fundamental concept, the bewildering varieties of teen-age behavior suddenly become comprehensible. Now the parent can understand why a teen-ager has a psychological need to like a different kind of music, wear his hair differently, dress differently, and in general behave in ways which are contrary to those approved by grown-ups.

As Mark Twain said: "When I was sixteen I thought my father was the stupidest man in the world. When I got to be twenty-one, I was amazed at how much the old man had learned in five years!"

Second adolescence is a transitional stage between childhood and adulthood. First adolescence is a transitional stage between babyhood and childhood. Both are full of storm and stress. Both involve negativism and rebellion.

It is important for a parent to see the *positive aspects* of this disequilibrium stage of development. Among sophisticated parents, this stage is known as the "terrible two's," and it is dreaded. But let's look at it this way. Take a "runabout baby" aged sixteen or eighteen months. He is still in the stage of babyhood. How can nature get him to become a three-year-old, with all of the personality maturity characteristic of being no longer a baby but a child? Mother Nature can steer him there only by breaking up the patterns of equilibrium he has achieved as a baby, albeit a "runabout baby." That's why, when our youngest boy started screaming *"No! No!"* at twenty months, we knew his patterns of equilibrium as a baby were breaking up.

Although your two-year-old's negativism and rebelliousness will cause you some difficult moments as a parent, remember that it is actually a *positive stage* in your child's development. Without it, he would remain stuck in the equilibrium of babyhood.

A friend who knew little about child psychology wrote to me many years ago when her little girl was about two and a half. She told me of an incident in which she was taking the little girl with her to the supermarket when suddenly the youngster abruptly squatted down on the pavement and refused to budge an inch. The mother was completely puzzled by this behavior because the girl had never done anything like that before.

She asked me, "Why is she acting like that?" Perhaps the simplest answer I could have given would be: "She's acting like that because she's two-and-one-half years old!"

Had this mother read the description of the two-and-one-half year old in Dr. Gesell's *Infant and Child in the Culture of Today*, she would have immediately known why her daughter was acting that way:

> If a group of nursery school parents should cast a secret ballot to determine the most exasperating age in the preschool period, it is quite likely that the honors would fall to the two-and-a-half-year-old, because he has a reputation for going to contrary extremes. The spanking curve therefore comes to a peak at about this time.[1]

The child at this stage is not a good member of any social group, and is not really ready for group relationships with his peers. He still needs mother. Mother is the sun around which he, the young planet, revolves.

He tends to be rigid and inflexible. He wants what he wants when he wants it, and he wants it *now!* It is difficult for him to compromise, to give a little, to adapt easily. Everything has to be just so. If a parent changes a word or leaves out a word in a favorite and well-known story of his, he may object violently. For any domestic routine he sets up a rigid sequence of events and insists that things be done exactly in that way. In this respect, he reminds you of a fussy, perfectionistic old bachelor, who is extremely set in his ways. But he can change his demands abruptly and violently 180 degrees. If you offer him juice in a glass, he wants a cup. If you offer him juice in a cup, he wants a glass.

He is domineering and demanding, and loves to give orders. He acts like the Little King, the ruler of the house. He may try to do something which he obviously cannot do, such as tie his shoes by himself, but he will furiously resist help. Then, when he finds out he can't do it, he will burst into tears and stage a violent scene, perhaps even berating you for not helping him.

This is a stage of violent emotions, storm and stress, and frequent changes in mood. It is an age of extremism. Often it is difficult for the child to make a simple, clear-cut choice and stick with it. He will shuttle back and forth between his contrary feelings: "I want it" to "I don't want it"; "I will" to "I won't." The simple decision of whether he wants to stop at the store to get an ice cream cone may bring out one of these violent decision-making shuttles in him.

He can be Mr. Broken Record. He will go on and on and on with some activity or speech pattern or word until mother is ready to climb the walls. It is often difficult to introduce new things to him, such as new foods or new clothes. He wants the security of the old and the familiar. This is why he likes rituals; everything must be done in just a certain way and in exactly a certain routine. The two-and-a-half-year-old is famous for his rigidity. And when a rigid two-and-a-half-year-old meets a rigid parent, watch out! The child at this stage makes strong demands on our patience. His ability to share, to wait, and to take turns is very limited.

From the positive view, a child at this stage is typically vigorous, enthusiastic, and energetic. If the parent is understanding of the nature of a child at this stage then she can enjoy his fascinating personality characteristics. And he *can* be charming at times, with his exuberance, his naivete, his wonderment at the new and unspoiled world as he sees it, his imaginativeness, his enthusiastic zest for life, and his generosity.

What is your child learning at this stage of development? The mother of a first adolescent might answer the same way the mother of a teen-ager answers: "I can't see that he's learning anything except how to be obnoxious and upset his mother!" And, let's face it, there's a certain amount of truth in the mother's anguished complaint!

But looking beyond the daily aggravations, you should understand that your child at this stage of development is learning *self-identity* versus *social conformity*. (This is a miniature version of the exact same developmental task he will go through much later in his teen-age years.)

Remember, your baby is born with no sense of "self" or "I." It takes him some time to learn to separate out the "me" from the "not-me" of his environment. This stage of development is the first one in which your youngster acquires a real sense of his own unique selfhood. And one of the things he has to do to establish his own individual sense of identity is to rebel against his parents, and become negativistic. In order for him to define who he is and what he wants to his own satisfaction he has to go through a stage of negating and defying what we want him to do.

In other words, *negative self-identity* is part of the struggle for *positive self-identity* at this age.

It is difficult to describe in words the difference between the sense of "selfhood" in a child in the stage of toddlerhood, and a child in the stage of first adolescence. There is a naive, innocent, one-directional quality of expansiveness in the toddler, for he is still basically a baby, though capable of locomotion. But the first adolescent has lost this naive, innocent, one-directional quality of his life. Life for him is not a one-way but a two-way street. For the first time in his young life he is struggling with massive contradictory tendencies within himself. By his behavior he is asking himself: "Hey, which way do I want to go? Do I want to go back to being a baby, or to move ahead to becoming a child? What do I want? Do I want to do what my parents tell me to do, or do I want to do what I want, which is just the opposite? Or is it really just the opposite? And who is the 'I' that wants to do these things? Who am I, anyway?"

An illustration from the teen-age years may clarify this typical "adolescent" behavior of the two-year-old. A fifteen-year-old high school girl went shopping with her mother to buy a new dress. She tried on a number of dresses but couldn't seem to make up her mind. Finally, she turned to her mother and asked, "Which one do you think I should get?" Her other said, "Well I think that blue one looks especially good on you." To which the girl snapped, "Oh, Mother—you're always trying to run my life!"

Several months later, the two of them were shopping again, this time to buy a new dress for a school dance. Once again the girl had trouble making up her mind, and once again she turned to her mother and asked her opinion. The mother, thinking she had learned a lesson from the previous shopping trip, replied, "I'm sure you'll be able to make a wise decision yourself, dear." To which the girl responded, "Oh, Mother—you never give me any help when I need you!" The mother was utterly bewildered, and when she related the story to me, exclaimed, "I guess I'll never understand teen-agers!"

Actually, once you have the key, it's easy to understand the girl's apparently contradictory behavior. Teen-age is a transition from childhood to adulthood. On the first shopping trip the girl was feeling mainly the wish to be adult and grown-up. So she didn't really want her mother's help in making a decision that day. The second shopping trip the girl was feeling the wish to be dependent and like a little girl again. She did want her mother's help that time.

First adolescence is like that also. Much of the time this stage is characterized by, "Please, Mom, I'd rather do it myself!" At times, the child will refuse his mother's help in dressing him, with the indignant comment, "I'll do it!" At other times he will go limp and proclaim that he is a baby and mother must do it all for him. Like the teen-ager, the two-year-old is swinging back and forth, from one hour to the next, or one day to the next, between his wish to be independent and his desire to hold on to his babyish dependence on mother. He is Mr. Yes-and-No. For this reason, rules and limits should be flexible for the first adolescent. It is a mistake for a parent to insist on one absolute set of rules regarding dressing, bath time, or anything else *for this age child*. Absolute and rigid rules simply don't fit this stage of development, because this stage is so full of ambivalent feelings and urges. In general, it *is* wise for parents to have consistent rules and limits, beginning when a child reaches approximately the age of three. But between the second and third birthday, parents could well adopt Emerson's wise counsel: "A foolish consistency is the hobgoblin of little minds."

The new developmental task for this age, then, is for

the child to *acquire a firm sense of selfhood*, of who he is. However, at the same time he must learn to conform to what society (mostly his parents, at this stage) expects of him.

There are two ways in which things can go wrong at this stage.

First, parents can make far too many demands for control and conformity, and the child can become over-controlled. I think of a boy I know who never went through the stage of rebellion typical of the two-year-old because his mother never let him. She trained him very strictly to be passive and obedient. She would tolerate none of the boyish impulsiveness and emotional outbursts so typical of this stage. Instead, she rewarded her son for being quiet, passive, and "nice." And it "worked," in the sense that far from being an unpleasant time for her, this stage of development was relatively easy. However, it did not "work" so well for the child. When he entered kindergarten the teacher reported that he was fearful, would not play with the other children, and kept to himself. Mother, it seems, had trained him all too well to be passive and quiet. And this behavior could easily cause him to become a timid, unaggressive adult, who will be afraid to venture out and try new things.

Not all children accept parental overcontrol as easily as this boy did. Temperamentally, some kids are more "feisty" than others. This type of parental overcontrol may be bitterly resisted by another youngster, who will fight to the death rather than give in. This whole stage of development then becomes a battleground of wills between parent and child. Regardless of who wins the battle, the child loses the potential gains of this stage of development.

Another possible variation with a child experiencing parental overcontrol at this stage is that outwardly the child appears to conform, but inwardly he seethes with hostility. He grudgingly does what is expected of him, but he becomes sneaky. Every chance he gets, when nobody is looking, he will loose a little hostility on his environment. He will break or destroy something, pinch his baby sister, or engage in some hostile or destructive act. He may grow up to be a self-righteous, narrow-minded moralist, outwardly full of pious moral rules, but inwardly full of hostility. This is the Pharisaical type of person described by Jesus as "like a white-washed tomb, which looks fine on the outside, but inside is full of dead men's bones and all kinds of rottenness" (Matthew 23:27).

Another problem of parental control which can emerge at this stage is that of the mother who is afraid to exercise control. When her two-and-a-half-year-old demands, she always gives in. When he refuses to abide by the limits she sets, she immediately relaxes the limits and lets him have his own way. Soon it is clear that the roles in this family have been reversed. The child is running the family instead of the parents. This produces the "Brat Syndrome." These children do not learn any of the lessons of conformity during this stage of development. They are going to have a difficult time of it when they enter kindergarten and find that their teacher and the other children require a reasonable amount of conformity to rules. They are unable to do this, because mother did not help them to learn a reasonable conformity during the stage of first adolescence.

Look around you at the adults you know. I'm sure you know some people who are terribly shy and timid. You know people who are overconforming and overcontrolled. They can never seem to allow themselves to relax and unbend. They are stiff and precise and stuffy. You also know other people who are always rebelling. You can count on them to take the opposite side of anything. As members of clubs and organizations they are always the ones who are causing trouble. Psychologically, they need to have something or somebody to fight against. Both overconforming and over-rebellious adults were probably mishandled back in their early childhood, usually beginning with this stage of first adolescence.

CHILD DISCIPLINE

Parental control brings us to the topic of discipline. Up to this stage of development, I think there is no need to speak of child discipline in the true sense of the word. There is no real reason a mother should have to discipline an infant or a toddler, if he has an environment suitable to his needs. But a child in the stage of first adolescence does require discipline, and a mother needs to know how to go about it.

In this chapter I'm going to speak of discipline as it relates to the first adolescent. But I think it is important that you get an overall view of child discipline. So before you read further in this chapter, please turn to Chapters 8 and 9 which deal with discipline, and read them. Then turn back and resume reading in this chapter.

If you are now reading this sentence immediately after reading the last sentence of the preceding paragraph, this means you fudged and didn't turn to Chapters 8 and 9 as I suggested. Naughty mother! You're resisting suggestions just like the child at the stage of first adolescence. Now, why not give it another try? *Really* turn to Chapters 8 and 9 at this time. Read them. Then come back to this chapter and you will get a great deal more out of it.

I suggest we begin discussing discipline for the first adolescent by dropping two words from our vocabulary: *strict* and *permissive.* These words only confuse parents, because parents are always asking, "Am I being too strict?" or "Am I being too permissive?" These are the wrong questions to ask, and the wrong words to use. The success or failure of discipline has little to do with how strict or how permissive you are.

The first thing a parent needs to do in dealing with a child, particularly at this stage of development, is to make a distinction between *feelings* and *actions.*

By *actions* I mean the outward behavior of a child. A child runs across the street when you have told him not to. A child hits another child when you have told him "No hitting." A child throws sand at another child when you have told him "No throwing sand." All these are actions.

By *feelings* I mean the internal emotions of a child: a child may be angry or happy or fearful or loving or shy.

It is important for parents to make this distinction between feelings and actions because a child can learn to control his actions; he cannot learn to control his feelings. A child's feelings, like his thoughts, come into his mind unbidden. He has no control over how he feels and when he feels it.

Take the feeling of anger. A child cannot help feeling angry or hostile at times. It is unreasonable to expect him to control the *feeling* of anger. But it is reasonable to expect him to learn to control *actions* which express this feeling by antisocial behavior such as hitting, throwing sand, or biting.

The first thing to do with a child in the phase of first adolescence is to help him set reasonable limits on his actions. Unfortunately, many parents have apparently misunderstood modern psychology by thinking that to set limits on a child is in some way to harm or restrict the development of his personality. Psychologist Eda LeShan tells the following story. A friend of her husband once called him on business, saying he was calling from a phone booth near his house. The friend went on to explain, "I can't make calls from home because Bobby keeps hanging up the receiver." Bobby was three.[2]

But what are reasonable limits for a young child? There is no hard-and-fast rule which can be given here. Begin by asking yourself: What are the absolute minimum of "no-no's" that I need for this age child? It may surprise you to write down such a list and discover that the minimum number is smaller than you think.

A patient once told me about her preschooler, who had many habits and mannerisms that annoyed her. One especially got to her. Instead of eating cake like her other children, he would peel off the icing, roll it up into a little ball, and eat it, leaving the rest of the cake on his plate. For some reason buried deep in her psyche, this infuriated the mother. She was consulting me about how to manage this child generally, and so she brought this up in one interview. I asked what she had done to change his unorthodox way of eating cake, and she said: "I've tried everything! Scolding him, slapping him, offering him money if he won't do it—nothing works." I then inquired why it was so important for her to get the child to give up his eccentric way of eating cake. Did it cause him more cavities to eat cake this way? Did it upset his stomach? "No, it upsets my stomach!" she said. "I just don't like to have him do it that way and waste the rest of the cake."

I suggested she try a little experiment in handling the child and his cake eating. The next time cake was served for dessert, sure enough, the little boy started peeling off the icing and rolling it up into a ball. Mother, guided by my instructions, said nothing. The boy was surprised.

"Hey, Mom—I'm peeling off the icing!" he said, feeling she must have missed the action somehow.

"I know," she said, gripping the arms of her chair tightly and bleeding internally.

"Ain't you gonna do something about it?" he asked.

"No," she answered.

So, in accordance with his usual procedure, the little boy peeled off the icing, rolled it up into a ball, ate it, and left the rest of the cake. He did the same thing the next four days. The mother continued to say nothing. The fifth day, to her immense surprise, he ate his cake the same way as the other two children in the family. When the mother reported this incident to me, she was astounded. "How come he changed?" she asked. "No actor puts on a play when the audience has left," I said quietly.

There are many insights that might be drawn from this little incident. But the one I want to emphasize here is how foolish it was for the mother to insist on the child eating his cake in an "orthodox" manner. Ask yourself, with regard to what you want your two-year-old to do: How important is it that he do this or refrain from doing that? Is it important enough to make an issue of it? There are enough *important* "no-no's" and limits for a two-year-old (such as hot stoves, going into the street, or throwing sand at other children), that we don't need to complicate our lives and his with a bunch of truly unimportant "no-no's."

Many parents believe that somewhere there is a magic list of correct limits which all parents should set for their children. Such a "magic list" cannot exist. For each set of parents have a different set of personality characteristics and life styles. One mother and father are relatively easygoing, with a few limits they consider important. Another set of parents is much stricter, with a larger number of limits. This second group of parents would be most uncomfortable allowing their children to do some of the things the first parents allow their children to do.

I'll tell you a secret. I don't think it matters much what limits you set on your child's *actions,* as long as these limits are reasonable and consistent, and you can justify these limits to yourself and your child.

On the one hand, it is certainly a mistake and an unnatural thing for a parent to set no limits at all on a child's actions. On the other hand, it will be a frustrating situation for you to attempt to set 3,481 limits on the actions of a two-year-old. Somewhere between these two extremes lies both parental sanity and child growth. But that "somewhere" will have to be defined individually by each mother and father.

Most parents are pretty sensible about the limits they set on the *actions* of their children. It is when we come to the *feelings* of their children that many parents go astray.

FEELINGS CANNOT BE IGNORED

To raise psychologically healthy children, with a strong self-concept, parents should allow children to express their feelings. The actual facts, unfortunately, are otherwise. Most parents *do not* allow children to express their feelings freely.

Take one example among hundreds that could be cited. I overheard the following conversation at a park. A mother was there with two children—a boy who looked to be about six and a girl about four. The boy, who was very angry at his sister about something, said, "I hate you, Susie!" Did his mother say: "Good, Tommy! Get those feelings out of your system! Tell your sister how you feel!" No. She actually replied: "Now, Tommy, that's your sweet little sister. You don't hate her. You love her." Now that's a lie, and the little boy knows it. His mother is trying to con him out of his feelings. Of course, she can't really change his angry feelings about his sister. All she can succeed in doing is to teach him to be dishonest about his feelings. She can teach him to bury his feelings underground, so that they will then come out in sneaky ways, such as hitting his sister when his mother isn't looking.

This example, and hundreds of others which might be cited, illustrates how parents generally do not allow children to tell us how they feel. Instead, we try to talk them out of their feelings. This is true for any feelings we consider "negative," such as anger, fear, shyness, hurt, or insecurity.

About the only feelings we do not try to talk our children out of are positive feelings of love and affection. I have never yet noticed a mother trying to talk a child out of his feelings when the child was saying, "I love you, Mommy!"

Why do we parents act this way? Why do we not allow our children to express their negative feelings? There is a very simple reason. Probably when we were children ourselves we were not allowed to express *our* negative feelings. And so, unwittingly, we pass on these same psychological inhibitions to our own children.

We need to allow our children to express their feelings—all of their feelings, negative as well as positive—freely. It is only when a child is allowed to express his *negative* feelings and get them out of his system that *positive* feelings can come in to take their place. If we don't allow him to express anger and hostility, and get them out of his system, then love and affection cannot come in.

Repressed feelings make for bad mental health. Children will generally express their feelings until we teach them not to. This is why two children on a block can be fighting bitterly in the morning, and be fast friends again by the afternoon. But the parents of those same children may hold a grudge against each other for months. One of the basic things that adults with psychological problems learn through psychotherapy is how to express their feelings adequately. But if we teach them to express their feelings adequately when they are little children, they will have good mental health when they become adults.

It is impossible for little children to repress only certain feelings such as anger and fear, without the repression spilling over to their other feelings as well. If we teach children to repress their feelings of anger and fear, we may end up unwittingly teaching them to repress their positive feelings of love and affection as well.

Children need not only to be allowed to express their feelings, but they need to know that their parents truly understand how they feel. When they are afraid, or helpless, or angry, or hurt, they want us to understand. How can you show your child you understand how he feels?

You can do it superficially by simply saying to him: "I know just how you feel." But that's too easy and glib, and will not necessarily convince a child. There is a better way of conveying to a child our deep understanding of how he feels. This way was first discovered back in the 1940s by a psychologist named Dr. Carl Rogers. He called it "reflecting feelings."

THE FEEDBACK TECHNIQUE

It works like this. You show another person that you truly understand how he feels by putting his feelings into your own words and reflecting them back to him, like a mirror. With two-year-olds this is easy to do, because, in reflecting back the feelings, you can often use the very same words they used to you in expressing the feelings.

For example, your two-year-old comes up to you, crying and indignant: "Jimmy (your five-year-old) hit me!" At this point, most parents give an agonized sigh and think to themselves: "Here we go again!" And you gather your two-year-old and your five-year-old together and begin the courtroom scene: "All right, now who started it?" But this new method of reflecting feelings gets you completely out of the role of referee. Instead, when your two-year-old says, "Jimmy hit me!" you can respond, with feeling: *"Jimmy hit you!"* or "You're mad because Jimmy hit you," or "That makes you angry because Jimmy hit you." You have put his feelings into your own words and reflected them back to him. I call this the "feedback technique" because you are feeding back to your child his own feelings, and thereby demonstrating that you do truly understand how he feels.

Several years ago a mother I had instructed in this feedback technique told me about an incident that illustrates the way this technique works. She belonged to a baby-sitting club and was baby-sitting for another couple. The other parents had just put Timmy to bed and gone off for the evening, when Timmy came out of his bedroom, tense and anxious, and said to her: "Mrs. Jones, there's a wolf in my room!" The mother told me that before learning this technique she would have mishandled the situation like most parents. She would have said: "Now that's ridiculous, Timmy—you know there's no wolf in your room." And she would have gone all through the room with the little boy showing him that there was no wolf to be found. Which would have done nothing to alleviate his fear. Instead of doing these commonsense (and wrong) things, she used a different approach. She fed back to him his own feelings.

She said: "Sit down here, Timmy, and tell me how you feel about that wolf." He told her how scared he was of the wolf. She fed him back his feelings, saying such things as: "You really feel afraid of that wolf," "That old wolf scares you a lot," and things of that nature. She didn't try to reassure him. She didn't try to talk him out of his feelings. She simply reflected back whatever feelings he expressed to her. He told her how afraid he was of that wolf, how he hated that wolf, and how he was going to push that old wolf off the cliffs down by the ocean. Finally, after about twenty minutes, in which she did nothing but reflect back his feelings, he turned to her and said: "Mrs. Jones, I think I can go to sleep now." She took him back to the bedroom, tucked him in bed, and in a few minutes, he was asleep.

She told me about it the next week and said: "Hey, it really works!" It really does. Try it. This technique has a built-in corrective factor. If you don't feed back the child's feelings correctly, he will usually tell you: "No, that's not how I feel."

This feedback technique is easy to understand but hard to put into practice. The reason it is hard to put into practice is that when we parents were children we were not raised that way. And we have spent many years of our lives trying to reassure other people, give them advice, or talk them out of their feelings, particularly if those feelings are negative. So this feedback technique goes against the grain of much of our own upbringing.

I have allowed my own children to express their negative and angry feelings to me. But I must confess that sometimes, when I am reflecting back some of their angry feelings, I find a little voice within me saying: "Don't you dare talk that way to me, young man: I'm your father!" That little voice is not the voice of my scientific knowledge of how to parent. It is the voice of my own father inside me, when I wasn't allowed to express my own feelings as a child.

This, in a nutshell, is the real difficulty we parents have in learning to use this feedback technique: If we were not allowed to express our feelings as children, we will probably have difficulties allowing our own children to express their feelings to us.

"But isn't this allowing a child to show disrespect for you, particularly if you let him tell you he hates you?" many mothers will ask. I don't think being allowed to express feelings has anything to do with true respect or disrespect. A child will respect a parent if he feels the parent knows more than he does, treats him fairly, and respects him. But, from time to time, that child will be angry at his parents. If that's how the child feels and the parents do not allow him to express his feelings, the child is going to be thinking the angry thoughts anyway. You may as well let the child express the angry feelings, because if you don't it is going to be that much harder for him to control his behavior. Expressing angry feelings is like letting off the steam in a boiler.

I have indicated that it is important for parents to make a distinction between feelings and actions. I have suggested we set reasonable limits on a child's actions, but that we allow him to express whatever feelings he has inside him. I have described the feedback technique as a way of showing him we truly understand how he feels. Now I want to use a concrete example from the two-and-a-half-year-old level to show how this distinction between feelings and actions works out in actual practice.

The following incident occurred several times when my oldest son was around the two-and-a-half-year-old level. I had taken him to the park where he was playing happily in the sand. Finally it came time to leave. I warned him a bit ahead of time, to get him ready for departure.

"Randy," I said, "in ten minutes we'll have to go."

Ten minutes later I said, "Randy, we have to go now."

"No—I dowanna go." (Why should I expect him to want to go? After all, he's having a great time!)

I reflected his feelings: "I know you don't want to go because you're having a lot of fun playing in the sand."

"I'm not gonna go!"

"You're having so much fun you don't want to budge at all!"

I reflected his feelings for a few more minutes. Finally I ended up picking him up bodily and carrying him over to the car, kicking and yelling, with me reflecting his feelings all of the way: "You're very mad at Daddy because you want to stay and play in the park and he's making you leave!"

Let's analyze this incident, because it is like a snapshot illustrating many aspects of the handling of a child in this particular stage of development. If I had allowed my son to intimidate me into letting him stay at the park when we really had to go, I would have been teaching him to become a little tyrant and refuse to submit to reasonable limits. I would not be helping him to incorporate within himself reasonable standards of social conformity.

On the other hand, if I had refused to let him express his feelings, I would have been negating his growing self-identity and sense of self-esteem. By allowing him to express his feelings and feeding them back to him I was, in effect, saying to him: "You have a right to be angry if that's how you feel. I would probably be feeling angry too if someone took me away from having a good time. You, as an individual, have a right to have these feelings and to express them."

This incident is typical of many that you will have to handle with your youngster at this stage. Give him a chance to express his feelings, but stand firm, and insist on his obeying reasonable limits in his actions.

What I have described is an *ideal* way to handle such a situation. This doesn't mean that I or any parent will, *in fact*, always handle it in such a manner. We parents have rights too! We have the right to have bad days and cross moments and angry feelings of our own. We will not always be able to "keep our cool" and handle things in a way that is best for the child. We will not always be feeling up to letting him express his feelings. Sometimes we will just bark, "Shut up! Mother's had it, and you kids had better settle down!"

Many times mothers feel badly if they lose their temper and scream at their children. There's really nothing so terrible about this, but somehow mothers have the impression they should always be calm and serene in dealing with their children. That's a nice ideal, but I've never yet met a real flesh and blood parent who was able to always live up to it. If we are trying to give our children a right to express their feelings, we should certainly give ourselves as parents that same right. So when you feel like yelling at your kids, yell at them. Then, having gotten some of the angry feelings out of your system, you will probably feel differently towards them. You can tell your child later: "Mother lost her temper. I'm sorry I was so mad a little while ago, but I feel better now." And your child will understand.

It may be comforting to state at this point that not all children are going to give us an equally hard time during the "terrible two's." There are definite constitutional differences among children. Each of our children is going to be biologically different from the other kids. Some children are more excitable, some are more easy-going. This means that piloting one child through the treacherous shoals of first adolescence is going to be easier than steering another child through those same troubled waters.

But all healthy, normal children are going to show some amount of negativism and rebellion during this stage. If you get discouraged during this stage, remember: he really will outgrow it! By the time he is three you will be amazed at how cooperative and easy-going he will become, in contrast to his behavior at two-and-a-half.

Any mother of a child at this stage knows that his favorite word is *no!* Incidentally, it shouldn't surprise us that a young child learns to say no long before he learns to say yes. After all, he has heard the word *no* from his parents many more times than he has heard the word *yes!* If we keep "no-no's" to a minimum during toddlerhood, we will probably hear fewer from him in the stage of first adolescence. But, regardless, we will still hear *no* from him, along with other manifestations of negativism, such as running away when we call him, kicking, going limp or rigid when we want him to do something, or full-scale temper tantrums. Ordinarily these types of behavior do not occur in toddlerhood. How shall we handle them now in this stage?

If you have read Chapters 8 and 9 on discipline, you will know that behavior which is reinforced tends to be repeated. If parents respond to negativism by getting upset, then, unwittingly, they are reinforcing negativism, and training the child to become still more negative.

But there are preferable alternatives to such negative reinforcement. First, we need to distinguish "verbal negativism" from truly negative behavior. We may say to a two-and-a-half-year-old: "Okay, we need to put your coat on to go outside." We begin helping him on with his coat. "No, I won't do it!" he says, meanwhile contradicting his words by assisting us in putting his arms through his sleeves. This is a good example of "verbal negativism." It's as if he is saying to his mother: "I know it's cold outside and I really do need a coat. And I know you're bigger than I am and you can make me put my coat on. But gee, Ma—recognize that I'm an individual too, and at least let me protest a little bit!" There is a playful quality about this negativism which indicates he is playing a sort of "disobedience game" with his mother. If the mother does not recognize the playful or game-like quality of the negativism, and reacts by becoming rigid about the situation, she may create a crisis of conformity where none really existed before.

True negative behavior, not merely verbal resistance, would be manifested in this same situation by running away or struggling violently against his mother putting the coat on him. If he does this, there are several courses of action open to the mother. If it's a question of his going outside to play in the yard, she might say: "Well, you'll need to have a coat on to play outside; maybe you'd rather stay in the house to play." If he really wants to play outside, chances are he'll reluctantly let her slip his coat on him. But it may be a different situation: for example, if mother is going to take him to the supermarket with her, and she needs to go right away she cannot afford to be so easy-going about it. Then she may need to reflect his angry feelings ("I know you don't want to put your coat on; I know it makes you mad") while she continues to stuff his arms into the sleeves of the coat!

Adults are not the only people to whom a "loss of face" is important. First adolescents do not like to lose face either. We can try to avoid all-out confrontations with a negativistic child, and throw in little face-saving gestures, such as offering a substitute activity, or giving him an extra hug or two, if we feel up to it. But above all, by reflecting his negativistic feelings we are preventing him from losing face. We are, in effect, saying to him: "I know you feel very negative about this, and it's quite all right to feel this way. I'm really sorry, because I know how you feel. But I'm afraid you'll have to comply with my request anyway."

HOW TO HANDLE TEMPER TANTRUMS

Temper tantrums are the ultimate in negativism. Here the child's rage is so enormous that all he can do is to cry, shout, scream, or throw himself on the floor, kicking and flailing. If you give in to his temper tantrum and do what he wants, you will reinforce it. You will teach him to throw more temper tantrums in order to get his way.

When my daughter was ten she asked a friend to go along with us on a weekend camping trip. The girl said her family had other plans for the weekend, but added:

"Don't worry, I can get to go. I'll just throw a big temper tantrum and my mother will let me go!"

If you get upset and angry at a child's temper tantrum you will reinforce it. Then he will know that he can get to you any time with a tantrum. Don't try to reason with a child in the midst of a temper tantrum or try to talk him out of it. He is a boiling sea of emotions. He is in no mood to listen to reason or logic. Above all, don't try to get him over a temper tantrum by the threat of a spanking. Haven't you overheard parents say to a child in the midst of a tantrum, "Shut up, or I'll *really* give you something to cry about!" That's like trying to put out a fire by pouring gasoline on it.

What should you do when your first adolescent throws a temper tantrum? What you want to convey to the child is that this tantrum is something he apparently has to go through, but that it will get him absolutely nowhere. How do you convey this to him? *You ignore the tantrum.* Each mother has to find the ways which are most comfortable for her to do this. Some mothers can stand there and say nothing and wait until the tantrum runs down of its own accord. Others will want to say: "I know you're frustrated and mad, but you'll need to go to your room until you've finished crying. Then when you're through I have something interesting to show you." Others will say sternly: "Go to your room!" Find the method of ignoring temper tantrums that suits you best and use it. But most of all, try to help your child save face by giving him a graceful way out of the situation, if at all possible.

A special word about the tantrums your child may throw in front of relatives, friends, at the market or drugstore or shopping center. The same basic techniques of handling the tantrum should be used, but you have a New Enemy which may get in the way of your handling the tantrum wisely. You now have an audience. "What will the neighbors think?" rears its ugly head. If your audience knows little about child psychology they may think you're terrible for not spanking the child and clamping down heavily on the tantrum. So what? Are you raising your child to have him turn out happy and psychologically healthy or to please the neighbors?

HOW CONSCIENCE DEVELOPS

But "the neighbors" do bring up an important aspect of first adolescence: the learning of social rules by *internalizing the limits and controls you teach him.* He will do this in the form of what is generally called his conscience. The conscience can be thought of as the internalized voice of the *Thou Shalt's* and *Thou Shalt Not's* of the parents. Conscience is not innate. No one is born with a conscience. We *learn* a conscience. And we learn it principally from our parents.

Some children grow up to be adults who have too little conscience. They are the psychopaths and criminals who can engage in various antisocial acts without feeling guilty about what they are doing. But some children grow up to be adults who have too much conscience. These are typically the adults we psychologists see in our clinical practice. They are far too worried, far too inhibited, far too fearful that they are bad or selfish or worthless people, far too eager to please others and worried about what other people will think.

We do not want our children to grow up to be like either of these extremes. We want our children to grow up to have a reasonable and healthy conscience. We can help a child grow this kind of conscience by being reasonable in our demands for social conformity.

You can actually see part of the growth of the conscience in the child's behavior at this stage. First of all, he may begin to say "no-no" out loud to himself, even while actually doing what he is not supposed to do. When my oldest boy was two and one-half I saw him standing in front of the bookshelves in the hall, saying "No! No!"—all the while engaged in the forbidden activity of pulling the books from the shelves! Some parents might get angry at this and think: "Well, if he can say 'no-no,' then he knows he's not supposed to do it. So why is he doing it?" The answer is that his conscience is just beginning to internalize the prohibition against pulling books from the shelves. But he has not yet developed sufficient impulse control to be able to heed his tender young conscience yet.

It is important for a parent to realize that the very fact

he is able to say "No-no" is the first step in the development of his conscience. Later, he will be able to say "No-no" to himself, and actually inhibit himself from pulling the books down.

The main function of a conscience is to *prevent* antisocial behavior, not merely to make a child feel guilty *after* he has done something wrong. But this preventive function of a conscience takes time to develop.

It will take all of the first five years of life for your child to develop his conscience, to learn to internalize the requirements of social conformity. Don't rush him. Language, of course, is a great help in internalizing the demands for social conformity. As he can put things into words to himself, he is greatly aided in his mastery of himself and the world. And it is at this stage of first adolescence that language takes a dramatic leap forward.

5

First Adolescence

PART TWO

In discussing toddlerhood, I pointed out that there are two phases of language learning: *passive language* (understanding) and *active language* (talking). Between a child's first and second birthday, the passive language phase predominates. But between his second and third birthday, the active language phase comes into prominence.

The second birthday, as far as language is concerned, is a point of transition and rapid development. Expressive jargon has now dropped out. The one-word sentences are still there, but increasingly the child is beginning to speak in more and more complex sentences. At eighteen months, the child was speaking in such sentences as "Come over!" or "Open door." Now at age two, he is using sentences such as "Where's Daddy gone?" or "Bring Daddy the paper!" or "I don't want to go to bed!" Pronouns are now beginning to be used a good deal, and often they are used correctly. Also the child's speaking vocabulary may show a dramatic increase.

If you have talked and interacted a great deal with your child, he will reap the language benefits in this new stage of development. What he has registered internally in the toddler stage will now begin to come out in speech. In general, the more you have talked to him, the more he will be able to talk. This doesn't mean that you need to jabber at him constantly, and drown him in a sea of words. But as a general rule, the more words he has heard you say, the larger his speaking vocabulary will be. This is verified by comparative research studies of children from poor homes compared to children from middle-class homes. Children from poor homes are spoken to very little, as compared to children from middle-class homes, where mothers generally spend a great deal of time talking and interacting verbally with their children. It is not surprising that there are enormous differences in favor of middle-class children in vocabulary and language development, even by the time the children are four years old!

Some children pronounce words sharply and clearly from the time they first begin to speak. Others' words remain almost incomprehensible to "outsiders" until much later ages; only the mother can interpret what the child is trying to say. Part of this is due to constitutional differences between children. But part of it is also due to how much you have talked with your child and how clearly you have pronounced your words.

If you saw the movie or the play *The Miracle Worker,* then you remember that a turning point in the life of blind and deaf and mute little Helen Keller came when her teacher was able to make her realize that *every object has a name.* Your youngster at this stage will experience that same kind of turning point when he first realizes that everything has a name, and that he can learn what that name is. This is a thrilling moment of discovery for a child. Knowing the names of objects in his environment gives the child a new kind of power over his world. Now, for the first time, he can *internalize his environment* and deal with it symbolically. He can manipulate the *names* of objects in his mind, without having to manipulate the actual objects in the outer world. This enables him to order his world. It is this new-found language ability which actually gives him his superiority over the lower animals.

Many years ago, two psychologists, a husband and wife team, raised a baby ape in their house, along with their young daughter. The delightful story of this is told in their book, *The Ape in Our House,* by Keith and Kathy Hayes.

Interestingly enough, at first the baby ape far surpassed their young daughter in various motor skills and physical tests of "intelligence" in the first two years of life. But about age two, their daughter suddenly took a dramatic mental leap forward, and began to far outclass the young ape in her skill and mastery of tasks. What caused the difference at this age? The *acquisition of language* by the little girl, who could now internalize and symbolize her world in ways in which the young ape could not.

With his new-found language abilities, your child can begin to conceptualize his world. He can reason with himself. He can project a simple future. He can play imaginatively. He can fantasize. His mental life has taken a giant step forward and landed on the moon.

Previously your child spent large chunks of time practicing motor skills such as climbing stairs. Now he will spend enormous amounts of time practicing the use of words. Ruth Weir, a linguist, studied the speech of her two-year-old son by making tape recordings of what he said to himself when he was alone in his bedroom just before falling asleep at night. She describes this fascinating research in *Language in the Crib*. Roman Jakobson explains in the introduction to this book that many of the child's recorded passages bear a striking resemblance to exercises in textbooks for self-instruction in a foreign language.

So by all means continue to play the "label the environment" game with your child. In this stage of development he is what Dr. Gesell calls "word hungry." You will find him an enthusiastic participant in this word game. Wherever you are and whatever you are doing with him, you can play this game. He will be proud that he knows the names of so many things.

ANSWERING A CHILD'S QUESTIONS

One new aspect of your child's language development at this stage is the "question-asking game." Some of his questions will be variations of the "labeling game." "What's this?" and "What's that?" will be typical questions. He will ask questions about everything and anything. When you feel overwhelmed by his torrent of questions, you can console yourself with the thought of how intelligent he is. Because the brighter he is, the more questions he will ask!

Here again, we find a difference between what is best for the child and what a real, flesh and blood parent can do. Ideally, a parent should answer all her child's questions. By doing so you help him with his language development, his vocabulary, his reasoning power, and his general intelligence. In actual practice, however, no parent is up to answering the questions of a first adolescent all of the time. Do the best you can. But don't feel you're ruining your child and stunting his intellectual growth if you say: "No more questions! Mommy's tired."

How we handle our child's questions at this age will depend in part on how important we view his questions as part of his intellectual development. I'm afraid that many mothers think of the questions of their two-and-a-half-year-old merely as nuisances. A mother often wishes her child would shut up and let her do her work. But if a mother realized how important these questions are and how important her answers, she would take a different attitude toward them.

Arnold Arnold, in a book called *Your Child's Play*, has a sequence showing two different parental attitudes to the same child and his questions. The scene: the kitchen. Mother, emptying an ice tray, has spilled an ice cube on the floor. Her young child comes over and picks up the ice cube and the following interchange takes place:

Child: Why is the ice cold?
Mother: Because it's frozen.
Child: Why is it frozen?
Mother: To keep it cold.
Child: What makes the ice cold?
Mother: The refrigerator.
Child: What makes the refrigerator cold?
Mother: It has a motor.
Child: Why?
Mother: To keep it cold.
Child: Why is the refrigerator cold?
Mother: Go away from the refrigerator.
Child: I want to know why the refrigerator is so cold.
Mother: So that the food doesn't spoil.

Child: Why does the food spoil?
Mother: Germs.
Child: What are germs?
Mother: Bugs.
Child: What are bugs?
Mother: Tiny little things.
Child: Can I see them?
Mother: No.
Child: Why not?
Mother: Because they are too small.
Child: Are they smaller than a mouse?
Mother: Much smaller.
Child: How much smaller?
Mother: Stay away from the refrigerator.
Child: But I want to know why it's so cold.
Mother: Will you stay away from the refrigerator?!!
Child: Why does it have a motor?
Mother: For the last time . . .
And so on.[3]

Then Mr. Arnold asks us to imagine a more responsive way of handling the child's eager questions. Same scene, same cast, but a different approach. The mother is just as busy, the child just as full of questions. But now the mother regards these questions as opportunities to aid him in his intellectual development, not as nuisances to be shunted aside as soon as possible:

Child: Why is the ice cold?
Mother: Ice is really frozen water. Did you know that it's so cold at the North Pole that the water there is always frozen? If you leave some meat outside at the North Pole it will freeze hard as a rock. When it's frozen like that, it can't spoil. Do you remember when I threw out that little bit of hamburger I forgot to put back in the refrigerator last week? I told you it had been spoiled.
Child: I remember. You said I couldn't give it to the cat. What does "spoiled" mean? Why couldn't I give it to the cat?
Mother: There are millions and millions of little animals, so small you can't even see them. They float around in the air. Some of them like to settle on food and eat some of it and grow on it. These animals

are called germs. They can give you an awful stomach-
ache if you eat them with your food. These animals
just hate the cold. When you keep food good and
cold, they stay away from it. When the food is in the
refrigerator, they don't spoil it. But too much cold
isn't good for anyone.

Child: Why isn't cold good for me?

And so on.[4]

The mother-child verbal interchanges which you will
have with your child in the course of everyday living are
the most important "classes" he will ever take. We can
call this class "Introduction to the Mysteries of the
World." Treat your child and his questions with the respect his growing little intellect demands. Your interest
and attention as you share with him your knowledge of
the world and its mysteries is one of the best gifts you
could ever give him.

TV AS AN EDUCATIONAL TOY

There is a "toy" your house probably possesses, which is
a complex and versatile teacher for your child. That toy is
the TV set.

Television has been heavily criticized in the last few
years as a vast "educational wasteland," and rightfully so.
Let us acknowledge that there are a lot of things wrong
with TV. I hate those inane shows and those stupid commercials as much as you do. Actually I watch TV relatively little myself, because the quality of the programs is so
low. Good children's programs are certainly few and far
between. Many children's programs consist of old animated cartoons in which the same familiar big animal
chases the same hackneyed little animal over and over
again. Also, many parents today are worried about the
depiction of violence on TV. (I will deal with this issue in
Chapter 10, "Your Child and Violence.")

Let us agree that many of these criticisms of TV are
valid, and that the quality of children's programs could be
vastly improved. Yet it would be a mistake to overlook
the fact that TV can be a valuable educational device for
your preschooler. For example, since the advent of televi-

sion in the American home, the speaking vocabulary of children entering kindergarten and first grade in our public schools has risen enormously over what it was before TV. Says Dr. Louise Ames of the Gesell Institute: "From three on, they're exposed to all kinds of things they wouldn't have seen a generation ago. Their knowledge is tremendously wide."[5]

Edith Efron, in an article "Television As a Teacher," comments: "First-graders who've done a stint before the set have vocabularies that are as much as a year or more ahead of those of non-viewing tykes. The brighter the preschooler, the more he sops up from the screen.... All in all, for babies—whatever their brain power—TV is an educational bonanza."[6]

The most thorough research study of the effects of TV on children in the United States was done by Dr. Wilbur Schramm, who studied 6,000 children. He established that the brightest children with the highest marks in school are heavy TV watchers. According to Dr. Schramm: "Typically, the bright children are early starters. They usually begin earlier to watch TV. In the early school years, they're more likely than the others to be heavy viewers of television."[7]

It would seem, therefore, that there is solid research evidence that television, in spite of all its obvious defects, is a healthy educational force in the life of your young child. There is no doubt that if children's programs were improved, TV could be an even better educational force for children. The new educational program "Sesame Street" is an example of television at its best for preschool children. This program was produced by the Children's Television Workshop and financed by grants from the Ford Foundation, the Carnegie Corporation, and the United States Office of Education. More than a hundred of the nation's leading educators, child development specialists, psychologists, teachers, film-makers, writers, artists, and communications professionals have collaborated to develop this imaginative breakthrough in early childhood education via TV. Through exposure to this program a preschooler will learn the letters of the alphabet and how to recognize them in words. He will learn numbers and how to count. He will begin to learn to use logic and reason. The Children's Television Workshop issues a parent's guide to the program. The first issue can be obtained free by writing to Children's Television Workshop, National Educational Television, Box 9070, St. Paul, Minnesota 55177. I enthusiastically recommend this program to all parents of preschool children. I hope more such programs will be produced. This is television at its educational best.

Please do not conclude from this that I advocate giving preschool children an unlimited diet of TV. Far from it. I believe in stimulating your child's development by a wide variety of activities, indoors and out. Your child should climb and run and ride tricycles and play in the sand and build with blocks and draw and paint and listen to records and have books read to him. But, I do believe that watching TV has its rightful place among those activities. Not a lion's share, but a reasonable place.

Since we are talking about the language development of children, this is a good place to raise the question: Should you teach your child to read? In Chapter 11, "School Begins at Home–Part One," I will discuss this question in detail and throw some surprising light upon it from new research studies. But let me briefly answer the question now by saying: Yes, I think it is a good idea to try to teach your preschooler to read. The research evidence points in that direction. But the crucial question is: When? One of the books which suggests that you "teach your baby to read" actually recommends to parents that two years of age is the best time to begin. This same book also states that "should you be willing to go to a little trouble, you can begin at eighteen months, or if you are very clever, as early as ten months of age."[8]

This is arrant nonsense. And I fear that many eager mothers, not knowing any better, have actually tried to teach an eighteen-month-old baby, or worse still, a ten-month-old baby, how to read. Such an attempt would be laughable if it were not so tragic. The time to try to teach a child to read at home is when he reaches the age of three, and not before. First adolescence is no time to attempt to teach the average child to read, for this is the time during which he is struggling with all of the ambivalent feelings and pressures to conform that I mentioned in the previous chapter. He hardly needs an additional pressure; so forget about teaching him to read at this age.

JEALOUSY IN CHILDREN

Next I want to discuss the perennial problem of jealousy in children, or, as we psychologists term it, "sibling rivalry." The term *sibling* is a word that has been coined to get away from the awkwardness of having to say "brother or sister, whichever the case may be."

Any time that a baby brother or sister comes into the family, your preschool child is going to have a definite reaction to that event. When a parent tells me "Tommy just loved his little sister from the day she was born," I don't believe it. It is psychologically impossible. Why? Let me use this analogy.

Suppose that tomorrow your husband informs you of the following delightful bit of news. "Dear," he says, "next week Roxanne my old girl friend will be joining us. Of course, I love you as much as I always have. And I will be with you on Mondays, Wednesdays, and Fridays. But on Tuesdays, Thursdays, and Saturdays I will be with her. Sundays we will put up for grabs." Furthermore, when this rival actually comes to take up residence in your house, you discover that she does not intend to lift a finger to help you around the house. All she does is loll around all day, reading women's magazines and drinking milk punches. How would you feel about Roxanne? Furious? Well, that's approximately the way a preschool child will feel when a younger brother or sister is born into his family. He feels gypped, hurt, out of it, and angry.

Typically, he feels abandoned by his mother when she goes away to the hospital to have this new baby. When she comes back home with the new baby, she seems to have little time for him. She seems engrossed with this intruder. Furthermore, all of the relatives and friends who come to visit *ooh* and *aah* over the new baby and how cute he is, and ignore the preschooler. Is it any wonder that a preschooler would have negative feelings toward a younger sibling?

You cannot *prevent* a child having negative feelings toward a younger sibling; but you can *minimize* these feelings.

You can tell your preschooler ahead of time about the forthcoming birth so that it will not come as a complete surprise. Do not tell him nine months ahead of time; that's too long for him to wait. A month ahead is sufficient. (Although he may find out about it sooner by overhearing conversations in the family.) You can also help your preschooler to play out his feelings about a new baby by presenting him with a sturdy, rubber baby doll, along with diapers, a crib, and a Bathinette. Depending on the age and sex of your older child, he may want to take care of the baby, thump the baby over the head, or express his feelings in various other ways with this doll-baby substitute for the real thing.

When you go to the hospital, you can hide some inexpensive presents around the house ahead of time. Then phone your child while you are at the hospital, chat with him, and tell him where he can find a surprise. This will make him feel less abandoned. He will know that you are really thinking about him, although you are away from him at the hospital. When you come home from the hospital, you and your husband need to make a special effort not to be so engrossed with the new baby that you neglect your older child. Take the time to give him some special love and attention.

In general, a preschooler will react to the birth of a younger sibling with two different sets of feelings and impulses. First of all, he will want to regress: to revert back to more childish and babyish ways of behaving. This is a typical defense mechanism all of us use from time to time in reaction to stressful situations. We become babyish and infantile. Most parents handle this desire of the preschooler to regress in exactly the wrong way. They try to point out to him the advantages of being older. He can't see these so-called advantages. All he sees is that while he has painfully learned to feed himself or to become toilet trained, this "little brat" of a baby now gets all the attention, as mother feeds it and changes its diapers.

It is as if the older child thinks to himself: "Hmmm—maybe if I acted like a baby again I could force Mother to give me some of that love and attention!" So he may revert to soiling or demanding a bottle or wanting to be held and rocked. What response do these tactics usually get from his parents? "Come on, Jerry—you're a big boy now; big boys don't act like that. Stop being a baby!" This reaction from his parents only makes him feel more hurt inside and causes him to want even more to act like a baby and be comforted like a baby!

What should you do? Give your older child the opportunity to regress if he wants to. When my first boy was born, our oldest girl was six. We were prepared for her wish to regress, and sure enough, she did. She asked for a bottle, which we gave her; and for four or five days, she drank her Coke or orange juice out of a bottle instead of a glass. After that time she voluntarily gave it up, as if to say: "Well, I don't need to do that any more. I guess it's really not such a big deal to be a baby and drink out of a bottle after all." We went through the same experience with my oldest boy when he was six and his younger brother was born. In both cases the older child regressed for a while and then gave up the regression when the temporary infantile need was satisfied.

Your older child will feel angry and hostile toward the baby. Unfortunately, most parents try to talk him out of these feelings. "Don't say those things about your little brother; that's not nice. Be nice to him—isn't he a cute little thing?" Instead of trying to con him out of his feelings, parents should allow the older child to express his anger and jealousy toward the baby. They can then feed back these feelings to the child: "You feel angry at little Jenny. You feel like Mother loves her more than you." It helps if parents can even go out of their way a little to criticize the baby to the older child (after all, you won't hurt the baby's feelings, since he doesn't understand what you're saying). You will thus give your older child the feeling that it's safe to criticize the baby. A good example of this is found in one mother's account of the reaction of a seventeen-month-old boy to the birth of his baby sister:

When I came home with Jenny, Mark stared at me at first as though I were a complete stranger. He cried bitterly when his father carried Jenny from the car to the house. He was somewhat aloof for several hours. I was prepared to see some jealousy in Mark, but somehow I thought it would be subtle, or directed against me. Not so at all! The first chance he got he went right for the baby, with the most agonized expression, and tried to sock her. He looked grimly determined to smash this little bundle of trouble, and yet he was obviously terribly upset by his own impulse and sobbed, "No, no" even as he went for her. ... The ice finally broke one day, perhaps a week after Jenny and I came home. I was diapering Jenny and Mark was watching from his grandmother's arms. Jenny made some little noise. I imitated her and said to Mark, "Doesn't that baby make *silly* noises?" Suddenly Mark smiled broadly and said, "Silly!" It must have been a revelation to him that I was on his side. Here we were together, laughing at the baby. From then on, there was almost no more trouble.[9]

It should be mentioned that sibling rivalry goes both ways, from older to younger, and vice versa. It is something that cannot be eliminated; *it can only be minimized.* Parents are always wondering why their own children bicker and fight so much, yet can play happily with a neighbor child without bickering. The answer is that with a neighbor child your youngster is not competing for the same parent.

Each child has moments when he wishes all of the other kids in the family would disappear and he could have mother and father all to himself. What can you do to minimize these feelings of jealousy between your children? *Try to spend some individual time with each child each day.* Let him know that this is his special time and no other child can get in on it. You say you don't have time to do that? The mother of John Wesley, the founder of Methodism, had eleven children, and she found time to do that with each of them each day!

Another helpful way to lessen sibling rivalry and jealousy on trips, outings, or even vacations is to arrange to take along a friend for one or more of your children. You'd be amazed at how this takes the pressure off, and reduces sibling bickering and infighting.

HOW TO TOILET TRAIN YOUR CHILD

Toilet training, in our culture at least, belongs in this stage of development. Let's begin by setting down a few basic psychological facts about toilet training. First, it is a fact that no parent can toilet train a child until the child is willing to be trained. You can lead a child to the toilet—and you can do it hundreds and hundreds of times—but if he isn't ready to be trained, you can't force him, no matter how much you cajole or pressure him.

Second, what motivates a child to give up his old carefree ways of elimination and learn what is a new and strange way of depositing his waste products? Only one thing can get him to do it. He wants to be rewarded by your love and attention for learning this new procedure. But he can only want your love and attention if you and he have a basically good relationship. If you and he have a poor relationship, you are probably going to have a difficult time toilet training him.

Third, if you start before your child is neuromuscularly capable of controlling his sphincter muscles, or if you put pressure on him to learn too fast, he is going to feel that too much is being demanded of him too soon. He is going to feel helpless, inadequate, and frustrated. That's why I have emphasized in previous chapters that you should not start toilet training your child until he is approximately two years old.

Fourth, to most parents, toilet training a child seems to be a very simple sort of procedure. While it may seem simple and easy to adults, viewed through the eyes of a two-year-old the process of toilet training is a complex learning task. When a mass movement of feces in the bowels produces pressure on the rectum, this causes relaxation of the rectal muscles, producing a bowel movement. For a child to be toilet trained, he must be taught to change this sequence of events. He must learn to suppress the evulsion response of his rectal muscles. He must learn to call to his parents. He must learn to walk to the bathroom, take down his pants, and sit on the potty chair, all the while suppressing the urgent evulsion response of his rectal muscles. And a child is not truly toilet trained until he can carry out this whole new sequence of events by himself.

Can you now begin to see why this is a complex learning task for a two-year-old? If his parents punish him or otherwise put pressure on him for "failures" or "accidents," very strong emotions will be aroused in the child. Fear, anger, defiance, and stubbornness may be aroused if this complex learning task is mishandled by the parents.

How, specifically, do you go about toilet training?

First of all, you need to distinguish between bowel training and bladder training. They involve different mechanisms and so should be handled differently. Bowel training usually comes first, so let's start with that.

Many parents begin bowel training by figuring out in their infinite adult wisdom that it's time to sit the youngster on the toilet and see if he can have a bowel movement. This procedure seems so logical to many parents that they cannot see the inherent absurdity of starting this way. Perhaps you can be helped to see the absurdity of such logic if I ask you the following question. Suppose right now, while you are reading this book, some ten-foot giant were to suddenly lift you up, transport you to the bathroom, and deposit you on the toilet, announcing in a loud and impressive voice: "It's time to have a bowel movement!" Suppose that he then were to force you to sit there for five to fifteen minutes. What would be your reaction? The same reaction your child would have in similar circumstances! Such an analogy is ridiculous you say? Think about it, and see if many parents do not disregard the biological needs of their children by proceeding in the fashion of that ten-foot giant.

Many years ago, in a classic book on raising babies, *Babies Are Human Beings,* Dr. Anderson Aldrich and his wife Mary Aldrich spoke of a far better method of training a child in bowel control:

> Our training often ignores one of the baby's most fundamental equipments, his physiologic plan for bowel control. When we fail to synchronize our habit-forming techniques with his own eliminative efforts as they appear naturally, we lose our greatest opportunity. . . . The physiologic plan for moving the bowels can be explained in a few words. . . . As in every other vital activity of the body, nothing is left to chance. The baby moves his bowels according to well-defined rules, automatically set up in his colon. . . . At intervals of several hours, a spectacular performance called the mass movement takes place. . . . All of the colon beyond the ascending portion segments into several long, sausage-like masses, which with startling suddenness slump down into the rectum. The pressure thus produced on the rec-

tum initiates the straining attempts of the abdominal muscles and the relaxation of those which close the rectum. At this time, and not at any arbitrary hour of our choosing, a bowel movement takes place in all babies who are allowed to use their automatic control unimpeded. The mass movement is apparently uncomfortable, for the baby fusses under its stimulation, strains vigorously, and then relieves himself. . . .

It is not long until the question of "training" comes up to throw a monkey wrench into the machinery. . . . The baby is placed on the "potty" chair and expected to evacuate. Usually he is not consulted at all as to the time chosen. On the contrary, he is expected to perform at some hour of the day which seems best suited to his regime, preferably just after breakfast. The fact that the baby has his own trigger mechanism, the mass movement, is ignored. When he refuses, the whole subject evolves into a battle between the baby and the mother, and true training is far from being achieved.

It is unhygienic to ignore the mass movement as an initiating force in the rhythm of evacuations, for when we ignore a natural activity long enough it tends to disappear entirely from our list of assets. This is what actually happens to most constipated children. Their internal stimulus has either disappeared entirely or has been disregarded so long it cannot be recognized as the automatic call to the toilet.[10]

The mistake of ignoring the child's own trigger mechanism, the mass movement, often has far-reaching consequences for the psychological development of your child. Your child will believe he's being expected to feel something inside himself (the desire to have a BM) which he doesn't actually experience, because the mass movement of his bowels is not present. This feeling tends to undermine his self-confidence. He will feel: "Maybe I'm not such a good judge of what's going on inside my own body after all. Mother seems to be telling me I need to have a BM because she put me on this potty. But it doesn't seem that way to me!" Or he may feel that you are pushing him around and just don't understand him at all.

Depending on how aggressive the mother is about this type of so-called toilet training and how compliant or rebellious the child is, all sorts of unfortunate psychological patterns may develop. A compliant child may become frightened over what he imagines you may do to him if he doesn't deny his own natural feelings and internal biological sensations with regard to his bowels. He will try very hard to please you; but the price he has to pay is to deny his own internal feelings, which undermines his self-confidence.

It is also possible that the child may become compliant in toilet training but take out his frustrations and tensions in some other area. He may suddenly begin to develop fears or shyness, or have nightmares. He may develop eating problems, or become generally balky and resistant. The mother may boast to her neighbors how easily he was trained, and see no connection between the toilet training and the other problems which have suddenly developed.

The child may not be so compliant. He may be a rebel. Suddenly he has learned that moving his bowels in certain ways seems to be the most important thing in the world he can do for you. If he moves them the way you want him to, he's your master, because then he seems to have the power to make you happy. If he doesn't move his bowels where and when you want him to, then he learns he can make you angry. Either way, he is learning that he can control you. The Battle of the Bowels has begun. Your child has formed a pattern of rebellion which will probably extend to many areas of his life and which will cause nothing but trouble for both of you. All of these unfortunate reactions can be avoided. *Simply respect your child's own biological signal that he needs to have a bowel movement.*

Now, let's be specific about what you actually do when your child is two years old and you decide to begin training him. Begin by teaching him words for what is happening to him. If you start bowel training at around age two this should be no problem. When you observe him straining and grunting some day, simply say to him casually, "Jimmy's having a BM in his diapers." After a number of repetitions of this phrase he will get the idea. Pretty soon he will announce it himself, as he has a bowel movement: "Mommy, I'm having a BM!" When he does this, you can take the next step.

Use a potty chair rather than a seat that fits over the toilet. I suggest this for several reasons. First, a child can get into it himself without any help. Second, children are sometimes frightened by the height of a toilet seat or the turbulence of a flushing toilet. For a few weeks before you plan to start toilet training, put his potty chair in the bathroom near the big toilet; but don't try to teach your child to use it yet. Your purpose at this time is simply to get him to feel familiar and comfortable with it. He can explore it all he wants and practice putting himself on and off it.

When you are ready to start the actual training, you can show him the potty chair. Tell him he's old enough to be able to sit down and have his BM's just like the grown-ups do. Young children love to imitate their parents and older siblings. Many parents, due to their own anxieties about toilet functions, do not make use of this imitation in training their child. If you can be free and relaxed about it, it will help your child to see your husband or you sit down on the toilet and have a bowel movement. It helps also if you have an older child around. The younger will want to imitate the older in just about everything he does. Having BM's is no exception.

Once you have shown him where and how to have a BM, then tell him he's getting bigger and doesn't need to wear diapers any more. Put training pants on him and leave it up to him. If he is mature enough to manage it, you can put a supply of training pants in a lower drawer or on a shelf that he can reach easily. That way he can change his own pants.

Since you are teaching him something new, you need to remember that punishment always interferes with the teaching of any new skill. *Punishment has absolutely no place in toilet training.* Let your child's own internal biological mass movement be the signal to him that he needs to go to the toilet. Then you should reinforce his first successes with your praise and affection, and ignore his failures.

It is a good idea to let your child use the grown-up toilet sometimes, as well as other toilet facilities. The importance of varying the toilet conditions is illustrated by my own experience on a family camping trip. We were driving along the road when my three-year-old boy suddenly announced, in urgent tones, that he had to go to the potty. Unfortunately, a gas station was miles away, so I stopped the car and took him out in the bushes by the road. "No, no," he said, "there's no bathroom here!" He was most unhappy about the whole procedure. Reluctantly he finally agreed to do the job. So don't let your child get so fixated on one set of familiar conditions that he can't function properly when these conditions are changed.

It is also important to wait until your child has gone away from the bathroom before flushing the contents of his potty down the toilet. Some sensitive children may, in their stage of primitive magical thinking, regard the toilet as a violent and noisy machine that makes things disappear. They may become frightened of it. To adults of course, this is a completely illogical way to think about a toilet. But remember—young children think differently about things than we do.

Even if your child is not afraid of the toilet, it is still puzzling to him when you flush his BM down the toilet. A young child regards his BM as a part of his body, and he values it. After all, haven't you made a big deal of it and shown that you value it too? Since he produces on the potty to please you, he thinks of doing this in the same way that an older child thinks of giving a gift to someone he loves. Since he gives you this "gift" of his BM because he loves you, it seems puzzling and strange to him that you should immediately flush it down the toilet. Wait until he leaves the room before you dispose of it.

TRAINING IN BLADDER CONTROL

Bladder control is generally harder for a child to establish than bowel movement control. Consequently it takes longer to achieve. There are several reasons for this. For one thing, the bodily sensations signaling to the child that he needs to urinate are at first less clear cut than the sensations of the mass movement in his bowels. Second, a child urinates initially as a reflex response to bladder tensions. The child must, therefore, learn to inhibit this reflex response. In contrast to this, once the stool has been formed by the mass movement, defecation requires only an act of expulsion. In other words, it is easier for a child to control himself when he has to make something happen than when he has to inhibit something from happening.

Bladder control has two aspects: waking control and sleeping control. Waking control usually comes first. Gesell has pointed out that waking control usually has three stages. First, the child becomes aware that he *has wet* himself. Later he becomes aware that he *is wetting*, and can announce that fact. Still later, he begins to anticipate that he is *about to wet*. Before you actually start bladder training, you can help your child to be able to put these stages into words. When you are changing his diapers you can tell him: "Billy is wet, see?" If you have an older child around you can use imitation to help train the younger one. Allow the younger one to see the older one urinate, and say: "Tommy is wetting now, see?" Father can be of help in the toilet training of a boy by letting the youngster see him standing up to urinate. If these suggestions make you feel at all squeamish, then don't attempt to use imitation as a method of training.

When you are ready to begin the actual training for waking bladder control, you can rely on the child's own biological signal that he needs to urinate, which is a full bladder. Put him in training pants and tell him that now he's a big boy and can wet in the potty. If it's a boy you are training, he may want to urinate in the big toilet just like Daddy. In this case, all you need is a small step on which he can stand in order to urinate standing up. Some books on child raising give the impression that boys and girls initially urinate sitting down. This is not a natural thing for a little boy to do at all, and is often due to the "bias" in his training given by the mother. It is more natural to teach a little boy to urinate standing up by imitating Daddy or older brothers. If your little girl wants to try to urinate standing up, let her try, until she discovers it doesn't work well for her.

You will need to teach the child a simple word, on his level, for these biological functions. BM is easy for a child to say. It seems to be the most universally used word nowadays for this function. Urination is beset with more semantic difficulties. The adult word *urinate* is generally too difficult for a young child to say. *Wet* is a very simple word to use for urination. But whatever you do, avoid all of the circumlocutions some parents use, due to their own squeamishness in talking about this subject. Teaching a child to say he has to "Go see Mrs. Murphy" when he has to urinate does nothing but confuse him.

It is also a good idea to get a child used to urinating in different places—including the great outdoors—so that he doesn't get too readily fixated on one place or on one set of conditions for urinating.

Training in bladder control will not happen overnight, but will follow a slow, off-and-on course, until it becomes finally stabilized. You should expect slow progress at first. Reward the child with your praise for his successes, and ignore his failures. Even after the child has generally established good urinary control he will still have occasional lapses when he is too engrossed in play or is overtired.

Sleeping control over the bladder can be established only when two conditions have been met. First, the child must have learned through daytime control to respond to tension in his bladder by tightening his sphincter muscles. Second, he must keep his sphincters closed without waking up. Naturally, this is going to make nighttime control more difficult to establish than daytime control. So it will take longer. What should you, the parent, do to establish nighttime control? Nothing. Absolutely nothing. The natural maturing of the child's bladder, plus the fact that he has learned from his daytime control that urine goes in the toilet, will take care of the situation sooner or later. When your child wakes up in the middle of the night with a wet bed, just change the bedding matter-of-factly. Say: "Next time maybe you'll stay dry all night," or "Next time maybe you'll wake up in time to go to the toilet."

A child who has been trained in bowel and daytime bladder control by the methods described in this book, and taught in a casual and relaxed way by his mother, should have no difficulty establishing nighttime control at a reasonable age. The child who will have difficulty with nighttime control is the child who has had various pressures put on him for daytime control and feels that toilet training is a big deal. This is the child who will take much longer to establish nighttime control, because he is generally nervous about the whole issue. Or the child may feel angry at the pressure put on him for toilet training. He will unconsciously take out this anger at his parents by wetting the bed at night, when he can safely disclaim responsibility for the action. It is important for parents to recognize that *the child is not wetting the bed deliberately*. After all, he is sound asleep! A child should *never* be punished for bed-wetting.

A small proportion of bed-wetting cases are due to physical causes. These cases are usually clear, because there are other symptoms, such as inability to control the urine in the daytime, which enable a physician to find out what is wrong. In the vast majority of cases, however, bed-wetting is due to psychological tensions in the child. If bed-wetting persists after the age of five, parents should refrain from trying the various home-grown remedies most parents unfortunately try. (Parents of bed wetters do the strangest things to try to get their kids to stop wetting the bed.) If you have a bed wetter past the age of five, then you should seek professional help, rather than try to correct the condition yourself.

You can lead a child to the toilet, but you can't make him go until he is ready. Suppose he isn't ready? Suppose after a week or ten days, your efforts at toilet training are simply not paying off? I suggest you conclude that your child is not ready to learn yet. Revert back to diapers, and wait a few months before you try again. We started the toilet training of our oldest boy when he was around two. After a week it became obvious that he wasn't the slightest bit interested in learning at that time. Rather than get into a long, drawn-out battle of wills, we put him back in diapers and tried again at two and one-half. Same results. He still wasn't ready. So we tried again about a month before he turned three. In approximately two weeks he was both bowel and bladder trained! With the youngest boy, we also started at two, found he wasn't ready, gave up and went back to diapers. We tried again at two and one-half and he was ready then, and was trained in about three weeks.

HOW MOTHERS FEEL ABOUT TOILET TRAINING

Let's look at a mother's feelings when she is trying to toilet train a child. (Many books on child raising seem to leave out this important topic.) Let's suppose a mother has decided to use the general methods of toilet training advocated in this book. She has now come to the "moment of truth" and put the youngster in training pants. What happens? Maybe nothing at all of a positive sort happens the first day, or the first few days. The child messes up several pairs of his training pants per day. That's all that happens! How does the mother feel? Usually she feels inadequate and helpless. She may think: "It seemed so easy when I read about it in the book! What's wrong with me? Maybe I'm not a very good mother. Maybe I'm just not good about things like this." Her feelings are natural and understandable, particularly if this is her first child. It will help her to remind herself that the crucial factor in the toilet training of a child is not what she does as a mother, but whether the child is ready to learn this new skill. If the child isn't really ready, he isn't going to learn it. She should remind herself that the way to learn any new skill is through making mistakes and then profiting from those mistakes. Toilet training works the same way. Your child will make lots of mistakes, and it will take time to learn.

So far the things I have discussed with regard to toilet training are entirely possible for a mother to accomplish, for they have to do with her *actions*. Now I want to talk about something that lies outside of the conscious control of the mother—her *feelings* about toilet training. We need to face frankly the fact that adults and young children feel quite differently about the waste products of the child's body. A young child is not bothered by a soiled diaper. He may even enjoy its odor and feel. Most mothers can't seem to work up the same degree of enthusiasm for the diaper. To a young child, his feces are only an interesting sort of "brown clay." He will uninhibitedly smear it around as he would any similar substance. He will even take a special kind of pride in this particular "brown clay" because he himself produced it.

Now, it is proper to teach a child to deposit this special brown clay in the toilet through a bowel movement, rather than use it for artistic ventures. But if at all possible, we want to avoid giving him an unnecessary set of negative feelings about it. This may be hard to do, because of all of the negative feelings we were taught about feces and urine (going back to the long-forgotten days when we ourselves were toilet trained). Our unconscious mind has not forgotten those days, however. That's why a mother will behave differently when cleaning a soiled child than when she is giving the child a bath. She is apt to show disgust in her manner and her facial expressions. She may even use such expressions as "Smelly diapers—ugh!" or "Smelly baby" or "Dirty boy."

If the mother communicates such feelings of disgust to the young child, he will feel he is "dirty" or "bad" for producing feces or urine. These attitudes can have a damaging effect on the sexual development of the young child. Since the organs of sex and the organs of elimination are in close proximity, attitudes acquired in the course of toilet training may unfortunately generalize to the sex organs. The child may come to feel that the organs "down there" are bad, nasty things. These attitudes of shame and disgust may cause difficulties in the development of healthy attitudes towards sexual functioning.

A mother cannot control how she *feels inside* when she is changing a diaper or cleaning up a soiled child. But as far as possible, if she has feelings of disgust or aversion, she should keep them to herself. A matter-of-fact attitude is best, if it can be achieved.

I have gone into toilet training in such detail because, over the twenty years of my clinical experience, I have been astounded at the ingenious ways in which parents can mess up what is, essentially, a *simple problem of teaching a child a new skill*. If you are not in a hurry, if you approach toilet training in a casual and relaxed manner, and if you have respect for your child's own biological signals of the need to empty bowels or bladder, then toilet training can be accomplished simply, without causing psychological problems.

PLAY EQUIPMENT FOR THE FIRST
ADOLESCENT

Let's turn to the lighter side of "first adolescence" and discuss learning through play. The play equipment I mentioned for the toddler in Chapter 4 will still, of course, be eagerly used by your first adolescent. But he is now ready for you to add new play equipment in keeping with his new level of maturity.

Since we are asking him to give up any "messing" he may have done with the products of his own body, we can offer him the opportunity to "mess" with sand, dirt, water, playdough, paint, and clay.

Water play continues to be important to a child of this age. He can use the kitchen sink or bathtub. He will love to dip sponges in the water and squeeze them out. He will enjoy filling and emptying small plastic glasses or pans or bowls. You would soon tire of repeating this over and over again, but a two-year-old does not. Parents are often amazed at how long water play can remain satisfying to a child of this age.

To add variety to the water play, offer him an eggbeater, or doll clothes or a handkerchief to "wash." He will also enjoy plastic straws, which he can use to blow air into the water and to perform little experiments in physics at his own primitive level. A handful of soap flakes will add variety and spice to water play. Producing soapsuds is like magic to a two-year-old. Various floating toys also contribute interest to water play.

Don't forget this age child actually *enjoys* cleaning up after making a mess through water play. The wise parent will make use of this particular personality quirk, because it is not characteristic of later stages! Give him a chance to mop things up with a sponge or large absorbent cloth.

A child of this age also loves to "paint" outside with water. A large paintbrush and a pail of water are all he needs. Creative materials such as playdough, plasticene, and clay are enormously satisfying to this age group. Playdough is probably the most preferred by mothers because it makes less mess than clay. You can buy playdough or you can make your own. Here is a simple recipe: Mix two cups of flour with one cup of salt. Add just enough water to make it the consistency of bread dough. If it becomes too sticky, simply add more flour. By varying the recipe you can get different textures of dough. You can sprinkle in food coloring or dried tempera paint for color. You can also add a little bit of baby powder or cinnamon or nutmeg or any other sweet spice to make it smell good. One or two drops of oil of cloves will preserve it for a long time. It can be stored in a plastic bag, and will keep for approximately a month.

When children of this age are using playdough, clay, or plasticene they are not making anything specific. They are interested in the material itself. They like to pound it, mold it, squeeze it, feel it, and shape it. To use any of these materials is very relaxing for this age youngster. The best tools are the child's own hands. But after he has had a lot of experience using his hands, popsicle sticks or tongue depressors will add variety to his experimentation.

Get your child a piece of plywood about two feet square. Waterproof it by varnishing. He can handle the playdough or clay on this board. Then put a piece of oilcloth on the floor, some newspapers on the table under the plywood, and he's ready to go.

Your youngster is now ready for an item of educational play equipment which will aid him all the way through his preschool years: a large blackboard, at least four feet square. You want it this large so your child can scribble or draw or print on it with full arm movements in an uninhibited fashion. (Surprisingly enough, few homes provide such a blackboard for this age child.) The blackboard can be nailed against a wall in his room. It will be one of the most versatile toys and learning devices you could possibly provide for your youngster.

Place both white and colored chalk in a shelf or box attached to the blackboard. He can then scribble on the blackboard to his heart's content. This should reduce the likelihood of his scribbling on your walls. However, it is doubtful if a rambunctious toddler or first adolescent will make it all the way through this stage of development without at least one foray against the walls of your house.

Scribbling is a prelude to writing and drawing. The child who has not had the opportunity to scribble freely will be delayed in the development of writing and drawing. No child is born with the ability to coordinate thumb and fingers in holding a pencil or pen. This small muscle development needs to be learned in order for your child to master the sheer mechanics of writing or drawing. The way your child learns to coordinate the small muscles needed to hold a pencil is by scribbling.

A blackboard has many advantages. It is something your child can use throughout his preschool and grade school years. It will be an enormous help to him in learning to print and write and draw in the years between three and six.

Crayons can now safely make their appearance. (You shouldn't give crayons to a one-year-old because he will probably eat them!) The paper must be big enough for him. Sheets of wrapping paper are good. You can even use your daily newspaper. Your youngster will draw and scribble on newspapers as happily as he will on plain white paper. A large rectangle of thin plywood makes a good drawing board. You can fasten the paper with big metal clothespins or clips. Crayons for this age child should be large and sturdy, not tiny, thin things.

Painting can now be introduced. You will need an easel. A wall easel is sturdier than a free-standing easel you buy in a store, which can be tipped over too easily. If you have the room for it, an inside easel on a wall, and an outside easel on a fence will both be appreciated by your child. You can make a wall easel out of a piece of plywood approximately two feet high by three feet long. This is large enough so you can hang open sheets of newsprint on it. Get two wooden blocks approximately two inches thick and attach them to the back of the plywood at the bottom corners, so your easel will have a slight slant when hung. Drill two holes at the top near the corners. You can use these to hang it from screws or nails driven into a wall or fence. A ledge with a raised lip may be attached to the easel to hold paint containers. Any kind of plastic container with a large screw-on top makes a suitable container for the paint. The child can dip right in the jar as he paints. The top can be screwed back on after he has finished painting. You will feel more comfortable if you provide a smock for your child to use while painting. One of Dad's old shirts with the sleeves cut short, worn back to front, will do nicely.

You will need water-soluble paints, which you can buy either in liquid or powder form, and a liberal supply of paper. The paper can consist of newspaper, blank newsprint paper, or wrapping paper. If you live near a newspaper office ask for a "core" of unused newsprint left over from a printing run. Most newspaper offices have a group of these cores standing round the room where the paper is run off.

This age child needs brushes which are easy for him to handle. Do not give him tiny brushes with tiny handles. He needs a brush with a long handle and with the bristle end about three-quarters of an inch wide. When you first start a child of this age on painting, present only one color to him at a time. When he becomes accustomed to that color and has worked with it a while, then you can add another color to his repertoire.

Some adults think of what a two-year-old paints as "pictures," and may ask "What is it?" This is a mistake. To this age child it is not a "picture" in the usual sense of the word. To him, it is an experiment in color and line. He is fascinated with the way he can cause marks and colors to appear. After he has finished working on it, a two-year-old is no longer interested in his "picture." To him the *experience* of working on it is all that matters. He is expressing important feelings through his painting for which there are no words as yet.

Which brings up a question you may have been thinking: what is the value of all of this messing about with playdough or clay or crayons or paints? Is it really so important for parents to go to all this trouble? Yes. Definitely! Your two-year-old has not yet learned to put into words all that he feels. These nonverbal activities such as working with clay or crayons or paints help him to express feelings for which there are no words as yet, as well as feelings for which he will never have words. These activities nourish and develop his feeling-life, and enrich his unconscious thinking and intuition.

The first adolescent will continue the vigorous outdoor play he began as a toddler. The Dome Climber will continue to be a favorite. A wagon to pull, a tricycle to pedal, large balls to roll and push, large hollow blocks to drag and build—all will help him develop his large muscles and build a strong and skillful body. Sand and water play will be as popular as ever.

A few comments should be made about the ability of a two-year-old to play with other children. A general mistake adults make is to expect too much of this age child in his ability to play with other children. Remember I said that the first adolescent is not yet ready to be a good member of any play group. So if an unsuspecting mother leaves several two-year-olds by themselves in the back yard, she is asking for mayhem. And it will not be long in coming!

One playmate at a time is a good rule for the two-year-old. His personality structure is not yet equipped to deal with the complexities of more than one set of personal relationships at a time. Interestingly enough, an older child of five or six is usually the best first playmate for a two-year-old. Not, however, the older brother or sister of the two-year-old! Materials which can be divided among several first adolescents without limiting the play of any are best. (They will tend to fight over one tricycle or a few trucks.) Sand, playdough, or blocks are better play materials if you can provide enough for each child.

Do not expect a two-year-old to be able to share toys with another child. Remember, your first adolescent is unskilled in playing with other children. A two-year-old will do well if he lasts out an hour of play with other children. You need to be nearby so you can watch out for signs of undue fatigue, intervene before disputes develop, and help end the play period at an appropriate time.

A brief look at the stages of development of the ability to play with other children might be helpful at this point.

First there is *solitary play*, in which the toddler has no ability at all to play with other children. To a youngster in the stage of toddlerhood, another baby or toddler is a plaything, not a playmate. A toddler will examine the other youngster carefully as he would a toy or any other interesting object by poking, pinching, or stroking, but not *playing* with the other child.

During first adolescence, the child makes the transition from solitary play to *parallel play*. This means that two or more children occupy the same geographical environment, but the play of one child will be unrelated to that of another, even though they may take pleasure in each other's proximity.

The next step up the ladder of play is what has been called *associative play*, in which all of the children do the same thing, such as playing in the sandbox, or making mudpies or pounding sticks on the ground. There is no real interchange among them.

Cooperative play does not come until the child is at the next stage of development, after the age of three. In cooperative play the children can discuss plans and assign play roles to each other. In playing house, they can assign different family roles to one another, or decide who will take turns pushing who in a wagon.

Don't expect much in the way of cooperative play from a child at the stage of first adolescence and don't expect him to be able to share. That comes in the preschool stage.

The first adolescent needs quiet play as well as active play. As his language development takes a giant step forward, he shows a heightened sensitivity to words, the building blocks of language. He loves to play with words, to imitate sounds, and to repeat familiar word rhymes. This is why this age loves nursery rhymes. When you read to him he delights in repetition, such as can be found in the *Three Little Pigs* or *Chicken Little*. It is the anticipation of what is coming next in the story that thrills him. Woe betide you if you change a familiar story or leave out part of it! He likes stories about his own experiences: going to the market, riding in an automobile, playing on a playground. He will love stories of this sort whether they come from a book or whether you make them up about some imaginary boy who sounds remarkably like him.

One of the best types of quiet play for a first adolescent is "The Silence Game." Call it by this name. Youngsters like to do most anything that you call a "game." Say something like this: "Harry, I have a new game for you and me to play. It's called 'The Silence Game.' Both of us will be just as quiet and silent as we can and listen. Shhh! Listen very, very carefully and tell me what you hear." He will then tell you whatever sounds he can hear that are occurring in the background where you are playing the game: perhaps a car down the street, the song of birds outside, or a radio playing in the house next door.

A variation of "The Silence Game" is to ask your child to shut his eyes and guess what sound you will make. You can strike a spoon on a glass, scratch a fingernail file, or do anything else that will make an interesting sound. Still another variation: "Now, Harry, listen just as quietly as you can and I'm going to whisper something to you very, very softly. See if you can hear it." Then whisper some simple direction he is to follow, such as: "Get up and walk over to the front door and touch it." After giving several such directions, you can conclude the game session by whispering to him where he can find some small surprise you have hidden for him.

"The Silence Game" is especially good for this age child. It helps train him to be quiet and to listen. It is also good therapy for a mother who is exhausted by an overactive youngster, and needs a gentle way to calm him down. "The Silence Game" is also a good way to induce a youngster inside for a meal when he doesn't want to come, or appeal to one who isn't very enthusiastic about bathtime or bedtime.

Another important aspect of developmental changes

during "first adolescence" is feeding. Feeding should never cause psychological problems if you will rely on your child's natural hunger to motivate his eating. Refrain from pushing or nagging him to eat. He will eat less than you probably think he should. But he will still eat enough to give him enormous amounts of energy each day! Set reasonably well-balanced meals before him and leave him alone. Don't insist he finish all of his food, or that he eat all of his main dish before you will let him have dessert.

One thing which sometimes causes difficulty with this age child is that parents begin to press for learning table manners. The parents are fooled by the child's newfound language ability. They mistakenly conclude from his new maturity in speech that he is capable of more mature behavior in other ways. First adolescence is no time to start teaching a child table manners.

I have mentioned that this stage is one in which the child loves rituals. So now is the time to establish a ritual for bedtime. Doing this has many advantages. Unfortunately there is no built-in "need to go to bed" in young children. (If there were, it would be much easier for us parents!) We need all the help we can get, and if a bedtime ritual will help, take advantage of it. What you want to accomplish with the bedtime ritual is to establish in his mind the idea that going to bed is as inevitable a thing as the setting of the sun.

Let me suggest a simple type of ritual. First, avoid a lot of rough-housing and active play after dinner because this will get him overstimulated and make it hard for him to settle down. You could begin the bedtime ritual by giving him a bath. Most mothers think of a bath purely in terms of cleanliness, but a child of this age thinks of it as water play. Give him enough water play and he will also get clean! Let him play in the bath as long as he wants and tell you when he is ready to come out. (If for some reason you are in a rush some night, you can speed up the process.) Let him have plenty of water play toys, and he will find this a relaxing and "quieting-down" time. After his bath he can go to bed and have a snack in his bed. By doing this you are reinforcing going to bed by pairing it with the psychological reward of food. While he's having his snack, you and he may want to have an affectionate and spontaneous little chat. Once again, going to bed is reinforced by the rewarding presence of you, his mother.

Following the snack can come a story or two, read to him in bed.

This is an appropriate point for father to enter the ritual. Some fathers may not enjoy reading a story to a young child. This is unfortunate. Don't insist, because the child will not enjoy it if he senses that father's heart is not in it. Some fathers may not arrive home in time to read a story before bedtime. If you are lucky enough to have a husband who enjoys doing this, it would be a fine thing to have father take over snack-time or story-time, or both, in the evening getting-to-bed ritual. I have done this with my three children and enjoyed it immensely. By reading to a child you are teaching him many things. You are teaching him that you like him by spending this time with him. You are teaching him you love books, and thereby teaching him to love books also. And you will probably find many spontaneous conversations growing out of this cozy reading time.

When you read to a child, hold the book so that he can see the pictures. They are important to this age child. Help him to learn to "read the details" of the pictures by asking him questions about different people and objects in the pictures.

This habit of reading to a child at bedtime is one which can be carried on until he is seven or eight, or until he actively tells you he doesn't want you to do it any more. Some parents stop reading to a child once the child has learned to read himself. This is a mistake. Even though he has learned to read, he will still enjoy the closeness and warmth of having you read to him for a few more years.

You will find a list of good children's books in Appendix C. I also want to refer you to a specific source that covers books for children of all ages and stages: *A Parent's Guide to Children's Reading* by Dr. Nancy Larrick, which is available in paperback. Dr. Larrick has done a magnificent job of creating a standard reference book for children's reading from babyhood through adolescence. I think every parent should own it. My own copy is pretty dog-eared by now.

If you or your husband enjoy making up stories of your own, they are fine for the bedtime ritual. This age youngster will especially like stories about an imaginary child, who can be himself, thinly disguised. If you've never told stories to a child before, this is a good age to begin. Your child audience at this age will love your stories no matter how you tell them! Put in lots of funny sounds if possible. These make a big hit at this age. Experiment with a simple trick of the public speaker: raise or lower your voice dramatically at times. This will be sure to capture your child's attention at both ends of the decibel scale. From time to time, ask your child: "And what do you think happened next?" He will tell you! Then you can say: "That's right, Johnny did find a puppy, and he brought him home with him."

Many children are afraid of the dark at this age. Why fight it and force a frightened child to grit his teeth and sleep in a darkened room? There is no reason why your child cannot have a soft light in his room which will eliminate his fear. The few extra cents that light costs you will be amply compensated by your child's psychological well-being. Don't worry that your child will grow up always needing a light in his room. As he grows older he will normally outgrow the need for a light and be able to sleep comfortably in a dark room.

There is also no reason why your child cannot continue to have an evening bottle to go to sleep by, even at this "advanced age" of two or two and one-half. Many of your neighborhood "experts" will frown on you if you do this, and say: "What—he's two and a half and he hasn't given up the bottle yet?" So what? What's the rush? If he still likes it as a security device, is there any reason why we have to insist he give it up at this age? All three of my children had a bedtime bottle. They didn't give up until they were between two and one-half and three years of age.

One of the important things about the evening bedtime ritual is that it should be a time of pleasure for your child. We want him to look forward to going to bed. He should not feel that bedtime is something unpleasant, where he is banished abruptly to a dark room, while the rest of the family does interesting things. The evening bedtime ritual should not only be a time of pleasure for the child, but for mother and father as well.

This brings me to the importance of a father's role with his children at this age. Recently I saw an ad in connection with Father's Day which ran something like this: "Okay kid. Now you do something for Dad. The dentist, summer camp, that set of drums. . . . He's pretty good to you, isn't he? Tell him so ... with something special from Ohrbach's." From the point of view of Ohrbach's, that was a clever and well-written ad. But what interested me, as a psychologist is the set of unwritten assumptions about a father's role which this ad contains. Father's role, according to this, seems to be to give material gifts to a youngster: dentist, summer camp, a set of drums. We would do well to remember Emerson's dictum: "Presents are not gifts. Presents are excuses for gifts. The only true gift is a portion of yourself." This is what father has to give: a portion of himself. He does this by spending time with his child, doing things they both enjoy. *Doing things that they both enjoy.* If father is grimly set on doing something with his child out of a sense of family obligation, but he doesn't really enjoy it, the child will sense this, and not gain much from the time they spend together.

For this reason, it is impossible to specify exactly what kinds of things a father can do with a child. Fathers vary enormously in what they enjoy. Hopefully, a father will like to do things with this age child such as reading books or telling stories, swimming or wading, or taking him to a park or playground. Or just going for a leisurely walk down the street. On such a walk the youngster can pick up rocks or pebbles, investigate ants in the grass, or engage in all of the little research activities which are fascinating to a child of this age. But each father will have to discover by experience what activities he finds enjoyable with this age youngster. If a father reads Gesell or other good books on child psychology (you will find a recommended list in Appendix E), he will get more out of his play with this age child. He will then be able to see landmarks in the child's emotional and intellectual growth he would not notice if he were completely ignorant of child psychology.

One final word before I close this chapter. In first adolescence, probably the most important aspect of a child's development is the *dynamic quality of a child's personality at this age.* Parents need to accept this dynamic quality of personality, to help the child establish his self-identity and build a strong self-concept at this particular stage of his development.

It is quite ironic that we want a child to grow up to be a strong and dynamic adult; yet all too often parents are not able to accept these very same dynamic qualities of personality when he is a two-year-old! A first adolescent is nothing if not dynamic! Who could fail to note his lusty protests against restraint, his hearty, rollicking, sensuous enjoyment of life, his demands for instant gratification, his enthusiastic and total commitment to the world as he experiences it. All of the activities which make him a genuine person have come about through this dynamic life thrust. Without this dynamic drive he would not have learned to sit, to crawl, to walk, or to learn a language. This dynamic quality of your child is a very important psychological resource. Do not be afraid of it. You do not want him to lose it. You need to foster this dynamic life force and treat it as an asset instead of something to be bleached out of your child.

A child at this stage of first adolescence needs the three Rs. No, I don't mean Reading, 'Riting, and 'Rithmetic. I mean Respect for the dynamic quality of his life at this stage of development. Rules suited to that dynamic quality. And our ability to Roll with the Punches. Give him these three Rs and you will aid him in adding the special lens of this stage to his self-concept eyeglasses.

6

Preschool

If you are still struggling through the stage of first adolescence with your youngster, it will come as a great relief to learn that Mother Nature has arranged for the next stage to be much easier on you.

I can distinctly remember living through the stage of first adolescence with my oldest boy. We were gritting our teeth and saying, "He's got to get better when he's three; he's just got to!" And sure enough, he did! Even though we knew that three would usher in a new and more pleasant stage of development, it was still hard to believe our three-year-old was the same boy we had known at two and a half.

For example, I distinctly recall one day shortly after he had turned three, he asked me, "Dad, may I watch television?" I almost fell over with shock, because he had never bothered to ask my permission to do anything during the previous year. But this behavior was indicative of this new stage of development—a stage during which a child goes out of his way to try to please and accommodate his parents. He actually takes pleasure in being cooperative, whereas in first adolescence, it often seems as if a child's sole pleasure in life consists of being uncooperative.

This next stage of development, the preschool stage, runs from roughly a child's third to sixth birthday. Unlike the previous stages, we cannot single out any one specific developmental task for this era. There are many developmental tasks that face your child in this stage. How he meets and masters these new tasks will determine his self-concept and personality structure, which will assume its stable form by the time of his sixth birthday.

Before examining these various developmental tasks, let's look at an overall survey of children in this stage, according to age groupings. You should have a rough idea of what a typical three-year-old, four-year-old, and five-year-old are like.

THE THREE-YEAR-OLD

Let's start with the three-year-old. He is in much better equilibrium with himself and the people around him. He has passed through the transition from babyhood to true childhood. He is no longer as full of anxiety as he was during the transition period. Consequently, he no longer needs the protection of rituals as much. He doesn't have to do everything in a certain precise way. He has a new spirit of cooperation and a desire to win the approval of his parents and even of his older brothers or sisters. Whereas in the previous stage he was the world's greatest nonconformist, he now actually takes pleasure in conforming and pleasing other people. His tantrums drop out, and parents discover they can actually begin to reason with him. (In the previous stage it must have seemed to parents that they couldn't reason with him about anything.)

He is also not so domineering, grasping, or dictatorial. No longer does everything have to be done his way—or else! He has abdicated as Emperor of the House—the little tyrant who likes to rule over everyone else. He is beginning to develop the capacity to share, to wait, to take turns. He is more able to work patiently at tasks instead of blowing his stack as he did at two and a half. In part this is due to a new confidence in himself, and in part it is due to the fading away of the anxieties of transition. He is more sure of himself in his motor control and muscular development. He is able to be more patient about trying to dress himself, or stack a bunch of blocks.

His improved language ability enables him to understand other people better and to have better control over his own impulses. He loves new words. As his intellectual horizons expand, a whole new world of imagination and fantasy opens up for the three-year-old. This is the time when he may develop an imaginary playmate, an invisible child or animal. He has a strong need for companionship at this stage. A child who must play alone much of the time is more likely to create this imaginary playmate for himself. This is nothing for parents to worry about. The playmate may be around for several years. Then he will vanish. Meanwhile, he is sort of a security device for the child who has created him.

Companionship with his peers also becomes quite important to the three-year-old. As a two-year-old, he was in the stage of parallel play. Now he has moved to a new play plateau of truly cooperative play. He is now developing the ability to interact with other children, to wait, to take turns, to share, to accept substitute toys.

Three is really a "Golden Age," a delightful time for both child and parents—a time when your youngster is at peace with his world. He loves life, he loves his parents, and he feels good about himself. Parents should take advantage of this enjoyable time, because the next stage of development is a buzz saw!

The three-year-old is in a stage of equilibrium. But Mother Nature is readying another stage of disequilibrium: the four-year-old. Once again, the child's behavior needs to loosen up in order to attain a new phase of integration. Four years is that time of loosening and breaking up the old equilibrium. The most succinct way I can describe the four-year-old is to say that he's like the two-and-a-half-year-old, only more mature, and not quite so difficult to get along with.

THE FOUR-YEAR-OLD

Four years is a period marked by disequilibrium, insecurity, and incoordination. The incoordination may be shown in many areas of behavior. The child who has been reasonably well coordinated at three, may now demonstrate motor incoordination by stumbling, falling, or a fear of heights. Tensional outlets are heightened at this age. The child may blink his eyes, bite his nails, pick his nose, play with his sexual organs, or suck his thumb. He may even develop a facial tic.

He also becomes a very social being. Friendships are important to him, although he may find it difficult to get along with his friends. He has difficulties with other children reminiscent of the two-year-old stage. He is bossy, rambunctious, and belligerent. Although a parent may suspect his behavior is a throwback to the two-and-a-half-year-old, it is really a period of adventurous thrust leading to a new plateau of achievement at five. Nevertheless, there is much in the four-year-old that will, at least superficially, remind the parent of the child he was at two and a half. He is given to the same type of emotional extremes: shy one minute, overboisterous the next. Many children are as ritualistic at this age as they were at two and a half. They become fixated in their routines of eating, dressing, or sleeping. It may be very difficult to get your child to tolerate any change in these routines. He will express his emotional insecurity by crying, whining, and frequent questioning.

Fours love to play together. But an anthropologist studying the social psychology and tribal life of a group of four-year-olds would have a field day. Social life among four-year-olds is no tea party; it is stormy and violent. Outsiders tend to be excluded once a clique has been formed. There is a good deal of commanding, demanding, shoving, and hitting. Bragging is the most common form of language among a group of four-year-olds. Name-calling is also popular. Four is crude and direct. Other people's feelings matter little to him.

Gesell suggests that the key word for the four-year-old is "out-of-bounds." He is out-of-bounds in his motor behavior. He hits, kicks, and throws fits of rage. Verbally he is out-of-bounds also. He is fascinated by words, and by the sounds of words. He is now learning for the first time that there is a whole class of words that do not ordinarily set too well with parents. Most of these words have only four letters. He discovers he can get quite a rise out of his parents by using one of these little gems, especially if company is around. The use of bathroom words is hilariously funny to him. A four-year-old will say: "Mommy, you know what I want for lunch? I want a sandwich and carrots and ice cream and—and—BM!" At which point he will dissolve into squeals of laughter, irresistibly overcome by his own excruciating wit. In accordance with the principles of reinforcement (see Chapter 8), the wise parent will refrain from reinforcing these four-letter words by getting upset and making a big deal over them. Instead, she will ignore them. Eventually they will fade away and be heard no more at age five.

The four-year-old is also out-of-bounds in his personal relationships. He loves to defy orders and requests. He chafes at restrictions, swaggers, boasts, and swears. "I'll sock you!" is a favorite threat he uses with other children. He also has a great spurt of imagination at this age. This is one of the factors which makes it difficult for him to sort out what is real from what is make-believe. The line between fact and fiction is not very real for him. He is full of tall tales, which he tells with a straight face. A parent should not make the mistake of calling him a liar at this age. To do so would be to ignore the fact that what he is really trying to do is to distinguish fact from fiction; however, his imagination gets out of control in the process. For example, he will assure his parents that he saw a "monster taller than our house" in the backyard, or that yesterday afternoon he "took a ride on a rocket ship to the moon."

He has no sense of property rights, except for his quaint belief that everything he sees is his property. But a four-year-old is no more a "thief" than he is a "liar." At this age, he thinks possession is ownership. A toy at a neighbor's house "belongs" to him because he was playing with it, put it in his pocket, and brought it home. Such is four-year-old logic about property.

His drive level is extraordinary. His motor drive is high. He races up and down stairs, runs exuberantly through the house, shuts doors with a crash and a bang. His drive to talk is also high. He is a great talker and loves to discourse about anything and everything. He is his own self-appointed commentator on the world, and sometimes his own audience. He has a tendency to run subjects into the ground. He loves to make up silly words, or to rhyme words. When one of my boys was four, we spent about a half hour on a drive rhyming words. The wise parent can use this new fascination with language to play all sorts of word games with the four-year-old. (See Chapter 11.) He especially enjoys humor, exaggeration, and nonsense rhymes. If you play along with this, a four-year-old will derive great amusement from your asking him questions such as "Do you have an elephant in your pocket?"

He loves to dramatize, and likes dramatic play. He can make good use of hand or finger puppets. He will engage in lengthy dramatic play indoors and out, with blocks, cars, trucks, trains, ships, dolls, or toy people.

A four-year-old reminds us forcefully of the man, described by Stephen Leacock, who jumped on his horse and rode off rapidly in all directions. Four never knows precisely where he is going. His high-drive level and fluid mental organization will lead him into unsuspecting alleys and byways. One four-year-old responded to a parent's question regarding what he was painting, with "How should I know? I haven't finished it yet!"[11] He may start to draw a turtle, but before he is through his drawing may have changed into a dinosaur or a truck. He is given to the same unexpected shifts of direction when he is reporting on some event.

As Gesell describes him: "He can be quiet, noisy, calm, assertive, cosy, imperious, suggestible, independent, social, athletic, artistic, literal, fanciful, cooperative, indifferent, inquisitive, forth-right, prolix, humorous, dogmatic, silly, and competitive.[12]

Because of the personality characteristics of this age group, four-year-olds need firmness. The weak or vacillating parent has had it with the four-year-old. "I can't do a thing with him!" complains one helpless mother of a four-year-old. The four-year-old thrives on variety. He needs a change of pace. A wise mother will have some new activity in mind to interest her four-year-old and lure him out of a potentially troublesome situation. His play and behavior can easily deteriorate into silliness if not controlled. The parent needs to anticipate when this is about to happen, and present him with a new and interesting activity.

Because of his stronger social drive and the greater importance of friendships at four than at three, isolation from the group is an effective discipline device at this age. The parent should say something such as: "You're not able to play very well with Tommy and Steve now, Joe. You'll need to play by yourself now. Perhaps soon you'll be able to come back and play with them. I will tell you when." That way, the mother is giving him a chance to "save face." She is also motivating him to want to shape up his behavior so that he can return to the group. If possible, she should try to say this in a matter-of-fact tone, without emotional overtones of punishment in her voice.

That's the four-year-old. Just about the time the parents have begun to feel that life isn't worth living with the little monster at this age—he turns five. Suddenly everything is different! Four was an age of disequilibrium; five is an age of equilibrium.

THE FIVE-YEAR-OLD

Five is a delightful age. The out-of-bounds behavior of the four-year-old is gone. Five tends to be reliable, stable, and well adjusted. Secure within himself, he is calm, friendly, and not too demanding in his relations with others. He tries only that which he feels he can accomplish, and, therefore, he can usually accomplish what he tries. Whereas four is fluid, five is more self-contained and in focus. By contrast to four, who often doesn't know what he's going to draw until he's in the process of drawing it, five has a definite idea in mind beforehand, and he completes the drawing he planned. Whereas four was not particularly bothered by incompleteness or change of direction, five likes to finish what he starts. Four rambles; five knows when to stop. In contrast to the expansiveness and out-of-bounds behavior of four, five shows an economy of motor movement and control.

The five-year-old is content to live in the world of here and now. He defines things pragmatically: "A hole is to dig; an ice cream cone is to eat." He is not in conflict with himself or his environment. He is satisfied with himself and others are satisfied with him. He returns to the spirit of cooperation and desire for the approval of others which he showed at three, only on a higher level. Mother is still the center of his world, and he likes to be near her, to do things for her and with her. He is usually content to obey her commands, which he may have resisted to the death at four. As he did at age three, he again enjoys being instructed and obtaining permission to do things.

In spite of his great love for home and mother, home is not quite enough for him. He is ripe for enlarged community experiences. He likes to play with friends in the neighborhood. If your school district has a kindergarten, he is ready for it and most eager to go to "school." Kindergarten is ideal for him because he is capable of a great deal intellectually, under the guidance of a skilled teacher. If your school system does not have a kindergarten, special thought should be given to his play day.

Gesell describes the five-year-old as follows: "He presents a remarkable equilibrium of qualities and patterns: of self-sufficiency and sociality; of self-reliance and cultural conformity; of serenity and seriousness; of carefulness and conclusiveness; of politeness and insouciance; of friendliness and self-confidence."[18]

Five is a remarkable balance of qualities contained in one all-inclusive package. All things considered, he is a delight to have around. Physically, he has gained poise and muscular skill. Emotionally he is well balanced. Intellectually he is full of curiosity and enthusiasm for learning. Five is that delightful age when a child takes life as it comes and is pretty content with it. We can let a five-year-old himself sum up in one word this stage of development. When asked, "What do you like to do best?" he answered, "Play."

You can see that there are enormous psychological differences between a three, four, and five-year-old. These differences need to be taken into account when you are interacting with them or disciplining them. Do not expect a four-year-old to be able to obey like a five-year-old. In spite of these differences, all three age groups have many things in common. That is why they are put together under one stage of development: The Preschool Stage. There are developmental tasks which run like a leitmotif in a piece of music throughout all three of these years. The leitmotif sounds different in the three-year-old than in the four-year-old, but the musical motif is still recognizable. What are these leitmotifs, these developmental tasks of the preschool years? What are the things the child must learn during these three years that will round out and complete his self-concept and his basic personality structure?

FULFILLING BIOLOGICAL NEEDS

First of all, your preschool child has to fulfill his biological needs for both large-muscle and small-muscle development. Your child has an innate biological drive to release energy: to run, jump, climb, wiggle, move, and in general to be on the go. Because parents are much more self-contained creatures biologically, we tend to overlook or underrate this dynamic biological aspect of the life of our preschooler.

Seated across from me in a restaurant one day, I noticed a young father and mother with their little boy, who appeared to be about four years old. He was restlessly wiggling around in his seat, shifting position several times every few minutes. The father exclaimed impatiently, "Can't you sit still?" I felt like saying to the father (but didn't, of course), "No, he can't sit still. He's only four years old. And you couldn't either, at that age!" In other words, that father was expecting a biological maturity of his four-year-old boy which was impossible.

Think of your preschooler as a biological factory. He takes in raw materials in the form of food and then uses these raw materials to manufacture vast supplies of energy. A psychologist once ran an experiment in which an hour-long movie was taken of a preschooler in action in an outside play yard. Afterwards, this movie was shown to a member of a college football team. He was instructed to go through the exact same motions for an hour that the preschooler had just performed. At the end of an hour the football player was exhausted!

This means you need to provide your preschooler with plenty of play space and play equipment both inside and out. This will allow him to work off his boundless energy and get in all of the practice he needs to develop control and skill with his large and small muscles. Children need to run and jump and yell. This often runs counter to adult needs for peace and quiet and order, which may make it difficult for us to cooperate fully in letting our preschooler work out his biological needs. However, if we don't give him constructive outlets for his immense energy, he will surely find destructive ones. Muscles and muscular coordination can't develop unless there is ample opportunity to use both large and small muscles. If a child has been forced to be too quiet and "good" during his preschool years, he is at a disadvantage with his classmates in grade school later. He lacks the basic foundation of muscular coordination which is necessary to develop reasonable skill in the games and sports (and hence in the social relationships) of grade school.

Moreover, to a much greater degree than most parents realize, motor skills are the foundation stones for later intellectual skills such as reading. Muscular coordination is made up of two basic factors: *laterality* and *directionality*. *Laterality* may be defined as the inner sense of one's own symmetry—our "leftness" and our "rightness." It is like a map of *internal space*. It is this internal map which enables a child to operate smoothly with either hand or leg, or with both hands and legs. *Directionality* may be defined as the projection into space of *laterality;* that is, your awareness of left and right, up and down, before and behind, in the world around you. This is like a map of *external space*. The sensations you feel inside your skin (which is your left side and which is your right side?) have their counterpart in the directionality of the world outside your skin.

These internal and the external maps depend upon muscular patterns and motor movements which must be learned by your child during his preschool years. They can be thought of as the "knowledge of the muscles."

"But what does all this have to do with intellectual skills such as reading?" you may ask. Much more than you realize. If a child has not developed a good sense of laterality, he will make letter and word reversals in reading. Notice, for example, that the only difference between the letter *b* and the letter *d* is one of laterality. If your child has not developed a good sense of laterality by age five or six, he is going to have trouble distinguishing those two letters. The importance of motor development and its relationship to later intellectual skills is treated very thoroughly in a book I strongly recommend called *Success Through Play* by D. H. Radler and Newell Kephart.

Give your child lots of opportunities to climb and crawl and build and run and tumble. Then you need not worry about his missing out on developing good laterality and directionality.

A CONTROL SYSTEM FOR HIS IMPULSES

During the preschool stage, your child is also learning to develop a control system for his impulses. A baby is born as a young savage who has no control at all over his impulses. As he advances to toddlerhood, his control is still primitive. If another child takes a toy from him, he will probably hit the other child to get it back. If he trips over a wagon, he will probably, in his frustration, kick the wagon. But between his third and his sixth birthday, your child will be actively working to establish a control system for his impulses. Developing control, however, will take time. It can not be achieved overnight. If you help him wisely and skillfully in these preschool years, by the time his sixth birthday rolls around your child should have a reasonably good control system established. This means that he will have developed the ability to effectively inhibit himself from hitting, stealing, or other antisocial behavior that might get him into trouble in grade school. It also means that from age six you should have relatively few occasions on which you will need to spank him throughout the rest of his childhood.

Some parents do not seem to understand that establishing a control system takes time. They seem to think that once you say no to a child he should obey that command instantaneously from then on. You will sometimes hear parents say to a child, "Don't you know what no means?" Certainly he knows what no means; but his control system isn't strong enough yet to deal with the no. Teaching a child to establish a control system takes a number of repetitions over the course of the preschool years before habits of inhibiting antisocial impulses are well established. Remember when your child was first learning to speak? He didn't start by speaking in complex sentences such as "Jimmy and I are going to go to the store to buy ice cream." He started speaking one-word sentences. Then he moved on to two-word sentences. Finally, he graduated to still more complex sentences. Parents are usually understanding and patient as the child's ability to handle language grows. They need to be equally patient as the child's ability to control his impulses grows and develops.

The child psychoanalyst Selma Fraiberg gives an amusing example of the difficulty a two-and-a-half-year-old had in learning to control her impulses and postpone a satisfaction. This little girl loved sweet things. When it came time for dessert she would usually get excited and bang on her high-chair tray with a spoon, shouting "Dzert! Dzert!" This time the dessert was ice cream, and her mother had to go downstairs to the freezer to get it. The clamor for "Dzert!" and the banging of the spoon got on the little girl's mother's nerves, and as she left to go downstairs she said irritably: "Oh, Jannie, have a little patience!" When the mother returned, she started in alarm because her little girl seemed to be having a convulsion. She was sitting rigidly in her high chair, fists clenched, eyes fixed, face beet-red, and she seemed not to be breathing. "Jannie! What's the matter?" her mother cried. Jannie exhaled and relaxed her fists. "I'm having patience!" she said.[14]

The postponement of an urgent impulse needed such exertion that the little girl had to summon all of her reserves of energy to oppose the impulse. This is why it takes so many years for children to be able to effectively inhibit their impulses.

Parents can make one or two major mistakes in teaching impulse control to preschool children. On the one hand, we can make no demands at all for impulse control, and the child at age six will then be pretty much the same as he was at age two. He will be unable to control his antisocial impulses. Most parents, however, are liable to make the opposite type of error, which is to pressure the child to learn to control his impulses too fast. This is why it helps for us to know in general what we can reasonably expect of a child of each age during the preschool years. A careful reading of Dr. Gesell's *Infant and Child in the Culture of Today* will help us do this. Then we will adjust our demands for impulse control to what a child of that age can reasonably manage. Parental pressure to learn to control impulses too fast causes many problems in childhood. Eating problems, dawdling, nail-biting, fears, nightmares—all of these things may be disguises for the child's response to too much pressure to control his impulses too fast.

Parents need to make gradually increasing demands on their child for control of his antisocial impulses. Three is a good age to begin, because three is a period of equilibrium and cooperation. By age three, the child has acquired enough language skill so that his command of words can help him to internalize controls through words. By allowing a child to put his feelings into words and express them, we are also helping him to be able to control his antisocial impulses and actions. By allowing him to say to his sister, "I hate you, Jennie!" we are making it easier for him to inhibit his impulse to hit her or to mess up her toys. We can also offer a child alternative outlets for his antisocial impulses. "No, you may not hit your sister, Charles. But I know you're mad at her and feel like hitting her, so you can hit this punching bag instead."

Dr. Ruth Hartley has offered a marvelous suggestion to parents for providing alternate outlets for a child's antisocial impulses. She suggests that you provide a child with what she calls "buffets." These are creatures specifically designed to take beatings without harmful effects. Buffets are basically sturdy rag dolls without bodies. The head can be made of canvas and stuffed, with features embroidered in colored thread. A woman's blouse or a man's shirt sewed to the neck completes the buffet. Make buffets which correspond to each member of your family: mother, father, and each age and sex child. These buffets can then safely be used to drain off antisocial impulses and disturbed feelings.

Dr. Hartley cites an example to show the usefulness of these little creatures: Marie was three when her brother was born. She immediately named the baby buffet "Tony"—her new brother's name. The day the real Tony came home from the hospital marked the beginning of Marie's favorite game, "spanking Tony." Every whipping was well deserved, of course. Tony was bad; Tony broke dishes; Tony cried at night. Toward the real Tony, Marie was sweet and motherly. The buffet was enough to drain off the jealous feelings.[15]

If your child can attend nursery school as a three and four-year-old, it will help him to develop a control system for his impulses.

SEPARATION FROM MOTHER

Your preschool child is also learning to separate himself from his mother. In the stage of first adolescence, your child is not yet ready to separate from mother. Mother is still the center of the two-year-old's universe, and he still needs her. This is why it is not a good idea to send a two-year-old to nursery school. Ordinarily a child of this age is not ready to leave his mother for three hours a day to play with other children under the supervision of a "strange" woman (his teacher). Of course, if a working mother has to leave a two-year-old at a day care center because of economic necessity, then there is no alternative. But ideally, a child should not begin nursery school until he is three years old.

When a child is three, he craves companionship in his play. He wants to separate from his mother and become more independent. The easiest way to help him to do this is to send him to a good nursery school. Even though a three-year-old wants to be separate from mother and get out into the world of his peers, he still has ambivalent feelings about leaving the security and protection of mother. It is only natural that he should feel this "separation anxiety," for mother has been "home base" for him for three solid years. Some children feel these separation anxieties more strongly than others.

Perhaps we can get some insight into how a three-year-old feels about separation from mother if we take a trip, in imagination, inside the mind of a three-year-old on his first day in nursery school. We can imagine the following soliloquy taking place inside his mind: "Mother has brought me to this new place. She said I'd like it and have lots of fun here, but I'm not so sure about that. Mother said that woman over there is my teacher. What is she like? Will she be nice to me? Will she take care of me? Who are all those strange children? I've never seen so many other new kids in one room together in all my life! Will they like me? Will they be nice to play with, or will they hurt me? I'm feeling scared. In fact, I'm not sure I like this place at all! Mother, don't leave me, don't desert me! I feel so scared I'm going to cry!"

And cry he does. If you visit a nursery school on opening day in September, you will find a number of crying children being held on teacher's laps and comforted.

All—I repeat, *all*—three-year-olds experience to some degree the feelings I have just tried to put into words. If the youngster is a secure and psychologically healthy child, he may feel them only fleetingly. Then he will let himself be led into the group of other children and started on an activity. But even if the child, without crying or making a big fuss, is able to start on an activity with the group, he will still feel somewhat ambivalent about letting mother go. Let's look again at the feelings that are taking place inside him: "I'm having fun with this clay, but—I miss you, Mommy. It feels strange here all by myself. Mommy, you said you'd be back later, but will you really? I think I'll phone you and find out." (At this point he picks up a toy telephone which the nursery school has thoughtfully provided for just such purposes.) "Hello, Mommy? Yes, I'm here. Yes, I'm playing with the clay. I like it. You'll be back soon? Okay, Mommy. See you later."

A child may express his feelings about separating from mother, not in words, but in a kind of "body language" of physical symptoms. When it's time to leave for nursery school in the morning, he may suddenly develop pains in his leg, an upset stomach, or dizziness.

It is also possible that a young child may have a delayed reaction to separation from his mother. Things may outwardly appear to be fine the first week of nursery school. He marches off to school, apparently without a care in the world. We don't notice it, but he's holding his anxious feelings in by keeping a stiff upper lip. But the anxiety finally catches up with him two or three weeks later, and he tells his mother that he's afraid to go to school. She is bewildered: "Why, he had no fear at all his first week at school!" Yes he did, but mother didn't see it because he repressed it. Finally he wasn't able to repress his feelings of anxiety any longer and they came flooding to the surface.

Separating from you and making it on his own with his peer group is a *big step* for your child. If he cannot attend nursery school, then you will need to help him accomplish the developmental task of separation from you by encouraging him to venture out into play with neighborhood children. This is ordinarily not as easy to accomplish, particularly with a shy child, as it will be if your child can attend nursery school. For in that case, a skilled teacher can help the child to separate from mother. However, you can still do it, and in Chapter 11 I will tell you how you can set up the equivalent of a nursery school in your own home.

THE NEW WORLD OF HIS PEERS

Your preschool child is learning the give and take of relationships with other children, his peer group, at this stage of development. The world of peer relationships is dramatically different from the world of his family. For example, one day at nursery school a little boy wanted to play with a toy truck which another child was playing with.

"Gimme that truck!" he demanded.

"I'm playing with it," retorted the other boy.

"Gimme that truck!" he repeated.

"I will not!" said the other.

"I'm sick—now gimme that truck!"

The other boy made no response. As you watched this interaction you could almost see the wheels go around in the first boy's head: "This works fine on Mother and she gives in to me—why doesn't it work with this boy?"

And so, sadly and joyfully, painfully and gently, the three-year-old learns that the world of peer relationships is a new world with a new set of rules and demands. In a child's first group experience, he comes face-to-face with both strengths and weaknesses in himself. He wins some acceptance and he suffers some rejection. He learns to give and to take.

In the world of his peers, a child needs to learn socializing skills. He needs to learn how to share, to wait his turn, to ask for something from another child, to put his feelings into words. He needs to learn how to stand up for his rights, to express feelings without fists, to participate as well as observe, to develop self-confidence in relation to other children. No child is born with these basic social and emotional skills. These skills in human relations must be learned in early childhood for them to be effective later.

Your preschooler will need to play with other children and learn these socializing skills during the ages of three, four, and five. Nursery school is an ideal place to learn them, because in nursery school the learning can be supervised by a trained teacher. In neighborhood play, the learning is hit or miss, trial and error. In neighborhood play, for example, there's no trained person to help a shy child integrate himself into a group and learn to build up his self-confidence and grow out of his shyness.

LEARNING TO EXPRESS FEELINGS

In the years between his third and sixth birthday, your preschooler is learning either to *express* or to *repress* his feelings. In the last chapter, I pointed out how important it is that we allow children to express their feelings rather than bury them underground, where they will come out in a disguised and harmful form. The years from three to six are years in which your child is going to establish some pretty basic attitudes about his feelings and emotions. Either he is going to come to believe that they are dangerous and he'd better keep them repressed, or he's going to learn to feel comfortable with all of his feelings, negative as well as positive.

If I could wave a magic wand and give all of the children in America one single gift that would improve their mental health overnight, it would be this: to banish from their minds the idea of "right" or "wrong," and "good" or "bad" as applied to *feelings*. They could reserve such concepts as "right" or "wrong," "good" or "bad" solely for *actions*. Even the law of the United States allows us this right, this distinction between our feelings and our actions. We can *feel* like killing somebody (we say, "I was so mad I could cheerfully have killed him!") and the law doesn't object to us feeling that way inside. It's only when we translate such a feeling into action that the law steps in and says "That is wrong." So why can't parents give their children the same right that the law of the land gives to all citizens? What prevents most parents from giving children this right is that we were not allowed to do that when we were children. So deep down in our unconscious mind we believe that somehow it is wrong to allow children to express themselves that way.

Try this example as a test. A mother has taken her two-and-a-half-year-old boy shopping with her. She has her groceries in the shopping cart, and the little boy is sitting in the cart also. An elderly woman comes over and gushes over him as follows: "Oh, aren't you a cute little uzzum-wuzzums boy!" The little boy looks up at Mrs. Gush and says loud and clear, "Go away. I don't like you!"

If you were the mother, how would you handle this incident? I'm afraid many mothers would say something to the boy such as: "Now that's no way to talk to this nice lady! Say, you're sorry." Or they might apologize to the woman and say: "He's only two-and-a-half and he doesn't know any better." In other words, many mothers would in some way indicate to the little boy that it was wrong for him to express his true feelings. I don't think that's a good idea. I think little children have a right to express their true feelings when they are preschoolers. It is bad for their personality development, their spontaneity, their authenticity as little people, for us to teach them to squelch their feelings in these early years.

I do not advocate allowing children *of all ages* to express their feelings anytime and anyplace that they feel like it. Children need to learn that other people have feelings too. They need to respect the feelings of other people and be gentle with them. But they can't learn to be gentle with the feelings of other people in their preschool period without paying the price of inhibiting their own spontaneity and verve. The two-and-a-half-year-old could not possibly learn to be gentle with the feelings of the gushy woman at his tender age.

The time to begin teaching children that other people have feelings is around the age of six, not in the preschool years. There will be plenty of time to teach a child from the age of six on that there are times and places to express feelings, and that sometimes you have to keep feelings to yourself or they can get you into trouble. In the grade school years we can teach children to discriminate where certain feelings may safely be expressed, and where it is not wise to express them. But the preschool years are the years in which we should encourage our children to express their feelings.

GENDER IDENTITY: MALE OR FEMALE

Your preschool child is also learning gender identity as a male or female. I said in earlier chapters that boys and

girls are sort of "genderless" in the early years up to about
age three. They play with the same kind of toys, and like
the same things. Boys, for example, in those early years like
to play with dolls and stuffed animals as well as girls do.
Of course, there are differences between girls and boys
even in these early years. Girls, in general, tend to mature
faster in many areas (such as language development) than
boys. Boys, in general, tend to be more aggressive and
physically active. But, all things considered, gender separation does not make its appearance in any decided fashion
until boys and girls turn three. From this time on, boys and
girls will be behaving differently, and viewing themselves
and the world differently. A recent book, distilling the
results of some 900 research studies, sums up the difference between little boys and little girls as follows:

> Little boys start more fights, make more noise,
> take more risks, think more independently, are harder
> to educate and are the more fragile of the sexes....
> More males than females die in the first year of life
> and in each decade after that. They are much more
> likely to stutter, to have reading problems and to
> suffer emotional quirks of every sort. They lag a year
> or more behind girls in physical development. By the
> time they start school, even their hand muscles are
> markedly less mature.
>
> In contrast, little girls are more robust and mature,
> yet much more dependent, passive, submissive, con-
> forming, unadventurous. They are more interested in
> people than in things, show more concern for others,
> and are more sensitive to their reactions and are
> more likely, by far, to remember names and places.
>
> Science has found no difference in IQ between
> boys and girls in childhood, yet their styles of think-
> ing and learning are quite different. Girls excel in
> verbal abilities ... they talk first, and later on they
> spell better and write more. Boys outclass them in
> abstract thinking, including math and science. Boys
> are also more likely to be creative.[16]

How do we explain these basic and early differences
between boys and girls? In all probability the differences
are due to hormonal and genetic factors, on the one hand,
and the way the children are raised, on the other hand.

Experts differ among themselves as to how much of the explanation to assign to biology and how much to assign to cultural teachings.

However, what concerns us as parents is to see to it that our boys and girls achieve a firm and solid gender identity during their preschool years. The achievement of a firm gender identity as a member of one's own sex is a very basic part of a child's self-concept and his mental health.

We need to remember that both boys and girls originally tend to identify with their mother, the most important person in a young child's life.

The boy, no less than the girl, since he loves his mother, wants to be like her. It is normal for a young boy of three to affirm to his mother that he is going to "grow up to be a mommy, just like you!" It is not unusual for a little boy to want to put on mother's shoes as well as father's shoes, or to use mother's lipstick or perfume. However, in the years from three to six, normally boys and girls begin to go their separate ways in their psychological development.

For one thing, the three-year-old is much more mature intellectually and is beginning to be aware of the sex differences between little boys and little girls. However, a preschooler may still be confused about this. One five-year-old boy was asked, when looking at a nude baby, if it was a boy or a girl. The boy replied, "I don't know—it's hard to tell with the clothes off!"[17]

Nevertheless, in one way or another preschoolers between the ages of three and six somehow manage to discover that a boy has a penis and a girl does not. This discovery marks a turning point in the lives of many children, although most parents seem to be blissfully unaware that this discovery means anything to a little child. The reason parents remain unaware of this is, of course, that this discovery is in the area of sex. And many parents suffer from great repressions which make them deaf, dumb, and blind to what little children are thinking or feeling about sex.

The healthier the family atmosphere is with regard to sex, the less psychological shock such a discovery will cause to a little boy or girl. The more repressed and guilt-laden the sexual atmosphere is in a family, the more difficulty a little boy or girl will have in assimilating this new and startling discovery. Regardless of the sexual atmosphere in the family, each individual boy and girl is going to react differently and in his own unique way to this discovery. However, we can still generalize about typical reactions of boys and girls to the discovery that boys have a penis, whereas girls do not.

The little girl is apt to feel she has been gypped, and is a sort of second-class citizen in this respect. Or she may believe that she was originally born with a penis, but has been deprived of it, perhaps as some sort of punishment. I know some of you are thinking "This is absolute drivel; I never heard of such a thing!" These ideas, however, are drawn from careful observation of thousands of small children by behavioral scientists. You can, if you are truly openminded, make the same kinds of observations of the play and talk and questions of your own preschooler. I remember, for example, my youngest boy saying to his mother when he was around three, "Mommy, where's your penis?" She replied, "Mommy doesn't have a penis; only boys and men have penises." "Yes you do!" our three-year-old insisted. "Where is it? Are you hiding it?"

If a mother will, with an open mind, observe the behavior of her preschooler she will find numerous instances of her child's reactions to his discovery of the anatomical differences between the sexes. Here is one incident from a mother's journal which describes the behavior of her three-year-old daughter:

Caroline envies the masculinity of her five-year-old brother, Billy, and she shows it in many ways. But the one way that's most obvious is that she tries to urinate as he does—standing up. This morning I watched her as she tried.

Caroline was alone with me in the bathroom. Caroline took off her panties and stood at the toilet as if to wet. She thrust her pelvis forward, as if aiming at the water below. Apparently she decided this wouldn't work, for she soon gave up.

Next, she grasped the skin above her crotch and tried to fold it into the shape of a penis; evidently she thought if she could create a make-believe penis in this fashion she could urinate through it. But this didn't work either, for there simply wasn't enough excess skin.

Once more, she stood at the toilet, trying to per-

form standing up. Then, gradually, she eased herself
up onto the toilet. In this position, sitting backwards
on the seat, with her face to the wall, she urinated.
And then she got down and put her panties back
on.[18]

Let's face it: little girls feel somewhat deprived, and
envious of boys. This doesn't mean, however, that they
necessarily have to develop a huge psychological trauma
about it. Usually, if the little girl has a healthy self-
concept she will adjust to the fact that she doesn't have a
penis. She will realize that there are many other things
about being a girl which more than compensate for the
lack of that particular appendage.

A mother may help a little girl build up her confidence
and self-esteem by explaining to her that while only boys
and men have a penis, she has something that boys do not
have: a uterus. Mother can explain that a uterus is like a
special little bag inside a girl or woman and that this is the
special place where babies grow. When girls grow up to be
women they can have babies but a boy cannot. I remember one little preschool girl whose mother explained this to
her who went around for days afterward, exclaiming
proudly: "I've got a uterus, I've got a uterus!"

Boys may react with psychological distress to the discovery that girls and women do not have penises. A little
boy may, in his primitive and unsophisticated thinking,
conclude that girls have had their penises cut off, and that
this type of punishment could be visited upon him also, if
he is not good. A five-year-old boy asked his mother
where she kept her penis. She reminded him she had told
him that boys and men have penises but girls and women
do not. The boy replied, "Yes, I remember now, that's
where someone axed you one!"[19]

In a home where the sexual atmosphere is open and
healthy and sexual organs are taken casually, a little boy's
fears that something might happen to his genitals by way
of punishment will soon subside. As a matter of fact, a
little boy generally takes considerable pride in his penis
and loves to show it off to his parents and peers. If a
mother is able to be relaxed about these things herself, she
will probably be able to enjoy the naive manner in which
a little boy will show off his newfound masculine charac-

teristic. The following incident from a nursery school teacher's diary illustrates this well:

Carl and Jennifer, both three years old, were building a house with giant blocks. Suddenly Carl looked up and said, "I gotta wet."

Jennifer continued her play.

Carl said, "Do you want to go to the bathroom with me and see me wet?"

Jennifer said, "Okay." She got up and followed Carl into the lavatory.

I casually moved along behind them and stood beside the open door where I could observe without intruding.

Carl opened his trousers and said proudly, "I got a penis."

Jennifer shrugged and said, matter-of-factly, "I know it."

Carl urinated and Jennifer watched. She seemed only mildly interested, nothing more.

When he had finished, Carl said, "I don't have to sit down like you do. I can wet standing up."

"That's nothing," Jennifer said stubbornly. "My brother does that too."[20]

What can a parent do to help a preschooler affirm gender identity as a boy or girl? The crucial factor is whether you and your husband accept the gender of your child. If you are happy he is a boy, chances are he will be happy with his gender. If you are happy she is a girl, she will also be happy with her gender.

But the little boy and the little girl also need models to imitate. In this respect, I think it is easier in our present society for little girls to accept and consolidate their gender identity than it is for little boys. Many factors have caused this. Contrast our highly metropolitan and suburban society today with what our society was like 100 years ago. At that time, most people lived on farms or in small towns. A little boy saw a great deal of his father. He tagged along after his father on the farm. Even if his father was a professional man, such as a lawyer in a small town, the father came home for lunch. Nowadays, many fathers leave early in the morning for their jobs and return late at night. A little boy may not see much of his father except on weekends.

One hundred years ago, there were few women teachers in our schools, and so both boys and girls had male teachers in their early grades. Nowadays a boy may not have his first male teacher until the fifth or sixth grade. We also must consider the effect of divorce on the presence or absence of male models for little boys. Usually it is the mother who is awarded custody of the children. This is easier on little girls, because they need a female model to imitate. But what about the little boy, who may see his father very infrequently under such circumstances? Where will he find a male model to imitate?

The cure for these situations is simple, but apparently not easy to achieve. It is for father to spend more time with his preschool boy. (Fathers need to spend time with preschool girls also; we shouldn't forget that.) I wish I knew some magical way to persuade fathers of preschool boys how important this is. Unfortunately, many men seem so driven by ambition and a compulsive need to get ahead that when their children are young they find little time to be with them. They usually rationalize this by saying they are really working these long hours so that the family can be better provided for financially in the future. Sometime in the future when the children are older, father believes he will have more time to spend with them. Unfortunately, it doesn't usually work out that way. If a father doesn't spend time with his preschool children and establish good relationships in these crucial early years, the children usually are not too interested in father in later years. And that is utterly sad.

There are several things even busy fathers can do for their preschool boys (and girls too) which do not ordinarily occur to them. One is to keep a supply of little cards or notes at his work, and send these cards or notes through the mail to his preschooler. Young children get very little mail, and they will be thrilled to receive a letter from Dad. He can also take time to phone his preschooler from work once in a while. A five-minute call can mean a great deal to his child.

Every father should arrange somehow to take his preschooler to see where he works and what kind of work he does. A father may need to give some thought to this. It is important that he explain his job to his child on a level the youngster can understand. Some jobs lend themselves more easily to explanation than others. Mother can encourage the child at home to act out in dramatic play "Daddy's job." Or the parent can help the child to create a book called "My Daddy's Job." I will describe in more detail how to create such books with your child in Chapter 11.

Preschool boys need dress-up clothes for dramatic play which express masculine activities and occupations, equally as much as preschool girls need feminine dress-up clothes. Yet if you investigate the average home you would probably find there are dress-up clothes for the little girls of the house, consisting of mother's old clothes and shoes and hats and jewelry. But usually there are no dress-up clothes for the boy. We need to provide a boy with father's hats, old jeans, old boots, army fatigues, army hats, and construction hats. A visit to the Goodwill or surplus store will yield these dress-up items of a masculine nature.

Most important, however, is mother and father's attitude to the little boy or girl. If mother glories not only in her daughter's femininity, but in her little boy's growing masculinity, everything will turn out well. Mother needs to allow for the fact that it is the nature of a boy to be feisty, mischievous, rambunctious, and crude. She should not try to make him over into a docile, sweet, quiet creature who is remarkably like a little girl. Reading a book such as *This Is Goggle* by Bentz Plagemann, which describes this boyish quality so well, might do more for a mother than reading ten dry-as-dust disquisitions on the subject by scientists.

And what of the father? He has a crucial role to play also. He can give a preschool boy the physical interaction and rough-housing that he needs. At the same time he can display the tenderness and softness his little girl needs to encourage her coquettishness and femininity.

It is also good for parents to keep in mind that no child is 100 percent masculine or 100 percent feminine. If they were, how in the world could they be expected to understand the other sex at all? We need to avoid gender stereotypes such as "being masculine means being tough and unfeeling," "boys don't cry," "girls don't need to think," etc. We want our boys to grow up to be men who are capable of showing such "feminine" traits as warmth and sensitivity to the feelings of others. And we want our little girls to grow up to be women who are less conforming, who are more original and daring, who can think as logically as any man.

For these reasons, we should not be rigid about what we convey to our children as "masculine" and "feminine" behavior. We need to allow our preschoolers to play out roles and feelings appropriate to the opposite sex as well as their own. It's not going to hurt a three-year-old boy to play house or for his mother to teach him how to cook simple dishes or bake cookies. And it's not going to hurt a three-year-old girl to play with trucks and fire engines if that's what she wants to do. Encourage your preschoolers in their gender identities, but don't be rigid and stereotyped about it.

7

Preschool

PART TWO

During the preschool stage your child is learning basic attitudes toward sexuality. In previous chapters I said that with a child up to the age of three all you had to do was to refrain from giving him *negative* sex education. It is time now to start giving your youngster a *positive* sex education. From this age on there are many things he is going to want to know and to need to know about sex.

As a psychologist who has been dealing with the intimate problems of people for more than twenty years, I am well aware that most parents, in their inner feelings, bear scars of misinformation, guilt, and fear about sex, which date back to when they were children. Only someone such as a psychologist can realize the incredible things so many people are hiding in their private heart of hearts about sex. Is it any wonder then, that many parents find it difficult to handle their children's questions and upbringing on this subject, which is for many so tender and delicate?

If we had been lucky enough to be raised on one of the South Sea islands things would probably be quite different. The adults on these islands have practically no cases of homosexuality, fetishism, peeping toms, or any of the

181

other sexual deviations and neuroses which are unfortunately so abundant in our society. The reason the adults in these societies do not suffer from these sexual deviations is simply that they were given healthy sexual upbringings when they were children.

Most of us were not so fortunate. I am very aware that whether you will be able to follow my advice with respect to the sex education of your children depends mainly on the kind of sexual education or sexual miseducation you yourself had as a child. Our ideal should be to treat the whole subject of sex as neutrally and as matter-of-factly as we would any other subject. Children are not abnormally concerned with sex nor obsessed with thoughts about it. It is grown-ups who teach them to be obsessed with sex. When children ask questions about sex, to them these questions are on the same level as their questions about why it rains, or where the sun goes at night, or what makes flowers grow. But when they get quite a different kind of reaction from us to their naive questions about sex, they sense that we grown-ups regard sex as something taboo and dirty, yet fascinating.

The first thing we need to do is to try to answer their questions about sex as openly and directly and honestly as we possibly can. These questions almost always seem to come out of the clear blue sky, at times when we have no way of anticipating them. The first question we will usually get from a three-year-old is, of course, the time-honored query, "Where do babies come from?" This can be answered very simply: "Babies come from inside the mother. They grow in a special place inside the mother called the uterus." That will usually suffice for that question, until the child wants a more elaborate explanation later. Give short and simple answers to children's questions about sex, as you do to their questions about other things. If your child wants a more detailed explanation, never fear, he will ask you more questions.

Incidentally, for some reason that I have never been able to fathom, mothers sometimes tell young children that babies grow in the mother's stomach. This, of course, is not only anatomically incorrect, but it gives rise to all sorts of fantastic misconceptions in the child's mind about other aspects of sex, such as How does the baby get into the stomach? How does the baby get out of the stomach? Tell your child about the uterus instead of the stomach.

Children are often afraid to ask questions about sex. And so, in addition to answering whatever questions about sex your youngster will ask you, you have to take a further step in order to provide him with a positive sex education at this stage of his development. You need to read a book to him which will give him, in more or less systematic form, an overall view of the sexual process and the way in which babies are born. There are three excellent books which do this and I would recommend that you buy at least one of them and read it to your child. All of them go at the subject from a slightly different angle, and it wouldn't hurt to use all three of them. I have read all three of them to my children when they were this age. The books I recommend are:

A Baby Is Born, Milton Levine and Jean Seligmann (Western Publishing)
Growing Up, Karl DeSchweinitz (Macmillan)
The Wonderful Story of How You Were Born, Sidonie Gruenberg (Doubleday)

Don't make a special thing of reading one or more of these books to your child. Don't wave the flag and say in hushed tones: "Tonight, Jimmy, we're going to read about sex!" Read these books to him as you would read any other book. Answer his questions as you would answer questions about any other book.

There is one thing, however, which makes the reading of these books on sex different from the reading of other books. Due to the anxiety-ridden and guilt-laden atmosphere about sex in our society, children can get more easily confused about it than they can about some emotionally neutral subject such as arithmetic or astronomy. For that reason, you may need to repeat explanations about sex that you have given previously and thought the child understood. One explanation in answer to a child's question about sex will not necessarily clear up his confusion about this area once and for all. For the same reason, it is a good idea to read these books to your child not just once but several times.

To be specific, I would read them to a child once when he is three, once when he is four, and once when he is five. The books can then be available in his own little library for him to consult later on after he has learned to read. The information found in these three books should take care of most of what a child needs to know about sex until he is on the verge of adolescence. At that point, a whole new era of sex education begins for him.

If you happen to be pregnant, you will have a special opportunity to teach your preschooler about sex and childbirth. At the appropriate time you can tell your preschooler that you have a baby growing inside you and that pretty soon he will have a baby brother or sister. (Incidentally, don't forget what we discussed in the last chapter about how to handle sibling rivalry at the time of the birth of a baby.) Your youngster is pretty sure to be interested in how this tiny baby is growing inside you, where it gets food, how it is going to get out, and so forth. This is the time to get out one of the books on sex you may have read previously and re-read it to your child. Or you may want to read to your preschooler and show him the photographs which are in a remarkable book, *A Child Is Born* by Lennart Nilsson (Delacorte). This book is sure to fascinate a preschooler, with its photographs of what babies actually look like growing inside the mother. Be sure to tell him how tiny he was when he started growing inside of you. He will be fascinated to see what he looked like at various stages of his development in the uterus.

One question that children usually have difficulty with is how the baby gets out of the mother. If your preschooler asks you this, before you tell him the correct answer, ask him to guess. The reason you ask him to guess is so that you can find out his misconceptions and clear them up before giving him the right answer. He may guess the baby comes out the "BM hole," or the belly button. You can tell him, "No, the baby doesn't come out the BM hole, that we call the rectum. And it doesn't come out the belly button. The mother has a special baby-hole, like a little tunnel. This baby hole is very stretchy. When it is time for the baby to come out, it can stretch big enough for the baby to come through the tunnel. After the baby is born, it can un-stretch, and go back to the way it was."

Now we come to that part of a healthy sex education for our preschoolers which is probably the most difficult for us parents to handle. What to do when a young child plays with his sexual organs? In various books on child raising this is referred to as "childhood masturbation," which is, I think, a most unfortunate word for it. It is not really masturbation at all. True masturbation does not take place until the teen-age years, because not until them is a child capable of having an ejaculation. To speak of a three-year-old boy fondling his penis in a bathtub as masturbating is incorrect and misleading. So let's simply call it playing with his sex organs. A younger child may do this purely out of curiosity, at a time when his sexual organs mean no more to him than his ears or his toes. But now, at the preschool stage, he discovers that they are a special kind of place. He discovers he can get a special kind of pleasure by fondling or caressing his sexual organs. In earlier times we believed that nothing like this occurred until teen-age days, but that Victorian era has passed. We now know that this type of sexual pleasure in playing with one's sexual organs is a part of normal development in the preschool stage.

How shall we handle it when our child does this? Ideally, it would be best to leave the child alone. After a while he will stop playing with his sex organs and move on to some other activity. If you are relaxed enough yourself in your own feelings about sex to let him do this, fine. But what if you're not? What if it just bothers you to death to have him do this? Then I think probably the best thing for you to do is to distract him by offering him some new and interesting activity he can engage in. But if you need to do it this way, try to keep your own cool and do it skillfully. Don't rush over as if you were going to put out a fire and breathlessly exclaim: "Here, Tommy—wouldn't you like to play a nice game of tiddlywinks with Mother?"

So far, I've talked about how to handle things when your child is playing with his sex organs by himself. But you may have to handle a situation when he and other young children are in the middle of sex play in a group. Usually, some form of group sex play is begun merely out of curiosity. This traditionally takes the form of the "doctor" game. One young child assumes the role of the doctor who is going to examine another "sick" little girl or boy. And the other children take their turns at examining or being examined. Once the initial curiosity is satisfied, this type of play will lose its fascination and disappear. No harm will come to any of the children from it.

If you happen to discover this type of sex play going on, you don't need to become frightened or panicky that you have a group of young sex fiends on your hands. You do not need to be punitive or harsh with them. In a matter-of-fact way you can tell them you know they were probably curious about each other's sex organs. Now that their curiosity has been satisfied, they can play some other games. Then get the group of children started on some new activity.

By handling things in this way, your child and the others will know that you have accepted their childish and normal ways of satisfying their sexual curiosity, but that they can now call a halt to their sex games with their peers. You need not probe to find out if your child is playing doctor at this stage in his development. Respect his privacy. You may never find out about his childish sex play with his peers. That's all right too. If your child's general sexual upbringing is healthy, he will not become obsessed with sex play.

Of course, it is always possible that the sex play may be discovered by some other mother, who phones you in a voice quivering with scandalized indignation. She informs you that your little Johnny, who is in her mind little more than a sex degenerate, has been leading her four-year-old daughter astray in the garage. How you handle that one will depend upon the general state of relationship between you and that mother. Try to realize, if you ever get on the receiving end of one of these tirades from an outraged mother, that she must have been very badly traumatized in the sexual miseducation she received as a little girl to be reacting this way as an adult. If some other mother gives your child a tongue-lashing for sex play, you will need to take your youngster aside at home. Explain that Mrs. Grundy was very upset at him, but that you don't feel that way about it. Yes, he and her daughter shouldn't have been playing with each other in the garage, but she needn't have made such a big fuss about it.

One final aspect of the sex education of young children concerns personal nudity in the home. In the Victorian period, parents would not have dreamed of letting their children see them nude or even partially nude. Bathroom doors were locked. Now the pendulum seems to have swung to the opposite extreme, and sometimes parents allow children to see them nude even when the children are in their pre-teens. What is best?

In general, I feel that today's more relaxed attitudes toward nudity in the home are a much healthier way of educating our children sexually. I think that for youngsters up to the age of six, a rather open policy toward nudity in the home is best. It makes for a more relaxed and healthy attitude toward sex and bodily functions for children and parents to be free to be nude or partially nude around the house while the children are preschoolers. After that, I think it is a different matter. Generally speaking, when children get to be seven or eight, they seem to develop a kind of instinctive modesty. We parents can help this along. At this later age, a child may want the bathroom door closed when he is taking a shower. We should respect his right to privacy. It is wise for the parent at this time to keep reasonably covered when bathing or using the toilet.

The reason for this change of attitude on the parent's part is that for a youngster of nine or ten years or older to see the parent nude may be too sexually stimulating for the child. This precocious sexual stimulation can lead to problems because it may be more stimulation than the child can comfortably handle.

A child of nine whom I was seeing in therapy provides a good example. In addition to seeing the child once a week, I saw the parents together once a month. Among other problems he had, the child was unduly preoccupied with sex. This is not normal at the age of nine. I inquired about the sexual atmosphere in the family and found that the mother, who prided herself on having outgrown mid-Victorian taboos about sex, often went around the house in bra and panties. The mother was surprised when I suggested she discontinue this because her boy was finding it too stimulating. "Surely he doesn't notice anything special about that, does he?" she asked. Her more realistic husband answered: "Honey, it turns me on, and I'll bet it turns him on too!" He was right.

My feeling is that both parents and children will naturally develop more modesty about nudity in the home during grade school days. Meanwhile, in the preschool stage, it is still the time for a much more relaxed attitude on both sides toward nudity.

THE FAMILY ROMANCE

Your preschooler during this stage of development is going through a normal stage which we call the "family romance." It works differently for boys than for girls, so I will need to describe each separately. Let's start with the boy.

Somewhere around the age of three, a little boy begins to discover that his father has a different relationship to his mother than he has. Up until then his intelligence has not matured sufficiently for him to discover this. Mother, of course, has always been the most important person in his young life. Whereas his previous relationship to her had been a babyish and dependent one, now his feelings about her change. Basically what happens is that he falls in love with his mother and develops new romantic feelings about her. He becomes a little suitor for her hand. This is normal. All little boys feel this way. Some boys may keep these feelings all to themselves. Other boys, particularly if they have been raised in a family where they are allowed to express their feelings freely, will express them openly.

The little boy wants mother all to himself, and begins to resent father, whom he now perceives as a rival to his 100 percent possession of mother.

When my oldest son was at this stage, we were on a family trip to the zoo one day. I was walking hand in hand with my wife, when he suddenly appeared behind us and pulled our hands apart, saying as he did so: "I break your love!"

Psychologist Dorothy Baruch tells an amusing incident which illustrates the new romantic feelings which arise in a little boy at this stage:

> Pat, who is five, is staging a scene of his own making in his older sister's doll house. He puts the father and mother to sleep side by side in their room. He puts the boy doll to bed in the room next door. "It's all dark," he says. Then, humming, "Silent Night," he makes the boy tiptoe into the parents' room, takes the mother out of the father's bed and transfers her into his own. At this point, Pat's tune changes to "Here Comes the Bride." Then he has the father

doll get up from his bed and leave the house. And with this he hums in merry triumph "Jingle Bells."

Pat's father, who had been curiously watching, wonders aloud: "Did you know what tunes you were singing?"

"Oh yes," answers Pat with a grin. "They're what the boy wants. He gives mother to be the bride. And father to be Santa Claus, who gives the mother to the boy for Christmas and then goes out to his reindeer and leaves."[21]

Boys will often be heard to say at this age that when they grow up they are going to marry mother. Or, as one five-year-old recently expressed it to his mother: "Gee, Mom, I wish you were younger and a lot shorter and not married to Dad!"

Instead of merely smiling indulgently at these "cute" sayings of children, we need to take them quite seriously. These feelings and fantasies run very deep in a little boy. They are Mother Nature's way of getting him ready for his eventual role as a husband to some future wife. This "family romance" in which he falls in love with his mother at this age is a very vital part of his development. His mother is the first woman in his life, his first romantic love figure. And his feelings toward his mother, on an unconscious level, will usually dictate his choice of a wife later on. He will want to marry a girl who in some ways reminds him of his mother. We even have an old song based on this childhood theme: "I want a girl just like the girl who married dear old Dad!" However, Mother Nature doesn't want him to get fixated on his mother forever. She wants him to get over it by the time he's six or seven, and most little boys do. However, in the years between three and six, these romantic feelings flourish within the heart of mother's miniature suitor.

The catch to all of this is that the "family romance" is also a "family triangle." The little boy not only feels deep and romantic fantasies toward his mother; he also feels rivalrous and jealous of his father. If the father does not realize what is going on (and many fathers don't, sad to say), then this development can throw him. I recall coming home from work one day and greeting my three-year-old affectionately at the door, only to be told by him: "Go away! I want Mommy!" Even though I knew what was going on at this stage of his development, it was hard for me not to take it personally and react with hurt feelings.

These feelings of rivalry with the father and hostility to him put the little boy on an uncomfortable spot. He loves his father and needs him. How can he feel at the same time that he wishes father would go away so that he can have mother all to himself? These ambivalent feelings toward his father are very difficult for the little boy to tolerate within himself.

Since the little boy feels these rivalrous and hostile feelings toward his father, by use of the defense mechanism of projection, he projects his own feelings onto his father. He begins to imagine his father also feels rivalrous and hostile towards him. Since father is so much bigger and more powerful, the little boy begins to develop fears that father will retaliate and punish him severely. This often results in the nightmares that are so typical for many children between three and six. The little boy projects his fears that father will hurt or punish him onto a tiger or lion or monster, who chases him in his dreams.

In a healthy family situation, the little boy gradually realizes that his fantasies of replacing father are not going to come true. This is part of one of his general intellectual tasks during this stage of sorting out reality from fantasy. (Remember how the four-year-old particularly has trouble separating reality from fantasy?) Usually it will take all of the years from three to six for the little boy to give up his romantic fantasies about mother and adjust to the reality that mother is father's woman and not his. Finally, however, he gets the idea and begins to adopt the attitude: If you can't lick 'em, join 'em. Since he can't *be* father, he decides he wants to be *like* father.

Now begins the process of identification with father. He uses father as a model and imitates him in many ways. Both of these processes (the gradual giving up of the romantic fantasies about mother, and the gradual giving up of the rivalry with father and replacing it with an identification with him) will take all of the three years of this developmental stage for the little boy to accomplish.

Our present society has made it harder in two ways for little boys to accomplish this important developmental task. First of all, father is such a distant and absent figure for many preschool boys today that they have difficulty identifying with him. This makes it harder for them to resolve the "family triangle" by giving up their fantasies about mother and wanting to be like Dad

Second, if a divorce takes place when a boy is between the age of three and six, this also makes it harder for him to resolve the family romance. He wants his mother all to himself and his father out of the picture. Then, with the divorce, it appears to him as if his wishes had magically been granted. The little boy now feels that maybe, in some way he cannot quite comprehend, he is responsible for the divorce. After all, that's just what he wanted to have happen, isn't it? And now it is a reality, and so he feels terribly guilty. Usually he tries pitifully to make up to both parents for what he feels he has brought about.

So if, through coincidence, you happen to go through a divorce during the time your little boy is in the preschool stage, be sure you help him to realize he is not responsible. Use the feedback technique I described in Chapter 4 to help him put his feelings into words, no matter how irrational they may be. Only after you give him a chance to put his feelings into words and mirror them back to him should you explain to him that he is in no way responsible for the divorce. You will also find *The Boys and Girls Book of Divorce* (described in Appendix E) extremely helpful to you and your child if you happen to go through a divorce when your child is a preschooler I recommend it highly.

In most healthy families, by the time the little boy is six he has resolved the family romance and passed through this very important phase of development. He now has within himself deep unconscious images of the type of woman he will later want to marry, as well as the type of husband he will be to such a woman. Without successfully resolving the family romance between the years three to six, he would not be able to find a marriage partner in later life.

Now let's turn to the little girl, because her family romance takes a somewhat different pattern. Notice that the little boy's first love figure was his mother He keeps that same love figure, though in a new romantic form, throughout the stage of the family romance. The little girl begins with that same first love figure· her mother. But, unlike the boy, the little girl now has to shift her love figure from her mother to her father This makes the phase of the family romance a more complicated thing for her.

As the little girl begins to become more independent and differentiate herself from her mother in the preschool stage of development, she now finds a new love figure within the family and falls in love with her father. As with little boys, some girls keep their feelings and fantasies to themselves, whereas others are quite open about them. Little girls can be very feminine and coquettish at this stage. When my daughter was five and coming out of the shower one day, she took her towel, and in the fashion of a shimmy dancer twirled it around her as she said to me, "Hey, Daddy, look at me!"

Little girls may be much more subtle than boys in the way in which they approach their aims during this period of the family romance. This is in keeping with the greater subtlety of females in personal relationships. In fact, the mother may not even realize how much her little girl is inwardly competing with her for father's love. You may just think she's delightfully trying to follow your example when she tries to learn to cook and clean, not realizing that in her inner feelings she's trying to demonstrate to her father how much better a wife she would make for him than you.

The little girl also faces a different situation than the boy in actual time spent with the romanticized parent. In our present society, mothers are present in the home most of the time, whereas fathers are mainly absent from the home. The little boy actually does get to spend a great deal of time with his romanticized love, his mother. However, the little girl must spend much of her day longing for her absent father. Her romanticized feelings for her father must be lived out more in fantasy than a little boy's.

The little girl feels rivalrous and competitive with her mother. These feelings trouble her in the same way that the little boy's rivalrous feelings toward his father trouble him. She is dependent upon her mother for love and affection and nurturing. How terrible of her, she feels, to wish that her mother would go away somewhere and never come back! In the same way in which the little boy projects his hostile feelings onto his father, she projects her hostile feelings onto her mother. She imagines her mother knows how much she wants to get rid of her, and therefore is equally angry with her and wants to punish her. Her dreams in this period are often troubled by nightmares in which she is pursued by some fearsome witch or monster, an unconscious disguise for the vengeful mother she imagines.

In a normal family, the little girl also learns that father belongs to mother and that she cannot have him. This learning extends over the whole period from three to six years of age. Gradually she renounces her romantic longings for her father, and replaces them in her mind with the general outlines of the man she will one day fall in love with and marry. Gradually, she identifies with her mother and, in her unconscious mind, fills in the general outline of what kind of wife she will become in later life. Thus the little girl, like the littly boy, resolves the family triangle.

Now for the important question: What can you and your husband do to aid your preschool youngsters in progressing normally through this family romance and resolving it by the time they are six or seven?

First, and most important, the state of your marriage relationship will be crucial in the ability of your children to work through their feelings and resolve their family romance. If you and your husband have a basically stable and loving relationship, your children will gradually realize the impossibility of their romantic fantasies and outgrow them during these preschool years. However, if your relationship with your husband is marked by deep-seated hostility and estrangement, this will make it difficult for your children to adequately resolve their family romance. If your marriage relationship is a shaky one, the best thing you could do to help your child work his way through the family romance would be to get yourself some marriage counseling! I mean this quite seriously.

Your preschool child will, of course, try to stir up arguments between you and your husband so that he can reap the supposed benefits. He will attempt, in his own childish way, to drive a wedge between the two of you. If basic difficulties exist in the marriage, the boy may succeed in getting mother to treat him more as a "miniature lover" than as a child. If mother revels too much in this kind of attention from a preschool son because she feels her husband pays too little attention to her, this is not a healthy thing for the boy. Mother will then tend to belittle the father to the son, instead of building him up to the son. Preschool daughters, of course, can play the same "divide and conquer" games, trying to pit father against mother.

Parents must be on the alert during this time not to let the child, finding chinks in their marriage, use these marital tender spots to play "divide and conquer." Both father and mother need to resist the temptation to respond to their youngster's romantic seductiveness by openly welcoming the child's advances. Instead, both father and mother should respond with what we may call "tender rejection." The parents should reject the romanticized relationship offered by the child. The mother needs to make it clear to the little boy that she loves Daddy and is Daddy's wife. She wants her little boy to love Daddy too. The little boy cannot marry her when he grows up because she is already married to Daddy and happy about it. But someday he will find a wife of his own and marry her. Meanwhile, he is her little boy and he is Daddy's little boy too.

Father should make it clear to the little girl that he loves her very much, but that Mother is his wife. No, she cannot marry Daddy when she grows up. He's already happily married to Mommy. But she is his little girl and no one can ever take the special place she has in his affections. But someday she will find a husband of her own and marry him.

There is no need for either mother or father to be brutal in disabusing a preschool child of his fantasies. You don't want to encourage him in the belief that his fantasies will come true. But you can let him down gently in presenting the realities of the situation to him. You don't want your child to feel ridiculous or foolish for having these fantasies. Remember, they are a normal part of his development, and a normal preparation for his future marriage. He shouldn't be ridiculed or shamed for having feelings which are a normal part of this stage of his development.

Above all, you should not actively encourage your youngster in these fantasies. To do so would be to promote an overly close attachment which he will have difficulty in breaking away from later on. All of us know men who have never been able to resolve their family romance, break away from their attachment to mother, find a woman to marry, and start a family of their own.

However, if you and your husband are reasonably mature people, with a healthy and happy marriage, your preschooler should pass safely through the ups and downs of the family romance by the time he is six or seven.

SENSITIVITY TO INTELLECTUAL STIMULATION

During the preschool stage of development, your child is going through a period in which he is particularly responsive to intellectual stimulation. With the proper kind of stimulation, he will develop basic skills and attitudes toward learning which he will carry with him the rest of his life.

A child's *intelligence* can be simply defined as "a child's repertoire of basic learning skills." Every time you increase a child's basic learning skills, you increase his intelligence. On intelligence tests for children you will find items testing the child's ability to follow directions, to listen carefully to a story, to summarize the meaning of a story, to remember the order or words in a sentence, to put together pieces of a puzzle, or to make a design out of blocks which will match the design on a card. These are examples of basic learning skills which a child can acquire in the years from three to six. These are the "learning how to learn" years.

How can you best insure that he receives an optimal amount of intellectual and emotional stimulation during his preschool stage? One of the best ways is to enroll him in a good nursery school when he is approximately three years old.

Perhaps I'd better define exactly what I mean by *nursery school,* since many parents seem to use "day nursery" and "nursery school" interchangeably, which is unfortunate. A day nursery or day care center is exactly what its name implies: a center in which young children between the ages of two and six whose mothers have to work can be cared for during the day while their mothers are working. These day care centers take children as early as six-thirty in the morning and keep them until six o'clock at night. Some of them are good, with well-trained teachers, ample equipment, and a good curriculum. Many of them are dreadful and are operated by ill-trained people who are in the business mainly to make as much money as they can as quickly as possible. The psychological care of the children in some of these centers is shocking. Unfortunately, these day care centers are listed in the Yellow Pages of the phone book under the same headings as "nursery schools" or "preschools." The naive parent may not be able to tell them apart.

A nursery school is quite a different matter. It is not designed primarily for the children of a working mother. It usually operates a half day rather than a full day. A nursery school will ordinarily not take children before they are three years old. Nursery schools are also known as "preschools." Nursery schools vary a great deal as to quality also, but one rule of thumb is that if the nursery school is operated in connection with a college or university, it is reasonably safe to assume that high standards prevail.

Another variation of the nursery school is the parents' cooperative nursery school. Here the school is staffed not by hired professional teachers, but by parents. Usually the director is a paid professional, and the rest of the teachers are mothers, who take turns in teaching the children.

Many otherwise intelligent parents are ignorant of the whole field of nursery school education, or, as it is now called, early childhood education. I have heard otherwise intelligent architects, bankers, lawyers, and their wives say: "Well, after all, nursery school is really nothing more than a glorified baby-sitter, isn't it?" To call a good nursery school nothing but a glorified baby-sitter is about as inappropriate as calling Harvard nothing but a playground for late adolescents. I have also heard otherwise intelligent mothers say, in all seriousness: "I don't really need to send my little boy to nursery school because he has lots of children to play with in our neighborhood." That same mother would not dream of saying: "I don't need to send my third-grader to school, because he has lots of children to play with in the neighborhood!"

If laymen are ignorant of much of what is going on in early childhood education these days, some of the professionals seem to be almost equally confused. Many books on child raising seem to assume that nursery school is good only for the *emotional* development of a child and has nothing to offer as far as his *intellectual* development is concerned. Several of the books on child raising pussyfoot around on the subject of whether you should or should not send your child to nursery school, with chapter titles such as "The Pro's and Con's of Nursery School." To me that is as ridiculous as having a chapter entitled "The Pro's and Con's of Grade School."

One of the best things you can do for your preschool child, if you can afford it, is to enroll him in a good nursery school when he turns three. You shouldn't send him to nursery school before that age, because he's not really ready to separate from mother until then. Of course, if you can't afford it, or if there is no good nursery school near you, you will have to make other arrangements. I will deal with this in Chapter 11 in which I describe in detail how you can set up the equivalent of a nursery school in your own home.

If you are able to afford it, however, how do you go about finding a good nursery school? As a psychologist who has had extensive acquaintance with nursery schools and early childhood education, I must report to you the sad fact that many mothers actually select a nursery school for their child mainly on the basis of the mother's convenience. The mother chooses the school because it is nearest to her home. Or because she knows of a carpool that is convenient to take her youngster to that particular nursery school. Frankly, I am amazed and appalled by this. Since most nursery schools in a given geographical area are within the same price range, it would be well worth the time of the mother to investigate and find the *best* nursery school, not merely the *closest*.

Nursery schools can be distinguished from one another by three points: (1) teachers, (2) equipment, and (3) curriculum. The most important is the teaching staff. A skilled, well-trained teacher, who is warm and relaxed and giving with children, is crucial to the learning experiences your child will have at nursery school. Don't hesitate, in talking with the teacher, to ask about her background and training in early childhood education. You have a right to know this. After all, it's *your child* you are entrusting to her care.

Most parents know little about nursery school equipment and curriculum. I would suggest that you read a good book on nursery school education. Several books which are good are the following:

The Nursery School, Katherine Read (W. B. Saunders Company)

The Guidance Nursery School, Louise Ames and Evelyn Pitcher (Harper and Row)

The Nursery School: Adventure In Living And Learning, Mary Rogers, Helen Christianson, and Blanche Ludlum (Houghton Mifflin)

Good Schools for Young Children, Sarah Hammond, Ruth Dales, Dora Skipper, and Ralph Witherspoon (Macmillan)

If you know little about nursery schools you will probably be amazed at the many different types of indoor and outdoor equipment that promote both emotional and intellectual development in the young child. See whether the nursery schools you visit have an abundance of educational toys and play equipment, or are trying to skimp by with as little equipment as possible.

With regard to curriculum, you should know that there is a good deal of dispute among authorities with respect to nursery school and kindergarten curriculum. One group favors the traditional arts and crafts curriculum, which helps the child in his emotional development. In this approach, the child has opportunities for large muscle development through outside climbing equipment, building with large hollow blocks and planks, and riding tricycles. Indoors, he works with clay, finger painting, paint, crayons, block building, dramatic play, and various other items of equipment which aid both his small muscle development and his creativity and emotional growth. Overall, the child is guided by his teacher in learning how to manage interpersonal realtionships with other children.

The other curriculum approach to nursery school and kindergarten we may label the "cognitive" approach. This approach says there is nothing at all wrong with the curriculum mentioned above, but that it should be supplemented. They believe the child should be exposed to various types of cognitive stimulation in these early years, without pressuring him or changing the relaxed atmosphere of early childhood into a formal classroom situation inappropriate to this age child. In this type of cognitive approach, new educational materials and techniques appear. I refer to such things as the Cuisenaire Arithmetic Rods, the Catherine Stern structural arithmetic, tape recorders, "talking typewriters," educational kits with which the child can learn to print, language development kits using puppets and other manipulative materials, and programmed materials which will teach the child to read.

Kindergarten teachers, no less than nursery school teachers, seem to be sharply divided on this issue. Some of the more traditional kindergarten teachers feel they should stick to such activities as block building, finger painting, and planting seeds. They believe that to teach a child to read in kindergarten is inevitably to pressure him and to "rob him of his childhood." Others insist that if a child is ready to learn to read in kindergarten, we should give him the chance.

I am firmly on the side of the "cognitive" curriculum group. I see no reason for the nursery school and kindergarten curriculum to stay the same as it was in the 1930s and '40s. Ten years from now we will look back in amazement that some educators actually thought we were "robbing a youngster of his childhood" if we taught him to read in kindergarten. We have accumulated a considerable mass of research evidence showing that it is important to give cognitive stimulation to preschool children if we are going to help them develop their maximum intelligence in later life. We have nothing but old wives tales to support the contention that we should refrain from giving cognitive stimulation to preschool children lest we damage them emotionally.

This controversy may have some bearing on the nursery school you select for your child. If the nursery school you select believes in only the "arts and crafts" type of curriculum, and it is otherwise a good nursery school, with well-trained teachers—fine. Your youngster will benefit greatly from it. But if you can find one of the newer type nursery schools which offers both cognitive stimulation as well as the arts and crafts type of curriculum, so much the better.

To make a wise selection of a nursery school for your child, take the time to actually see it in operation. Arrange for a babysitter and visit the school by yourself for the complete session. Do not take your youngster with you. If you do, you will find yourself riding herd on him instead of getting a chance to observe what his potential teacher is like. Do not tell the school ahead of time that you will be visiting. This way, you will get a genuinely unrehearsed look at the kind of teaching that the school provides. If the school won't allow you to visit and observe in this way, I would distrust it.

You will probably need to pick up some information about teacher techniques and methods by browsing through one of the books on the nursery school that I mentioned previously. Otherwise you may not know good nursery school teaching when you see it in action! The skilled nursery school teacher may talk very little and remain in the background much of the time, intervening only if some crisis seems about to erupt. The uninitiated parent may be apt to think, "Why she's hardly doing anything! What kind of teaching is that?" This parent would be missing the skill and subtlety with which the teacher is guiding the group.

However, you should be able to judge *one* important aspect of the school without any technical knowledge of nursery school teaching techniques. This is the emotional atmosphere in the classroom. Is it a warm and relaxed atmosphere, in which the children feel free to be themselves? Or is it a tense or scolding or moralistic atmosphere, in which the teacher may shame a child, or send him to stand in the corner, or say things like "That's not a nice boy, Tommy." You certainly don't want to put your child into a room where he will be subjected to that kind of judgmental emotional atmosphere for three hours a day.

Whether you are able to send your child to nursery school or you set up the equivalent of a nursery school in your own home, the more you know about good nursery school techniques, the better off you will be in guiding your preschooler. If you like any of the books on nursery school techniques you find in your library, it would be a wise investment to buy it as a reference book.

Kindergarten is a most crucial year of learning for your child. Since kindergarten offers such marvelous opportunities for learning, and since the five-year-old is so ripe for learning, it is a shame so many children in the United States at this writing do not have the opportunity to go to public kindergarten. This deplorable situation is due to the fact that there are no kingergartens in their school district, or they have been turned away for lack of space.

What should you do if there is no public school kindergarten in your school district for your child to attend?

My answer is unequivocal: If you can at all afford it, find a good private kindergarten for your child and enroll him. I would even borrow the money if I had to. Parents will cheerfully borrow money to send a child to college, but very few parents ever seem to think of borrowing money to send a child to kindergarten. Yet the early years of learning are so important I think it would be better to borrow for kindergarten than college if you were forced to choose between the two. All of the things I said about finding a good nursery school apply equally to finding a good kindergarten.

You also need to know something about the curriculum your child is likely to have in kindergarten. For the more traditional kindergarten approach, two good books are:

The Kindergarten Teacher, Helen Hefferman and Vivian Todd (Heath)
Kindergarten: A Year of Learning, Marguerite Rudolph and D. H. Cohen (Appleton-Century)

For the newer "cognitive" approaches in kindergarten, see:

New Directions in the Kindergarten, Helen Robison and Bernard Spodek (Teachers College Press, Columbia University)

If your school system does have kindergarten, you and your child are fortunate. How can you get him ready for kindergarten? If you follow through on the suggestions I will give you in Chapter 11, "School Begins at Home—Part One," your child will be amply prepared for kindergarten. You might also want to consult a book expressly written for the purpose of helping you prepare your child for kindergarten. It is *Your Child and the First Year of School* by Bernard Ryan, Jr. (World Publishing Co.).

If your school system does not have a kindergarten, the suggestions I will give in Chapter 11 will not take the place of a well-run kindergarten, with the opportunities for interaction with other five-year-old children. But they are the next best option I know of.

We have covered a lot of territory in this chapter. That's not really surprising because in the years from three to six an enormous amount of development is taking place in your child. Let's summarize what has happened in these important years.

During the preschool stage, your youngster has had a number of crucial developmental tasks to work through. Look at what he has learned during this stage:

He has fulfilled his biological needs for both large and small muscle development.
He has developed a control system for his impulses.
He has separated himself from his mother.
He has learned the give and take of relationships with his peers.
He has learned to express or to repress his feelings.
His gender identity as a male or female has become stabilized.
His basic attitudes toward sexuality have been formed.
He has worked his way through the resolution of the "family romance."
He has gone through a period of development in which he is particularly responsive to intellectual stimulation, and hopefully, he has received an optimal amount of such stimulation.

So here he is. He has spent five years as a traveler on this spaceship Earth. If you have followed through on the suggestions given in this book, your child should now have a strong self-concept and a healthy and stable personality structure. If things have gone well, your child will have developed a basic sense of trust, good self-confidence, and a strong sense of self-identity. Your most important work is completed in helping him to build a solid foundation in the first five years of his life.

Having taken you through this chronological survey of the first five years of your child's life, in the next two chapters I will focus in detail on a subject which is vital to your handling of him not only in these first five years, but as long as you have him in your care. That subject is the perennially important one of child discipline.

8

Can You Teach a Dolphin to Type?

Discipline is a particularly vexing subject today because so many mothers are confused by conflicting opinions from all sides. One magazine article says one thing; another says the opposite. One book says to do this; another says not. One neighbor advises one course of action; another swears by the opposite. Mothers are continually asking themselves silent, internal questions such as: "Am I being too strict? Am I being too permissive? Was it wrong of me to spank Jimmy this morning? I certainly felt like it, but I'm not sure I did the right thing."

First of all, what exactly do we mean by the word *discipline? Discipline* is a word with many meanings and connotations. Webster's unabridged dictionary defines it as: (1) "to instruct, educate or train" and (2) "to chastise, or punish." As synonyms Webster suggests "to train, form, educate, instruct, drill, regulate, correct, chastise, and punish." If you interviewed a group of mothers at random, chances are that many of them would tend to think of discipline as something you do to get a child to behave properly. In the minds of many people, discipline is almost synonymous with punishment, as a means of getting a youngster to behave.

I would like to suggest a far broader definition: "training." The word *discipline* is related to the word *disciple*. When you discipline your child you are really training him to be a disciple of you, his teacher.

We parents must ask ourselves: "What is the ultimate goal we are working toward in the training of our children?" If we reflect deeply on this question, most of us would answer that our ultimate goal is to produce an adult who has learned *self-regulation*—who has learned to make his own choices and regulate his own behavior, who has learned to exercise his freedom in a responsible way.

Thousands of psychological experiments with animals ranging from white rats to dolphins have provided insights into how to achieve this goal with our children. Please, mothers who are reading this, don't bristle! I'm not saying there's no difference between your child and a dolphin! But in the same way that physicians have learned a great deal about life-saving drugs and vaccines by first using them on lower animals, we have learned many things about training children by experiments in training lower animals.

For example, a psychologist wanted to study the effectiveness of different types of teaching methods with animals. He ran two different groups of white rats through a maze, one at a time, with food at the end. The purpose was to use two different methods of training the rats to run the maze, and to find out which method proved more successful. One group of rats was guided through the correct path to the food, each in a little "rat" wagon pulled by the psychologist. The second group of rats was simply put in the maze, again one at a time, and each was allowed to find its way through by trial and error twenty times. These two groups of rats were then paired, two at a time, and allowed to run the maze. The second group won paws down because the rats in the first group didn't have to think actively about the maze when they were being pulled through in the rat wagon.

You can see the relevance of this experiment to the modern "discovery" method of teaching. Learning is much more firmly imbedded in a child's mind if he has discovered ideas for himself, rather than having them handed to him in a verbally prepackaged form by a teacher. An experiment such as this says a lot about how to teach a child to become self-regulating.

If mothers and fathers actually had some first-hand experience in teaching and training animals, it is doubtful that they would make the usual mistakes in training their children. This may seem like an extreme statement, so let me give you an example of what I mean.

Mothers and fathers all over the United States are busily training their children to be obnoxious. These well-meaning parents do not, of course, think of it this way. But the attention, approval, and affection that a parent gives to a child are powerful reinforcers. Any behavior of a child producing attention and response in the parent is likely to be reinforced or strengthened.

Consider the following typical scene in a market. A child asks for something in a quiet voice; his mother doesn't respond. She is busy talking to a friend or the clerk. The child's voice gets louder and whinier and more insistent. Finally the mother responds. Unwittingly, she has taught the child that the louder his voice gets, and the more unpleasantly he insists on something, the more likely he is to get his way.

Without being aware of it, his mother has followed a perfectly designed procedure for teaching her child to be obnoxious. It's as if she said to herself: "I want little Jimmy to learn to be obnoxious, to ask for things in a most irritating and unpleasant way. Every time he asks for something in a nice way and a quiet voice, I will be too engrossed in some adult activity to pay attention to him. I will only reward or reinforce him with my attention if he asks for something in an obnoxious way, if he whines or pouts or demands loudly or throws a temper tantrum."

An eight-year-old boy, whom I was seeing for therapy, had a knot in his shoelace one day. He asked me to untie it for him. I said, "I'm sure you can untie it yourself, Richard."

"No I can't. You'll have to do it for me."

"I know it's hard to get the knot untied, but I feel sure you can do it," I said.

"I'll get my mother to do it for me if you won't!" With that, he opened the door to the waiting room and ran out to where his mother was sitting.

"Mother, Dr. Dodson is mean and won't untie my shoe for me. You do it!"

His mother stood firm at first, following the general instructions I had given her in the past about teaching him independence.

"No, Richard, you can untie the knot yourself."

"I can't, I can't! You've got to do it for me!"

"You'll be able to do it yourself if you try."

At this point, Richard threw a tantrum. He fell to the floor and began kicking and screaming, "I can't, I can't! You've got to do it for me!"

His mother caved in. "All right, Richard," she said disgustedly, "I'll do it."

I decided it was time to intervene. "Mrs. Goodwin," I said, "you would be making a mistake to do this for Richard now."

She stopped, thought about it a minute, and said, "No, Richard, I'm not going to do it for you; you can do it for yourself."

Richard continued to yell and pound the floor for a few minutes. Then, as he saw she really meant it this time, he suddenly got up from the floor and rushed back into the playroom. I followed and closed the door behind us. He sat in a corner of the room with his back to me for a few minutes, silent and sullen. Then he turned around, gave me a sly smile and said, "You want to play checkers?" I answered, "Sure. Why don't you get that shoelace tied, and then we'll have a game."

The management of Richard's youthful and very human behavior is an example of how not to reinforce bad habits. It has its parallel in the training of animals. But, of course, the more important side of training is that of positive reinforcement.

Suppose you tell an eight-year-old child: "I'd like you to say words out loud as fast as you can think of them, one after the other. It doesn't make any difference what words you say. Just any words that come into your mind. Go ahead."

You have decided ahead of time that each time he says the name of an animal you will say "good." But you will keep silent after whatever other words he says. The child, of course, doesn't know you have decided to do this. He starts saying words. Each time he says the name of an animal, regardless of what animal it is, you say "good."

Try this little experiment and keep careful records. You will find the number of "animal words" will gradually increase. Notice an interesting fact: the child will not even be aware that this is happening! But he will be saying the names of more and more animals. Why is this? Because you are reinforcing him with your attention and that little word of praise ("good") each time he says the name of an animal.

Just for fun, you might try this at the adult level. The next time you are conversing with another person or a group, decide to reinforce some subject whenever it is discussed. It doesn't matter what the subject is: children, clothes, politics, gardening ... you name it. Whenever that subject comes up, reinforce it by showing great interest. Make comments such as "That's interesting" or "I never realized that before" or "Tell me more about that." Whenever the other person is talking about any other subject, keep silent. You will find the same kind of results with adults as you find with eight-year-old children. In fact, we are almost always reinforcing different types of behavior with other people.

Think of children all over the world, brought up in quite different cultures with different languages. At the age of six months or so, all children begin babbling. And the babbling sounds pretty much the same whether the child is English, Russian, Chinese, Arabian or Bantu. But by the time these children are two years old, some of them will be speaking English, some Russian, some Japanese, some Tagalong, some Arabic, and so forth. How is this possible? No child is born with genes that enable him, when he matures, to speak a particular kind of language. Children the world over learn to speak their distinctive languages through well-established psychological principles of learning.

First of all, children imitate the sounds they hear around them, whether English, Russian, Chinese, or whatever. In addition, the parents of these children reinforce the different sounds the baby makes, depending on whether the parents are English or Russian or Chinese or Arabic. For example, in the United States a young baby is lying in his crib, babbling away happily. Sooner or later he says something that sounds like *ma-ma-ma-ma,* because this is one of the easiest sounds for his young vocal cords to manage. But what usually happens when he is babbling away with these sounds of *ma-ma-ma-ma?* If his mother is within earshot, chances are she will jump up delightedly, hug the baby, and say, "He said 'mama'! He knows me; my baby knows me!" In other words, through her attention and affection she gives him powerful reinforcement for making the particular combination of babbling sounds that to her mean "mama." And, in line with well-established reinforcement principles, the baby is soon saying that particular combination of sounds more and more frequently.

Parental reinforcement is a powerful influence in shaping the behavior of babies and children. You need to become aware of what types of behavior you are reinforcing in your children. Though it may have sounded farfetched to you when I first mentioned it, you can now see the relevance of reinforcement training with animals.

Let's look at nine important lessons science has taught us from years of research in reinforcement psychology:

1. *The animal must be in a condition for learning.*

Animal trainers do not try to teach an animal when he is tired, sick, or otherwise avoiding the learning situation. The animal must be ready to hear what the trainer has to say.

In one fascinating experiment a psychologist recorded signals from the brains of cats. These signals indicated that a sound had been transmitted along the auditory nerve and had arrived in the brain. Every time a little click was produced near the cat's ear, the nerve record in the brain showed a specific change. Then the experimenter put in front of the cat a glass jar containing some live mice. He sounded the clicker again. This time the brain record showed no change. The cat did not hear what had previously been a perfectly audible sound. It never got into the higher centers of the brain.

Too many times we try to teach children something when they are in no condition for learning. For example, think of the little "lectures" we often give when the child is in tears after some misbehavior or family crisis. Little Jimmy has just hit his sister with a block and has been spanked for it. While Jimmy is wailing away like a banshee, Mother chooses this inappropriate moment to give a little lecture. "How would you feel, Jimmy, if your sister had hit you with that block?

Can't you learn to have some consideration for the feelings of other people?"

Let's take a tip from the reinforcement psychologists. Do not attempt to teach a child when he is tired, fussy or cranky, upset, or otherwise avoiding the learning situation. It's foolish to try to teach a child anything unless he is in condition to learn.

2. *The animal must be able to perform the task you want him to learn.*

Animal trainers are realistic. They know they can teach a dolphin to jump through a hoop. They also know they can't teach a dolphin to type. So they don't try.

Elementary, you say. But think of all the things parents attempt to teach children which are as impossible for a child to do as for a dolphin to learn to type. To become toilet trained at nine months. To sit still in a restaurant at two years. To be polite and mind his manners at four years. To obey at two years the same way he can obey at five years. The list is endless.

Many parents expect children to learn things which are way above their capacity to learn, the equivalent of trying to teach a dolphin to type. The reason we do this is often simple lack of understanding. Many parents are ignorant of the nature of children at different ages and stages of development. We tend to expect far more than the child is actually capable of at his stage of development. That is why parents usually do a better job of raising a second child or third child. The parent has learned what you can reasonably expect of a child at different stages of development.

3. *Animal trainers avoid punishment except as a last resort or to prevent the learner from being killed or seriously hurt.*

Of course we need to be realistic about this. If you've got a two-year-old who repeatedly runs into the street, your only alternative may be to use punishment. Administer a pat on the bottom low and hard until he learns to stop this dangerous behavior. You have to impose your more mature judgment on the youngster until his judgment becomes mature enough to handle the situation. But in the main we can teach our children most of the things we want them to learn without having to resort to punishment.

Why avoid punishment? Because the only real effect of punishment is to suppress a response temporarily. No permanent weakening of the punished behavior has taken place. When the suppression effect wears off, as it is bound to do in time, the behavior will recur.

For example, a psychologist has trained a white rat to press a lever in his cage to get food. Then the lever is wired so that every time the rat presses it he gets a small electric shock. The rat withdraws from the shock and stops pressing the lever. But eventually, when he gets hungry enough, he will return and press the lever again. The lever-pressing behavior has merely been suppressed temporarily, but not eliminated. When the punishment is no longer continued, the rat begins to press the lever again as if nothing had happened.

There are additional reasons for using punishment as little as possible when teaching a child. Whether teaching a child or an animal, whenever we punish the learner we are teaching him to hate us and fear us. We do not want to teach our children hate or fear unless it is absolutely necessary for self-protection.

Whenever a teacher punishes a learner, he becomes an "aversive stimulus," just like an electric shock. The learner will want to avoid contact from then on with both the teacher and whatever he is being taught.

I once treated a physicist who had come into the field and obtained his Ph.D. rather late in life. Strangely enough, he had avoided science courses all through college. It wasn't until years later in the course of his therapy with me that he learned why he had done this. It went back to his first contact with science in his third grade class with a teacher we shall call Miss Pruneface. He still had vivid memories of Miss Pruneface and the little experiments he did with bell jars and electric currents. What he remembered most vividly about Miss Pruneface was her thin, tight-lipped, grim face and her mean, sarcastic ways with children. She belittled the children and poked fun at the students who were deficient in their work. She represented "science" to my patient. Since she was such an aversive stimulus he learned to avoid the subject of science for many years.

4. *Instead of punishment, when you want to get a child to stop doing something undesirable, use "extinction techniques."*

When a psychologist wants an animal to stop doing something he merely stops reinforcing the animal. If he is rewarding a white rat with a food pellet for pressing a lever, and he wants to stop the animal from pressing the lever, he merely stops giving him the food pellet. Sooner or later, when the reinforcement stops, the animal will stop pressing the lever. It works the same way with a child.

Take a four-year-old who has discovered the electrical effect that the use of four-letter words can have on his parents. He comes home with these four-letter words for the first time. Does he get reinforcement for them? You bet he does! In fact, his mother usually acts as though she's been given the special job of reinforcing these four-letter words so that her four-year-old will continue to use them. (Though of course this is the last thing in the world she really wants.) By acting so upset when her four-year-old uses "bad words" she is actually reinforcing him. Her attention acts as a reinforcer.

How can she get him to stop? Merely stop reinforcing him. Ignore the four-letter words and play it cool. Sooner or later, when her little boy sees that he doesn't irritate mother any more, he will stop using them.

5. *The teacher must have reinforcement for the learner.*

For animals, the reinforcement is food. For children, it is your love and attention. But there is a

catch to this. In order for your love and attention to
be reinforcing, you must be fun and pleasant to be
around. You need to spend some time with your child
just having fun to make it rewarding for your child to
seek your love and affection. Ask yourself: How
much time do I spend with my child that is just
fun—where I am not requiring anything of him? If
the answer is "very little," then perhaps you are not
offering enough of an incentive to want your love and
attention.

For example, a seventeen-year-old boy I had in
therapy was discussing his feelings toward his father,
and he said: "The first fifteen years of my life I
practically saw my father only on Sundays. He was
so busy working he didn't have time to spend with
me. Now that I've got these problems, he's making
the big scene to be a pal and take me places. He
wants me to get over these problems and quit causing
trouble in school. But I feel like, 'Forget it, man!
Where were you all those other years?' "

We need to have the kind of relationship with our
children that makes them want to get our love and
attention.

6. *Reinforce whatever you want the child to do and
pay no attention to what the child does that you
don't want him to do.*

For example, a patient of mine who was unaware
of this principle once unwittingly discouraged his sister from writing poetry. He was away at college
when his younger sister was in high school. She sent
him a poem she had written and asked him for a
critique of it. He knew nothing of reinforcement
psychology, so he went over the poem line by line,
writing to her exactly what he liked and disliked
about each part of the poem. He said things like,
"This is a very good phrase"; "That is awkwardly
put"; "I like your wording here"; "This is a cliché—
it's terrible." The result of his earnest effort to evalu-
ate his sister's poem was that she never wrote another. Why? She was discouraged by all the negative
things he said about her first attempt at writing
poetry.

How should he have handled this, according to reinforcement techniques? He should have told her all the specific things he liked about this first poem. That would have been quite honest. There were many positive things he liked about the poem. He should have ignored what he didn't like and made no comment at all on the parts needing improvement. If he had done this, the behavior of "writing poetry" would have been reinforced by his attention and praise, and she would have continued to write more poetry.

As you read this, the thought may be occurring to you, "Hardly any of the teachers I had in school ever treated me that way. They didn't just praise the positive things. They always pointed out my mistakes and errors." Unfortunately, this is all too true for many of the teachers throughout our educational systems.

The tragic fact is that animal trainers are much better at teaching than many of the teachers in our nation's schools. This is one of the reasons why many parents have such a hard time teaching their children to pursue the goals they would like the children to follow. We ourselves have not been taught by the wise use of even the most elementary type of reinforcement techniques. We have no models to imitate when we start trying to teach our own children.

7. *Reinforce every move in the direction of the goal. Do not wait for your child to get all the way to the goal before you reinforce him.*

For example, a nine-year-old boy I was working with in therapy was a behavior problem at school because he kept hitting other kids. He had gotten *F* in citizenship.

When he first came to me he was smacking other children about ten times a month. After three months of treatment, he was in trouble only two or three times a month. Yet, when his next report card came out, he still got an *F* in citizenship. The teacher explained to the mother: "Well, I had to give him an *F*, because he's still hitting other children on the playground."

This was a most unfortunate way of looking at it.

The teacher was saying to him: "Johnny, I can only reward you with a good grade in citizenship when you reach the final goal of not hitting a single child on the playground." She was ignoring the fact that she was doing nothing to reward him for slowly moving toward that final goal.

The boy, of course, felt angry and let down. He had genuinely been trying, with my help, to stop hitting other children. "What good does it do me, Doc, to get better? I only hit three kids this month, but I still got the same lousy old *F* in citizenship!" And psychologically he was right! He was getting no reinforcement from the teacher's grades for improving and moving toward the final goal.

Whether your child is learning to read, ride a bike, play a musical instrument, have better manners, or stop hitting other children—whatever the goal— praise him every step of the way. Reinforce every bit of positive behavior with your attention.

We can always find a reason to praise our children if we try hard enough. One little boy in a nursery school was a holy terror to his teacher and the other youngsters in the class. We had a hard time figuring out something we could praise him for which would move his behavior in a more positive direction.

Finally we hit upon the solution. During rest period one day, he happened to be resting quietly (probably tired that morning from giving his parents a hard time the night before). His teacher seized upon his unexpected behavior and said, "Larry, you're the best rester in the group today." He told his mother proudly when she came to pick him up that day: "My teacher says I'm the best rester in the class!" And the next day he also rested quietly!

When our children are being good and well mannered, we often pay little attention to them. They're not bothering us, so we ignore them. We are doing nothing to reinforce their good behavior. But when the child acts up, he gets our immediate attention! In other words, we immediately reinforce undesirable behavior. The remedy for this is to take the time to reinforce the desirable behavior of our children, instead of ignoring them when they are behaving well.

This is particularly important if you have a very rambunctious, feisty, difficult-to-manage boy on your hands. During the times when he is playing quietly, you can come over to him, ruffle his hair or give him a hug, and say something like: "It's very nice sometimes, isn't it, to have a quiet play time?"

8. *In the early stages of training, it is important to reinforce every desirable response. Once learning is well under way, the reinforcement may be spaced out.*

You don't need to reinforce every single desirable response. It's hard for a busy mother to have that much time. If she spaces out her reinforcement, she will still be helping her child move in the direction of the desired behavior.

9. *Arrange for the prospective learner to be successful in the initial stages of the activity that is to be learned.*

Start him with easy tasks or tricks and work up to hard ones. I do this with my own four-year-old. For example, I was playing checkers the other night with my ten-year-old boy, when my four-year-old wanted to play also. Of course I promised I would play with him next. Have you ever tried to play checkers with a four-year-old? To play by the strict rules would be very frustrating for him, as this would demand too much from his four-year-old level of maturity. And yet he was eager to "play checkers with Daddy."

What was my solution? How did I arrange for him to be "successful" in playing checkers with me? Easy—I adapted the rules to his four-year-old level. We "played" checkers by simply moving the pieces around the board in a haphazard fashion. First he moved a piece, and then I moved a piece. I helped him to jump some of my men, and pretty soon the game was over and he had "won." He triumphantly announced to his mother: "I beat Daddy in checkers, Mommy!" I had helped him to be successful in the initial stages of learning to enjoy playing checkers.

If I could wave a magic wand tomorrow and get all parents to begin using these nine principles, they would be much less frustrated. The use of these nine reinforcement principles would go a long way toward raising happier and more self-confident children.

9

Discipline Through
Self-Regulation

We have discussed reinforcement methods of discipline or training which have been derived from experiments on various animals. Now we come to methods of training which are unique to children, which cannot be used with dogs or dolphins or parakeets. These methods center around strengthening the self-concept of the child. A dog or a dolphin does not have a self-concept. Your child does.

Your child's self-concept is the mental image he has of himself. How successful he will be in school and in later life will depend upon how strong and positive his self-concept is. Remember that our ultimate goal in disciplining a child is to help him become a self-regulating person, and that the extent to which he will become self-regulating will depend upon the strength of his self-concept.

What can you as a parent do to help strengthen his self-concept and move him toward this ultimate goal? You can make use of the following teaching methods:

☐ *Using "environmental control" makes the environment minimize the need for other methods of discipline.*

Suppose you visited a nursery school or kindergarten and found the room stripped down, with no educational or play equipment whatsoever. No blocks, no trucks, cars, wagons, crayons, paint, paper, clay—nothing for the children to play with. When you went out on the playground you observed the same thing: no climbing equipment, no slides, large hollow blocks, tricycles or wagons. If a teacher actually tried to teach youngsters in such a barren and unstimulating environment, she would have her hands full of discipline problems.

Look at your own house and backyard. Is it one which has little in the way of play equipment for a young child? Is is full of adult things which he must not touch? If so, you will probably have a number of needless discipline problems on your hands. But if you provide an interesting and stimulating environment in your home and back yard, you will be using environmental control to prevent discipline problems.

Think of long vacation trips in a car with small children. I know of parents to whom such trips are nightmares, simply because they provide nothing for young children to do during such a long trip. They don't take along games or art materials or surprises to introduce when the sibling rivalry gets sticky. They don't plan the trip so that they can stop once in a while at a park or open space where the youngsters can get out and run around for a bit. Then the parents wonder why their youngsters are fighting, whining, and making the trip miserable. An ounce of environmental control for such a long trip is worth a pound of discipline after the trouble starts.

Environmental control is something parents need more of. The more adequately we can arrange the environment of the child, the fewer discipline problems will arise.

□ *An individualized approach to each child promotes a good self-concept in that child.*

Intellectually, parents know their children are unique. Yet in practice, parents often try to use the same discipline methods on all of their children, as if one were like the other. Obviously our children are not the same. They start out with different combinations of genes. Biologically, one child is more high-strung, one is more easy-going.

Even though each child is raised in the same family, he is in effect raised in a different environment, due to his position in the family. The first child grows up in an all-adult environment until the second child is born; he is the one by whom his parents learn how to raise children. (This probably accounts for the fact that first children outnumber all other children who come to psychologists' offices and child guidance clinics throughout the country!) The second child always has one ahead of him to whom he looks up, who is usually stronger and knows more because he is older. If a third child is born, the second child now becomes the middle one. He doesn't have the advantages which go with being the oldest, nor the advantages of being the "baby." He is Unlucky Pierre, the man in the middle. The third child will then be the baby of the family, with a special set of attitudes from his parents by virtue of this position. And so it goes: no matter how many children there are in a family, each child grows up in his own unique environment.

The combination of genes plus family position means that each child in your family will be different. Therefore, you need to use different teaching methods with each. You should handle a highstrung child differently from the way you handle an easy-going one. Unfortunately, most parents do not do this. They look for universal and absolute methods of discipline which will apply to all children. Yet, strangely enough, the only universal methods which *do* apply to all children are twelve negative methods which promote a poor self-concept! These twelve negative methods promote a poor self-concept in *all* types of children, regardless of their personalities. But when we deal with the positive methods which promote a good self-concept, we need to individualize these methods. This means we need to take the time to study the individual characteristics and the "growing edge" of each of our children, whether they be introverts or extroverts, happy-go-lucky carefree children or serious, introspective youngsters.

☐ *Giving a child freedom to explore his environment and assume self-regulation as soon as he is able at each stage of development builds a positive self-concept.*

When he first grabs a spoon and indicates to you that he wants to feed himself, give him the chance. What difference does it make how much of a mess he makes at this age? He is learning self-regulation. If you continue to feed him, you are going to slow down the development of his independence and self-regulation. It's the same with all of his other activities. As soon as he can dress himself, turn on his own bath water, or brush his teeth, let him do these things by himself.

To allow a child to do these things calls for patience. There is no doubt it is much faster for us to do these things for a small child than to let him do them. But it is much more beneficial if he does them himself.

Children and adults view dressing quite differently. We think of a zipper as something to be closed when a child is getting in or out of a garment. A child views a zipper quite differently. To him it is a sort of toy.

> A zipper to my Mommy,
> Is a thing that fastens clothes.
> To me it's a tiny railroad track,
> That goes and goes and goes.

We view a bath as something to get us clean. A child thinks of a bath as a delightful opportunity to play with water. So we need to exercise patience and give a child time to do things his own way.

To allow a child to do things on his own requires a genuine desire on our part for our child to grow up. Whenever I hear a parent consistently refer to a child over the age of two as a "baby," it's clear that unconsciously the parent still doesn't want that child to grow up. Many times we still hesitate to let a child do various things on his own because, way deep down, we don't want to see him grow up. And yet what great things we can do for our children if we respect their urge for freedom and give it room to develop!

□ *Treating the feelings of your child differently from the way you treat his actions builds a positive self-concept in a child.*

(Review our discussion of this in Chapter 4.)

□ *Relying on the powerful force of unconscious imitation is a great builder of a positive self-concept in a child.*

Children are terrific imitators. And because of this, we have a powerful teaching tool at our disposal: we can furnish living models of positive personality traits and good habits. Our children will learn from us by unconscious imitation.

Understanding this concept will save us needless coercive battles with our children. If we show good table manners by our own example, our children will imitate us when they grow old enough. Not at two years or at four years, but later. If we are persistent in what we attempt and do not give up at the first signs of difficulty, our children will imitate our persistence. If we want our children to respect the rights and feelings of others, we must begin by respecting the rights and feelings of our children. A good example is the most powerful way we can teach them. When we nag a child to respect the feelings of others, thus showing that we do not respect his feelings, our actions are teaching him far more powerfully than the words we speak.

A sixteen-year-old patient had seen his father fly off into rages, hurl bottles around the house, strike his mother, and knock her across the room. Finally the mother divorced the father. What brought the boy into therapy was the fact that he was repeating this same type of behavior with his mother. When he got angry with her, he would throw books at her, or hurl a Coke bottle through the window in his frustration. Child see, child do!

Not only does the child unconsciously imitate the behavior of a parent, but he will absorb the general atmosphere of his home: friendly and cooperative, hostile and antagonistic, or concerned with social status. The atmosphere of the home is the stage setting for whatever else we try to teach by way of discipline. So it behooves parents to look to that general atmosphere, as well as to the specific models we are furnishing our children, if we want them to grow up in desirable ways. Every day we are teaching them through the silent language of our own behavior. We are giving them models which they are unconsciously imitating.

☐ *Emotional support from his parents helps a child to overcome feelings of inadequacy and to build a strong self-concept.*

All children have feelings of inadequacy because of their size and their lack of experience in dealing with the world. Many adults overlook these two factors and the feelings which children have as a result of them.

Children are small and helpless and vastly inferior to their parents and other adults in strength and power to cope with the world about them. If you don't believe it, try this experiment. Walk around on your knees for a while. See how you feel looking up at those giants of the adult world. The feelings of helplessness you would have if you tried this little experiment is what all children experience. This is why *all* children need emotional support and encouragement from their parents, in order to allay these feelings of inadequacy.

As I indicated previously, the most important way we can give emotional support to a child is to use the feedback technique and show him we truly understand his feelings. This is the single most reassuring thing we can do for a child. Amazingly enough, the very fact that an adult shows him he truly understands how insecure he feels causes the child to feel more secure.

Unfortunately, many adults think of childhood as a carefree, happy-go-lucky time. So we tend to play down the importance of children's feelings of insecurity and fear. We tend to think the things that upset our children are "little problems" compared to the "real problems" we have in coping with adult life. One six-year-old patient of mine summed this up very well. Speaking about something that had upset him greatly, but which his father had told him was "nothing to cry about," he said: "To him it was a little thing—but to me it was a big thing!"

When a child is confronted with some new task which makes him feel inadequate, we can first convey to him a genuine understanding of his feelings of inadequacy. Then we can give him emotional support by showing him that we believe he can do it, and that we are his ally. This can be done in many ways. Mostly it is accomplished by conveying to the child the feeling that he is not alone. Whenever he has need of us, he can turn to us for help. This quality of "being there" is not something about which a parent can fool a child. The parent may be physically present in a house with the child, but the child senses that the parent is not truly "there," in the sense of being available when he needs support and understanding.

Parents can give emotional support to their children by physical demonstrations of affection. Children never outgrow this need for physical demonstrations of love. A hug, a kiss, an arm around the shoulder, being tucked in bed at night are all important nonverbal ways in which a parent says to a child: "I'm here, and I'm on your side whenever you need me."

Another way often overlooked by parents which conveys our emotional support to a child is to say those three magic words: I love you. Sometimes a parent will feel, "I show him I love him through my actions; why do I need to put it into words?" If you feel this way, then let me ask you this question: Though you know through his actions that your husband loves you, would you be content to go through the rest of your married life without ever hearing him say those three magic words to you? Of course not. Well your child feels the same way. He needs to hear those three words from you.

One word of caution. You should *never* try to show physical affection to your child or say "I love you" when you are not genuinely feeling that way inside.

Don't try to be demonstrative or affectionate just because you think it would be good for your child. If you do, your child will sense the phoniness of it. He will know your words or gestures of affection are not matched by your real feelings underneath. This will confuse and upset him, because he will sense he is receiving a double message from you. With your words or gestures you are saying "I love you," but with your inner feelings you are saying "I don't love you." So if you don't feel especially affectionate to your child at a particular time, it is far better to say or do nothing than to be phony about it.

☐ *Letting your child learn by natural consequences helps to build a strong self-concept.*

This is one of the most powerful tools we parents have to enable our children to learn things. Unfortunately, it is a tool few parents use. Let's see how natural consequences works.

A child doesn't eat the food on his plate at breakfast. He dawdles and fools around and does everything but eat. Mother does not get angry and threaten the child with punishment. Instead, she merely removes the food from the table at the end of the meal and lets the natural consequences take over. Before too long the child will probably want a snack. Mother can then say, "I'm sorry you're hungry. We will have lunch at twelve o'clock. It's too bad you have to wait so long." The hunger the child experiences is a natural consequence of not eating his breakfast. It promotes a far faster change in his actions than any amount of scolding or punishment by his mother would do.

One of the problems many parents have mentioned to me over the years has been the problem of children procrastinating in getting ready to go to school. Mothers have told me the hassle this is for them, morning after morning. They feel emotionally drained each day when they finally succeed in getting the child off to school. At each step of the way, the child is resisting, and they are nagging.

I point out to these mothers that they really need to do only three things. Have the child decide what he is going to wear the night before and lay out his clothes ahead of time. Wake him up when it's time to get up. And have his breakfast ready at a reasonable time. Everything else is up to the child. He can get washed and dressed. He can eat his breakfast. He can get his things together and get off to school.

Almost invariably, when I present such a plan to a mother, she will say, in a defeated tone of voice, "I know what will happen if I try it."

"All right—what will happen?"

"He will fool around and fool around, and miss the school bus."

"So?"

"Well, if he misses the bus, I'll have to drive him to school."

"Why would you do that?"

"If I didn't drive him, he'd be late for school."

"So what? What if he had to walk to school?"

"That's a terribly long walk, and he'd be tired."

"So what?"

"That would be embarrassing for him to get to school so late."

"So what?"

I keep asking her questions, such as So what? and What would happen then? I want her to see that if she would refrain from protecting her child from the natural consequences of his actions, the natural consequences themselves would be very powerful teachers.

If the natural consequences are pleasant, the child will usually continue to act that way. If the natural consequences are unpleasant, the child will be motivated to change his actions—unless we parents step in and protect him from the natural consequences of his actions. Unfortunately this is usually the case. When parents step in and prevent the child from experiencing the unpleasant natural consequences of his actions, the child loses the educational value of those unpleasant natural consequences. He depends upon his parents to intervene and protect him from the unpleasant natural consequences of any of his actions. This is bad for his self-concept. It prevents him from learning to stand on his own two feet.

Of course, you need to use common sense in utilizing this concept of natural consequences. If you let a toddler experience the natural consequences of running out into a busy street, you might end up with a dead child. So you step in and prevent him from running into the street. In other words, where the natural consequences of a child's actions might result in serious or fatal injury to your child, you intervene and prevent these natural consequences from taking place. But where natural consequences will result merely in unpleasantness for the child, you step aside and let these natural consequences take place.

It would be nice if we could rely entirely on the natural consequences of inadequate behavior to discipline a child. Unfortunately, natural consequences are not always sufficient. Sometimes we must find artificial or arbitrary consequences to apply to the behavior of a child.

There are three main methods we can use:

1. *We can deprive the child of something important to him.*

Suppose your five-year-old scribbles on your living room walls with crayons. Such behavior is "normal" for a two-year-old. But it is an act of hostility for a five-year-old. Unfortunately for your discipline, there are no unpleasant natural consequences for the child as a result of scribbling on the walls of your house. You have to create some artificial and arbitrary consequences which will set firm limits to the child, and, in effect, say to him: "No more of this!"

If you feel sufficiently angered when you discover it, you may immediately spank him. That is one type of artificial but unpleasant consequence for him. Or you might deprive him of some privilege, perhaps saying, "Danny, you're old enough to know not to draw on walls with crayons, so I guess you won't be allowed to use your crayons for three days. That will help to remind you that crayons are to be used on paper, not on walls."

2. *We can use social isolation by sending the child out of his social group or to his room.*

Suppose your four-year-old is disrupting the play of a group of children in your back yard. You might say to him, "Charles, I see you are not able to play well with the other children right now. You keep hitting them and causing trouble. You'll have to go to your room and play by yourself until you tell me that you're able to control your actions."

Whenever you use social isolation as a means of discipline, it is important you make it an open-ended rather than a closed-ended affair. Don't just send the child to his room, as if he had to stay there forever. The purpose of sending him to his room is not to incarcerate him indefinitely, but to enable a change in his behavior to take place. Always let him know that when his behavior is able to change and he is able to play reasonably with the other children, he can come back and play.

3. *We can spank a child.*

I want to make it clear that there is a "right" kind of spanking and a "wrong" kind. By the wrong kind I mean a cruel and sadistic beating. This fills a child with hatred, and a deep desire for revenge. This is the kind that is administered with a strap or stick or some other type of parental "weapon." Or it could also mean a humiliating slap in the face.

The right kind of spanking needs no special paraphernalia. Just the hand of the parent administered a few times on the kid's bottom. The right kind of spanking is a *positive* thing. It clears the air, and is vastly to be preferred to moralistic and guilt-inducing parental lectures.

Some of you may have heard the old saying "Never strike a child in anger." I think that that is psychologically very poor advice, and I suggest the opposite: "Never strike a child *except* in anger."

A child can understand very well when you strike him in anger. He knows you are mad at him and he understands why. What a child cannot understand is when he disobeys mother at 10 A.M. and she tells him, "All right, young man—your father will deal with you when he gets home!" Then when Dad arrives home he is expected to administer a spanking which will "really teach the boy a lesson." That's the kind of cold-blooded spanking a child cannot either understand or forgive.

What I advocate is the "pow-wow" type of spanking: your "pow" followed by his "Wow!" Spank your child only when you are furious at him and feel like letting him have it right then. Too many mothers nowadays seem to be afraid to spank their children. They talk and nag a great deal as a substitute; they try to negotiate with a child. This is a huge mistake because it reduces their authority as parents.

What you should do is to tell your child once or perhaps twice what you want him to do or to stop doing. Then, if he refuses to obey your reasonable request, and you have become frustrated and angry, let him have it right then and there!

After spanking, your first immediate reaction may be frustration and guilt. It may bother you that you've blown your cool.

Courage, Mother, all is not lost!

You can always say to your child, in your own way: "Look, Mommy goofed. I lost my temper, and I'm sorry I did." Then you can go on from there. You don't have to be "stuck" with the guilt and the frustration and the unhappy feelings.

Wait until you really feel better about the situation and about your child. It might be five minutes or five hours later. But if you feel you have blown your stack, *it's important to admit it to your child.* Above all, don't pretend to him that the sole reason you spanked him was for his benefit. That's as phony as a three-dollar bill, and he will know it.

The main purpose of spanking, although most parents don't like to admit it, is to relieve the parent's feelings of frustration. All of us need to do this from time to time when our kids get on our nerves.

If we were 100 percent perfect parents, we would all be so mature we would never need to spank our kids except in unusual or extreme situations (such as when a child runs out into the street). The point is, we are not such 100 percent perfect parents. We are not able to administer discipline calmly and serenely all the time. It would be nice if we could. But life doesn't seem to work out that way. We get fed up when our kids misbehave and we lose our cool and swat them. But that's nothing to feel guilty about. We feel better and they feel better, the air is cleared.

Both parent and child get a chance to begin again. Having gotten angry feelings out of your system, you can once more feel positive toward your child. You can then assume your rightful role of parental authority.

Some of you may feel uncomfortable with the notion I have just advanced that the main purpose of spanking is to relieve the frustrated feelings of the parent. You may still be under the illusion that the purpose of spanking is solely to influence your child in a better direction. In this case, I refer you to one of my favorite cartoons, which shows a father whaling the tar out of his little boy, saying as he whales him, "That'll teach you to hit people!" (He's right—it will!)

Nevertheless, we parents are human, and so I say "spank away" if you need to. But, hopefully, if you follow the constructive suggestions I have made on child discipline, you will find you need to spank far less frequently than you otherwise would. And as your child grows older and becomes increasingly capable of self-regulation, you should have to spank far less often.

If you are quite honest with yourself, you will find that there are times when you will lose your temper, fly off the handle at your child, and yell at him or spank him—only to realize afterwards that what he did actually should not have elicited such a violent outburst from you. You were really mad at your husband or your neighbor. Or just cranky for some unknown reason. And you took it out on your child.

What can you do in such a situation? Well, you could pretend you are a holy paragon of virtue and that your child fully deserved the scolding or spanking he got. Or you can have the courage to say something like this to your child: "Danny, mother got mad at you and scolded you. But I can see now that you didn't do anything that was really that bad. I think I was really mad at something else and I was sort of taking it out on you. So I'm sorry."

Your child will feel a wonderful warm feeling toward

you for admitting you are human and fallible. This will do wonders for his self-concept—and yours!

Let's stop a moment and see where we are. I have said that the natural consequences of a child's misbehavior may have to be supplemented by artificial consequences. But even though these consequences of a child's misbehavior are artificial rather than natural, there are still some basic principles governing their use.

1. *The artificial consequences should be reasonably consistent.*

The same consequences should follow the same behavior. If your child is deprived of his crayons one day for scribbling on the wall, but is laughed at indulgently the next day for doing the exact same thing, it will be very difficult for him to learn to stop scribbling on walls.

2. *The artificial consequences should be immediate.*

The more closely related in time a consequence is, the more it will help a child to learn new behavior. When the unpleasant results follow after a considerable delay in time, it is difficult for a child to see the connection. For instance, if your child has misbehaved in the middle of the morning, let the unpleasant consequences begin right then. Don't put off the punishment until Dad gets home that night. Say: "All right, Jimmy—I'm afraid you're not going to be allowed to watch TV the rest of the day, beginning right now."

3. *If you deprive a child of something important to him, the amount of time the deprivation lasts should be reasonable.*

To deprive a five-year-old of watching TV for a month is unreasonable. The punishment then becomes meaningless to him. He has no incentive to improve his behavior so that he may be allowed to watch TV again. To deprive him of watching TV for a few days is a meaningful punishment, and does give him the incentive to improve his behavior.

4. *Never deprive a child of something really crucial to him as a punishment.*

I have known parents who deprived a child of a birthday party as a punishment. Or of a special trip to an amusement park which he had been looking forward to for a long, long time. Such deprivations accomplish little in the way of true behavior change. The child reacts to them only with deep hostility and a desire for revenge. As a child sees it, to deprive him of something like a birthday party constitutes "cruel and unusual punishment." And he is right.

5. *The unpleasant artificial consequences should be as relevant as possible to the misbehavior.*

If a child has scribbled on the wall with crayons, it is *relevant* for him to be deprived of the use of his crayons for several days. And he will recognize the relevance and the justice of such a punishment.

It would be nice if we could rely on all of the positive reinforcement techniques I mentioned in the last chapter and all of the natural consequences of misbehavior that I mentioned earlier in this chapter as our sole discipline methods. Unfortunately, it doesn't usually work out that way. From time to time most of us need to use some of these artificial consequences which we call "punishment" when a child misbehaves.

6. *Give your child a positive model for what he should do.*

If you followed mothers and their children around all day long, you would discover that many of them spend a fair amount of time actually telling their children what *not* to do! If this last statement sounds strange, consider the following example. I know a puppet master named Preston Hibbard who gives Punch and Judy shows for children. He understands the psychology of children very well. That's why children are so delighted with his shows. At one point in the show, Punch is riding on a horse, and the puppet master tells the children, "Now don't say 'giddyap,' because every time the horse hears the word *giddyap*, he will buck and throw Punch off. Remember—don't say 'giddyap' to the horse!" Hardly has he finished admonishing the children what *not* to say, than the children are joyously shouting "giddyap"! Many mothers do not seem to understand the effects of telling a child *not* to say "giddyap." They are surprised and unhappy when their child starts shouting the psychological equivalent of "giddyap" to them.

We need to phrase our instructions to a child so that we tell him *what to do,* and refrain from telling him what *not* to do. Instead of saying, "Stop throwing sand," you can say, "Sand is for playing in, not throwing." Instead of saying, "Don't hit Larry with the block!" you can say, "Blocks are for building, not for hitting."

7. *Handle danger situations wisely.*

By danger situations for a preschool child I mean such things as crossing a street, fires, boiling water, sharp knives, and poisons. The wise use of environmental control will keep some of these dangers inaccessible to your child. If your child has a fence around his back yard, you do not need to worry about him getting out in the street. If all potential poisons are where he cannot get at them, you do not need to be concerned about him poisoning himself.

But environmental control will not do the complete job. The key to helping your child learn to cope with danger situations is to teach him a healthy respect for the danger, without developing excessive fears in him. Allow him to experience the minor unpleasant consequences of his actions in stiuations which are not dangerous. He will then be more likely to be cautious and to listen to you as a reliable guide to danger than if you have overprotected him and prevented him from experiencing the natural consequences of his actions.

With regard to fires, for example, I think it is wise

to teach a child to light matches and to respect the nature of fire as soon as he can manage it. Let him learn to use matches to start a fire in the fireplace or on the stove. This is much better than keeping a child away from matches altogether. Then matches and fire may become a "taboo" area for him. He may want to play with matches and fire just because they have been forbidden.

The use of these seven positive methods will do wonders to strengthen your child's self-concept and help him to become a self-regulating person. But I feel it is important also for parents to know what teaching methods they should avoid: the teaching methods that weaken a child's self-concept and keep him from becoming a self-regulating person.

Before I describe to you the teaching methods you should avoid using with your child, I want to make it clear that all of the parents I know, myself included, have used some or all of these undesirable methods at one time or another. And we will probably use them again before our children are raised and off on their own. (Like tomorrow, maybe?) Sometimes we will use them out of ignorance, not knowing that this is a bad teaching method to use with a child. Sometimes we will know better, but use the method anyway because of the state of our own frustrated feelings. However, I want to list these undesirable methods so that at least no parent reading this book would use one of these methods out of sheer ignorance. Here, then, are twelve *Thou Shalt Not's* for parents:

Thou Shalt Not belittle your child.

We may say ,"Now that was a bright thing to do, wasn't it?" or "How could you be so dumb?" or "Haven't you got any sense?" Each time we unleash one of the belittling statements we are chipping away at our child's self-concept.

Thou Shalt Not use threats.

Threats weaken a child's self-concept. We say, "If you do that one more time, you're going to get it!" or "If you hit your brother again, Mother is going to spank you so hard you'll remember it for a long, long time!" Each time we threaten a child, we teach him to feel uneasy about himself. And we teach him to fear and hate us.

The psychological effect of *threats* on a child is bad. But this does not mean that *firm limits* are bad. Mothers sometimes misinterpret this concept and think it means you should never say "no" to a child. Far from it. When a child gets out of line, and you have to enforce a limit, even if you have to enforce it with a spanking, do it. But don't tell your child ahead of time what you are going to do if he is bad. Threats deal with the future, but children live in the present. Therefore, threats are useless in improving the future behavior of a child.

Thou Shalt Not bribe a child.

The most enormous bribe I personally know of was offered to a teen-age patient by his father, who promised him a Porsche when he graduated from high school if he maintained a *B* average. What is the effect of such a bribe? It removes the incentive from internal to external. Instead of a child wanting to learn for self-satisfaction and positive self-concept that he acquires from what he learns, the child is now learning only for the sake of external reward.

If you visit a market where mothers have taken young children shopping, you will hear a variety of bribes offered and accepted almost every day. The child is upsetting mother by taking down packages and cans and getting into things on the shelves. Finally, in desperation she promises him: "If you'll be good and not touch anything, I'll buy you a toy." If the mother wants to teach him to manipulate people, starting with her, that bribe is a fine method. However, it's not very helpful for building a good self-concept in the child, for teaching him to be a self-regulating person, who is respectful of the rights of others.

Thou Shalt Not extract promises of better conduct from a child.

The sequence of events runs something like this. Little Willie has done something he shouldn't. Mother blows her stack. "Now Willie, promise me you will never, never do that again!" Willie is no fool. He promises. A half hour later he has done it again. Mother is hurt and furiously accusatory: "Willie—you promised!" She doesn't know that promises are meaningless to children. A promise, like its older brother, a threat, deals with the future. But small children live only in the present. If a child is a sensitive youngster, extracting a promise from him will merely teach him to feel guilty if he breaks it. Or, if he is not so sensitive, it will merely teach him to be cynical, and substitute verbal behavior for true behavior change.

Thou Shalt Not use overprotective supervision with a child.

This undermines his self-concept. When a mother excessively supervises a child's behavior she is teaching him: You can't do much for yourself. I'll have to stand over you and see that it gets done. Most parents seem to have far too little confidence in a child's ability to do things for himself. We should try to adopt as our motto: Never do anything for a child that he can do for himself.

Thou Shalt Not talk excessively to a child.

Excessive talking conveys this message to a child: "You aren't very capable of understanding things, so you had better listen to what I have to say!" Two comments from the small fry set illustrate their reaction to the excessive talking of adults. One preschooler asked his father, "Daddy, why do you always give me such a long answer when I ask you a short question?" Another preschool youngster was overheard threatening a playmate at nursery school in this fashion: "I'll hit you! I'll cut you up in little pieces! I'll—I'll—I'll *explain* it to you!"[22]

Thou Shalt Not insist on blind and instant obedience with a child.

Suppose your husband said to you, "Dear, drop what you're doing and get me a cup of coffee, right now, immediately!" I'm sure you would feel like letting him have a cup of coffee—in the chops, maybe? Well, your youngster feels the same way when you insist he drop what he is doing *immediately* and do what you tell him.

The least we can do is give our young children some advance warning of what we are going to ask of them. "Jimmy, in about ten minutes you're going to have to come in for lunch." And we can also allow them the freedom to grumble a bit before obeying us. "Aw gee, Mom—do I have to stop playing right now?" Blind and instant obedience may fit in well with the self-concept of a puppet or a member of a totalitarian state, but it has no place in our repertoire of teaching methods if we want to raise independent and self-regulating persons.

Thou Shalt Not pamper and overindulge a child.

Pampering and overindulging is what many parents actually mean when they speak of "spoiling" a child. At its root, overindulging a child means that the parents are afraid to say no to him, to be firm in their limits. This gives the child the feeling that all rules are made of rubber and that if you push hard enough they will stretch. That may work in the bosom of the family, but the child is in for a sad awakening in the outside world. Overindulging a child means that we are really depriving him of the opportunity to grow in his ability to become resourceful, independent, and self-regulating.

Thou Shalt Not use inconsistent rules and limits with a child.

On Monday mother is feeling very relaxed about things and lets her child break all the rules. On Tuesday, when the child does the exact same thing he was doing Monday, she lands on him like a ton of bricks. The effect of these inconsistent signals on the child is roughly akin to how successfully you would learn to drive if on Monday, Wednesday, and Friday red meant "stop" and green meant "go." But on Tuesday, Thursday, Saturday, and Sunday, red meant "go" and green meant "stop." A child needs to have some uniformity and reliability in knowing what is expected of him, and these inconsistent signals do not provide that.

Thou Shalt Not use rules which are inappropriate to the age of the child.

If you expect your two-year-old to obey like a five-year-old, he can only feel inadequate and full of hatred for you. You are expecting a maturity of behavior of which he is not capable at his age, and this has a very bad effect on his self-concept.

Thou Shalt Not use moralizing and guilt-inducing methods of discipline.

Such methods promote a poor self-concept. A guilt-inducing method of discipline is one which conveys by words or actions this sort of message to your child: That wasn't nice what you did. You're not a very nice boy for doing it. How could you have done such a thing after all that Mommy does for you?

The next time you feel the temptation to launch into a little moralistic lecture to your preschooler, why not instead speak a few sentences of Spanish or German or French or even doubletalk? It will do him fully as much good as the little moral lecture in English! But it will avoid filling him full of guilt, as the little moral lecture will.

Every day hundreds of thousands of words of disapproval are loosed against hapless children by their parents. If hidden tape recorders took down verbatim this verbal barrage of disapproval, and the tapes were played back, the mothers would be shocked to hear what they actually say to their children every day. The tapes would record the little moral lectures, the bawlings out, the scoldings, the ridiculing, and the name-calling.

An interesting thing happens to a child who is exposed to this verbal barrage: his ears drop off! He develops the only defense he can muster against this flow of words. He learns to tune out. Of course he is not able to tune out altogether. He registers all too well the negative implications of this verbal barrage on his self-concept.

Verbal disapproval does little to change a child's behavior. All it does is to undermine his self-concept.

Thou Shalt Not give any command to a child that you do not intend to enforce.

Here is a typical sequence of events. Mother says to her preschooler, "Don't climb on the chair." The child continues to climb on the chair. "Richard, I told you, don't climb on the chair!" The child, ignoring his mother, continues to climb. "Richard—did you hear me? I said stop climbing on that chair this instant!" The child continues to pay no attention to what mother is saying. Mother makes no attempt to stop Richard from climbing; all that she does is teach him to ignore her requests and commands. To avoid this kind of negative teaching, never make a request or give a command to a child that you are not able to enforce.

We have covered a good bit of ground in discussing the subject of discipline. And I want to review for you what I have been trying to say in these two chapters.

You want your child to become an adult who will be able to manage completely by himself; who will be in short, a self-regulating person. But in the years from toddlerhood through adolescence, your child needs parental discipline in order to guide him in the direction of self-regulation.

I have defined discipline as essentially a *teaching process* on the part of the parent, and a *learning process* on the part of the child. Since discipline is a teaching/learning process, it is subject to basic psychological principles which we have discovered govern the learning of both animals and human beings.

There are psychological principles of teaching and learning which apply equally well to both animals and people. It is wise for us as parents to learn what these are and to use them intelligently. If we don't, we will end up being more frustrated in trying to teach our children than animal trainers will be in trying to teach tricks to a dolphin.

But there are other psychological principles of learning which apply specifically to human beings, and it behooves us parents to be familiar with these also. Otherwise we will find ourselves using methods which are doomed to failure and which produce only frustration in both our children and us.

If we use teaching methods which have been demonstrated through scientific research to work effectively, then we can teach our children *from toddlerhood through adolescence* to regulate themselves without the need of any external regulation from us.

What will be the result if we learn to use the successful teaching methods and avoid the unsuccessful ones? Will we then raise a "model child"? I hope not. As a psychologist I am not too impressed with "model children." A "model child" is neither a happy child nor a self-regulating child. He is a child with a facade. He has been intimidated into a certain outward conformity, but there is considerable emotional disturbance hidden inside him. If we end up with a preschool child who is quiet and respectful of adults at all times; who never rebels or gets out of hand; who is pleased to do whatever adults want him to do without complaint; who has no negative feelings about anything or anyone; who has no interest whatever in sex; who never lies; who never hits his brother or sister or friends; who is moral, unselfish, and of high ethical principle; who is conscientious, clean, and respects private property—then we are not really dealing with a child at all. We are dealing with a person who has been intimidated into being a miniature little adult masquerading as a child.

While we are disciplining our children and guiding them toward our ultimate goal of self-regulation, let us not forget they are still children. One of my favorite cartoons shows a mother walking along the street, dragging a little child by the hand and saying to him, "Stop it, Jimmy—you're acting just like a child!" Yes he is, and let's give him the right to act that way!

Our methods of discipline should enable the dynamic quality of childhood to be channeled into socially approved ways of expression. But our methods should never eliminate that vital and dynamic quality which makes children act like children!

10

Your Child and Violence

After the tragic events of recent years, parents are concerned about violence and their children. We have seen assassinations, rioting, and mob action in cities throughout the United States. Witnessing these events on TV has emphasized vividly the existence of violent impulses among people in our country. None of us wants our children to grow up to become violent persons. How do we prevent this?

Too many people these days speak of "violence" in a vague and general way. A recent book on violence, for example, spends 356 pages on the subject without once defining exactly what the author means by violence! To me, violence is really the emotion of anger or hostility, in an intense and destructive form. I would define it more precisely as "anger, expressed in an intense form, with the intent to physically hurt or destroy a person."

We must make a distinction between violent *actions* and violent *feelings*, for the two are not the same. You will notice that the definition of violence clearly refers to violent or hostile *actions*. We want our children to be able

239

to control violent actions, during childhood and later when they grow up.

Two children are playing together at nursery school. One child wants to play with a truck. The other child refuses to give it to him. The first child picks up a wooden block and angrily hits the other over the head. This is a violent *action*. We do not want our children to act this way.

Last week in the Los Angeles area where I live, a judge and his wife were having a bitter quarrel in the middle of the night. At the climax of the quarrel, the judge stabbed his wife several times with a knife. Ordinarily, a judge is not the type of person one associates with violence, but that was certainly a violent *action*. We do not want our children to be unable to control their impulses in this fashion when they grow up to be adults.

Most of us, when we think of violence, think of someone stabbing or shooting another person. But there is another type of violence we often overlook. Last year in a small suburban town near where I live, the mayor took his own life. This is fully as much an act of violence as the judge who stabbed his wife. An act of violence against the self is still a violent *action*.

Violent *feelings*, on the other hand, are different. We cannot control our feelings. I have tried to emphasize throughout this book that feelings come into our minds unbidden: feelings of joy and happiness, feelings of depression and sadness, feelings of love, feelings of anger and hostility. In this respect violent feelings are no different from any other types of feelings. They are not subject to conscious control.

If we are truly honest with ourselves, we will admit that from time to time we do *feel* violent. From time to time, husbands and wives feel violently angry at each other. When a child does something that infuriates us, we feel violent. Show me a mother who says she has never had a violent feeling toward her child and I'll show you a mother who is kidding herself. I have certainly had violent feelings toward my children from time to time. It is *normal* to have such feelings. (Of course, if you find that you feel violently toward your children *most of the time*, you probably need professional help in order to be able to deal with your feelings and your relationship to your child.)

Our children feel violent also. And it is *normal* for them to do so. When a child is having a temper tantrum, yelling and screaming out his anger, there is no doubt he is feeling violent at that moment.

It is most important that we make this distinction between violent *actions* and violent *feelings*. Once we do, we can see clearly that we cannot prevent either ourselves or our children from having violent feelings. These are normal. Violent feelings are merely anger which is felt deeply and intensely. While we cannot control our feelings or those of our children, we can learn to control our actions, and to refrain from engaging in violent actions.

One of the things we are proud of in the United States is that every four years we elect a president peacefully and without violence. Ballots, not bullets, decide the issue. We would not want to be like countries which change their leaders from time to time by violence and bloodshed.

It is the same with respect to relationships among individuals and groups in our country. Violence is a very poor method of resolving conflicts between people, whether those people are husband and wife, college students and administration, or whites and blacks. The violence which has erupted in recent years in the United States has had a sobering effect upon us all. We do not want this violence to continue. We want people to resolve their differences and conflicts without resorting to violence and the law of the jungle. And so we must do all we can to help our children and ourselves to control violent actions.

We do not merely want to overcome the *negative* aspect of violent actions in our children. We also want to teach them the *positive* values of love, cooperativeness, sincere interest in the welfare of other people, and compassion for suffering. We want them to learn to use reason and negotiation as methods of resolving conflicts between people.

How do we do this? How do we prevent our children from resorting to violent actions to resolve their conflicts with other people? There is no research evidence suggesting that human beings are innately violent. People *learn* violence. Of course, the people who teach them to be violent are by no means aware they are teaching them. *The sad fact is that violent children and violent adults are mainly taught to be that way by their parents.* Of course no parent deliberately and consciously sets out to teach her child to be violent. Nevertheless, it happens.

There are several ways by which a parent teaches a child to become violent. One way is to be violent himself. The child will then learn to be violent by identifying with his parent and imitating him. Child see, child do! The clearest example of this I have personally seen was the case I mentioned in Chapter 9 of the teen-ager who threw pop bottles at his mother. Having seen his father do the same thing, he was merely duplicating his father's behavior. A violent chip off the old violent block. (In most such cases of parental imitation of violence, it is the father rather than the mother who is the violent person.)

I'm concerned that some mother reading this may have lost her temper recently and may be thinking at this point: "Oh, my goodness—maybe I'm a violent person! And maybe I'm having a terrible effect on my child because of this." If such thoughts are occurring to you, relax. Losing your temper or throwing something once in a while does not make you a violent person.

I think of an incident involving a friend of mine. It was one of those days when everything went wrong. The hot water heater went out. The kids gave her a bad time. You name it, and that day it went wrong.

She and her husband were having company that night, and she was making a salmon loaf for dinner. Just about the time her husband got home from work, the salmon loaf burned. That was the last straw. She took the pan out of the oven and threw it against the wall, where it splattered all over. Her husband walked in as she was cleaning up the mess. His response, when she told him what happened, was to say, "Now, dear, was that the reaction of a rational human being to a frustrating situation?" I asked her how she felt when he said that. "If I had had some salmon loaf left I would cheerfully have thrown it at him!" she said.

Now I know that woman quite well. She is not a violent person. But that day she had really had it. She lost her temper. So what? It was unpleasant and inconvenient to clean up the kitchen and to scrape the salmon loaf off the wall. But no one was hurt and no great harm was done. So let's not confuse occasionally losing your temper with being a truly violent person.

Another way a parent teaches his child to become violent is to condone his child's violence by not setting firm enough limits against hostile actions.

When the child hits other children, for example, the parent may not set firm enough limits for him. Often what happens is that the mother will say to the child, "Now don't do that, Timmy!" but not follow through by actually stopping the child. The child knows that mother does not intend to follow through, and so he keeps on hitting. Finally, mother does follow through, and he stops hitting. But meanwhile his mother has, in effect, reinforced him for hitting.

I have even known of cases where parents have allowed their child to strike them. If they forbade the child something, he would get angry and strike or kick them. When he hit her, his mother might say, "Now that's not nice to do that, Billy," but she would not physically prevent the child from hitting her. In cases such as this the parents often use supposed "child psychology" to rationalize their fear of saying no to their child and setting firm limits for him. Often they will say they don't want to inhibit their child.

Well, children need to be inhibited in some actions! They need to be inhibited about hitting other children or hitting or kicking their parents. They need to be inhibited about being cruel to animals or destroying property. They need to be inhibited about stealing money from mother's purse or stealing things from stores. Parents make a sad mistake if they do not teach children to be inhibited about such actions. What we do want our children to be uninhibited about is their *feelings*. That's good common sense as well as good psychology.

If a parent does not set firm limits on physical expressions of hostility and violence, the child cannot internalize these limits and develop a control system for his violent impulses. Make no mistake about it. A child *wants* to be able to internalize firm limits against physical violence. It scares him that his own violent impulses may get out of hand and run away with him. When the teen-ager who threw pop bottles at his mother came to me for therapy, he very desperately wanted me to help him control such hostile impulses. They scared him. He said: "It kind of spooks me when I get mad and throw things at my mother. What if I got so angry I hit her with something and actually killed her? It scares me to think about that." In other words, he could not control his violent impulses, and he was begging someone outside himself for help. Since his mother, by her passivity, was not able to help him control his hostile actions, he was begging me to help him. If ever a kid needed firm limits it was that boy!

When I say *firm limits*, this does not necessarily mean that a parent needs to spank a child. Spanking a hostile child often looks suspiciously like meeting violence with violence. (Remember the cartoon of the father swatting his child and yelling, "That'll teach you to hit people!") Spanking a hostile child for hitting or being physically destructive is certainly better than hiding your parental head in the sand, ostrich-fashion, and completely ignoring such antisocial behavior. But there are better ways to handle the situation than spanking.

Suppose your preschool child is hitting or being physically destructive. If you are in control of your own actions and can "keep your cool," then grab your child's arms, hold him firmly, and immobilize him. While you are doing this, look him firmly in the eye, and say sternly to him something like this: "You must not do that! I cannot let you hit your brother (or friend). You can tell him you are mad at him, but you *must not hit!*"

Children vary greatly as to how easy or how difficult it is to teach them to set firm limits on their violent actions. Generally speaking, girls are not as prone to violent actions as boys. But some boys are much easier to teach than others. Some strong-willed and determined boys may take months or even years to learn to internalize limits on their violent and hostile impulses.

Sometimes parents unconsciously approve of their child's hostile and antisocial actions. A youngster will defy his parents, hit other children, take things, and then run away from his parents if they try to discipline him. Secretly the parents are amused, and unconsciously they egg him on. "He's a real holy terror, isn't he?" a father or mother may say admiringly. "Of course, he gets out of hand sometimes, but you've got to admit, he's got lots of spunk!"

This type of parental behavior usually means that unconsciously the parent wanted to be rebellious and antisocial when he was a child, but felt he was too goody-good. Now he is unconsciously encouraging his child to act out the rebellious and antisocial actions he was too afraid to try when he was little. Unconscious parental encouragement reinforces a child for being hostile and violent in his actions. The lesson is clear. If you don't want your child to grow up hostile and violent in his actions, set firm limits to his hostile impulses and help him internalize these limits.

Strangely enough, a third way in which a child may be taught to become a hostile adult is caused by a vastly different type of child raising than these first two types. In this third type of child rearing, the parents are very firm in their limits on hostile and violent actions. This is good. But, unfortunately, the parents also attempt to prevent any expression of hostile and violent *feelings*. This is a mistake. Children cannot help having hostile and violent feelings from time to time. But the parent allows the child no outlets at all for such feelings. The parent assumes that by being strict about not allowing the child to express hostile feelings, she will be teaching the child not to have such feelings. This is impossible. The child will have the feelings anyway. All that the parent is doing is teaching the child to repress these feelings and push them down into his unconscious mind.

What happens in such cases is that the parent teaches the youngster to become a "model child." The child is outwardly sweet, kind and polite. But inwardly he is seething with hostile and violent feelings for which he has been allowed no outlet. He is like a boiler with no safety valve. The feelings build up and up, until finally he explodes into violent action.

A few years ago a high school student who was planning on becoming a minister shot and killed his mother and father. The neighbors were shocked and dumbfounded. He had a reputation in the community of being an "ideal" teen-ager who was quiet and obedient and respectful of his elders. This was the outward "front" that the neighbors and church people saw. What they couldn't see were the angry and hostile feelings boiling beneath the surface.

Allow your child a safe outlet for his angry and violent feelings. Let him express these feelings and put them into words. Or give him some socially acceptable substitute: "I know you're mad at your brother and feel like smacking him. I can't let you do that, but you can hit your punching bag or your buffet instead."

From this short trip through the Land of What Not to

Do, you are probably beginning to have a pretty good
idea of some of the things you *should* do in order to
prevent your youngster from growing up to be a violent
person.

> Don't be a violent person yourself, or your child will
> imitate you.
> Make a distinction between violent *actions* and vio-
> lent *feelings*.
> Set firm limits on your child's hostile and violent
> *actions*.
> Give him outlets for expressing hostile and violent
> *feelings*.

Encourage him to express these feelings in words. Use the
feed-back technique described in Chapter 4 to help him
handle these feelings.

Now we need to discuss two topics about which parents
are concerned: dangerous weapons, and violence in fantasy.

First, dangerous weapons. Let me say flatly that it is
not good to have dangerous weapons around the house.
They are not only a potential source of tragic accidents,
they are a potential incitement to violent actions.

It is a sad and frightening thing to contemplate how the
United States seems involved in an internal arms race, to
see how many of our citizens can buy the most guns.
According to recent statistics, the number of adults in the
United States purchasing guns is increasing at an alarming
rate. Most of these guns are supposedly bought for self-
protection. The reasoning of the person who buys the gun
runs something like this: "Having the gun in the house
will protect me and my family if someone should try to
harm us." This is foolish reasoning, based mostly on irrational fear. It is the kind of thinking that the father in the
novel *Johnny Get Your Gun* used in explaining things to
his son:

> . . . he remembered the evening when he had sat
> beside his strong and wise father and had first been
> shown the gun and had it explained to him. "A gun
> is a good thing," his father had said. "Because some-
> time you might have to protect yourself or your ma.
> Maybe sometime two or three of 'em will come at you

and you won't have a chance. Then the gun makes you the boss; when they see a gun they stop real quick. When you've got a gun, nobody's gonna give you no trouble."[23]

Instead of protecting the occupants of a house against invaders, the presence in the house of a gun, particularly a loaded gun, is merely an invitation to tragedy and bloodshed. The presence of a deadly weapon is an invitation to violent action when estranged parents are quarreling, or to a tragic death when children are playing with a supposedly "unloaded" weapon.

It is unfortunate that it is so easy for anyone to buy a gun. Would any parent hand out loaded revolvers to a group of two-year-olds playing in his backyard? Of course not. Yet our present society makes it easy for persons with no more emotional control than a two-year-old to get ahold of a gun. Under present laws, assassins, snipers during riots, criminals, juvenile delinquents, estranged husbands and wives, and mentally disturbed persons easily buy guns. It is easier to buy a firearm today than it is to buy a prescription at a drug store. This is truly an insane situation, hardly conducive to the raising of children in a nonviolent atmosphere.

The history of private ownership of firearms in this country begins with the fourth article of the Bill of Rights, which declares ". . . the right of the people to keep and bear Arms shall not be infringed." In 1776 the need for the general populace to have the right to private ownership of firearms was essential to the welfare and safety of this young nation, which at that time had a total population of only three million. But the unrestricted ownership of firearms by a population of over 200 million in our complex industrial society is unrealistic and downright dangerous.

In 1967, for example, over 5,600 Americans died of gunshot wounds. In contrast to this number, thirty died in Great Britain, twenty in France, and twelve in Belgium. Great Britain, France, and Belgium, as well as Japan, Norway, Sweden, and Canada have far stricter laws regulating firearms than we have. My advice is that unless father is a hunter and owns a hunting rifle, it would be best not to have a gun, especially a loaded gun, around the house.

There is no doubt that many mothers today are terribly upset about violence erupting in our society. One reaction that many mothers have is to forbid any outlets for violence in fantasy by their children. They will not allow their children to play with toy guns, toy soldiers or to watch TV or movies in which violence can be found. Some parents even go to the ridiculous extreme of forbidding their children to watch television cartoons in which "violence" occurs; in which animals zonk each other over the head or shoot at each other. At a recent Punch and Judy puppet show at a nursery school approximately 200 families attended. The nursery school staff were amazed to find that two mothers phoned afterward to complain of the "violence" their children had been exposed to during the puppet show!

Fear of fantasy violence on the part of mothers has been aided and abetted by a spate of recent articles in women's magazines about toy guns and violence on TV, including cartoons. These articles are not written by psychologists and psychiatrists who could be expected to bring a professional point of view to the subject, but by journalists with a layman's viewpoint. And I think they have unduly alarmed many mothers. This enormous fear of violence in fantasy on the part of many parents is out of proportion. These parents are not being properly protective of their child against violence. They are being unhelpfully overprotective.

What causes this type of overprotection on the part of a parent? The parent is afraid of her own angry feelings. She is afraid that they will get out of hand and will erupt into violent and hostile actions. She is probably not aware that she feels this way; these feelings are unconscious. Every single bit of fantasy this parent sees on TV or in a movie triggers the fear: What if my own angry feelings erupted and I hurt my husband or my children? Because these feelings are so frightening to her, the parent projects them onto her child, and assumes that the child feels the same way. For this reason, such parents are afraid of letting their children see any fantasized violence on TV or in the movies, or participate in fantasy violence through playing with toy soldiers.

This is a mistake. Children need socially acceptable fantasy outlets for their hostile and violent feelings. If the parents do not allow the child such outlets, he will often create the fantasy outlet himself. If Mother forbids all toy guns, the child will create a "gun" out of a piece of wood, a stick, or his own thumb and forefinger: "Bang, bang, you're dead!" Children for centuries have liked to play with toy soldiers. They will improvise their own, if they are forbidden by overprotective parents to buy them.

By sheer coincidence, as I am typing these lines on a Saturday morning in the family room of our home, my four-year-old boy is playing on the floor with a set of plastic toy soldiers he bought at the toy store. He has decided the blue soldiers are the "bad guys" and the green soldiers are the "good guys," and he is happily zapping the bad guys with the good guys. He is not a violent child, and he is not going to grow up a violent adult. We have not done the things that will teach him to be either a violent child or a violent adult. He is a peaceful, but normally aggressive, young boy.

It is very important that we make a distinction between a child's being *violent* and a child's being *aggressive*. These two characteristics are often confused by parents. *The opposite of violent is peaceful. The opposite of aggressive is passive.*

We don't want to teach our children to grow up to become violent adults. But we do want to teach our male children to grow up to become aggressive adults. It is not good for an adult male to be passive. He is handicapped in his masculine role if his parents have reinforced passivity in him. A parent who is hysterically overprotective of her child against any type of fantasy violence is not being helpful to her child. A parent who forbids her boy to play with toy soldiers or toy guns, who does not allow him to watch "violent" cartoons on TV or at the movies, is molding him to be like a passive little girl. She is not helping him to be a strong, adequate, aggressive little boy who can handle himself with other boys his own age.

I have seen many passive boys in my clinical practice. They are usually brought in for therapy because other boys pick on them, and they cannot stand up for themselves. It is really ironic. In their overprotection against "violence," the parents unwittingly train the boy to be passive and ineffectual in his male role. Then when they see the unfortunate results of this in his relationship with other children, they bring him in for therapy, saying, in effect:

"Please, Mr. Psychologist, undo the effects of my training on my boy!"

Now please, don't misunderstand what I have just said. Don't feel that you have to go to the other extreme and let your child buy *any* sort of toy gun. If your boy has listened to the hard sell on television of a "chrome-studded reinforced plastic, self-destructo, bloodthirsty night fighters, guerrilla submachine gun with plastic bullets which splatter plastic blood when you shoot them at the Christmas tree," don't feel obligated to buy this monstrosity for him!

I would not buy a child any toy gun that actually shoots anything. A plastic bullet could blind another child. I would not buy any toy gun or toy of "violence" I considered offensive and in poor taste. I would not buy my child a Do-It-Yourself Crucifix, consisting of a plastic cross to which the child would then nail the Christ figure. The advertisement for this "toy" in a toy magazine, believe it or not, states that this is the "World's first Crucifix model kit." The ad describes it as "inspiring, beautiful, authentic," and goes on to say, ". . . this easily assembled crucifix is a prized, welcome and tasteful addition to any Catholic home"![24] A mother should use her common sense and good taste in what type of toy guns or toy soldiers she allows her child to buy.

Merely allowing a boy to play with toy soldiers and toy guns and watch "violent" cartoons or shoot-em-up westerns will not in itself produce a boy who feels comfortable and adequate in his male role. It is a parent's respect for the exuberant, feisty, dynamic quality of boyhood which will cause him to feel good about his male role. When a mother can say, "He's all boy!" and be proud of it, the seal of her approval is set on this dynamic quality of maleness in her young son. When he is rewarded for being independent, outgoing, not letting others push him around, he will be a normal aggressive boy, and grow up to become an adult who is healthily aggressive, but not violent.

It is important that we do not confuse hostility and violence with being aggressive. We want our boys to grow up to become aggressive and forceful males. But we also want them to grow up to be peaceful persons, who will use reason and peaceful means to resolve conflicts, rather than resorting to violence.

Many fathers, in their heart of hearts, feel that their

wives have gone to extremes in forbidding their boys to play with toy guns or toy soldiers. But they keep their real feelings to themselves about this. This is most unfortunate, because a woman wants her man to be a strong and adequate person on whom she can lean when she needs support. Overprotecting little boys against normal expressions of violence through fantasy will not help the boy to grow up to be that kind of a strong adult male.

Adults allow for discharge of hostile and violent feelings through socially acceptable outlets. Fantasy is one of these outlets. Adults watch football and ice hockey games, yell "Kill the umpire," read murder mysteries, and watch fantasy violence on movies and television.

Children need these fantasy outlets as much as adults do. Let your child play with toy soldiers and toy guns if he wants; it will do him no harm. If you forbid him *all* toy soldiers and *all* toy guns, you will create a taboo area in his mind. This will make this type of play fascinating for him, and he will engage in play of this sort behind your back.

Now we come to the problem of violence in the media. Let us assume you are following the general advice on child raising in this book. You are meeting your child's basic psychological needs, so there is little reason for him to feel enormously frustrated and hence full of hostility and violence inside. You are providing him with an interesting and stimulating environment in your home, so that he has ample opportunity to play inside and outside, to read, to engage in art activities, and to do many other interesting and creative things besides watching television. You do not let him sit "glued to TV" for four or five hours a day. You restrict his TV viewing to a reasonable amount of time each day. You reward or reinforce him for watching good children's programs such as "Sesame Street," "Captain Kangaroo," "Misterogers Neighborhood," "H. R. Pufnstuff," or "The Friendly Giant." Because you do these things you should have little to worry about if your child sees shows on TV in which violence is portrayed.

The fallacy which needs to be exposed here (which appears in many magazine articles on children and TV violence) is that children learn to become violent persons by seeing violent actions portrayed on TV. There is no research evidence which supports this. Children learn to become violent when parents teach them by the means I have described in this chapter.

> Children learn to become violent when parents frustrate their psychological human needs and fill them with rage and violence inside.
> Children learn to become violent when they imitate violent parents.
> Children learn to become violent when parents reinforce them for violent actions and do not set firm limits against their hitting other children or destroying property.
> Children learn to become violent when they are not allowed to release violent feelings.

If you avoid these ways of teaching your children to become violent, you have little to fear from the TV tube.

Sometimes parents act as if violence on TV is something new, and children were never before in the history of mankind exposed to fantasy violence. This is simply not true. The Bible is full of violence. So is Shakespeare. So are children's fairy tales, in which ogres and monsters existed centuries before they were seen in children's TV cartoons.

There is often a vast "generation gap" between an adult who is excessively afraid of violence and a child who has no such fears. Children often seek out fantasy which is violent and scary because it is a way of helping them master, through fantasy, their own inner feelings of hostility and violence. This generation gap between adults and children was illustrated recently when the book *Where the Wild Things Are* was published. The reviews of many children's librarians condemned the book, saying that it was a terrible book to put in the hands of children because of its story and its vivid pictures of a little boy's fantasies of ogres and monsters. Young children, however, love that book! It is in tune with their inner needs. It helps them deal with their inner world of violence and hostility.

Your child knows well the difference between violence in fantasy on a TV or movie screen, and violence in action when he hits another child, is cruel to an animal, or destroys property. We need to set firm limits for the violent actions of a child, but we need to give him socially acceptable outlets for his violent feelings. For example, a four-year-old boy in therapy got angry at me one day. Before I could stop him, he had hit me with his fist, saying, "I hate you, stupid!" I told him firmly: "Tommy, you can tell me you're mad and call me stupid or whatever names you want to call me. But I will not let you hit me." Later in that same therapy hour, he played out a war with toy soldiers in the sand box, bombing and blasting the "enemy" with his troops. If I had not set firm limits when he hit me, I would have been encouraging him to engage in violent actions. Allowing him to play out his violent *feelings* in fantasy with the toy soldiers was good for him, and did not encourage him to be a violent person. By allowing him to express his hostile feelings through fantasy, I gave him a chance to get them out of his system. Then warm and positive feelings could come in. You can use the same principles with your child. Set firm limits on his violent actions, but give him socially acceptable outlets for his violent feelings.

I am in favor of reducing the general level of violence and sadism in television and movies. But too much sadism and violence is not the only thing wrong with TV. TV programs are uncreative, hackneyed, and oriented to instant financial acquisitiveness. ("This lucky contestant wins a new refrigerator, a brand new Buick hardtop, and an all-expense vacation to beautiful downtown Burbank!") When you think of the rich cultural and educational possibilities of TV for both children and adults, and then look at what is actually available on TV, it makes you shudder. Given what is actually available on TV now, we have to use our common sense and good judgment when our children watch it.

We must resist the temptation to scapegoat television as the cause of all the violence we see in America today. Remember that there is violence in the world even in places that have never seen a TV set! Too many articles in women's magazines have unduly alarmed mothers and caused them to go to ridiculous extremes in trying to protect their children from anything remotely resembling violence on television.

I have saved until last the discussion of the most effective preventive measure of all which you can use so that your child will not grow up to become a hostile and violent adult. We call this preventive measure *love*.

We should never forget that hostile and violent adults

are persons who have been deprived of genuine love in childhood. Adults who injure and kill others are sick and twisted persons. They are full of hatred and violence because they have been deprived of love.

The most effective inoculation we can ever give our children against the virus of violence is our love and affection as parents. Instead of spending a major part of our time trying to prevent some virus of violence in the environment from infecting our children, we should spend our time in building strong and healthy and loving relationships with our children. We should not merely avoid teaching sadism to our children; we need to teach them the positive values of warmth, compassion, and a genuine interest in being helpful and considerate of other people.

We need to reinforce their youthful idealism. We need to point out to them the horrors and tragedy of war. We need to enlist our children and young people in what the psychologist William James called the "moral equivalent of war"—an aggressive attack on the current problems of mankind: poverty, environmental pollution, race hatred, and war. We need to teach them to love their neighbors as they love themselves.

The soil in which a genuine and loving concern for other people can grow in the minds of our children is our own genuine and loving parental concern for them. If we use, with love, the science of parenting, we will do the most important thing to insure our children's growing up to be psychologically secure and peaceful adults, instead of violent and hostile persons.

11

School Begins at Home

PART ONE

The concept of "IQ" is a mysterious one to many parents. They read about experiments and methods designed to raise a child's IQ and wonder just how this could be done. If, instead of "IQ," we speak of "basic learning skills," the whole subject would be clearer.

For example, last year I attended a six-week course in backpacking and mountaineering given by the Sierra Club. As a result of that course my camping and backpacking IQ was raised considerably. It would sound a bit confusing if you described it that way. However, if you said that as a result of the course my basic learning skills in camping and backpacking had increased that would be more understandable. You would know that I had learned such basics as reading a topographic map, using a compass, rock climbing, and building a snow cave.

Intelligence or IQ tests are good predictors of whether or not a child will be successful in school because of a simple fact: the intelligence test samples the repertoire of basic learning skills which the child has acquired. The larger the repertoire of basic learning skills, the higher the

IQ, and the greater the probability of success. The child
who enters kindergarten or first grade with a large repertoire of learning skills will learn more rapidly than one
with a small repertoire of those skills, and will receive
more positive reinforcement from his teacher. Thus, the
first child, with the larger repertoire of basic learning
skills—and, therefore, the larger IQ, is the more likely to
succeed in a scholastic situation—and in life as well.

Remember that these skills can be *learned*. So the
purpose of this chapter is to explain how you can teach
them to your preschool child, so that he will have the best
possible start open to him.

For many years, professionals working with children
have known that the first five years are the most important for the emotional development of a child, since these
years shape the basic personality structure of the adult. It
is only recently that research has shown that the first five
years are the most important years for intellectual development as well as emotional development.

Since we can experiment with lower animals to a degree
which is impossible with human beings, a mass of research
evidence now exists which demonstrates the effect of early
stimulation on adult behavior in such diverse animals as
dogs, cats, rats, monkeys, ducks, and birds. Numerous
experiments have shown that when animals are given
stimulation in infancy, they develop at a more rapid rate
and become more intelligent than others which are not so
stimulated.

Research at the University of California at Berkeley
done by a team of two psychologists, a biochemist, and an
anatomist has shown that *an enriched early environment
in white rats cannot only develop superior problem-solving
adult animals, but can actually produce changes in the
anatomy and chemical characteristics of the brains of the
rats*. Dr. David Krech, professor of psychology, describes
one of the standard experiments done by this research
team:

At weaning age, one rat from each of a dozen pairs
of male twins is chosen by lot to be placed in an educationally active and innovative environment, while
its twin brother is placed in as unstimulating an environment as we can contrive. All twelve educationally
enriched rats live together in one large, wire-mesh

cage in a well lighted, noisy, and busy laboratory. The cage is equipped with ladders, running wheels, and other "creative" rat toys. For thirty minutes each day the rats are taken out of their cages and allowed to explore new territory. As the rats grow older, they are given various learning tasks to master, for which they are rewarded with bits of sugar. This stimulating educational and training program is continued for eighty days.

While these animals are enjoying their rich intellectual environment, each impoverished animal lives out his life in solitary confinement, in a small cage situated in a dimly lit and quiet room. He is rarely handled by his keeper and never invited to explore new environments, to solve problems, or to join in games with other rats. Both groups of rats, however, have unlimited access to the same standard food throughout the experiment.[25]

Tests of the rats in later life showed that those which received early stimulation were more intelligent and could solve problems better than their nonstimulated litter mates. Then the rats' brains were studied. This standard experiment, repeated dozens of times, indicated that as the fortunate rat lives out his life in the educationally enriched environment, his brain expands and grows deeper and heavier than his culturally deprived litter mate. The brain cortex showed an increasing number of certain types of brain cells, with more branching between cells than the brains of the unstimulated rats. Important chemical changes took place also. A greater amount of two important enzymes were found in the brains of the stimulated rats than in their unstimulated litter mates. Comments Dr. Krech: "We have demonstrated that these structural and chemical changes are the signs of a 'good' brain. . . . We have created superior problem-solving animals."[26]

Research at a human level confirms the fact that stimulation or lack of stimulation in the early years has an important effect on adult behavior and intelligence. Dr. Benjamin Bloom, professor of psychology at the University of Chicago, has summarized a mass of research which shows that children develop 50 percent of their intelligence by the age of four. This accounts for the fact that disadvantaged children of poor parents actually enter kindergarten or first grade considerably behind in intellectual ability as compared with the children of middle-class parents. And the poor children never catch up, due to the lasting effects of the lack of intellectual stimulation in their early years. This is why the Head Start programs attempt to give these children enough intellectual stimulation in their early years so that they will not be hopelessly educationally handicapped throughout their school careers.

What does all this research mean for your child?

It means that the more intellectual stimulation you can give your child in the first five years of his life, *without pushing or pressuring him*, the brighter and more intelligent he will become, the higher IQ he will have as an adult.

TEACHING YOUR CHILD TO THINK

The most basic learning skill we can possibly teach a child, is *how to think*.

What is thinking? The late John Dewey, a famous professor of education, suggested that "thinking begins with a felt difficulty." Dewey stressed the point that *we do not think unless there is some difficulty or problem we are confronted with.*

Let me quote a marvelous example of thinking on the four-year-old level:

A group of four-year-olds were playing house in a large packing box. They had built a number of crude pieces of furniture out of their blocks, but as space within the box was limited, it was necessary to move about with extreme caution in order to avoid knocking things over. Clumsy and excitable Jimmy found this well-nigh impossible. After half a dozen accidents, the "father" of the family announced in the tones of one who has just made a thrilling discovery: "We gotta have a dog too! Jimmy, you be the dog! You have to stay outside and bark whenever anybody comes by the house. Bark loud!"[27]

This example shows that there are three steps in the thinking process. The first step is a problem or a difficulty, a disequilibrium in your life. In the children's example, the problem was that clumsy Jimmy kept knocking things over in the play house. The second step in thinking is a hypothesis or idea that will solve the problem. The "father" of the family comes up with the idea: "Jimmy, you be the dog." (That'll get you out of the playhouse, buddy, and you'll stop knocking things down!) The third step is the conclusion or solution to the problem, when Jimmy accepts the role of the dog. Although this example illustrates the thinking of children, the three basic steps are the same for all thinking, from the most primitive to the most sophisticated.

There are also two basic kinds of thinking—what Dr. Jerome Bruner, professor of psychology at Harvard University, calls the "thinking of the right hand" and the "thinking of the left hand." By the "thinking of the right hand" he means logical, analytical, rational thinking— thinking which we do with our conscious mind and which proceeds carefully, step by step, to a logical conclusion. This is the kind of thinking with which schools and colleges are concerned and make an effort to teach to children. But there is another kind of thinking, often neglected by the schools. This is the "thinking of the left hand," which is intuitive and hunchy, and which involves access by the thinker to his unconscious rather than his conscious mind. It is this thinking which gives rise to great scientific discoveries or to creative breakthroughs in the world of business or politics. Thus we need to teach our children how to do *both* kinds of thinking.

"THINKING OF THE RIGHT HAND"

What can we do to teach our preschooler the thinking of the right hand? We can provide raw materials for him to use, the most basic of which are sensory experiences.

Parents may be classified into three groups, depending upon how they encourage their children to relate to sensory experiences. First, there is the "No-No" Parent, who actively discourages exploration through sight, hearing, touch, taste, and smell: "Get away from that!" "Keep your hand off that—it's dirty." Second, there is the "Neutral" Parent, who takes an essentially passive and neutral atti-

tude toward sensory exploration by her child. Third is the
parent who actively encourages her child to experience the
world as fully as possible through his senses.

I hope you will be one of the third group. Encourage
him to feel things, to become aware of different textures.
Help him to listen to all of the varied sounds of his
environment and become more aware of them. Help him
to truly *see*—to see beauty in commonplace things: the
peeling paint on a garage wall, the intricate pattern of
cracks in an asphalt driveway, the configuration of water
as you hose down a car. Try to help your child to be
aware. As the late Victor Lowenfeld, professor of art
education at Pennsylvania State University, put it:

> You can encourage him to use his eyes, ears and
> hands continually. . . . You can make him conscious
> of the beauty of a row of tulips in a garden, of the
> difference between the long, flowing leaves of a weep-
> ing willow tree and the green-and-silver symmetry of
> a silver maple leaf. Encourage him to touch the
> rough, ridged bark of an old oak tree and the smooth,
> mottled bark of a sycamore. Let him feel the texture
> of wool and velvet and rayon in your clothes and in
> his own. Make him conscious of the way the cat's
> fur feels. . . . A simple statement like, "Johnny, do
> you smell the burning leaves in the wind?" can open
> up a rich sensory experience to a youngster, an ex-
> perience which might go quite unnoticed but for you.
> Even the sounds of the wind through the trees, the
> call of a robin in the early morning, the bubbling of
> brook water against smooth stones for a young child
> can be springboards to an expanding sensitivity which
> will enrich his entire life.[28]

The time to start a child on the road to awareness is
when he is a preschooler. *A true awareness of the sensory
world is his most basic foundation for thinking.*

In addition to providing a wide range of sensory experiences for our children, we need to provide a variety of
materials which they can use as stimuli for their thinking—
materials which your child should have between the ages
of three and six. He should have available lots of paper;
crayons, felt pens or watercolor pens; scissors with blunt
ends; stacks of old magazines; cardboard of various shapes

and sizes; a blackboard with white and colored chalk; a scrapbox for collage, containing all kinds of scrap wood, fabric and paper; glue; wooden blocks of various sizes; dress-up clothes and costumes; a record player or tape player; inexpensive records he can play by himself; good records you play for him; Lego or similar types of construction toys; playdough and clay; books. Your child should have a set of plastic, magnetic alphabet letters and numerals and a metal blackboard they can stick to. Without the above-mentioned materials, your preschooler would be as handicapped in his thinking as a college student with no textbooks.

You should also provide a bulletin board on which you can tack up the artistic and printed productions of your child. Having a place to display what he has done gives him a sense of pride in his work and rewards him for his accomplishments.

Another important aspect of early intellectual development is to give your child as wide a range of firsthand experiences as you possibly can.

Many persons are not very powerful thinkers because they have had little firsthand experience. Their minds are full of the opinions and thoughts of others, instead of opinions and thoughts originating within themselves. If you think I exaggerate, ask yourself or others this question: Do you spend even a half hour a day in quiet meditation listening to the voice of yourself? Or is all of your day taken up with the voices of others, whether the voices are those of other people, a television program, or words on a printed page?

In his remarkable *Autobiography*, Lincoln Steffens, the famous crusading journalist, suggests a project for becoming an original and discriminating critic in the field of art. However, his suggestion has wide ramifications. He suggests you visit an art museum and pick the three works of art you like best in the entire museum. Go back the following week and again pick the three works you like the best. Keep doing this each week for six months. At the end of that time you will probably not pick the same three that you picked at the beginning. You will, in effect, have put yourself through a small course in art appreciation by the changing and developing taste you have acquired by forcing yourself to pick those three works of art. At the end of six months you might pick the same three works of art that an art critic would choose as the best. The point is that you would have chosen those three out of your own genuine firsthand experience. Not because somebody else told you they were great works of art.

This suggested project by Mr. Steffens is a model for what we can use with our children. Give them lots of opportunity to experience things for themselves, rather than through somebody else's eyes and thoughts and feelings.

Our child's experience should not only be *firsthand*; it should be as *broad* as possible. Thinking is based on the extent of a child's experience; it can extend no further than his experience. Thus you want to make sure your child's experience is as broad as possible.

One of the best ways to broaden your child's firsthand experience is to take him on what schools call field trips into the community. Every community, whether it is a small town or a large city, has a number of fascinating places which can enlarge the experience of a preschooler. My own preschoolers were excited by trips to such places as a fire station, a police station, a dairy, a foundry, a library, an airport, a newspaper, a shoe repair shop, a bakery, a welding shop, a body and fender shop, a bank, and a pie factory.

The place which fascinated my children most was the foundry. When they saw how this red-hot material was formed into shapes and cooled, they had a much better idea of how things were made out of metal. And this aroused their curiosity about how other things were made.

You will probably discover it is great fun for an adult to go on field trips such as these with a child. Usually we adults don't get a chance to do things of this nature. We feel a little shy about going to the fire house and asking the fireman, "Can I look over your fire engine?" But your child is your ticket to all sorts of adventures within a half hour's drive of your house. I have found that even the gruffest men love to show a small child around their factory or place of work.

There are many ways to extend your child's experience after you have taken the field trip. You might read from the *Let's Go* books published by G. P. Putnam, which include such titles as *Let's Go to a Post Office, Let's Go to a Zoo, Let's Go to a Bank,* and many others. When you get back from a trip, you can encourage your child to draw pictures and make up stories about the trip. He can even "write a book" about the trip.

When you select the means to enrich your child's knowledge, don't overlook the obvious. Museums are a great way of broadening his experience, although you need to expose a preschool child to a museum in small doses. (Remember his short attention span.) Travel, of course, can extend your child's experience greatly, particularly if you are fortunate enough to be able to travel to a foreign country. And books, records, tapes, movies, and TV programs are invaluable aids to broadening your child's horizons. Remember the words of the psychologist Piaget: "The more your child sees and hears, the more he wants to see and hear."

It is important to let your child's abstract thinking arise out of concrete experiences. Young children are not capable of much abstract thinking unrelated to concrete materials, but they are capable of a great deal of abstract thinking when it arises out of concrete materials they can see and touch and manipulate.

This awareness of the importance of "tactile education" was part of the genius of Maria Montessori, and it is one of the reasons for the rebirth of the Montessori movement in the United States recently. Montessori said she presented the children with "materialized abstractions." By this she meant that she presented abstract ideas in a concrete form, which the child could manipulate through an activity. She designed a whole series of educational play equipment which a child can manipulate and so learn mathematics, physics, reading, writing, and other skills.

Other specialists in childhood education have followed Montessori's lead. There are well-designed educational toys on the market which can lead your child into abstract thinking through the use of concrete materials which he can manipulate. You will find these listed in Appendix A, but I want to give you one example now.

Georges Cuisenaire, a Belgian, was one of those who followed Montessori's lead. He invented a set of materials by which young children can learn arithmetic and mathematics—the Cuisenaire Rods. These are a series of wooden rods of various lengths and different colors. They are the best way yet devised to teach a child arithmetic and math. The child can learn to add, subtract, multiply, and divide. He can learn to check his own work to see if it is correct.

Using these rods, he can actually go into algebra in a small way. The Cuisenaire Company of America sells a special Parents Kit, with a complete set of rods, plus step-by-step instructions for parents to teach their children how to use them (see Appendix A).

These types of educational toys are based on the principle of allowing a child to discover things for himself. Things he discovers for himself are much more forcefully imbedded in his mind than things you explain to him. Take a very simple example. You are letting your child experiment with painting different colors. You might tell him how he can mix yellow and blue and get green. But if you tell him, that robs him of the thrill of self-discovery. Why not do it a different way? Let him have yellow paint and blue paint. Then say: "Why don't you mix them together and see what happens?" He will try it, and his face will light up: "Hey, it makes green!"

It is hard for parents to use self-discovery as a teaching method with our children because we are so accustomed to telling them things. I remember that when one of my children was three he asked me, "Daddy, if I plant a stick in the ground will it grow into a tree?" My first immediate reaction was to answer, "No, it won't." Instead, I used the method of self-discovery. I said, "Let's do an experiment. Let's plant a stick in the ground and see if it will grow." We did, and a few days later he commented, "I guess it won't grow." Then we planted some seeds, and he learned by firsthand discovery what will grow and what will not grow when planted.

Aid your child to develop key concepts which help him organize and make sense out of his world.

Children are bombarded with information from their environment. They are constantly trying to relate and test one bit of information against another in order to make sense out of their world. They are trying to discover cause and effect relationships and to classify and put in order information about what they see, hear, and feel in their environment.

Fostering Intellectual Development in Young Children by Kenneth Wann, Miriam Dorn, and Elizabeth Liddle will give you a good deal of background information so that you can help your child develop key concepts. By a *key concept* I mean an idea which helps a child integrate a number of different phenomena and make sense out of his environment. Among the examples of key concepts which can be understood by preschool children are the following:

"Gravity is an invisible force that pulls things down to the ground."

"All animals have some sort of protection against their enemies."

"Friction takes place when two things rub together, and friction makes things hot."

Once a child truly understands one of these key concepts, he can understand a whole group of phenomena in his environment.

You can explain key concepts to a child by reading a book which presents such concepts on a level he can understand. *Gravity All Around* by Tillie Pine and Joseph Levine is such a book. (A list of other books will be found in Appendix C.) You can also explain the concepts to him by simple demonstrations from everyday life. Gravity can easily be demonstrated by showing that when you let go of something, it falls to the ground instead of going up in the air. You can explain that in outer space there is no gravity, so people would just float around in space unless they happened to be on a planet where gravity pulled them to the ground.

Learn to play educational games with your child. All children like to play games. (Many of the educational toys listed in Appendix A are in the form of games.) But with preschoolers, you don't have to go out and buy games; you can make up your own.

There are many simple yet educational games you can play with your child. A good choice for a four-year-old is the "Rhyming Game." You think of a word and he thinks of another word that rhymes with it. Then he thinks of a word and you think of a rhyming word. (Be liberal in your interpretation of what a "rhyming word" is.) This is a very simple game, yet one which he will enjoy playing.

Another good game is "Wouldn't It Be Funny If. . .?" Tell him: "I've got a new game we can play. It's called 'Wouldn't It Be Funny If. . . ?' Here's how you play it. I'll start. Wouldn't it be funny if people walked on their hands instead of their feet? Now it's your turn." All sorts of interesting concepts may develop: Wouldn't it be funny if cars ran on water instead of on gasoline? Wouldn't it be funny if children gave shots to doctors? By playing this type of game you are helping your youngster learn to think in a novel fashion. You are encouraging him to create new ideas, and you are helping him to develop his imagination.

A variation of this game is "What Would Happen If. . . ?" What would happen if cars ran on water instead of gasoline? The family would save money because water is cheaper than gasoline. There would be much less smog. You would have to stop at a water station instead of a gas station.

An important principle to use in playing these games with your preschooler is to accept whatever ideas he comes up with. Do not be critical of his ideas and say things like: "No, that couldn't happen" or "That's not true." This will discourage him from coming up with ideas and take away the fun of the game for him. Don't worry. He will learn to be more precise and accurate in his ideas as he grows older. All you want to do at this stage is to encourage him to *produce* ideas, regardless of how scientifically accurate they are.

Another useful game is the "Statement Game." A statement is any sentence that states something. You can start a statement game with a statement such as this: "This car is colored white." Then you ask questions about the statement.

"Is this car colored green?"

"No."

"Is this car colored red?"

"No."

"Is this car colored white?"

"Yes."

Here is a slightly more complicated one:

"All dogs have four legs. Monkeys have two legs. Is a monkey a dog?"

"No."

"How do you know?"

"Because it doesn't have four legs."

Your purpose is to show the child that you can create an infinite number of questions which can be answered yes or no starting with any statement. This game, played at a preschooler's level, is a powerful foundation for logical thinking.

Use your imagination to make up your own games with your preschooler. Try it and you will see that the list of activities which can be turned into "games" for a young child is literally endless. See, for example, what "games" you could invent out of a trip to the market with your child.

"THINKING OF THE LEFT HAND"

Now we turn to the "thinking of the left hand." Here what we are trying to do is to help your child develop the intuitive, imaginative, unconscious part of his mind as well as the rational, logical, conscious part. How can you help him do this?

First, you can encourage his creativity.

It is unfortunate that the word "creativity" has become a cliché these days. Every toy manufacturer is getting into the act and labeling the most pedestrian and uninspired junk as "creative" toys. We need to get back to the original meaning of the word.

When your child creates something it means that out of unstructured materials he is forming a structure, which originates inside his mind. For example, contrast using a coloring book with using crayons and blank paper. When your child colors a coloring book, the structure is already there in the book. Your child creates nothing. The only value to him is that he is learning to keep within the lines. There is absolutely no creativity involved. But when your child draws with crayons on a sheet of paper, he is creating his own structure, which originates within his mind, out of the unstructured materials: the crayons and the paper.

This is why it is so important for your child to have access to *unstructured* materials. These can be crayons, paint, clay, playdough, paper, collage, blocks, Legos, sand, dirt, and the like. None of these materials has any structure in itself. It is the mind of your child which creates the structure.

A word of caution here. Sometimes parents misunderstand this emphasis on aiding a child's creativity, and think: "Well, that's not so terribly important, because I doubt if my child is going to grow up to be an artist." They have missed the point. You are not trying to teach your child to be an *artist* by using these unstructured materials. You are trying to teach him to be *creative*. You are giving him a chance to build up his self-confidence by seeing that he can impose order and structure on unstructured materials. You are increasing his sensitivity, his awareness, his originality, and his powers of flexibility. These creative qualities will be needed in whatever field he chooses in later life.

I have already indicated how important it is for the mental health of your child that you allow him to express his feelings. It is also very important for the maximum development of his intellect. You can help your child develop access to his unconscious mind by encouraging his expression of feeling. You need to teach him that there is no such thing as *right* or *wrong, good* or *bad* when it comes to his feelings or thoughts. *Right* and *wrong, good* and *bad* are confined to actions, to outward behavior, not inner thoughts and feelings. One of the main things that prevents unconventional ideas or ways of doing things from popping into the mind of an adult is that as a child he was taught that certain ideas or feelings are bad or wrong. Yet, the more easily unconventional, new, and creative ideas can pop into an adult's mind, the more successful he is going to be in his chosen work.

As David Ogilvy, one of the most creative and successful advertising men our country has produced, points out:

The creative process requires more than reason. Most original thinking isn't even verbal. It requires a groping experimentation with ideas, governed by intuitive hunches and inspired by the unconscious. The majority of business men are incapable of original thinking, because they are unable to escape from the tyranny of reason. Their imaginations are blocked.

. . . I have developed techniques for keeping open the telephone line to my unconscious, in case that disorderly repository has anything to tell me. I hear a great deal of music . . . I take long hot baths. I garden . . . I go for long walks in the country. And I take frequent vacations, so that my brain can lie fallow—no golf, no cocktail parties, no tennis, no bridge, no concentration; only a bicycle. While thus employed in doing nothing, I receive a constant stream of telegrams from my unconscious, and these become the raw material for my advertisements.[29]

The way you will help your child become this kind of a creative adult is to *encourage* his expression of feeling. It is through his *feelings* that a child or an adult has access to his unconscious mind. And from the unconscious come the creative hunches and ideas that are so important to us. A dry, pedantic, stodgy adult has no access at all to his unconscious mind because he has shut the doors on his feeling-life.

We want to open the doors of the feeling-life while our children are young, and to keep them open.

You need to feed your child's imaginative life. Our age tends to go overboard on the side of fact as opposed to fantasy. Although there are many good books on factual subjects for children, truly fine books of fantasy are scarce. But fantasy needs to be cultivated, not eliminated. A child who has grown up without having his parents read to him from books such as *Winnie-the-Pooh*, *Alice in Wonderland*, or *The Little Prince*, or a modern classic such as *Charlie and the Chocolate Factory* or *The Twenty-One Balloons* is a child who has missed a very rich part of childhood fantasy and imagination. (You will find a list of recommended books of fantasy for preschoolers in Appendix C.)

We can feed a child's imagination not only through books on fantasy but through nonverbal activities such as music, dance, and art. These nonverbal activities give a child a chance to express his feelings and to develop his imagination and his fantasy life.

We can help a child develop his imagination by telling him stories and encouraging him to tell stories. There is a difference between a story you *read* to a child and a story you *tell* a child. When you yourself tell a story to a child, you are helping him to believe that he can also learn to make up a story.

Children take particular delight in stories 'you tell them about your own experiences as a child, particularly when you were a child of their age, or close to it. Feel free to stretch the "literal" truth in elaborating your story so that it becomes more interesting to your child. (I used to tell stories about a little girl named Summer Woomer Bow Bow, who invented a gigantic chocolate cake that grew until it burst through the roof of her house.)

When you tell a story to your child, vary your pace. Speak rapidly for certain parts of the story and very slowly and dramatically in other parts. Vary the volume of your voice: loud in some parts, and down to a whisper in others. Whenever possible, use sounds and sound effects, because preschoolers love them: "The bee went zzzz" or "The big old train went *chug, chug, chug!*"

One of the best ways of encouraging your child to learn to tell a story himself is to use a picture as a springboard for the story. Get an interesting picture from a magazine, and show him how it's done by making up a brief story about the picture. Then show him a different picture and let him try.

Another way to help develop your child's imagination is for you to tell the first part of a story and let your child supply the ending. With several children in a family, the whole family can make up a round robin story. One person tells one sentence of the story, the next person contributes the next sentence, and so on.

But you may think: "I couldn't do things like that. Let's face it—I'm no storyteller!" If that's how you feel, I've got encouraging news for you. You can be the most clumsy and inept storyteller in the world, and your preschooler will still think you're great! You couldn't ask for a more appreciative audience. So relax and try it. You're bound to be a hit with your own little preschool audience. If you want to consult a helpful book to aid you in telling stories to your child, read *The Way of the Storyteller* by Ruth Sawyer.

One final thing which aids a child to develop a vivid imagination is his parents' ability to take a playful approach to life. Parents, of course, vary widely in this ability. Some are more staid and dignified. Some are more playful and zany. *Be yourself*. Don't try to be something you are not; but the more zany you can allow yourself to be with a preschooler, the more you help him to give his imagination free rein. A friend of mine used to cut the birthday cake for his children, not in conventional wedge-shaped pieces, but in the shapes of circles, squares, rectangles, and diamonds. "Makes it more interesting that way," he said.

You should help your child to develop positive *imagos*. By an *imago* I mean an unconscious mental image. In the old version of the Wechsler Intelligence Test for Adults, the arithmetic subtest used to be introduced to the subject in these words: "Now let's see how good you are in arithmetic." My experience in giving that old form of the arithmetic subtest was that every time I said that to a woman, she usually said something like: "Oh, I just know I'm going to do badly on this—I was always terrible in arithmetic!" In other words, her unconscious mental image of arithmetic was a negative one, due to her previous negative encounters in childhood with the subject. You want to help your child to have positive rather than negative imagos of the various subject areas of learning.

How can you do this? You see that his first encounter with a subject area occurs in a setting of fun and pleasure.

Take chemistry, for example, which lends itself beautifully to preschool "experiments." Mixing salt and water or sugar and water can be a "chemistry experiment." Baking simple cookies can become a "chemistry experiment." Actually use the word *chemistry* with your preschooler and suggest various experiments he can try. The "laboratory" for your child's experiments can be the kitchen sink or back porch sink. When your child first meets the subject of chemistry in grade school or high school, he will then have a very positive imago of it. You can do much the same thing with physics, foreign languages, mathematics, or most any subject that you introduce to a preschooler in a setting of fun and games.

12

School Begins at Home

PART TWO

HOW TO STIMULATE YOUR CHILD'S
LANGUAGE DEVELOPMENT

There are two aspects to your child's language development: his *oral language* and his *written language*. And there are various things you can do to stimulate the development of each.

The first thing you can do to stimulate your child's language development is to read to him.

You can begin to take him to the library and help him select books when he is around three years old. Introduce him to the children's librarian, and help him make a friend of her. You would be amazed at how many parents do not know the children's librarian in their library. (If your library is a small one, it probably has only one librarian, but she, too, will be knowledgeable about children's books.)

A librarian can be of immense help in suggesting books, in teaching a child to use the library's many services, and in helping a child feel at home in the library. Ask her to take your child on a personal guided tour of the library facilities, and let him know about special programs, such as a preschool story hour. He will be intrigued by the

272

tour, and you may be surprised at some of the services that are now available.

Get in the habit of making regular trips to the library to borrow books. (Incidentally, preschool children sometimes have difficulty understanding that the books have to be taken *back* to the library. Make allowance for that.) Be patient with your child's limited understanding of the difference between buying a book and borrowing it for two weeks.

But you should not confine your child's reading merely to library books. Begin to buy him his own books. If your budget is limited, these can be paperback books, as many good children's books are now coming out in paperback. The best thing is to go to a bookstore and browse among the children's books to get an idea of what's available.

Many parents believe that what kind of books they get for a preschooler aren't too important. They casually pick up a random selection of cheap twenty-nine-cent books at a supermarket or drugstore. I think this is a mistake. The kind of books you read to your child and buy for him *are* important. You will find an annotated list of especially recommended books for preschoolers in Appendix C.

There are special techniques for reading to very young children. First of all, hold the child on your lap or sit close to him. This makes reading more than an intellectual affair. Reading becomes a warm and cozy relationship between the two of you. Before you read a book to your child, tell him the author and title and the publisher and year of publication. If the book is illustrated, and the name of the artist is given, tell him that too. You are reinforcing in him the idea that a person needs to pay attention to who wrote the book, who illustrated it, who published it and when. This habit will come in handy later on in school, when he will need to learn to pay attention to important details.

Hold the book so that your child can see the pictures when you are reading. Point out details in the pictures. "See the mouse down in the corner? What do you think he's doing?" Encourage *him* to point out details in the pictures. You will sharpen up his powers of observation, and make the reading of the book a much more meaningful experience, than merely listening passively to words.

Don't read a book to a child in an unvarying and

monotonous tone of voice. Be dramatic. Let your voice rise and fall in different parts of the story for emphasis.

Read to only one child at a time. Trying to read to several children of different ages at the same time is very difficult. I don't recommend it.

How often should you read to your child? As often as you feel like it. Do try, however, to read to him at least one story or one very short book each evening.

There are a number of series of books which are designed for beginning readers, such as the Dr. Seuss Beginner Books by Random House or the Let's Read and Find Out Science Books by Crowell or the *True Book* series by Children's Press. I call these "double-duty" books. You can first read them aloud to your child when he is a preschooler. Then in kindergarten or first grade when he learns to read, he can use them himself. These books will help him in learning to read, for he has heard their content many times and probably knows much of it by heart. The books will be like old familiar friends— and much easier for him to learn to read than completely new and strange ones.

In addition to buying selected books for your child, you will also find it helpful to subscribe to a children's magazine. Young children get very little mail, and it is always a thrill for them to get a letter or package. There are two particularly good magazines for children under the age of six. One is *Humpty Dumpty Magazine*, published by Parents Magazine Publications, Bergenfield, New Jersey. The other is *Jack and Jill*, published by Curtis Publishing Company, Independence Square, Philadelphia, Pennsylvania. I recommend you get either or both of these magazines for your child, beginning to subscribe when your child is three. They contain stories you can read to him, puzzles he can do, jokes, cartoons, and a variety of written material of interest to a young child. You will want your child to get in the habit of reading magazines as he grows older, and one of the best ways to insure that he will enjoy reading magazines, as well as books, is to get him started in his preschool years.

As for joining a children's book club, I would generally advise against it. That may surprise you, but I think you can probably do a better job of selecting books from a bookstore than an impersonal book club can. Remember what I have said about parents using their own very valuable common sense? Why not use it here? After all, you know your own child, with his unique tastes and preferences. You should be able to select books which will fit his individual tastes and needs. If you live far from a bookstore, you could choose from a very good selection of children's books in the Sears and F.A.O. Schwarz catalogs.

The second thing you can do to stimulate your child's language development is to teach him to print.

Begin when he is around three and one-half years old. Get an alphabet book which has the letter in both upper and lower case—not just upper case. Also get a felt tip pen, which is easier for him than a pencil, pen, or crayon. Start with upper case or capital letters first, because it is easier for your child to learn to print the upper case, capital letters, than the lower case, small letters. Sooner or later a child is going to have to learn both types of letters, but you may as well begin with the easiest ones while he develops confidence in his ability to print.

Certain people (like kindergarten or first grade teachers) may tell you that there is a "right way" to teach children to make letters. Don't you believe them. There isn't any one "right way." Any way your child can make the letter is the right way for him. After all, he's not necessarily going to make the letter that way the rest of his life!

You don't have to teach him the letters beginning at *A* and going through to *Z*. Start with the letters that are the easiest to make. Then go to the harder ones. Here is one possible order you might want to use in teaching him the capital letters: *I, L, X, T, H, F, E, A, M, V, N, P, U, C, W, O, Q, D, Y, Z, B, K, J, R, S, G*. There's nothing sacred about this order; it is merely one which starts with letters that are easier to make and moves to letters which are generally harder. Remember that this order of letters is for children in general. And your child is not "children in general." So he will probably have a different order of letters, which go from easier to harder *specifically for him!*

It will take a child some time to learn to print these letters. He will find some letters easier than others. As I have said, different children find different letters easy. But be patient; show him how the strokes go to make up the letter, and give him *lots of time* to learn. It may take as long as a year to teach your child to print the capital letters, if you begin when he is three and a half. It depends on the child. But there is no rush! Your child has a whole lifetime ahead of him. So don't *you* rush him!

When your child has learned to make the letters which make up his name (and you might want to change the suggested order so that you can teach him the letters that make up his name first), show him how to print his name. This is a thrilling event in the life of a preschooler—learning to print his own name! Your child may also like to print the names of other people. Perhaps MOMMY or DADDY or the name of some special friend. He may want you to show him how to print his name the very first thing. He may pester you to teach him the letters that make up his name as *his very first letters*. If this is what interests him, do it! A basic rule of teaching: Whenever a child is interested in learning something, forget whatever else you were planning. Teach him what he is interested in learning *right then*.

The lower case letters are with some exceptions quite a bit harder to learn. Don't try to teach them until your child has learned all of the upper case letters—unless, of course, he (not you) specifically wants to learn some lower case letters. When you get to the lower case, begin by showing your child that he already knows *nine* of them. These are exactly the same as the upper case, only smaller: *c, i, o, s, u, v, w, x,* and *z* (except that *i* has a dot over it).

It may take your child another year to learn to print the lower case letters. That's quite all right. You've got lots of time. There's no rush. Even at this relaxed pace, he will still enter kindergarten or first grade knowing how to print both capital and lower case letters.

There are educational aids you can use to help your child learn the capital and lower case letters. Creative Playthings has a set of capital and lower case letters made of wood (see Appendix A). There are magnetized plastic capital and lower case letters—available in most toy stores—which can be attached to the metal board that goes with the set or to any metal surface. The door of your refrigerator, for instance, can be a fun place to leave little "words" for your youngster as he is becoming familiar with the shapes of the letters. You can also make sandpaper letters. Cut the letters from medium-textured sandpaper and glue them onto a rectangular piece of cardboard. Then have your child trace the shape of the letter with his fingers.

With the three-dimensional wood or plastic or sandpaper letters, you can play a game with your child in which you give him a letter to feel with his eyes closed. Then he identifies the letter. When you play this game, start with the capital letters, then move on to the lower case letters. Don't mix the two. Your child will find this confusing.

The third thing you can do to stimulate your child's language development is to teach him to make his own books.

Making books is one of the most exciting things you can ever teach your child. Pick a time when both he and you are in a good mood and tell him: "We're going to make a book. Mother is going to show you how. It's going to be your own special book!" To do this you will need raw materials: old magazines, especially those with lots of pictures, such as *Life* and *Look*; scissors; paper; staples or string (to bind the pages of the book together); cardboard for covers; felt pens; and crayons.

There are two kinds of books you can make: the kind he dictates for you to print and, as he learns to print, the kind he prints himself. You start, of course, with the kind he dictates to you. As with most of these learning games, a good time to begin is when he is three years old—three is generally an age of equilibrium, a more cooperative age than the stage of first adolescence between two and three.

What will his book be about? That's up to him. It depends on what your child is interested in. He might want to write a book about dogs, or trucks, or dolls, or dinosaurs, or a trip to his grandmother's or his pet turtle . . . anything! That's the beauty of it. You don't have to worry about choosing the subject of the book because it is going to be *his very own book*. Tell him: "A book is just talk, written down. You're going to talk and I'm going to write it down. We're going to make a book."

For example, here is the beginning of an actual book, as dictated by a three-year-old to his mother, who asked him what he wanted to write a book about.

"Batman."

"OK—fine. What do you want to say about Batman?"

"He's a good guy."

"Fine. That will be the first page of the book."

His mother printed slowly and carefully, in large letters, on page one: "Batman is a good guy." She didn't happen to have any pictures of Batman handy at the moment, so she left room on the page for the boy to draw or glue pictures of Batman later. Then she asked: "What do you want to say next about Batman?"

"Batman turns in bad people to the police."

She printed that on the next page. Each page had one sentence on it. Whatever he said, she printed. She didn't worry about whether he might have chosen a "nicer" book to write, or said things in a better way. She wrote down whatever he said, because it was *his* book, not her book.

"What do you want to say next about Batman?" his mother asked

"His best friend is Robin."

She printed that on the next page. And so it went. He dictated and his mother wrote it down.

That's all you have to do. As long as he's interested in dictating, you write it down. When his interest flags, then you know you have come to the end of the book. Figure out an appropriate way to end it and stop. Print it with capitals and lower case letters, just as you would find in a real book, even though he isn't able to read it yet. Don't use all capital letters. You would not find it printed that way in a real book.

After you have finished, you can read it out loud to him. In fact, he will probably demand that you read it over to him two or three times. This book will have great meaning for him, because he has produced it. It is genuinely *his own book*.

The title of this first book should contain your child's name: "Danny's Book." Print this on the cover, which you can make out of cardboard. Then beg, borrow, or steal a Polaroid camera. Take his picture and glue it on the cover. It is better to do this with a Polaroid camera because you are producing something from the camera at the very same time you are writing the book. That makes it more exciting. If you don't have access to a Polaroid camera, use a snapshot you have around the house. One way or another, get his picture on the cover. That will give this first book the uniqueness it deserves. The other books you and he do after this one can have titles derived from the subject matter, such as "My Pet Turtle" or "A Visit to My Grandmother's" or "Dinosaurs"; but the very first book should be titled by his name. Each book should say, after the title, the words "by Danny Jones," since your child is the author.

There is probably no single activity you could do with your child which does more to build his self-confidence in oral and written language than this method of writing his own books.

At first he will dictate the books to you. Later on, when he has learned to print well enough, he can print the book himself, with you telling him how to spell the words. When he is at the stage of printing the words himself, it is important that you not make any criticisms of turned-around letters or the way he divides words up when he comes to the end of a line and finishes the word on the next line. Pointing out any type of error will only discourage him at this point in his writing career. Your role at this stage is merely to accept and praise what he is able to do.

It is important that the subject matter and the sentence structure be entirely his, not yours. For example, when my oldest boy was four and had learned to print the whole alphabet, he wanted to write his first sentence. What do you think it was? Did he write "See Dick and Jane?" or "See Spot run?" No. His first sentence was about his older sister. His first sentence read: "Robin is a bad girl!"

When the subject matter and the form of the sentences truly comes from inside the child, he has a very powerful motive for wanting to write a book about that subject matter. You are sure it is something that interests and pleases him. As he learns he can first dictate a book to you and later print a book of his own, he becomes highly motivated to continue to develop both his oral and written language, because he wants to write more and more books.

If you have access to a Xerox or copying machine at a nearby library or business office, you can add something unique to the book-making process. Your child will be fascinated to find out that he can make copies of the pages of his own book! Now he will have extra copies to give to a friend, to send to his grandparents, or to take to nursery school. The praise he will probably get from other people to whom he sends his book will further motivate him to continue his preschool writing career. There is nothing dearer to the heart of an author, whether he is three or forty-three, than the praise of an audience!

The fourth thing you can do to stimulate your child's language development is to arouse his curiosity about words and the meaning of words.

This should be part of your everyday living with him. On trips to the store you can point out words on cereal packages or cookie packages or ice cream. Whenever you see a sign, you can call his attention to what the words say on the sign: Stop, No Left Turn, No Parking, For Sale, Toy Store, Ice Cream, Restaurant, and so forth. When you are watching TV with him, call his attention to words that are flashed on the screen. (This will help make some of the commercials bearable!) If you call his attention to words naturally and matter-of-factly in his everyday living, it will not be long before he will start asking you what a word says. Then you will know you have been successful in arousing his curiosity about words. This will become part of his motivation for wanting to learn to read.

TEACH YOUR CHILD TO READ

The fifth thing is to offer your child the potential opportunity of learning to read.

The single most important skill your child needs throughout his whole school career is reading. No matter what subject your child is studying, he has to be able to read. How well he reads and how much he likes to read will be a significant factor in how well he does in all his subjects.

Probably you are aware that there has been a great deal of controversy about the whole subject of learning to read. One aspect of the controversy concerns whether you should wait until children are six years old and in the first grade before teaching them to read, or whether they should be taught to read earlier. Another aspect of this controversy concerns whether a parent should try to teach a child to read before he enters school or whether only a schoolteacher is qualified to teach a child to read. Research by Dr. Dolores Durkin may throw some light on the answers to both these questions.

Dr. Durkin studied children who had learned to read before they entered school. She wanted to find out how these children had learned before being exposed to any formal reading instruction at school. She studied 5,103 first-grade children in the public schools of Oakland, California. Out of this group, forty-nine children had already learned to read at home before they entered first grade.

She followed the children through five grades, testing their reading achievement in each grade. This group of early readers stayed ahead of other children for all five grades. (This research finding would seem to refute the old wives tale that it does not do any good to teach children to read early since children who learn to read later catch up to them anyway.) Dr. Durkin's research furnishes evidence that the children who learn to read later do not catch up to the early readers, at least through the fifth grade, which is as far as she tested them.

How did these early readers get to be that way? Dr. Durkin found that they were not necessarily any different from other children in their intelligence or personality. *The difference was not in the children but in the parents, and specifically in the mothers.* The mothers provided a more stimulating home environment for their children. That's how they learned to read early. To take one specific example, every one of those forty-nine mothers had provided a blackboard in their home for their child to use, to draw and print on before he entered school.

In a second study in New York City, Dr. Durkin divided the children into an experimental group and a control group. The experimental group was composed of thirty children who had learned to read *before* they entered first grade. She compared them with a control group of thirty children who were not early readers, who could not read when they entered first grade. The two groups were matched individually for intelligence, as measured by the Stanford-Binet Intelligence Test. Since the two groups were equal in intelligence, that ruled out the possibility that one group learned to read early because those children were more intelligent than the children in the second group.

Once again, she compared the reading achievement of the early readers to the equally intelligent group of nonearly readers. The reading achievement of the early reader group was significantly higher. Moreover, they maintained this lead in reading achievement throughout the first three grades of school, which was the test period.

Here were two groups of children, both equal in intelligence. And Dr. Durkin asked herself the question: why does one group of children learn to read before first grade and the other one does not?

Is it the personalities of the children? No—Dr. Durkin obtained teacher's ratings on the personalities of the children, and found that children in both groups had the same kind of personalities. In fact, Dr. Durkin could not find *any* way in which the children in one group were basically different from the children in the other group. What was the difference between the two groups then? Why did one group of children learn to read early and the other one did not? Here we come to Dr. Durkin's significant finding: *the difference was not in the children at all; the difference was in the mothers of the children*. The mothers of the early readers provided a more stimulating home environment for their children than the mothers of the nonearly readers.

What did the mothers of the early readers do more of for their children at home than the other mothers did?

They read to their children before the children entered school.

They had materials around the home that stimulated their child's interest in reading. They had paper and pencils and felt pens for the child to scribble, draw, or print with. They had books, both bought and from the library. They had a blackboard in the home.

They stimulated their children's curiosity about the meaning of words. They would do this on trips to the market, while watching television together, or in other aspects of everyday living.

They explained the meaning of words to their children.

They helped their children learn to print.

These mothers were different from the other mothers not only in what they *did* with their child, but in *their beliefs*.

They believed that parents should give help with skills like reading to preschool children.

They challenged the belief that only a trained teacher should teach a child to read.

To put it a different way: The mothers of the children who did *not* learn to read early believed that only teachers in the schools should teach reading. The mothers of the early readers believed that it was a good thing for a mother to teach reading to her youngster in the home before he entered school.

All of the findings I have cited were quantified and expressed in the form of percentage differences between the two groups of mothers. These differences were found to be statistically significant. However, there was another important finding of Dr. Durkin's which could not be quantified so easily, but which Dr. Durkin found to be a genuine difference between the two groups of mothers. The mothers of the children who did *not* learn to read early characterized themselves as "busy." That word cropped up again and again in the way they spoke of themselves and their lives. They said they were too busy to do special things with their children. The mothers of the early readers did not speak of themselves in this way. However, when Dr. Durkin compared the two groups of mothers, she found that the mothers of the children who did not read early did not actually do more or have any more responsibilities than the mothers of the early readers.

The mothers of the early readers seemed to get a great deal of fun out of the things they did with their children. As one mother put it, "Gee, I enjoyed that child!" For example, a mother of a child who did not read early might take her youngster shopping and concentrate entirely on buying groceries. Basically her child was a nuisance who was interfering with her getting her shopping done quickly and efficiently. The mother of an early reader might have exactly the same responsibilities—buying groceries for the family—but she would make shopping a kind of adventure for her preschool child. She would say things like: "Let's see what these words say on the different cereal boxes. That one says Captain Crunch, and that one says Lucky Charms, and that one says Cocoa Puffs."

Dr. Durkin's research has shown that children *can* be taught to read early at home. She has shown that early readers forge ahead of other children in their classes and stay ahead in reading achievement, as far as she tested them in grade school (fifth grade). She has demonstrated that early readers are not some special kind of child. In personality, intelligence, and everything else, you can not tell early readers from nonearly readers. Rather, *early readers have a special kind of mother.*

The results of Dr. Durkin's research are thrilling in their implications for mothers of preschool children. They mean that if you want your child to become successful in school, you can do it! They mean that if you provide a stimulating environment for him in his preschool years, the probabilities are that he will become successful in school. I'm sure it did not escape your attention that the things the mothers of early readers did for their children are exactly the same things I have suggested in this chapter that you do for your child at home in his preschool years!

READING AND THE PRESCHOOL CHILD

Our society has tended to rigidly restrict the teaching of reading to our children who are six years old and in the first grade; yet there is clear research evidence that some children are mature enough to learn to read at age four, some at age five, some at age six, and some not until age seven or eight.

Given the fact that it is *possible* to teach children to read before first grade, the next question is: should you?

Since 1967, we have offered reading instruction to our kindergarten class at La Primera, using a unique set of programmed materials developed by Dr. W. A. Sullivan of Palo Alto. Our educational philosophy at La Primera Preschool is that children should not be pushed or pressured. We believe in what we call the "cafeteria theory" of education. As in a cafeteria, the child is free to choose or to reject whatever educational "dishes" appeal to him. Instruction in phonics, language development skills, and reading is merely one of a variety of educational dishes offered.

Thirteen children attended kindergarten at La Primera in 1967. All but one learned to read by the end of the year. It was not mandatory that a child learn to read in our kindergarten; we merely offered reading instruction.

Fifteen children attended our kindergarten in 1968, and all but two learned to read by the end of the year. By *learned to read* I mean that they could at least read on a first-grade level, and some of them could read up to third-grade level.

Last year we offered an experimental class in reading for four-year-olds. We specified to all of our parents that the class was definitely "experimental." Fourteen children were in the class. Two of them learned to read, one at first-grade level, and one very gifted child at fifth-grade level. The very least that the other twelve children gained were some word attack skills and background in phonics.

This year my youngest son, Rusty, is in the experimental class. Frankly we don't know whether he will learn to read by the end of the year or not, but we do know that he loves the class and hates to miss school if he is sick. I do know that he said to me the other day as we ate lunch at a family-type restaurant, "Daddy, Smorgasburger starts with *s!*"

I believe there are definite advantages, both intellectual and emotional to offering reading instruction to four and five-year-olds.

First, when a child learns to read at that age, it gives a terrific boost to his independence, self-reliance, and self-regulation. He can then read all kinds of signs and instructions and messages from our culture. This was amusingly illustrated by my son Randy when he first learned to read in kindergarten six years ago. We were out shopping and he developed an urgent call of nature. He announced proudly, pointing to the sign over the door, "That says 'men's room,' and I can go all by myself!"

Second, learning to read opens many intellectual doors for a child. He then has independent access to a great deal of information and enjoyment which was closed to him before he learned to read.

Third, if you expose a child to reading instruction at age four and again at age five before he enters first grade at age six, you may actually take pressure off him! How? Well, nobody demands that a four-year-old learn to read. Nobody demands that a five-year-old learn to read. But in our culture when a child reaches the magic age of six, our society, in effect, insists that he learn to read *during that one year!* If he does not, he feels like a failure. Isn't that pressure? If it is bad to pressure a child at age four or five, is it suddenly all right to pressure a child at age six?

Fourth, four and five-year-olds find phonics fun. They like repetition and they like playing with the sounds of language. Remember what I said in Chapter 6 about how fascinated the four-year-old is by language, words, and sounds? Four and five-year-olds can enjoy phonics training and repetition. But the same phonics materials that they welcomed enthusiastically at age four may be sheer drudgery when they are six.

The concept of "reading readiness," which was a very useful concept twenty-five years ago, has taken on mystical overtones. At the present time it often gets in the way of clear thinking. The following quotation from Dr. James Hymes, a leading authority in the field of early childhood education illustrates what I mean. Dr. Hymes has written many valuable books and articles on early childhood education. I enthusiastically recommend one of his books in Appendix E of *How to Parent*. I have heard him speak, and he is a great person. However, I must disagree with him when he says this:

> Inside of us there is a timetable. Our own personal rate of growing. . . . You couldn't keep him from crawling . . . not when he was one month but when he was old enough to crawl. You couldn't keep him from going up stairs . . . not when he was six months, but when he had grown enough to climb. You couldn't keep him from talking, not when he was ten months old, but when he had grown old enough to jabber. The same will hold true with reading.[30]

This quotation, which is typical of the position of many people in the field of early childhood education, speaks as if readiness to engage in crawling, walking, talking, or reading is due to some kind of mystical readiness inside a child. It totally ignores the influence of the environment on the development of a child's ability to learn these various skills.

The plain scientific truth is that you *can* delay a child's crawling. Remember Dr. Dennis' researches on the orphanages in Teheran from which I quoted in Chapter 2 on infancy? The bleak and stultifying orphanage environment did delay the crawling and walking of those infants. If we do not present a child the opportunity to learn some new skill, such as finger painting, riding a tricycle, or reading, we will at the very least delay his learning that new skill. But let's not say the reason he doesn't learn the skill is that he has not yet developed "readiness" for it. Let's admit that perhaps he hasn't learned the skill because we have not tried to teach him!

Many in the field of early childhood education say: "What's the rush? Why teach a child of four or of five to read when he has no 'readiness' for it? Why rob him of his childhood?" I want to point out that this argument is a double-edged sword. Suppose someone said (but no one has dared to!): "What's the rush about teaching a six-year-old to read? Maybe he doesn't have readiness yet either! So we'll continue to let him do other things in first grade, but we won't try to teach him to read." Would you buy that? I wouldn't. And I don't think a lot of other people would either. But the double-edged argument on "readiness" is exactly the same for the six or seven-year-old as it is for the five-year-old. "What's the rush?"

I infer from various scientific facts that there are intellectual advantages to teaching a four or five-year-old to read. But there are emotional advantages as well. Learning to read is a great boost to a child's self-concept. It increases his feelings of adequacy and self-confidence. This new skill enables him to read books, read signs, understand directions, and comprehend his world in a way he had not been able to do before.

So I say to those of the "What's the rush?" school of thought: *check your presuppositions!* We are viewing the same set of *facts*, but coming to different *conclusions*. One group comes to the conclusion that it is unwise to teach a preschooler to read even though there is scientific evidence it can be done. The group of which I consider myself an adherent concludes that on the whole it is a valuable thing to teach a preschooler to read, both for intellectual and emotional reasons. The two groups come to different conclusions from the same set of facts because the two groups begin from different presuppositions.

I feel quite comfortable in saying I believe it is a good thing to offer reading instruction to preschoolers in nursery and kindergarten. However, I must admit that I have reservations when it comes to the question of *parents* teaching their children to read.

It is bad to pressure a child to do anything, even to finger paint! And I know all too well there are many parents today pressuring their children for early academic achievement. They start this pressure even in the preschool years. I know this well because I have worked with children in therapy who have been academically pressured by their parents. As a consequence these children are under-achievers in school, as a way to unconsciously punish the parent for the early pressure. This kind of pressure can really backfire, with sad results for the child.

Some years ago, I happened to be browsing in the children's section of a local bookstore. A young mother came in and asked the clerk for "that book on how to teach babies to read." The clerk didn't know about the book, and I overheard the mother saying, "I've heard you can start teaching your child as young as ten months, and my little girl is already a year old!"

I had frightening fantasies of this mother just itching to get the book so she could start cramming reading down the throat of her year-old baby, and I mentally winced. It is ridiculous to try to teach a child that young to read. Even though I know the book, I didn't volunteer the information to the young mother.

If a mother tries to pressure her child into reading or into other forms of intellectual activity, she will end up doing more harm than good. This phenomenon was amusingly illustrated in a recent vignette called "My Life Story" by Sheila Greenwald:

> From the day I was born my parents have seen to it that I am a winner.
>
> When I was two years old I was taken to a cubicle in New Haven where they taught me to type. Two-year-olds can learn such things, and if they don't they merely waste their time. When two-year-olds who don't know how to type meet two-year-olds who do know how to type, they are overwhelmed and fall behind and are losers from then on.
>
> At two-and-a-half I was sent to a school where I play with learning equipment. I excell in carrot grating. My play time is not frivolous or wasted. I learn about textures and colors and relationships.

At three my mother taught me to read. Children of three can learn to read and if they don't they waste their time. They fall behind in school from the start and they are losers.

My parents never neglected the social side of my development. I have been exposed to children constantly. After school I attend play group. Relationships with one's contemporaries cannot start soon enough and are vital in the child's development. If these exposures to one's contemporaries don't begin soon enough, the child cannot cope with them when he starts grade school. He falls behind. He is a Loser.

I began to attend rhythm classes at three-and-one-half. I play drums and run like a pony, which strikes me as frivolous, but it instills something in me and I'll be a winner, rhythmically speaking.

Now that I'm four, I feel sure of my ground. When I enter the kindergarten of my choice in the fall, it will be with a sense of purpose and readiness to cope with all situations. I will be on my way as a winner.

When I grow up, I would like to be a garbage man.[81]

The delightful humor of this satire is not quite so humorous when you think of children across the United States whose anxious parents are subjecting them to pressures for early learning so that they can become a "wonder kid." I hope you will resist the temptation to pressure your child when you provide him with intellectual stimulation. You might succeed in pressuring a child into reading at an early age, only at the price of giving him emotional problems which bring him to a psychologist's office later. When in doubt, leave the kid alone!

MATHEMATICS STIMULATION FOR YOUR CHILD

In addition to language, mathematics is a vital area in which your child needs stimulation in his preschool years.

Unfortunately, when we get to this subject, we often run headlong into massive parental anxieties. Most parents feel quite comfortable in teaching their preschooler to print, sound out the letters of the alphabet, and so forth. They are on familiar ground doing these things.

But when it comes to math, many parents, unless they happen to be engineers or scientists, feel distinctly uneasy. Particularly since the arrival of the new math in the schools. Parents have heard about things like "set theory" and "base two" and "modular arithmetic" and other things that are entirely new to them. Their children, even in grade school, are learning to do arithmetic by methods which are quite different from the methods the parents learned when they were children. The net effect of this is to cause many parents to feel distinctly uneasy about the whole area of mathematics.

But you can relax. The way I'm going to suggest you teach math to your preschooler is one which assumes you know *nothing at all* about the subject. I'm going to suggest you teach math to your preschooler by using a parents' kit designed especially for that purpose. It is called the Cuisenaire Rods Parents Kit and can be obtained from the Cuisenaire Company of America (see Appendix A). You can begin using this kit when your child is three years old. You will find it a delightful and fascinating thing to use—you will probably even wish you had learned math and arithmetic when you were a child by playing games with different colored rods the Cuisenaire way.

HOW TO TEACH YOUR CHILD TO COUNT

In addition to the use of the Cuisenaire Rods kit, you can teach your child to count. But this is by no means as simple as it seems.

Many parents are under the illusion that they have taught their preschool child to count. They say: "Show Uncle Jimmy how you can count to twenty, Richard!" Richard will obligingly reel off the numbers from one to twenty and Uncle Jimmy will be duly impressed. But if Uncle Jimmy placed twenty buttons in front of Richard and said, "Richard, let's see if you can count these buttons from one to twenty," Mother and Dad would quickly realize the vast difference between genuinely teaching a child to count, and merely teaching him to sound off the numbers from one to twenty! Teaching a child to mimic words like *one, two,* and *three,* without really understanding what he is saying, is not the same as teaching him to count.

Counting is such a basic operation in arithmetic and mathematics that it is very much worth taking the time and trouble to teach your child this important skill. As with teaching him to print, you can begin when he is about three years old. The original ideas for the method I am going to explain to you were obtained from Siegfried and Therese Engelmann's excellent book, *Give Your Child a Superior Mind;* I wish to acknowledge their gracious courtesy in permitting me the use of their material.

You will need some objects such as buttons, poker chips, or blocks. Suppose, for example, we use buttons.

Spread three buttons (no more) in front of your child, leaving a lot of space between them, so they are easy to see and he doesn't get confused. Explain to your child the rules of this new game, which you can call "The Counting Game." (Remember I have said that it is always wise to present a learning situation to a child in the form of a game.) Tell your child: "You must touch each button with your finger, but you can only touch it one time. When your finger touches a button you must give it a number."

"Okay, let's start. We want to find out how many buttons we have here. I put my finger on the first button and say, 'one.' Next, I move my finger to the next button and say 'two,' and then on to the next and say 'three.' So we have three buttons. We see three; we touch three."

"Now we are going to do it again. But first we are going to move the buttons around and mix them all up. The reason I'm moving the buttons around is so that you will not think that 'one' or 'three' is always the name for this red button or this green button. 'One' is always the name of the *first* button we touch, regardless of what color or size it is. And 'two' is always the name for the *second* button we touch, regardless of what color or size it is."

Incidentally, be sure to always count the buttons from left to right, because that is the way we read and count in English, from left to right on a page.

Continue playing this counting game several times. Then let the child do it himself, with a little help from you. Take his finger and place it on the button and count "one." Have him say "one" out loud. After doing it together a few times, let him try it alone. If he doesn't succeed, help him once again, until he has mastered the counting procedure. Praise him, but don't force him or pressure him. Play the game for about five minutes or so, no longer, even if he is learning very quickly.

Try to play the game with him once a day. After the child has it down pat with three buttons, gradually add buttons, until he can count to ten.

Whenever there is an opportunity to play the counting game with other things, do it. Take advantage of any spontaneous opportunities that present themselves to count things. But be sure that things you count, such as keys or apples or oranges, are all physically present at the same time. Otherwise the counting game will be too difficult for your child. For example, to count the stop lights or the number of trucks you pass on the road as you are driving is too difficult. All of the objects are not present at the same time. Stick to counting things such as the oranges or apples or boxes of cereal you buy in the market.

After you have been playing the counting game for three or four months, add a new rule to the game. Have your child pick up each item, while he is counting, and put it in a pile. If he does this correctly, all of the items will be gone from their original position and be in a new pile. First you show him how to do this, and then let him try it by himself.

After he has mastered this variation of the counting game, introduce a new twist on the game. Place ten buttons on the floor. We want him to stop counting at five. Show him how to do it. Pick up one, two, three, four, five buttons, counting each one aloud as you pick it up.

Then say: "Okay, now it's your turn. Count to five and stop after you say 'one,' 'two,' 'three,' 'four,' 'five.'" If he is successful, praise him. If not, show him one more time, and let him have one more turn. Your child may have trouble with this new aspect of the counting game, but be gentle and patient with him and he will gradually catch on.

Counting from six to ten is harder for a child of three than the early phases of "The Counting Game" you played with him. Don't worry; it will come, with practice on his part and patience on your part. By using concrete objects he can manipulate in learning to count, your child will be able to learn the basic principles of counting. If you begin teaching him at age three, by the time he is four he will probably have mastered the basic principles of counting.

Notice that both of the mathematical games you have been playing with your preschooler ("The Cuisenaire Rods Game" and "The Counting Game") have been based upon concrete objects that he can manipulate. Preschool children can learn a great deal of math when it is based upon the manipulation of concrete objects and materials. But their ability to learn math in the abstract at this age is quite limited. One of the reasons why so many children and adults have trouble with arithmetic and math is that they were expected to learn it by manipulating abstract numbers and symbols on a piece of paper. They should have had previous years of experience in manipulating concrete objects and materials.

Notice the difference between children learning language and children learning mathematics. Children generally have much less trouble with language than they have with math. And there are two reasons for this.

First, language involves thinking with words, whereas mathematics involves thinking with numbers and shapes. One reason language is easier for children is that children are given much more practice in thinking with words than in thinking with numbers and shapes. If we gave our children anywhere near the time and practice in thinking with numbers and shapes that we gave them in thinking with words, our children would all be much more proficient in math than they are. Our children are subjected to a "verbal bombardment" of words from our culture in the form of television, radio, newspapers, magazines, and books. The bombardment of numbers and shapes is much, much less than the bombardment of words.

Second, we expect our children to learn arithmetic and math without giving them adequate experience in manipulating concrete materials and objects, out of which they can learn the abstract principles of arithmetic and math. Children who have played with the Cuisenaire Rods and counted out buttons for several years as preschoolers are much better prepared to learn arithmetic and math than children who have not had this type of concrete experience with mathematical objects and materials.

LEARNING THE NUMBER SYMBOLS

Now you can show your youngster how to write the number symbols he is counting. I suggest you do this when your child is about four years old or a few months before.

Write the symbols 0 through 10 on a large piece of cardboard and hang it in your child's room. You can also write the number symbols on his blackboard, or in crayon on a large piece of paper. Help him to learn to identify the symbols and then to write them himself.

If you live where your child can watch "Sesame Street" on television, you can coordinate teaching him the numbers with the timing of the teaching of the numbers on the program. They do a superb job of teaching the numbers up to ten on that program.

(Incidentally, you as parents should be aware that there is a difference between a *number* and a *numeral*. Your child will learn about this difference when he studies the new math in grade school. I have not gone into this difference here, because there is no real need for parents to explain this difference to a preschool child. It is a difficult distinction for a preschooler to grasp, but one which he can grasp easily in grade school. Even if you happen to know that we should really speak of the "numeral 3" or the "numeral 6" rather than "number 3" or "number 6," don't try to explain it to your preschooler. Let him find out about that abstract concept when he is older and in grade school.)

Give each symbol its name. "The name of this symbol is 'one.' "

It is especially helpful to a child learning the number symbols to have concrete materials to work with. Creative Playthings has a set of wooden numbers (Appendix A) which your child can use. He can trace around the wooden number symbols with his pencil and can feel the shape with his fingers. You can also make sandpaper number symbols like the sandpaper letters. Cut the symbol out of sandpaper and glue it onto a cut out piece of cardboard and have the child trace the shape of the symbols with his finger.

Help your child learn to write the number symbols on paper with a felt pen or crayon, or on the blackboard with chalk. Point out the distinguishing characteristics of each symbol:

0 looks like the letter *O*.

1 looks like a small letter *l*.

2 is curved on top and has a flat bottom.

3 is made up of two backwards letters *C* on top of each other.

4 is like a letter *l*, with a funny arm on one side.

5 is flat on top and curved on the bottom.

6 is a big curve, with an *O* at the bottom.

7 is flat on top, with a diagonal slash below the top.

8 is like an *O* at the top, with another *O* beneath it.

9 is like an *O* at the top, with a big curve underneath it.

10 is a one and a zero side by side.

Many of these number symbols are going to be harder for your child to learn to write than many of the alphabet letters. The configuration of the number symbols is more complicated than most of the alphabet letters. Be patient with him as he struggles to master these new symbols— particularly when he makes the common mistakes which preschool children make, such as confusing 6 and 9.

While the child is learning to write the symbols, you can play games with him in which he locates and identifies the symbols. Use the cardboard with all of the symbols on it. Point to different ones and say: "What symbol is this?" If he gets it, say: "That's good." If he misses, say: "That's a seven," and move on to another symbol.

Vary the game by asking him to locate the symbols. "Find me a four. Good. Now find me an eight."

The final step in learning the number symbols involves taking the symbol out of its familiar context. Now, instead of using all ten symbols printed in a row, use only a blackboard and chalk, or crayons and paper. Say: "I'm going to write a number down. See if you can tell me what it is." If he gets it, say "Good." If he misses, say: "No, that was a four. Let's try another one."

It is very important that your child grasp the fact that

zero is a number. Many parents are not clear about this, and think *zero* and *nothing* or *none* mean the same thing. They do not. This can be seen quite clearly if you think of the difference between the number 43 and the number 403. In 43 there is "nothing" between the four and the three. So the number symbol stands for four tens and three ones. In 403 there is a zero between the four and the three. So the number symbol stands for four one hundreds and three ones. Quite a difference!

The use of rhymes like the following will help you explain to your child the concept that zero is a number:

> Five enormous dinosaurs
> Letting out a roar;
> One went away
> And then there were four.
>
> Four enormous dinosaurs
> Crashing down a tree;
> One went away
> And then there were three.
>
> Three enormous dinosaurs
> Eating tiger stew;
> One went away
> And then there were two.
>
> Two enormous dinosaurs
> Having lots of fun;
> One went away
> And then there was one.
>
> One enormous dinosaur
> Afraid to be a hero;
> He went away
> And then there was—zero!

You can also ask your child humorous questions which will help him to grasp the concept that zero is a number. For example, ask him: "Billy, how many tigers do you have in your pocket?" or "How many alligators are there sitting in the living room?"

One of the best ways to teach number concepts to

children is through games involving the use of dice. One good game is Skunk, which uses a special set of dice which have a skunk where the *1* spot on the dice should be. Parcheesi or Sorry or other board games which involve the use of dice and counting to move players across a board are also helpful. If you are playing Parcheesi with your preschooler, he may shake a two and a four on the dice and then count out "one," "two," and then "one," "two" "three," "four," as he moves his marker six spaces. But before you know it he has learned to say "six" after rolling the dice, without the intermediate counting steps he used at first.

You can make your own homemade dice and marker game. Buy a pair of dice. Then get a large sized piece of cardboard or posterboard, say two feet by three feet. Decide with your child what kind of a game you and he want to make. Suppose, for example, he likes race cars. With a felt pen, you can lay out on the cardboard a racetrack, divided into segments, with a segment labeled "Starting Line" and one labeled "Finish Line." At odd intervals print instructions on some of the segments such as "Go back three spaces," "Go ahead four spaces," or "Go to the finish line." Purchase some small metal automobiles at a toy store for markers and you are ready to go. Your child will love the game because he and you made it yourselves, and he will learn much arithmetic playing it.

Roulette and bingo are two other games from which a child can absorb basic mathematical concepts quite painlessly. When playing bingo, call out the numbers in this fashion: "twenty-three; that's two, three."

If you play Cuisenaire Rod games and counting and dice games with your youngster between the ages of three and six, he will enter first grade with a great deal of experiential background in arithmetic and mathematics. This rich background should help him greatly with his math in grade school.

In this chapter, I have tried to suggest a number of things you can do with your child in the preschool years to maximize his intellectual development, to expose him to a stimulating intellectual environment, without making him feel pushed or pressured. Now let's look at the parental problem of teaching technique.

TEACHING TECHNIQUES FOR PARENTS

How can you, as a parent, know if you are, in fact, pressuring your child? A good rule of thumb is this: When a child indicates lack of interest in any game or activity, drop it immediately. To continue with a game or activity beyond that point is to pressure the child.

Preschoolers have short attention spans. For that reason, many of the intellectual games I have suggested in this chapter should not be played for more than five minutes at a time. Your idea of time and his are two entirely different things. Keep the game time short and he will continue to enjoy it. Of course, if it is quite clear that he is thoroughly enjoying playing a particular game and he protests loudly at stopping, it's all right to go over the five minutes and continue the game. You can rely on common sense about when to stop in such cases. The main point I'm trying to make is this: It is better to err on the side of making the game too short, than dragging it out for too long with an unwilling child whose attention span has lapsed.

Punishment has absolutely no place when you are teaching a child something. Never scold or punish your child for making mistakes or not understanding something you are trying to explain to him.

If you are presenting some task or concept to your child and he doesn't seem to understand it, don't worry about it. Decide that one of two things must be happening. Either he is too young to understand that concept or task at this time, or you haven't presented it to him in a form that he can understand. Don't keep at him with that task or concept, but move on to something else.

Above all, remember that learning should be fun. Don't give your child the feeling that everything you and he do together has to be "educational" or to improve his mind. If any of the things I have suggested in this chapter turns out not to be fun for you to do with your preschooler, forget it. You will not be doing either him or you a favor by mentally gritting your teeth and continuing with the activity, all the while thinking to yourself: "I hate doing this, but I've got to, because it's helping to give him a higher IQ!" The things you and your child do together should be mutually enjoyable. As the poet John Masefield says: "The days that make us happy, make us wise."

13

How to Select Toys, Books, and Records for Your Child

Parents are concerned with what is being taught their children. The school curriculum is an area bitterly contested by parents, yet it is astounding that those same vitally concerned parents seem uninterested in the "curriculum" of the home. Their lack of interest is shown by the rather haphazard manner in which they select toys and books and phonograph records for their children. If you think about it, the curriculum of the home is as important as the curriculum of the school. Before your child enters kindergarten or first grade, the curriculum of the home is the only curriculum he has.

A basic research discovery of psychologists and educators is that your child is learning something *all* the time, not just the time he spends in so-called formal learning in school. A second basic research discovery is that the main way in which preschool children learn anything is through play. Therefore, it is important to select with care the toys, books, and records we give him to play with. Toys and books and records are the textbooks of the preschool years.

Since your child is learning all of the time, what he will

learn in his home play will depend upon what kind of play equipment you provide, how much you know how to play with him, and how much you know how to teach him to play by himself. That second point will come as a shock to many parents: the idea that either parents or children need to *learn* to play. Most parents take for granted the idea that their child knows how to play. Psychologists do not take this for granted. Psychologists say that children need to learn how to play. A three-year-old does not have the innate ability to build complex and interesting structures in his block play, or to build towns and cities cooperatively with another youngster in block play. This is something he has to *learn* to do.

It is undoubtedly much easier for a young child to learn to play by himself or with other children than for a parent to learn to play with that young child. The parent needs to get off his adult high horse and get down to the child's level in play. This is not easy for many parents. We need to learn to play games with a young child, to make up spontaneous games, to tell stories and read books to him. There is an art to all of these activities. They are learned skills.

But there are few activities more enjoyable than learning the art of play. Most of the time, it will be a two-way street. When we play with a young child, we learn from him and he learns from us. For many parents, playing with a young child offers a wonderful opportunity to recapture things they missed in childhood.

One of the first things a parent needs to learn is how to buy toys for her child. Parents in the United States spend more than two billion dollars annually on toys. Unfortunately, much of this money is wasted. Why?

First, many toys are poorly designed, produced by people who know little about children, psychology, or education.

Second, the truly creative toy designers are handicapped by merchandising and marketing pressures from large firms. A friend who is a creative toy designer says he gets a headache every year when he goes to Chicago for a preview of his firm's toy line by a particular mass merchandiser. The mass merchandiser will say, "That toy's too expensive; you've got to cut the price down by two dollars." To do so may knock out many of the creative features of the toy, but the mass merchandiser could care less.

Third, it is hard for the small-but-good toy manufacturers to compete with the giants in the field and their mass advertising techniques. I think, for example, of a small firm such as Princeton Educational Toys, which has very creative and wonderful toys designed by Eugène de Christopher. How difficult it is for a small but creative firm like this to compete with the giants in the field of toy making.

Fourth, the toys may be good toys, but the parent doesn't know enough about child development to give the right toy to the right child at the right age. For example, a father gave his three-year-old son an Erector Set. The Erector Set is a good toy, but it should be given to a child when he is eight or nine. A three-year-old does not have the small muscle dexterity to cope with an Erector Set. The child, after trying a number of times to put the pieces together, became frustrated and gave up. The next Christmas, when his father got him Baufix, a wooden construction toy quite suitable for a four-year-old, the boy would have nothing to do with it. He remembered his frustrations with the Erector Set, and he wouldn't touch any construction toy that remotely resembled that Erector Set.

What is a "good toy"?

First of all, a good toy is safe. It does not have sharp edges or toxic paint. It is not made out of material that is easily shattered or splintered. It does not have small pieces on which a child can choke.

Second, a good toy is durable. The durability of a toy depends on the age and personality of the child who plays with it. But, in general, plastic and tin toys are the least durable; wood and sturdy metal, the most durable. However, you have to discriminate among different kinds of wood. I think of some expensive imported wooden toys which will splinter and break after two or three rough play sessions with a preschool child. The hardwoods, of course, are more durable than the softwoods. A visit to a good nursery school would be very educational for a parent who wants to learn about the durability of toys. Toys in nursery school get a lot of hard play and rough treatment. They *have* to be durable over years of play.

Third, if 90 percent of the play is in the child and 10 percent of the play is in the toy, it is a good toy. If 90 percent of the play is in the toy, and 10 percent of the play is in the child, it is a poor toy.

Contrast a push-button, battery-operated toy with a set of wooden blocks. A little boy is given a battery-operated dog which will walk across the floor and wag its tail when the button is pushed. Here 90 percent of the play is in the toy. All the boy can do with the toy is to push the button. (Except to take the toy apart and destroy it, which is usually the next step in playing with such a toy.) With a set of blocks the situation is quite different; here, 90 percent of the play is in the child. The blocks are not so rigidly structured that the child can do only one thing with them. The possibilities of what the child can make out of the blocks are almost endless.

This third criterion of a good toy indicates a whole new approach to toys that parents need to grasp. The more the child has to do and the less the toy does for him, the more the child develops his self-confidence and creativity, and the more the child learns by playing with the toy. The less the child has to do, and the more the toy does for him, the less the child develops his own creativity and self-confidence, and the less the child learns by playing with the toy.

Once you have grasped this principle, you can see why a large cardboard box, big enough for a child to crawl into, is such an ideal toy. The box is abstract rather than specific, so it can be many things—a boat, a fort, an igloo, a submarine, an airplane, a robot. It stimulates and enriches a child's powers of inventiveness. He can use it as it comes originally. He can cut holes in it at appropriate places. He can color it with crayons or paint it. There are few toys which you can buy in a toy store with the play value of a large cardboard box; yet how many parents make regular trips to a market or furniture store to take home, at no cost to themselves, such a large cardboard box?

Fourth, a good toy is fun. A toy may be educational, but if it's not fun, it's not a good toy. We must distinguish between immediate fun and fun over the long term.

There is no doubt that a push-button, battery-operated toy is a source of immediate fun for a preschooler. He will push the button and delightedly watch the car or animal zip around the room or do whatever it does when its button is pushed. However, a few hours of this and the fun has vanished; the lure of that toy has worn off. A set of wooden blocks, however, can be fun to play with day after day after day; they are fun in the long-term sense.

Fifth, the toy must be suitable to the age and stage of development of the child. Here a parent needs knowledge of what sorts of toys suit youngsters in general at a certain age and stage of development. This is the type of information to be found in Gesell's *Infant and Child in the Culture of Today* and in Goldenson and Hartley's *The Complete Book of Children's Play*.

But a parent needs to know more than what kinds of toys children in general like at certain ages. She also needs to know *her particular child*, and her child's likes and dislikes. Her four-year-old is not four-year-old-children-in-general. He is like no other four-year-old on this planet. Each parent needs to ask herself: "Does it suit his age and stage of development? Is it suitable for his sex, as a boy or girl? Does it fit his individual set of play interests? Is it suitable for his physical size? Can he handle it himself or is it a toy he will need help with?"

When you are selecting toys for a preschooler, remember that the smaller the child, the bigger the toy should be to suit his immature stage of development. Preschoolers, in comparison to older children, need bigger blocks, bigger and fatter crayons and pencils, bigger paint brushes, and bigger nuts and bolts to unscrew on construction toys. (In Appendix A you will find a list of toys classified according to children's ages and stages of development. This should help you select toys for your child.)

When buying toys for their children, many shy away from certain good toys because the parent feels the toy is too expensive. We need to think clearly about exactly what an "expensive" toy is. If you buy a ninety-eight-cent plastic truck for your child, at first glance that seems to be an inexpensive toy. But if twenty minutes after you give it to him your child has managed to break it so that further play is out of the question, then that ends up being an expensive toy you bought for him.

If a parent adds up the cost of all the cheap, easily broken plastic toys that she buys at a market or drugstore, she would be surprised at the amount. For the same amount of money she could purchase a number of durable, well-built, creative but "expensive" toys. Six ninety-eight-cent plastic toys that last a week cost the same amount as one $5.95 durable wooden or metal toy that can last for years.

For example, suppose that you had $60—and only $60—which you could afford to spend for toys for your preschooler for a period of three years. I would advise you to buy only two toys with that money—the outdoor Dome Climber and the Indoor Gym House for $29.95 each. A toy priced at $29.95 is not a cheap toy. But when you consider all the play value that is in those two toys over a period of several years, those toys are cheap at the price.

Approximately 40 percent of all the toys parents buy for their children are bought at Christmas. As all of us parents know if we are really honest with ourselves, we tend to overbuy toys at Christmas. This holds true not merely for wealthy families, but for families with incomes all the way up and down the economic scale. Go ahead and buy the number of toys you are accustomed to buying for your children for Christmas. I wouldn't deprive you or myself or any parent of the fun of doing that. But don't give your child all of these toys at Christmas. Save about 40 to 50 percent of them and give them to him at spaced intervals in the next two or three months after Christmas. (He will still probably have plenty of toys at Christmas, when you consider the toys he will get from grandparents and relatives.) He will get more play value out of these toys if they are spaced out after Christmas than he could possibly get by having them added to the huge oversupply of toys spread around him on the floor Christmas day.

Don't forget that the most important "toy" in the life of your child, the "toy" he likes to play with more than any other, that will influence him more powerfully than any other is that unique, flesh-and-blood toy—you! His play with you means a thousand times more to your child than his play with any toy. Hundreds of wonderful and shining toys are no substitute for emotionally satisfying times when you and he play together.

As I indicated in Chapter 5, the second most important "toy" in the life of your child will be found in your living room or family room. It plugs into the wall, has a picture tube and different channels, and it is called a television set.

As I have mentioned earlier, I am aware of the inane and mediocre fare of many TV programs, and I want to see the violence on TV kept at a low level. Nevertheless, with all of the furor about what's wrong with television programs, it is important we not overlook the positive values a child can reap from watching TV. Television, for example, is excellent for raising a child's vocabulary level and stimulating his language development. Research studies have shown that the oral language vocabulary of children entering kindergarten and first grade has increased enormously since the advent of TV in the American home. These are positive values and should not be overlooked by parents. If even the low quality of today's TV shows stimulate a preschool child's vocabulary and language development, how much more could be accomplished by really top-notch television shows for preschool children such as "'Sesame Street"?

Even with all of its shortcomings, television is still a marvelous educational toy for your child, and it is a mistake to take a completely passive attitude toward it as so many parents do. Take the time to watch some TV programs with your child and find out which programs are the best. In addition to "Sesame Street," I think of excellent programs such as "Captain Kangaroo," "Misterogers Neighborhood," "Friendly Giant," and "H. R. Pufnstuf." Find ways to psychologically reinforce your child for watching good TV programs such as these. Your being with him to watch the program together is one kind of reward or reinforcement. What you are doing, in various subtle ways, is teaching your child to be *selective* in watching.

Now don't go to extremes about this and give him the impression you think it's a federal offense to watch a program you happen to think is junk. By a little judicious reinforcement you can steer his watching in certain directions. Television is too potentially valuable an educational toy to take a completely laissez faire attitude toward it. When you encounter good TV programs, write a brief fan letter to the show and the sponsor. Your votes, in the form of fan letters, help to keep good children's shows on TV.

SELECTING BOOKS FOR CHILDREN

Let's talk about how to select books for children. Some of you may feel: "Why make such a big production out of this? You just get your child some books he'll enjoy reading, and read them to him, and that's it. What difference does it make what kind of books you select for him?"

A study done by Dr. George Gallup shows you what a difference it makes. Dr. Gallup studied the book-reading and book-buying habits of adults in the United States, and he came to the conclusion that adult Americans do not particularly like to read or buy books.

He studied a representative sample of three groups of people: those who were high school graduates, those who had attended college but not graduated, and those who were college graduates. He found that 50 percent of the high school graduate group had not read a book during the previous year. Forty-six percent of those who had attended college but not graduated had not read a book during the previous year. Approximately one-third of the college graduates had not read a book all the way through during the previous year. Dr. Gallup comments: "These figures give small comfort to those who defend the present system of education in America."[32] Furthermore, when the book-reading habits of the people of the United States are compared with those of Great Britain, Germany, Holland, Switzerland, France, and the Scandinavian countries, the United States stands at the bottom of the list.

In another research sampling of adults in the United States, Dr. Gallup found that nearly two-thirds of the adults reported that they had not read a single book all the way through during the previous year (excluding the Bible and textbooks). Furthermore, only one adult out of six could think of any recently published book he would especially like to read.[33]

The book-buying habits of the American public are also an indication of how well Americans have been taught a love of reading and of books. At first glance, it would seem that America is a country of avid book readers, if you merely consider the impressive number of both hardcover and paperback books sold in America. However, when you examine the figures closely, you find that in reality one adult in five accounts for more than 80 percent of all books bought and read in the United States. What these figures show is that a small proportion of adults in the United States love books and reading. If this situation is to be changed, as Dr. Gallup puts it, "Interest in books, for most persons, must be carefully nurtured."[34]

It is in the first five years of life that the basic foundations of a love of books and of reading can be established. That is the time to begin the careful nurture of the book-reading and book-buying habit.

Among the things American schools are supposed to teach children is the habit of reading and enjoying books. From Dr. Gallup's figures, it is clear that, in fact, the American school system fails miserably in doing this with a large percentage of school children. Therefore you cannot rely upon the schools your children attend to do the job. If your child is to develop the habit of reading books and to continue this habit when he becomes an adult, you as a parent will have to get this habit started and see that it continues. The most important time in which to get this habit started is in those all-important first five years, before your child even sets foot in school.

Teaching your child to love books follows the same basic principles of learning we talked about in earlier chapters. Your child will learn to love books and to enjoy reading and buying books if you reward and reinforce him for doing these things.

From this follows a very basic principle: "Don't worry what your child is reading as long as he's reading. Any piece of printed matter that your child wants to read and enjoys reading, whether it is a book, magazine, newspaper, or comic strip, is good for him to read. This particularly holds true for children beyond the age of six. Parents sometimes feel: "Oh, he's just reading trash—comic books and trashy novels—I want him to read good literature." Don't worry about it—the "trash" he's reading must satisfy some psychological need in him at this time, and that's okay. As long as he continues reading, his taste will gradually improve. Of course, the so-called problem of reading trash doesn't arise in the preschool years, because what he "reads" will be what you select to read to him. (Or, if he learns to read before the age of six, what you select for him to read himself.) And what you select to read to him in these preschool years will have a great deal to do with how much he loves to read in later life.

How should you select books for him? Select a balance of nonfiction and fiction to read to him. (In Appendix C you will find a list of excellent books of both nonfiction and fiction.) He needs a balanced diet of books just as he needs a balanced diet of food. Reading only nonfiction leaves his creative imagination underdeveloped. Reading only fiction and fantasy neglects the use of reading as an avenue of understanding the real world he lives in.

He needs to strike a balance between borrowing books from the library and buying books of his own for his growing home library. Many parents make the mistake of confining all of the books their child reads to library books because it saves them money that way. Those same parents who are "saving money" by not buying books for their child, will buy toys for him at Christmas. If a parent does this, whether she is aware of it or not, she is teaching the child: "Toys are more important than books, because we buy you toys to keep, but we never buy you books to keep." And a child, particularly a preschool child, needs books to keep—books he can feel are his very own.

It is difficult for a child to grow up really valuing books if he never has any books of his own, never enjoys the thrill of building up his own personal library as he adds to it book by book over the years. Just as a child has special toys that he loves to play with again and again, so should he have the opportunity to have special books that he reads over and over. When a child is sick and has to stay home from school, it is then that he likes to play with old familiar, favorite toys. It is at such a time that he should also be able to read old familiar, favorite books. No matter what your economic circumstances are, some part of the money you spend on your child should go for books for him.

If you have taught your child to discover all of the pleasure that he can get through reading, he will open his books again and again and again. Even if you could only afford to buy your child five paperback books a year, buy him those books and let them become a part of his growing little library. If you bought him only five books a year, and continued this habit until he graduated from high school, at that time he would have eighty-five books in his personal library. And that would be eighty-five more books than a lot of American children have in their own library when they graduate from high school!

Due to the electronic revolution wrought by television, it is harder to develop a love of books and reading in children today. When I was a young boy there was no such thing as TV. And I loved to read books. But if I had a choice of going to the neighborhood movie or reading a book, it was no contest. The movie won hands down. Only now the "neighborhood movie" is in the home, instantly available, and we call it television. Parents have to take more time and effort to see that their children love to read books than they did in the days before TV.

One of the best ways of insuring that your preschool child loves books and everything connected with them is to make certain that the library and your local bookstore are places he associates with pleasure and good things. He should think of the librarian and the owner of the bookstore as friends. The personal touch is important to preschool children. It is worth your while as a parent to see that the librarian and the bookstore owner take a personal interest in your child. You want to associate a visit to the library or bookstore with pleasant things in your child's mind.

Many parents today are frankly confused and bewildered by the vast array of children's books from which they are expected to select books for their child. I have taken this into account and provided in Appendix C a comprehensive list of books which are excellent for preschool children. I want to emphasize that you should not use this list of recommended books, or any other list, in a blind fashion. Before you buy any book on this list for your child, or even before you get one of these books out of the library for him, look it over yourself first. *Probably the single most important criterion of selecting books to read to preschoolers is that the parent should like the book herself.* If the book "speaks" to you, it will speak to your child. But if you don't enjoy it, chances are your child won't enjoy having you read it to him. In this sense there can be no infallible list of recommended books for children, because not only is each child unique in his taste, but each parent is unique in her taste.

Sometimes parents are horrified to find that children's

hardback books are priced at $3.95 and $4.95 and up. They think: "That's an awful lot of money for a short book that my child is going to read only once." That's where the parent is wrong. A young child may take his beloved Mother Goose book to bed with him and look at the pictures and have you read it to him for months. A four-year-old may want to have you read *Horton Hatches the Egg* by Dr. Seuss over and over again. Children get a great deal of mileage out of a book they really cherish.

This brings me to another topic related to books and their cost. Perhaps it is due to the cost of children's books. Perhaps it is due to some kind of reverence for the printed word. But many times we parents tend to expect a child to be very adult in his care of the books we buy him. We expect him not to mark the book, get it dirty, or tear it. Why is this? When we buy a preschooler a toy, we fully expect that it will be given hard usage. In fact, the more beloved the toy, the more wear and tear it will get. Why can't we learn to feel that way about books too? The books our preschooler loves the most will be the ones which will show the most wear and tear. That's as it should be. If we are constantly after our child to keep his books looking spotless, we will discourage him from becoming familiar and comfortable with his books.

One factor that will help us keep the cost of children's books at a manageable level is the growing number of quality paperback books for children. However, even though more and more publishers are putting out good quality paperback books for children, it is still difficult for many parents to find them because only a few stores carry them. If you do not live near a bookstore which carries a good selection of children's paperbacks, your solution may be to buy by mail. You can deal with Scholastic Book Services, 904 Sylvan Avenue, Englewood Cliffs, New Jersey, or 5675 Sunol Boulevard, Pleasanton, California. Ask for their free Reader's Choice catalog, which lists more than 500 good paperbacks for children.

We should provide bookshelves in our child's room for his growing library. The easiest type to construct are those built, from the floor up, of concrete blocks or bricks, with boards laid across the bricks for shelving, making it easy to adjust the height of the shelves to suit the books. Such construction is particularly helpful with a bookcase for preschoolers, since children's books are often large or out-sized and do not fit in a conventional bookcase. Also, you can easily take this bookcase apart and move it if you need to.

Books can have a tremendous impact on a preschool child. When you read him a book, what goes in one ear does not come out the other. It stays imbedded in his memory. A research study by Dr. George Gallup found that children who are read to regularly by their mothers at an early age do better in school than those who are not read to at an early age. Dr. Gallup studied 1,045 mothers and found that 79 percent of high-achieving first graders were read to regularly in their early years, as compared to 49 percent of low achievers in first grade.[35]

Your youngster's years of childhood are limited. You can't read *The Tale of Peter Rabbit* to a ten-year-old; he is beyond it. He has missed it for life unless you have read it to him in his early years. This is why your wise selection of books for him in his preschool years is so important to his education and development.

SELECTING RECORDS FOR A CHILD

Next we come to an area where many parents feel very unsure of themselves: the area of children's records. Parents buy far fewer records and tapes for their children than they buy toys and books, because the average parent feels on much shakier ground in selecting records for her child than in selecting toys or books.

But before we talk about how to wisely select records for your child, let's talk about his record player. Remember, I suggested that you buy your child a simple "push-in" type of record player or tape player, along with a number of inexpensive records. Don't worry too much about the quality of these records; you can't get much quality for twenty-nine cents or eighty-eight cents. The purpose of these inexpensive records and record player is so that your child can play these records by himself, whenever he wants to. He does not need your help to play the records. Also, you don't have to worry about whether he scratches the record or how he handles it.

However, there should be good long-playing records,

which you should play for your child on the family record player or tape player. Do not let him play these records. These are records that *you* play for him. These are the records that you need to select carefully.

It is a sad fact that most of the children's records bought by parents are what I call "kiddie records." The kiddie records are designed and packaged to appeal to parents, not children, since the record manufacturers know all too well that it is parents who buy the records. However, these types of "cute" records do not do much for children. Typically, they are too fast, trite, and over-orchestrated, with a large orchestra or chorus. If you browse in the Children's Records section of the average record store, you will find, unfortunately, that many of the records are of this sort.

What are the criteria you should look for in buying children's music records? First, the music should be simple, rather than elaborate or ornate. Second, it should not be too cluttered up with orchestration or big choruses. Third, the tune or rhythm should be catchy and appeal to children.

In Appendix D you will find a list of recommended records for preschoolers. As you listen to these records with your child, analyze them in terms of these three criteria. The criteria will become more meaningful to you as you can hear them illustrated and exemplified in the records.

What are some of the different categories of records for preschool children?

First, folk songs. A good folk song for children will meet all of the above criteria, and folk singers such as Sam Hinton, Pete Seeger, and Tom Glazer have excellent albums of children's folk songs.

Second, music of other cultures. Do not restrict yourself to records found under the category of Children's Records in a record shop. The preschool years are an ideal time to expose your child to the music of other cultures, before he has acquired hardening of his musical arteries and can understand and enjoy only music of the United States. Let him hear Polynesian drums, African drums, Balinese gongs and gamelin, Japanese koto, Greek bouzoukai, Mexican mariachi, Guatemalan marimbas, and the like. Your preschool child will probably like any music of another culture which has a strong beat and rhythm.

Third, miscellaneous music records. I reserve this for records not easily classified under the first three categories. For example, Walt Disney's *It's a Small World*, an excellent record with a catchy tune, takes a child on a musical geography trip.

Fourth, activity records. These are records which involve some specific muscular activity or fantasy acting out that the child can engage in as the record plays. The *Dance-a-Story* record is an example of a particularly fine activity record.

Fifth, intellectual stimulation records, which are the equivalent of nonfiction books. This category would include nature and science records, history records, counting and math records, etc. An example would be *Space Songs* by Tom Glazer. Included on this LP record are such songs as "Rocket Ship," "What is the Milky Way?" "Why Does the Sun Shine?" "Friction," etc.

Sixth, storybook and record combinations. These are fiction books, faithfully and simply narrated in the form of a record. These can be used to get a preschooler interested in the book on which the record is based. It can also be used after he has had the book read to him. He can experience the meaning and message of the book in a different form, and through a different sense modality. An example of a good story book and record combination would be *Fox in Socks* and *Green Eggs and Ham*, an LP record in which Marvin Miller narrates and dramatizes two of the Dr. Seuss Beginner Books.

If you are fortunate enough to have a shop with an adequate stock of good children's records near you, you can obtain any of the records listed in Appendix D. If you do not have such a record store close enough to where you live, your solution is to purchase by mail. You will find listed in Appendix D the address of Children's Music Center, a store which specializes in children's records and music supplies.

All right; let's say you have bought several good children's records—now what to do with them? This is where many parents make their mistake. They simply play the record "cold" for the child. They say, "Here's a nice record Mother just bought for you; let's listen to it." The child listens to it and seems uninterested. A few such experiences and Mother concludes (wrongly) that little

Susie just doesn't take to children's records, so there's no sense buying any more. This mother doesn't understand that preschool children need to be prepared to understand and enjoy a record.

Rather than speak generally and abstractly about how children should be prepared to understand and enjoy a record, I'm going to take a few specific records and illustrate the process of preparing a child to listen to them. First of all, you can't prepare a child for a whole LP record—it simply doesn't work that way. You have to deal with one song at a time and prepare the child for that.

On a very fine children's record by Pete Seeger called *Sleep Time* (Folkways) is the folk song "Abiyoyo." How do you prepare your child to understand and enjoy this song?

First, listen to it yourself. You should never play a record for your child that you have not listened to yourself. Having familiarized yourself with the song, you could tell your child something like this: "I'm going to play you a song about a big giant. (Preschool children always love songs and stories about giants.) What kind of a giant do you think he is?" (Your child will tell you his ideas of the giant, in answer to your question.) Then you tell him: "This was a special kind of giant because he liked to listen to a ukulele! As you listen to the record, see if you can remember what kind of hair the giant had, and what kind of teeth he had, and what kind of claws he had. This song is about this giant and a father who was a magician and a little boy." By now your child is very curious to hear the record and find out more about this special kind of giant who likes ukulele music. "Okay, now I'm going to play the record for you. Listen carefully and see if you can tell me all about this giant when we finish hearing the record."

Then play "Abiyoyo." After you have played it, ask your child some questions. "Now let's see what you remember about Abiyoyo, the giant. How tall was he? (Tall as a house.) What kind of claws did he have? (Long claws, because he didn't cut them.) What kind of hair did he have? (Matted hair, because he didn't comb it.) What kind of teeth did he have? (Slobbery teeth, because he didn't brush them.) "What kind of musical instrument did the little boy play? And what was his father? What kind of a magician was he—what could he do?" Then guide your child into telling you what happened in the story. Do not tell him the answer if he can't remember, but say: "Let's listen to the record again and see if we can find out how tall Abiyoyo was or what kind of teeth he had."

If you listen to records in this way with your child, you will develop in him a much greater understanding and enjoyment. In addition, you are painlessly teaching him valuable skills in listening and paying attention, which he will need later on in grade school.

Let's take another excellent record for children: *Whoever Shall Have Some Good Peanuts*, by Sam Hinton (Folkways).

First listen to the "Frog Song" on the record. Then you might say something like this to your preschooler: "This is a song about a little boy who went for a walk in the swamp. The little boy was just about your age. He heard some frogs. Do you think frogs can talk? If frogs could talk, what do you think they would say to each other? Let's listen and see."

After you and he listen to the record together, you might ask questions, such as: "What sorts of noises did the frogs make?" You and he might imitate the different noises the different frogs made, or listen to that part of the record over again. Then you could ask him: "What did it sound like the frogs were saying to each other? What did the little green frog say? What did the big old bullfrog say? And what did the great big old frog with great big old green eyes say?" If your child doesn't remember what the frogs said, you can play the song over and let him hear it again.

Perhaps the next song you might listen to on this record would be "The Barnyard Song." You could prepare your child in this fashion: "This is a song about a farmer who had a lot of animals. Listen and see if you can tell me what kind of animals he had. Each animal is going to make a different kind of sound. Listen carefully now, and see if you can make the sound that the animal makes." After you play the song, ask him what animals the farmer had on his farm and what sounds they made. Then you can play the record over, and you and he can make the sounds of the different animals along with the record. Preschoolers love to imitate the sounds of things, and this song will be a favorite.

One final example from this Sam Hinton record: "A Horse Named Bill." This is a humorous song, but preschoolers need to be *told* that a song is a funny song. So whenever you play a humorous song or tell a humorous story to your preschooler, tell your child in so many words that this is a funny song or story. Here's how you could do it: "Now I'm going to play you a really funny song. This is so funny and silly, it'll just make you want to laugh. It's about a funny horse named Bill. He ran into a barber shop. Isn't that silly? Did you ever see a horse in a barber shop? It also tells about a whale named Lena, who does all kinds of funny things. Let's listen to the record and find out what kinds of silly and funny things that whale does." Listen to the record and ask your child questions about it. Don't get too elaborate with your questions on this song, because some of the humor and the plays on words are a little advanced for a preschooler to grasp.

These examples should give you an indication of the three-step-process of playing a record for a child: (1) Prepare your child to listen to the record; (2) Listen to the record with him; (3) Talk with him about the record after he has heard it. When you use a record in this way with a child, you change record listening from a *passive* to an *active* experience for him. You have aroused his curiosity before playing the record so that he is eager to hear it. By asking him questions about the record before playing it, you have motivated him to listen actively to the record so that he can answer your questions. All of this makes listening to records a very pleasurable learning experience for a child; this is quite different from simply playing the record "cold" for him.

Records are not only effective learning devices for small children, they can be used to head off a discipline problem. Playing a record for your child can become part of the environmental control for effective discipline that I spoke of in Chapter 9.

For example, your child is hungry, but dinner won't be ready for a while. You can easily forsee that he is going to pester and annoy you to give him something to eat in that half hour as you are going about fixing dinner. What to do? Play a record!

Remember to give him a brief "buildup" for the record: "Remember that record we played last week about the monster who liked to listen to the ukulele? Let's listen to that record now, and when it's finished you can draw a picture of the monster." By getting him involved in listening to the record you are "buying time" for yourself to fix dinner, and thus heading off a potential discipline problem.

Listening to a record can calm a child who has become overstimulated. Perhaps he is playing with some other children, and you see that the play is getting out of hand and he is becoming wild and overstimulated. Use a story record rather than a music record for the purpose of calming him down. Give him a brief buildup to get him motivated to listen to it, and then play it for him. You can use the story record to take your place at a time when you are too busy to read to him. If he has the book that goes along with the story, he might want to look at the pictures in the book while he listens to the record. That's why it's a good idea to keep the books that go with story records close by the record player so they are easily available.

In other words, records are not only invaluable learning materials for children, they can be used by a wise mother to rescue her from potential "difficult times" with a child—just before dinner, for example, or just before bedtime. Or when you are forced to keep a child inside the house due to bad weather or sickness. At these times, records can come in very handy.

There are two inexpensive sources of records. The first is your local library, if it is large enough to have a record collection. You can borrow records just as you borrow library books. But many parents do not take advantage of the record collection of their local public library. The second is your tape recorder. You can make your own tapes of your child's favorite books. Simply get an empty tape or cassette and record the book on tape by reading it out loud. Or, if you have an older child in your family, he might like to record a book on tape.

We have had our ten-year-old boy record simple books on tape this way. He enjoyed doing it and listening to the tape afterwards, and this helped to increase his skill in oral reading. And his four-year-old brother loved to listen to the "special books" recorded on tape by his older brother.

Let me summarize this chapter. Your child is enormously influenced by the curriculum of his school. But before he enters school, he is even more powerfully influenced by the "curriculum" of your home. Toys, books, and records constitute the curriculum of your home. Take the time and the effort to select them wisely.

14

A Baker's Dozen for Parents

Since we began our conversation about your child in
infancy, we have covered a tremendous variety of topics.
We have talked about everything from temper tantrums to
learning to read to a recipe for playdough.

If you and I were sitting down having coffee together
while we discussed all of these topics, this could be a real
two-way conversation. We would be sharing our experiences about parenting. You would be telling me about
your child, and I would be asking you further questions. I
would be talking about the science of parenting, and you
would interrupt me from time to time. You would say: "I
don't understand why you said that," or "I disagree with
that," or "What you said a moment ago kind of rubs me
the wrong way," or "When we were talking about the
stage of toddlerhood you never mentioned such and such.
How would you handle that?"

A book, unfortunately, is a one-way proposition. I have
attempted to put myself in your place and imagine what
questions you might have at various points, and then try
to answer them. But possibly I have not answered some
questions you have about raising your child. If you do

have questions which I have not covered fully in this book, you can write to me in care of my publishers, Nash Publishing Company, 9255 Sunset Boulevard, Los Angeles, California 90069. I will answer additional questions in my future book, *Questions Parents Ask*, as well as in the revised edition of *How to Parent*.

We have covered many diverse topics in the thirteen chapters of this extended conversation about the first five years of your child's life. Perhaps by now you may not be able to see the proverbial forest for the proverbial trees. To clarify the view, let me summarize the main ideas of this book for you, the most important things to remember about child raising. Here is a Baker's Dozen Guideline.

1. Raising a child is a human relationship, and human relationships cannot be reduced to a set of rules. So don't dogmatically follow any rules—including these! Rules are only guidelines. You and your child are unique. You and he have a special relationship, which is different from the relationship of any other two people on this planet. Don't make the mistake of trying to fit this relationship into any generalization.

2. The years before six are the most important in establishing attitudes and habit patterns which will last throughout life. The relationship established with your child in his preschool years will determine your relationship with him throughout the rest of his life. For example, to prevent a teen-ager from becoming a defiant juvenile delinquent, take the time to establish a solid relationship of affection and mutual respect when he is a preschooler.

3. You can learn many scientific facts about children, but if you don't have the *feel of childhood* you will not guide your child wisely. You will know the *words* of parenting, but lack the *tune*. To acquire the feel of childhood re-establish contact with the child within yourself. That is your best single guide to bringing up your own children.

4. Each of your children is a unique combination of genes which has never existed before on this planet and never will again. He is also growing up in a unique psychological environment because of his position in your family. This combination of unique genes plus unique environment means that, in the strictest sense of the word, each child in your family is as unique as his fingerprints. He deserves to be treated that way. You need to respect

his uniqueness. Don't try to fit him into some preconceived mold of what you think he should be. The most important thing you can do for your child is to stand back and allow him to actualize the unique and potential self which is unfolding within him.

5. In order to achieve self-actualization, your child needs to grow up in a stable family—one governed by adults. Your child needs a strong leader running the government of his family; he needs strong, loving parents who will guide him, but not coerce or tyrannize him.

6. In guiding the behavior of your child it is important that you make a distinction between internal *feelings* and outward *actions*. It is reasonable to expect a child to learn to control his outward actions, according to his age and stage of development. It is *not* reasonable to expect a child to control his feelings, for thoughts and feelings come unbidden into the mind.

7. Decide on limits and reasonable rules for the control of your child's actions. Then enforce these limits and rules consistently. There is no *one* magic set of rules which is right for every family or for all children. It depends on which rules you feel are important, and which rules you feel comfortable in enforcing.

8. Although, as a parent, you assume responsibility for teaching your child to control his actions, it is equally important to allow him the freedom to express his feelings. Giving your child this right will in no way lessen his respect for you. On the contrary, it will increase it. For he will recognize that you feel secure enough in your position as a parent to allow him the democratic right to express his feelings as a junior member of the family. Allowing your child to express his feelings gives him the same type of democratic rights in your family that you have as a free citizen of your country.

9. The best way to keep your relationship with your child strong and meaningful is to show him that you genuinely understand how he feels about things. You can do this most convincingly not by glibly saying "I understand how you feel," but by putting his feelings into your own words and feeding them back to him. By doing this you will be actively trying to put yourself in his place and see the world through his eyes.

10. In guiding your child toward self-regulation, reinforce his positive moves toward worthwhile goals. Ignore

actions which are not in the direction of worthwhile goals. Behavior which is reinforced tends to be repeated. Reinforce your child when he acts independent, self-assertive, creative, and loving. Do not reinforce him when he acts timid, whining, uncooperative, violent, or destructive. You then become a powerful influence in helping your child to become a mature and self-regulating person.

11. School begins at home. The "curriculum" of your home is fully as important as the curriculum of the schools your child will attend. He needs a wisely chosen curriculum of toys, books, and records, for these are the textbooks of his school at home.

12. Your child needs stimulation for his intellectual development. The intellectual stimulation you give him, particularly in the first five years of life, is of crucial importance for the optimal development of his intelligence. Stimulating his language development, teaching him to become interested in words and to love books, teaching him to print, playing games which teach him to think logically and grow in his understanding of mathematics—all of these are part of the rich intellectual heritage you can give to your child by the time he is six years old.

13. Parents have rights too! Raising a child is no easy task. It demands more maturity than most parents have at times. All of us, from time to time, fall short of the ideals we set for ourselves. If we give our children the right to be imperfect children, we should also give ourselves the right to be imperfect parents! If we allow our children the right to express their feelings, we should certainly keep that same right for ourselves. A parent who feels she is sacrificing herself for her child is not doing that child any favors. So in order for us to be good parents we must first of all aim at being self-actualizing, genuine human beings ourselves.

One of the best ways to learn to become self-actualizing persons is to understand the child within ourselves. The feelings we have as children are not outgrown once we reach the age of twenty-one. Childhood feelings are still there, hidden behind our adult facade. All of us contain within ourselves the child we once were, at each stage of our development. If we did not contain within ourselves the children we once were at earlier stages of our development, we would be unable to understand or communicate at all with children. We would be completely encapsulated

in our adult world, unable to put ourselves in our child's
place and see the world through his eyes.

Some parents are almost completely unable to understand children because they are so out of touch with the
child within themselves. The memories of their own childhood and adolescence are so repressed that it is as if they
never experienced a childhood or adolescence. It's as if
these parents were born at the age of twenty-one. This is
tragic. It is only by getting in touch with the child within
ourselves that we can truly acquire the feel of childhood.

Ray Bradbury has captured the feel of childhood in an
incident in his book *Dandelion Wine*. Douglas Spaulding,
age twelve, is trying to persuade Mr. Sanderson, owner of
Sanderson's Shoe Store, to sell him a pair of tennis shoes
for a dollar less than the asking price. In exchange for a
dollar reduction, Douglas proposes to work free for Mr.
Sanderson, wearing his tennis shoes. He urges Mr. Sanderson to try on the tennis shoes to see how they feel.
Reluctantly, Mr. Sanderson agrees and puts on the tennis
shoes, which look "detached and alien down next to the
dark cuffs of his business suit." Douglas now speaks:

> "Please! . . . Mr. Sanderson, now could you kind
> of rock back and forth a little, sponge around, bounce
> kind of, while I tell you the rest? It's this: I give you
> my money, you give me the shoes, I owe you a dollar.
> But, Mr. Sanderson, *but*—soon as I get those shoes on,
> you know what *happens*?
>
> Bang! I deliver your packages, pick up packages,
> bring you coffee, burn your trash, run to the post
> office, telegraph office, library! You'll see twelve of
> me in and out, in and out, every minute. Feel those
> shoes, Mr. Sanderson, *feel* how fast they'd take me?
> All those springs inside? Feel all the running in-
> side? Feel how they kind of grab hold and can't let
> you alone and don't like you just *standing* there?
> Feel how quick I'd be doing the things you'd rather
> not bother with? You stay in the nice cool store while
> I'm jumping all around town! But it's not me really;
> it's the shoes. They're going like mad down alleys,
> cutting corners, and back! There they go!"

Mr. Sanderson stood amazed with the rush of
words. When the words got going the flow carried
him; he began to sink deep in the shoes, to flex his

toes, limber his arches, test his ankles. He rocked softly, secretly, back and forth in a small breeze from the open door. The tennis shoes silently hushed themselves deep in the carpet, sank as in a jungle grass. . . . He gave one solemn bounce of his heels in the . . . yielding and welcoming earth. Emotions hurried over his face as if many colored lights had been switched on and off. His mouth hung slightly open. Slowly he gentled and rocked himself to a halt, and the boy's voice faded and they stood there looking at each other in a tremendous and natural silence.[36]

Mr. Sanderson had lost the feel of childhood. He could only view tennis shoes from an adult perspective. He had lost the feel of what tennis shoes mean to a twelve-year-old boy.

Douglas helped Mr. Sanderson recapture the feeling of his own childhood. And this is what your own child can do for you. All of the scientific facts we learn about childhood will do us little good if we do not have the feel of childhood. But if we can, in imagination, put ourselves inside the skin of our child and see how the world looks to him, feel how the world feels to him . . . then a lot of what puzzles us about children and how to raise them will fall into place quite easily and naturally.

One of the things that may be helpful in acquiring the feel of childhood is to work with some of the materials your child is using. Pretend for a short while that you are a three or a four-year-old. Sometimes you can do this by yourself; sometimes you can do it with your child. Try your hand at painting at the easel, not to make definite "pictures" of anything, but merely to experiment with colors the way a three-year-old would. Try coloring with crayons, especially pastel crayons. Do not try to draw pictures of anything in particular. Just scribble, playing around with colors and lines. Work with clay and playdough, and see how they feel to you. Put on a record of another culture, and dance around and express your feelings to Polynesian drums or Guatemalan marimbas. Go out in the sandbox and get the feel of the sand. Spend some time just letting it run through your fingers and enjoying the texture of it. See if you can recapture how sand felt to you many years ago when you enjoyed sand play. Then build some sand creations yourself: castles or houses or roads or tunnels.

Our family once spent a summer vacation at Cannon Beach, Oregon. One of our happiest memories of that vacation is the annual Sand Castle contest, held every year at Cannon Beach, in which we participated as a family. We had a wonderful time constructing our sand castle, with each member of the family contributing his part to the overall design.

From time to time at our nursery school we hold what we call a Phun Phling for Parents. At this event, we provide our parents with all of the materials their children use in nursery school: paper, paint, crayons, wood, collage, glue, clay, music and rhythm instruments. Then we turn them loose. For one evening those parents are preschoolers again. They love it! They really get involved with the materials, even though they may never have done anything like that before in their adult lives. As one father put it: "I think I understand what nursery school is all about, now that I've had a chance to do some of the things my little boy has been doing." You will probably share that father's feelings, if you give yourself a chance to experiment with the things your child will be doing in his preschool years.

THE FEEL OF CHILDHOOD

This is the emotional foundation upon which all the scientific knowledge about your child's growth and development must rest. Without the feel of childhood, adults will misuse and distort the scientific facts. We will be viewing them entirely through adult eyes. When we acquire the feel of childhood, then everything will fall into place. For, in the truest and simplest sense, your emotional grasp of your own childhood is the real key to the adventure of parenthood. Good luck!

A FINAL WORD

This book has been full of the science of parenting. I hope it has also been full of the common sense of parenting. To speak only of the science of parenting underestimates the *intelligence* of a mother. To speak only of the common sense of parenting overestimates the *information* of a mother.

I want my closing word to be one which goes beyond both science and common sense. My closing word is a word of feeling . . . a word of love.

The love of a mother for her child is more important than all of the scientific information she may acquire about how to raise that child. And the love of a mother for her child is more important than all the common sense she may have about how to raise that child.

As Santayana puts it in one of my favorite sonnets:

> It is not wisdom to be only wise;
> And on the inward vision close the eyes.
> *But it is wisdom to believe the heart.*

So mother, in the final analysis, believe your own heart! You may be unsure of how to handle some particular situation with your child. Science may tell you one thing and your own heart may tell you something else. Believe your own heart! Common sense may tell you one thing and your own heart may tell you another. Believe your own heart!

People over thirty call it "heart." Those under thirty call it "soul." But whatever name you use, it is the same thing. Perhaps we should try to bridge the generation gap and call it "heart and soul." But "heart and soul," as anyone knows, is a code word for "love." So why don't we call it by that simple and universal word: *love*.

Science is important in raising your child. Common sense is important also. But love is the most important of all.

> Science, common sense, and love . . . these three.
> But the greatest of these is love.

Appendix A

TOYS AND PLAY EQUIPMENT FOR CHILDREN OF DIFFERENT AGES AND STAGES

I. **The Stage of Infancy** (from birth until creeping and walking begins, usually around the end of the first year):

This is the time for *sensory toys*. The first year of life is a powerful year of learning. The young child is doing basic research on the sensory qualities of his universe. He spends all his waking hours seeing, hearing, tasting, smelling, touching everything he can manage to make contact with. Years before he acquires the language ability to name objects, he is busy creating in his mind inner models of all these objects. He manipulates the hardness, softness, and shape of the object. He mentally compares it with other objects. He measures it, matches it, puts it in his mouth, or smells it. He is endlessly manipulating his environment. What toys does he need to help him in this all-important sensory exploration of his early environment?

1. Crib mobiles, bought or homemade
2. Cradle gym
3. Rattles
4. Rubber squeeze toys
5. Anything your imagination can think of that you can hang securely from his crib or playpen, which is interesting and colorful and will not be potentially dangerous to the baby
6. Soft cuddly animals

329

7. Inquarium (Creative Playthings). Plastic, hang-up aquarium containing live fish
8. Teething toys
9. Gumby (for use as a bendable teething toy)
10. Small, soft texture ball
11. Texture Pad (different textures of cloth sewn on a two foot square piece of rubber matting)
12. Soft thick cord, knotted at ends and at intervals, too short for a baby to get tangled in
13. Common household objects of various sorts
14. Water
15. Bath toys, plastic and rubber
16. Sponges for bath play
17. Music boxes
18. Trash basket of discarded junk mail
19. Crawligator (Creative Playthings). Crawling board, mounted on ball casters that swivel freely, having a contoured body that cradles the baby comfortably, while he maneuvers with his hands and feet
20. Musical carrousel or musical mobile

II. **The Stage of Toddlerhood** (approximately from onset of walking to second birthday):

The basic developmental task of this stage is *active motor exploration of his environment*. The child can now get around on his own two feet, and he's "into everything." He is either developing self-confidence and assertiveness as he tries to explore his environment, or he is developing self-doubt and learning to fear his own eager curiosity. What kind of toys and play equipment will help him to develop his self-confidence?

A. Play Equipment for Large-Muscle Development (mostly outdoor play equipment)
1. Dome Climber (Creative Playthings)
2. Slide
3. Tyke Wagon (Playskool)
4. Tyke-Bike (Playskool)
5. Baby Walker or Ride 'em Horse (Creative Playthings)
6. Cardboard hollow blocks
7. Wooden hollow blocks

8. Boards, small but sturdy
9. Sandbox and sand toys: cups, spoons, pie pans, sifters
10. Small metal cars and trucks for sand play
11. Hard plastic animals and people for sand play
12. Dirt
13. Water toys for outside water play: plastic boats, coffee cans, measuring spoons, etc.
14. Old coffee percolator
15. Small but sturdy shovel for dirt digging and sand play
16. Large wooden or metal outdoor trucks and cars
17. Pull-toys of various sorts
18. Outside playhouse, bought or, preferably, homemade
19. Large cardboard boxes big enough for him to get inside
20. Pets: a dog, not a cat

B. Indoor Play Equipment
1. Open shelves (rather than toy chests) for toys and books
2. Modular blocks twelve inches square, with one side open, for building and for toy storage
3. Riding horse on springs (Wonder Horse)
4. Indoor Gym House (Creative Playthings)
5. Cardboard boxes of various sizes
6. Beanbags
7. Stacking toys of various sorts
8. Hammering toys (Playskool and Sifo)
9. Large beads to string
10. Soft cuddly animals
11. Balloons
12. Form boards (Playskool, Creative Playthings)
13. Very simple puzzles (Playskool, Sifo, Simplex)
14. Rubber animals, domestic and jungle (Creative Playthings)
15. Rubber beach ball
16. Small rubber ball
17. Tiny metal cars and trucks (Tootsietoy, Midgetoy)
18. Coordination board: Go 'N Play (Mattel). (Particularly useful on trips, since it comes in carrying case)

19. Large size wooden or metal cars and trucks (Creative Playthings, Great Lakes Toys, Tonka)
20. Dolls
21. Tea sets
22. Dress-up clothes (Goodwill, Salvation Army)
23. Gumby and Pokey
24. Water and water play toys: soap flakes, floating objects of many kinds
25. Corrugated fiberboard blocks
26. Large wooden hollow blocks
27. Foam blocks
28. Various miscellaneous toys made for this age group by Playskool, Sifo, and Creative Playthings. (You will rarely go wrong on any toy made by these three companies.)

C. Books
1. Hardboard or cloth books. (He will probably explore these first by putting them in his mouth!)
2. Block Books (Western Publishing)
3. Sears or Ward Catalog
4. Blue Chip Stamp Catalog
5. Toy catalog
6. *Best Word Book Ever*, Richard Scarry
7. *Cat in the Hat Dictionary*, Dr. Seuss
8. Other books which have large pictures of objects or people, with words naming the object or person, to help him label his environment and stimulate his language development
9. *Mother Goose*
10. Very simple picture story books, such as *Goodnight Moon* by Margaret Wise Brown

III. The Stage of First Adolescence:

The basic developmental task of this stage is *self-identity versus social conformity*. In his ladder of "play maturity" your child has now reached the stage of *parallel play*. The toys and play equipment you provided for him in the previous stage of toddlerhood will continue to be used with eagerness and gusto by your child. But he is now ready for new types of play equipment. For example, you did not provide crayons and chalk and paint in the stage of toddlerhood because he might eat them. He has reached a new developmental level and can now handle these media. He is also now ready for a whole new group of unstructured creative play equipment which he could not handle in the previous stage of development.

A. Play Equipment for Large-Muscle Development
   The same toys and play equipment of the toddler-hood stage will continue to be enthusiastically used by your child for his large-muscle development.

B. Indoor Play Equipment
   1. Blackboard, four feet by four feet, and white and colored chalk. (The single most basic item of play equipment you can get for him at this stage of development. He will continue to use his blackboard throughout his preschool years and even into grade school.)
   2. Small-size desk or table for him to draw and paint on. (This will also be used for many years.)
   3. Small-size, sturdy chair
   4. Bulletin board (celotex) to pin up his scribblings, drawings, and printing
   5. Painting easel (wall type is best)

C. Unstructured Creative Play Materials
   1. Paper: various shapes, sizes, textures, including newsprint and newspaper
   2. Crayons
   3. Watercolor felt pens
   4. Paint, liquid or dry
   5. Finger paints
   6. Playdough, bought or homemade
   7. Clay
   8. Plasticene
   9. Outside easel for painting. (Make one that will go on a fence in your yard; use cut down milk cartons for paint containers.)
   10. Hardwood or softwood blocks. (Get a small set, since at this stage your child will not do much more than stack them and become familiar with them. In the next stage you can add a much larger set of blocks, since your child will then be ready for more elaborate block building.)
   11. Various types of put-together toys (Playskool, Sifo, Creative Playthings)

    12. The Learning Toy Series by Grolier
    13. Lego beginner set

D. Toys Dealing with Sounds and Music
    1. Rhythm instruments: drums, pans, cigar boxes,
       cymbals, triangles, etc., bought or homemade
    2. Special sounds: toy xylophone, accordion, etc.
    3. Inexpensive "push-in" type of record player or
       tape cartridge player
    4. Inexpensive records he can play himself
    5. Good family record player
    6. Good records you play for him (See Appendix
       D)

E. Miscellaneous Toys and Play Equipment for This
   Stage
    1. Unbreakable six-inch polished steel mirror
       framed in wood (Creative Playthings). (It en-
       courages development of self-image and self-
       identity.)
    2. Giant Ride 'em Tractor-Trailer
    3. Giant Ride 'em Flatbed Truck
    4. Giant Ride 'em Open Van Truck
    5. Giant Ride 'em Bus
    6. Giant Ride 'em Train
       Items two through six are all available through
       Creative Playthings. They are expensive, but
       they are excellent wooden toys for this age.
       Your child can actually ride on these toys, which
       are designed to hold his weight. He will get
       enormous play value out of even one of these
       durable toys. They should last throughout the
       preschool years.
    7. Jumbo Steam Roller
    8. Jumbo Fire Truck and Fire Ladder Trailer
    9. Jumbo Automobile
    10. Jumbo Diesel Train
    11. Jumbo Bus
    12. Jumbo Cargo Carrier
        Items seven through twelve are all available
        through Creative Playthings. They are not quite
        as costly as the Giant Ride 'em toys. Excellent
        durable wooden toys for this stage, they will
        provide play value for years and years.

13. Giant magnifier on stand (Creative Playthings). Lens, specially mounted so it will not break, on heavy three-legged wood framework. (It introduces your child dramatically to the phenomenon of magnification.)

14. Big I, little i Lenses (Creative Playthings). Lens set which contains a concave reducing lens and a convex magnifying lens. (Your child looks through each lens separately to compress or enlarge his world. He can combine the lenses to play additional tricks.)

15. Lens comparer (Creative Playthings). Triangular wood box into which your child can put various tiny objects for viewing. On each side of the box are embedded concave, single convex, and double convex lenses. (Your child will discover changes in size when objects are viewed through the different lenses.)

16. Play Puddle (Creative Playthings). Reinforced yellow fiberglass, light and portable for use indoors or outdoors. Sculptured surface suggests lakes, islands, mountains, streams. (It is expensive to buy. However, you can sculpture your own out of concrete very inexpensively.)

17. Picture Lotto

18. Pounding toys (Playskool, Sifo)

19. Puzzles (Playskool, Sifo, Simplex)

20. Hard plastic animals: domestic and farm animals, dinosaurs

21. Hard plastic people: astronauts, cowboys and indians, toy soldiers

IV. The Preschool Stage (ages three through five):

These are years of enormous development for your child, both emotionally and intellectually. Your child has now reached the stage of truly *cooperative play* with other children. He is particularly responsive to intellectual stimulation. The closer your home comes to having the kind of indoor and outdoor play equipment that is found in a good nursery school, the richer an environment, both emotionally and intellectually, it will provide for your preschooler. If there is a good nursery school nearby, visit it. Pay particular attention to both the inside and outside play equipment, and see how you can duplicate this in your home. Much of this equipment you can make yourself, with a little ingenuity.

A. Play Equipment for Large-Muscle Development
   1. Abstract tree house, built low to ground, with ladder and slide
   2. Tricycles
   3. Wagons
   4. Rope ladders or cargo netting
   5. Large hollow blocks
   6. Boards
   7. Balancing boards
   8. Walking and balancing board, consisting of a two by four, with wooden supports which will allow it to be used either flat or on edge for walking or balancing.
   9. Tunnel of Fun (Creative Playthings, F.A.O. Schwarz). A crawl-through play tunnel.

B. Play Equipment for Small-Muscle Development
   1. Crayons, pencils, felt pens, and paper
   2. Scissors (left-handed ones for left-handed children)
   3. Glue and paste
   4. Various fit-together coordination toys (Playskool, Sifo, Creative Playthings)
   5. Push-in pegboard toys (Playskool Peg Village, Sifo)
   6. Hardware tools: hammer, nails, saw, etc. Not make believe, but real tools which a child can use under supervision.
   7. Pounding toys

C. Construction Toys
   1. A large number of wooden blocks which can be used for elaborate block building by an individual child, extension of field trips through block building, or cooperative block building by several children
   2. Playskool Village
   3. Wooden cars and trucks for play in the block cities children will create
   4. Tiny hard plastic people and animals for use in connection with block play or sand play

5. Metal cars and trucks, bulldozers, cranes, etc. (Tonka)
6. Very small metal cars and trucks (Tootsietoy, Midgetoy. Matchbox, Corgi)
7. Skaneatles wooden trains and interlocking tracks (Playskool, hard to find, but available through Creative Playthings and F.A.O. Schwarz)
8. Jumbo transportation toys (Creative Playthings)
9. Wooden animals
10. Bendable family doll set
11. Crane sets pulley, etc. (Creative Playthings)
12. Rubber animals (Creative Playthings)
13. Put-together construction toys
    a) Bilofix
    b) Baufix
    c) Brio
    d) Tinkertoy
    e) Tinker Zoo
    f) Lego
    g) Tog'l Blocks (Mattel)
    h) Crystal Climbers
    i) Playplax

D. Role-Playing and Creative Fantasy Development (especially for four and five-year-olds)

1. Puppet stage, bought or handmade. (Try using one side of a homemade playhouse as an outside open puppet stage.)
2. Hand puppets
3. Finger puppets
4. Bendable family dolls
5. Costume box: dress-up clothes (Salvation Army, Goodwill)
6. Doctor kit, hospital kit
7. Flannel cutouts and flannel board
8. Play store. (It is expensive to buy, but you can make a simple one yourself.)

E. Homemaking Corner and Dollhouse Play for Girls
1. Stove, sink, refrigerator, bought or homemade
2. Child-size pots and pans, tea set, silverware
3. Dolls and dollhouses. (Avoid the electronic won-

der dolls. Make your own dolls. They will probably be better than anything you can buy.)

F. Creative Arts and Crafts
1. Playdough
2. Plasticene
3. Clay
4. Large crayons
5. Paint
6. Large paintbrushes. (Avoid small ones for this age.)
7. Colored tissue paper for collage
8. Glue and collage. (Don't throw anything away; you can always use it in the collage box!)
9. Gummed paper cutouts for abstract collage
10. Wood block print set
11. Rubber abstract shapes for block printing. (Cut them out of inner tubes or other kinds of rubber.)
12. Various materials for block printing: lemons, oranges, cutout potato, key, wire, leaf, etc.
13. Inexpensive prints for your child's room to expose him to good art
14. Mobiles for your child's room. (You and he can make them.)
15. Etch-a-Sketch (Ohio Art Company)
16. Wonder Art (Pressman). "Finger painting" without mess

G. Cognitive Stimulation Toys and Equipment
1. Reading and language development
   a) Wooden alphabet letters and numerals (Creative Playthings)
   b) Magnetic letters and numerals
   c) Sandpaper letters and numerals
   d) Fit-a-Space and Alph-a-Space (Lauri Toys)
   e) Rubber stamps you make of letters and numerals
   f) Cardboard signs with familiar words you print on them
   g) Materials to make his own picture book by gluing cutout pictures from magazines. (He dictates to you and you print what he says.)

    h) Puzzles of all sorts (Playskool, Sifo, Simplex)

    i) Peg Time Clock (Playskool)

    j) Dominos

    k) Matching games (matching colors, shapes, etc.)

    l) Teach Key, Beginners (3-M)

    m) Teach Key Math (3-M)

    n) Teach Key Reading (3-M)

    o) Listen and Learn with Phonics

2. Mathematics and numbers

    a) Cuisenaire Rods Parents Kit (Cuisenaire Company of America)

    b) Sum Stick (Creative Playthings)

    c) Mosaic geometric shapes (Playskool)

    d) Wooden time clock, or clock blocks for learning to tell time

    e) Wiff n Proof. Math and logic games for very bright five-year-olds, most six-year-olds, and on up through grade school. (Note: You have to read the directions and teach them these math games. They cannot learn them by themselves.)

3. Science

    a) Magnets

    b) Ant farm

    c) Other good science toys from the science section of the Creative Playthings catalog.

    d) Phonograph records on science: The Motivation Records series (see Appendix D for more elaborate description)

    e) Books on science to be read to preschoolers

        (1) *Let's Read and Find Out Science Books* series, Crowell

        (2) *True Book* series, Children's Press

        (3) *Science Is What and Why Books* series, Coward-McCann

4. Foreign Language

    a) Various phonograph records for teaching foreign language to young children (see Appendix D)

    b) Berlitz books: *Spanish for Children, French for Children,* etc.

    c) *Cat in the Hat Beginner Dictionary* in Spanish and French

H. Music and Dance Toys
  1. Rhythm instruments
  2. Activity and participation records (see Appendix D)

I. Field Trips to Local Places of Interest
  1. Fire station
  2. Police station
  3. Newspaper
  4. Dairy
  5. Bank
  6. Bakery
  7. Foundary, etc.

J. Secret Toys You Carry Inside Your Head
  1. Stories you make up
  2. Stories your preschooler makes up
  3. Round robin family stories
  4. Wouldn't It Be Funny If . . .
  5. What Would Happen If . . .
  6. Solid, Liquid, or Gas
  7. Person, Place, or Thing
  8. Twenty Questions: animal, vegetable, or mineral

Sources for Toys and Play Equipment
  1. Creative Playthings, P.O. Box 1100, Princeton, New Jersey 08540
  2. Community Playthings, Rifton, New York 12471
  3. Childcraft, 155 East 23rd Street, New York City, 10010
  4. Childplay, 43 East 19th Street, New York City 10003
  5. Novo Education Toy and Equipment Company, 11 Park Place, New York City
  6. Musicon Inc., 42-00 Vernon Boulevard, Long Island City, New York 11101
  7. F.A.O. Schwarz, Fifth Avenue at 58th Street, New York City 10022
  8. Cuisenaire Company of America, 12 Church Street, New Rochelle, New York 10805

You can get a free catalog by writing to these companies, and it would be well worth your while to do so. You will quickly see the difference between the excellent selection of educational toys in these catalogs and the toys in your local toy store. Most of these companies carry extensive lines of play equipment for both outdoor and indoor play during the preschool years. You can also make your homemade version of many of the items you see in these catalogs.

Appendix B

FREE AND INEXPENSIVE CHILDREN'S TOYS
FROM A TO Z

Every week our children are deluged with TV enticements
to get them to buy toys, toys, and more toys. This TV
campaign, as any battle-scarred parent knows all too well,
rises to its annual frantic crescendo just before Christmas.

Parents often lose sight of the fact that the toys children may get the most play value from can be fashioned
out of free, or at least inexpensive, materials. These free
or inexpensive toys will do much more to develop a child's
inventiveness and imagination than expensive push-button
gadgets.

So let's take a trip through our alphabet of inexpensive
toys and toy materials.

A is for Art Materials. We are usually much too restrict-
ed in our thinking as to what our youngsters can use for
art materials. We tend to think only of paint and crayons
and paper. We may overlook such things as old egg
cartons, paper bags, discarded buttons, broken rubber
bands, tin cans, used matches, toothpicks, popsicle sticks,
and a thousand and one such items. Children can use these
things for collages, constructions wired or glued together,
or papier-mâché.

B is for Blocks. Sure, you can buy them in a toy store if
you want to. But why not try your hand at making your
own? The houses or apartments being built near you, or
the scrap box at a nearby lumber yard or cabinet shop
will yield materials for blocks of all sizes. Sand them

342

down, and your child will have a large supply of one of the best play materials he could ever use.

C is for Collage, the art technique of gluing different materials onto paper, cardboard, fabric, or masonite. Almost anything can be used in an interesting way in a collage: colorful bits of old fabric, leaves, twigs, buttons, odd pieces of colored paper, old Christmas cards. Protect the work surface with layers of newspaper or a large sheet of plastic you can buy at a dime store. Then pour some Wilhold or Elmer's Glue in an old pie pan, give your child an inexpensive brush to brush on the glue, and stand back!

D is for Dolls. Who decreed that all dolls must be very expensive electronic beauties which are capable of talking, whistling, or dancing the rhumba when the appropriate button is pushed? Give your little girl a chance to make her own dolls, with a little help from you, out of wood, discarded bits of fabric, cardboard. Decorate them with a few deft touches of crayon or paint. With these dolls, the play will be in the child, not in the doll.

E is for Empty Boxes. Your local market is an untapped gold mine of these. Get small ones and build houses for toy cities. Or make animals or people out of them. Get a huge box (like the kind a refrigerator comes in) and make it a playhouse for several children, or a fort or a pirate ship or many, many things. Or just present the empty box to your youngster without any suggestions from you at all. He'll find uses for it that you never dreamed of!

F is for Felt Pens, or water color felt markers. These colorful pens are one of the greatest inventions of the twentieth century in encouraging very young children to draw or to learn to print. Young children like them because they glide easily over the surface of the paper and are easy to manipulate. Be sure to get the water color type of felt pen, rather than the indelible kind of felt marker.

G is for Games. With a piece of sturdy cardboard, you can make any kind of Parcheesi-type game you want. Mark off the path the game will take with different squares. Every once in a while write on the square things like: "Go back three spaces" or "Advance to the Old Haunted House." Then all you need is a pair of dice and some markers for each player, and you've got a game. You could personalize the game around your own family's special set of interests or activities.

With some marbles and a large piece of plywood you can make a marble game. Bore holes in the plywood, with different scores for the different holes. You can make a bingo game, a homemade roulette game, or whatever you like. Homemade games have a special fascination for small children, particularly if they are given a voice in the planning and construction of the game.

H is for Hollow Blocks. Every good nusery school has a set of these, but how many homes have them? One reason few parents buy them is that they are so expensive. Why not make them yourself? You don't have to be a top-notch carpenter to nail six boards together! It helps the child to grip the hollow block if you leave an open space between two boards on one side of the block. Sand the block down to remove splintery surfaces. You can varnish or shellac the blocks if you want, but it's not absolutely necessary. You will be amazed at the play value your youngster will find in a group of hollow blocks and a few small-size boards in his back yard.

I is for Imagination. This "material" is absolutely free and can be found in the mind of a parent who will take the trouble to develop it. With the priceless gift of imagination, a parent can find "toy materials" for a young child out of almost anything in her house. A refrigerator door becomes a metal bulletin board for teaching a child his ABC's with magnetic letters. An old coffee percolator becomes a fascinating manipulative toy. An old, beat-up broom becomes a "magic horse" to ride. And so on. Mix the contents of your house with imagination, shake well, and you have many, many unsuspected toys and play materials for your preschooler.

J is for Junk. The wise mother learns to take her preschooler to the Goodwill, Salvation Army, Army and Navy surplus stores, or garage sales. Things that we adults find of no value may be utterly fascinating to a young child. Junk mail, for instance. We throw it away, but our child may be very happy to play with it, opening the envelopes and restuffing them. Put up an old mailbox in your backyard, and you have a marvelous center for dramatic play, using junk mail.

K is for Kittens. Somebody is always giving away free kittens somewhere. Of course they do eat food, so they're not entirely free. But they make fine pets, as do puppies or any other free animals that are given away. Pets are good ways of bringing out the tenderness and spontaneity of a young child.

L is for Lumber. Lumber is expensive to buy new, but scrap lumber is free. The list of toys you can make out of lumber scraps is endless. Wooden toys don't have to be elaborate or elegantly finished. Simple, chunky boats, houses, cars, and trucks can be built out of wood scraps. Decorate them with crayon or paint, or leave them unpainted if you prefer. Chunky animals, people, or even robots can be made out of wood. The inexpensive wood toys of this sort that you make will probably be more durable than many expensive toys you might buy in a store.

M is for Macaroni. Macaroni comes in many different sizes and shapes and is one of the least expensive and most interesting collage materials your child could use. He can color it with tempera or water color after he has glued it on the backboard.

N is for Newspapers. That's right—just plain old ordinary newspapers! Who said that children could only paint or crayon on plain paper? Actually there is nothing to prevent them from using crayons or paints on old newspapers, and they will get interesting effects that way. Newspaper can also be used for papier-mâché. Tear the newspapers into strips about one inch by two or three inches and glue them on whatever object you want to papier-mâché. Or glue them on a piece of cardboard or wood, and then color them with crayons or paint, making an abstract painting.

O is for Old Clothes. Don't throw away your adult old

clothes: use them for dress-up clothes for your preschooler. You can also pick up old shoes, hats, dresses, jackets, etc. at the Goodwill or Salvation Army for your preschooler's dress-up wardrobe.

P is for Puppets. Hand puppets can be made out of many materials. They do not need to be elaborate. You can make them out of cloth, with embroidered features. You can cut them out of cardboard, or saw them out of wood with a jigsaw. You can even make them out of little wooden ice cream spoons. Draw a face on the spoon with crayon or paint, and you have a puppet! A simple puppet stag can be made out of a few pieces of wood nailed together. Presto! The door has been opened for a new world of dramatic puppet play by your child.

Q is for Quiz Games. Children love these on television—why shouldn't you design your own homemade quiz games? You can play them anywhere: at home, in the car, on a boat, at a picnic. Make them easy at first for your small child. "I'll bet you can't guess what I'm thinking of. It's red and you like to eat it." The quiz can increase in complexity and difficulty as your child grows older.

R is for Rubber Stamps. Any old piece of rubber will do: an old inner tube ... anything Cut out shapes or letters from the rubber with a sharp knife; then glue them on to a piece of wood big enough for your child to grasp easily. Now he has a rubber stamp he can use to make designs on paper. You can also use large rubber erasers and cut designs into them. You can use ink pads or make your own stamp pads out of a foam rubber sponge soaked with tempera paint.

S is for Serendipity. This word means "the art of unexpectedly finding something you weren't looking for." If you can manag to loosen up your personality and get out of your mental ruts, you can allow serendipity to work for you Suppose you see something interesting at a junk sale but don't know what you could possibly make out of it. The object intrigues you. and it is inexpensive. Buy it! We once bought very cheaply a hundred or more plywood range markers at a Naval Surplus Depot. We didn't know what we were going to make out of them at the time we bought them, but they looked interesting. We ended up making puppet faces out of them.

Here's a good recipe for serendipity in the family. Write down a bunch of interesting and zany things to do and put them in a box. Some weekend when you can't think of what to do, pick one of them out of the box and do it, whatever it is!

T is for Toothpicks. You can make a collage from these on paper, cardboard, or wood. You can use them to teach a child the capital letters, putting them together in sand or gluing them on a background. You can glue them together to make houses or forts. There are all sorts of things you can do with the lowly toothpick!

U is for Useless Things. By now you have gotten the message: There is no such thing as a "useless thing" for a preschool child. If you have imagination, you or he can find a use for this hitherto "useless" object. If you can do nothing else with it, use it in a collage!

V is for Visits. Visits to a bank, a newspaper, a filling station, a garage, a fish cannery, a bakery, a fire station, a police station ... the list is endless. Your preschooler hasn't seen these places, and the visit will greatly expand his intellectual horizons.

W is for Water Play. Your child can use water play outside in the summer, and inside in the sink all year round. Water play in the bathtub in connection with his bath is always enjoyed by a child. Let him have different-size cans or plastic bottles, plus sponges, or plastic boats and floating objects. Sometimes vegetable coloring makes for a very special kind of enjoyable water play.

X is for Xylophone. Buy an inexpensive one from the store, or make your own at home. The basic principle is simply that of different tones produced by different sizes and lengths of metal or wood. You can use different lengths of old copper tubing or steel pipe, or you can use different lengths and thicknesses of wood. Lay the metal or wood pieces out flat on a big piece of foam rubber or hang them up with sturdy fishline like chimes.

Y is for Yarn. This can be bought very inexpensively at the Goodwill or Salvation Army or surplus store. Your child can use it with sewing cards, which you make by punching holes in cardboard. You punch the holes in the shape of a design or alphabet letters, and he sews the yarn onto the card. He can do the same with any old IBM cards you find. Yarn can also be used in collage.

Z is for Zoo Animals. Children love to play with toy animals, and your child will especially like it if you have made the animals. You can cut them out of cardboard. If you have a jigsaw or coping saw you can cut them out of wood. But whether you make them of wood or cardboard, be sure to glue or nail them onto a flat piece of wood for a foundation, so they will stand upright. Color them with crayons or paint. You don't have to be an artist to do this project. The shape of the animal can be very crude indeed, and your child won't mind. Whatever the shape of the animals, he will love them. They are his own private zoo, made for him by his own parent.

Appendix C

A PARENT'S GUIDE TO CHILDREN'S BOOKS FOR THE PRESCHOOL YEARS

Warning: Do not buy any book from this list or any other book list without a first-hand inspection of the book. Browse in a library or a bookstore and look the book over before you decide to buy it. If it is a book *you* are going to read to your child, you should like it yourself.

This list of books is arranged according to ages and stages of development in the preschool years. Since there is such a profusion of good books for preschool children, I have starred (*) the ones I think are especially good.

I. **The Stage of Toddlerhood** (approximately from first to second birthday):
   A. Books for "Labeling the Environment"

At this age a "book" is not something that contains a continuous narrative story, but something with pictures of people or objects, and words labeling those people or objects. Books are useful devices at this age to help your child play the "label the environment" game we discussed in the chapter on toddlerhood.

Books for this age should be sturdy affairs, of cardboard or cloth, because the first thing your toddler will probably do with these beginning books is put them in his mouth.

*1. *Golden Block Books* (Western Publishing). These extra sturdy cardboard books are shaped like building blocks. They are too strong to tear, too solid to bend, and just the right size for the tiny hands of a toddler. Each page has a simple caption and a full-color picture of a familiar object easily recognizable by a toddler. The four books in the set include *Here I Am, All My Friends, Time to Eat,* and *Animal Friends.*

2. Sears or Montgomery Ward catalog, Blue Chip Stamp catalog, or toy catalog. Although ordinarily not thought of as a book, these catalogs are ideal for playing the "label the environment" game. And who cares if a few pages get torn out here and there?

*3. *Best Word Book Ever*, Richard Scarry (Western Publishing). This book is one of the best investments a parent could ever make for a toddler. When you have finished playing the "label the environment" game with this book, with its 1,400 gaily illustrated objects with words to match, your child will have a vocabulary of 1,400 words. A terrific boost to his language development! Uniquely appealing animals are pictured in all kinds of activities related to a young child's experience and interest. This book can be used for several years with a young child.

*4. *The Cat in the Hat Beginner Book Dictionary*, Dr. Seuss (Random House). Another excellent picture dictionary to play "label the environment." Funny pictures and a phrase show the meaning of 1,000 words in Dr. Seuss's inimitable style. You can read it to your child when he is a toddler. And he can read it himself in the first three grades of school.

5. *My First Book* and *My First Toys* (Platt and Munk). Extra sturdy, vividly colored books. Each page clearly pictures three objects you can point to and teach your toddler to name.

B. Mother Goose Books

There are a tremendous number of Mother Goose books on the market. You should browse and find one most suited to your own taste. I recommend three for special consideration.

*1. *Mother Goose*, Brian Wildsmith (Franklin Watts). I must confess I am a dyed-in-the-wool fan of this wonderful British artist. That's why I would personally choose his book, with the authentic nursery rhymes illustrated in vivid and striking colors.

2. *The Puffin Book of Nursery Rhymes,* Iona and Peter Opie (Penguin [paperback]). Two hundred rhymes in related sequence.

3. *Hi Diddle Diddle* (Scholastic). Contains very simple rhymes. There is also a small 33⅓ rpm record, *Hi Diddle Diddle,* which parallels the book and will aid in introducing your child to Mother Goose.

Incidentally, a parent often does not need to wait until her child's first birthday to start reading Mother Goose, but may begin when the baby is nine or ten months old. A baby this age will delight in the rhythmic repetition of sounds in simple nursery rhymes.

C. Other Books for the Toddler

*1. *Pat the Bunny,* Dorothy Kunhardt (Western Publishing). On each small page there is something for baby to do: look in the mirror, play peek-a-boo, smell the flowers, or pat the felt-lined bunny. A delightful book for a toddler.

*2. *The Giant Nursery Book of Things That Go,* George Zaffo (Doubleday). Boys especially love this book. Large action pictures of boats, trains, trucks, planes . . . things that go.

3. *Baby's First Book,* Garth Williams (Western Publishing). A picture book on cardboard pages. Excellent for baby to begin with, as are Garth Williams' *Baby Animals* and *Baby Farm Animals.*

4. *First Things,* George Adams and Paul Henning (Platt and Munk). A stunning picture book of things that are familiar. Done in beautiful, natural color.

5. *Anybody at Home?,* H. A. Rey (Houghton Mifflin). Toddlers will delight in finding the surprise picture under the flap of each page.

6. *Farm Animals,* Irma Wilde (Grosset and Dunlap). Young children love to look at books about animals. This book of farm animals will exert a great appeal.

7. *Things To See*, Thomas Matthiesen (Platt and Munk). Beautiful color photographs depict things a little baby will recognize.

8. *Who Lives Here?*, Pat and Eve Witte (Western Publishing). Peek under the flap and see who lives here. A charming book. Little ones love it.

9. *The Touch Me Book*, Pat and Eve Witte (Western Publishing). This touch and feel book will fascinate toddlers. With a flick of a finger they can work a seesaw, turn a bicycle wheel, move a giraffe's head, and operate many other objects.

D. Bedtime Books for the Toddler

*1. *Goodnight Moon*, Margaret Wise Brown (Harper and Row). A toddler's classic. All of my children loved it. Old fashioned illustrations of a little bunny saying goodnight to everybody and especially to "nobody."

*2. *A Child's Goodnight Book*, Margaret Wise Brown (W. R. Scott). This delightful book, geared to a toddler's level, describes bedtime.

3. *Bedtime for Frances*, Russel Hoban (Harper and Row). Russel Hoban is one of our finest writers for young children, and his series of books about Frances, the irresistible little badger, is particularly fine. This one tells of Frances' clever ways to stay up past her bedtime. If you should find this a little too advanced for your toddler, wait a bit and try it out on him in the next stage of First Adolescence, when he will be sure to like it.

II. **The Stage of First Adolescence** (approximately second to third birthday):

The age ranges in this book list are not to be taken rigidly and absolutely. A book that hits one two-year-old "just right" may be too advanced for another two-year-old, or too babyish for another. Your child is unique and the book must meet him "where he is." Some of the books that were his favorites in the Stage of Toddlerhood will continue to be his favorites in this stage. Some of the books that are listed in this book list under the Preschool Stage would be too advanced for many First Adolescents. Other First Adolescents will be delighted by them and beg you to read them again and again. This or any other book list is only a rough and ready guide to selecting books for different age children. *Your child is the final arbiter of what book is appropriate for him. Be guided by his response.*

A child in this stage is fascinated by words and word play. And so he will continue to love nursery rhymes, with their rhythm and repetition of sounds. This age child loves to repeat something until he feels he has mastered it. He likes the repetition in familiar nursery tales such as *The Three Little Pigs* or *Chicken Little*. He likes to recognize what is coming next in the story and chant it with you as you read it to him. He also loves sounds of all sorts, particularly unusual or funny sounds. When you read books of sounds to him, emphasize the sound.

He also enjoys stories about the "here and now" of his everyday world: going to the market with mother, riding in a car or bus, playing in a park, going to a zoo. Animal stories are especially popular at this age.

Reading to a First Adolescent should be a cooperative affair. He likes to look at the book and touch it. He likes to be asked to find things in the illustrations. Sometimes he likes to join in the chant of a familiar repetition from a well-loved book.

He often has favorite books he will want you to read him day after day. Woe betide you if you dare to change a phrase in a familiar book! Sometimes it is difficult to get him to listen to a new book.

A. ABC and Counting books

*1. *Brian Wildsmith's ABC*, Brian Wildsmith (Watts). An Animal ABC book done in Wildsmith's usual stunning colors.

2. *ABC of Cars and Trucks*, Anne Alexander (Doubleday). Instructs a child in his ABC's by using cars and trucks.

3. *ABC of Buses*, Dorothy Shuttlesworth (Doubleday). Another ABC book with a definite appeal to boys.

*4. *Bruno Munari's ABC*, Bruno Munari (World). A highly original alphabet book with beautiful illustrations.

*5. *Dr. Seuss's ABC*, Dr. Seuss (Random House). A wonderful ABC book done in Dr. Seuss's inimitable style.

*6. *Brian Wildsmith's 1 2 3's*, Brian Wildsmith (Watts). A unique counting book for young children. A visual delight.

7. *One Snail and Me*, Emily McLeod (Little Brown). A child learns to count in a most delightful way—in a bathtub.

8. *Counting Carnival*, Feenie Ziner and Paul Galdone (Coward-McCann). A clever way to stimulate number awareness.

9. *Brown Cow Farm*, Dahlov Ipcar (Doubleday). A thoroughly enjoyable book about counting up to 100. Excellent illustrations.

*10. *The Nutshell Library*, Maurice Sendak (Harpers). Young children are fascinated by miniature things, and these tiny, tiny books have an irresistible appeal. This nutshell library of four books includes a counting book, an alphabet book, a book about the months.

B. Books About Sounds, Which Help to Develop a Child's Perceptual Acuity

As I mentioned above, a child of this age is fascinated by sounds, and particularly the repetition of sounds. Margaret Wise Brown has probably done more books of this nature than anybody. Here is a selection of several of her books which will appeal to the First Adolescent.

1. *The Noisy Book*, Margaret Wise Brown (Harper and Row).

2. *The Indoor Noisy Book*, Margaret Wise Brown (Harper and Row).

3. *The City Noisy Book*, Margaret Wise Brown (Harper and Row).

4. *The Country Noisy Book*, Margaret Wise Brown (Harper and Row).

5. *The Seashore Noisy Book*, Margaret Wise Brown (Harper and Row).

6. *The Summer Noisy Book*, Margaret Wise Brown (Harper and Row).

7. *The Winter Noisy Book*, Margaret Wise Brown (Harper and Row).

8. *Bow Wow! Meow! A First Book of Sounds*, Melanie Bellah (Western Publishing). A good introduction to sounds for the First Adolescent.

9. *Listen to My Seashell*, Charlotte Steiner (Knopf). Another good book of sounds for the young child.

C. Nursery Tales

* *Tall Book of Nursery Tales*. Illustrated by Feodor Rojankovsky (Harper and Row). Twenty-four of the most popular nursery tales, with superb illustrations by Rojankovsky. Children particularly like the repetition found in tales such as *The Little Red Hen, The Three Little Pigs,* and *The Three Bears.*

D. Animal Stories

Animal stories are popular with this age. This age child often identifies more closely with animals than he does with children.

*1. *The Tale of Peter Rabbit*, Beatrix Potter (Warne). This classic tale has been going strong since it was first published in 1903. It is doubtful if children will ever get tired of the story of Peter, who set out to do precisely what his mother told him not to do: go into Mr. McGregor's garden. Has a particular appeal to the negative nature of the First Adolescent!

*2. *Millions of Cats*, Wanda Gag (Coward-McCann). A very old man and woman wanted a cat—just one cat—but soon they had "millions and billions and trillions of cats." Your child will soon be chiming in as you read: "hundreds of cats, thousands of cats, millions and billions and trillions of cats!" Wood-block illustrations of great distinction by the author.

*3. *Make Way for Ducklings*, Robert McCloskey (Viking). Another animal story that has become a children's classic. A family of mallard ducks in Boston find a home and are befriended by a policeman. The bold illustrations by the author are excellent.

*4. *Little Bear*, Else Minarik (Harper and Row). The delightful adventures of a little bear and his many antics. Depicts the warmth of feeling and the special companionship that exists between a small child and his mother.

*5. *The Duck*, Margaret Wise Brown (Harper and Row). Gorgeous photographs by Ylla and a simple text by the author tell the story of a duck that visits the zoo and sees many animals.

*6. *Harry the Dirty Dog*, Gene Zion (Harper and Row). A white dog with black spots gets himself so dirty his owners don't know him. Finally he has an amusing struggle to get clean again. Distinctly appealing to the love-to-get-messy nature of the First Adolescent.

*7. *The Story About Ping*, Marjorie Flack (Viking). The story of a fluffy yellow duck who lives on a Chinese riverboat.

*8. *Swimmy*, Leo Lionni (Pantheon). Swimmy, a black fish, decides to explore the unknown depths of the ocean. The full-color illustrations are stunning. This book will introduce a young child to good art.

Speaking of books to introduce a young child to good art, here is a marvelous threesome by Brian Wildsmith. Animal books with spectacular full-color illustrations.

*9. *Brian Wildsmith's Birds* (Watts)

*10 *Brian Wildsmith's Fishes* (Watts)

*11. *Brian Wildsmith's Wild Animals* (Watts)

12. *Johnny Crow's Garden*, Leslie Brooke (Warne). A delightful story of Johnny Crow and the growth of his garden.

13. *Bread and Jam for Frances*, Russel Hoban (Harper and Row).

14. *A Birthday for Frances*, Russel Hoban (Harper and Row). Two more amusing adventures of Frances, the lovable badger.

15. *The Runaway Bunny*, Margaret Wise Brown (Harper and Row). A nice story of a naughty little bunny and his understanding mother.

16. *Whatever Happens to Puppies?*, Bill Hall (Western Publishing).

17. *Whatever Happens to Kittens?*, Bill Hall (Western Publishing).

18. *Whatever Happens to Bear Cubs?*, Bill Hall (Western Publishing).

*19. *Where Have You Been?*, Margaret Wise Brown (Hastings [hardcover]), (Scholastic [paperback]). Fourteen animals answer the same question. Children love the repetition.

*20. *The Cat in the Hat*, Dr. Seuss (Random House). A nonsense story in verse about an unusual cat and his tricks. A modern classic for children. Also by the same author: *The Cat in the Hat Comes Back*.

E. Books About the Child and His Familiar Everyday World

1. *This Is the Way Animals Walk*, Louise Woodcock (Scott). The author of *The Life and Ways of the Two-Year-Old* really knows this age. A simple repetitious text which children of this age will like, together with humorous pictures.

*2. *All Falling Down*, Gene Zion (Harper and Row). Young children like this because of its repetition and also its reassuring surprise ending. Various things are falling down: leaves, snow, the block house. But then comes the ending: "Daddy lifts him up and tosses him in the air. *He doesn't fall* . . . (Italics added) Daddy catches him."

3. *Play With Me*, Marie Ets (Viking). A little girl needs someone to play with and tries to get a grasshopper, frog, turtle, chipmunk and other animals to play with her.

4. *Just Me*, Marie Ets (Viking). A little boy can walk like a cat, hop like a rabbit, and wriggle like a snake. However, his greatest joy is in running "just like me," when his daddy calls.

*5. *Umbrella*, Taro Yashima (Viking). A young Japanese girl in New York wants it to rain so she can use her new umbrella and red rubber boots. Gorgeous illustrations by the author.

6. *Big Red Bus*, Ethel Kessler (Doubleday). The everyday story of what the big red bus does. Boys will especially like this.

*7. *A Friend Is Someone Who Likes You*, Joan Walsh Anglund (Harcourt Brace and World). A modern classic—a book of friendship and kindly feelings, with delicate illustrations by the author.

8. *While Susie Sleeps*, Nina Schneider (Scott). What happens when I sleep is a question asked by young children. Nice story about what goes on at night.

*9. *Daddies: What They Do All Day*, Helen Puner (Lothrop). A wonderful book. Children need to know and understand what daddies do.

*10 *The Carrot Seed*, Crockett Johnson (Harper and Row). Charming story of a little boy with faith.

11. *Where's Andy?*, Jane Thayer (Morrow). Mother and Andy play hide-and-seek.

12. *The Day Daddy Stayed Home*, Ethel and Leonard Kessler (Doubleday). A delightful story about things a daddy can do when he has to stay home.

*13. *When You Were a Little Baby*, Rhoda Berman (Lothrop). Children at this stage love to hear about what they were like when they were tiny babies. This book has great appeal for that reason.

*14. *Here Comes Night*, Miriam Schlein (Whitman). A bedtime book that tells about the night.

15. *Saturday Walk*, Ethel Wright and Richard Rose (Scott). Large, vivid pictures of cars, ships, and trains. Especially appealing to boys.

16. *Everybody Eats and Everybody Has a House*, Mary McBurnery Green (Scott). An illustrated book showing what animals do and eat.

17. *The Night When Mother Was Away*, Charlotte Zolotow (Lothrop). Daddy takes care of his little girl, who doesn't want to sleep.

*18. *The Hole Book*, Peter Newell (Harper and Row). An old book which never loses its fascination. Small children love to look through the hole and see where it leads to next.

III. **The Preschool Stage** (approximately third to sixth birthday):

These are years of enormous intellectual potential for your youngster. Research studies have shown that how much a child is read to during these years correlates highly with how successful he is in school. We need to read both nonfiction and fiction to the preschooler. Nonfiction provides him with key concepts which help him understand his world; fiction enlarges his imagination and his creative thinking.

A. Nonfiction
1. "Double-Duty" Beginning to Read Books
These books do double duty for both the child who has not yet learned to read and the child who is just learning to read You can read the book to your child in his preschool years before he has learned to read. Later, as he is learning to read in kindergarten or first grade. these books will aid him in learning this vital skill. He will regard them as old familiar friends rather than frightening "newcomers," full of unfamiliar words. His familiarity with the book will build confidence in his ability to master this strange new task of learning to read.

Rather than break these books down into specific categories of subject matter, I have listed them by publisher to make it easy for you to become familiar with the Beginning Reader series of each publisher. Although I have listed them under nonfiction, in actuality the Beginning Reader books contain both nonfiction and fiction. However, it seemed best to list all of them at one time according to publisher.

a) Harper: I Can Read Books
*(1) *Doctors and Nurses: What Do They Do?*, Carla Greene

(2) *Soldiers and Sailors: What Do They Do?*, Carla Greene

*(3) *Railroad Engineers and Airplane Pilots: What Do They Do?*, Carla Greene

*(4) *Policemen and Firemen: What do They Do?*, Carla Greene

*(5) *Little Bear*, Else Minarik

(6) *A Kiss for Little Bear*, Else Minarik

(7) *Little Bear's Visit*, Else Minarik

(8) *Little Bear's Friend*, Else Minarik

(9) *Father Bear Comes Home*, Else Minarik

*(10) *No Fighting, No Biting!*, Else Minarik

*(11) *Danny and the Dinosaur*, Syd Hoff

(12) *Sammy the Seal*, Syd Hoff

(13) *Julius*, Syd Hoff

(14) *Chester*, Syd Hoff

(15) *Oliver*, Syd Hoff

(16) *Little Chief*, Syd Hoff

(17) *Stanley*, Syd Hoff

(18) *Last One Home Is a Green Pig*, Edith Hurd

(19) *Hurry Hurry*, Edith Hurd

(20) *Stop Stop*, Edith Hurd

(21) *No Funny Business*, Edith Hurd

(22) *Emmet's Pig*, Mary Stolz

*(23) *Harry and the Lady Next Door*, Gene Zion

(24) *The Fire Cat*, Esther Averill

(25) *David and the Giant*, Mike McClintock

(26) *Morris Is a Cowboy, a Policeman, and a Baby Sitter*, B. Wiseman

*(27) *A Picture for Harold's Room*, Crockett Johnson

(28) *Tell Me Some More*, Crosby Bonsall

(29) *Who's a Pest?*, Crosby Bonsall

(30) *The Happy Birthday Present*, Joan Heilbroner

(31) *This Is the House Where Jack Lives*, Joan Heilbroner

(32) *Little Runner of the Longhouse*, Betty Baker

(33) *What Spot?*, Crosby Bonsall

(34) *The Secret Three*, Mildred Myrick

(35) *Grizzwold*, Syd Hoff

(36) *Lucille*, Arnold Lobel

(37) *Red Fox and His Canoe*, Nathaniel Benchley

(38) *Tom and the Two Hands*, Russel Hoban

(39) *Three to Get Ready*, Betty Boegehold

(40) *Johnny Lion's Book*, Edith Hurd

(41) *Oscar Otter*, Nathaniel Benchley

(42) *Amelia Bedelia and the Surprise Shower*, Peggy Parish

*(43) *Magic Secrets*, Rose Wyler and Gerald Ames

*(44) *Spooky Tricks*, Rose Wyler and Gerald Ames

(45) *Truck Drivers: What Do They Do?*, Carla Greene

*(46) *Animal Doctors: What Do They Do?*, Carla Greene

(47) *I Am Better Than You!*, Robert Lopshire

(48) *Small Pig*, Arnold Lobel

b) Harper: I Can Read Science Books

*(1) *Seeds and More Seeds*, Millicent Selsam

(2) *Plenty of Fish*, Millicent Selsam

(3) *Tony's Birds*, Millicent Selsam

*(4) *Terry and the Caterpillars*, Millicent Selsam

*(5) *Greg's Microscope*, Millicent Selsam

(6) *Let's Get Turtles*, Millicent Selsam

*(7) *Benny's Animals and How He Put Them in Order*, Millicent Selsam

*(8) *When an Animal Grows*, Millicent Selsam

(9) *The Bug That Laid the Golden Eggs*, Millicent Selsam

*(10) *Hidden Animals*, Millicent Selsam

(11) *Red Tag Comes Back*, Fred Phleger

*(12) *Prove It!*, Rose Wyler and Gerald Ames

(13) *The Toad Hunt*, Janet Chenery

*(14) *Ants Are Fun*, Mildred Myrick

(15) *Wolfie*, Janet Chenery

(16) *Catch a Whale by the Tail*, Edward Ricciuti

(17) *The Penguins Are Coming*, R. L. Penney

c) Harper: I Can Read History Books

(1) *The Pig War*, Betty Baker

(2) *Indian Summer*, F. N. Monjo

     *(3) *Sam the Minuteman*, Nathaniel Benchley
- d) Harper: I Can Read Sports Books
  - (1) *Here Comes the Strikeout*, Leonard Kessler
  - (2) *Kick, Pass, and Run*, Leonard Kessler
  - (3) *Last One In Is a Rotten Egg*, Leonard Kessler
- e) Harper: I Can Read Mystery Books
  - (1) *The Case of the Hungry Stranger*, Crosby Bonsall
  - *(2) *The Case of the Cat's Meow*, Crosby Bonsall
  - (3) *The Case of the Dumb Bells*, Crosby Bonsall
  - (4) *The Strange Disappearance of Arthur Cluck*, Nathaniel Benchley
  - (5) *A Ghost Named Fred*, Nathaniel Benchley
  - (6) *The Homework Caper*, Joan Lexau
  - (7) *The Rooftop Mystery*, Joan Lexau
  - (8) *Big Max*, Ken Platt
  - (9) *Binky Brothers, Detectives*, James Lawrence
- f) Harper: Early I Can Read Books
  - (1) *Albert the Albatross*, Syd Hoff
  - (2) *Who Will By My Friends?*, Syd Hoff
  - (3) *Cat and Dog*, Else Minarik
  - (4) *What Have I Got?*, Mike McClintock
  - (5) *Come and Have Fun*, Edith Hurd
- g) Crowell: Let's Read and Find Out Science Book Series

It is difficult to praise this series of books too highly. The scientific information is accurate and up-to-date, for the editor of the series is Dr. Franklyn Branley, Coordinator of Educational Services for the American Museum-Hayder Planetarium. In addition, Dr. Branley himself has written a number of books for the series. Educationally, the books are superb and meet the child on his level, for the special adviser of the series is Dr. Roma Gans, Professor Emeritus of Childhood Education at Teachers College, Columbia University. The format of the books is splendid, and the illustrations are eye-catching. A parent will thoroughly enjoy reading any book in this series to her child.

*(1) *Before You Were a Baby*, Paul Showers and Kay Showers
*(2) *A Baby Starts to Grow*, Paul Showers
*(3) *Your Skin and Mine*, Paul Showers
*(4) *The Wonder of Stones*, Roma Gans
 (5) *Why Frogs Are Wet*, Judy Hawes
*(6) *What the Moon Is Like*, Franklyn Branley
*(7) *What Makes Day and Night?*, Franklyn Branley
*(8) *What Makes a Shadow?*, Clyde Bulla
*(9) *Watch Honeybees With Me*, Judy Hawes
*(10) *Upstairs and Downstairs*, Ryerson Johnson
*(11) *A Tree Is a Plant*, Clyde Bulla
*(12) *The Sun: Our Nearest Star*, Franklyn Branley
 (13) *The Sunlit Sea*, Augusta Goldin
*(14) *Where Does Your Garden Grow?*, Augusta Goldin
 (15) *Starfish*, Edith Hurd
*(16) *Straight Hair, Curly Hair*, Augusta Goldin
 (17) *Spider Silk*, Augusta Goldin
*(18) *Snow Is Falling*, Franklyn Branley
 (19) *Shrimps*, Judy Hawes
*(20) *Seeds by Wind and Water*, Helene Jordan
 (21) *Sandpipers*, Edith Hurd
*(22) *Salt*, Augusta Goldin
*(23) *Rockets and Satellites*, Franklyn Branley
*(24) *Rain and Hail*, Franklyn Branley
*(25) *North, South, East, and West*, Franklyn Branley
*(26) *My Hands*, Aliki
*(27) *My Five Senses*, Aliki
*(28) *The Moon Seems to Change*, Franklyn Branley
*(29) *A Map Is a Picture*, Barbara Rinkoff
*(30) *Look at Your Eyes*, Paul Showers
*(31) *The Listening Walk*, Paul Showers
 (32) *Ladybug, Ladybug*, Judy Hawes
*(33) *It's Nesting Time*, Roma Gans
*(34) *In the Night*, Paul Showers
*(35) *Icebergs*, Roma Gans
 (36) *Hummingbirds in the Garden*, Roma Gans
 (37) *How You Talk*, Paul Showers
*(38) *How Many Teeth*, Paul Showers

*(39) *How a Seed Grows*, Helene Jordan
*(40) *High Sounds, Low Sounds*, Franklyn Branley
*(41) *Hear Your Heart*, Paul Showers
 (42) *Glaciers*, Wendell Tangborn
*(43) *Follow Your Nose*, Paul Showers
*(44) *Floating and Sinking*, Franklyn Branley
*(45) *Flash, Crash, Rumble and Roll*, Franklyn Branley
 (46) *Fireflies in the Night*, Judy Hawes
*(47) *Find Out by Touching*, Paul Showers
 (48) *The Emperor Penguins*, Kazue Mizumura
 (49) *Ducks Don't Get Wet*, Augusta Goldin
 (50) *Down Come the Leaves*, Henrietta Bancroft
 (51) *The Clean Brook*, Margaret Bartlett
*(52) *Where the Brook Begins*, Margaret Bartlett
*(53) *The Bottom of the Sea*, Augusta Goldin
*(54) *Birds Eat and Eat and Eat*, Roma Gans
 (55) *Birds at Night*, Roma Gans
 (56) *Big Tracks, Little Tracks*, Franklyn Branley
 (57) *The Big Dipper*, Franklyn Branley
*(58) *Bees and Beelines*, Judy Hawes
*(59) *Animals in Winter*, Henrietta Bancroft and Richard Van Gelder
*(60) *Air Is All Around You*, Franklyn Branley

h) Follett: Beginning Science Books Series
*(1) *Air*, John Feilen
*(2) *Airplanes*, Edward Victor
*(3) *Animals Without Backbones*, Robin Pfadt
*(4) *Ants*, Charles Schoenknecht
*(5) *Astronautics*, Julian May
 (6) *Bats*, Richard Van Gelder
*(7) *Birds*, Isabel Wasson
*(8) *Butterflies*, Jeanne Brouillette
*(9) *Climate*, Julian May
 (10) *Deer*, John Feilen
*(11) *Earth Through the Ages*, Philip Carona
*(12) *Electricity*, Edward Victor
*(13) *Fishes*, Hubert Woods
*(14) *Friction*, Edward Victor
 (15) *Frogs and Toads*, Charles Schoenknecht

*(14) *Motion*, Seymour Simon

j) Children's Press: The True Book Series

This fine series of books will provide your child with valuable information about science and the world he lives in. Each book is scientifically accurate, well written, and illustrated to appeal to a small child. The series has been prepared under the general direction of Illa Podendorf of the Laboratory School of The University of Chicago. She has done an outstanding job.

*(1)   *African Animals*, John Purcell
*(2)   *Air Around Us*, Margaret Friskey
*(3)   *Airports and Airplanes*, John Lewellen
*(4)   *Animal Homes*, Illa Podendorf
*(5)   *Animal Babies*, Illa Podendorf
*(6)   *Animals of Sea and Shore*, Illa Podendorf
*(7)   *Animals of Small Pond*, Phoebe Erickson
*(8)   *Automobiles*, Norman and Mary Carlisle
*(9)   *Bacteria*, Anne Frahm
 (10) *Birds We Know*, Margaret Friskey
*(11) *Bridges*, Norman and Mary Carlisle
*(12) *Chemistry*, Philip Carona
*(13) *Circus*, Mabel Harmer
 (14) *Cloth*, Esther Nighbert
*(15) *Communication*, Opal Miner
*(16) *Conservation*, Richard Gates
*(17) *Cowboys*, Teri Martini
*(18) *Deserts*, Elsa Posell
*(19) *Dinosaurs*, Mary Lou Clark
 (20) *Dogs*, Elsa Posell
*(21) *Energy*, Illa Podendorf
*(22) *Farm Animals*, John Lewellen
 (23) *Flight*, E. Blandford
 (24) *Freedom and Our U.S. Family*, Paul Witty
 (25) *Health*, Olive Haynes
 (26) *Holidays*, John Purcell
*(27) *Honeybees*, John Lewellen
 (28) *Horses*, Elsa Posell
*(29) *Houses*, Katherine Carter
*(30) *Indians*, Teri Martini
*(31) *Insects*, Illa Podendorf
*(32) *Jungles*, Illa Podendorf
*(33) *Knights*, John Lewellen
 (34) *Little Eskimos*, Donald Copeland
*(35) *Maps*, Norman and Mary Carlisle

* (5) *Hop on Pop*, Dr. Seuss
* (6) *Green Eggs and Ham*, Dr. Seuss
* (7) *One Fish, Two Fish, Red Fish, Blue Fish*, Dr. Seuss
* (8) *Dr. Seuss's Sleep Book*, Dr. Seuss
* (9) *Foot Book*, Dr. Seuss
* (10) *Ear Book*, Dr. Seuss
* (11) *Fox in Socks*, Dr. Seuss. (This is an especially good book for a child just learning to read. With it, he can practice his phonics in the most painless way possible. Read it to your youngster in his preschool years, and let him read it to you as he is learning how.)
  (12) *Go Dog Go!*, P. D. Eastman
  (13) *Don and Donna Go to Bat*, Al Perkins
  (14) *A Fish out of Water*, Helen Palmer
  (15) *Do You Know What I'm Going To Do Next Saturday?*, Helen Palmer
  (16) *The Digging-est Dog*, Al Perkins
  (17) *Cowboy Andy*, Edna Chandler
* (18) *Book of Riddles*, Bennett Cerf
* (19) *Book of Laughs*, Bennett Cerf
* (20) *Animal Riddles*, Bennett Cerf
  (21) *The Big Jump*, Benjamin Elkin
  (22) *The Big Honey Hunt*, Stanley and Janice Berenstain
  (23) *The Best Nest*, P. D. Eastman
  (24) *The Bear's Picnic*, Stanley and Janice Berenstain
  (25) *The Bear's Vacation*, Stanley and Janice Berenstain
  (26) *The Bear Scouts*, Stanley and Janice Berenstain
* (27) *Are You My Mother?*, P. D. Eastman
  (28) *Ann Can Fly*, Fred Phleger
* (29) *Inside Outside Upside Down*, Stanley and Janice Berenstain
  (30) *The Whales Go By*, Fred Phleger
  (31) *Summer*, Alice Low
  (32) *Snow*, Roy McKie and P. D. Eastman
  (33) *Sam and the Firefly*, P. D. Eastman
  (34) *Robert the Rose Horse*, Joan Heilbroner
* (35) *Put Me in the Zoo*, Robert Lopshire

(36) *Off to the Races*, Fred and Marjorie Phleger

(37) *The King's Wish and Other Stories*, Benjamin Elkin

(38) *King Midas and the Golden Touch*, Al Perkins

(39) *The King, the Mice, and the Cheese*, Nancy and Eric Gurney

*(40) *I Was Kissed by a Seal at the Zoo*, Helen Palmer

*(41) *Hugh Lofting's Travels of Doctor Doolittle*, Al Perkins

*(42) *Hugh Lofting's Doctor Doolittle and the Pirates*, Al Perkins

*(43) *How To Make Flibbers, etc.*, Robert Lopshire

*(44) *Why I Built the Boogle House*, Helen Palmer

l) Grosset and Dunlap: Living Science Books

*(1) *Air and Water*, Woods Palmer

(2) *Plants*, Leslie Waller

*(3) *Mountains*, Leslie Waller

*(4) *Light*, Leslie Waller

(5) *Gems and Rare Metals*, Leslie Waller

*(6) *Energy*, Jordan Moore

*(7) *Continents and Islands*, Leslie Waller

(8) *Plains and Prairies*, Woods Palmer

(9) *Birds*, Woods Palmer

*(10) *Animals*, Leslie Waller

m) Grosset and Dunlap: Early Start Preschool Reader Series

A particularly good series of books to use to teach your youngster to read in the preschool years. They have the smallest vocabulary of any of the early reader books, ranging from sixteen words to thirty-nine words for an entire book. They are definitely on the level of a preschooler, and young children like them.

*(1) *Happy Day*, Anne DeCaprio

*(2) *Dinosaur Ben*, Anne DeCaprio

*(3) *Willy and the Whale*, Anne DeCaprio

*(4) *The Tent*, Dorothy Seymour

*(5) *The Sandwich*, Dorothy Seymour

*(6) *The Rabbit*, Dorothy Seymour

*(7) *The Pond*, Dorothy Seymour

*(8) *Poems*, Tony Lazzaro
*(9) *On the Ranch*, Dorothy Seymour
*(10) *One, Two*, Anne DeCaprio
*(11) *New Bugle*, Anne DeCaprio
*(12) *Lion and the Deer*, Anne DeCaprio
*(13) *Jumping*, Karen Stephens
*(14) *Crate Train*, Dorothy Seymour
*(15) *Bus From Chicago*, Anne DeCaprio
*(16) *Bill and the Fish*, Dorothy Seymour
*(17) *Big Beds and Little Beds*, Dorothy Seymour
*(18) *Ballerina Bess*, Dorothy Seymour
*(19) *Ann Likes Red*, Dorothy Seymour
n) Grosset and Dunlap: Easy Reader Series
   (1) *Will You Come to My Party?*, Sara Asheron
   (2) *When I Grow Up*, Jean Bethell
   (3) *What's Going On Here?*, Mary Elting
   (4) *A Train for Tommy*, Edith Tarcov
   (5) *The Three Coats of Benny Bunny*, Sara Asheron
   (6) *The Surprising Pets of Billy Brown*, Tamara Kitt
   (7) *A Surprise in the Tree*, Sara Asheron
   (8) *The Surprise in the Storybook*, Sara Asheron
   (9) *The Secret Cat*, Tamara Kitt
   (10) *Question and Answer Book*, Mary Elting
   (11) *Petey the Peanut Man*, Jean Bethell
   (12) *Old Man and the Tiger*, Alvin Tresselt
   (13) *Mr. Pine's Purple House*, Leonard Kessler
   (14) *Mr. Pine's Mixed Up Signs*, Leonard Kessler
   (15) *The Monkey in the Rocket*, Jean Bethell
   (16) *Miss Polly's Animal School*, Mary Elting
   (17) *Little Popcorn*, Sara Asheron
   (18) *Little Gray Mouse Goes Sailing*, Sara Asheron
   (19) *Little Gray Mouse and the Train*, Sara Asheron
   (20) *Laurie and the Yellow Curtains*, Sara Asheron
*(21) *I Made a Line*, Leonard Kessler
   (22) *Hurry Up Slowpoke*, Crosby Newell

*(23) *How to Find a Friend*, Sara Asheron
*(24) *How the Animals Get in the Zoo*, Mary Elting
 (25) *Hooray for Henry*, Jean Bethell
 (26) *The Fox Who Traveled*, Alvin Tresselt
 (27) *The Duck on the Truck*, Leonard Kessler
 (28) *The Clumsy Cowboy*, Jean Bethell
 (29) *The Boy Who Fooled the Giant*, Tamara Kitt
 (30) *The Boy, the Cat, and the Magic Fiddle*, Tamara Kitt
 (31) *Billy Brown Makes Somthing Grand*, Tamara Kitt
 (32) *Billy Brown, the Baby Sitter*, Tamara Kitt
 (33) *The Big Green Thing*, Miriam Schlein
 (34) *Barney Beagle Plays Baseball*, Jean Bethell
 (35) *Barney Beagle and the Cat*, Jean Bethell
 (36) *Barney Beagle*, Jean Bethell
 (37) *Adventures of Silly Billy*, Tamara Kitt

o) Grosset and Dunlap: Easy to Read Books
*(1) *The Dinosaur and the Dodo*, Anne DeCaprio
*(2) *The Hippopotamus*, Bobbi Herne
*(3) *The Train*, Jean Fritz
 (4) *The Dog and the Wolf*, Anne DeCaprio

p) G. P. Putnam's Sons: See and Read Biography Books series
A most unusual series of biographies of persons important in the history of our country. They can be read to a preschooler, and a first grader can read them himself.
*(1) *Christopher Columbus*, Helen Olds
*(2) *George Washington*, Vivian Thompson
 (3) *Nathan Hale*, Virginia Voight
*(4) *Daniel Boone*, Patricia Martin
 (5) *Andrew Jackson*, Patricia Martin
*(6) *Abraham Lincoln*, Patricia Martin
*(7) *Jefferson Davis*, Patricia Martin
*(8) *John Fitzgerald Kennedy*, Patricia Martin

q) Follett: Beginning to Read Books series
*(1) *Abraham Lincoln*, Clara Judson
 (2) *All Kinds of Cows*, Madeline Dodd
 (3) *Animal Hat Shop*, Sara Murphey
 (4) *Barefoot Boy*, Gloria Miklowitz
 (5) *Benny and the Bear*, Barbee Carleton

(6) *Big Bad Bear*, Zula Todd

(7) *Big Bug, Little Bug*, Jean Berg

(8) *Big New School*, Evelyn Hastings

(9) *Bing-Bang Pig*, Sara Murphey

(10) *Birthday Car*, Margaret Hillert

*(11) *Boy Who Wouldn't Say His Name*, Elizabeth Vreeken

*(12) *Christopher Columbus*, Clara Judson

(13) *Come to the Circus*, Margaret Hillert

(14) *The Curious Cow*, Esther Meeks

(15) *Danny's Glider Ride*, Don Snyder

(16) *A Day on Big O*, Helen Cresswell

(17) *The Dog Who Came to Dinner*, Sydney Taylor

(18) *The Elf in the Singing Tree*, Sara Bulette

*(19) *The First Thanksgiving*, Lou Rogers

(20) *Funny Baby*, Margaret Hillert

*(21) *George Washington*, Clara Judson

(22) *Gertie the Duck*, Nicholas Georgiady and Louis Romano

*(23) *Grandfather Dear*, Celentha Finfer, Esther Wasserberg, and Florence Weinberg

*(24) *Grandmother Dear*, Celentha Finfer, Esther Wasserberg, and Florence Weinberg

(25) *Have You Seen My Brother?*, Elizabeth Guilfoile

(26) *Henry*, Elizabeth Vreeken

*(27) *The Hole in the Hill*, Marion Leyton

(28) *In John's Back Yard*, Esther Meeks

(29) *Jiffy, Miss Boo and Mrs. Roo*, Aileen Brothers

(30) *Kittens and More Kittens*, Marci Ridlon

(31) *Let's Ride in the Caboose*, David Burleigh

(32) *Linda's Airmail Letter*, Norman Bell

(33) *Little Quack*, Ruth Woods

(34) *Little Red Hen*, Jean Berg

(35) *Little Runaway*, Margaret Hillert

(36) *Mabel the Whale*, Patricia King

(37) *The Magic Beans*, Margaret Hillert

(38) *Mr. Barney's Beard*, Sydney Taylor

(39) *My Own Little House*, Merriman Kaune

(40) *The No-Bark Dog*, Stanford Williamson

*(41) *Nobody Listens to Andrew*, Elizabeth Guilfoile

(42) *No Lights for Brightville*, Letta Schatz

*(43) *One Day Everything Went Wrong*, Elizabeth Vreeken

*(44) *Our Country's Flag*, Nicholas Georgiady and Louis Romano

(45) *Our National Anthem*, Nicholas Georgiady and Louis Romano

*(46) *This Is a Department Store*, Nicholas Georgiady and Louis Romano

(47) *Our Statue of Liberty*, Thelma Nason

(48) *Peter's Policeman*, Anne Lattin

*(49) *Picture Dictionary*, Alta McIntire

(50) *Piggyback*, David Burleigh

*(51) *Beginning to Read Poetry*, Sally Clithero

*(52) *Beginning to Read Riddles and Jokes*, Alice Gilbreath

(53) *Shoes for Angela*, Ellen Snavely

(54) *Shoofly*, David Burleigh

(55) *Snow Baby*, Margaret Hillert

*(56) *Something New at the Zoo*, Esther Meeks

(57) *Spark's Fireman*, Anne Lattin

*(58) *This Is a Newspaper*, Lawrence Feigenbaum and Kalman Siegel

*(59) *This Is an Airport*, Richard Bagwell and Elizabeth Bagwell

*(60) *Three Bears*, Margaret Hillert

*(61) *Three Little Pigs*, Margaret Hillert

(62) *Three Goats*, Margaret Hillert

(63) *Too Many Dogs*, Ramona Dupre

(64) *Uniform For Harry*, Caary Jackson

(65) *Wee Little Man*, Jean Berg

(66) *Who Will Milk My Cow?*, Janet Jackson

(67) *Yellow Boat*, Margaret Hillert

*(68) *This Is a Town*, Polly Curren

*(69) *This Is a Road*, Polly Curren

r) The Bowmar Early Childhood Series

A unique series of beautifully illustrated picture books with only a few sentences per page. With each book there is a record, so that your child will be able to hear again and again the stories from the picture books. These books are ordinarily sold to schools and libraries and are not available in the average bookstore. Your bookstore would have to special order them for you.

*(1) *Father Is Big*, Ruth and Ed Radlauer

   (2) *Watch Me Outdoors*, Ruth Jaynes
*(3) *Follow the Leader*, Marion Crume
   (4) *Benny's Four Hats*, Ruth Jaynes
*(5) *My Friend Is Mrs. Jones*, Nancy Curry
*(6) *Friends! Friends! Friends!*, Ruth Jaynes
   (7) *Where Is Whiffen?*, Ruth Jaynes
*(8) *What Is a Birthday Child?*, Ruth Jaynes
   (9) *Funny Mr. Clown*, Marion Crume
  (10) *Watch Me Indoors*, Ruth Jaynes
  (11) *That's What It Is!*, Ruth Jaynes
*(12) *How Many Sounds*, Marion Crume
*(13) *An Apple Is Red*, Nancy Curry
*(14) *Do You Know What . . .* Ruth Jaynes
  (15) *The Biggest House*, Ruth Jaynes
  (16) *A Beautiful Day for a Picnic*, Nancy Curry
  (17) *Let Me See You Try*, Marion Crume
  (18) *Three Baby Chicks*, Ruth Jaynes
  (19) *A Cowboy Can*, Beth Clure and Helen Rumsey
  (20) *The Littlest House*, Nancy Curry
*(21) *Colors*, Ruth and Ed Radlauer
  (22) *I Like Cats*, Marion Crume
  (23) *A Box Tied With a Red Ribbon*, Ruth Jaynes
*(24) *What Do Your Say?*, Marion Crume
  (25) *Do You Suppose Miss Riley Knows?*, Nancy Curry
  (26) *Furry Boy*, Marion Crume
  (27) *Melinda's Christmas Stocking*, Ruth Jaynes
*(28) *My Tricycle and I*, Ruth Jaynes
*(29) *Tell Me, Please! What's That?*, Ruth Jaynes
*(30) *Morning*, Marion Crume
*(31) *Evening*, Ruth and Ed Radlauer
*(32) *Listen!*, Marion Crume

s) McGraw-Hill: Science Books by Tillie Pine and Joseph Levine
*(1) *Air All Around*
*(2) *Friction All Around*
*(3) *Gravity All Around*
*(4) *Heat All Around*
*(5) *Light All Around*
*(6) *Sounds All Around*

* (7) *Water All Around*
* (8) *Weather All Around*
* (9) *Electricity and How We Use It*
* (10) *Magnets and How to Use Them*
* (11) *Rocks and How We Use Them*
* (12) *Simple Machines and How We Use Them*
* (13) *The Egyptians Knew*
* (14) *The Chinese Knew*
* (15) *The Eskimos Knew*
* (16) *The Incas Knew*
* (17) *The Indians Knew*
* (18) *The Pilgrims Knew*

t) Franklin Watts: The Let's Find Out Books series

* (1) *Bread*, Olive Burt
* (2) *Weather*, David Knight
* (3) *Air*, Martha and Charles Shapp
* (4) *What Electricity Does*, Martha and Charles Shapp
* (5) *What's in the Sky*, Martha and Charles Shapp
* (6) *Water*, Martha and Charles Shapp
* (7) *Wheels*, Martha and Charles Shapp
* (8) *The Moon*, Martha and Charles Shapp
  (9) *Snakes*, Martha and Charles Shapp
* (10) *The Sun*, Martha and Charles Shapp
  (11) *Fishes*, Martha and Charles Shapp
* (12) *Winter*, Martha and Charles Shapp
* (13) *Fall*, Martha and Charles Shapp
* (14) *Summer*, Martha and Charles Shapp
* (15) *Spring*, Martha and Charles Shapp
* (16) *Wheels*, Martha and Charles Shapp
* (17) *What the Signs Say*, Martha and Charles Shapp
  (18) *Birds*, Martha and Charles Shapp
* (19) *Animals of Long Ago*, Martha and Charles Shapp
* (20) *Animal Homes*, Martha and Charles Shapp
* (21) *What's Big and Small*, Martha and Charles Shapp
* (22) *What's Light and What's Heavy*, Martha and Charles Shapp
* (23) *Houses*, Martha and Charles Shapp
  (24) *Firemen*, Martha and Charles Shapp

(25) *Policemen*, Martha and Charles Shapp
(26) *Cowboys*, Martha and Charles Shapp
(27) *Indians*, Martha and Charles Shapp
*(28) *The United Nations*, Martha and Charles Shapp
*(29) *Abraham Lincoln*, Martha and Charles Shapp
*(30) *Daniel Boone*, Martha and Charles Shapp
(31) *Mars*, David Knight
*(32) *Magnets*, David Knight
*(33) *Telephones*, David Knight
(34) *Earth*, David Knight
*(35) *Insects*, David Knight
*(36) *Addition*, David Whitney
*(37) *Subtraction*, David Whitney
*(38) *The President of The United States*, David Whitney
*(39) *Milk*, David Whitney
*(40) *Color*, Ann Campbell
(41) *Boats*, Ann Campbell
*(42) *Farms*, Ann Campbell
(43) *The Red Cross*, Valerie Pitt
(44) *The City*, Valerie Pitt
*(45) *The Clinic*, Robert Froman
(46) *Eskimos*, Eleanor and Ted Wiesenthal

Well, there they are! Twenty different series of "double-duty" books. If you read only a small number of these books to your preschooler, he (and you!) will absorb an amazing amount of information about science and the world we live in.

I am going to list other books which can be read to your preschool child to stimulate his intellectual development. These books are listed under different categories, according to what aspect of intellectual or emotional development the book deals with. Since books cannot be categorized precisely in certain instances, you may find a particular book listed in more than one place.

2. Books That Deal With Intellectual or Emotional Development
   a) Development of Sensory Awareness and Perceptual Acuity

*(1) *The Silly Listening Book*, Jan Slepian and Ann Seidler (Follett)

*(2) *An Ear Is to Hear*, Jan Slepian and Ann Seidler (Follet)

*(3) *Bendemolena*, Jan Slepian and Ann Seidler (Follett)

*(4) *The Hungry Thing*, Jan Slepian and Ann Seidler (Follett)

*(5) *Ding-Dong, Bing-Bang*, Jan Slepian and Ann Seidler (Follett)

*(6) *Do You Hear What I Hear?*, Helen Borten (Abelard-Schuman)

*(7) *Do You See What I See?*, Helen Borten (Abelard-Schuman)

*(8) *Do You Move As I Do?*, Helen Borten (Abelard-Schuman)

*(9) *A Picture Has a Special Look*, Helen Borten (Abelard-Schuman)

(10) *Bow Wow! Meow! A First Book of Sounds*, Melanie Bellah (Western Publishing)

*(11) *Of Course, You're a Horse!*, Ruth Radlauer (Abelard-Schuman)

*(12) *Good Times Drawing Lines*, Ruth Radlauer (Melmont)

*(13) *The Headstart Book of Looking and Listening*, Shari Lewis and Jacqueline Reinach (McGraw-Hill)

b) Concept Formation: Relationships

*(1) *Let's Find Out What's Light and What's Heavy*, Charles and Martha Shapp (Franklin Watts)

*(2) *Let's Find Out What's Big and What's Small*, Charles and Martha Shapp (Franklin Watts)

*(3) *The Very Little Boy*, Phyllis Krasilovsky (Doubleday)

*(4) *The Very Little Girl*, Phyllis Krasilovsky (Doubleday)

(5) *So Big*, Eloise Wilkin (Western Publishing)

(6) *The Up and Down Book*, Mary Blair (Western Publishing)

(7) *Nothing But Cats*, and *All About Dogs:*

> *Two Very Young Stories*, Grace Skaar (William R. Scott)

    (8) *Hi Daddy, Here I Am*, Grete Hertz (Lerner Publications)

  *(9) *High Sounds, Low Sounds*, Franklyn Branley (Crowell)

 *(10) *Fast Is Not a Ladybug*, Miriam Schlein (Scott)

  (11) *It Looks Like This*, Irma Webber (Scott)

c) Concept Formation: Classification
  (1) *Classification by Color*
    a. *All the Colors*, Saint Justh (Grosset and Dunlap)
  *b. *Let's Find Out About Color*, Ann Campbell (Franklin Watts)
  *c. *Colors*, Ruth and Ed Radlauer (Bowmar)
    d. *Ann Likes Red*, Dorothy Seymour (Grosset and Dunlap)
  *e. *The Color Kittens*, Margaret Wise Brown (Western Publishing)
    f. *What Is Red?*, Susanne Gottlieb (Lothrop, Lee and Shepard)
    g. *Is It Blue as a Butterfly?*, Rebecca Kalusky (Prentice-Hall)
  *h. *Let's Imagine Colors*, Janet Wolff (E. P. Dutton)
    i. *My Slippers Are Red*, Charlotte Steiner (Knopf)
    j. *I Like Red*, Robert Bright (Doubleday)
  (2) Classification by Shape
    a. *Round and Round and Square*, Fredun Shapur (Abelard-Schuman)
    b. *Square as a House*, Karla Kuskin (Harper and Row)
  *c. *Shapes*, Miriam Schlein (William R. Scott)
    d. *A Kiss Is Round*, Blossom Budney (Lothrop)
  *e. *Squares Are Not Bad*, Violet Salazar (Western Publishing)
  *f. *Hello! Do You Know My Name?*, Cecile Jeruchim (Putnams)

*g. *The Wing on a Flea*, Ed Emberley (Little, Brown)

h. *Round and Square*, Janet Martin (Platt and Munk)

i. *On My Beach There Are Many Pebbles*, Leo Lionni (Ivan Obolensky)

(3) Classification by Time

*a. *It's About Time*, Miriam Schlein (Scott)

*b. *Let's Think About Time*, Jane Hart (Hart)

(4) Classification by Number

a. *One Is No Fun, But Twenty Is Plenty!*, Ilse-Margret Vogel (Atheneum)

b. *One, Two, Three: A Little Book of Counting Rhymes*, pictures by Norah Montgomerie (Abelard-Schuman)

*c. *Ten Black Dots*, Donald Crews (Scribners)

*d. *Over in the Meadow*, John Langstaff (Harcourt Brace)

e. *Counting Carnival*, Feenie Ziner and Paul Galdone (Coward-McCann)

f. *I Can Count*, Carl Memling (Western Publishing)

*g. *Brian Wildsmith's 1, 2, 3's*, Brian Wildsmith (Franklin Watts)

*h. *Little 1*, Ann and Paul Rand (Harcourt, Brace and World)

i. *Now I Can Count*, Dean Hay (Lion Press)

(5) Classification by Seasons of the Year

*a. *Let's Find Out About Fall*, Charles and Martha Shapp (Franklin Watts)

*b. *Let's Find Out About Winter*, Charles and Martha Shapp (Franklin Watts)

*c. *Let's Find Out About Spring*, Charles and Martha Shapp (Franklin Watts)

*d. *Let's Find Out About Summer*, Charles and Martha Shapp (Franklin Watts)

*e. *The Year Around Book*, Helen Fletcher (McGraw-Hill)

d) Concept Formation: Basic Scientific Concepts Which Tie Together a Large Number of Events in One Basic Concept

*(1) *Friction All Around*, Tillie Pine and Joseph Levine (McGraw-Hill)
*(2) *Gravity All Around*, Tillie Pine and Joseph Levine (McGraw-Hill)
*(3) *Heat All Around*, Tillie Pine and Joseph Levine (McGraw-Hill)
*(4) *Friction*, Howard Liss (Coward-McCann)
*(5) *Heat*, Howard Liss (Coward-McCann)
*(6) *Motion*, Seymour Simon (Coward-McCann)
*(7) *Atoms*, Melvin Berger (Coward-McCann)
*(8) *Molecules and Atoms,* Edward Victor (Follett)
*(9) *Friction*, Edward Victor (Follett)
*(10) *Heat*, Edward Victor (Follett)

e) Problem Solving
*(1) *What Makes Day and Night?*, Franklyn Branley (Crowell)
*(2) *What Makes a Shadow?*, Clyde Bulla (Crowell)
*(3) *Why I Built the Boogle House*, Helen Palmer (Random House)
*(4) *How Do You Get From Here to There?*, Nicholas Charles (Macmillan)
 (5) *How Do I Go?*, Mary Hoberman (Little, Brown)
*(6) *Are You My Mother?*, P. D. Eastman (Random House)
*(7) *The Shadow Book*, Beatrice DeRegniers (Harcourt, Brace and World)
*(8) *What Can You Do With a Shoe?*, Beatrice DeRegniers (Harper and Row)
*(9) *The Upside-Down Day*, Julian Scheer (Holiday House)
*(10) *Why Can't I?*, Jeanne Bendick (McGraw-Hill)

f) Scientific Method for Preschoolers
*(1) *Prove It!*, Rose Wyler and Gerald Ames (Harpers)
*(2) *Benny's Animals and How He Put Them in Order*, Millicent Selsam (Harpers)
*(3) *Greg's Microscope*, Millicent Selsam (Harpers)

* (4) *How Can I Find Out?*, Mary Bongiorno and Mable Gee (Children's Press)
* (5) *The Learning Book*, Susan Dorritt (Abelard-Schuman)
* (6) *What Could You See?*, Jeanne Bendick (McGraw-Hill)
* (7) *The Headstart Book of Thinking and Imagining*, Shari Lewis and Jacqueline Reinach (McGraw-Hill)

g) Alphabet And Learning To Read

* (1) *Curious George Learns the Alphabet*, H. A. Rey (Houghton Mifflin)
* (2) *Don Freeman's Add a Line Alphabet*, Don Freeman (Golden Gate)
* (3) *We Read: A to Z*, Donald Crews (Scribners)
* (4) *Richard Scarry's Great Big Schoolhouse*, Richard Scarry (Random House)
* (5) *Picture Dictionary*, Alta McIntire (Follett)
* (6) *Cat in the Hat Picture Dictionary*, Dr. Seuss (Random House)
* (7) *The Headstart Book of Knowing and Naming*, Shari Lewis and Jacqueline Reinach (McGraw-Hill)

h) Richard Scarry

Richard Scarry is so unique and wonderful he deserves a category all by himself. He has a series of absolutely enchanting books, which teach children what happens in school, what people do all day, and the occupations of people all over the world. I would advise buying all of these books for your preschooler. He will use them for years and receive enormous intellectual stimulation from them.

* (1) *Richard Scarry's Great Big Schoolhouse*, Richard Scarry (Random House). Getting ready for school, the routine of school, the alphabet, counting, measuring, shapes, the hours of the day, colors, the months of the year, and learning to print and write. A marvelous book!
* (2) *What Do People Do All Day?*, Richard Scarry (Random House). All of the various activities that go on inside a city: the

different workers in the city, building houses, the postal system, the work of mothers, ships, the police department, the fire department, the hospital, building a new road, and many other aspects of the city of Busytown.

*(3) *Busy, Busy World*, Richard Scarry (Random House). Amusements and occupations of people all over the world: Paris policemen, Norwegian fishermen, Greek painters, New York firemen, and many more. The most painless lessons in geography your child could ever have.

i) Mathematics

*(1) *Let's Find Out About Addition*, David Whitney (Franklin Watts)

*(2) *Let's Find Out About Subtraction*, David Whitney (Franklin Watts)

j) The Self-Concept

*(1) *My Book About Me*, Dr. Seuss and Roy McKie (Random House)

*(2) *My Hands*, Aliki (Crowell)

*(3) *My Five Senses*, Aliki (Crowell)

*(4) *Who Am I?*, June Behrens (Elk Grove Press)

*(5) *Umbrellas, Hats and Wheels*, Ann Rand (Harcourt, Brace and World)

(6) *Look at Me*, Marguerita Rudolph (McGraw-Hill)

(7) *Just Like Everyone Else*, Karla Kuskin (Harper and Row)

*(8) *Inside You and Me*, Eloise Turner and Carroll Fenton (John Day)

*(9) *Your Body and How It Works*, Patricia Lauber (Random House)

*(10) *What's Inside of Me?*, Herbert Zim (Morrow)

*(11) *A Boy and His Room*, Ogden Nash (Franklin Watts)

*(12) *Jack Is Glad, Jack Is Sad*, Charlotte Steiner (Knopf)

(13) *Katie's Magic Glasses*, Jane Goodsell (Houghton Mifflin). For a child who wears glasses.

k) Relationships Within the Family and With Peers

 *(1) *My Family*, Miriam Schlein (Abelard-Schuman)
 *(2) *The Don't Be Scared Book*, Ilse-Margret Vogel (Atheneum)
  (3) *It's Not Your Birthday*, Berthe Amoss (Harper and Row)
 *(4) *It's Mine—A Greedy Book*, Crosby Bonsall (Harper and Row)
 *(5) *If It Weren't for You*, Charlotte Zolotov (Harper and Row)
 *(6) *When I Have a Little Girl*, Charlotte Zolotov (Harper and Row)
 *(7) *When I Have a Son*, Charlotte Zolotov (Harper and Row)
 *(8) *Stevie*, John Steptoe (Harper and Row)
 *(9) *Mommies Are for Loving*, Ruth Penn (Putnams)
*(10) *Mommies*, L. C. Carton (Random House)
 (11) *Mommies at Work*, Eve Merriam (Knopf)
*(12) *Daddies*, L. Carton (Random House)
*(13) *Daddies—What They Do All Day*, Helen Puner (Lothrop)
*(14) *My Sister and I*, Helen Buckley (Lothrop)
*(15) *My Grandfather and I*, Helen Buckley (Lothrop)
*(16) *My Grandmother and I*, Helen Buckley (Lothrop)
*(17) *Animal Daddies and My Daddy*, Barbara Hazen (Western Publishing)
 (18) *When I Grow Up*, Lois Lenski (Henry Z. Walck)
 (19) *Animal Babies*, Tony Palazzo (Doubleday)
*(20) *When You Were a Little Baby*, Rhoda Berman (Lothrop)
 (21) *Everybody Has a House and Everybody Eats*, Mary Green (Wm. R. Scott)
*(22) *The Little Girl and Her Mother*, Beatrice DeRegniers (Vanguard)
 (23) *Polar Bear Brothers*, Crosby Bonsall (Harper and Row)

(24) *Whose Little Bird Am I?*, Leonard Weisgard (Warne)

*(25) *Mommies Are That Way*, Ruth Radlauer (Abelard-Schuman)

*(26) *My Daddy's Visiting Our School Today*, Myra Berry Brown (Watts)

*(27) *Grandmothers Are to Love*, Lois Wyse (Parents Magazine Press)

*(28) *Grandfathers Are to Love*, Lois Wyse (Parents Magazine Press)

*(29) *Keep It Like a Secret*, Sandol Warburg (Little, Brown)

*(30) *Ice Cream for Breakfast*, Myra Brown (Watts)

*(31) *Company's Coming for Dinner*, Myra Brown (Watts)

l) The Community and Community Helpers

*(1) *My Favorite City*, Willma Willis (Elk Grove Press)

*(2) *The March of the Harvest*, Irma Johnson (Elk Grove Press)

*(3) *What Is a Community?*, Edward and Ruth Radlauer (Elk Grove Press)

*(4) *A Walk in the Neighborhood*, June Behrens (Elk Grove Press)

*(5) *I Know a Policeman*, Barbara Williams (Putnams)

*(6) *I Know a Fireman*, Barbara Williams (Putnams)

(7) *I Know a Garageman*, Barbara Williams (Putnams)

(8) *I Know a Mayor*, Barbara Williams (Putnams)

(9) *I Know a Bank Teller*, Barbara Williams (Putnams)

*(10) *I Know a Librarian*, Virginia Voight (Putnams)

*(11) *I Know a Postman*, Lorraine Henriod (Putnams)

*(12) *I Know a Teacher*, Naoma Buchheimer (Putnams)

(13) *I Know a House Builder*, Polly Bolian and Marilyn Schima (Putnams)

(14) *I Know an Airline Pilot*, Muriel Stanek (Putnams)

*(15) *I Know a Zoo Keeper*, Lorraine Henriod (Putnams)

(16) *I Know a Nurse*, Marilyn Schima and Polly Bolian (Putnams)

(17) *Policeman Small*, Lois Lenski (Walck)

*(18) *The "Where's That?" Book*, Blair Walliser (Grosset and Dunlap)

*(19) *The "Who's What?" Book*, Blair Walliser (Grosset and Dunlap)

*(20) *How Do You Get From Here to There?*, Nicholas Charles (Macmillan)

(21) *The Little Fire Engine*, Lois Lenski (Walck)

(22) *The Truck and Bus Book*, William Dugan (Western Publishing)

(23) *Planes, Trains, Cars and Boats*, Muriel and Lionel Kalish (Western Publishing)

(24) *Rides*, Virginia Parsons (Doubleday)

*(25) *What Do People Do All Day?*, Richard Scarry (Random House)

*(26) *Whose Tools Are These?*, Ed and Ruth Radlauer (Elk Grove Press)

*(27) *Get Ready for School*, Ruth Radlauer (Elk Grove Press)

(28) *Airports U.S.A.*, Lou Jacobs, Jr. (Elk Grove Press)

m) The Larger Community: The World

*(1) *People Around the World*, Rozella Donan and Jane Hefflefinger (Elk Grove Press)

*(2) *Where in the World Do You Live?*, Al Hine and John Alcorn (Harcourt, Brace and World)

*(3) *Money Around the World*, Al Hine and John Alcorn (Harcourt, Brace and World)

*(4) *You Will Go to the Moon*, Mae and Ira Freeman (Random House)

*(5) *A Book of Astronauts for You*, Franklyn Branley (Crowell)

n) Children's Emotions or Special Problems

(1) *Timid Timothy*, Gweneira Williams (Scott). It's a mother's job to help her

child enjoy new experiences, and mother cat does a good job with Timothy.

*(2) *Lost and Found*, Kathryn Hitte (Abingdon). Getting lost is often a frightening experience. This is a reassuring book to read to a child about this subject.

*(3) *Will I have a Friend?*, Miriam Cohen (Macmillan). Will I Have a Friend? is a silent question children often ask on their first day in school. Though they are afraid to ask this question out loud, they nevertheless want to have it answered. This charming story will help your child ask this question.

*(4) *Curious George Goes to the Hospital*, Margret and H. A. Rey (Houghton Mifflin). Curious George always has high adventures and this time the adventures are in a hospital.

*(5) *The Really Real Family*, Helen Doss (Little, Brown). A special book about adoption which covers the topic as a child would see it.

*(6) *Where Is Daddy? The Story of a Divorce*, Beth Goff (Beacon). This book will help a child understand what it is like when parents get divorced. Excellent.

(7) *Benjy's Blanket*, Myra Berry Brown (Watts). Benjy's Blanket is a security item. This is the delightful story of how he learns to give it up.

(8) *First Night Away From Home*, Myra Berry Brown (Watts). Sleeping over the first time is an experience that always has both good and bad features. This is a delightful story which covers both sides of the experience.

*(9) *The Dead Bird*, Margaret Wise Brown (Scott). A very sensitive story which deals with death and how a group of children experience the problems of death.

*(10) *Dumb Stupid David*, Dorothy Aldis (Putnams). Big brother's jealous reaction to a new baby and how it is overcome.

*(11) *This Room Is Mine*, Betty Wright (Whitman). It is always hard for brothers and sisters to share. This delightful book describes how two sisters work out their problems of sharing.

(12) *Big Sister and Little Sister*, Charlotte Zolotov (Harper and Row). A picture book of love between sisters.

*(13) *The Quarreling Book*, Charlotte Zolotov (Harper and Row). An authentic picture of sibling relations in most families—a book greatly enjoyed by preschool children.

*(14) *Amy and the New Baby*, Myra Berry Brown (Watts). A warm and understanding story of how Amy's jealousy of the new baby eventually is overcome.

*(15) *Love Is a Special Way of Feeling*, Joan Walsh Anglund (Harcourt, Brace). All of Mrs. Anglund's books are beautifully done, and this one is no exception.

(16) *Judy's Baby*, Sally Scott (Harcourt, Brace). Happiness is not always a new baby, and this little girl has problems with the "intruder" who comes into her family. This is the story of how she struggles through these problems.

*(17) *The Man of the House*, Joan Fassler (Behavioral Publications). Four-year-old David tries to become the grown-up protector of the house while his father is on a business trip.

*(18) *All Alone With Daddy*, Joan Fassler (Behavioral Publications). A little girl tries to take her mother's place when her mother is away.

*(19) *My Grandpa Died Today*, Joan Fassler (Behavioral Publications). A little boy learns about death for the first time.

(20) *The Boy With a Problem*, Joan Fassler (Behavioral Publications). A little boy discovers that the best way to cope with a problem is to talk about it to someone who really listens.

*(21) *Don't Worry, Dear,* Joan Fassler (Behavioral Publications). A very little girl with an understanding mother grows out of her thumb-sucking and bed-wetting habits.

*(22) *One Little Girl,* Joan Fassler (Behavioral Publications). Because she is somewhat retarded, Laurie has been called a "slow child." Laurie learns that she is only slow in doing some things and that there are other things she can do quite well.

*(23) *The Angry Book: My ABC of Mean Things,* Robin King (Norton)

*(24) *The Thinking Book,* Sandol Warburg (Little Brown)

o) The Magic of Words and the Magic of Books

  *(1) *Books!,* Murray McCain and John Alcorn (Simon and Schuster)

  *(2) *Ounce, Dice, Trice,* Alastair Reid (Little, Brown). This book is so unique it deserves a special mention. It will help your child to love words. Although written for older children or adults, you can still use it with a preschooler. Begin when your child is four, because he is so fascinated by language at that age. Read parts of this book to him in small doses. Do not attempt to read the whole book to him at once. It can be read to your child throughout grade school. A book designed to be read aloud, it particularly lends itself to family reading. I dare you to check this book out of the library and not become so fascinated by it that you end up buying it!

  (3) Nonsense Poems

    A good way of getting a preschooler fascinated by words and language at an early age. Four is an especially good age to begin reading nonsense poems to a child. Here are some particularly good books of nonsense poems.

    *a. *The Pobble Who Has No Toes and Other Nonsense,* Edward Lear (Follett)

    b. *Calico Pie and Other Nonsense,* Edward Lear (Follett)

*c. *The Scroobious Pip*, Edward Lear, completed by Ogden Nash (Harper and Row)

d. *Silly Songs and Sad*, Ellen Raskin (Crowell)

*e. *Lear's Nonsense Verses*, Edward Lear (Grosset and Dunlap)

p) Painless Etiquette and Manners for the Preschooler

*(1) *What Do You Say, Dear?*, Seslye Joslin (Scott). For the preschooler, but with a delightful touch of whimsy.

*(2) *What Do You Do, Dear?*, Seslye Joslin (Scott). More painless manners for your preschooler.

q) Books About Religion for Preschoolers

Sad to confess, good books about religion for preschoolers are mighty scarce. Here are a few. There should be more.

*(1) *A Book About God*, Florence Fitch (Lothrop). The mathematicians use the word *simple* to mean elegant. In this sense, this religious book for preschoolers is both simple and elegant. Gorgeous illustrations by Leonard Weisgard enhance its value even more.

*(2) *Once There Was a Little Boy*, Dorothy Kunhardt (Viking). A lovely and charming story of the Christ Child.

(3) *Told Under the Christmas Tree*, Association For Childhood Education International (Macmillan). All you need to know about Christmas, and Hanukkah— beautifully and simply done.

*(4) *One God: The Ways We Worship Him*, Florence Fitch (Lothrop). Protestants, Catholics and Jews, and the way they worship. Although not written on a preschool level, it is a book to grow on. A good book for any family to have in their home library, it will answer many questions about the three major religious faiths in America for your child in grade school.

(5) *A Child's Grace*, Ernest Claxton (Dut-

ton). A child's prayer simply and beautifully written and easy for a preschooler to learn by heart.

(6) *Children's Prayers for Every Day*, Jessie Moore (Abingdon). Everyday prayers on a preschool level for both Christians and Jews.

(7) *Mary Alice Jones*

Mrs. Jones has written a series of excellent books on religion for children. Highly recommended.

*a. *God Is Good*, (Rand McNally)

*b. *My First Book About Jesus*, (Rand McNally)

*c. *Tell Me About God*, (Rand McNally)

*d. *Tell Me About Jesus*, (Rand McNally)

*e. *Tell Me About the Bible*, (Rand McNally)

*f. *Tell Me About Christmas*, (Rand McNally)

*g. *Prayers and Graces for a Small Child*, (Rand McNally)

r) Other General Books on Science Not Previously Listed

*(1) *Science in the Bathtub*, Rebecca Marcus (Watts)

*(2) *Let's Look Inside Your House*, Herman and Nina Schneider (Scott)

*(3) *Let's Go to the Brook*, Harriet Huntington (Doubleday)

*(4) *Let's Go to the Seashore*, Harriet Huntington (Doubleday)

*(5) *Let's Go to the Woods*, Harriet Huntington (Doubleday)

*(6) *Let's Go to the Desert*, Harriet Huntington (Doubleday)

*(7) *Let's Go Outdoors*, Harriet Huntington (Doubleday)

(8) *Sound*, Solveig Russell (Bobbs Merrill)

*(9) *A Book of Astronauts for You*, Franklyn Branley (Crowell)

*(10) *A Book of Planets for You*, Franklyn Branley (Crowell)

(11) *The Honeybees*, Franklin Russell (Knopf)

*(12) *In the Days of the Dinosaurs,* Roy Chapman Andrews (Random House)

(13) *To Be a Bee,* Ellsworth Rosen (Houghton Mifflin)

(14) *Insects Do the Strangest Things,* Leonara and Arthur Hornblow (Random House)

*(15) *Finding Out About the Past,* Mae Freeman (Random House)

*(16) *Mammals and How They Live,* Robert McClung (Random House)

*(17) *A Book of Stars for You,* Franklyn Branley (Crowell)

(18) *A Book of Moon Rockets for You,* Franklyn Branley (Crowell)

(19) *Catch a Cricket,* Carla Stevens (Scott)

(20) *Animal Habits,* George Mason (Morrow)

*(21) *The First People in the World,* Gerald Ames and Rose Wyler (Harper and Row)

*(22) *Nabob and the Geranium,* Judith Miller (Golden Gate)

*(23) *There Was a Time,* Susan Morrow (Dutton)

B. Fiction and Fantasy

If you have skimmed this appendix thus far, you have definitely gathered the impression that there is an enormous number of good nonfiction books for a preschooler. Unfortunately, the number of really excellent books of fiction for preschoolers is far, far fewer. But here are a selected number of excellent works of fiction and fantasy for preschoolers, with the cream of the crop starred (*).

*1. *The Story of Babar,* Jean De Brunhoff (Random House). Everyone knows and loves Babar, the wonderful elephant. This book could easily be called a classic.

*2. *Madeline,* Ludwig Bemelmans (Viking). Madeline always has a good time. This time it's in Paris.

3. *The Five Chinese Brothers,* Claire Bishop (Coward-McCann). Once upon a time there were five Chinese brothers, and they looked exactly alike. Around these remarkable characteristics is woven a most ingenious tale.

*4. *The Little House,* Virginia Burton (Houghton

Mifflin). Urban development as told on the preschool level. A delightful story.

5. *Springtime for Jeanne-Marie*, Francoise (Scribners). Gay and stylized illustrations will delight a young child's eye as he enjoys the adventures of a little French girl and her white sheep.

6. *Corduroy*, Don Freeman (Viking). The art and the story are direct and just right for the very young who like bears and escalators.

*7. *The Biggest House in the World*, Leo Lionni (Pantheon). In this gorgeously illustrated picture book, a small snail has a very large wish. He wants the largest house in the world.

8. *Little Leo*, Leo Politi (Scribners). Soft colors and lovely double page pictures of villages and children enhance this delightful story.

9. *Spectacles*, Ellen Raskin (Atheneum). A picture book done with imagination and humor. May be useful with a child who is resisting glasses which he needs.

*10. *Rain Makes Applesauce*, Julian Schneer (Holiday). A really unique picture book which a young child will want to look at again and again.

11. *Caps for Sale*, Esther Slobodkina (Scott). A tale of a peddler, his caps, and some monkeys who combine to produce a bit of delightful monkey business.

12. *The Biggest Bear*, Lynd Ward (Houghton Mifflin). A story of a boy and his pet bear and the masterful task this boy must perform.

*13. *Theodore Turtle*, Ellen MacGregor (McGraw-Hill). The amusing story of a turtle who forgets where he leaves things. Any similarity to children you know is more than coincidental.

14. *The Little Family*, Lois Lenski (Doubleday). Lois Lenski writes of a little family—especially for small children.

15. *The Little Auto*, Lois Lenski (Walck). All of Miss Lenski's books are simple and appealing to young children.

*16. *Gwendolyn the Miracle Hen*, Nancy Sherman (Western Publishing). Gwendolyn can lay

Easter eggs. A modern story with a folk tale flavor.

*17. *Where the Wild Things Are*, Maurice Sendak (Harper and Row). Great pictures of wild things by Maurice Sendak, with a story to match. A little boy's dreams help other children to deal with their fears on a child's level and thus overcome them. An enormous favorite with little children, particularly boys.

*18. *A Little House of Your Own*, Beatrice Schenk DeRegniers (Harcourt, Brace and World). Every child likes to have a small and secret place of his very own. This book is a great favorite with little children.

*19. *Mike Mulligan and His Steam Shovel*, Virginia Burton (Houghton Mifflin). Boys love the story of Mike and his steam shovel. A charming modern classic.

*20. *The Little Red Computer*, Ralph Steadman (McGraw-Hill). A modern day story of a dunce at computer school.

*21. *Little Toot*, Hardie Gramatky (Putnams). An old, old favorite describes the adventures of a small tug boat in New York harbor.

*22. *A Rainbow of My Own*, Don Freeman (Viking). A small boy looks for a rainbow to own.

*23. *The House on East 88th Street*, Bernard Weber (Houghton Mifflin). The funny adventures of Lyle the Crocodile.

*24. *Crictor*, Tomi Ungerer (Harper and Row). Such fantasy. Would you believe a boa constrictor with his own bed and a sweater for the snow? Just great!

*25. *And to Think That I Saw It on Mulberry Street*, Dr. Seuss (Vanguard). One of Dr. Seuss' first and best—a classic.

*26. *The 500 Hats of Bartholomew Cubbins*, Dr. Seuss (Vanguard). A fun fantasy with never-ending hats. A great favorite of small children, not to mention their parents.

27. *Crow Boy*, Taro Yashima (Viking). The tender story of a shy Japanese Boy.

*28. *Ferdinand*, Munro Leaf (Viking). Who does not know of this venerable children's classic of the bull who preferred to smell flowers rather than fight in the bull ring? Your preschool child probably does not, so read him the book and let him discover Ferdinand also.

*29. *Inch by Inch*, Leo Lionni (Obolensky). All of Leo Lionni's books are beautiful. This one teaches the concept of measuring.

*30. *Lentil*, Robert McCloskey (Viking). Charming— like all of McCloskey's. A small boy, Lentil, plays music on his harmonica and becomes a hero.

*31. *Make Way for Ducklings*, Robert McCloskey (Viking). Another children's classic about a family of ducks on Beacon Street in Boston.

*32. *One Morning in Maine*, Robert McCloskey (Viking). A wonderful story about the loss of the first tooth. Homey illustrations of slow, easy family life.

33. *Timothy Turtle*, Alice Davis (Harcourt, Brace and World). A delightful picture story of what happens to a turtle who gets turned on his back and how his friends manage to rescue him from his plight.

*34. *The Alligator Case*, William Pene DuBois (Viking). Mr. DuBois writes fun and fantasy for young children. A little boy plays detective.

*35. *Burt Dow, Deep Water Man*, Robert McCloskey (Viking). More of Mr. McCloskey's imaginative work. You have heard of adult exaggerated "fisherman's tales"—well here is a preschool fish "tail."

*36. *Horton Hatches the Egg*, Dr. Seuss (Random House). Poor Horton sits on an egg while a silly bird goes away.

*37. *The Snowy Day*, Ezra Keats (Viking). Beautiful illustrations. A charming, very simple story of a small boy in the snow.

*38. *Staying Home Alone on a Rainy Day*, Chihiro Iwasaki (McGraw-Hill). What to do on a rainy day? Answer: Day Dream!

*39. *Switch on the Night*, Ray Bradbury (Pantheon). The famous science fiction writer turns his hand to a child's book with delightful results.

40. *A Tree Is Nice*, Janice Udry (Harper and Row). A delightful story of a tree.

*41. *Where Have You Been?*, Margaret Wise Brown (Hastings). Fourteen different animals answer the same question. Your child will enjoy joining in and repeating the gay poetic lines of this book as you read to him.

42. *Anatole*, Eve Titus (McGraw-Hill). The wonderful adventures of a mouse who decides to work for a living and becomes head taster for a cheese factory in Paris.

*43. *Frederick*, Leo Lionni (Pantheon). A field mouse rescues his friends from the long, cold winter by his word pictures of sunshine and colors. The usual vivid illustrations we have come to expect from Mr. Lionni.

*44. *Casey, the Utterly Impossible Horse*, Anita Feagles (Scott). The amusing tale of a talking horse who expects much from his pet boy—as many children expect much from their parents.

*45. *The Happy Lion*, Louise Fatio (McGraw-Hill). A happy lion manages to escape from the zoo in a French town, only to find that people run away from him.

46. *Space Cat*, Ruthven Todd (Scribners). A cat goes by rocketship to outer space.

47. *Pedro, the Angel of Olivera Street*, Leo Politi (Scribners). A lovely story of a small Mexican boy who celebrates Christmas on Olivera Street.

48. *Gilberto and the Wind*, Marie Ets (Viking). A charming picture book about a little Mexican boy who has trouble with the wind.

49. *Little Pear*, Eleanor Lattimore (Harcourt). A modern classic about a little Chinese boy.

*50. *May I Bring a Friend?*, Beatrice Schenk DeRegniers (Atheneum). The fantasy adventure of a little boy who visits the king.

51. *Angus and the Ducks*, Marjorie Flack (Doubleday). Angus, a feisty scotch terrier, has trouble with some smart ducks.

*52. *Harold and the Purple Crayon*, Crockett Johnson (Harper and Row). A great favorite with small children. Harold is a most unusual artist.

*53. *Emile,* Tomi Ungerer (Harper and Row). The story of an octopus who can do great things.

54. *A Hole Is to Dig,* Ruth Krauss (Harper and Row). A delightful story of words and what they mean as viewed by a small child.

*55. *Olaf Reads,* Joan Lexau (Dial). Learning to read can be funny, as you will discover with Olaf.

*56. *The Brave Cowboy,* Joan Walsh Anglund (Harcourt, Brace). Another delightful story of a preschool cowboy.

*57. *The Lively Adventures of a Burly Woodcutter, A Pint-Sized Inventor, Two Pretty Pastry Cooks, and a Gang of Desperate Criminals,* Hilde Jenzarik (Harper and Row). Does any parent really need to do more than read the title of this book to know that it is a wonderful book of fantasy for children? (And parents!)

*58. *Blueberries For Sal,* Robert McCloskey (Viking). More of wonderful Mr. McCloskey. A little girl helps her mother pick berries.

*59. *Old MacDonald Had an Apartment House,* Judith Barrett (Atheneum). A delightful fantasy of a modern-day four-story farm.

*60. *From Ambledee to Zumbledee,* Sandol Warburg (Houghton Mifflin.) Bugs from A to Z.

C. More Advanced Books of Fantasy

The preceding books of fantasy and imagination can safely be read to preschoolers. The books in this next category, however, may be too advanced for some preschoolers, but just right for others. In general, the books in this next group will be suitable for five-year-olds, although some four-year-olds will relish them as well.

One word of warning: don't feel you have to read your preschooler *every word* of the books in this next category. These books are really written for older children. You may have to adapt and abridge them somewhat for a preschooler. If you notice that your youngster's attention is flagging, do not hesitate to do just that. You may even conclude that the book is a trifle too advanced for him and wait until he is older.

If you read these books to your child when he is a preschooler, he will read them himself as he grows older.

At that time he will understand many of the subtle nuances and innuendoes he missed as a preschooler. The books in this next category can be enjoyed by a child up to the age of twelve. (Also by adults—I must confess I enjoyed reading them to my preschoolers more than any other books I read to them!)

*1. *Charlie and the Chocolate Factory,* Roald Dahl (Knopf). A modern classic. Five children get to see the mysterious machinery in the marvelous chocolate factory of Mr. Willy Wonka. Mr. Wonka's fantastic inventions will delight all small children.

*2. *James and the Giant Peach,* Roald Dahl (Knopf). Another delightful fantasy by Roald Dahl. "Fabulous unbelievable things" happen to James inside the giant peach.

*3. *The Talking Machine,* James Kruss (Universe). Professor Prendergast and his nephew Martin have invented a fabulous Talking Machine which can make instant translations of animal languages into several human languages, and vice versa. With a beginning like that, what book could possibly go wrong?

*4. *Stuart Little,* E. B. White (Harper and Row). The whimsical first sentence of this book reads: "When Mrs. Frederick C. Little's second son was born, everybody noticed that he was not much bigger than a mouse." In fact, he *was* a mouse! The rest of the book describes his fascinating adventures. A modern classic.

*5. *Charlotte's Web,* E. B. White (Harper and Row). Another wonderful tale of whimsy and imagination by E. B. White. Charlotte, the spider, saves the life of her friend, a doomed pig, by spinning messages in her web. Another classic.

*6. *Winnie-the-Pooh,* A. A. Milne (Dutton). Be sure to get the original edition of this and not the watered-down Walt Disney version. As the episodes are generally too long for a typical preschooler's attention span, you will probably have to abridge your reading of these delightful tales even for a five-year-old. Don't hesitate to skip ahead in reading the story if your preschooler becomes inattentive. It is very worthwhile to read this book to your child in his preschool years, abridging as you go, for you are laying the foundation for a deeper appreciation of the subtler nuances of the book at a later age. If you have an older child, he may enjoy listening to it also, while you read to a preschooler. Originally written by A. A. Milne for his own son Christopher Robin, this is one of the most wonderful children's classics ever written.

*7. *Just So Stories*, Rudyard Kipling (Grosset and Dunlap). Another children's classic that will never grow old. A delightful collection of humorous animal fantasy tales, such as "How The Leopard Got His Spots." and "How The Whale Got His Throat." One of the few books you can read simultaneously to children of all ages, from preschool through twelve. Adults enjoy these stories as much as children do.

*8. *Mary Poppins*, P. L. Travers (Harcourt, Brace and World). Disney's wonderful movie Mary Poppins has spread the fame of the fabulous nursemaid of the Banks children. Wherever Mary Poppins is, magic is sure to be in the air. As with Winnie-the-Pooh, you may have to skip at times in your reading to allow for the short attention span of a preschooler.

*9. *Mr. Popper's Penguins*, Richard and Florence Atwater (Little, Brown). Mr. Popper, a paper hanger with a passion for the Antarctic, is given a penguin by an explorer. The one penguin becomes twelve, and the twelve penguins proceed to turn upside down the lives of the entire Popper family. Hilarious whimsy.

*10. *The Twenty-One Balloons*, William Pene DuBois (Viking). This is the book that I personally enjoyed the most reading to my children when they were preschoolers. Professor William Waterman Sherman goes adventuring in a flying balloon which lands on the amazing island of Krakatao, where twenty families live in secluded luxury. The inventions of the families of Krakatao will delight both a preschooler and his parents.

*11. *Chitty Chitty Bang Bang, the Magical Car*, Ian Fleming (Random House). Walt Disney has also popularized this one. Boys particularly will love to hear the story of Commander Crackpot and his marvelous car, which can swim, fly, and communicate with people.

*12. *The Enormous Egg*, Oliver Butterworth (Little, Brown). A twelve-year-old boy finds a huge egg which hatches into a dinosaur.

*13. *The Wind in the Willows*, Kenneth Grahame (Scribners). This book is really too advanced for most preschoolers. Your youngster may be six or seven before he is old enough to appreciate it, but I could not close this bibliography in good conscience without mentioning this marvelous children's classic. It is the story of Mole, Badger, Water Rat, and Toad, and their life along the banks of the Thames river. They have such delightfully human characteristics.

I agree 100 percent with A. A. Milne, who said in his introduction to the book: "One does not argue about *The Wind in the Willows*. The young man gives it to the girl with whom he is in love, and if she does not like it, asks her to return his letters. The older man tries it on his nephew, and alters his will accordingly. The book is a test of character. We can't criticize it, because it is criticizing us."

D. Collections of Stories, Tales, or Folk Tales

*1. *Told Under the Green Umbrella*, by the Association for Childhood Education International (Macmillan). Folk tales for young children.

*2. *Castles and Dragons: Read-to-Yourself Fairy Tales for Boys And Girls*, compiled by the Child Study Association of America (Crowell).

3. *Read-to-Me Storybook*, compiled by the Child Study Association of America (Crowell). Modern stories and verses.

4. *Fables From Aesop*, Retold by James Reeves (Walck). Famous fables told with modern-day language.

*5. *The Book of Greek Myths;* Edgar and Ingri
      D'Aulaire (Doubleday). Forever good. Out-
      standing book and a must.

E. Poetry for Preschoolers

*1. *Something Special,* Beatrice Schenk DeRegniers
      (Harcourt, Brace and World). Begin reading
      poetry to your preschooler with this book and he
      will love poetry. And if you are not much for
      poetry yourself, begin reading poetry to your
      preschooler with this book and *you* will learn to
      love poetry! Free verse, rhymed verse, and a
      chanting game: "What Did You Put In Your
      Pocket?" Begin with the chanting game and
      work forward and backward from there, at your
      pleasure.

*2. *I Can't, Said the Ant,* Polly Cameron (Coward-
      McCann). The scene: the kitchen. The hero: an
      ant. The time: now.
          "Teapot fell," said the dinner bell.
          "Broke her spout," said the trout.
          "Push her up," said the cup.
          "I can't," said the ant.
          "Please try," said the pie.
      Your preschooler will be delighted with this tale
      in verse.

*3. *I Met a Man,* John Ciardi (Houghton Mifflin).
      One of America's foremost poets proves that a
      poetry book written in a limited vocabulary for
      beginning readers doesn't have to be dull or
      trite. These verses sparkle. Your preschooler will
      love to have you read him "The Man That
      Lived in a Box," "The Man From Nowhere,"
      and other poems in this delightful book.

 4. *Cricket Songs,* Harry Behn (Harcourt, Brace and
      World). A group of Japanese haiku, poems of
      nature.

 5. *Sung Under the Silver Umbrella,* Association For
      Childhood Education International (Macmil-
      lan). Good selection of poems for children from
      preschool through third grade.

*6. *Whispers and Other Poems,* Myra Cohn Living-
      ston (Harcourt, Brace and World). A small
      book of poems which gives a child's view of

such things as riding on a train and going to the zoo.

*7. *Poems to Read to the Very Young*, Josette Frank (Random House). A well-chosen collection of poems, with charming illustrations.

*8. *Hailstones and Halibut Bones*, Mary O'Neill (Doubleday). A stunning collection of poems about colors, with beautiful illustrations by Leonard Weisgard.

9. *People I'd Like to Keep*, Mary O'Neill (Doubleday). Gay verse about nice people.

10. *Nibble Nibble*, Margaret Wise Brown (Scott). A lovely book. Poems about nature and things that fly, crawl and swim.

*11. *You Read to Me, I'll Read to You*, John Ciardi (Lippincott). A unique poetry book in which poems for adults to read aloud to children alternate with those which children can read aloud to adults.

12. *Cricket in a Thicket*, Aileen Fisher (Scribners). Nature study is a fond love of young children. These poems will delight the young child.

13. *All Around the Town*, Phyllis McGinley (Lippincott). Happy poems for the city child.

14. *Don't Ever Cross a Crocodile*, Kaye Starbird (Lippincott). Poems filled with humor and a delightful appreciation of a small child's experiences.

*15. *A Child's Garden of Verses*, Robert Louis Stevenson. There are several versions, but I strongly suggest you get the one illustrated by Brian Wildsmith (Watts). Some of these poems seem a little dated, but others will never grow old. A classic.

16. *The First Book of Poetry*, Isabel Peterson (Watts). A first-rate selection of poems for young children, but the illustrations could be considerably improved. If Brian Wildsmith or Leo Lionni did the illustrations for this book it would be superb!

*17. *When We Were Very Young* and *Now We Are Six*, A. A. Milne (Dutton). These classic poems for children, written in the 1920's, will never grow old. Thus it seems only fitting to close our section on poetry for young children with them. They are my favorite poems to read to preschoolers. Children particularly love Milne's use of nonsense words like "wheezles and sneezles." And who could resist the wonderful rhythm of:

James James
Morrison Morrison
Weatherby George Dupree
Took great
Care of his Mother,
Though he was only three!

If you have not yet discovered these wonderful poems which Milne wrote to amuse his own son Christopher Robin, rush right out to a bookstore or library! Get the books and read them to your child. After you have put your child to bed, read them over once again to yourself just for the sheer delight of it!

Appendix D

A PARENT'S GUIDE TO CHILDREN'S RECORDS

We need a consumer revolution in the field of children's records. If you mothers care enough, you can bring it about.

I'll tell you how you can pull off this revolution in just a minute, but first I want to tell you why we need it.

Most music stores all over the country unwittingly discriminate against young children. They have a good selection of records for teen-agers and adults, but their selection of records for young children is terrible. Oh, they have a section marked Children's Records, of course. But most of them are the type of records I have called "Kiddie Records." You will probably not find a single record in the Children's Record section by the record company that in my opinion makes the best records for children—Folkways Records.

Folkways has put out the record I would buy if I were allowed to get only one record for my own children. It's called *Whoever Shall Have Some Good Peanuts*, and it's by Sam Hinton, my favorite folksinger for children.

I may be a little biased because I think Sam is such a wonderful, genuine and down-to-earth fellow. Besides being an oceanographer, (he makes his living that way) he sings folk songs for fun. Sam knows and loves children. He enunciates very clearly so that very young children can understand what he says even when he is singing a very fast song.

I *know* children love to hear him sing because we have had him sing to children and their parents at our nursery school, La Primera Preschool in Torrance, California. If you haven't heard Sam Hinton's wonderful, wonderful record, *Whoever Shall Have Some Good Peanuts*, you have a treat in store.

If you lived in West Los Angeles, you would have no trouble buying that Sam Hinton record or other Sam Hinton records. In fact, you would have no trouble buying literally thousands of good children's records. You could simply drive over to the Children's Music Center at 5373 West Pico Boulevard, talk with Mrs. Sherman, the owner, and browse through their extensive collection of children's records.

Every once in a while, I take the time and trouble to drive all the way over there just for the privilege of doing exactly that. Children's Music Center does sell to parents and schools by mail order, but I like to go over and buy records in person, because Mrs. Sherman and her entire staff are very knowledgeable about children's records.

As a matter of fact, Mrs. Sherman and her staff were very helpful to me in preparing this section.

I spent several days browsing through their entire stock of records in order to prepare this section.

Another reason I like to buy records at Children's Music Center is that they are old-fashioned enough to have a record player so you can listen to the record first to see if you want to buy it.

That's the kind of old-fashioned courtesy I appreciate.

About that consumer revolution. Parents don't need to take this situation lying down. If you go to your local bookstore, they usually have at least a smattering of good children's books. So why do you parents put up with a situation where local music stores and record shops have such poor selections of children's records? Children's Music Center, as far as I know, is practically one of a kind.

Here is my point. You can demand that your local music store carry a better stock of children's records (such as the ones listed in this appendix). Then you will be able to buy those records when the store responds to your consumer demands. You mothers really have the unused power to get your local music store to resemble Children's Music Center! (Reread Chapter 8 on reinforcement techniques!) Incidentally, Children's Music Center puts out a free catalog. They list a lot of records that space prevented us from listing in this appendix.

If enough mothers around the country descend on their local music stores, then the store will change its policies on children's records. After all, the owner of the music store is surely enough of a businessman to want to sell records, whether they are children's records or adult records.

If one mother does it, the owner will be startled, but he will pay attention! If two mothers do it, well ... that's one more consumer he has to reckon with. But if a whole bunch of mothers descend on their music stores, then as Arlo Guthrie says, "Friends you've got a Movement!"

Mothers of the United States, let your voices be heard! And record men, be properly warned: Never underestimate the voice of a consumer who is also a mother!

Watch out, record men, the mothers are coming!

The women's clubs mothers ... the PTA mothers ... the church groups mothers ... the nursery school mothers ... the Head Start mothers ...

They are coming, record men, and you'd better get ready!

This ends the fun-and-games introduction. Now to get to the more serious business of choosing records for your preschool child.

Children's records are usually purchased for entertainment; they are not recognized as valuable learning devices. This is unfortunate, because children's records are great teaching aids as well. Any good record can be used for training the memory, building listening skills, training the ear, teaching thinking, building the vocabulary, and providing a child with information.

When you play a record for your child, ask him leading questions about the story or song. Suppose, for example, you play him a record of *The Three Little Pigs*. After he has heard the record ask him:

If the Three Pigs had neighbors, who do you think they would be?

What kind of house would they live in?

Do you think they would live in a city or a town?

What kind of voice did the big bad wolf use when he first knocked on the door?

Which pig was the best architect?

Questions such as these will give the child experience in all of the above-mentioned skills.

Young People's Records:

This is a terrific, but little-known "double value" series for children. One side is a delightful story and song. The second side contains classical music. Young People's Records publish a catalog which is broken down by age groups. Therefore, I have listed only a few of their best.

> *Carrot Seed*
> *The Little Fireman*
> *Aladdin*
> *My Friend*
> *Funniest Song in the World*
> *Me, Myself and I*
> *The Waltzing Elephant*
> *Drummer Boy*
> *Little Indian Drum*
> *Build Me a House*
> *Clock That Went Backwards*

Dance, Body Movement and Rhythm:

Most young children move freely to rhythm and music. It is only later that they become self-conscious and inhibited. These records give an opportunity for your young child to experience that wonderful feeling of movement.

Dance-A-Story About, Anne Barlin, is a unique type of dance record series. One side of a record is narrated, with possible movements suggested to go with the melody. The second side is melody alone. Your child is free to interpret the music as he feels it.

Rhythmic Songs, Grette Agatz (Peripole Records)

Come Dance With Me, Anne Landry (James H. Heineman, Publishers)

Let's Play a Musical Game, Tom Glazer and Others (Columbia)

Listen, Move and Dance, Volume I, arranged and directed by Vera Gray (Capitol)

Marching Across the Green Grass and Other American Children Game Songs, Jean Ritchie (Asch Records)

Activity Songs, Marcia Berman (Tom Thumb Records)

Activity Songs for Kids, Marcia Berman (Folkways)

Drummer Boy (Young People's Records)

This Is Rhythm, Ella Jenkins (Folkways)

Rhythms of Childhood, Ella Jenkins (Folkways)

Songs and Rhythms From Near and Far, Ella Jenkins (Folkways)

You'll Sing a Song and I'll Sing a Song, Ella Jenkins (Folkways)

Rhythm and Game Songs for the Little Ones, Ella Jenkins (Folkways)

Country Games and Rhythms for the Little Ones, Ella Jenkins (Folkways)

Introducing the Rhythm Instruments, Lois Raebeck (Classroom Materials Records)

Exploring the Rhythm Instruments, Lois Raebeck (Classroom Materials Records)

Our First Rhythm Band, Lois Raebeck (Classroom Materials Records)

Rhythm Instruments With Folk Music From Many Lands (Rhythm Productions Records)

Rhythms for Today, Album #29, Carrie Rasmussen and Violette Stewart (Activity Records)

Dance, Sing and Listen Again and Again, Miss Nelson and Bruce, Volume 3 (Dimension 5 Records)

Dance Music for Preschool Children, arranged by Bruce King (S&R Records)

OLATUNJI, Drums of Passion (Columbia)

More Drums of Passion (Columbia)

Strictly Percussion, Daniel Barrajanos and his drummer (Hoctor Dance Records)

Misterogers:
Misterogers is a well-known television personality who

runs a wonderful program for children. He has some delightful and unique records dealing with the feelings of children. For example, he sings about how frightened a child feels when it thunders; what he should do when he feels angry; how he can control himself if he feels like biting. Here are some of his records.

You Are Special (Small World Records)

Won't You Be My Neighbor (Small World Records)

Misterogers Tells the Story of Josephine the Short-Neck Giraffe (Small World Records)

Let's Be Together Today (Small World Enterprises)

Self and Body Image (for exceptional children):

Although these records were designed for slow-learning children of grade-school age, they are also valuable learning aids to the normal young child. What will help a slow-learning child of eight or nine with self and body image learning is often just right for a normal child of preschool age.

Songs For Children With Special Needs, #1, collected by Frances Cole (Bowmar)

More Learning As We Play, selected and arranged by Winifred Stiles and David Ginglend (Folkways)

Story Records:

A story record is a child's equivalent of reading a book. Television leaves no room for a child's imagination; it gives the child little opportunity for make-believe. A story record, however, gives him the opportunity to imagine things for himself.

Caedmon Recordings of the Spoken Word (Leading modern poets and well-known actors and actresses have recorded children's classics).

A Gathering of Great Poetry for Children, Volume 1.

Let's Listen, four children's stories by contemporary authors.

Miracles: Poems Written by Children, collected by Richard Lewis.

Mother Goose

Puss in Boots and Other Fairy Tales from Around the World

The Three Little Pigs and Other Fairy Tales
Hans Christian Andersen's Fairy Tales
Hans Christian Andersen's The Ugly Duckling and Other Tales
Madeline and Other Bemelmans, Ludwig Bemelmans
Nonsense Verse of Carroll & Lear, Lewis Carroll and Edward Lear
Pinocchio, Carlo Collodi
Petunia, Beware!, Roger Duvoisin
The Reluctant Dragon, Kenneth Grahame
The Jungle Book: Mowgli's Brothers
A Child's Garden of Verses, Robert Louis Stevenson, narrated by Judith Anderson
Mary Poppins, P. L. Travers
Mary Poppins Comes Back, P. L. Travers
Mary Poppins and the Banks Family, P. L. Travers
Mary Poppins Opens The Door, P. L. Travers
Mary Poppins from A to Z, P. L. Travers

Other Good Stories:
Winnie The Pooh and Christopher Robin, Frank Luther (Decca)
The Original Sound Track of Hansel and Gretel (RCA Camden)
The Little Engine That Could (RCA Camden)
Dr. Seuss Presents Bartholemew and The Oobleck (RCA Camden)
Abiyoyo and Other Story Songs for Children, Pete Seeger (Folkways)

Foreign Language for Preschoolers:
Songs in Spanish for Children, Elena Travesi (Columbia)
Songs in French for Children, Lucierne Vernay (Columbia)
Folksongs for Children of All Ages, sung in Spanish and English by Jerry Vincent (Cantemos Records)

Lullabies:
Lullaby and Goodnight, Giselle MacKenzie (Pickwick Records)
Lullabies for Sleepy Heads, Dorothy Olsen (RCA Camden)

Lullabies from Round the World, Marilynn Horne and Richard Robinson (Rhythm Productions)

Golden Slumbers—Lullabies from Near and Far (Caedmon)

Lullabies and Other Children's Songs, Nancy Rowen (Joan Lowe Recordings)

Lullabies and Other Children's Songs, Nancy Rowen (Pacific Cascade Records)

Songs for the Quiet Time, Dorothy Olsen (Camden)

Folk Songs:

Abiyoyo and Other Story Songs for Children, Pete Seeger (Folkways)

The Wandering Folk Song, Sam Hinton (Folkways)

Whoever Shall Have Some Good Peanuts?, Sam Hinton (Folkways)

Through Children's Eyes, The Limelighters (RCA Victor)

Birds, Beasts, Bugs and Bigger Fishes, Pete Seeger (Folkways)

Birds, Beasts, Bugs and Little Fishes, Pete Seeger (Folkways)

Songs To Grow On, Woody Guthrie (Folkways)

Songs To Grow On for Mother and Child, Woody Guthrie (Folkways)

Woody Guthrie Children's Songs, Bob and Louise de Cormier (Golden Records)

Book and Record Combinations:

All of the records listed below are by Columbia Children's Book and Record Library.

The Elephant Who Forgot, Lloyd Moss

Furry Gets Ready, Carole Danell

The Little Drummer Boy, Lloyd Moss

Little Red Bird, Bonnie Sanders

Winter, Spring, Summer, Fall, Barbara Hazen

Custard The Dragon, Arnold Stang

I Know An Old Lady, Gilbert Mack and Carillon Singers

The Lollipop Tree, Burl Ives

Can't, P. T. Bridgeport and the Carillon Singers

No!, P. T. Bridgeport and the Carillon Singers

Laughing Time, William Jay Smith

Around My Room, William Jay Smith

Grandmother Ostrich, William Jay Smith
Dogs are Friends to Owls, and Cats Aren't, George Rose
Drummer Hoff, Mack Gilbert
The Sorcerer's Apprentice, Marshall Izen

Music of Other Cultures:

Bouzoukee—The Music of Greece, Iordanis Tsomidis, Bouzoukee, others
The Koto Music of Japan, Master Hagiwara, Master Hatta, Master Kitagawa, Master Kukusui
Caledonia! The Macpherson Singers and Dancers of Scotland
The Pennywhistlers, Seven young women sing folk songs from Bulgaria, Czechoslovakia, Hungary, the U.S.A., the U.S.S.R., Yugoslavia
The Real Mexico in Music and Song, recorded in the State of Michoacan by Henrietta Yurchenco, E. Ramos and T. Naranjo
A Heritage of Folk Song from Old Russia, Maria Christova
Music of Bulgaria, Soloists, Chorus and Orchestra of the Ensemble of the Bulgarian Republic
The Real Bahamas in Music and Song, Peter K. Siegel and Jody Stecher
Classical Music of India, John Levy
Tahiti: The Gauguin Years, Francis Maziere
The Toshiba Singing Angels, Japanese Children's Choir

Intellectual Stimulation:

If you do nothing more than just play these records for your child, he would be gaining a great deal of information. If you take the time to discuss them with him, he would be getting a wealth of information!

It's A Small World, Disneyland Boys Choir (Disneyland Records)
Note: *It's A Small World* can be enjoyed simply for the melody and songs, but it is also a very interesting geography lesson.
Sing A Song of Home, Neighborhood and Country, Roberta McLaughlin and Lucille Wood (Bowmar)
Our House Is Upside Down, Marais and Miranda (Periscope Records)

Noisy and Quiet, Big and Little, Tom Glazer (Camden)

Why Mommy? Tom Glazer and Paul Tripp (Columbia)

Listening Skills for Pre-readers, Volume I

Listening Skills for Pre-readers, Volume II

Listening Skills for Pre-readers, Volume III

Listening Skills for Pre-readers, Volume IV (Classroom Materials Records)

Sounds for Young Readers, Volume I (Classroom Materials Records)

Acting Out The ABC's—A child's primer of alphabet, counting and acting out songs (Disneyland Records). (Illustrated book and LP record)

Counting Song and Alphabet Song (Peter Pan Records)

Give Your Child A Headstart, Shari Lewis with Lambchop (Camden)

Let's Play School With Kay Lande (Leo The Lion Records)

Learning The ABC's and How To Count (Columbia)

Show and Tell, Joan Lamport and Jackie Reinach (Golden)

Play and Learn, Suzy Mallery (Singalong Educational Records)

Singing Sounds, Album 1 (Bowmar)

Singing Sounds, Album 2, Simplified phonics set to music (Bowmar)

Winter, Spring, Summer, Fall (Columbia)

Do You Know How You Grow Inside?, Isabel Abrams and Roxana Alsberg (Folkways)

Do You Know How You Grow Outside?, Isabel Abrams and Roxana Alsberg (Folkways)

Musical Experiences For Basic Learning Readiness: Who Am I?, Lois Raebeck (Classroom Materials Records)

Finger Play Songs and Games (Classroom Materials Records)

Dance, Sing and Listen with Miss Nelson and Bruce (Dimension 5 Records)

Developing Body-Space Perception Motor Skills, Album #1 (Classroom Materials Records)

Learning Basic Skills Through Music (Educational Activities)

Science:

All of the records listed below are Motivation Records.

Space Songs, Tom Glazer and Dottie Evans

Weather Songs, Tom Glazer

Nature Songs, Marais and Miranda

More Nature songs, Marais and Miranda

Experiment songs, Dorothy Collins

Energy and Motion Songs, Tom Glazer and Dottie Evans

Appendix E

A SURVIVAL KIT FOR PARENTS

A Basic Book List for Parents to Aid Them in the Raising and Education of Their Children

When it comes to being a parent, I agree with Charlie Brown: "We need all the help we can get!" This book list should be of great help to you. Some of these books are for all parents, because they deal with aspects of child raising which are universal. Others will apply only to parents with special situations, such as parents of twins, adoptive parents, or divorced parents, or a situation where there has recently been a death in the family.

I heartily recommend each and every book on this list. That does not mean that I agree 100 percent with everything in the book, but that, on the whole, I regard the book as a wise and thoughtful discussion of parenting. Since I am covering so many books in this annotated bibliography, I fear that a parent reading it may suffer from an "embarrassment of riches." For that reason I have starred (*) the most basic and indispensable books. I refer to the hardcover edition of each book, unless I specifically note that it is out in paperback also.

Books Covering the Stages of Development in Children

*1. The Parent's "Bible": A basic series of books by Arnold Gesell, M. D., Frances Ilg, M.D., and Louise Ames, Ph.D.

*a. *Infant and Child in the Culture of Today* (Harper and Row, 1943). Covers the child from birth to five years. The most typical traits and growth trends of each age are summarized in a behavior profile and a behavior

414

day. The behavior profile gives a quick thumbnail sketch of the behavior and growth patterns of a child of that age. The behavior day describes a "typical" day in the life of a youngster of that age, using such categories as sleeping, eating, self-activity, sociality, play and pastimes, etc.

*b. *The Child From Five to Ten* (Harper and Row, 1946). Does the same for the years from five to ten.

*c. *Youth* (Harper and Row, 1956). Covers ages ten through sixteen.

If parents were allowed to buy only three books to aid them in raising their children, these are the three I would suggest they buy. These books do not tell you what to do in raising or disciplining children. But they do tell you what to expect from your child at different stages of development. Not all aspects of development are equally well covered. The books suffer more from errors of omission than from errors of commission. The discussion of childhood sexuality in all three is inadequate. New research findings on the importance of intellectual stimulation in the early years of childhood are not included in *Infant and Child in the Culture of Today*, since this is an old book, published in 1943. For this reason, these books should be supplemented by other books describing the developmental stages of childhood.

*2. *The Magic Years*, Selma Fraiberg (Scribners, 1959). An interpretation of the first five years of life from a psychoanalytic point of view. An excellent book; but take with a grain of salt her belief that parents should not spank children.

3. *The Child Under Six*, James Hymes (Prentice-Hall, 1963). Another splendid book, which covers the development of the child through the first five years.

*4. *Baby and Child Care*, Benjamin Spock (Pocket Books, 1968 [paperback]), *Baby and Child Care* (Meredith, 1968 [hardcover]). It is doubtful if any book will ever replace Spock for a splendid and thorough coverage of the medical and physical aspects of infancy. However, it is unwise to use Spock as a complete guide to raising children, for many significant aspects of child raising are left out. Spock is particularly deficient in discussing the intellectual development of children in the first five years and the importance of intellectual stimulation during those crucial early years. A careful glance at the index of Spock's latest revised edition will show you the general medical orientation of the book and what important subjects are left out. For example, the index contains one reference to erythroblastosis, three references to hernias, four references to hexachlorophene soap..., but there is not one single reference to intellectual stimulation, cognitive development, or kindergarten!

*5. *Childhood and Adolescence*, Joseph Stone and Joseph Church (Random House, 1968). A college-level textbook covering birth through adolescence. It is scientific and comprehensive, but it is also *readable*, which makes it one of the most unusual college textbooks in existence. This is the single most complete reference book on the development of children from birth to adolescence. You may find that you will want to skip over some of the early sections of the book; they go into considerable physiological detail, which is of little practical meaning to parents. As one mother put it, "Some of those early sections tell me more than I need to know about babies!" Once past those sections, the rest of the book is clear sailing.

6. *The Nursery Years: The Mind of the Child from Birth to Six Years*, Susan Isaacs (Schocken, 1968 [paperback]). This book, by the English psychologist Dr. Isaacs, is not very well known in the United States. More's the pity, because it is a real gem. It covers the years from birth to six years, and packs an amazing amount of insight into its 134 pages. If you read it, you will quickly see why it has become such a "classic" in England and why it has been reprinted so many times.

7. *Growing Up With Children*, Maria Piers (Quadrangle Books, 1966). A wise, practical, and down-to-earth discussion of the stages of children's growth from birth through adolescence. The discussion of toilet training is good, but I think the specific timetable Dr. Piers gives is rushing things quite a bit.

*8. *How to Give Your Child a Good Start in Life*, Leland Glover (Collier, 1962 [paperback]). Based on the exact same premise as *How To Parent*: that the first five years of life are the most formative years. The late Dr. Glover gives excellent advice to parents who want to give their child the best possible start in life. This book is carefully grounded in research, written in a very clear and down-to-earth manner: a splendid book, and a terrific bargain at ninety-five cents.

9. How to Guide Your School-Age Child, Leland Glover (Collier, 1965 [paperback]). Another fine book by Dr. Glover. For some reason which I have never been able to understand, good books dealing with children between the ages of six and thirteen are very scarce. This is one of the few. It is based on the same careful scholarship as Dr. Glover's previously mentioned book, and contains the same clear and down-to-earth writing. Another real bargain at ninety-five cents!

10. The Intelligent Parents' Guide to Raising Children, Eve Jones (Free Press, 1959 [hardcover]), (Collier, 1961 [paperback]). A splendid guide to raising children from birth through adolescence. I especially like the author's major guiding principle for a mother's interaction with her baby. The baby is the boss in regard to his own inner biological needs such as sleeping, eating, and bowel movements. Mother is the boss in regard to social or cultural things like table manners, going to bed, and washing regularly. The chapter on unreasonable expectations parents have of babies and young children is a must for all parents. All in all, this is an excellent book covering the emotional development of children from birth through adolescence. The most glaring omission in the book is that little mention is made of the intellectual development of children.

11. The Emotional Care of Your Child, David Abrahamsen (Trident, 1969). Another excellent guide to the emotional development of children from birth through adolescence. Dr. Abrahamsen stresses particularly the role of *unconscious feelings,* which more than any other factor shape both the child's and the parents' attitudes and behavior. One of the unique features of this book is the way Dr. Abrahamsen skillfully interweaves cases from his clinical practice into his discussion of a particular stage of child development. As with Dr. Eve Jones' book mentioned previously, the most glaring omission in this book is the completely inadequate coverage of the intellectual development of children. Nevertheless, an excellent book.

12. Your Child Is a Person, Stella Chess, Alexander Thomas, and Herbert Birch (Viking, 1965 [hardcover]), (Parallax, 1969 [paperback]). This book is unique among books on the stages of development in children in that it stresses the *individuality* of each child. It covers the years from birth to first grade. It points out the important psychological fact that child raising is a two-way street. Not only do parents influence the child, but the child influences the parents. There are many excellent things about this book due to its focus on the temperamental individuality of children. However, the section on toilet training is, in my opinion, not handled at all well. The idea of using *any* type of punishment in connection with toilet training, as the authors of this book advocate, is psychologically completely wrong. Although there are other points at which I feel the book goes astray, on the whole I think it is a splendid book. It wisely counsels against trying to fit the highly individualistic life style of a child into some abstract and general rule.

*13. *The Family Book of Child Care*, Niles Newton (Harper and Row, 1967). This book is not nearly as well known as it deserves to be. It covers the development of a child all the way from the fetal stage through the grade school years. What I especially like about it is Dr. Newton's down-to-earth advice about many practical problems of child raising which other books leave out. For example, the chapter entitled "Preparing for the First Important Weeks of Baby's Life" is a gem. As with so many books on stages of development, the *emotional* development of a child is covered very well, but the *intellectual* development of the child is neglected. Nevertheless, an excellent and helpful book for any mother.

Books Which Help Parents Understand the World From a Child's Point of view

*1. *Summerhill: A Radical Approach to Child Rearing*, A. S. Neill (Hart, 1966). (Available in both hardcover and paperback). The subtitle describes the book accurately: a radical book on child raising and education, discussing the author's theories and experience with children at his school, Summerhill, in England. I do not agree with all of Mr. Neill's theories; for example, I believe he overplays the role of sex in causing neurosis. Nevertheless, I think it is a book every parent should read. It shakes up parental complacency and gives some basic insights into the way children look at the world. I make a practice of rereading it *once a year*. I feel I am more sympathetic toward and understanding of my children for at least a week after I have read it!

2. The Complete Book of Children's Play, Ruth Hartley and Robert Goldenson (Crowell, 1963). I have already recommended this book most enthusiastically in the body of my book. It is exactly what its title says it is: *the single, most complete guide to understanding children's play from birth through adolescence*. It is a magnificent book, which all too few parents know about. The authors obviously have an immense background in the scientific literature on play, a thorough knowledge of children, and the capacity to write in a simple and interesting manner. A gold mine of practical information for parents concerning all aspects of your child's play. You will refer to it again and again.

3. Your Child's Play, Arnold Arnold (Essandess Special Edition, 1968 [paperback]). This is a revision of Arnold's classic book *How to Play with Your Child*, now, unfortunately, out-of-print. A sensitive, down-to-earth book which can help a parent understand the play of her child and participate in that play. A splendid book.

4. *Child's Play: A Creative Approach to Playspace for Today's Children*, David Aaron and Bonnie P. Winawer (Harper and Row, 1965). Another excellent book, which will illuminate the meaning of children's play for adults. Includes a fine section of instructions for a parent who wants to build a backyard playspace for his children.

5. Play and Playthings for the Preschool Child, Elizabeth Matterson (Penguin, 1967 [paperback]). A really fine book. Similar to Hartley and Goldenson's book in that Mrs. Matterson stresses the importance of play for the intellectual and emotional development of children in the preschool years. She shows how natural materials and improvised playthings in the home are far superior to "gimmick" toys.

6. *Your Inner Child of the Past*, Hugh Missildine (Simon and Schuster, 1963). Written mainly as a book for adults to help them understand themselves, this book can help a parent see the connection between different patterns of child raising and their effect on the adult personality. It should also help a parent get in touch with the child within herself, thus aiding her in acquiring the "feel of childhood," as I suggested in Chapter 13.

7. *Dibs: In Search of Self*, Virginia Axline (Ballantine, 1967 [paperback]). This book has become a classic. It is the moving story of the psychotherapy of a little boy, told

with great sensitivity by Dr. Axline. It should help any parent acquire more of the "'feel of childhood."

Books on Child Discipline

*1. *Between Parent and Child*, Haim Ginott (Macmillan, 1965 [hardcover]), (Avon, 1969 [paperback]). If you had to buy only one book on child discipline, buy this one. It was on the *New York Times* best seller list for over a year, and deservedly so. It is particularly helpful in getting across to parents that they should not take literally everything their child says, but should instead try to emphatically translate the "foreign language" he is speaking through his behavior as well as his words. An excellent book; however, I disagree with his belief that parents should not spank their children.

*2. *Children: The Challenge*, Rudolf Dreikurs (Duell, Sloan, and Pearce, 1964). A really splendid book on discipline, full of examples which illustrate well the points made in the book. You will see yourself and your children in this book many times. Up until the publication of Ginott's book, this was the best single book on child discipline. This book is basically a revision of Dreikurs' earlier book *The Challenge of Parenthood*, which is still a good book to read.

*3. *New Ways in Discipline*, Dorothy Baruch (McGraw-Hill, 1949). As I mentioned in my acknowledgments, the late Dorothy Baruch has been one of the most important influences on my own thinking about parenting. She has never written a poor book for parents, and this is one of her best. Her writing is always informed, practical, down-to-earth, and lively.

*4. *Living With Children: New Methods for Parents and Teachers*, Gerald Patterson and Elizabeth Gullion (Research Press, 1968). This is a unique book. It is a programmed book, which means it is like a teaching machine in book form. This makes it particularly easy to read. It is based on the same principles of reinforcement that I discussed in Chapter 8, "'Can You Teach a Dolphin to Type?" You will find it most useful.

*5. *Play Therapy*, Virginia Axline (Ballantine, 1969 [paperback]). This book is really written not for parents, but for child therapists. Fortunately, however, Dr. Axline writes in a clear and down-to-earth manner so that any parent can read it and profit. It describes the "feedback" technique, or "reflection of feelings" technique, of Dr. Carl Rogers as applied to children in play therapy. By using your imagination you can see how this same technique can be applied in the home.

Practical Suggestions for the Preschool Years

*1. *Your Preschool Child: Making the Most of the Years from 2 to 7*, Dorothy Burnett (Holt, 1961 [hardcover]). The best, and by far the most comprehensive, handbook for parents of preschoolers. A treasure trove of practical suggestions and handy hints: a boon for the harrassed mother.

2. *Home Play for the Preschool Child*, June Johnson (Harper and Row, 1957). Similar to Burnett's book, but not as comprehensive.

3. *838 Ways to Amuse a Child*, June Johnson (Harper and Row, 1960 [hardcover]), (Collier, 1963 (paperback]). Another excellent book by Mrs. Johnson, a school teacher and the mother of several children. Even more comprehensive than her first book.

4. *What to Do When "There's Nothing to Do,"* Members of the Staff of the Boston Children's Medical Center and Elizabeth Gregg (Delacorte Press, 1968). Similar to June Johnson's books mentioned previously. Contains 601 tested play ideas for young children. These play ideas answer the question: How can a mother keep young children happily and safely occupied when there is housework to be done or when bad weather keeps the children cooped up at home? A great help for the harassed mother of a preschooler.

*5. *The Playgroup Book*, Marie Winn and Mary Ann Porcher (Macmillan, 1967). This is an absolutely indispensable book for *any* mother of a preschool child to own, treasure, and use. It is even *more* indispensable (if such a thing is possible) if the mother lives too far away from a good nursery school or is not able to afford to send her child to nursery school. The book gives step-by-step directions for setting up the equivalent of a nursery school in your own home, with your own child and other children in the neighborhood. With this superb book, plus the directions in Chapter 12 of *How to Parent*, you can create your own do-it-yourself preschool at home.

When Your Child Is Ill

*1. *When Your Child Is Ill: A Guide to Infectious Diseases in Childhood*, Samuel Karelitz (Random House, 1969 [hardcover]). A thorough and comprehensive book. Not to be used as a substitute for a doctor, but as an aid which answers the questions parents ask both before and after the doctor's visit. More than 1,000 specific questions which parents ask repeatedly are answered in this book.

2. *Young Children in Hospitals*, James Robertson (Basic Books, 1958). A psychological analysis of the experiences of young children in hospitals, with suggestions for minimizing their anxiety and distress.

3. *Play for Convalescent Children in Hospitals and at Home*, Anne Marie Smith (A. S. Barnes, 1960). Stresses the value of play in the recovery of a convalescent child. Gives many practical suggestions for play activities suitable for convalescent children.

4. *Johnny Goes to the Hospital*, Josephine Sever (Houghton Mifflin, 1953). The story of Johnny, whose stomach hurt and who needed to go to the hospital to have it taken care of. A good book to read to preschool children to allay their fear of the strange world of a hospital.

5. *Johnny Visits His Doctor*, Josephine Sever (Children's Medical Center [300 Longwood Avenue, Boston], 1955). A thirty-two-page pamphlet for parents to read to their preschool child before a visit to the doctor's office.

6. *Johnny's First Visit to His Dentist*, Josephine Sever (Children's Medical Center [300 Longwood Avenue, Boston], 1957). Another thirty-two-page booklet to read to a preschool child before his first visit to the dentist.

General Books on Parenthood

*1. *The New Encyclopedia of Child Care and Guidance*, Sidonie Gruenberg (Doubleday, 1968). Over one million copies of the first edition of the *Encyclopedia of Child Care and Guidance* have been purchased by parents, teachers, and other people who work with children. It is easy to see why. This new revised edition should have the same type of sales record. It is a must for every parent. The people who have written articles for this new edition sound like a *Who's Who* of experts in child psychology and education. Many of the people whose books I recommend in this bibliography have written articles for this encyclopedia. It is the most comprehensive book available covering the full range of a child's development. The book is arranged so that whatever information the parent needs can be found easily. However, the authors have presented the information so that the reader can see it as a "many-sided solid" rather than as a "flat outline." For example, if a parent looks up Thumb-sucking, she will find good coverage of that particular question. In addition, at the end of the article are suggestions for related topics, such as Bottle-Feeding, Breast-Feeding, Sucking, Self-Demand, and Tension, and reference to the chapter on infancy and the chapter on the years from two to five. This way the mother is encouraged not to view thumb-sucking as some isolated problem, but to see thumb-sucking in the total context of the child's age, stage of development, and early experiences, and also in the context of the underlying needs which are satisfied by thumb-sucking. It would be difficult to praise this authoritative, comprehensive, and unique encyclopedia too highly.

*2. *Child Behavior*, Frances Ilg and Louise Ames (Harper and Row, 1955 [hardcover]), (Dell, 1955 [paperback]). Over one million copies of the paperback edition of this book have been sold, and it is not difficult to understand why it has become such a classic. Chapter two on ages and stages gives a very helpful summary of different stages of development in children from birth to ten—a much abbreviated condensation of the material found in *Infant and Child in the Culture of Today* and *The Child from Five to Ten.* The rest of the book discusses various areas of child development which are important to parents: eating, sleeping, elimination, fears, mother-child relationship, father-child relationship, brothers and sisters, school, sex behavior, and others.

As with the original three volumes coming from the Gesell Institute, this one leaves something to be desired in its treatment of sex. There is no mention whatsoever of the "family romance" which children go through between the years of three and six, which is discussed so well in Dr. Eve Jones' and Dr. David Abrahamsen's books.

The importance of a stimulating intellectual environment for children in the first five years of life is also left virtually untouched. The rest of the book is splendid. The paperback version at sixty cents is one of the best bargains a parent could ever find!

*3. *Parents Ask*, Frances Ilg and Louise Ames (Harper and Row, 1962 [hardcover]), (Dell, 1962 [paperback]). The authors state: "Here is a book which to a large extent was written by our readers." This book is based upon questions raised in letters by parents to the daily newspaper column written by the authors. The book is noted for its practical, down-to-earth advice concerning a child who is having difficulty in some aspect of his daily living. It covers an enormous range of topics, from how to raise an intellectually gifted child to sex education, television, and comic books. The book is dedicated to Dr. Arnold Gesell, "Who did so much to reassure us that our children were no worse than anybody else's." This is the general tone which pervades the book. Parents who read it should acquire the same feeling of assurance. The paperback version is another terrific bargain for parents at ninety-five cents.

*4. *Dialogues With Mothers*, Bruno Bettelheim (Free Press, 1962). This is a most unique book in the literature on child raising. It is *not* a how-to-do-it book or a practical guide to child raising. Instead, it is a chance to listen in on what were, originally, tape-recorded discussions between Dr. Bettelheim and a group of mothers of normal children, who were full of questions about the behavior of those children. What Dr. Bettelheim hopes parents will obtain from these discussions is a *method* of investigating the whole situation when they run into trouble. This method of finding out "what is going on" in the child can then serve the parents in all situations they might encounter in raising their child. A very valuable book and one I would recommend every parent read.

*5. *Dr. Spock Talks with Mothers*, Benjamin Spock (Houghton Mifflin, 1961 [hardcover]), (Fawcett, 1961 [paperback]). This book begins where Dr. Spock's *Baby and Child Care* leaves off and discusses various aspects of the behavior of children from infancy through adolescence. The basic material in the book was taken from articles Dr. Spock wrote in the *Ladies' Home Journal*. The advice is sound, down-to-earth, and reassuring to parents.

Dr. Spock has taught parents something very valuable about young children. In the pre-Spock era, parents had a saying, "Children should be seen and not heard." Dr. Spock, along with others, helped to change that. He taught us that children are human beings and that they have a right to be heard. Dr. Spock helped to end the "authoritarian" era of child raising, and bring in what has come to be called the "permissive" era. He taught us that parents should be seen and heard, and that children also have a right to be seen and heard.

But what Dr. Spock failed to make clear is that *children are not parents*. This, in my professional opinion, is the fatal flaw running like a leitmotif through all of Dr. Spock's writings. He, and others who have followed in his footsteps, have failed to make clear that it is impossible for *both* children and parents to run a family. In my opinion, the failure to make clear that parents, not children, should be running a family, is the most serious error Dr. Spock has made in the various books he has written. *Dr. Spock Talks with Mothers* and *Problems of Parents* unfortunately both contain that error.

6. Problems of Parents, Benjamin Spock (Houghton Mifflin, 1962 [hardcover]), (Fawcett, 1962 [paperback]). Like *Dr. Spock Talks with Mothers*, this book is also based on articles originally written for the *Ladies' Home Journal*. This book, however, focuses more on parents and their feelings than Dr. Spock's previous books. He discusses such topics as the quarrels of mothers and fathers, their guilt over favoritism of a child, their resentment at interfering grandparents and difficult neighbors, and their difficulties in talking about death and sex with their children. This book won the Child Study Association of America annual Family Life Book Award, and it is easy to see why. Once again, his advice is warm, compassionate, and down-to-earth. However, once again his presentation, in my professional opinion, is flawed by the same crucial error I mentioned in discussing *Dr. Spock Talks with Mothers*. Dr. Spock never gets down to the real nitty-gritty question of *where the locus of authority is in the family*. One minor indication of this is that one will search in vain in the index of both *Dr. Spock Talks with Mothers* and *Problems of Parents* for the topic "spanking." If you stop to think deeply about it, this is really incredible, for spanking is probably the one subject parents feel most strongly about, pro or con, when they are searching for answers to questions about discipline.

7. *Mothers and Daughters: A Lifelong Relationship,* Edith Neisser (Harper and Row, 1967). "There is only one person a girl hates more than her mother and that is her eldest sister." This statement, attributed to George Bernard Shaw, is, unfortunately, all too true in many families. Mrs. Neisser has written a wise and comprehensive book which will help you to prevent this happening in your family. The relationship between mother and daughter can be one of the deepest and most satisfying relationships in a woman's life. This book will give you some sound advice on how to achieve such a relationship with your daughter.

8. *Brothers and Sisters,* Edith Neisser (Harpers, 1951). Mrs. Neisser has done the same kind of thoughtful and comprehensive analysis of the brother-sister relationship in this book that she did for the mother-daughter relationship in her previous book.

Parties For Children

*1. *The Gesell Institute Party Book,* Frances Ilg, Louise Ames, Evelyn Goodenough Pitcher, and Irene Anderson (Harpers, 1959 [hardcover]), (Dell, 1959 [paperback]). Would you know the difference between planning and giving a birthday party for a two-year-old, a three-year-old, and a four-year-old? If you are not sure (and most parents are not), this is the book for you. Discusses the planning and giving of parties for children in relation to their age and stage of development.

A Guide to Baby-Sitters

*1. *A Parent's Guide to Better Baby-sitting,* Faye Cobb (Pocket Books, 1963 [paperback]). A really excellent book, which I recommend enthusiastically to all parents. It discusses how to find a good baby-sitter and how to work with her in helping her to become a better baby-sitter. Part two of the book is a Baby-sitter's Manual. The parent can ask the baby-sitter to read this so that she can do a better job for you and your child. A "must" for all parents and a real buy at fifty cents.

Exploring Nature With Your Child

*1. *Exploring Nature With Your Child*, Dorothy Shuttlesworth (Hawthorn, 1952). If you are at all interested in the world of nature, camping or hiking, I cannot recommend this book too highly. We have used it on many camping trips with our family. I have learned a great deal by using the book to educate my children! Mrs. Shuttlesworth has a magnificent way of opening up the world of nature and living things in a clear, down-to-earth, and fascinating manner.

Books to Help Parents in the Education of Their Children

*1. *Give Your Child a Superior Mind*, Siegfried and Therese Engelmann (Simon and Schuster, 1966). An absolute must for parents interested in the intellectual development of their children in the crucial preschool years. Concentrates exclusively on the intellectual development of the child, and does not deal with emotional or social development. I like especially how specific and realistic the authors are in telling parents how to go about providing a stimulating environment for their child. For example, in telling parents how to teach a preschool child to differentiate left from right, the Engelmanns point out that this is one of the most difficult concepts imaginable to teach a young child. They suggest specific ways to teach the child this important concept; but they state that it may take him a year or more to learn it. This is typical of the down-to-earth nature of the Engelmanns' advice. They give very specific teaching instructions to parents, including the amount of time to spend teaching each concept. They avoid extravagant claims and specious promises.

*2. *How to Raise a Brighter Child*, Joan Beck (Trident Press, 1967). Another very fine book instructing parents in how to provide a stimulating intellectual environment for their children in the first five years of life. Packed with information for parents, it is an excellent supplement to the Engelmann book. Mrs. Beck is a journalist rather than a behavioral scientist, and for that reason at some points in the book she is a little naive. For example, in the chapter on the Montessori method, she is apparently unaware that good nursery schools in the United States have for many years been working with young children in ways which Mrs. Beck thinks are exclusively a monopoly of Montessori schools. Nevertheless, it is still an excellent book, and I would recommend it most highly.

3. *Revolution in Learning: The Years from Birth to Six*, Maya Pines (Harper and Row, 1967). The Engelmann and Beck books contain specific practical suggestions which parents can use in stimulating the intellectual development of the preschool child. Mrs. Pines' book is more an overall view of the newer movements in early childhood education, such as the method by which Dr. Omar Moore has taught preschoolers to read with his "talking typewriter," the rebirth of the Montessori movement in the United States, Project Head Start, whether parents should teach their children to read at home, and other important and controversial aspects of the new interest in early childhood. Mrs. Pines' discussion of all these topics is informed and sophisticated, and she writes well. A parent will get a great deal of useful information from reading this book.

4. *Fostering Intellectual Development in Young Children*, Kenneth Wann, Miriam Dorn, and Elizabeth Liddle (Bureau of Publications, Teachers College, Columbia University, 1962). A little known classic describing the intellectual development of children in the preschool years. It demolishes the old wives' tale that preschool children can't learn much of anything except sandpile and finger painting until they get to kindergarten or first grade. Although the language tends to get a bit cumbersome and dry at times, the book is full of handy hints for parents and teachers of young children.

*5. *A Parent's Guide To Children's Education*, Nancy Larrick (Trident Press, 1963 [hardcover]), (Pocket Books, 1968 [paperback]). Although this book is available at lower cost in paperback, I strongly advise buying it in hardcover. This is *the* guide to the education of your child through the elementary grades. It tells you what your child will be learning in the different subject areas at school. It is also full of specific suggestions as to how you can enrich his education at home. The most basic reference book any parent of a grade school youngster could own. The only weakness of the book is in the section on the new math, which is short and inadequate, and that the new English is not covered at all. Dr. Larrick writes clearly and interestingly. This book has deservedly become a classic in its field.

6. *Mathematics Enrichment: Program A, Program B, and Program C,* George Spooner (Harcourt, Brace and World, 1962). These three books are all programmed books (teaching machines in book form), similar to *Living with Children,* mentioned previously in the appendix. Very few parents have ever heard of these books, and the reason is not hard to discover. They are actually written for sixth-graders, not for parents! However, if you are a mother who feels shaky about the new math, and wants to keep ahead of your child in math, at least through the elementary grades, these books are for you. An utterly fascinating and painless way for a parent to learn the new math so that she can understand her grade school child when he speaks of "base four," "binary arithmetic," or "the number line."

*7. *Thinking Is Child's Play,* Evelyn Sharp (E. P. Dutton, 1969). A real educational bonanza for parents. The first part of the book is devoted to a theoretical overview of how young children learn to think, based on the work of the French psychologist Piaget, and Americans such as Jerome Bruner of Harvard, Robert Karplus of the University of California, and Patrick Suppes of Stanford. The second part of the book contains twenty-two beginning games and eighteen advanced games which will teach logical thinking to young children. These mind-stretching games can be played by a mother and child using the most ordinary materials, such as playing cards, babyfood jar tops, scotch tape, paper plates, napkins, string, and spools. This book is on a par with the Engelmanns' book, and is recommended just as enthusiastically.

8. *How to Help Your Child in School,* Mary and Lawrence Frank (New American Library, 1954 [paperback]). Covers the same basic territory as Dr. Larrick's book. A clear and detailed explanation of how children learn in school and how parents can help them.

*9. *The Modern Family Guide to Education,* Benjamin Fine (Doubleday, 1962). An excellent and comprehensive guide to education from preschool all the way through college.

10. *The Do-It-Yourself Parent,* Richard and Margery Frisbie (Sheed and Ward, 1963). An unusual and helpful book for parents who want to enrich the education their

child receives at school. Written with a delightful sense of humor. These three sentences sum up the book's point of view: "This book is dedicated to the proposition that all a parent can expect his child to get out of school is exposure to reading, writing, arithmetic, and chicken pox. If your child attends a mediocre school, his education will be largely in your hands. If he attends a superior school, the efforts you make to assist in his education will bear fruit all the more abundantly."

*11. *Tested Ways to Help Your Child Learn,* Virginia Warren (Prentice-Hall, 1961). Along with Dr. Larrick's book, this is the most comprehensive and helpful book for parents that I know of. It is an encyclopedia of specific suggestions for children from preschool through high school. It is a book you will be referring to again and again for your child.

12. *Help Your Child Learn How to Learn,* Marie Avery and Alice Higgins (Prentice-Hall, 1962). Similar to Virginia Warren's book, except that this one focuses on the preschool years. Contains a wealth of detailed suggestions to parents of preschoolers.

*13. *Success Through Play,* D. H. Radler and Newell C. Kephart (Harper and Row, 1960). I have already enthusiastically recommended this volume in the body of my book, but it deserves repetition in this annotated bibliography. This book is the result of an effective collaboration between Newell Kephart, a psychologist, who has given the book a solid base in scientific research, and D. H. Radler, a professional writer, who has made it fascinating to read. It deals with helping children learn perceptual and motor skills which are the foundation for future success in school. It is addressed to parents of preschoolers so that they may enable their children to acquire these skills in the normal course of development. It can also be read with profit by the parents of grade school youngsters who are having problems in school due to perceptual or motor difficulties. The book concludes with a series of specific games which parents can play with their children to help them develop basic motor and perceptual skills.

*14. *87 Ways to Help Your Child in School,* William Armstrong (Barrons Educational Series, 1961 [paperback]). A great deal of value is packed into 169 pages for parents of children from grade school through high school. Has a particularly good section for junior high and high school students on how to study and prepare for examinations.

15. *How to Get the Best Education for Your Child,* Benjamin Fine and Lillian Fine (Dolphin Books, 1962). Another small but excellent volume. In many ways this book is a condensation of their hardcover book *The Modern Family Guide to Education,* already previously recommended in this bibliography.

16. *Your Child and the First Year of School,* Bernard Ryan (World, 1969). I have already recommended this volume in the main body of my book. A good book to help parents understand what their child will be learning in kindergarten.

For Parents With a Gifted Child

1. *Helping Your Gifted Child,* Ruth Strang (Dutton, 1960). Parents of intellectually gifted children often need special help in understanding and raising these children. Dr. Strang has had considerable experience with gifted children, and her book is jam-packed with specific and down-to-earth suggestions for parents.

2. *Your Gifted Child: A Guide for Parents,* Florence Brumbaugh (Collier, 1962 [paperback]). Another excellent book for the parents of a gifted child.

Parents' Guide to Books

*1. *A Parent's Guide to Children's Reading,* Dr. Nancy Larrick (Trident Press, 1969 [hardcover]), (Pocket Books, 1969 [paperback]). Absolutely indispensable for parents! The most comprehensive available guide to books for children up to twelve years of age.

*2. *Your Child's Reading Today,* Josette Frank (Doubleday, 1969). Equally as good as Dr. Larrick's book. Unfortunately not available in both hardcover and paperback as Dr. Larrick's is. More comprehensive than Dr. Larrick's book, in that it covers the adolescent years adequately.

*3. *Best Books for Children,* Patricia Allen (R. R. Bowker, 1969 [paperback]). This book includes adult books for adolescents and 3,700 titles of books currently available, annotated and arranged by age and grade level.

An indispensable guide for parents in buying books for their children.

Parents' Guide to Children's Art

*1. *Art for the Family*, Victor D'Amico (New York Graphic Society and Museum of Modern Art, 1954). This book deserves to be far more widely known than it is. It is the best single book on children's art, as well as family art projects; and it is modestly priced.

*2. A series of books by Harvey Weiss (Young Scott Co.)
   a. *Paper, Ink, and Roller*
   b. *Sticks, Spools, and Feathers*
   c. *Clay, Wood, and Wire*
   d. *Pencil, Pen, and Brush*
   e. *Ceramics from Clay to Kiln*

These books are written for grade school children. Adults can also use them for wonderful times with their children. Or adults can use them for their own pleasure and instruction. They are the most unique how-to-do-it books on art in existence. They encourage real creativity in both children and adults, rather than following rigid step-by-step formulae.

3. *Creative Crafts for Everyone*, G. Alan Turner (Viking, 1959). Contains hundreds of ideas you can use for art projects with your child.

Parent's Guide to Children's Music and Dance

*1. *Children Discover Music and Dance*, Emma Sheehy (Holt, Rinehart, Winston, 1959). Thorough, comprehensive, and practical, this book covers preschool through the elementary grades. Suggests how you can introduce singing, various instruments, phonograph records, and dance forms into the day-to-day experience of children. The most basic book of its kind.

Teaching Young Children to Swim

*1. *Teaching an Infant to Swim*, Virginia Newman (Harcourt, Brace and World, 1967). Mrs. Newman majored in physical education and minored in psychology in college. She has been a private swimming instructor for many years and has an ideal background to write this book. She believes it is valuable for children to learn to swim as early as possible, because of the child's safety in and around water. In addition, learning to swim early will build the child's self-confidence and open up to him a lifetime of enjoyment in the water. An excellent book.

2. *Teaching Young Children to Swim and Dive*, Virginia Newman (Harcourt, Brace and World, 1969). In this sequel to her earlier book, Mrs. Newman deals this time with the child from five to ten. She provides step-by-step instructions for teaching swimming and diving to children of these ages. All of her advice is psychologically sound. She starts by explaining how to get a child used to the water, then how to teach him the "dog paddle," and how to move on to the Australian crawl, the backstroke, and a simple forward dive. Excellent.

Sex Education in the Home

*1. *New Ways in Sex Education*, Dorothy Baruch (McGraw-Hill, 1959). By all odds the best book available for parents on how to handle the sex education of their children at home. Highly recommended.

The following are a group of books for parents to read to preschool children or for grade school children to read themselves. All of them are excellent.

*2. *A Baby Is Born*, Milton Levine and Jean Seligmann (Golden Press, 1962).

*3. *Before You Were a Baby*, Paul Showers and Kay Showers (Crowell, 1968).

*4. *Growing Up*, Karl de Schweinitz (Macmillan, 1965).

*5 *The Wonderful Story of How You Were Born*, Sidonie Gruenberg (Doubleday, 1952).

*6. *Being Born*, Frances Strain (Meredith, 1954).

The group of books listed above will give your child all of the basic information he needs on sex up to the age of puberty. At puberty a whole new area of sex is going to open up, and he needs a different type of book to help him deal with it.

There have been numerous books for puberty-age children on sex, but in my opinion most of them have been very poor. Recently two excellent books for puberty-age children have appeared, and I would recommend them enthusiastically. Both are by Dr. Wardell Pomeroy, a psychologist. One is called *Boys and Sex* and the other is called *Girls and Sex*. Both are published by Delacorte Press. I strongly suggest you read them yourself before giving them to your adolescent to read. Dr. Pomeroy pulls no punches in either book. He "tells it like it is." If you are prudish, you may find some of the things he says rather shocking; however, your adolescent girl or boy will find them not shocking, but helpful.

For Parents of Twins

1. *Twins: Twice the Trouble, Twice the Fun,* Betsy Gehman (Lippincott, 1965). Although there are over four million twins in the United States there is precious little available in written form to help a parent raise twins. It should be obvious that the psychological job of raising twins is *not* the same as that of raising two siblings who are not twins. Mrs. Gehman stresses the theme of individuality as the key to raising twins, asserting that individuality is what twins value above all else. I agree with her 100 per cent that this is the key to raising twins in a psychologically healthy manner. Her book is full of practical and down-to-earth suggestions, all the way from the easiest ways to feed twins when they are infants, to the address of the National Mothers of Twins Club. No parent of a twin should be without this book.

For Parents of a Handicapped Child

*1. *Caring for Your Disabled Child,* Benjamin Spock and Marion Lerrigo (Macmillan, 1965 [hardcover]), (Fawcett, 1967 [paperback]). A most excellent and comprehensive book for parents with a child who is blind, deaf, crippled, or in any way handicapped. Contains a useful annotated bibliography to which parents may turn for further help in understanding their particular child and his disability. Highly recommended.

2. *Physical Disability: A Psychological Approach,* Beatrice Wright (Harpers, 1960). This book was written for professionals rather than laymen. It does not communicate as well as the Spock and Lerrigo book, which was specifically written for parents. However, parents of handicapped children will find a good deal of insight into the

feelings of children afflicted by various types of disabilities. Parents will find much in the book which can help them aid their child in coping with his particular handicap.

3. *How to Help the Shut-In Child: 313 Hints for the Homebound Child*, Margery McMullin (E. P. Dutton, 1954). A compendium of games, entertainments, and activities to wile away the difficult hours of a bed-ridden or homebound child. Very helpful.

4. *The Directory for Exceptional Children: Education and Training Facilities*, Porter Sargent (Porter Sargent, Publisher, 1962). A very basic aid for parents of handicapped children. Lists 2,000 programs for the training and education of exceptional children, including 1,100 clinics. Gives information on associations, societies, foundations, and federal and state agencies which are directly concerned with handicapped children.

The Child With Speech Problems

1. *Your Child's Speech Problems*, Charles Van Riper (Harpers, 1961). Discusses home treatment of speech defects in children. Especially helpful if you live far from a speech clinic.

The Mentally Retarded Child

1. *When a Child Is Different*, Maria Egg (John Day, 1964). Parents of a mentally retarded child are often unwilling to face the true physical and psychological facts about their child. Consequently they are greatly handicapped in guiding his emotional and intellectual growth. This is a splendid book, full of wise counsel and specific suggestions for parents.

2. *Child in the Shadows: A Manual for Parents of Retarded Children*, Edward French and Clifford Scott (Lippincott, 1960). Another excellent practical guide for parents.

3. *Play Activities for the Mentally Retarded Child*, Bernice Carlson and David Ginglend (Abingdon, 1961). Discusses how to help a mentally retarded child grow and learn through games, music, arts and crafts, and other play activities.

For Parents Planning to Adopt a Child

1. *If You Adopt a Child*, Carl and Helen Doss (Holt, Rinehart, and Winston, 1957). A complete handbook for childless couples planning to adopt a child. The Dosses themselves are adoptive parents, and they cover just about everything a couple planning to adopt a child needs to know.

*2. *The Adopted Family*, Florence Rondell and Ruth Michaels (Crown, Revised Edition, 1965). Contains two books: Book I—*You and Your Child: A Guide for Adoptive Parents* gives excellent and specific advice on all phases of adoption and after. Book II—*The Family That Grew* is a picture book and story to read to the adopted child and to use in explaining the situation to him. I think all adoptive parents should buy this book.

*3. *Adoption and After*, Louise Raymond (Harper and Row, 1955). Covers all phases of adoption and its aftermath, including specific procedures for telling the child he is adopted. Excellent.

For Divorced or Separated Parents

*1. *The Boys and Girls Book of Divorce*, Richard Gardner (Science House, 1970). This book reminds me of a sign on the wall of a research laboratory: "The solution to the problem, once we have managed to find it, will be obvious." In our increasingly divorce-ridden society, it seems obvious that someone should have written a book like this years ago. Nobody did until Dr. Gardner achieved this breakthrough. The author, a child psychiatrist, writes out of a sensitive and perceptive knowledge of the divorced parents and their children he has had as patients. It is an excellent book. It is written for children themselves to read, yet parents can also read it with great profit for an insight into how children feel about divorce. I recommend it most highly for any divorced family where the children involved are five years or older.

*2. *Explaining Divorce to Children*, Earl Grollman (Beacon Press, 1969). A most helpful book for divorced parents in explaining divorce to the children involved and helping them to accept it. It is a comforting book in that it helps divorced parents learn that all is not lost. It abounds with specific suggestions for them as to what to say and do with their children. It reports research showing that, contrary to popular opinion, there is significantly less juvenile delinquency among children of one-parent homes than among children of intact homes. Dr. Evelyn Pitcher's chapter on explaining divorce to young children is a particularly helpful one.

3. *Children of Divorce*, J. Louise Despert (Doubleday, 1953 [hardcover]), (Dolphin, 1962 [paperback]). This book will be very helpful to parents confronting the problem of their child's emotional adjustment during the process of divorce and afterwards. Excellent psychological insight into the world of divorce as seen through the eyes of children.

*4. *Raising Your Child in a Fatherless Home*, Eve Jones (Free Press, 1962). A very thorough, wise, and comprehensive book for the divorced or widowed mother who must raise her child temporarily or permanently by herself. Covers all aspects of the subject in great detail. Marred somewhat by a curious strain of hidden Puritanism which creeps into the discussion of sex. Otherwise, a good book.

*5. *Parents Without Partners: A Guide for Divorced, Widowed, or Separated Parents*, Jim Egleson and Janet Egleson (E. P. Dutton, 1961). One of the organizations I have been recommending for many years to friends or patients who are divorced or going through a divorce is Parents Without Partners. All parents of intact homes indulge in a kind of informal "group therapy" when we get together with other parents and "talk shop" about our children. Divorced parents need to do this also, for the world of the "parent without a partner" is different from the world of the two-parent home. A single parent needs the experience of belonging to a group of parents who will understand her unique problems. Parents who are not divorced have great difficulty truly understanding the situation of single parents. This book tells the story of the Parents Without Partners groups throughout the United States, and contains many helpful suggestions for single mothers and fathers.

*6. *The World of the Formerly Married*, Morton Hunt (McGraw-Hill, 1966). A "must" for every divorced parent. More than any other book I know, it helps you to understand your psychological situation as a divorced person and a single parent. I used it in a course I once taught for divorced parents and it received high praise from all the parents taking the course.

7. *The Successful Stepparent*, Helen Thomson (Harper and Row, 1966). Many divorced families are inevitably confronted with the problems of the relationship between stepparents and stepchildren, as well as between stepsiblings. Stepparents face a difficult job in defining the new roles and relationships among the divorced parents and children concerned, and working out a satisfactory adjustment to those new roles and relationships. This book is a thoughtful and comprehensive analysis of all of the many problems that arise in such a situation, such as: Who takes care of discipline, and how? Should children be adopted by the new stepparent? How can friendly ties of affection be created between stepsiblings? Psychologically it is harder to be a stepparent than any other kind of parent. This book gives insight and guidance which will make the task of the stepparent easier.

What to Tell Your Child in Special Situations

*1. *What to Tell Your Child About Birth, Death, Illness, Divorce, and Other Family Crises*, Helene Arnstein (Bobbs-Merrill, 1960). A comprehensive book which discusses various crises which may arise in the life of a family and suggests how to handle these crises with your children. Covers such topics as illness and disability in the family, a divorce, when a mother needs to go to work, the remarriage of a parent, death, a family financial crisis, and when a parent is mentally ill. Happily, the book avoids pat formulas or superficial rules for meeting such critical situations. Instead, the author suggests new ways of looking at problem situations, which will stimulate the thinking of parents to face crisis situations constructively with their children.

DR. DODSON'S WHIZ-BANG, SUPER-ECONOMY PARENTS' SURVIVAL KIT FOR $11.60 (Plus Tax)

If you have skimmed over this entire list of books, your reaction right now may be: "Wow! I'd like to buy scads of those books, but my family budget won't stand it!" I have considered that very important financial factor and come up with the following list of thirteen paperback books which will form a basic home library for parents at the relatively modest cost (considering today's inflation) of only $11.60 for all of them. Here they are:

1. *Baby and Child Care*, Benjamin Spock (Pocket Books), $.95.

2. *How to Give Your Child a Good Start in Life*, Leland Glover (Collier, 1962), $.95.

3. *The Intelligent Parents Guide to Raising Children*, Eve Jones (Collier, 1961), $.95.

4. *How to Guide Your School-Age Child*, Leland Glover (Collier, 1965), $.95.

5. *Between Parent and Child*, Haim Ginott (Avon, 1969), $1.25.

6. *Child Behavior*, Frances Ilg and Louise Bates Ames (Dell, 1960), $.60

7. *Your Child's Play*, Arnold Arnold (Essandess Special Edition, 1968), $1.00.

8. *Play Therapy*, Virginia Axline (Ballantine, 1969), $1.25.

9. *A Parent's Guide to Children's Reading*, Nancy Larrick (Pocket Books, 1969), $.50.

10. *A Parent's Guide to Children's Education*, Nancy Larrick (Pocket Books, 1963), $.50.

11. *Summerhill*, A. S. Neill (Hart, 1966), $1.95.

12. *Accident Handbook*, Children's Hospital (Children's Medical Center [300 Longwood Avenue, Boston, Massachusetts], 1950), $.25.

13. *A Parent's Guide to Better Baby-sitting*, Faye Cobb (Pocket Books, 1963), $.50.

TOTAL COST: $11.60

A Magazine For Parents

I cannot end this list of recommended readings for parents by referring exclusively to books. I want to recommend one valuable magazine which I feel all parents should subscribe to. This is *Parents Magazine*. You can subscribe by writing to *Parents Magazine*, Bergenfield, New Jersey. As with any magazine, the articles published in it are uneven in quality, but on the whole they are very well done and helpful to parents. I recommend it highly.

QUOTES AND REFERENCES

1. Arnold Gesell and Frances Ilg, *Infant and Child in the Culture of Today* (Harper and Row, 1943).
2. Eda J. LeShan, *How to Survive Parenthood* (Random House, 1965).
3. Arnold Arnold, *Your Child's Play* (Essandess Specials, Division of Simon & Schuster, Inc., 1968). (Original Title: *How to Play With Your Child*, 1955).
4. *Ibid.*
5. Edith Efron, "Television as a Teacher," *TV Guide*, October 25, 1969.
6. *Ibid.*
7. *Ibid.*
8. Glenn Doman, *How to Teach Your Baby to Read* (Random House, 1963).
9. Joseph Stone and Joseph Church, *Childhood and Adolescence* (Random House, 1968). Copyright © 1968 by Random House, Inc.
10. C. Anderson Aldrich and Mary M. Aldrich, *Babies Are Human Beings* (Collier-Macmillan Books, 1962). Reprinted with permission of The Macmillan Company. Copyright © 1954 by The Macmillan Company.
11. Theodore Lidz, *The Person, His Development Throughout the Life Cycle* (Basic, 1968).
12. Gesell and Ilg, *Infant and Child.*
13. *Ibid.*
14. Selma Fraiberg, *The Magic Years* (Scribners, 1959).
15. Ruth Hartley and Robert Goldenson, *The Complete Book of Children's Play* (Thomas Crowell Co., 1957).

16. Stanley Yolles, "How Different Are They?" *New York Times Magazine*, February 5, 1969, p. 64. Copyright © by The New York Times Company. Reprinted by permission.
17. Lidz, *The Person.*
18. Leland Glover, *How to Give Your Child a Good Start in Life* (Collier-Macmillan Books, 1962). Reprinted with permission of The Macmillan Company, Copyright © 1954 by Leland E. Glover.
19. Lidz, *The Person.*
20. Glover, *Give Your Child a Good Start.*
21. Dorothy Baruch, *New Ways in Sex Education* (McGraw-Hill, 1959). Copyright © 1959 by Dorothy W. Baruch. Used with permission of McGraw-Hill Book Company.
22. Stone and Church, *Childhood and Adolescence.*
23. John Ball, *Johnny Get Your Gun* (Little, Brown and Co., 1969).
24. "Precision Hobby Kits" Advertisement, *Toys and Novelties*, February 1959.
25. David Krech, "The Chemistry of Learning," *Saturday Review*, January 20, 1968, p. 50. Copyright © 1968 by Saturday Review, Inc.
26. *Ibid.*
27. Florence Goodenough, *Developmental Psychology* (Appleton-Century-Crofts, Educational Division, Meredith Corporation, 1945).
28. Viktor Lowenfeld, *A Source Book for Creative Thinking* (Charles Scribners and Sons, 1962).
29. David Ogilvy, *Confessions of an Advertising Man,* Copyright © 1963 by David Ogilvy Trustee, Reprinted by permission of Atheneum Publishers.
30. James Hymes, *The Child Under Six*, Copyright © 1963, 1961 by James L. Hymes, Jr. (Prentice-Hall).
31. Sheila Greenwald, "My Life Story," Copyright © 1966, by Harper's Magazine, Inc. Reprinted from the July 1966 issue of *Harper's* Magazine by permission of the author.
32. George Gallup, *The Miracle Ahead* (Harper and Row, 1964). Copyright © 1964 by George Gallup.
33. *Ibid.*
34. *Ibid.*

35. George Gallup, *Report on Education Research* (Capitol Publications, Inc.) November 26, 1969, p. 5.
36. Ray Bradbury, *Dandelion Wine* (Doubleday Publications, 1957).

Index

There is no index to this book. There never will be. But in fairness to the reader, I think I should explain why.

If the book has an index, some parents are going to read the book "backwards" by using the index, a procedure somewhat akin to the tail wagging the dog. If a mother is worried about her child's temper tantrums, she will look up *temper tantrums* and follow the advice given there. If the child is wetting the bed, she will look up *bed-wetting*, and read that particular section. Many mothers have read Dr. Spock's book in exactly this fashion. I do not want a similar fate to befall this book.

If a mother reads a book on child raising this way she tends to see each problem as an isolated incident. But a child can't be raised in sections; he is a total personality. Each individual child has gone through certain stages of development in his past, and is at a particular stage of development now. In order to understand your child, you have to see him in the totality of his growth pattern.

You can't understand a movie if you arrive in the middle. And you can't understand a child's bed-wetting or sibling rivalry or any other problem, unless you understand his total development.

This book was meant to be read as a unified whole. It contains an integrated psychological approach to understanding and raising children. *You cannot understand a child unless you understand what has happened to him in the development of his self-concept, beginning at birth.*

I don't want to put any roadblocks in the way of a parent reading this book as a coherent and unified whole. An index might provide precisely that kind of roadblock for some parents. So read the book as a whole. Digest its educational philosophy of parenting. Don't try to cut it up into little isolated chunks as "cookbook answers" to specific problems.

Fitzhugh Dodson